RUINS OF BONE

For Mom and Dad

You've given your lives to raising a family and loving us well, and I'm forever thankful! Over the years, you've sown so much into my life in time, energy, and prayer. And you passed on your love for literature, which laid the foundation for my life as a writer.

Mom—thank you for teaching me how to read and for being the first person who said you thought I'd write a book one day. You were right!

Dad—thanks for giving me the love of fantasy and spending hours reading aloud the Chronicles of Narnia and Lord of the Rings series to me as a child. Those remain very special memories for me!

SERIES READING ORDER

For the optimal reading experience, the *Blood of the Fae* series should be read in sequential order, starting with *Whispers in the Waters*.

Primary books:
 Whispers in the Waters (prequel)
 Tattoo of Crimson
 Ruins of Bone
 Binding of Silver
 Mirror of Argent
 Shades of Obsidian (coming October 2026)

For novelettes and bonus materials, visit the link below.

https://go.sarahchislon.com/botf-series

CHAPTER 1

How might a lady oppose a high fae in possession of power enough to destroy her family, her city, and quite possibly the kingdom to which she belonged? Through the long night since my encounter with said fae, I'd considered the impossible conundrum and concluded: only by exercising the cunning of a serpent while appearing to possess the innocence of a dove. Perhaps then she might hope to attain some small advantage.

Or perhaps she deluded herself.

One should not attempt the impossible, but I found myself with no choice—I'd need any advantage I could gain to thwart the attempts of Lord West to acquire Kilmere. None of our lore suggested mortals could stand against high fae in any circumstance, and so far, no true plan to deter him had presented itself.

Yet I'd no intention of surrendering the inheritance entrusted me, one that, according to Ibbie, held vital information about the relationship between the Otherworld and my own. It wasn't a matter of seeking abstract knowledge, but of understanding my own peculiar nature and burgeoning abilities —and the threat represented by the as-yet-hidden incursion of the Otherworld into the mortal one.

My worries drowned out the soft swirl of conversation at the breakfast table. For the protection of my family and the trust, I required time to gather information and mount some sort of defense, which meant persuading Aunt Caris we should not remain at home this afternoon when she knew full well an eligible gentleman had announced his intent to call. At the best of times, I didn't favor the endless niceties of formal calls, but when the gentleman in question was in fact high fae, the matter became less one of personal preference and more one of surviving the encounter unscathed. Lord West had satisfied himself with the merest hint of compulsion before the Magister yesterday—with the insistence he'd call today to sort the matter. If I continued to resist his efforts to coerce me to sell Kilmere, he'd surely bring more power to bear.

Perhaps I might achieve my escape and collect information all in one endeavor—a trip to Fortham & Co. Certainly if any bookshop in Avons held obscure information on how one might prevent the sale of a property, it would be Fortham's. If I could find some legal means by which I could temporarily excuse myself from selling, perhaps it would buy enough time to form a true strategy.

I shook myself from my musings and looked up. My sisters had absented the table, leaving me alone with Aunt Caris to present my argument. I set down my cup, the tea swirling in the bottom. "Aunt Caris, may I use the carriage this afternoon? I'd like to visit Fortham & Co."

"My dear, have you forgotten Lord West means to call?"

"Indeed not, but it isn't our ordinary at-home day. Why should we give the impression we're overeager to receive him? He was already bold enough with his advances."

"I suppose." A slight frown tugged at her lips. "Yet one does not slight a man of his consequence, particularly one interested enough to call after only a single encounter."

"His interests lie in the ruins of Kilmere alone."

"Be that as it may, one must make the most of opportunities that present themselves."

Just how much encouragement did she intend to give him? A chill swept my body. Lord West would exploit any angle open to him, but if Aunt Caris welcomed him with open arms, he could harm my entire family. Jade, my enormous black cat, leapt into my lap and nuzzled my chin, a reassuring gesture.

"I cannot think he's taken enough note of our calling days to recognize a change in plan—yet if he did, doubtless he'd be flattered." Aunt Caris folded her linen napkin and placed it alongside her plate. "Save your errands for the morrow, my dear, and receive him today."

I looked into the dark depths of my cup. I could not fail Ibbie in this, and if I did not have time to marshal my defenses, I'd no hope of success. My throat tightened. However little I wished to expose my pain, Aunt Caris would understand that at least, and her concern for my well-being took precedence even over her deep desire to see me wed. "I cannot receive him, not yet. If I must speak to him about Ibbie, about the plans she had for Kilmere . . . I'm not ready."

"Of course, all this must be a painful reminder." Her deep green eyes darkened, as if with remembered losses of her own, then she reached over and patted my hand. "Perhaps you're right. It shan't hurt Lord West to wait, and Holden can inform him of our next at-home day. I'll come with you to Fortham's, then we'll go calling afterward."

"Thank you, Aunt Caris." I pressed to my feet. Despite the concession I must make to social rounds afterward, I'd won my escape from Lord West.

In the early afternoon, I descended from the carriage onto the footwalk outside the bookshop with a light step, the sun sylph Asrina fluttering by my shoulder, concealed either by her innate glamour or some working imparted by Riven when he'd left her with me. Large arched windows separated by fluted sovstone columns formed a pleasing facade, and the gold-scripted *Fortham & Co.* above the door promised treasure within.

Jade emerged just behind me, her dark pupils slitted and the white starflower patch on her chest gleaming in the bright afternoon light. She kept pace with Aunt Caris and me as we stepped over the threshold.

I breathed in the familiar mineral scents of ink and aged parchment. They mingled with the soft orange fragrance of the shelf polish Fortham's favored to form a heady perfume. The flicker from Asrina brightened—evidently, it pleased her also.

The well-lit front chamber, which stretched the full length of the building, offered a wide selection of popular titles and drew the interest of ladies and gentlemen alike, who often did as much visiting as book selecting, a fact which doubtless helped reconcile Aunt Caris to our visit. Fortham's encouraged browsers to linger and become buyers by placing spindled chairs at intervals around low tables where patrons could rest and read or converse.

Yet it was the warren of rooms hidden beyond this one that held the true wealth of the bookshop. I looked askance at Aunt Caris. "Do you mind?"

The fine lines at the corners of her eyes crinkled, and her full lips curved into a smile. "Of course not, my dear. I knew what I was getting into when I allowed you to wheedle me here, and it will be my turn soon enough."

When she pressed me into hours of calls. Still, it was a small price to pay to avoid Lord West, even if only for a day. I wove between stacks of books and towering shelves to where the oldest volumes were kept. As an avid antiquarian, Ibbie had regularly patronized Fortham's, and she'd introduced me to the hidden gems within.

A now-familiar ache sank bone-deep. I'd give anything to have her exploring the stacks alongside me again. Jade pressed against my ankle, her presence a comfort—and her nudge a reminder of the fact that I'd little time to waste. Aunt Caris wouldn't wait forever.

I skimmed my fingers across the embossed leather spines of a range of obscure titles, none of which appeared to have any bearing on my current situation, while Jade leapt onto one shelf, then another. She worked her way to the topmost ledge, which was well above my head—not a difficult feat, given my stature.

She perched there and gave a soft *mrow.*

Hmm.

I rolled the wheeled ladder over and climbed up to examine the books surrounding her. She pawed at the end of the row, and I pulled down the books she'd nudged, but she ignored them all, burrowing her nose into the dark crevice they'd left. I pulled down several more tomes, and in the gap they left, I found a short, squat volume hidden behind the others. It was titled *Alchemickal Workings: A Treatise.*

I tilted my head to regard Jade. This wasn't the first time she'd unearthed something of import, yet I couldn't afford to consider it in greater detail now, not when Aunt Caris might fetch me away at any moment.

Instead, I flipped the book open. A dry must smell tingled my nose. The title page contained no date for the work, so I examined it as Ibbie might have. It wasn't what I'd sought, but it was old; that much was clear from the antiquated spelling of *alchemical,* and the use of a simple walnut dye on the leather, a long-outdated practice. The alchemists of our day held their secrets close. Might this book provide insight into their practices? Some believed the stronger alchemists of old could stand against fae, so perhaps it could even suggest a means of resisting Lord West.

I clutched the book beneath one arm and started to descend the ladder. Before I reached the floor, a prickling sense of Other swept over me, pebbling the skin along my arms.

The fur on Jade's back rose, and Asrina's presence dimmed to a near-imperceptible shimmer.

Something—or someone—Other had entered Fortham's, and I'd left Aunt Caris vulnerable. Forgetting propriety, I raced back to the front of the store, rounding the corner just in time to see Lord West bending over Aunt Caris's hand.

She beamed at him, and why not? Thanks to his glamour, he appeared every inch the perfect gentleman, dripping with charm and innate appeal.

If not for the as-yet-unknown fae influence that allowed me to peer through his glamour and perceive the power, the *Otherness*, seething within, doubtless I'd have fallen into his snare also. Whatever his true age, he appeared no more than thirty, a man in his prime. Nothing in his elegant attire, fine-sculpted features, or close-cropped hair suggested fae. Only what he concealed beneath it all . . . a far wilder beauty and near-boundless might.

"Ah, there you are, my dear!" Aunt Caris brightened. "Lord West was just inquiring after you."

With Aunt Caris at his side, he strode toward me, the sharp scent of something as cold and ancient as mountain stone wafting round him.

Asrina abandoned her post at my shoulder and fluttered down into the crevice between two books on the shelf just behind.

That didn't bode well.

Lord West stopped just an arm's length away and offered a small, perfectly correct bow. "I feel most fortunate to have stumbled upon you here after missing you at your home."

Stumbled upon us, indeed. I'd no doubt he'd tracked us here, using whatever arcane methods fae possessed. Though I'd hoped those had been unique to Riven, it appeared otherwise.

Jade interposed herself between us, her tail twitching as she fixed her gaze upon Lord West.

Aunt Caris gave me a speaking look, a not-so-subtle reminder that ladies should *always* encourage the attentions of eligible gentlemen. His glamour had evidently driven all my reservations about this encounter from her mind. "We're delighted that you did."

I forced a smile, feigning the pleasure that came naturally to Aunt Caris. If I hadn't already betrayed myself when I resisted his compulsion in the Magister's chambers, no sense doing so now.

Aunt Caris gestured toward the nearest cluster of chairs, her soft red-gold curls gleaming in the afternoon sunlight that poured through the bank of windows into the room. "Won't you join us a moment?"

"Nothing would delight me more." His wolf-sharp smile flashed, bright and gleaming and hungry.

On unsteady limbs, I moved to the farthest chair and perched upon its edge. I must find a way to bring this encounter to an end—and soon.

Lord West chose the seat nearest mine. Many gentlemen would have appeared awkward perched in the spindled chair, yet he occupied it as if it were a throne, with regal grace. The skin-pricking sensation of Other intensified when he gave me a nod. "Miss Jessa, I must beg pardon for addressing you in court yesterday and not considering the strain such an unaccustomed task must have placed upon you. You will forgive me, I trust?"

A compulsion laced the words, an order to forgive and forget, a suggestion that we welcome him into our good graces.

Aunt Caris softened further. "Of course. You need think no more about it, my lord."

"Ah, but I must. My eagerness to acquire Kilmere led me to forget my manners." The sun illumined his face, but shadows pooled behind him—a touch darker than they should be, perhaps. "It's of both sentimental and academic interest to me, so I'd hoped—but there, I've started again."

His words were so very polite, so inane that he might have been any society gentleman observing the required pleasantries. And yet, when he turned his obsidian gaze upon me, something seized within my chest, as though a shadow-fist gripped it.

Jade gave a low growl and glared at him through slitted eyes, as though contemplating the manner of his demise.

I stroked her, seeking her calm as well as my own. If she struck out at a high fae, the outcome might well be disaster. "Lord West, about Kilmere, I'm afraid—"

"Don't spoil the moment with business. We've only just begun to get acquainted. There'll be time enough for that later. For now, I wish to know all about you." He held my gaze, and his voice dropped low, weighty with glamour. "When I sought Kilmere, I did not expect to find its keeper so intriguing."

If he meant to pretend interest in me, then he'd succeeded, at least as far as Aunt Caris was concerned. She practically glowed, becoming as radiant as the sunbloom she'd always reminded me of. Dear Aunt Caris needed no glamour to imagine I might catch the eye of the finest gentlemen. She might have shared Aunt Melisina's fears that my eccentricities would drive them away, but the first hint otherwise brought hope to full blossom.

Perhaps she believed that if I granted his request to purchase Kilmere, he'd be even more inclined to regard me with favor. As it stood now, all that Ibbie left me remained locked in trust so it would prove no lure to fortune hunters. From Aunt Caris's perspective, this made my inheritance of no value, perhaps even a detriment to my future, given that Kilmere represented antiquarian studies. Yet if Lord West acquired Kilmere and paid suit to me, it would address her two greatest concerns—my lack of matrimonial prospects and my undesirable bent toward academics—in one fell swoop.

Only I knew better. Lord West sought to acquaint himself with his opponent, nothing more. And perhaps a good deal less, for what fae believed a mortal could offer any opposition? Most likely, he sought to entertain himself at my expense before wresting the ruins from me. I clutched the book tighter as he and Aunt Caris exchanged polite niceties.

What could he perceive of my nature? In the Magister's

chambers, he'd taken note of Asrina, which meant whatever glamour or working that kept her concealed from mortals did not hide her from him, and he'd not ignore the oddity of her presence. Yet would he note the unknown element of Other that influenced my soul? Not fae-touch, as I'd once feared—at least so Riven had assured me—but something that remained inexplicable.

I pressed back my fears. Lord West didn't appear to view me as anything out of the ordinary, so I must move forward as planned and lean into the perception of mortals as weak. When I'd faced Uros, he'd discounted me as a threat, scorning my mortality, focusing his attentions on Riven and Nikol, never considering I could act against him. If Lord West were like the rest of his kind, he'd share that sentiment.

Even as he engaged in easy conversation with Aunt Caris, something cold and unyielding pressed against my soul, urging me to favor him, to surrender to his charm . . . to do whatever he asked of me.

I inhaled deeply of the sweet-grass scent of Jade's fur, a homely, welcoming fragrance that cleared my mind. Unless I was much mistaken, he'd seek to press his advantage soon, and I needed to retain full possession of my wits.

He turned toward me. "Miss Jessa, do you enjoy gardens?"

The gleam in his eyes suggested he'd not have asked without knowing the answer. Just how much had he learned about me already? I offered a small smile. "I enjoy growing things, yes."

"And she has an uncommon talent for design. It's due to her ideas that we have such lovely grounds, both in Avons and at Caldwell House," Aunt Caris said.

"Beautiful and gifted. How rare."

I didn't try to hide the rising flush, one that might be interpreted as maidenly modesty rather than suppressed indignation. He intended to beguile me with his words, charm me with glamour, and then force Kilmere from me.

That was bad enough, but what would he do when I must

refuse him? I pulled Jade close, her formidable frame offering a bulwark against his attentions. If he brought even a portion of his power against me, I would have no hope of stopping him. I needed to make him believe his glamour influenced me, without surrendering to his wishes—a task as difficult as keeping stonecrop from rooting through one's entire garden.

"I noticed a fine prospect across the way." He lifted one brow ever so slightly. "Would you be so kind as to join me, Miss Jessa?"

The edge of compulsion to his words sent an unpleasant tingle down my spine, yet I gave a small nod. "I'd be delighted. Only let me purchase this book first."

With effort, I kept my hands steady as I withdrew the coins from my canvas-lined reticule and handed them to the clerk, ever aware of the pricking sense of Other at my back. What now?

With Aunt Caris as our shadow, Jade draped in her favorite position like a stole over my shoulders, and Asrina—who'd reluctantly emerged from hiding—fluttering with the dullest of gleams near my left shoulder, Lord West and I entered the garden.

Though small, Ashton Park offered a respite from the oppressive sense of power emanating from him. Soft white lilacs murmured a soothing song, spreading their gentle fragrance on the breeze, while sprightly sweet briar sparked determination with a militant murmur. Surely I could convince Lord West I wasn't immune to his glamour while keeping Kilmere from him.

I must.

Aunt Caris dropped back a considerable length, fulfilling the requirements of her role as chaperone, while allowing Lord West the opportunity to converse freely.

He surveyed the shrubbery, the coldness in his eyes belying the warmth of glamour in his voice. "Miss Jessa, I'm given to understand you not only have an interest in gardens, you've a passion for the study of herbalism."

"You understand correctly, my lord." Perhaps I could deflect him with a barrage of useless information. I inclined my head toward a stand of star-shaped yellow flowers. "For example, Saint-John's-wort has many purposes, including quieting the disposition of those inclined to nervous disorders and inducing more restful sleep."

It was also believed to deter fae, though he gave no indication of being discomposed by their presence.

"Is it?" His tone conveyed absolute disinterest.

So much the better. I was a boring mortal, no more. "And lavender is also quite soothing for—"

"I'm afraid I don't intend to pass our time together discussing botanical life. I only mentioned it so you might know I understand passionate interest in one's area of study." He continued at a leisurely stroll. "I have many such interests, including the sort of ruin Lady Dromley left to you."

I matched his pace, though I'd much rather have fled the park. "I see."

"Good. Now you will listen."

A low rumble emanated from Jade, as though the edge of compulsion in his statement riled. Silently, I willed her not to lash out.

The breeze picked up, snatching at leaves and scudding a few across the path before us. He trampled them. "I require Kilmere, and it's in your best interests to grant it to me. We'll draw up the contract today, and you'll accept my offer."

As before, power wove through his words, forming a demand to consent—and this time it came with far greater force, strong enough to snatch breath.

Why *not* sell Kilmere? It wasn't an unreasonable request, not coming from one so generous—wait, no.

I skimmed my fingers across the hawthorn hedge bordering the path and drew upon the quickening strength it offered. The fierce, protective murmur surrounded me like a shield against the crushing weight of glamour he'd turned on me. Still, I found

I didn't need to summon breathiness into my voice. "Lord West, I appreciate your generosity and your . . . passion for your interests. I find I can scarcely think."

"There's no need for thought, only action. Say you agree."

I pressed a hand to my head—not a feigned gesture, for it throbbed relentlessly. Would devotion to a loved one provide any ordinary person with the means to fend off glamour? I could only hope so. "Of course. But I think—I cannot—that is, someone very dear to me left Kilmere in trust. To sell to anyone would betray her final wishes. I don't wish to disappoint you, but I cannot sell."

The veil of glamour around his features lifted a bit more, revealing their sharpness, the hard gleam in his obsidian-dark eyes, the cruel twist to his beautifully formed mouth. He halted abruptly.

Upon my shoulders, Jade tensed, as though poised to spring, while behind us, Aunt Caris placidly turned aside to address an acquaintance.

I clutched at the hawthorn boughs, and their fierce murmur became a roar in my ears as Lord West closed the distance between us.

His voice came colder now, the strands of power laced in it far stronger. "I'm afraid you're mistaken. You'll sign Kilmere over to me this day—and in exchange, I will grant you what you most desire."

What I most desired? My mind clouded slightly, then filled with vivid images of Mother, vibrant and alive, as she should be.

"You'll give your consent now," he said. "The mortal contract will follow."

All he needed was my agreement to form a binding bargain, one which would become graven upon my skin like the shimmering silver mark on Ainslie's arm. The written contract would satisfy the conventions of my world, but once I gave my word, once a bargain was formed between us, there would be no undoing it.

A shadow, streaked with silver at its edges, snaked from his fingers and crept toward me, its motion mesmerizing—and terrifying.

I pretended I could not perceive it and looked up at him wide-eyed, after the manner I'd seen debutantes adopt. "A contract? I . . . I cannot possibly enter into a contract for Kilmere."

The shadow branched into multiple coils and writhed along the crushed stone path toward me. "You can, and you will."

I shrank back against the hedge. I *must* make him believe his glamour had swayed me, and it was only the law that kept me from compliance. I'd desired a substantive legal barrier, and now I must fall back on the only excuse that presented itself, one far too flimsy for comfort. "I don't wish to disappoint you, my lord, but truly I cannot. I'm only twenty—not yet of age, so I must have the consent of my father and my trustees before making any such agreement."

As soon as the words left my mouth, I regretted them. While true, they could make Father or my trustees a target—although, since the nature of the trust meant they couldn't sign it away from me and that Lord West would require my agreement along with their own, perhaps that would protect them from his wrath. And what else might I have said? He'd taken from me the opportunity to craft a better defense.

A sparrow chirped merrily from its perch in a linden tree, the ordinary sound jarring. Somehow, I mustered a smile. "My father has gone on a short trip, but perhaps after he returns and I secure his permission, we might speak again?"

It was a considerable stretch of the truth, since the short trip was merely a jaunt to the library, but I hoped Lord West would not take note, nor suspect I made a bid to buy time and deflect him long enough to form a plan for our protection.

He gave a clipped nod, and the shadows coiled back toward him. "I will call upon you in three days. You will speak to your father and your trustees before then."

Evidently, he knew enough of mortal conventions to understand the nature of a trust and accept my explanation. I tilted my head. "He may not be back—"

"You'll see that he is. Even if you must summon him." The words slapped with a near-physical force.

"I . . . I'll see that he is." I echoed his command as I'd seen others do when under the influence of glamour.

Aunt Caris had finished her conversation and now approached.

"Very good. I'll leave you to the keeping of your aunt." With a slight nod, he departed.

I hadn't deterred him, only bought a bit of time. What would happen when I refused him again? He'd surely force the matter, unless I could find some way to stop him.

I had three days.

CHAPTER 2

A dense blanket of cloud shrouded the sun the following morning, casting a grayish pall over the dining room when we gathered to break the fast. Yet when Lovell unexpectedly appeared—as he was prone to do at any hour of the day or night, treating our house much as his own—his jaunty grin lifted my spirits.

After all, the very fact that he'd survived after being marked by Uros was proof that sometimes mortals *could* elude the stratagems of Otherkind.

"Morning, all." He snatched up a thick slice of ginger cake, then turned to me. "What trouble are you brewing, Jess?"

He might only be a cousin, but he'd made himself more of a brother to Ada, Ainslie, and me, and he never hesitated before inquiring into our affairs.

"None whatsoever." Yet there *was* trouble, even though I wasn't the one responsible—and worse still, I'd made little headway toward a solution since my distressing encounter with Lord West. Aunt Caris had kept me out all afternoon, and then I'd fallen asleep last night over the dense, archaic prose of the book on alchemy, which was long on theory and short on practical implementation, leaving me none the wiser as to a strategy of defense.

"No? I heard there's a new suitor." His dark hair, in the longer style that some gentlemen had begun to favor, fell over his brow as he leaned forward to snatch a sausage.

I stirred my tea with rather more vigor than required, the warm scent of vanilla failing to soothe. "I'd rather not discuss it."

"My dear, you shouldn't be so swift to dismiss Lord West. I found him perfectly delightful," Aunt Caris said.

"Do I get to meet this paragon of virtue and determine if he's indeed satisfactory?" Lovell asked.

Ainslie spread butter across a scone, then pointed the knife toward him. "After you chase off Lord Bradford. He won't leave Ada be."

Ada, fatigued by a late evening ball, hadn't joined us for breakfast, but Ainslie lost no opportunity to champion her twin's cause.

His eyes clouded. "Wish I could. Mother's dead set on him, and none of my attempts to get through to her have made a bit of difference."

Aunt Caris shook her head. "One would think him a repulsive creature, instead of a wealthy young lord, with the way Ada has taken him in dislike."

"Can't marry someone you don't get on with."

"Perhaps, but nor can she afford to be overly choosy. She's been out long enough that she should have accepted an offer." Her gaze distant, Aunt Caris touched the locket at her neck.

"I'm not saying she should hold out for some notion of a love match—it's not as if any of us have much hope of that." Lovell stabbed at his sausage, his fork clinking against the china plate. "But if she truly can't tolerate him, then it's a great deal to ask."

To wed for love—as Mother and Father had done—was far less prevalent among the gentry than the common folk. Yet Lovell had never appeared concerned with it before. Had some lady deemed unsuitable by Aunt Melisina and Uncle Milton caught his eye? As a gentleman, he'd more liberty in choosing a bride than a lady did her husband, yet if he chose his own course, he could find himself disinherited.

Never mind that. I set down my cup as the conversation swirled around me. I couldn't afford to grow distracted. Last night I'd determined my best chance of stopping Lord West lay in ascertaining why he desired Kilmere. To do that, I must better understand the nature of the ruin and what it might hold—and the best place to acquire that information was the Avons Antiquary Society, a repository for relics and research alike, with members who shared the passion Ibbie held for the past.

Yet since Aunt Caris believed I'd abandoned the family and all propriety to go on a botanical expedition after Lovell had been marked by the Crimson Tattoo Killer, any chance of slipping out had become impossible. Aided by our butler, Holden, she kept a close watch over all our comings and goings—mine in particular. She'd surely forbid an unattended excursion, even to a place as staid as the Antiquary Society.

But perhaps Lovell would agree to serve as escort. I slipped a bit of sausage to Jade, who perched on the chair next to me. "Do you have plans this morning, Lovell?"

"I promised Father I'd consult with the estate steward. He's come up from the country with his reports—thrilling stuff." Lovell helped himself to another slice of cake. "Why?"

"Only a small errand I wished to run." Even with a chaperone, Aunt Caris would likely object to the Antiquary Society, for a lady did not engage with such studies—unless she wished to be branded a bluestocking. If it meant protecting all Ibbie had entrusted me, it didn't matter to me, but both my aunts would view it as tarnishing the family name. I took a sip of the strong black tea, bolstered by its richness and the hints of vanilla. "Since you're occupied, I'll check with Father. I believe he means to attend a lecture this morning. Perhaps he'll accompany me."

Before Aunt Caris could inquire further, I slipped from the

dining room. Fortunately, Father proved amenable to my suggestion to leave me at the Antiquary Society and return to fetch me after his lecture. In his abstraction, he ignored the fact it would leave me unchaperoned in mixed company, precisely what Aunt Caris wished to avoid. Should I suggest we take Lianne, our lady's maid who served as companion upon occasion?

As much as it chafed, I must admit Aunt Caris wasn't entirely wrong. I needed to appear ordinary long enough for my sisters to marry—long enough to come of age. Until then, I must avoid any appearance of impropriety or eccentricity, and more importantly, conceal the influence of the Otherworld, which, if revealed, would bring the Vigil down upon us.

If I succeeded, then perhaps I could retreat to the isolation of Thornhaven, the small estate Mother had left in trust for us. Given its distance from civilization, I might more readily conceal my peculiarities there. And if I was particularly fortunate, I could draw upon the funds left by Ibbie to provide a quiet, modest life.

Yet I'd have no future whatsoever if I couldn't elude Lord West, and if Lianne overheard the questions asked at the Antiquary Society and reported back to Aunt Caris, I'd lose my hope of stopping him. So I discarded the notion and hurried after Father into the carriage, where he immersed himself in an unbound manuscript.

Jade rested her head on my lap, and I stroked the patch between her ears, considering my limited options.

To surrender Kilmere was unthinkable. Even if I was willing to break faith with Ibbie, if she'd been right about the nature of Kilmere, it held information vital to the future of Byren—and my own. I couldn't blindly surrender it to Lord West to do with as he pleased. Yet I needed to consider all possibilities, even those I did not favor. If I did grant him Kilmere, what then? Would it guarantee the safety of my family? Now that I'd drawn his attention, I couldn't believe he'd simply leave us in peace. Not when it was clear that he enjoyed toying with mortals.

Asrina dropped to my shoulder, and her light flickered in rapid succession, the ordinarily golden threads pulsing with darker tones, deep umbers and russets. Her colors had changed after Lord West's arrival yesterday—a sign of fear? Or frustration?

Not for the first time, I wished I could understand her. But she communicated with flickers of light I found indecipherable —even though she clearly understood every word I spoke to her.

If only Riven were here . . .

I leaned against the sun-warmed leather seat and closed my eyes. In the small hours of the morning, I'd considered sending Asrina to fetch him, but I could find no way to justify it. Unlike when Uros threatened Avons, this wasn't a problem that impacted both worlds. How could I expect Riven to involve himself, to take on this conflict as his own? It was entirely unreasonable; we'd only had a tenuous—and temporary—partnership of necessity.

If he came, he'd likely advise signing Kilmere over to Lord West and staying clear of fae altogether, much as he'd advised me to flee Avons and avoid Uros before.

Even if I could persuade him to help, then according to fae economy, I'd owe him a great debt—and there were few things more dangerous to a mortal than being indebted to a fae. I opened my eyes and stared unseeing through the carriage window.

It was better to avoid drawing the Otherworld further into our lives. I'd find a way out myself.

If I hadn't earned the enmity of Alchemist Lyons and received firm instruction not to return to the Avons Sanctum, I might have consulted the alchemists within the city. Perhaps the more advanced ward-stones could provide some defense . . . but I didn't truly believe it, not after all I'd witnessed in the Otherworld.

If I were to stand against Lord West, I'd have to find some way to outwit him or perhaps turn his own desire against him. I could never match his power, but perhaps I could find some sort of leverage to wield. But to do so required a great deal more understanding about his motives and his desires.

Why did he want Kilmere? What had drawn his notice at this particular moment? Whatever his reasons, his interest didn't bode well for our world. The brief glimpse beneath his glamour assured me he was more like Mocvar than Riven, which meant danger.

Outside the carriage window, Kelforth Cloister—the home of Avons's Sisters of Verity—swept arched roofs toward a clearing sky, reminding me of the fae-touched who sheltered within. How did Dreda fare? With the removal of the dread-aught, had she fully recovered? I'd like to see her again, and Sister Margery. Perhaps if I managed to extricate myself from Lord West, I could return.

If not . . . it didn't bear considering. I clenched my reticule so tightly that my fingers numbed within my leather gloves.

Jade nudged at my arm until I released my grip, and then she clambered into my lap, the rumble of her purr low and soothing.

Unbidden, the question I'd been avoiding slipped softly from my lips. "What are you?"

An unbearable pressure built in my chest as I awaited— what? Even if she'd been influenced by the Otherworld, she could scarcely explain her plight to me. Yet surely she'd show some sign.

Her purr continued unabated. She didn't so much as twitch an ear or look up at me. Was it possible that I was mistaken, that she wasn't touched by Other in some way? I struggled to believe she was an ordinary cat; everything about her receptiveness and the ease with which she'd navigated the Otherworld defied it. But if she was not, she clearly intended to hold her secrets close.

As I did mine.

I glanced at Father, but he'd taken no note of my question. His head remained bent close to the pages before him, his spectacles perched near the end of his nose. He muttered something under his breath. Evidently, we shared the unfortunate habit of self-conversation.

Jade chuffed, and I tugged her closer.

A few moments more, and our driver halted in front of the Tresforth Building, the east wing of which housed the Antiquary Society. After a quick goodbye to Father, I hurried that direction and ascended the wide, well-polished sovstone steps.

A small brass plaque by the door read *MEMBERS ONLY.* That didn't bode well for my mission, yet I straightened and marched inside.

The scent of all things aged swirled round me—the slight hint of must and tinge of old wood, warmed by the fragrance of beeswax and resin. Display shelves on the adjacent wall housed a magnificent collection labeled *Inish burial cairns* that held a wide assortment of artifacts, including blue-daubed vases, carved marble miniatures, flint blades, even stones graven with old runes.

Ibbie had spoken with great delight of her involvement in the assembling of this collection, and to see it now . . . I wrenched my gaze away.

Across from the door stood an imposing burled desk with a suitably ancient doorkeeper. He creaked upright, unfolding his body bit by bit, then regarded me with eyes the rich brown of frost-opened chestnuts. "I don't believe I recognize you, miss. If you tell me your name, I'll find you in the roster."

Before him, a registration book sprawled with black-inked names in orderly lines scripted across its surface. They must require members to sign in each time.

He lifted a smaller book, undoubtedly the roster, and began to page through it, with hands that were all thin skin stretched over knobby bones and vine-like veins.

"I'm Miss Caldwell, but I'm not a member yet. How does one join?"

He lowered the book. "You must have two current members

vouch for your knowledge of antiquities, and you must submit an original written report demonstrating your knowledge of antiquarian matters."

That would be difficult. I'd learned a great deal in assisting Ibbie, but antiquarian studies were her passion, not mine. And though I knew the names of some of Ibbie's fellow members from her correspondence, they didn't know me—certainly not well enough to vouch for me.

"I see." I took a small step closer. "Do you ever allow the public to access your records?"

He hobbled back to his seat. "Oh, no, miss. Most of our documents, books, and artifacts are from private collections, kept here only by the assurances of strictest protection. If we allowed them to be handled by common rabble, they'd be pulled at once."

Jade bristled, and I gave her a reassuring pat. I'd never been called common rabble before, but his denial wasn't truly a surprise. These sorts of societies thrived upon exclusivity. Yet somehow, I must gain access. Ibbie had held a membership for decades, and even aside from what records the society might hold, she might well have spoken to some of its members about her views on Kilmere or her experiences there.

"I appreciate your caution, but I hope you can find a way to assist. I'm calling on behalf of a former member—Lady Isabel Dromley. Her estate, at least as it pertains to antiquarian matters, was left in my hands."

"Ah, yes, Lady Dromley." His hoary head bowed. "We all grieved at her passing."

"As did I." As I would for months and years to come—perhaps always, though the biting edge of grief might lessen.

"If you've come to see about the return of her belongings, the request must be submitted in writing to the president of our society." He riffled through the stack of papers before him and emerged with an ink pen, which he held aloft. "I would be happy to supply the required items should you wish to leave him a note."

"I wasn't aware she'd left items here." Did I have a legal right to request the items? Her will had granted me all her research and papers as well as personal antiquities. If she wanted them here, I'd rather they stayed, but I couldn't afford to overlook any source of information. "Would it be possible to speak to the president or someone else about them instead? I don't wish to delay."

"I'm not certain . . ."

"Will you at least ask?" I couldn't keep the note of pleading from my voice. I couldn't afford to wait for an audience, not when Lord West would return in a matter of days. If I left a note, the three days and more might pass before I received a reply.

"If you'll wait here, miss, I'll go see." He unfolded himself slowly from the chair once more and then tottered down the corridor.

When he vanished from view, I eyed the register. On the chance I couldn't gain an audience with anyone today, I required another avenue of investigation. I tugged it closer to examine the names therein. Several I recognized, including that of Ibbie's longtime friend Thea Darrington. If all else failed, I could perhaps call upon her. Given the affection between them, she might be willing to offer her assistance, might even possess some knowledge of Kilmere.

It was rare to find any sort of society that accepted women, save those devoted strictly to ladies' affairs, and Ibbie had told me how Mrs. Darrington had paved the way into the Antiquarian Society through her generous patronage. Ibbie had followed the precedent she'd set, also garnering membership. I could hardly hope to match their financial or academic contributions, so I might well have to find another path, if the powers that be refused cooperation.

I shoved the register back to its proper location, brushing

against the iron ward-sigil affixed to the front of the desk. It sent a chill even through my glove, a sharp sensation adjacent to pain.

I rubbed my hands together as if I could chase away both the sensation and the disquieting thoughts it provoked. Riven had told me I was not fae-touched, but he'd refused to speak of what I might be—leaving me to conjure all sorts of possibilities.

The sting of the ward-sigil afforded an unpleasant reminder of all my speculations, including the one I feared most. Though they hadn't repelled me, the tremendous ward-stones within the Alchemists' Sanctum had produced a stomach-churning sensation, and now this repeated response to iron . . .

Was it possible that—

"Miss Caldwell?" The doorkeeper's quavery voice emerged from the vicinity of my shoulder, and I jumped. "I'm afraid our president is out, and none other can provide consent. If you'll return tomorrow, perhaps he'll see you then."

"Very well. Thank you." My shoulders tightened with frustration. It wasn't his fault—he only carried out the duties entrusted him. But I couldn't afford to sit idle until then. I slipped from the building, denying myself the pleasure of giving the door a harder thud than necessary. Such a display would do no good.

Father had told me he'd fetch me at half past two, which gave me several hours to investigate further—more than enough time to speak with Mrs. Darrington, if she was at home to receive me.

Perhaps I would answer for it later, but for now, I'd gained my first moment of liberty since my return from the Otherworld. I'd best put it to use. With Jade at my side, I stepped onto the stone footwalk and flagged a hack.

CHAPTER 3

When I arrived at Crestridge Court, Mrs. Darrington's butler greeted me. He was a man with hair as silvery pale as birch bark and a bearing as upright as the slender bole of the same, despite his age. In the way of his kind when faced with unexpected guests, he politely bid me wait in the entry while he ascertained if his lady was at home.

He disappeared beneath a grand arched doorway that mirrored the one I'd walked through. A magnificent staircase curved upward in an elegant spiral toward a dewdrop chandelier that glistened above the entry, each gemlike piece of crystal polished to perfection. None of the elegance on display put me at ease.

I waited so long, I feared Ibbie's name had not proved sufficient inducement to receive an unknown. If Mrs. Darrington sent me away, what then?

Just as I'd prepared for the worst, the butler swept back in and announced, "Mrs. Darrington would be delighted to have you join her for tea. This way, please."

Jade, Asrina, and I followed him into the drawing room, a space adorned in pale blues and ivories and golds. The simplicity of the decor lent an understated beauty to the space and formed the perfect backdrop for the stunning antiquities scattered through the room. Upon the mantel sat marble figurines that dated back several centuries—I'd sketched similar ones from Ibbie's collection—alongside a tall vase with etchings of ancient runes down the side. Fragments of an old map pieced together in a gilded frame formed part of a collection upon the far wall, and countless other treasures formed an intriguing hint at the interests Mrs. Darrington possessed.

Before I could examine any of it more closely, a tiny wisp of a woman with hair as white and fluffy as milkweed floss hobbled into the room. Though she leaned rather heavily on a carved ivory cane, her eyes were bright and her demeanor cheery. "Good day, Miss Caldwell. I'm quite pleased you've come. Ibbie always spoke so highly of you."

The bitter taste of loss flooded my mouth, but I managed the expected response. "Thank you, Mrs. Darrington—she was very kind."

"None of that now. You may as well call me Thea. Ibbie always did. And she never offered unmerited praise. She believed it no kindness, as you must know, given your close acquaintance." She gestured to a small round table appointed with an elegant silver tea set and a tiered tray that was adorned with queen cakes and other rich pastries. "Will you take some tea?"

"Thank you, yes." I accepted the cup she offered, the delicate floral aroma soothing. "I don't know if you're aware, but Ibbie left Kilmere and her research to me."

Thea situated herself on the settee, with an enormous pile of embroidered cushions to rest against. "I hadn't heard it, but I'm not surprised. She was deeply concerned about the fate of her life's work should she pass to the Final Haven, though why she worried so much about it, young as she was, I could never fathom."

To a woman of Thea's advanced years, no doubt Ibbie had seemed young, even in middle age. Had Ibbie worried about her will even before the killer marked her? Given that Wyncourt held connections to the Otherworld, and that she'd once been wed to a fae, she'd had cause. I sipped my tea, then returned it to its saucer. "She liked to be prepared."

"To be sure, she did." She handed me a small plate heaped with pastries, holding on to it a moment longer than necessary before she relinquished it into my grasp. "And she trusted you implicitly, young lady. She believed you had backbone. Do you?"

I nearly overset the plate. "I . . . I certainly hope so. I intend to do what's right by all she left me."

"Excellent. Then we are in accord." Thea gave a brisk nod. "And I imagine this isn't just a social call?"

Clearly, Thea appreciated plain speaking, which was a great deal easier than trying to obscure my purpose behind polite niceties. I could see why she and Ibbie got on so well. "I never asked Ibbie about Kilmere, and now I have a number of questions about it. I'd hoped that given your long-standing acquaintance and shared membership in the Antiquarian Society, you'd have some knowledge of its history, and perhaps how Ibbie acquired it."

"Ah. Kilmere." Her hands quivered slightly, and a drop of tea spilled over the edge of her cup, staining the silver as it trailed downward. "To explain, I'll have to return to when I first became acquainted with Ibbie."

Jade's ears pricked. I leaned forward slightly, and Asrina settled upon the edge of the table, her light shifting to a softer white.

Thea returned her cup to its place, her cornflower-blue gaze growing distant. "Ibbie was young when I met her, younger even than you. Her mother was concerned about her interest in the world of antiquaries and how it might influence her ability to find a suitable husband."

Small wonder then that Ibbie had offered such sympathy and support to me. I rubbed at the knot forming in my chest.

"Her mother was a shrewd woman, one determined to have

her way in all things. I've long believed that Ibbie got her intellect from Aubrey, only the woman forced herself to confine her interests to socially acceptable matters—such as managing her daughter. As you might imagine, their relationship was tempestuous." Thea shook her head. "To see Ibbie secure a match to make all the other mamas in Avons envy became her sole aim. It would be a feather in her cap, of course, but also security for the family's future, since Ibbie was their only surviving child. So she did something I considered most ill-advised. She asked her husband to acquire the ruins of Kilmere—a site Ibbie had long been fascinated with—and hold it in keeping as a wedding present. She thought the prospect of receiving the ruins would induce Ibbie to take matrimony more seriously."

"And did it?"

"It's difficult to say. Ibbie was furious at the time. She'd spent years researching Kilmere and had become convinced it held important information about our past. She stormed and raged, but her mother remained unmoved. She'd have it when she wed —or not at all."

Oh, Ibbie. To have a loved one use your dreams as a weapon for control . . . It was no surprise she'd not opened up readily in later years. But how did all of this fit with the appearance of Edward on the scene? I nibbled at a queen cake, delicately flavored with almond and rosewater, more from politeness than hunger. "I can't imagine that improved relations between them."

"It didn't, but then that was never Aubrey's aim—only the perfect marriage, as she envisioned it," Thea said. "I suppose she could have induced Ibbie's father to force a match, but the man never liked to exert himself, nor do most gentlemen want an entirely unwilling bride. Besides, Aubrey wanted Ibbie at her most charming, in order to ensure the best prospects, which required her cooperation. Ibbie was quite the beauty, and whenever she deigned to engage in society and conceal her interests, she attracted a great deal of attention. Wealth and beauty have ever made an attractive prospect."

Yet the combination made it likely Ibbie wouldn't have been sought for herself—but rather for what she could offer.

"Whether the coercion would have been sufficient remains unknown, but once the social season began, Edward Dromley came to Avons. He made Ibbie the immediate object of his attentions, and he captivated her at once."

Doubtless thanks to his use of glamour. Never mind pretending to savor the pastries. I leaned forward. "Was it widely known that Kilmere was to be her wedding present?"

"I'm not certain." Thea drew her lace shawl a bit closer around her shoulders. "Does it matter?"

"Perhaps." I found it difficult to believe it was a coincidence that Edward, a high fae in mortal guise, had taken interest in Ibbie shortly after her father had acquired a property that could shed light on mortal and Otherworldly relations—assuming her theory had been correct. Yet sometimes life held odd twists. Perhaps I sought meaning where there was none.

"Regardless, they had a whirlwind romance." She sighed softly. "It seemed everyone was happy—Dromley was titled and wealthy and charming, which pleased Ibbie's mother, and he supported Ibbie's academic interests, which delighted her."

Only it had all proven false, and he'd hurt her, so very deeply. The entries in her diaries proved that, even though the compulsion he'd placed on her made it impossible for her to share details.

"But something changed after they wed. Ibbie wasn't the same. Her passion for Kilmere, even for life itself, appeared to wane. She became a shadow of herself, and I . . . I feared for her."

"What do you believe changed?" I asked quietly. Did Thea know of Edward's true nature? Had she suspected marriage was responsible for the alteration in Ibbie?

"It was the curse, no doubt."

A sudden spider-skittering sensation crept down my spine. "The curse?"

"One should never attempt to cross such things. Ibbie thought it a bit of fiction at first, but after her entire team died while excavating the ruins, she said she'd never return."

In her letter, Ibbie had referred to painful memories associated with Kilmere—but this? Everyone who'd worked to study and excavate the ruins had died? My hand stole to the pendant at my neck, and it pulsed warm to the touch. "How did Ibbie escape?"

"She wasn't there the day the curse claimed them—or so the stories say. She refused to speak of it even to me, nor would she discuss any part of the excavation, but anyone could see she suffered deeply. She felt responsible." Thea's voice quavered. "It was wrenching to see her becoming a shadow of herself, all the while insisting she was fine. Perhaps it's for the best that she's not here to witness the curse striking again."

I blinked. "What do you mean?"

"You don't know?" Thea asked. "I thought that was why you'd come."

"No, I knew nothing of it. What have you heard?"

"A great deal more than I'd prefer. I keep abreast of the news from Withern-at-Sea, the town nearest the ruins of Kilmere. In fact, I've a long-standing correspondence with Lady Denby. She was the one to inform me the curse has woken again, thanks to a Mr. Tibbons prodding about the ruins." She gave me a sharp glance, one that showed a keen mind still concealed within the fragile frame. "Do you know of him, at least?"

I shifted uncomfortably. "Only that he investigated rumors about Kilmere at Ibbie's request. I instructed him to carry on as she'd ordered, but last I heard he'd gone to the Fens region to follow up on a lead, not to Kilmere."

"Men. Always mucking about and stirring trouble." She rapped her ivory-handled cane on the edge of the table. "If he *is* to blame for reawakening the curse, he has much to answer for."

"Such as?"

"Two deaths, to start."

My pulse roared in my ears. When Mr. Tibbons mentioned the curse in his letter, I'd thought it no more than a rumor, some way to explain ill luck or perhaps misfortune brought on by incursions of the Otherworld—but two dead?

Jade gently nudged my chest, a reminder to breathe. I wanted to bury my face in her fur, but I couldn't afford to betray how much Thea's words had discomposed me. I forced an even tone. "Who died? And how?"

"A cousin of Lady Denby, for one. Though they were not close, she was understandably distraught. And an elderly woman whose roots go back to the beginning of Withern-at-Sea. The authorities claim the victims were poisoned. They think nothing else could have caused such protracted, excruciating deaths." Her lips tightened, the lines about them drawing furrows in her face. "Of course, they refuse to listen to those who have occupied the region for generations—those who know the power of the curse and of Kilmere, when it's angered."

I lifted my cup and sipped mechanically at the floral tea, not trusting my voice. I'd intended to uncover why Lord West might have interest in Kilmere, but to learn of death and destruction was more than I'd bargained for. A gentle breeze stirred the boughs of the flowering laburnum beyond the windows, and I opened the hedge within, that its cheery song might flood my soul, bringing comfort. Then I addressed Thea once more. "You feel confident these deaths are part of a curse at work?"

"Ibbie was no shrinking violet. If something frightened her away from Kilmere these many years, it wasn't an imagined threat—it must have been real."

Yet danger could have come in many forms, including that of her own husband. If only I could venture to Kilmere to determine the truth myself—but I could only imagine how Aunt Caris would greet that suggestion.

"The ruins are ancient. Who is to say that some remnant of Otherworldly power wasn't trapped within?" Thea asked. "Certainly, rumors of the curse are well-documented in our records. As I said, when Ibbie first began to study Kilmere, she encountered many such stories, but she dismissed the tales as legend—tragedies that had taken on a life of their own, till every misfortune became attributed to a malevolent force about the ruins. Yet after she did some preliminary excavation, which resulted in the deaths of those working there, she sealed the ruins and abandoned her endeavors. She refused to discuss it further, except to say it wasn't safe. But all those who have dwelt in Withern for generations, including Lady Denby's family, hold the curse as fact, and the deaths a consequence of meddling. Now Kilmere has been tampered with again, and more have died. It's no great stretch to find a connection there."

Had Ibbie believed in the curse? Or was there another explanation for her deeds? And if she *had* believed in it, why leave Kilmere to me—unless she felt the importance of its secrets outweighed the dangers?

But then, her reasons for sending Mr. Tibbons to investigate became murkier. Why now? Was it because her experiences with her husband had given her enough understanding of the Otherworld to recognize its recent mysterious encroachment into our own? Had she sought a countermeasure to whatever dangers lurked within Kilmere so she might safely resume excavation?

She wasn't here to ask, and the weight of all she'd left me bowed my shoulders.

"Are you well, Miss Caldwell?"

"I didn't expect such a report, and I must admit it dismays me to hear it." I folded my hands in my lap. "And I wonder very much what Ibbie wished me to do."

She'd mentioned continued excavation in her letter, which surely she would not have done if she believed it too dangerous —yet she'd left no instruction on precautions. Perhaps she'd run out of time . . .

"As do I." Thea's milkweed-floss brows lowered with concern. "But I must know—if you did not come to learn about the curse, then what prompted your visit?"

"I'm looking into the past of Kilmere because someone has taken an unusual degree of interest in purchasing it from me, and I wish to understand why."

If Kilmere truly held some dark power, then perhaps that explained why Lord West desired it. Only it was all speculation at this juncture.

"How peculiar." The seams of her face deepened. "And just when the curse has struck again. I don't imagine it's coincidence."

"Nor do I."

"Who is this mysterious buyer?"

I hesitated, but it would perhaps draw her interest more if I avoided a name, so I said, "One Lord West."

"I'm not familiar with him, and I know most of the prominent families within Byren."

"I believe he hails from a distant region." Just how distant, she didn't need to know. "I must say I wouldn't recommend making his acquaintance. He's not particularly pleasant."

"Hmm." She shifted slightly, and the multitude of cushions behind her crinkled. "I don't imagine so, if he's attempted to harass you into selling your inheritance. Do you believe he holds some past link to the place?"

"I'm not certain what to think, only that I'm ill-informed and must remedy that if I've any hope of routing him."

Her wrinkled lips lifted into a smile, and a chortle of delight escaped. "Oh, I do love a good rout! And information makes an excellent weapon. You know Ibbie kept much of her records on Kilmere at the Antiquary Society."

"I went there first, but they denied me entrance."

"I can't say I'm surprised, but if you'll meet me there tomorrow morning, I'll see that you're granted access." She gave a decisive nod. "I'd accompany you this afternoon, only I'm expecting my solicitor shortly, and we must attend some pressing matters of business."

"Thank you, but I was told that since I wasn't a member, it would be impossible—"

"Stuff and nonsense. You may not be a member, but you're as good as the daughter of one." A militant light kindled in her eyes. "Just let me put it to rights. It would do me good to bestir myself from this house."

We agreed to meet at ten in the morning, though I did not know how I'd prevail upon Aunt Caris to release me once more.

I took my leave, and together with Jade and Asrina, entered a hack. In visiting Mrs. Darrington, I'd gained more questions than answers. Lord West had taken interest in Kilmere at the same time the so-called curse became active once more. Or perhaps it wasn't the curse at all, but only Lord West. Could he be behind the deaths? Might he have taken advantage of the legends to kill without drawing notice?

But why? Unless he meant to frighten me into accepting his offer by making Kilmere appear dangerous . . . But no, he couldn't have suspected his attempts to glamour me into selling would fail. So what would he gain from the murders, save sheer perverse pleasure in the taking of lives?

I couldn't discount it. Though not all Otherkind were so cruel, I'd seen it in Uros.

Whatever caused these deaths, I must stop it. With Ibbie gone, someone had to take responsibility for Kilmere—and who else would, if I did not? Only I couldn't help but fear the cost.

As the hack waited at a crossroads, I peered out the window. Shadows pooled deep between the shrubbery along the road, a reminder that curse or no curse, Lord West would bring suffering enough if I could not find a means of defense.

Surely this notion of a curse, one that hinted of power within Kilmere, must relate in some way to why he desired it. Yet how could I use it against him?

CHAPTER 4

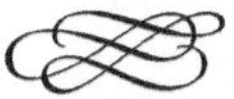

The question continued to plague me as I paced the walk in front of the Antiquary Society, awaiting Father. If I could uncover the truth behind the so-called curse, could I find a means of protecting the ruins and whatever information they might hold—as well as those I loved—from Lord West?

Certainly, I could do nothing without learning more first. I halted at the edge of the building, turning to traverse its length again.

With feline grace, Jade jumped atop the low wall alongside me, her pace matching my own. Even the soft call of a collared dove from some nearby tree failed to distract her. I did not deserve such constancy, yet it lifted my spirits.

I rubbed my hand along her back, and her rumbling purr greeted me. We would find a way. If the Antiquary Society held no further evidence, then perhaps the Cloister library would, assuming I could convince the Brothers to allow me access again after I'd unintentionally led a Vigilist to their sanctuary. And while I awaited admission into the Antiquary Society, I'd seek further answers within the alchemical book. After Ibbie's death, I'd found alarming hints of what might best be termed the

Forgotten War, for it had passed out of general mortal recall. Yet if we'd once engaged in open conflict with the Otherworld, we must have had some means of defense, else we'd have been destroyed. Or had I entirely misinterpreted the scraps of information I'd unearthed on the topic?

However improper, I settled onto the low wall next to Jade, weary in body and soul. The skies had clouded over once more, threatening a storm, so I hoped Father wouldn't delay. If I could have taken a hack home, it would have been much simpler—but it would have provoked a great deal of distress from Aunt Caris. She and Aunt Melisina had held one too many closeted conversations for my comfort of late, and I didn't want to give her cause to restrict my movements further.

Still, time slipped by without bringing Father, and I was left uncertain. Should I await him or make my own way home?

When the oratory bells rang across Avons, marking half past three—a full hour beyond our appointed meeting time—and a mizzling rain began to fall, I abandoned hope. Perhaps he'd immersed himself in conversation with a colleague or, mind awhirl with new information, he'd gone home without stopping by the Tresforth Building first. Either way, it appeared he'd forgotten me.

Or—what if Lord West had grown impatient and sought him out? The cold touch of the rain on my skin drew a shiver. Surely he was safe, else Lord West would have already returned to me with fresh demands.

Regardless, I must return home before my protracted absence raised concern. If I exercised care, perhaps I could slip in without attracting notice—though Holden might well report to Aunt Caris that I'd come in unaccompanied. Without further delay, I hired another hack.

When I arrived home, a stately carriage awaited before our row house, and an elegant lady descended our stairs and ensconced herself within. Only after her carriage departed did I climb from the hack and hurry toward the house. No sense betraying my improprieties before what might be a prominent member of society.

Holden admitted me with a nod, offering his usual gracious welcome before taking my damp hat. Snatches of conversation drifted from the drawing room into the entry. Abruptly, Aunt Melisina's strident tones rose above the rest. "Ada, what ails you? You scarcely engaged with Lady Bradford at all. One would think you didn't care to make a favorable impression upon your future mother-in-law."

"Now, Melisina," Aunt Caris interjected. "Even if Ada was quieter than usual, I'm certain she made a positive impression."

"Positive? I scarcely think so. She didn't say two words put together. Lady Bradford deigned to call today in order to become acquainted with the lady her son intends to marry. If that's not a reason to be at one's best and brightest, then what is? She may exert herself to change his mind, if she's displeased."

"Come, Mother." Lovell's voice emerged low and soothing as he made his usual attempt to quiet the refined tempest that was Aunt Melisina. "Lord Bradford knows his own mind—and Ada does hers."

Could I slip up the stairs without drawing notice? Or should I attempt to lend support to Ada? She did have Ainslie and Lovell to take up her part, but—

"Your aunts have requested your presence upon your return, Miss Jessa," Holden said.

Blight and rot. I marched toward my inevitable fate as Ainslie spoke. "Lovell is right. Ada does know her mind, and she does *not* wish to marry Lord Bradford."

"Mind your own affairs, child, and let me mind Ada." When I stepped over the threshold, Aunt Melisina arched an imperious brow. Instantly I became aware of how the damp had left my dress limp and made my dark curls even more unruly than usual.

"Ah, Jessa, you're here at last." She looked beyond me. "But where is Alden? We require him to talk sense into Ada."

"I . . . I'm not certain."

"Caris said you left in the carriage with him this morning." Aunt Melisina rapped the floor with the handle of her parasol. "Was that false?"

"I did, but—"

"But what?"

"He forgot to fetch me home. If he's not here, I suppose he's still at his lecture."

Behind me, Holden cleared his throat. "If I may, Lady Stanford, your brother did return, only long enough to fetch one of his portfolios before going out again."

Then he'd not fallen victim to Lord West, not yet. Some of the tension coiled in my shoulders eased.

Aunt Melisina's lips pulled into a tight line, but before she could speak, Aunt Caris said, "Thank you, Holden." Then she looked at me and sighed. "Do I want to know how you came home?"

"It began to rain, so I hired a hack."

"You took a hack? Alone? If word got out . . ." Aunt Melisina's features pinched. She straightened her already picture-perfect posture further. "This is why a proper chaperone is needed, Caris. At once. There can be no further delay."

"I suppose you're right," Aunt Caris murmured.

A chaperone? If someone kept watch over my every move, in order to report any impropriety to my aunts, how in the Crossings was I to fend off Lord West and investigate Kilmere? If my aunts had even the slightest hint of how I'd occupied myself of late, they'd never allow me to leave the house again.

"Surely there's no need." Ainslie smoothed her skirts, though nothing needed rearrangement—she was as refined as usual. Given her concealed work as P. Smith, she'd not welcome watchful eyes any more than I did. "Between the two of you, we have chaperones enough for any society event we could wish to attend. And Lianne has made no complaint about attending us on simple errands when you cannot."

Lovell, who shared the P. Smith persona with Ainslie,

hastened to chime in. "And I can squire them around any time it's needed."

As Aunt Melisina regarded him, the rigid lines of her face softened. If anyone could induce her to change her mind, it would be her beloved son. Yet her lips firmed. "It's time you looked to your own future, and you cannot if you're forever dancing attendance on your cousins."

"But Mother, I—"

"Nor should their lady's maid be required to take on a task outside the scope of her duties. Certainly, she cannot always chase Jessa about Avons, as she plunges from one unsuitable occupation to another."

The edge in her words cut deep, and I lowered my gaze. Jade rumbled, a low, threatening sound.

"Aunt Melisina, it's not as bad as you say." Despite the gentleness in Ada's tone, Aunt Melisina refused to calm.

"Your father should have forbidden Jessa her pursuits long ago, not to mention taken action to secure all of your futures. Since he has not, Caris and I will do what we can to preserve your reputations and ensure you wed well. You'll thank us one day."

I'd not last long enough *to* thank her, if Lord West had his way. But Father would agree to almost anything Aunt Melisina suggested—including the installment of a chaperone—if only she would leave him in peace. Which made Aunt Caris my only hope. I turned to her. "Surely you don't think this necessary."

"My dear, I know you wish Avons was like Upper Northlea, and you might ramble about alone as you did in the country-side, studying your plants and herbs, but it's not—and it never will be." Faint shadows were gathered beneath her eyes, dulling their brightness. "If you don't take care, your reputation will soon be irrevocably tarnished. There's already been gossip about your appearance before the Magister, even garnering censure in the social column."

"But I'm no one of significance. Why would they bother to mention me?"

Ainslie's cheeks bloomed with color, making her appear more like a queen's glory rose than ever. "Perhaps because society loves to mud-sling and has more than its reasonable share of old cats who like nothing more than to disparage those who don't adhere to their wishes?"

What had nettled her into such unusual outspokenness? Some difficulty she'd run into while attempting to gather information for the articles she crafted with Lovell?

Aunt Melisina stiffened, the silk of her gown rustling. "Really, Ainslie! I might expect such an uncouth comment from Jessa, but from you?"

"I apologize for my tone, but you must see it's true. They wish to set the standards and retain their positions, so they must condemn all who step beyond the bounds they've placed."

"True or not, there's no need for hasty actions." Ada attempted once more to calm the troubled waters. "I'm sure once Jessa understands—"

"It's not Jessa alone. You've persisted in rejecting Lord Bradford, though he's one of the most eligible gentlemen in Avons, as you have those who came before him. If you continue to ignore his attentions also, you might well be regarded impossible to please."

Ada touched the engraved sapphire ring on her right hand, a bequeathment from Mother. Perhaps she sought strength in the reminder. "I don't wish to engage his attentions, and I've tried to make it plain from the beginning. If he thinks I've encouraged him, then that's his own misbelief. We'd never suit."

"Pish, child." Aunt Melisina waved her hand in dismissal. "You're hardly of an age to know your own mind. You must trust us to find a proper match for you."

"But we need not discuss it further now." Aunt Caris cared no more for conflict than Ada did. She patted Ada's shoulder. "And you must not be overconcerned about the matter of the chaperone, my dears. We'll find someone whom we can regard as part of the family. In truth, with the three of you needing oversight and Melisina often occupied, I should have engaged one some time ago."

Jade leapt upon my lap and touched her nose to my chin. At once, my thoughts returned to the Kelforth Cloister, and an unexpected notion presented itself. "I have a suggestion for the chaperone position."

Full silence fell as they all turned to regard me.

Aunt Melisina sniffed slightly. "I cannot imagine you know a suitable individual."

"Her name is Dreda, and she's dwelt within the Kelforth Cloister for a time, so you may inquire of the Sisters of Verity regarding her character." Though I'd last seen her in a state of extreme distress and oppression, from which I could only hope she'd recovered. Why had I thought this a good idea? The assurance that had come with the notion rapidly faded.

"A respectable woman, then." Aunt Caris smiled. "We should invite her for an interview. What do you say, Melisina?"

"I'm in favor of Ermenhild."

"And I cannot abide her. She's far too sour-tempered. Don't forget, sister, I must share a house with whomever we engage."

Aunt Melisina pressed to her feet. "Then I suppose we will interview this Dreda and see what references she can provide."

"I'm certain if the Sisters of Verity recommend her, she will suit," Aunt Caris said.

But would they, or had I stirred further trouble? No, the Sisters would not expose the truth about Dreda. If she'd not made a full recovery, it was likely they'd suggest another woman in her stead—and anyone they favored would be an improvement over an individual loyal only to Aunt Melisina.

Jade gave a low, satisfied *mrow*. Had she—I shook off the notion and stroked the starflower patch on her chest.

Any chaperone would prove difficult, even one sent by the Sisters. If Dreda accepted the position, would she feel bound to report my investigation to my aunts? I would conceal whatever I could, but still . . .

And what if she told my aunts how we'd met? What I'd done? Surely she wouldn't want to condemn herself by exposing her secret, unless she assumed I'd already told them. I tugged Jade closer.

None of it would matter, neither chaperone nor threat of the Vigil, if I couldn't stop Lord West—a task that my aunts had just made exponentially more difficult.

CHAPTER 5

Two more days and Lord West would return. I woke with the knowledge burning through my limbs like frost on early blossoms, making further rest impossible. I climbed from bed and drew back the drapery.

Early morning light crept into my bedchamber, the charcoal-and-umber dawn foreboding. I'd not be able to simply deflect Lord West again; I must find some actual means of defense—a near-impossible task.

I collected the alchemical book from my dressing table and pulled a chair over to the window that I might overlook the gardens while I read. The soft murmur of the plants reached me even through the glass, a reminder that my Other senses—whatever they were—strengthened.

I paged through the book until I found my place. Jade settled on my lap, and Asrina perched on the arm of the chair, her long wings as vibrant as banners of flame, their flickering light an encouragement to continue.

So I plunged into the difficult text, finding little of practical value. The small book presented a history of vague theories and experimental dead ends that marked the beginnings of alchemy. At last, however, the record came to the point.

It laid out as fact what I'd never even heard other lore hint—that in addition to their innate abilities, fae enhanced their magics by wielding objects of power.

Once, I might have dismissed such a notion. Certainly, I'd seen no indication that Riven or Nikol used such devices. And yet, I bore one such artifact about my neck: the pendant that contained power to repel low fae. Though limited in scope, it had proven effective.

According to this record, the concept of objects with the capacity to hold Other power became foundational to alchemy and provided its first successes. Alchemists learned mortals could craft a shell of the device, using undisclosed practices, but they required something Other, something of innate power from which alchemy could draw to accomplish its intended aim. An improperly crafted device or improperly forged source, and the item would spectacularly fail.

Some sort of water damage marred the next section of the book, rendering the words illegible, so I leafed through to the final third, entitled *On Defense in Our Time*.

Here the author appeared to respond to an argument of his day, suggesting that the making of potions and wards was not enough. For mortals to protect themselves from fae, they must wield some measure of true power. The conclusion? Alchemists must implant Otherworldly elements or devices within mortals. Whatever the controversy, the attempt had been made. Experiments were conducted that resulted in the same outcome each time: death.

My mouth went dry. With cold fingers, I turned the page.

Such was the fear of an Otherworldly onslaught that the alchemists continued, rather than abandon the attempt. This time, they chose those whose bodies they deemed more resilient.

Children.

A flare of heat burned away the chill in my limbs. How dare they consign the young and innocent to such a grim fate? They'd condemned children—who couldn't have possibly understood what they would suffer, let alone consent to it. And what of their parents? How had they allowed such a thing?

Oh.

The alchemists had chosen the poor, those who had no hope, those guaranteed to leap at the prospect of a better life for their children, reassured by the glowing accounts the alchemists offered. Or they sought the orphaned, who had none to speak in their defense.

My stomach churned as though I'd been cast upon a storm-tossed sea.

I'd condemned the cruelty of the fae in creating the ghouls I'd found trapped in Wyncourt, for deceiving mortals with promises of immortality and making them monsters instead, but this was an act just as vile. In their quest to protect the kingdom of Byren, the alchemists had counted no cost too great.

Jade nuzzled the corner of the book, an invitation to stroke her head, which I accepted, her presence a calm to the storm within.

Had these abominable practices forced the abandonment of alchemy, in the end? No one I knew had ever ventured an explanation for why it had been lost for centuries, then rediscovered in the past few decades. For the knowledge to have simply died out made no sense—unless a public outcry had forced it. Or something had happened to *all* the alchemists.

I skimmed my fingers over the age-tattered pages. How had this book come to be concealed within *Fortham & Co.*? Alchemists sought and enjoyed public favor—they'd not want such rumors to escape. Of course, they could claim it a false, unverified account, speculations of an age long gone.

Seeking greater understanding, I returned to the account and learned that their efforts had paid off. Two of the children survived the procedure. On them, the writer pinned his hopes for the future.

Jade stretched, her eyes gleaming, then sprang to the floor to prowl the bedchamber.

I traced the outline of my ribs beneath the muslin of my nightgown. Could the alchemists have performed a similar working upon me? Could that be the source of my peculiar abilities? But no, if I'd been ripped open, and something Other, something powerful, had been placed inside . . . surely I'd remember; surely it would have left scars.

Besides, the alchemists of our day didn't possess power as great as their forebears. So much had been lost. Since the revival of alchemy two decades ago, they'd made great strides, but primarily in healing potions and other mortal aids, while their defensive mechanisms against fae, which they claimed so strong, had proven limited in scope—not that the general public was aware of that fact.

And unlike the parents of the children chosen for experimentation in the past, my own had no reason to agree to the implanting of a device.

Which left the more plausible, equally terrifying explanation—

Jade knocked over the tin of dried fish on my bedside table with a clatter, and I startled. "I take it you're hungry?"

A loud *mrow* confirmed it. I placed some dried fish into her bowl, contemplating the veracity of this account—or lack thereof. The experiments from centuries ago, the erasure of alchemical knowledge, and its slow revival . . . it must have some significance. But what?

I returned for the final few pages, which concluded that our one hope of survival as a species was to incorporate objects of power into mortals. Though the deaths of those experimented on provided a compelling counterargument, the author ignored this point. Whatever arguments the book might advance, surely our mortal frames were not meant to contain such abilities; they had not been designed in such fashion. Prolonged exposure to Other could lead to fae-touch and madness; Riven had confirmed as much.

Which did not bode well for the two children who had

survived the procedures. The entire account left me troubled—and no closer to a solution for my current predicament.

Jade had finished her portion of fish, and she returned to groom herself in a warm patch the sun cast on the rug.

"What am I to do?" I whispered.

Asrina pulsed light in an irregular cadence, almost like the beats of speech, yet entirely undecipherable. Even if she could communicate in a way I could understand, what could she say to change the situation? I'd no power to match Lord West, and he'd return soon.

Yet whatever Kilmere meant to him, it meant more to me—a connection to Ibbie and the answers I must have, a possible means of protection for my kingdom and those I loved who dwelt within it.

And that was its own strength.

I stood and tucked the book in the depths of my wardrobe. When I turned, a stack of letters atop the dressing table caught my eye.

Gaile must have brought them up yesterday, and I'd been too weary to notice. I riffled through them. One bore the crabbed handwriting of Mr. Heard, and it appeared rather worse for wear, stained in places and creased on one edge, as if it had fallen into some out-of-the-way crevice. Perhaps that explained the delay.

I broke the seal, and the faint scent of pipe tobacco wafted from within.

Miss Jessa,

You asked about fae-touch and the killer. Can't say it's impossible—fae-touch can drive a fellow to some of the blackest deeds, altogether unaware.

It's a plaguey matter. Best not delve too deep. The protectors of such information are none too friendly.

Its protectors—the Vigil? Had Mr. Heard ever experienced conflict with them?

Same goes for Otherkind preying on mortals in our world. Facts are sparse, opinions bountiful. Only ones that matter are those of the Vigil, leastwise we're told.

If you asked the wrong person, they might tell you of an erroneous theory—that something governs the relations between the Otherworld and our own, else they'd have overrun us long ago. That it's not our own efforts as have spared us in past. And that something has gone amiss in the present. Of course, you'd know better than to listen to such heretical ideas. Ha!

Only goes to show, you'd best not ask questions of the wrong sort. Best to keep your eyes open and your knowledge right close. If you ever return to Milburn, call on me. I expect we have much to discuss.

Regards,
Leofric Heard

P.S. Mill thriving. Niece still has no sense, but she's taken to assisting Mrs. Hopkins on occasion, so mayhap her wits will rub off on said niece.

I folded the letter, the paper crinkling in protest. If I understood aright, his theories on the current encroachment of the Otherworld agreed with my own . . . and he believed them dangerous theories to hold.

Because of the Vigil?

He'd also suggested that mortals hadn't possessed any greater means of defense against Other in the past, but relied on some other protection, some mediating force. What did that mean, when it came to the Forgotten War? And what did it mean for me now, in facing Lord West?

The door burst open, and I jumped, thrusting the letter into the folds of my nightgown. But it was only Ada and Ainslie, still clad in dressing gowns, their hair in long plaits down their backs.

"Good, you're awake," Ainslie said.

They swept into the room, and Ada softly secured the door behind them.

"Yes, but I'm surprised you are."

"Pressing matters required an early morning. It's high time we held a council of sisters." Ainslie plopped onto the bed. "This situation with Ada's suitor has gone on long enough."

Ada sank more gracefully onto the edge next to her. "Yet I cannot make Aunt Melisina listen, nor Lord Bradford, for that matter."

"Then we should go to Father and make him listen. Surely he'll put a stop to it, if he knows Ada is truly unwilling." I tucked the letter into the drawer of my dressing table, until I could find a better spot to secure it. I'd rather no one else read the missive and question why I corresponded with a loremaster about fae.

Ada shook her head. "I tried."

"And he didn't listen?"

"I went to him last night." Ada traced her finger along the floral pattern of the bedquilt. "But Aunt Melisina had reached him first. She'd persuaded Father it's a good match—and that Lord Bradford is a good man. That it's only maidenly fears of marriage that keep me from considering him. Now he's asked that I spend time getting to know Lord Bradford and seriously consider his suit."

"Father said all that?" I perched on the end of the mattress. "It's not like him."

"From what he said, Aunt Melisina rang a peal over him about our futures and what our fate will be if we're unwed and he dies, since Caldwell House and much of its resources will pass on to the male line. He seemed—afraid. Afraid of letting Mother down, and us also, if he does not see our futures secured."

Ainslie shoved a sleep-tousled curl from her face. "She always did know how to get under his skin."

"It's a reasonable concern, but Mother left us Thornhaven." Which would require a sum to maintain. Yet if I understood the nature of the trust Ibbie left correctly, we had other options when I came of age at four and twenty. I needed to learn its exact terms, rather than leave it to chance. If I could not muster a sufficient annuity to live removed from society, then my plan to avoid scandal and protect my family from the Vigil might well fail.

Whatever the appeal of a love like that my parents had shared, I couldn't afford to consider marriage. Not when my nature must remain hidden. Even if a man could bring himself to accept it, it would blight his future as well as my own. Better to become known as an eccentric spinster who preferred to dwell in the wilds near a Crossing—its proximity explaining any oddities that transpired about me—than to be branded as fae-touched and locked away forever, condemning those I cared about in the process.

Only the fate would be a lonely one.

"Jessa, are you attending?" Ainslie pitched her voice loud enough to break through my reverie.

"I'm sorry, I was just . . . considering the situation."

"What if Aunt Melisina is right?" Ada's delicate features drew tight. "What if it *is* my responsibility to accept him, for all our sakes? It would please Father and our aunts, and if I wed well, whoever I married would surely make provision for both of you, should the situation require—"

"I cannot think Lord Bradford cares for anything beyond his own desires." Ainslie sprang from the bed and paced the room. "And the idea of you wed to someone of his disposition is unthinkable."

"I agree." I leaned over to squeeze Ada's hand. She needed someone kind and principled, not an unfeeling man bent on satisfying only his own desires. He'd crush her, and then move on to his next conquest, while she remained bound to him.

"Then we cannot allow this to continue," Ainslie said. "Ada *does* wish to wed, and as long as Lord Bradford hangs about, he'll discourage all others."

"You said you've made your disinterest plainly known?" If only I'd forced myself to attend more events with my sisters, I might have a better understanding of the situation.

"I haven't been rude, but I've made it clear I don't desire his attentions." She smoothed the fabric of her gown, clearly ill at ease. "He pays no heed. I rather think he . . . relishes the prospect of forcing my hand."

Jade rumbled low, her thrum of anger matching my own. "Then we must find a way to force his instead."

"Precisely what I think!" Ainslie said.

If Lord Bradford intended to be difficult, then we must shift the perspective of our family instead. "If Father and our aunts can be shown why Lord Bradford is unsuitable, then surely they'd abandon the idea of a match. From what you've said of his proclivities, he must have some secrets."

"And you propose we dig them up?" Ainslie's eyes sparkled.

"Ordinarily, I wouldn't—and I don't suggest we spread them about—but if we find some evidence to show he's lacking in character, then Aunt Melisina will withdraw her support."

"You're right. However difficult she may be, she wants our best." A soft smile restored some of the missing brightness to Ada's countenance. "And whatever fears of the future Aunt Melisina instilled, Father would never press a man of dubious character on me."

"If by chance that doesn't work, Lovell and I could always write a scandal-mongering article about him," Ainslie said.

"You'll do no such thing." Ada gave her a stern look. "We mustn't be unjust."

Ainslie dimpled. "I'm only jesting."

Yet her jest provided the opportunity I'd sought since

learning her secret from Lovell. "Does anyone aside from Ada and me know the two of you are P. Smith?"

She sobered. "No, and I must swear you to secrecy. If anyone found out . . ."

They'd face a great deal of censure. Society viewed news reporters as common, even vulgar, given the unsavory places they must go and low topics they must discuss. Of course, a lady shouldn't even consider such things, let alone speak or write about them—and particularly, she should not speak or write the sort of political commentary I'd noted P. Smith favored. But a gentleman reporter would receive his share of condemnation as well, for engaging in an occupation beneath his dignity. If Lovell were exposed, he might not face the same degree of judgment as Ainslie, but he'd still endure repercussions.

"I won't tell anyone, but I've wondered—what made you and Lovell pursue reporting?"

"It was a way to . . . speak about what I found interesting." Ainslie lifted her slim shoulders. "I'm not like you, Jessa. I enjoy society, and I've no wish to be cut off from it, only to expand my horizons a bit. It seemed to offer an opportunity for both."

That meant the occasional comment she'd made on matters of state represented wider interests than I'd known she possessed. How many other things did I remain blind to within my own household? "What of Lovell, then?"

"He sought purpose, but refused to discuss his reasons. It's my opinion that he experienced some sort of heartbreak and needed distraction. I noticed when we first came to Avons— when you and Aunt Caris still remained at Caldwell House, Jessa —that he wasn't quite himself."

Ada shifted, drawing her legs onto the bed and leaning against the frame. "I thought so too, but he insisted all was well when I asked."

"He fed me the same story, but I determined that I'd find out what troubled him, whether he wished to speak of it or not. He confessed very little, only that he was determined to make a change. He said he wearied of being a gentleman of leisure, but he didn't have a desire for the tedium of estate management—which his father is still perfectly capable of handling." Ainslie extended a hand to Jade, who pointedly ignored the overture, as she had all others. "One thing led to another, and, well, I proposed P. Smith. Editors would never work with a lady in such a role, so Lovell provided the masculine front when needed. Not to mention he's quite a skilled writer."

His correspondence had always been engaging, so I could believe it.

Ainslie shrugged and withdrew her hand. "I find it quite easy to gather facts and make connections when attending events. People will talk a great deal around a young lady whom they believe understands little. We thought perhaps our articles could bring about change, in time."

She felt deeply about this. How long had she kept her passion for news and politics and shaping the world around her hidden? I could certainly understand why she'd felt she must conceal her socially unacceptable pursuits. A sudden chill prickled my arms. What if she hadn't been able to fully conceal it from an interested party? What if the fae who'd forced her into a bargain sought to use whatever knowledge she'd collected?

The sleeve of her dressing gown concealed the binding mark, but it wouldn't vanish until she fulfilled whatever she'd sworn under glamour. What had she promised? Might it be some sort of ongoing exchange? I rubbed my pebbled skin. I'd no reason to think so, and I must keep my fears in check.

Ada patted her arm. "You know we support you—we always will."

"*I* know that, but does Jessa?"

"Do I what?"

"Know that we would support whatever endeavors *you* undertake."

The two of them regarded me. Whatever their differences in personality, a near-perfect accord and understanding that transcended the spoken word had always existed between them, perhaps by virtue of their nature as twins. And it seemed they'd entered harmony of purpose in their intent to question me.

"You've always encouraged my interests, even when our aunts feared they'd mark me a bluestocking." I spoke slowly. Would the evasion satisfy them? "I have no reason to believe that's changed."

"And yet, you're holding something back." Ainslie closed the distance between us, as though she could draw the answers from me by force of will alone. "We don't believe that you actually left Avons on a botanical expedition when Lovell received the mark. You may care about your plants, but not to the exclusion of all else—you'd never have sought a pleasure excursion with him in danger. So what were you about?"

Jade's ears pricked, and Asrina fluttered up to her post at my shoulder. I tucked my hands together to still them, to conceal the sudden unsteadiness of my limbs. Ainslie's secret might generate scandal, but mine would force them to turn me over to the Vigil—or face the consequences. It was my burden to manage, not their danger to risk.

"Well?"

I struggled to find words. What might I offer to satisfy them?

"Ainslie, we should respect Jessa's wishes." When Ada turned toward me, my breath caught. In her gentle gaze, I caught a hint of the way Mother used to regard me. "But I hope you know you can trust us."

"Of course I do. And you're right." A deep ache hollowed my chest. If I continued to deny everything, they'd watch over me with greater care. I must tell them enough to ease their minds, while still keeping them safe. "I didn't go on a botanical expedition. It was all so much—Ibbie, the inheritance, the killer, then Lovell being marked. I wanted to find a way to help, and I found some . . . information in Wyncourt. The authorities refused to consider it, so I thought perhaps I could find further evidence on the killer—it's why I left Avons."

Ada gave a soft gasp. "Oh, Jessa, that was a tremendous risk. If somehow you'd encountered him—it's a mercy the authorities found him first."

"I was certainly relieved when I heard the report. And now that's behind us—"

"But something still troubles you?" Somehow Ada's gentleness was harder to resist than Ainslie's demands. "We can help, you know."

I sighed. Perhaps asking for a bit of assistance would provide them the peace of mind required to drop the matter. "As it turns out, there are unresolved matters related to Ibbie's estate. I need to return to the Antiquary Society this morning to resolve them, but I'm uncertain how Aunt Caris will receive the request after yesterday."

"Then we shall sway her." Ainslie offered a warm smile. "Let's dress and go at once."

We separated to prepare, and I made short work of my morning toilette. The little I'd offered had satisfied them for now. But how long before the strengthening element of Other within couldn't be concealed?

BETWEEN THEM, Ada and Ainslie did indeed sway Aunt Caris in favor of my outing, her only stipulation that I use the family carriage and bring Lianne, whom they'd assured they could do without for the day. One obstacle had been removed, yet countless others remained.

If my errand went exceedingly well, I might gain enough insight on what power rested within Kilmere to attempt to bargain with Lord West. If it did not . . .

No, I refused to consider it.

When we halted in front of the Tresforth Building, Jade twitched her tail, as though she prepared for imminent conflict.

I turned to Lianne. "Why don't you wait in the carriage?"

She tilted her head, her brown-black eyes pools of doubt. "I don't know if your aunt would be best pleased."

"I'm meeting Mrs. Darrington, and she'll serve as chaperone while I remain within." I rummaged in my portfolio and withdrew a book. "I brought this to occupy you while you wait, if you'd like it."

I offered her the newest Keswick novel, a shameless bribe. Novel reading was her not-so-secret indulgence, and if she'd only embrace the unexpected opportunity for leisure, I'd have the freedom to properly investigate.

"If you're sure she'll be there . . ."

"She's given her word to meet me."

"I'll not complain, then." A smile lilted across her face like a sunbeam across a poppy. "Thank you, Miss Jessa."

Most chaperones wouldn't be so readily dissuaded from their duties, though Dreda might prove an exception, if my aunts chose her. Regardless, I'd make the most of the opportunity before my aunts made their selection. With Jade and Asrina, I hastened up the stairs and into the Antiquary Society.

"Ah, Miss Caldwell." The ancient doorkeeper greeted me with a nod. Then he lifted a linen envelope and held it aloft. "I've a message for you, delivered with the morning post."

A message left here? Something sank within me—it could mean nothing good. "Thank you."

The brief note read:

Miss Caldwell,

> *I write on behalf of my employer, Mrs. Darrington. She took ill in the night and remains abed today. Her physician has ordered the strictest confinement, therefore she'll not be able to visit the Antiquary Society with you. Once she recov-*

ers, she will call on you, and she hopes to offer her assistance then.

She sends her deepest regrets.

Respectfully yours,
Miss Everby

The words blurred slightly beneath my gaze. "Does Mrs. Darrington employ a Miss Everby?"

"Yes, Miss Caldwell. She serves as secretary, and she's attended the society with Mrs. Darrington on occasion, though Mrs. Darrington's health doesn't permit her to come as often as she once did."

Then perhaps I refined too much upon a coincidence. I folded the letter. "Mrs. Darrington was to meet me here today. She'd assured me she could grant me access to the archives, yet it seems she's taken ill. Might I speak with your president?"

"I'm sorry, but he's been called away for a few days. If only you'll be patient, I'm certain he'll sort matters upon his return."

Jade's pupils slitted.

An unexpected trip and a sudden illness? Perhaps I saw nefarious forces at work where none existed, but I couldn't help but feel someone conspired against me. Either way, I'd certainly write to inquire after her health later. For now, I needed the information held within. "I'm afraid I cannot wait. It's of pressing importance that I examine the records left by Lady Dromley. If I cannot go within, I require my property returned to me at once."

He faltered. "I don't think that can be done, miss, not without permission."

"Then I must speak with someone who does know." It pained me to press him while he only sought to carry out his duties, yet what choice remained?

"We have some members present, but they have no authority—"

"Then someone with authority must be found." Fear of what might happen if I could not obtain leverage to stop Lord West instilled steel in my spine. I straightened. "If they're not turned over to me, I'm afraid I'll have to summon a friend of mine, Stratesman Burke. I'm certain he'd come at once, if he heard the society unlawfully retained possession of personal property."

"A stratesman, here?" He gave a rasping, half-strangled sort of cough. "The president would be most displeased if any sort of scandal were attached to the society."

"I don't think there's any need for stratesmen or scandal." I softened the words with a smile. "Surely there's someone who can grant permission for the release of my belongings?"

"I'll see what I can do, miss." He tottered to his feet.

Even if I could secure Ibbie's personal collection, the artifacts and records the society held would remain barred to me. Still, it would be a great deal more information than I possessed now, and—

The forceful beat of leather boots upon polished stone broke the hush of the society halls. A stick of a man marched down the corridor toward me, his mustache as fine and pale as old man's beard blossoms in full tuft—and his demeanor suggested he meant to cause as much irritation as its acrid sap. The door-keeper bobbed along behind him.

"Is this the young woman in question?" he barked.

"Yes, sir, but—"

He stalked toward me and jabbed his walking stick in my direction. "I don't know what you think you're about, but you don't belong here. I suggest you leave at once."

Unlike the doorkeeper, I didn't feel the slightest qualm about opposing this gentleman, since he appeared intent on intimidating me into submission. Unfortunately for him, he posed far less a threat than the fae. I lifted my chin and met his gaze—never mind the impropriety. "If you wish to make matters difficult, I'll be happy to oblige. I shall summon my solicitor to produce a copy of the will and request Stratesman

Burke oversee the transfer of all Lady Dromley's property at once."

"You certainly shall not." He sputtered, and Jade gave a quiet chuff, as though amused. At least someone found this entertaining. His gaze lowered to her. "And you will remove that creature at once."

"I'll be happy to take her and go as soon as my property is restored. Of course, if you wish the records to remain here, you have only to grant me access to the archive so I can study them in place. One of your members, Mrs. Darrington, intended to accompany me today, only she was taken ill—"

"I hardly intend to add one irregularity to another. You must wait until our president returns."

"As I've told your doorkeeper, this business cannot wait."

His frown deepened into a glower. "I'll warn you: if you insist upon pressing the matter, the society will be inclined to look unfavorably upon any future requests."

I studied him. What mattered to him? I knew little of his desires, aside from the fact he belonged to the society. If he was like other members, he'd care about its aims. And he'd be more likely to withdraw if I presented him a favorable out, one he could appear to consider and accept with the grace of a gentleman. I softened my tone. "I do hope that's not true, since I'd much prefer to share with the society anything I discover at Kilmere, in honor of Lady Dromley. I know how much the society meant to her. Perhaps a special display would be in order?"

"You intend to excavate at Kilmere?" He stroked his mustache.

"It's under consideration, which is why I require further information. I can make no promises yet, you understand." I leaned forward. "But the society does stand to gain if excavation moves forward."

"That does change things. Rightly the president should agree, but as he's gone, I will take responsibility."

"How very kind of you." I summoned a smile.

"I can't grant admittance, but I'll send for the records." He spoke with the air of one offering a grand concession. "If you call once more when our president has returned, he'll consider the case for your admittance."

Though the encounter had left my emotions as tangled as aspen roots, I murmured thanks. No sense making additional enemies—I possessed enough already.

Not long after, several servants emerged from the depths of the building with leather-bound cases, which they deposited into our carriage.

Once sequestered within, I leaned back and released a sigh. Blessedly, Lianne remained silent, immersed in the world within the pages she held.

I longed for nothing more than a quiet haven in which to examine the boxes, for silence and peace, for . . . Wyncourt? The seed of an idea took immediate root. Where better to examine the records Ibbie had left than the study in which she'd conducted much of her research? If I could not have her, I could at least take shelter where we'd shared so many pleasant moments before her passing. And it was past time I checked in with the servants to make sure nothing else odd had transpired after Riven departed.

I requested our driver take us to Wyncourt, and as we rattled down the street, Jade sniffed curiously at the boxes. Her eyes narrowed to gleaming slits.

What did she sense inside?

CHAPTER 6

When Ibbie had still lived, I'd often experienced a slightly out-of-kilter feeling when I regarded Wyncourt, a sensation which I now attributed to its nature as a fae demesne in the mortal world. This time, as I crossed the threshold, a gentle warmth rose up to surround me, almost like an embrace, and the tension coiled inside unwound.

Danvers offered a warm welcome and ordered a footman to assist us with bringing in the boxes.

While I waited, I wondered. What did the change mean? Did it have anything to do with my choice to relinquish the cage of thorns which I'd used to hold captive any sensation of Other? Had Wyncourt always felt this way, and I'd just been unable to sense it? Or had it embraced me as I'd embraced Other?

If Riven were here . . .

I shook my head. I needed to stop thinking of him—he was fae, and no true partnership had ever developed between fae and mortals. Yet he *had* left Asrina so that I could contact him, if there was a need.

But what constituted a need? Lord West had done nothing besides what all fae sought to do—take what they pleased from mortals. Riven had no reason to involve himself, and every reason not to take the part of a mortal above his own kind. I couldn't afford to grow distracted, wishing otherwise.

Mrs. Peters joined us in the entry. She still wore the unrelieved black of mourning, not a requirement for her position, but a token of her deep feeling for Ibbie. "Will you take tea, Miss Caldwell?"

"In the study, thank you. The boxes can go there also." I moved across the polished marble floor, my imagination conjuring an image of Ibbie bustling to greet me, describing a new antiquity that had arrived and the sketches she wished made. My surroundings blurred.

Jade nudged my ankles, and I lifted her into my arms, holding her close.

In short order, the footman delivered the boxes and Mrs. Peters fetched tea. Then she ushered Lianne belowstairs, where they might take refreshments together, as proper.

Even now, the faintest hint of Ibbie's damask-rose fragrance lingered in the air, and it strengthened my resolve. I would honor her in this and protect Kilmere from the fae, as she'd sought to do with Wyncourt.

I reached for the first box, then hesitated. Now that Riven was gone, who would protect the servants from the Other nature of Wyncourt? With the ghouls removed, did they even need protection? Ibbie had attempted to maintain some sort of ward by scripting runes on the walls at regular intervals, which suggested a need for some sort of barrier to keep its Other nature from influencing the mortal inhabitants of the house.

Before I left I'd have to ask Danvers and Mrs. Peters if they'd had any more trouble, but for now, I needed to examine the evidence at hand. I removed my gloves, setting them on Ibbie's desk, and opened the first box. Then an ominous creak issued from the fireplace. I froze.

Were Wyncourt an ordinary house, I'd suspect the sound was due to wind gusting down the chimney. Yet the plants in the garden beyond the sash windows remained still, untouched by the slightest breeze—and this was no natural manor.

Riven had removed the ghouls, yet we'd had no time to explore further. Could some other sinister creature lurk in the depths? Uneasy, I surveyed the room and found nothing out of place.

So I bent back over the records. And a creak issued from the hearth, followed by a sort of gusting sigh. I whirled round. No fire blazed within the hearth, not even a bed of embers, so no change in temperatures caused the sounds. What then?

Jade padded over to the fireplace, her ears pricked forward. Yet the fur on her ruff remained smooth. Did that mean there was no threat?

If some Otherkind intended to emerge from its place of concealment, I was better equipped to deal with it than the servants—but that wasn't saying much.

I marched over to the hearth and snatched up the iron poker. It was the best defense the room offered against Otherkind, but the chill of it crept up my arm into my shoulder, a sharp, searing sensation. My grip faltered, and it clattered to the ground.

Blight and rot.

I didn't want to consider what that meant.

My senses swirling, I returned to the desk to fetch a letter opener crafted of silver, its sharp point held at the ready. The stylized dragon on the haft dug into my skin as I strode back to the fireplace and peered up the chimney.

Nothing.

No pricking sensation of Other, at least no more than Wyncourt itself ordinarily held. No sign of a passing prism or fae lurker or even a household nisi. Nothing except a slight warming to the air.

Had Wyncourt merely sought to attract my attention? And if so, why?

Jade stalked past me, then nosed about the bricks of the

hearth. At last she stretched up to her full length, her head reaching the top of the mantel.

Her gaze fixed on the intricate carving of a serpentine form —a wyvern, perhaps, or some other dragonish sort of Otherkind. I switched the letter opener to my left hand and touched the beast. Other than the air warming further, nothing changed.

I drew back, considering.

The workings woven into Wyncourt gave it some degree of awareness, perhaps even sentience, though I was unclear precisely how fae demesnes worked and even less clear on how one might operate when constructed in the mortal world. Riven had indicated that the force of Other might strain mortal materials and that the construction of a half-fae, half-mortal demesne could have unknown implications. Might it seek to communicate with me?

And if so, to what end? I'd uncovered multiple hidden spaces within the manor already, so perhaps another existed. Could Ibbie or Edward have hidden something here?

Since the study was Ibbie's sanctuary, I considered her the more likely candidate. If she was responsible, it was a point in my favor, since I'd not have to manipulate a fae-working to gain access.

Given all Ibbie had faced, she'd ample reason to desire secrecy. She'd used a hidden compartment in her bedchamber secretary to sequester away her diaries, so why not a concealed space in her study to hide sensitive information?

Surely Wyncourt wouldn't have drawn my attention here for no reason. If this hiding place followed mortal conventions, then it would use some sort of concealed lock mechanism, likely accessed by a pattern of pressing or shifting the mantel carvings.

Yet after a quarter hour of attempting various sequences, I'd accomplished nothing. The intricacies of the carvings meant hundreds of possible combinations, assuming I was even right and hadn't invented the whole scenario.

A slight gust of air puffed through the room, as though Wyncourt itself sighed.

Well.

I *was* trying to understand what it sought, however insufficient my abilities.

"I don't suppose you could lend assistance?" I touched the serpentine form again. A slight creak sounded. Then I tried a rose vine. Nothing.

Perhaps the sequence relied upon the individuals in the carving, rather than the scenery? I pressed upon the first figure—receiving a confirmatory creak—and then the second.

Nothing.

I skipped ahead to the third. The creak sounded again—I was making progress.

Bit by bit, Wyncourt and I worked out the sequence, and when I touched a figure near the bottom, the stonework shifted and a section of the mantel opened.

In a small niche in the stone, a thin stack of papers rested, bound by a golden cord. I fetched them out, and Ibbie's familiar script greeted me.

How did one address a fae demesne planted in the mortal world—one that had given a tremendous gift? I clutched the papers to my chest and stroked the mantel. "Thank you."

A little puff of air gusted from the chimney and swirled my skirts, warm and gentle. Then I retreated to the settee. Jade curled up beside me, while Asrina flickered at my shoulder.

Wisps of unease brushed the back of my neck, delicate as the branches of a willow. Did I want to uncover more secrets? I traced the cord with a finger, its nubbly edges rough to the touch. If Ibbie had concealed this, it wasn't something innocuous.

But I couldn't afford to remain in the dark. I tugged the cord and pulled it away, then surveyed the title page.

The Maiden and the Monster

A Faerie Tale

I inclined my head. What was this? Ibbie had written fiction? It didn't fit what I knew of her, but then, she'd kept much concealed.

I turned to the next page.

> *Once there was a girl named Isabel, whom some deemed a princess. She possessed a great deal that others valued—a fortune, a favored position in society, and even a castle, one left in ruins.*
>
> *One some claimed was cursed.*
>
> *She didn't mind the tales of the curse, only resented that she could not determine their veracity until she wed and the castle became properly her own.*
>
> *She believed many years might pass before she found a suitable partner, but soon a prince presented himself as a candidate for her hand. In little time, his charm enchanted her, and she fell in love.*
>
> *Only the prince turned out to be no prince at all, but a monster.*

As though strangle-root twined about it, my chest tightened, and my breathing shallowed. In her diary, Ibbie had referred to a compulsion that made it impossible for her to speak of what her husband had done—of what he'd forced her to do. Could this have been her way of circumventing the compulsion, by creating a faerie tale that communicated her truth? Would that have been sufficient to overcome the geas he'd placed upon her?

> *When they wed, he revealed his true nature. He lusted for power; he savored the infliction of pain. Though he'd already amassed strength beyond measure, he craved still more. And he believed he'd find it within the castle ruins.*
>
> *It suited him to use the princess's knowledge and her*

servants to study the castle and prize out its secrets—and however much she desired to do so, she soon found she could not resist. He had ways of forcing compliance and punishing every infraction.

The princess had always believed the wealth of the ruins rested in the secrets they might contain about the past. The monster believed otherwise—he sought antiquities of great power, supposedly hidden within.

In short order, he enthralled her servants also, binding them to his will.

This too pleased him, for the monster did not like to dirty his own hands. He existed not to serve, but to be served. And since the castle ruin rejected him, he must rely on them to do his bidding within. They warned him of the dangers, yet he paid no heed. What were their lives to him?

Since they were bound, no choice remained. They delved further than safe, despite the warnings of the curse, despite the evils within. No matter how they feared, they must continue to search, for he compelled them.

They found magnificent objects to delight his heart, though nothing could satisfy his insatiable desires.

Then the princess sought a way to keep from him what he desired most.

Bindings leave little room for infraction. Yet she found the tiniest of loopholes, whereby she might keep concealed the heart of the ruin, might ensure it remained intact. Perhaps it contained what he sought. Perhaps it did not. It was a small act of vengeance, one that carried a greater cost than she anticipated.

For eventually he believed the ruin spent and the servants of no further use. He left the princess no choice. She must betray her servants. Must lock them within the ruins, abandon them to death. For them, there would be no escape.

Nor was there for her. Ever after, their fate haunted her by day and by night.

A tear dripped from my cheek and onto the page. I swiped at it before it could wash out the ink and forced myself to continue.

The monster was pleased. He'd mined from the depths all he sought. And from the princess, he'd taken everything that mattered.

He'd received his happy ending, while the princess was left with only ruin and darkness and pain—and one small burning ember of hope, that of future justice.

The End

Oh, Ibbie. The strangle-root sensation strengthened, as though its powerful coils wove about me, constricting to the point of pain. How had Ibbie endured? How had she kept this locked inside all these years?

If I'd known what she'd suffered, I . . . In truth, I could have done nothing, except offer sympathy and a listening ear. For her husband was long dead and gone.

Was his death justice enough for all he'd done? For all he'd forced Ibbie to do? It didn't feel like it. Not when he'd deliberately inflicted suffering upon the helpless mortals in his path . . .

And who were the servants in the tale? The team Ibbie sent to excavate the ruins, perhaps? The ones Mrs. Darrington said all died.

To consider Ibbie betraying them stung. But was it truly betrayal when she could do nothing else? When fae power snared her in a compulsion impossible to resist? It was *wrong* that Otherkind could force mortals to carry out their will, that one mistake, one bargain, could cause so much suffering and destruction.

I sprang up and walked to the window, thrusting open the sash. The gentle fragrances of morning-rose and lavender swirled into the room, and a strand of the ivy in the pot nearest the door swayed toward me, brushing my hand and imparting its ever-green strength.

I couldn't do anything about Edward Dromley and whatever he'd done to Ibbie in the past, but I could stand against Lord West and prevent him from claiming whatever he sought within Kilmere.

If Ibbie had managed to conceal whatever she referred to as its heart by some unknown means, then did more objects of power remain hidden within? Presumably Lord West had heard rumor of their existence and now sought to claim them. Why else would he desire a mortal ruin?

I absently stroked the ivy, its resolve matching my own. Just as it delved into rock with its delicate rootlets, over time defeating even stone, so perhaps could mortals stand against fae . . . if they found the right path and used the right tools.

But what of the curse? Had the tales arisen due to whatever was concealed within the ruins? If I understood the narrative correctly, Ibbie had caused the deaths of her team at the bidding of her husband. If true, that meant they'd not fallen victim to some curse of old as Thea had speculated.

Either way, Ibbie had felt responsible. In her final journal entry, she'd written: *I would rather go to my grave than live with more deaths on my conscience.*

I'd thought she simply feared bringing others to the attention of the Crimson Tattoo Killer, but it seemed she'd meant far more. What precisely had she done to them? She'd spoken of abandoning the servants to the ruin, as though Kilmere itself brought about their deaths. Might there be some fae-working or alchemical object of power within Kilmere that had become known as the curse? That would fit with her reference to the *evils within.*

If so, what did that mean about the two recent deaths? It stretched the bounds of credulity that their fates had nothing to do with all of this. I didn't believe the victims had succumbed to a mortal poisoner, but to something Other—whether some power associated with Kilmere or the actions of Lord West or another interested fae.

While I didn't want to consider that Kilmere had caught the attention of additional Otherkind, the possibility couldn't be eliminated, not yet.

The mantel clock chimed, jolting me from my reverie. I shut the sash window and returned to the sheaf of papers to copy the tale within my sketchbook. Then I returned the bundle back to its hiding place. With Lord West skulking about, I didn't want to chance them falling into his hands.

As I turned away, the whole of Wyncourt seemed to shudder, the air charged with hostility.

My breath caught, and I pressed up against the wall.

Jade roused from slumber, the fur on her scruff standing on end. Her eyes glowed like embers, and a low growl sounded deep in her chest.

Had I angered Wyncourt?

I touched the wall behind me, and it warmed in response. The immensity of Wyncourt impressed itself upon my mind, all the workings woven within it awake and alive, bristling against some outside force, some *intruder*.

The word brushed at the edge of my mind. Pressure built in the air, and my ears popped. Then it ebbed, along with the tightness in my chest. A watchful, discomfiting sensation remained. I waited, one minute stretching into two, then three.

When no further assault came, I pulled away from the wall. What might have triggered such an alarm? Would it have vanished if a threat remained? I moved toward the door, straining for any out-of-the-ordinary sounds beyond, yet I caught nothing. Perhaps Wyncourt had sensed some Other presence nearby—a disturbing possibility, but one that meant I was most safe remaining within these walls.

After a few more quiet moments, I abandoned my post at the door. Though a nagging sense of unrest tugged at me, I must try to attend to the records before I lost my opportunity to examine them. I settled myself at the desk, then opened the first box and pulled out its contents.

Ibbie had been as meticulous with her research and antiquities as she was untidy with her other belongings, so it was no surprise to find the documents within the first case well-ordered. What I found first was no ancient record, but recent correspondence from Mr. Tibbons on the matter of the curse.

I read through the letters he'd sent Ibbie, in which he chronicled various events he'd heard attributed to the curse over the years.

Mysterious illnesses.

Crop failures.

Disappearances.

But mostly strange, terrible deaths.

Ibbie had made a note that the accounting of the curse occurred predominantly in oral lore, and very few written records referenced it. She mentioned sending Mr. Tibbons to one Sir Alfred, rumored to possess documents on the matter.

Oh.

This was the failed expedition of which Mr. Tibbons had written to Ibbie, the letter that had arrived after her death and therefore came into my keeping instead. Only why would she have assigned Mr. Tibbons to investigate the curse when she'd already partially excavated Kilmere? Surely she must have had some knowledge about what it concealed. Had she considered reopening her excavation in search of secrets hidden within its heart? Or had she merely sought to understand what she'd encountered all those years ago?

I leaned back into the chair, yearning for Ibbie. If only I could ask her . . .

Yet I'd no time for *what-ifs*, only forward progress. I paged through a few of her notes, which indicated the legend of the curse dated back as far as the founding of Kilmere.

Hmm.

Perhaps I'd better start there. While Jade prowled about the windows, as though keeping watch, I sorted through the three small boxes, assembling a timeline of sorts.

Asrina fluttered to the edge of the desk, casting her golden glow over the papers as I assembled a sort of chronology. Then I moved to the beginning and began to read.

According to Ibbie's research, Kilmere had been constructed by a family who'd lived in the region for time out of mind. The purpose of the construction wasn't particularly clear, given they already possessed an ancestral home nearby, adjacent to the town now known as Withern-at-Sea. While ordinarily a seaside fortress might have protected against invaders, no record existed of conflict at the time it was built—wait.

Might its construction relate to the Forgotten War? I'd previously found references to the war and the so-called Dark Era in three obscure locations—a book on the history of the Vigil, old letters procured by Ibbie for Lord Blackburn, and an ancient logbook in the keeping of the Brothers of Fidelity. None of the references had dates attached, so I could only guess by their apparent age, but certainly both Kilmere and the Dark Era belonged to our far-distant past.

Ibbie had believed Kilmere held secrets about the interactions between our two worlds. Could it have been created in response to fears of a possible fae invasion? No Crossings existed near Kilmere, but perhaps then they'd understood what had fallen out of common knowledge in our day, that some fae could create passings wherever they pleased. They didn't require fixed Crossings to move between worlds, not like mortals. Unless there was some fear of danger, the construction of a fortress in a time of peace appeared peculiar. Was the Forgotten War the link? I set down the page I held. "Or perhaps I seek connections where none exist."

Jade's ears pricked, and she regarded me with her steady green gaze.

"Yes, I'm aware that talking to myself is a less than desirable trait, but surely I may address you and Asrina?" If only they could respond and lend their insight. I picked up another paper. "If the ruins have no connection to the Dark Era, then what did Ibbie find within that made her believe Kilmere could give insight on relations between fae and mortals?"

For now, I could only speculate. I tucked aside my theories for later consideration and returned my attention to the information before me. According to Ibbie's notes, lore held that the lord had built the fortress at the request of his wife. Perhaps the fears were hers.

Whatever the case, she'd died while the foundations of Kilmere were being laid—some said she'd passed away while on site, the cause unknown. I shoved a curl out of my face. Perhaps from that tragedy, the legend of the curse had sprung?

I desired more details; however, it was remarkable that Ibbie had collected as much as she had, since written records from this time were relatively sparse.

Ibbie had noted that the brokenhearted lord sold the site, and the individual responsible for completing construction remained unknown, along with any record of its ownership. The next clear record indicated that it had fallen into the hands of the crown, as its previous holder had died without leaving an heir.

Yet by this time legends of the curse ran strong, and no one wished to purchase it, so it sat falling into ruin for generations.

Ibbie had recorded a snippet from a journal with an account from this time.

One of our party, Sir Yarbrough, ventured into the ruins of Kilmere, being much curious about its lore. He did not return for a full day and night, and when he did, he'd a peculiar air about him. He did not seem to realize how much time had passed. The morning next, he fell ill.

Such pain came upon him that he could not walk. And his speech made no sense, mumblings and mutterings impos-

sible to understand. We summoned a doctor to the inn, and he concluded that Yarbrough must have encountered some toxin, mayhap a miasma of air or water within the ruin or that he'd eaten the fruits of some poisonous plant.

The doctor believed it would pass. Yet Yarbrough grew worse, such pain as I've never seen, along with swellings of his abdomen and discoloring of his skin. And then he began to cough blood.

Not a day after the blood appeared, he passed, the death a mercy compared to his fortnight of agony. Whatever the doctor might say, the locals believe he fell to the curse of the ruins. They blame him for his folly of venturing therein and look on us with suspicion, as if we would follow his footsteps, when in truth we cannot depart the region quickly enough.

Though the writer described a grim fate, the account intrigued me, for the physician had counted this Yarbrough as a victim of poison, at least at first.

I moved to the next document, which indicated that some years before Ibbie had developed an interest in the ruins, a well-known antiquarian became fascinated by its lore.

Yet after he purchased the site, he fell gravely ill and could conduct no further study. His writings on Kilmere and his collection of research, done prior to purchasing the ruin, had sparked a passion in Ibbie. And eventually, Ibbie's father had bought it from his estate, which in turn set her life on a course she could not have imagined. "If she'd known, would she have chosen differently?" I murmured.

Jade gave a soft *mrow*, as if in reply.

How I wished I could ask Ibbie about all of this. My neck protested my bent posture, and I tilted my head upward to relieve the tired muscles, my gaze catching the clock.

It was well into the afternoon now, and though I'd looked over every document, I'd come no closer to an answer of how to stop Lord West, though I'd gained insight on why he desired it —and why he must not have it. With the knowledge of the destructive power within Kilmere, I couldn't justify any bargain that would hand part of it to him. He'd only use it to make mortals suffer.

I collected the papers and returned them to their boxes. Perhaps I should leave them at Wyncourt, where I might be assured they'd have protection. I tucked them into the space beneath the desk, where they seemed to fade into the shadows, ready to be forgotten.

As the Dark Era of our own history had been. How did it all fit together? I needed more connecting pieces to construct this puzzle. Lord Blackburn had an interest in the conflict between our world and the Other, and he possessed relics from that era. Might he hold more information? Certainly, he had the wealth to collect other documents of the sort he'd commissioned Ibbie to procure, and perhaps he'd done so. Though Riven and I had called upon Lord Blackburn in less-than-favorable circum-stances, suspecting him of connection with the Crimson Tattoo murders, we'd parted on good terms. If I shared some of what I'd discovered, perhaps he'd divulge what he'd learned.

I withdrew stationery from the top drawer, and using the remnants of ink in the bottle atop the desk, I jotted a message to him, telling him I'd found information related to the letters Ibbie had procured for him. If he was interested, might he call at his convenience?

Seeking Danvers, I emerged from the study. When I handed the letter to him, he assured me he'd see to its delivery and sent for Lianne, who emerged from belowstairs, her novel tucked under one arm.

With Jade and Asrina at my side and Lianne trailing behind, we stepped out of doors. A fierce shock of Other blazed across my skin, raising the hairs along the back of my neck. Abruptly, I halted, and Lianne nearly crashed into me as I sought the source.

Lord West.

He'd not waited. Instead, he stood across the street, his arms crossed over his chest. Power coiled about him in dark tendrils, scarcely concealed by glamour. A chill crept into the air between us, and a bitter, metallic tang filled my mouth. Had his presence caused the upheaval in Wyncourt I'd sensed earlier? Had he sought to force his way in?

Teeth bared, Jade snarled softly.

His demeanor remained that of a gentleman, his face cold and impassive, yet something seethed beneath the surface, a force emanating from him to fill the air between us. Implacable as stone, it pressed against my chest.

At my back, Wyncourt snapped to life, a rushing murmur like wind channeling through the corridor behind. The door-frame sparked beneath my fingers, and I stepped back toward the shelter it promised—not soon enough.

A shadow shot from Lord West and hit Asrina, rapid as a serpent's strike.

She plummeted down onto my shoulder, clutching at the collar of my gown. What had he done to her? I staggered back through the doorway, and Wyncourt engulfed me.

Her light pulsed unsteady, as ragged as the beating of my own heart. Distantly, I was aware of Lianne speaking as I surveyed Asrina. Like a warped form of lacework, dark lines spread across her gleaming wings, then faded. She clung to the muslin at my shoulder, her form quivering. I wanted to examine her more closely, but I couldn't, not with an audience.

I lifted my gaze to Lord West. He tipped his head to me, and a small smile played about his mouth as he regarded Asrina.

Why had he struck her? What could he possibly gain from it, unless it was the perverse pleasure of the strong inflicting its will upon the weak?

Jade prowled about my ankles, then seized upon my skirt, tugging me deeper into the entry. I motioned for the bewildered Danvers to shut the door, and he blotted Lord West from view.

But he wouldn't give up. How was I to return home?

CHAPTER 7

When I turned from the closed door, Danvers hovered only a few paces behind me. "Is something wrong, Miss Caldwell?"

"It's only—I wish to avoid the gentleman across the street. He was working with Mr. Broward to attempt to claim the inheritance Ibbie left me. Now he intends to force me to sell, if he can manage it."

"Well." Danvers drew himself up to an impressive height. "If you'll allow me, I shall send him on his way."

"Thank you, Danvers. You're most valiant. But I don't wish to antagonize him further, simply avoid him." I offered an attempt at a reassuring smile as Jade twined between my ankles. Wyncourt offered the best shelter within Avons, yet I could not remain forever. "Perhaps I'll continue working in the study until he wearies of waiting. Lianne, you may take your leisure as you choose."

A smile lilted across her face. "That I will, miss."

I slipped back into the study and returned to the settee, where I gently lifted Asrina from my shoulders, cradling her tiny form in my hands. I'd never attempted to hold her before, never believed she'd permit it. Her glow steadied, yet her light held umber tones, and she shivered. Was she in pain?

Danvers opened the door, and I nearly dropped her. I forced myself to lower my hands to my lap, as though I did not cup a precious form within. I must appear ordinary, somehow—as though a cruel fae lord did not lurk just out of doors nor an injured sun sylph shelter within my embrace.

"Forgive the intrusion, Miss Caldwell."

"It's no trouble." At least, it wasn't as long as Asrina's glamour held.

"That gentleman—he wished to purchase Wyncourt?"

"No, he was interested in the ruins of Kilmere."

"Ah, I see." He turned to go.

"Why do you ask?"

"Our kitchen maid believed someone tried to gain access to Wyncourt last night. I'd wondered if perhaps this lord had sent someone to try something underhanded, and if so, I thought you should know about it. But if he's not interested in Wyncourt, that seems unlikely. And she's prone to fancies, as I've said before."

Only I knew they were no fancies, and who was to say Lord West hadn't decided he'd like to acquire the demesne also? I straightened the embroidered pillow alongside me. "Have you noticed anything else amiss within Wyncourt of late?"

"Nothing more than reports of odd noises on occasion, but I rather think it's more due to overfertile imaginations than anything else."

"I see. Thank you." After he left, I reached out and skimmed my fingers across the wall closest to me. "You'll bear in mind that they're mortal, won't you? And keep from them that which might harm them?"

The softest of sounds, almost like a low hum, thrummed through the air. I'd take that as agreement—for I possessed no other means by which to protect those who inhabited Wyncourt.

I glanced down at Asrina. I'd thought all Otherkind looked

down on mortals, yet she'd seemed to welcome contact. I gently smoothed her gauzy skirts, which held the warmth of a summer day, and she nestled into my own.

Though possessed of innate power, she was nearly as vulnerable to Lord West as I was. The water sprites in Milburn had feared high fae, and now I understood why. He'd had no loyalty to her as a fellow being of the Otherworld; he'd struck her without regard.

Why? And why now?

Something had changed. Had Lord West discovered I'd deceived him about Father's absence? Regardless, the fact he'd sought me at Wyncourt suggested he'd lost patience—or perhaps it was only that he wished to toy with me, to strike at those I loved bit by bit until I was forced to surrender. In any case, I doubted he'd accept further stalling tactics.

But if I openly refused to sell, it would reveal beyond doubt that his glamour could not influence me. And if thwarted, he could kill my family, Jade, me, as easily as he'd struck down Asrina. The knowledge seared my soul. There *must* be a way to stop him, yet I'd run out of time to find it.

What would he do next?

Though I'd now encountered several high fae, I'd no idea the true scope of their powers nor precisely what display of dominance was most likely. Our lore gave them all sorts of abilities, ranging from peculiar ones like the manipulation of dreams or snatching breath, to ones I now knew to be true—the capacity to bend elements such as light and shadow to their will, to wield crushing glamours, to bind and enslave mortals.

Jade perched beside me, and I absently stroked her fur. What else did I know as fact? When he'd wanted to stay in Wyncourt, Riven had bargained. He might have kinder sentiments toward mortals than most fae, but Mocvar certainly did not, and he had also been forced to bargain with me. Which meant what?

That Mr. Heard was right and some sort of rules governed the interactions between fae and mortals, some precepts that offered us a measure of protection—albeit one fading fast? What I'd witnessed appeared to confirm it, else why hadn't Lord West simply killed me and taken Kilmere from the beginning? Why bother to bargain? Unless it was for entertainment.

Tension knotted my shoulders and sent a dull pain through the base of my neck. Could I gamble my life and those I loved on such speculation?

I glanced at Asrina, her wings still, her small form tucked into a ball on my lap.

No.

I didn't know enough, and Lord West had already lashed out at her. If we'd not been tucked into the shelter of Wyncourt, might he have wielded his power directly against me—or the servants? I might choose to risk my own life, but to endanger others without their knowledge? It was untenable.

Yet I couldn't give him Kilmere. So what choice remained? Only to seek Riven.

He might not come. And even if he did, he might tell me to surrender Kilmere to Lord West, and then I'd be worse off than before—for I could not accept such counsel, and I'd have angered not only one but two high fae. Still, with Lord West even now lurking outside, I must take the risk.

At least I had greater justification now that Lord West had harmed Asrina. She served Riven; surely he'd want to see her well.

I shifted back, taking care not to jostle her. "Lovely sylph, I believe we must request Lord Riven's aid."

Her glow dimmed further, but she pushed herself upright.

"Will you ask him to come?"

Her light flickered in a ragged pattern, like the cadence of speech. Clearly, she tried to communicate, but I was no closer to understanding than before. I'd never heard the slightest vocalization from her. Perhaps sun sylphs had no voice and must communicate with patterns of light?

Though an interesting prospect, it wasn't helpful since I'd no means of interpretation.

Whatever her own capacity for communication, she'd no trouble understanding that of others. She'd responded to my voice before—and to Riven's spoken instruction.

Jade leapt upon Ibbie's desk and gave a loud *mrow*. Then she nudged the inkwell and looked at me expectantly.

Hmm.

Perhaps it would work. If Asrina could understand me, then I only needed a way to comprehend her response in return. Before I could overanalyze, I gently deposited her on the desk and snatched up paper and ink.

I wrote *yes* in large block letters on one half of the page and *no* on the other. In case my assumption that she could read was incorrect, I informed her what each one said in turn. "Now, most lovely one, I'm going to ask you a few questions. You have only to shed your light upon the correct answer."

I could perhaps have asked her simply to nod or shake her head in response, but her fluttering movements and flickers of light came with such frequency that I could easily mistake a cue. This would offer greater accuracy.

And it appeared to please her, for she brightened a bit at the compliment, her preferred form of currency. I ventured the first question. "Will you fetch Riven?"

Her light fell upon *no*. I sank into the chair. If she refused, what path remained? "Are you able to contact him?"

No.

How badly had Lord West injured her? I swiped at a dried fleck of ink on the desk, wishing I could remove him from our lives so readily. "Is it because of what Lord West did to you?"

Yes.

What *had* he done? I turned the whole of my attention to her, opening my senses. As though a web of glamour had been whisked away, I could *see*. Her whole frame sprang into sharp relief, and as it did, I perceived strands of silver-black woven through her flame-like wings.

I swallowed hard. "Does it hurt?"

She cast light between the two words.

"A little?"

Yes.

"Does it prevent you from flying?"

Yes.

It was unclear to me which fae could create passings and which relied on Crossings or passing prisms, as Uros had done. "Do you require a Crossing to access the Otherworld?"

Yes.

If she must use a Crossing, that would explain why she could no longer reach Riven. For me to bring her to one would require extensive travel, an impossibility in our current predicament.

Blight and rot.

Perhaps Lord West had sensed her connection to Riven—or he'd merely made an educated guess that a sylph wouldn't follow a mortal unless ordered by another fae. While he'd even less reason to believe Riven would offer aid than I did, he certainly wouldn't want another of his kind to take interest in the ruin. Had he meant to ensure she could not carry any reports of his presence?

"My apologies, most magnificent of sylphs. I didn't know he'd try to hurt you."

No.

Hmm.

"Was he trying to hurt you?"

No.

What then? My stomach lurched with a sudden realization. "He was . . . trying to kill you?"

Yes.

I clasped my pendant, a protective talisman that couldn't keep us safe from high fae. Perhaps Wyncourt had offered shelter enough to prevent the working from causing her death. Still, she'd sustained an injury while watching over me.

She'd served as Riven bid her, and I'd never stopped to consider if she could have said no or if the sun sylphs must serve the high fae without question. Certainly, everything in the Otherworld followed a hierarchy of power. Had she any choice in the matter?

Either way, I'd brought her into Lord West's path . . . and now she suffered for it.

I extended my hand toward her, and she sank wearily into it. Something twisted in my chest. Though Other, she was vulnerable. And I'd give anything to keep her safe.

Jade chuffed, as if in approval.

A glorious warmth stirred within, and at once, the sounds of the plants within the gardens surged into my senses, a rich multilayered song, tinged with expectancy, almost as if they awaited . . . what?

Could I somehow offer her aid? I tilted my head to better inspect the working that blighted her wings. Though I could perceive its structure, I'd no notion how to unravel it, for it was woven into the very fabric of her wings.

Jade sniffed at Asrina, then her hackles rose slightly.

That wasn't promising.

Nevertheless, ever so gently, I touched her wings, willing the working to release, much as I'd willed the dread-aught to detach from Dreda.

But nothing changed.

Her lovely head drooped.

"Should I try something else? Perhaps some sort of salve?"

No.

What then? I sought a yes or no question. "Could I cause more damage, if I try to remove the working?"

Yes.

Her light pulsed rapidly, with darker tones. Perhaps she was as frustrated as I—or as afraid.

Would the working kill her in the end, if I could not remove it? Riven could tell me, but I had no way of reaching him. I shouldn't have allowed myself to think otherwise, to hope that another would intervene.

I struggled to my feet, Asrina cupped in my hand. I was on my own when it came to Lord West—and he held all the power.

~

AFTER AN HOUR PASSED, the prickling watchfulness of Wyncourt subsided. I waited a bit longer, then ventured slowly out of doors, Jade at my side, Asrina tucked up against my shoulder, firmly gripping the muslin of my collar, and Lianne trailing behind. This time, no sense of Other crept over me, and no trace of Lord West remained. Why would he leave?

He'd only withdraw if it gave him some advantage, some other way to hurt me.

My family.

The stinging lash of fear struck like a blow from a whip, and I stumbled in my rush to enter the carriage, where I urged our driver to hurry.

"Is everything well, Miss Jessa?" Lianne asked.

I murmured reassurance I did not feel. I folded my hands in my lap, clenching them so tightly that pinpricks of pain shot up my arms. If he'd sought them, while I'd sheltered in safety . . .

At last we halted before our row home. Forsaking propriety, I flung open the carriage door without awaiting assistance. As I ascended the stairs, I glanced over my shoulder, seeking Lord West. I couldn't find him, and yet . . . that pricking sense of Other crept up my spine and tingled along the back of my neck.

Holden opened the door.

"Do we have company?" I asked.

"Indeed, Miss Jessa. How did you know?"

Ignoring him, I hastened to the drawing room, where Lord West sat with my aunts and sisters, taking tea.

When I entered, his lips curled into a predatory smile. "Welcome home, Miss Jessa."

The words dripped satisfaction. I'd been right—my time had run out.

Jade bristled, while Asrina nestled into my neck as though she could hide. I fought the urge to snatch her up and run. What had he done to my family in my absence?

Though my limbs felt numb, I forced myself to move forward. "Lord West. What a surprise. I did not expect you here until tomorrow."

"I confess I grew impatient." His eyes glinted as though he perceived my discomfort—my fear—and reveled in it. "I learned your father had already returned, so I saw no reason to wait."

"You spoke with Father?"

"Indeed. We had a delightful conversation." He leaned forward, his voice almost a purr. "I expressed my desire to grow better acquainted with you, and he gave his consent."

What in the Crossings? I'd expected Lord West to threaten my life, my family, to make me suffer—but this? I remained rooted in place. "You . . . what?"

Aunt Melisina gave me a subtle nudge. "Lord West has paid you a great compliment."

So I hadn't mistaken his meaning. Instead of pressing Father about Kilmere and forcing the sale, he'd suggested he was interested in calling on me. What could have possibly moved him to change tactics? He held every advantage already. Unless what he'd perceived at Wyncourt gave him to understand I wasn't an ordinary mortal. Perhaps he sought to exploit not only Kilmere, but the oddities I presented. Or perhaps it was only a game to him, one he sought to prolong for his own entertainment.

I drew back slightly, struggling to maintain a calm facade. "Forgive me, I was only surprised. We are so little acquainted, and—"

"It's a situation I intend to remedy." His obsidian gaze locked into mine, challenge clear. "If you're willing."

"Of course she's willing," Aunt Melisina said.

"Then it's settled. I'll call for you tomorrow—perhaps a stroll in Calcot Park would suit?"

Aunt Melisina gave a decisive nod. "A lovely idea."

With several pleasantries and a smile that did not reach his eyes, Lord West took his leave.

"This is a most delightful turn." Aunt Caris beamed upon me, at ease in her favorite chair, unaware she'd welcomed high fae into our home.

I collapsed onto the settee and clutched a cushion to my chest. "I cannot see it so. I don't believe his attentions are sincere."

"Whyever not, my dear?" Aunt Caris asked. "He seemed very taken with you from the first. I guessed it might come to this when he requested to stroll the park with you. Most gentlemen have little interest in gardens, except as they offer an opportunity to steal a quiet moment with a lady who has caught their eye."

"You're much mistaken. He'd no thoughts of courtship that day. We spoke mostly of Kilmere." I tugged the cushion closer, the pressure failing to ease the knot inside. "Since I've made it clear I won't sell, I believe he intends to acquire it another way."

My aunts exchanged a speaking glance. I'd never convince them, not when they wished nothing more than to see me make a suitable match, but it was the only theory that made sense. He'd entertain himself with me, then force me to surrender Kilmere.

"Nonsense." Aunt Melisina rapped her fan against the table. "What plagues you and your sisters that you must imagine every suitor has a nefarious purpose? In my day, young ladies accepted the attentions of well-established gentlemen without refining too much on whatever quirks they might possess."

A deep frown creased Ainslie's face and she opened her mouth, but when Ada shook her head slightly, she subsided.

I clasped my hands together, checking hasty words of my

own. Being fae was hardly a *quirk*, though in fairness, Aunt Melisina knew nothing of his nature. The desire to confess burned in my chest, yet if I did, the cost would be far too great.

She continued, "His interest in antiquities should endear him to you, given your close connection with Lady Dromley's affairs. He might even be more tolerant of such interests than other men."

"Aunt, I—"

"I'll admit, I thought we'd have to exert ourselves a bit more to attract a desirable suitor for you, yet it seems that your looks have stood you in good stead and proven sufficient to overcome your other deficiencies."

Only Aunt Melisina could so skillfully weave together compliment and insult. I rubbed my aching temples. "I still don't believe he's truly a suitor—"

"Pish. What does it matter? You must take advantage of his interest to ensure he becomes one." She gave a brisk nod. "If a gentleman of Lord West's fortune and position wishes to show you his attentions, you must do all within your power to encourage them. In a discreet, ladylike fashion, of course."

Did she imagine I'd interpret her counsel as instruction to fling myself into his arms? I shuddered. I'd rather fall into the embrace of a wyvern. "Do you agree, Aunt Caris?"

"I do, my dear." Aunt Caris poured a cup of tea and offered it to me. "The match would hold countless advantages. If you wed—"

I choked on the tea and struggled to regain my composure.

Ainslie patted my back. "It's far too soon to speak of a wedding or even a betrothal. Jessa's only ever seen him thrice, and once before the Magister. She may not even like him."

"And what does that have to do with it, pray tell?" Aunt Melisina arched a brow.

For once, Ainslie appeared bereft of words.

Ada rested a hand on her arm. "Of course Jessa will take

time to become acquainted with Lord West, as requested. Surely we need leap no further ahead?"

Aunt Caris, who shared Ada's peacekeeping tendencies, nodded. "You're quite right, my dear. Gentlemen can be fickle. We must not expect too much so soon, only see what comes of furthering his acquaintance."

If Ibbie's faerie tale held true, it would bring nothing but death and destruction. But if I proclaimed that, they'd truly believe I'd taken leave of my senses. So I sipped at the tea Aunt Caris offered and sought to form a new plan—one that did *not* involve accepting courtship from a malevolent fae.

CHAPTER 8

The morning brought no new wisdom, only a deep, soul-level fear, impossible to shake. Lord West meant to entertain himself with me, and he'd think nothing of destroying us in doing so, then collecting his reward from the rubble. Meanwhile, I'd have to feign acceptance of his courtship. How difficult would he make it? I stared unseeing out my bedchamber window, considering the multitude of ways he might inflict pain while appearing to pay suit.

Yet perhaps his desire to amuse himself at my expense presented an opportunity. In his arrogance, he'd given me time to discover something to use against him, if such a weapon existed. Though he might suspect some element of fae had touched me, he'd not believe any mortal capable of scheme or subterfuge against the mighty fae, not if he held to the views of his kind. It was my one advantage.

Asrina rested upon the windowsill, her wings motionless. The sight sent a wave of heat through my body. What if the pretense was not enough? What if he chose to strike Asrina again —or Jade, or my family? What then? I pressed my lips together tightly.

Steady and sure, the song of the oak in the gardens below

surged into my awareness. And I opened to it, the steadfast strength reassuring. I pressed my face to the glass pane of the window between us.

Below, at the base of the house, ivy swayed gently in the breeze, its evergreen melody weaving together with the stately song of the oak. And I remembered.

When Uros had attacked, the potted ivy within my bedchamber had surged from its place and twined round his legs, as if it sought to mount a defense.

Could I replicate such a feat? I needed to find out, because if I could not deceive Lord West, if he forced his will upon me, I must mount some defense. I could no longer afford to wait for the safety of Thornhaven and the isolation it offered to experiment; I must make an effort now. Of course, I couldn't hope to match his strength, yet perhaps I might surprise him enough to buy a chance of escape for those I loved.

I hurriedly dressed, then with Jade at my side and Asrina clinging to my shoulder, I dashed into the garden.

Early morning dew still glossed each leaf and blade of grass, burnishing them until they shone like jewels in the brilliant sunlight or glinted dark in the shade. I felt as though those very grasses danced and swayed within my stomach. Surely this was folly—to consider that I might do more than sense plants, that I might bid them as I desired.

At times before, they'd appeared to respond to my emotions. But was that something I could control? Something I should control? I'd finally begun to feel at ease with the Other sensations botanical life provoked, but this . . . What if my attempt went dreadfully awry? What if it awoke something in me, or the world around me, that I could not control, leaving me exposed?

Asrina shifted on my shoulder, a perch she should not require. For her sake, I would try—and trust I'd not be overcome.

Only I'd best start small.

Heedless of the dew staining my gown, I settled on the path

of crushed stone. A small sprig of ivy had popped up its head amid a stand of calendula, its dark green stark against the paler stems and vibrant flowers of its neighboring plants. Still, it kept so low to the ground, I might not have taken note except for its determined song, a vibrant thrum in the background.

Jade stretched out on the path alongside me, her gaze fixed upon my face.

The sensation of grasses swaying in my stomach intensified. Yet I must try. I lightly brushed my fingers across the stiff, glossy leaf of the ivy.

Its determination bled into me, no longer a whispered song but a delighted declaration. It burned new strength into my veins, not only that of the little sprig, but also of the mother, far distant, from which it had sprung, and her countless offspring, their roots burrowing throughout the garden, their shoots popping up as they pleased.

Evergreen.

Persistent.

Rooting even through stone.

The leaves beneath my fingers rustled as though my touch pleased them, as though they wished to be *bid*.

I sat, letting the tide of sensation flow through me. Though strong, the current did not carry me away, only immersed me so that every other part of my surroundings faded—as if this one sense had become so strong as to obscure all others.

No other sight or sound pierced the weave of green-gold glory surrounding me.

Come.

I bid the ivy, and it swirled up and around my fingers.

Dimly, my skin sensed its touch, and something else, something within, exalted at the connection.

It crept up my arm, gentle loops and swirls coiling to my elbow until I whispered *stop*.

And it did.

Had the vibrant determination of the ivy surged less strong, perhaps fear might have taken root, but now I could only *feel* all the glorious life at my fingertips, thrumming through my frame, and—

Wait.

Something nudged at my shoulder. Asrina? No, the nudge became a spike of pain, one that drove back the swell of green-gold.

Jade.

She'd nipped my shoulder. Why?

A voice called from the path just behind me, breaking through the song of the ivy that still swirled in my ears. "Jessa? Jessa!"

Oh, please no. Not Aunt Caris.

I turned to face her, the ivy falling from my arm. She'd come dangerously near, had called my name perhaps more times than I'd realized. How long had Jade attempted to rouse me? What had Aunt Caris seen? The sun was higher in the sky now; most of the dew had burned off the grass. How long had I sat, lost in a world of new sensations?

"My dear . . ." Her face was blanched of all color, her rich copper hair blazing in contrast. "Are you quite well?"

What had Aunt Caris perceived in me that sparked such fear? Had she witnessed the response of the ivy? My connection to it?

"Yes, of course. I was only . . . thinking." Suddenly cold, I wrapped my arms around my middle. I should have waited, should have found somewhere I'd not have risked exposure. But if I had, if her arrival hadn't provoked an interruption, what might have happened? Would I have lost myself forever?

"You . . . you didn't hear me. Not until . . ." She reached for me, then drew back her hand. "Are you certain you're well? You don't look yourself."

"Please forgive me, Aunt Caris. I'm a great deal distracted by Lord West."

She fidgeted with the lace near her throat, her face still

matching its pallor. "You didn't seem distracted. You seemed like you'd . . . gone. I thought something had happened to you."

What could I say? My heart thrummed in my chest, and all the emotion surging within me poured into my voice, causing it to ring with a discomfiting tone. "You needn't worry, Aunt Caris. I'm quite well; there's no cause for concern."

She drew a shuddering breath, then relaxed. "If you're quite well, I needn't worry. There's no cause for concern. Silly of me."

My pulse hitched. What had I done? I dug my fingers into the crushed stone, the edges abrading my skin. Had I just— surely I could not. Only I must have? She'd *echoed* my words. I pressed to my feet. "Aunt Caris, I'm so sorry. Please, I never meant . . ."

Never meant to glamour you with whatever fae influence works in me. I choked back the confession, but with such evidence, I could no longer deny it. Fae blood might well run through my veins. Had Riven suspected?

I was trembling from head to toe, and I tucked my hands within my skirts in a vain attempt to conceal their unsteadiness.

Jade nudged my ankle, but I denied myself the comfort of cradling her, a gift I did not deserve. Not when I'd somehow glamoured one I loved.

"No harm in making me come to the gardens, my dear." Aunt Caris blinked as though coming back to herself. "We've had word from Dreda. She's accepted our invitation for an interview this morning at ten. I thought you might wish to attend, only you're all over grime."

"I . . . I can change." Mechanically, I brushed at the traces of soil left by the ivy. "I'll go now."

Before I lost any remaining scrap of composure, I fled to my bedchamber, shut the door, and slammed the bolt home. I pressed a hand to my stomach, but could not still its churning.

Collapsing on the edge of the bed, I drew one ragged breath after another.

It was one thing to allow the sensations liberty, quite another to try to govern what I did not understand. What if I'd lost myself altogether? What if I'd done something more noteworthy than coil ivy up my arm, something that could not be explained away to passersby? If they chanced to see me arm-deep in ivy, it would not seem too peculiar, for everyone knew of my love for gardening. But if I'd altered the landscape—or hurt someone, unaware—could I even do such things? I didn't know, which meant what I'd done was far too dangerous.

Jade leapt onto my lap, her purr a low rumble. Yet for once, it failed to console. How could it, when I'd glamoured Aunt Caris, unthinking—when I'd enacted the sort of fae-working I abhorred most, for the easy way it allowed them to manipulate mortals.

From the basin, I dashed cold water over my hands, and then my face. Still, I felt as though fire burned through my veins, hot and unsettled and tumultuous.

If I had some amount of fae blood, could it cause these abilities? Everything in me rebelled at the notion. Fae were cruel, merciless in their dealings with mortals and those weaker than them.

I wanted no part of that heritage, and yet . . . an echo of the ivy's vibrant song swirled about me, stirring longing.

I curled up in the chair, and Jade planted herself on my lap once more, this time with a plaintive *mrow.* She ran her face alongside my chin, her warmth offering consolation, her sweet-grass scent filling the air.

However much my hands shook, I forced myself to stroke her fur, to calm and to *think.* I could no longer avoid considering the possibilities that had lurked at the edges of my mind, the ones I'd shoved aside since my return from the Otherworld. They'd cropped up as persistent and pervasive as knotweed, no matter how I'd tried to thrust them aside. Now I must confront them.

If I had fae blood, how had it come to pass? Could Mother

or Father be fae? Or was I some sort of changeling, and not the natural child of either?

To consider the possibility cut through me like a scythe through winter wheat. If I shared no ties to those I loved most . . . I couldn't bear to consider it, yet I must.

Mother had carried three children in relatively quick succession—including one set of twins—and Riven had said fae women didn't bear children easily. Surely that suggested she wasn't fae.

As for Father, he seemed an even less likely candidate. He'd fallen so easily to Riven's glamour, although I supposed it could have been an act. But no, I simply couldn't credit it. If he'd known Riven was fae, he'd never have allowed me to enter into perceived danger. He would have acted, found a way to dismiss the glamour without raising suspicion or addressed me later.

But what if . . . what if both Mother and Father were mortal, and I was the child of a bargain like the one Mocvar had attempted to force on me? What if Mother had fallen into the clutches of fae who'd misused her—and I was the result?

I buried my face in Jade's fur. It would explain the melancholies Mother had suffered—and the fact my sisters appeared unaffected.

Given what I knew of fae, it was the most likely explanation. Only, if true, why would any fae, having gone to the trouble of securing a child, allow said child to escape his claims?

Mother. She was quick-minded and fierce in her love for her children. Even if she'd been forced to carry me against her will, even if I was a product of shame and suffering, tainted in a different way than I'd ever imagined, she wouldn't have surrendered me to the fae. She'd have sought my protection.

What if that had led to her death?

I pressed a hand to my stomach, yet could not find calm. The room seemed to swirl around me, and I closed my eyes.

If I was right, only my sisters could be called my own, and

the tie only that of half-blood. Yet wasn't family more than blood? Didn't love and devotion also bind us?

Perhaps, but if I revealed my speculations, it would surely sever those cords. Every mortal feared fae, and if I was partly Other, their only sensible choice would be to cut ties, before they found themselves victim to some dreadful fate—whether from the Otherworld or our own Vigil.

I burned unbearably hot. My lungs tightened, and I could not take in enough air. Was *I* a danger to them? On instinct and without forethought, I'd glamoured Aunt Caris.

And with the benefit of hindsight, I knew she wasn't the first. It had started in Milburn, with the innkeeper, the instinct to glamour stubbornly working its way to the surface at times when my emotions rose. Could I control it? Or would the fae blood in me also give rise to the cruelty they often displayed, the power gradually corrupting me?

I was shaking now, my head throbbing, the room about me wavering. The song of the oak surged tempestuous into my senses, seething with turmoil to match my own, as did that of the ivy below—

A sharp pain stung my arm, bringing me back to the room, back into my own body.

Jade.

She'd drawn one claw along my wrist—the tiniest of scratches, from which a single drop of blood welled.

The clamor of the gardens subsided. I sank back in the chair, cold and exhausted.

With unblinking eyes, she watched me for one moment, two. Then she curled up in my lap.

With trembling fingers, I stroked her head. I must focus. I couldn't afford to lose myself in wild speculation. One thing I knew—I had abilities of no mortal origin. The evidence seemed to favor fae blood, but alchemical alteration remained a slim possibility, though such a prospect had many marks against it.

Somehow, I must find the truth. But how could I, with Mother gone?

The mantel clock chimed softly ten times.

Oh no—I was late. I cast off my gown, flinging it onto the chair, and rummaged in my clothes press for a new one.

I glanced into the mirror, the faint foxing at the edges bleeding toward my face. A number of dark curls had escaped to bound down my neck, and my eyes appeared an even darker shade of blue than usual, deep shadows in the spectral pallor of my face.

Somehow, I needed to collect myself. I attended to evening my breaths and to the sensation of Jade, warm and steady within my arms.

Then I descended to the morning room, where my aunts waited, where I must pretend all was well.

A woman of middling age sat before them—Dreda—though she bore little resemblance to the distraught soul I'd encountered within the Cloister. Smooth, nut-brown curls, only just touched with gray, framed a face with features too sharp to be deemed beautiful by society. Her hands rested in her lap, slim and elegant, no longer drawn into twiggy claws. She was well— which meant some good *had* come of my abilities.

Aunt Melisina frowned at me. "So kind of you to join us, Jessa."

"Please forgive my tardiness. I'd been in the garden, and I thought I'd best tidy up before I joined you."

"I see." Aunt Melisina turned back to Dreda. "I think you've some idea of what you must work with. Would you find the task too onerous?"

"Of course not." With the ragged edge of terror absent, Dreda's voice was soft and melodious. "It would give me great pleasure to serve as chaperone for your nieces."

What had they discussed? What rules did they expect Dreda to enforce? If I'd not allowed my emotions to overtake me, I might have participated in the conversation from the beginning.

I glanced at Dreda. Would she be kindly disposed toward me still? Or would she feel responsible to report all to my aunts?

Dreda offered me a tentative smile. "In fact, I'm indebted to Miss Jessa for her kindness when last we met."

Aunt Caris clasped her hands, appearing as pleased as she always did whenever one of us received praise. "Excellent. We will pay you as discussed, and of course, you'll receive your room and board, as well as any clothing required to attend events."

"When can you start?" Aunt Melisina asked.

"If you'll allow me the day to collect my things and offer my thanks to the Sisters for their aid, I can return tomorrow."

Aunt Melisina nodded. "That will do."

After a few more moments of polite conversation, Dreda took her leave, Holden escorting her from the room.

"I must say, my dear, I think she'll suit our household quite well." Aunt Caris patted my hand, any trace of her earlier unease absent. "She's quiet, but well-mannered, and she bears an excellent reference from a Sister Margery, who commends her fortitude in the face of trial and her readiness to serve within the Cloister after her recovery from illness."

Illness—so that was how Sister Margery termed the incident of the dread-aught that had brought Dreda to them. And indeed, it was a sort of illness, for which Dreda could not be faulted, though many would disagree—the Vigil in particular. "I'm glad she's pleased you."

And even more glad that she suffered no lingering ill effects from her oppression.

"I still think the stronger hand of Ermenhild would suit better," Aunt Melisina said. "Miss Twells appears a rather gentle soul."

"We don't require someone overbearing, only one who understands and carries out what's expected." A slight frown crossed Aunt Caris's face. "Besides, I cannot abide the thought of listening to Ermenhild's endless strictures all day. Even you must admit they grow tiresome."

"Perhaps a trifle—"

"And I'll remind you I have to live with any chaperone we engage."

Aunt Caris valued peace and harmony in her home above all —even enough to temporarily oppose Aunt Melisina, it seemed.

"Very well, have it your way. I only hope you don't have cause to regret it." Aunt Melisina stood, looking down upon me. "As for you, Jessa, it's of paramount importance that Lord West think you a proper young lady. Of course, either Caris or I will accompany you whenever you are with Lord West, but you *must* take Miss Twells on any other excursions. You are not to roam Avons without her, not even to take a stroll down Camden Row."

"I understand."

"And do not ramble on about your herbs and books and sketches with Lord West."

"I have no intention of doing so."

"Nevertheless, I'll return to oversee his call this afternoon." With that, she glided from the room.

His call. With all that had transpired, I'd pressed it from my mind, but I still must face Lord West this afternoon, must pretend to welcome his attentions long enough to find some way to escape them—if there was one.

CHAPTER 9

Somehow I maintained my composure through luncheon, though I wanted nothing more than to flee to the privacy of my bedchamber—or perhaps immerse myself in a mundane task such as sorting Father's correspondence—but I couldn't risk Lord West stealing another moment alone with my family.

So, after the meal, I retired with my aunts and sisters to the morning room to await his call. I immersed myself in my sketchbook, a storm-tossed meadow taking shape beneath my pencil, a matching tumult in my thoughts. When Lord West arrived, I needed no announcement from Holden to recognize his presence. Even with his fae nature heavily veiled by glamour, Other pricked against my awakened senses, along with the distinctive current of power I'd come to associate with Lord West. The sensation settled about my chest like a band of iron.

Asrina shuddered and sank into the space between my skirt and the arm of the chair.

I couldn't risk him hurting her again. As Aunt Caris instructed Holden to admit Lord West, I tucked Asrina inside my reticule. She nested atop my lace handkerchief, her light flaring a bit brighter. When she made no attempt to climb out, I drew the strings to seal her in, leaving a small gap at the top for air to flow. It was a fragile shelter, but the best I could offer.

Then Lord West entered the room, and I rose with the others, offering a smile in greeting, attempting to appear like a young lady who received her suitor with pleasure.

My efforts gained a slight nod of approval from Aunt Melisina. "Lord West, I trust you are well?"

"Indeed. Better than ever." He closed the distance between us. "Shall we explore Calcot Park this afternoon, Miss Jessa?"

"What a pleasant suggestion." I lowered my gaze to conceal my feelings, but Jade made no attempt to disguise hers—she glared at Lord West, her teeth bared.

"Would you mind some additional company?" Ainslie dimpled up at him. "We rather thought we'd all take advantage of the lovely day for a stroll."

Part of me wished to embrace her in gratitude; the other part wanted to urge her to flee. Clearly my comments yesterday had revealed enough of my sentiments to prompt her intervention. Would she have felt so inclined if she knew the danger I'd drawn into our lives? Or the threat I might represent?

An answering smile spread across his features, one with just the slightest edge of malice. "I'd be pleased to have such lovely companions. Miss Jessa?"

He extended his arm, and I'd no choice but to accept or cause a scene. Yet when I took it, the pricking sensation of Other swept up my hand, pebbling my skin. A sharp, slightly metallic scent—like that of long-buried stone—assaulted me, a reminder that he represented a force as ancient and implacable as mountains of granite.

At the door, Holden handed over parasols to each of the ladies. Then we swept from the house onto the broad footwalk of Camden Row, Jade close on one side, Lord West on the other. While he exchanged pleasantries with my aunts, I willed myself to calm, to present the facade of an unsuspecting innocent, altogether ignorant of his schemes.

If our encounter at Wyncourt had roused his suspicions, this was my chance to allay them. I must remain steady, must not suggest I could perceive his true nature. With a touch of good fortune, perhaps he'd decide that whatever oddities he'd noted stemmed from Wyncourt itself, not from me. Surely he must have perceived its fae nature.

"Don't you agree, Miss Jessa?" Lord West's voice broke into my awareness.

What in the Crossings had he said? "I . . ."

Ainslie intervened again. "Jessa favors Enderly above Calcot, I believe."

"An interesting choice."

His gaze burned into me, and I struggled to keep my face expressionless. A lady never showed she was ruffled, after all. "I find it offers a greater variety of blossoms for sketching."

Would he believe that excuse? Or did he know Enderly had once been touched by Other, when Uros preyed upon Avons? His face gave no sign.

As we neared Calcot, he slowed his steps so that we trailed behind the others. A common maneuver among gentlemen who sought to gain private conversation while maintaining all expected propriety. We meandered through the gently arched entrance to the park, and the wisteria draped over its gate brushed my arm as we passed, lending its strength.

Yet alongside the whispers of wisteria threaded something more subtle, a pulse of charm surrounding Lord West, one which drew attention to the finely sculpted features of his face, the strong lines of his body . . .

No—he might be beautiful, as were all fae, but he was also cruel, and if given opportunity, he'd destroy us. Clinging to this thought, I shook off the strands of glamour that sought to draw me to him. Then I offered a shy smile, as though they'd had their way. "It's a pleasant day for a stroll."

"The company makes it so." His lips quirked upward. "I've anticipated this moment since our conversation yesterday."

"How very gracious you are." The temperature in the air surrounding us seemed to drop, and I angled my parasol to allow more sun to filter onto my face. "Yet I'm surprised that you feel so, considering how little time we've spent in each other's company."

"It doesn't take me long to determine what I want." The planes of his face sharpened, his glamour thinning. "Nor the best means by which to acquire it."

"And if you cannot?"

He laughed, a rich, full, mocking sound, before which the ordinary thrum of the park about us faded. "I always achieve my ends."

At what cost to those around him? The oppressive sense of his power swirled about me, and I stumbled over a stone. "Then you're very fortunate. Not many can make such claims."

"It's not a matter of good fortune, but understanding the game at hand and stacking the elements in one's favor." He steered us down a narrow path, one closely lined with boxwood. "Any obstacle must be turned into an advantage—or eliminated."

"That sounds exhausting."

"It's how the game is played."

To which game did he refer? That of courtship and match-making played in our world—or the cat-and-mouse game of fae-and-mortal those of the Otherworld pursued? Either way, his intent was clear.

Before I could collect myself, he leaned closer. "You must have been on very friendly terms with Lady Dromley, for her to leave so much to you."

"Indeed. We shared a close bond and a common view of the world." The boughs of the trees overhead bent toward me, offering shelter, consolation for both my pain and my fear, and I almost reached for them. But no, not now—not in front of Lord West. I tightened my grip on the handle of my parasol. "We both enjoyed exploring mysteries, though Ibbie particularly favored those of the past. What of you? Do you enjoy the prospect of solving a good puzzle?"

"I enjoy claiming answers. The truth cannot remain hidden long, if one knows where to look." The sun overhead cast his shadow in sharp relief, lengthening it beyond its natural proportions. "As a matter of fact, I find you somewhat of a mystery, Miss Jessa—but I don't intend that you'll remain so long."

Warmth crept up my neck. I'd hoped to assess him; instead, he'd brought me here to assess me. Had it been his purpose all along? Not only to entertain himself with my discomfort, but to unearth my secrets and seek to turn them to his advantage?

"I'm afraid you'll be disappointed." The resinous scent of the boxwood tinged the air around me, reassuring. "I come from a very ordinary family. But I must confess I find you a bit puzzling also."

"Why is that?" The faintest of compulsions laced his words, bidding me to share my thoughts.

And so I would—only not the ones he wanted, but those I hoped would reveal information I desperately needed. I looked up at him. "You desire Kilmere, yet you've been good enough not to press me further for it. Why?"

"Ah, Miss Jessa. You underestimate your charms." His smile gleamed white in the sun, yet it did not touch his eyes; they remained dark and hungry, those of a predator seeking to draw blood. "As it turns out, there's more I want than Kilmere."

"I see." What did he seek? Was it Wyncourt? Or did he think, like Mocvar, it would be convenient to use a mortal woman to produce an heir? Something sharp as thorns twisted inside.

With one vow, he could bind me to him—and claim everything belonging to me, Kilmere, Wyncourt, and my entire future. He'd said it himself: he relished the prospect of total victory. To force me into marriage provided such a path.

"You're still uncertain of your feelings." His voice dropped low, threaded with power. "But that uncertainty will fade. We've not yet had time to become properly acquainted, but you'll find we have a great deal in common."

A glamour, strong and compelling, commanding me to succumb. Caught off guard, I did not respond quickly enough. A sense of overwhelming pressure built in my chest. The fur on Jade's neck stood on end; her eyes glowed an impossibly brilliant green.

His eyes narrowed till they resembled shards of stone. "You'll tell your aunts you've taken ill, and I'll offer to escort you home. Then you will come with me."

I nearly buckled beneath the power crackling in his words, a compulsion laced with the unyielding strength of stone. A metallic taste flooded my mouth; my thoughts fogged.

I threw open my senses to the song of the boxwood along the path, its ever-greening strength filling my ears, drowning out the allure of Lord West's glamour.

He was testing me. If I resisted the compulsion, I'd confirm I wasn't an ordinary mortal. If I agreed, he could take me where he pleased. And unless I missed the mark, he'd take me to the Otherworld, where any fragile protections the mortal world might offer would be stripped away.

I blinked up at him as though bewildered. "You know it wouldn't be proper, Lord West. Not without a chaperone."

"And are you always so very proper, Miss Jessa?" His voice lowered. "I have a suspicion you violate the rules when it pleases you, in ways you'd rather remain hidden."

Jade rumbled deep in her chest.

And I stumbled to a halt, releasing his arm. "Lord West, I—"

"Consider before you speak." When the light caught in his eyes, little glints of silver appeared amid the obsidian, and they appeared ancient—far too shrewd and canny to belong to any mortal. "I believe the Vigil takes great interest in cases such as yours."

My mouth went dry. How had he guessed what worried me?

Perhaps he was simply experienced enough with our world to know the Vigil was an effective threat. The bitter, biting taste of fear intensified, and try as I might, I couldn't force a response.

"They might find the company you keep noteworthy." His fingers brushed against my reticule. If he chose, he could wrap his hand about it and crush Asrina in an instant. Instead, he bent a shadowed glamour about us and lifted his hand to trace the links of the chain that held my pendant. "Or the jewel you bear about your neck."

My pulse throbbed at the base of my throat. *Don't flinch.* For once, I wished Aunt Melisina close enough to chastise his impropriety, though doubtless the glamour would have kept her from witnessing it. Somehow, I managed to speak, though my voice sounded distant to my own ears. "The Vigil keeps busy protecting Byren from Otherworldly threats. I've never heard that they concern themselves with ladies' fripperies or social lives."

"Is that so?" He reclaimed my hand, settling it once more upon his arm. His half-smile mocked me. "Come, you must attempt to look pleased with my company. Your aunts desire it, after all."

I couldn't restrain a shiver, never mind that he'd feel it. When he found me unswayed by glamour, he'd chosen a mortal sort of weapon—threatening me with the conventions of my own society.

"Will you accept my suit?" he asked.

His words held a trap. One misstep, and I'd find myself bound in a fae bargain, from which there was no release.

I forced myself to keep putting one foot in front of the other, slow and steady, as though untroubled. Every plan I'd made so far had failed—he'd been one step ahead each time. He'd forced a revelation of my resistance to glamour; he knew there was something Other about me. Yet not *what*, unless I was much mistaken. If he already held that answer, then I didn't think he'd continue playing the game. He'd make his final move, not string out the process, unless for the pure joy of it.

So what now? I could not consent. Nor could I expose weakness.

"I know what you are." With difficulty, I kept an even tone. "And I'm not afraid. Nor am I minded to agree with your demands."

"You are young and ignorant. But you will learn what it means to fear—and I will take pleasure in teaching you."

Jade growled and wheeled to face him.

I willed her to remain quiet, my pulse throbbing at the base of my throat. Could he perceive it? The fear I denied, yet scarcely kept in check. If he sought to take my life in this moment, I couldn't stop him.

With her eyes gleaming, Jade stalked toward Lord West. And I bent to snatch her up, welcoming the opportunity to free myself from his grasp.

"Meantime, you have secrets you wish kept. I require your cooperation to do so." His tone was unyielding. "Do you accept?"

"I can make no commitment regarding my future, but I'll not turn you away when next you call." Even that concession galled. Yet he'd forced my hand, and he knew it. The Vigil needed no prompting to examine an individual for fae-touch, and once they began to look at my life, they'd find more than enough peculiarities to condemn me. And were I to turn around and accuse him of being high fae, it would only strengthen the case against me—because everyone believed high fae couldn't enter Avons.

"It will do, for now."

With that, my concession became a bargain. The thinnest thread of shadow coiled between us and wove around my upper arm, where it settled, silvery-smooth and bitter cold against my skin.

We'd rejoined the main path, my aunts and sisters distant

enough that they'd not overhear our conversation, yet close enough to satisfy convention. He bent low to murmur in my ear, "But I'll warn you. When I uncover the truth—and I will—you may wish you'd taken my first offer."

Which meant what? He required this pretense of courtship for now, but what he uncovered about me might change that? I offered no reply, for what could I say?

"One thing more. If you're so very ordinary," he continued smoothly, "you won't mind if I verify, will you?"

I wanted to deny him, rather than give my consent to some unknown binding, but he'd laid his snares well. Even if some protection for mortals existed, limiting how he maneuvered, he did not need his powers to pose a threat. He'd determined I feared the Vigil, that I'd cooperate to avoid being taken in. So I'd no choice but to say, "Of course not."

"Excellent."

The binding mark shimmered, then shifted slightly, as though my agreement changed the nature of the bargain between us. My stomach roiled, and I pressed my lips together.

Ahead, Ainslie had immersed herself in conversation on the green with a short, rather stout lady, while my aunts and Ada continued to stroll down the winding paths. Ada glanced back at me, the slightest of frowns crossing her face.

"Smile." Even as he issued the command, another sinuous shadow wove through the air between us, only this one sliced deep into my arm, sharp as a dagger. "Your sister appears concerned."

Though a shard of pain spiked down from the binding mark, I summoned a smile and waved to Ada. Like a blade, the shadow slid deeper. I stifled a gasp. I'd not give him the satisfaction of a response.

Yet it did not matter. Still, he took his pleasure, his gaze fixed on my face, as if he absorbed every alteration in it.

Then he gave a nod. "I regret I must take my leave. *Moreland* is playing at the Crescent Theater Friday. I'll fetch you at seven. Be ready."

When he departed, the dagger-like sensation ebbed slightly. I sank onto a bench, releasing an unsteady breath. A stalwart black walnut tree spread its branches overhead, its bright, rich melody steadying the rapid pulse of my heart, the churning turmoil within.

With her usual grace, Jade hopped onto the bench. She nuzzled the binding mark, and I flinched as it sent another sharp pang down my arm.

A low rumble emanated from her.

"I didn't know what else to do, didn't expect him to choose the course he did," I whispered. "I failed. Badly."

Jade curled herself in my lap, her warmth reassuring. Yet the tension coiled in her body refused to leave, even when I stroked her head. She was troubled too.

Ainslie rushed toward me, and I worked to school my features, to hide my pain.

She settled onto the bench next to me. "You'll never guess! I've just unearthed something about Lord Bradford."

With effort, I wrenched my thoughts from Lord West, but my arm throbbed with an ever-present reminder. "How?"

"By talking with Mrs. Pickering. She's an inveterate gossip with a rather vulgar tongue, so with the proper prompting she confessed all she knew of him." She lowered her voice. "It seems he has a habit of fathering natural children and abandoning them."

Then Ada was right in her assessment of his nature. While it wasn't discussed openly, it was no secret that many of the gentlemen of Byren kept mistresses. Yet Father would never support such an act, particularly not when it involved the abandonment of children. It wasn't his way, however common it might be, and certainly not what he'd wish for Ada. It was a small comfort to think we might have rid ourselves of one unwanted suitor.

"Well done, Ainslie."

"You don't seem very pleased." Ainslie lowered her parasol. "Was your stroll unpleasant?"

"It did not go as I hoped."

Along my arm, a bruise of deepest black formed. I willed it to escape notice, discreetly tugging at my sleeve, though it was not long enough to conceal the spreading shadow. It had become so dark that it completely concealed the binding mark.

What had Lord West done?

CHAPTER 10

By the time the household prepared to retire for the night, my arm had grown numb to the fingertips, save for the occasional sharp pang. While it was clear Lord West had taken pleasure in my pain, he'd also sent the shadow right after I'd consented to a test. What did he seek to assess?

If only I could ask Riven.

He'd also desired to understand the peculiarities about my person, yet unlike Lord West, he'd not forced a working upon me, not pressed or coerced me into bargaining further, even when what I'd confessed to him offered him every opportunity.

I cradled my bruised arm to my chest. I needed to stop thinking of Riven. I couldn't reach him, and I couldn't afford to dwell upon the impossible. Lord West was my problem to manage, and for now, I must do something about the injury he'd inflicted.

Whatever it was, I'd no doubt it posed a danger—and I didn't want to find out what would happen if it was left unchecked. With Jade at my side and Asrina perched on my shoulder, I crept down to my compounding chamber.

A fae-working held Other power. What did I have to match

it? Amelior, perhaps? I'd collected the translucent plant with its inverted-pipe blossoms from near a Crossing, and it held Other properties. When used in a salve, it had healed our cook Estine from a severe burn.

Yet I could not tell if some part of the shadow-working remained or only the injury it had caused. Unlike with Asrina's wings, I could perceive no lingering strands of power, but perhaps they'd sunk below sight.

Either way, fresh amelior would be more effective than the small amount I had dried. After I gathered some cuttings from the glasshouse, I returned to the compounding room. I set Asrina upon the table, nesting her on a small pile of linen scraps. The dark lines upon her wings hadn't spread, but nor had they faded. And her fatigue appeared to grow.

Her pain pricked at me, sharp as a nettle. She hadn't wanted me to interfere with the working, but perhaps if I found an effective salve—and tested it on myself first—she'd consider it.

The thought sent fresh strength into my weary limbs. On instinct, I drew the heavy mortar and pestle from the shelf. I didn't have time to infuse the amelior as I ordinarily would and could only hope, since it was Other, infusion wouldn't be required.

As I ground the leaves with the pestle, I turned over in my mind what I required, and the sensation of Other swept over me, not a painful pricking, but something warm and gentle. The leaves released their oils, and their translucent white transformed to a rich golden hue in the gaslight.

Then I fetched a heartsease-and-calendula-infused oil from the shelf above. Moving to the kitchen, I melted beeswax on the still-warm stove and then mixed all the components into an aromatic salve.

As soon as it cooled, I spread the salve down my arm in long strokes, envisioning the golden richness of the life within melting away any remnant of the shadow-working.

The gentle fragrances swirled around me, and my skin

warmed, the numbness receding and the bruise fading from the deepest of blacks to a bluish-brown, through which the finer threads of the binding mark shone.

I let out my breath. Somehow, it had worked—and I'd take any victory I could obtain, no matter how small. Perhaps it would open the door to a greater one, if I could heal Asrina.

I turned to her. "I know you didn't wish me to keep trying to remove the working before—that you feared I'd make matters worse. But this salve has eased my pain, and perhaps it will yours also."

She gave the smallest tilt of her head, then crossed the table to stand before me. I gently worked the salve into her flame-like wings. She brightened, and when I finished, she gave her wings a tiny flutter.

Then she collapsed, and her light went dim.

It hadn't been enough—the lines still marred the fine material of her wings—and her attempt at movement evidently caused a great deal of pain. "I'm sorry, lovely one."

Why hadn't it worked on her? Was it because her nature as a sun sylph differed from my own? I possessed no more plants with Other properties, unless one counted the goldhearts, but they lent themselves to the strengthening of souls, not bodies.

I collapsed into the wooden chair and closed my eyes, exhaustion binding me in place. I'd assuaged my own pain, but not Asrina's, and somehow that felt worse than if I'd done nothing at all.

When next Lord West came, he'd be sure to note that I'd healed from the damage the shadow-marking had left. Had that been the test all along? What would he do in response? I pulled my knees to my chest, wrapping my arms tight about them.

What did I know of him? The familiar exercise brought some measure of calm. He saw this as a game, one in which the victor took all. Yet he was fae, which meant he didn't see mortals as worthy opponents, but victims.

Before it had felt like an advantage; now it felt *true.* How could I change that?

If I couldn't match his power, then I must either offer something more compelling in bargain, something that he'd consider worth abandoning his plans over—which I could not fathom—or find a weapon I could use to rout him.

I traced the wood grain on the arm of the chair. This had all started with Kilmere. Would the ruins hold the insights I needed to free myself of Lord West? If I explored it, might I find the object of power he craved—if that was indeed his purpose?

Yet what would I risk in so doing? Not only my own life, but possibly those in Withern, if tales of the curse held truth.

A faint rattle of canisters broke the stillness of night as Jade prowled among them.

And I was bound to receive Lord West when he called. Even if I managed to sway Aunt Caris, would the binding allow me to depart for Kilmere? And what of my family? If I *could* leave Avons, would Lord West follow? Or would they remain vulnerable to him?

To start, I would send for Mr. Tibbons. I needed a full account of everything that had taken place when he explored Kilmere, needed to understand if the deaths were connected to it in some way and what might lurk within.

Meanwhile, I'd continue to seek the truth about the curse. I had several possible approaches, but given how helpful Mrs. Darrington had been, I thought perhaps I should write to others with whom Ibbie had held long acquaintance and inquire into their knowledge. Certainly it couldn't hurt—and if I could find a way to excavate Kilmere safely, it might change the game. It had brought Lord West into my life; perhaps it would help me remove him.

But for now, weariness clouded my thoughts. I lifted Asrina onto my shoulder, and together with Jade, we returned to my bedchamber. Asrina nestled on the edge of my pillow that night, and Jade curled up close to me, her head resting on the binding mark as though by concealing it, she could make it vanish.

Tomorrow, we would try again.

THE NEXT MORNING, I found I couldn't endure the notion of light conversation over breakfast, so instead, I slipped down to my compounding room, attempting various combinations of salve for Asrina—and coming up short each time.

Finally, she pulsed a bright flare of light, then stamped her foot, as though her patience had come to an end.

As had mine. It seemed clear that the supplies at hand weren't sufficient. We abandoned the compounding room and ventured abovestairs. The house was now quiet, and Holden informed me Aunt Caris and my sisters had left to visit the milliner, which left me free to compose a message to Mr. Tibbons.

From the secretary in the morning room, I withdrew several sheets of paper, then uncorked a bottle of ink.

The familiar mineral smell wafted about me, comforting. I jotted a note asking Mr. Tibbons to return to Avons as soon as possible. After a moment of hesitation, I penned one to my trustees as well, asking if they would approve expenses for a trip to Kilmere. I didn't see a clear way forward, but if I could remove possible obstacles, then perhaps . . .

Holden glided into the room, as imperious and unruffled as ever.

"Miss Jessa, Mr. Burke has come to call," he announced. "I informed him you were not at-home to callers, but he proclaimed it Magistry business. If you wish to wait until your aunt returns—"

Jade lounged at my feet, half-asleep, but still one of her ears pricked toward Holden.

Surely I could justify welcoming a stratesman on official business, even without a chaperone. "I'll see him now."

"As you wish, Miss Jessa." Only a slight tightness about his lips hinted at disapproval, but when he escorted Mr. Burke in, he left the door standing wide and offered no refreshments.

"Mr. Burke, how delightful to see you." It wasn't a social pleasantry. The knot in my chest, present since my last encounter with Lord West, eased as he entered the room. "What brings you here?"

One corner of his mouth lifted, and his gray eyes brightened. "Would you believe it was the pleasure of your company?"

His words startled a laugh from me. "I'd be hard-pressed to do so."

"I thought as much." Though he sat, he maintained his ever-vigilant posture, and he assessed me with his kestrel-sharp gaze. "Have you been well since your recent trip?"

"I've suffered no ill effects from it. And you?"

"I've fared well enough." He leaned forward slightly, and the familiar, very mortal scents of bergamot and clove filled the air. "The Magister was quite pleased with the outcome of the case."

"I'm glad." Although his efforts alone hadn't brought the killer to justice, he'd gone far beyond what most would have done in seeking the protection of Avons—and for that, he deserved commendation. "But I cannot think you've called to offer a report on the case, either."

"Then you'd be correct." Mr. Burke hesitated, then drew a hand over his jaw.

I stilled. Was something wrong?

"What do you know of Kilmere?" He became very still, as though intent on my answer.

"You're here about the ruins?" A peculiar sort of numbness crept across my middle. How had he known? My shoulders tightened. "Do you still have men following me?"

"What? No, of course not." He gave me a sharp look. "Should I?"

Warmth crept up into my cheeks. I'd lowered my guard when he arrived, and now I'd betrayed too much. "It's only that your mention of it surprised me, because Kilmere has been much on my mind of late. I've considered excavation, but I'm attempting to learn more about it first."

"I think that wise." His eyes darkened to a stormier gray. "I've heard rumors that I'd like to investigate, if you'll grant access."

"Rumors about the deaths?"

"You know of those? I suppose I shouldn't be surprised." He shifted toward me. "Is that what troubles you?"

"What do you mean?"

"You don't look quite . . . yourself."

"A gentleman doesn't remark on such things."

He chuckled quietly. "And you're now a stickler for proper behavior?"

I sighed. "I passed a difficult night, if you must know. There have been troubles with Ibbie's estate, and it's weighing on me."

"Is that all?"

He'd not readily give up—I had to offer him something more. The truth burned on the tip of my tongue, a confession about Lord West and Kilmere and the bargain binding me. Thanks to the affair of the Crimson Tattoo Killer, Mr. Burke knew more about the Otherworld and my involvement in it than anyone aside from Riven.

But if I spoke, I'd make him a target for Lord West. In the end, he could do nothing to help, yet he'd feel honor bound to try. I'd dragged him into Otherworldly danger before, and I'd not do so again. I weighed my words. "Only personal matters—nothing to involve the Magistry."

"I see." He straightened, his expression becoming more formal. "In that case, I'll not trouble you overlong. Are you willing for me to investigate Kilmere?"

And risk his death haunting me as the others had Ibbie? I folded my hands in my lap. "I'm concerned about the dangers.

Are you aware of the legends of the curse? If the rumors are true, even in part—"

"I'll be careful, but it's my job to take such risks."

Perhaps it was his responsibility to protect the citizens of Byren from mortal threats, but if the danger originated from the Otherworld, what then? As if sensing my agitation, Jade roused and climbed into my lap.

I pulled her close. Could my objections stop him from going? Likely not. If the Magistry had sufficient cause for concern, they could press the point and make things difficult. If I asked Mr. Burke to let Kilmere alone, I believed he'd respect my wishes, but the Magistry might then assign another, one who'd refuse to listen, who would enter the ruins completely blind to the danger.

At least Mr. Burke would consider a warning—and I could trust him to share what he found there. "If I agree to grant access to Kilmere, will you tell me everything you find?"

His voice lowered. "You're a great deal concerned about this."

"I am." Unexpectedly, my eyes burned, his kindness threatening to undo my fragile composure. "If I was at liberty to do so, I'd have already traveled to Kilmere myself. It would be a comfort to know you'll share what you discover."

"Then you have my word."

But it wasn't enough. I couldn't in good conscience send him without clearer warning. He'd kept my involvement with the Crimson Tattoo Killer from the Vigil before. I had to trust he'd do so with any hints of Otherworldly intrigues now. I toyed with the chain of my pendant, and the jewel warmed in response. "As I said, I've been investigating Kilmere, and the tales are troubling. I think something dangerous lurks within."

His brows drew together. "You give credence to the curse theory?"

"This is only speculation, so please don't share it, but records Ibbie left suggest fae had interest in Kilmere and that it might contain some element of Other within. If true, I believe it could have given rise to the stories of the curse."

He said nothing.

"You don't think it possible?" After what we'd witnessed together, I'd not expected him to balk at the notion of an Other-worldly murderer—even if I could not share about Lord West.

"I'll not deny the possibility." Mr. Burke steepled his fingers. "Yet I find it more likely that someone has taken advantage of old legends to provide cover for their own desires for murder or vengeance."

It wasn't an impossibility, yet something about his reluctance to consider Otherworldly involvement troubled me. Perhaps I was being equally stubborn in my own insistence that the deaths must be of Other origin. There could be more than one element at work, and the deaths in Withern might have nothing to do with Kilmere or Lord West.

"You disagree?" he asked.

"I feel otherwise, but feelings are not facts."

"Might your sentiments on the matter have been influenced by all that happened when you sought Lady Dromley's killer?" He let the silence stretch a moment, then continued. "Or is there something you're not telling me, Miss Caldwell?"

I tried not to flinch under his scrutiny. "As you say, recent events—and my experience with Uros—have weighed on my mind."

"Is there anything else? Anything . . . Other?"

He wouldn't come out and ask *have you encountered other high fae invading our supposedly fae-proof city?* Which gave me enough room to demur. "I've nothing else to report."

He didn't appear satisfied—nor was I. Before he could press further, I changed course, taking the offensive. "You must have reason for your certainty a mortal committed these murders. Will you share it?"

"You know I cannot discuss cases in detail."

"But with two dead—"

"Three." He exhaled. "Three dead, one more poisoned and suffering. I cannot divulge details, but there's an individual with the means and motive to have poisoned the victims in question."

Four victims . . . How many more would be claimed? The tension in my shoulders crept down my back. "If the authorities believe they've found the responsible party, then why investigate Kilmere?"

"Given the history of the region, we must make sure," Mr. Burke said. "Don't you agree?"

"It seems I have little choice."

"I'll let you know what I find."

Before I could respond, a sharp sense of Other sliced across my senses, cold and implacable. Asrina slid down between two cushions.

Oh no.

Holden materialized in the doorway, his mouth set. "Lord West, Miss Jessa. He said he was quite certain you'd receive him."

Before I could speak, Lord West filled the doorframe. "Miss Jessa, I didn't know you had another caller."

He surveyed Mr. Burke coolly, and Mr. Burke held his gaze without wavering. The last thing I needed was the two of them at odds.

Somehow I needed to usher Mr. Burke out before he could recognize any hint of Other within Lord West. I didn't believe our time in the Otherworld had given him any particular insight, but I wasn't willing to take the risk.

I stood abruptly, displacing Jade. "Lord West, I didn't expect you so soon."

A half-smile, tinged with mocking, pulled at Lord West's lips. "I found I couldn't be parted from you long."

Mr. Burke raised a brow, and a tide of heat burned up my chest. Whatever impression it gave, I couldn't reject Lord West —my bargain bound me to acceptance.

"Clearly you have matters to discuss," Mr. Burke said. "I'll trouble you no longer."

Part of me wanted to plead with him to stay and provide a buffer from the unwanted attentions of Lord West, yet the greater part willed him to go, so I'd not be responsible for dragging anyone else into danger. "Thank you for calling. Do you plan to leave Avons soon?"

"Tomorrow." He gave a curt nod to Lord West, and a small bow to me, and then he stalked from the room, leaving me to Lord West.

All I could think of was escape. My acceptance of his visit had proven enough to satisfy our bargain—even now the binding mark faded. If only I could be rid of him so readily. With Jade at my heels, I turned toward the door leading to the garden. "Will you join me out of doors?"

"Not today, I think. My call will be short."

"Oh?" I couldn't imagine why he'd deprive himself of the pleasure of tormenting me. I glanced at Holden. He was sure to report this conversation in full to Aunt Caris and, absent a chaperone, appeared to have no intention of abandoning his post.

Lord West's eyes narrowed at him. "It's time you left."

Holden blinked beneath the force of glamour in his words, then stumbled from the room without protest, an act utterly unlike him. I swallowed hard. What harm might have been done?

"That's better." Lord West stretched out on the chair Mr. Burke had vacated, lounging at his ease. "I can't linger long because business calls me away, but never fear, I'll return in time for *Moreland*."

Business. Could it have anything to do with Kilmere and the deaths in Withern? Fae couldn't lie. Perhaps I needed to ask him.

A cold smile flicked across his face. "As it happens, I've also made the acquaintance of one Lord Bradford."

That couldn't have been accidental. I situated myself in an armchair away from Asrina and as far from Lord West as was reasonable.

"He suggested we make the theater a family affair and has extended an invitation to share his box."

"How thoughtful. But I cannot think—"

"I took the liberty of accepting on behalf of you and your sisters. You prefer your family close, I believe, and it would please me to deepen my acquaintance with them." His obsidian eyes flickered. "I shall leave it up to you to persuade them to accept this plan."

Somehow he knew Ada did not favor Lord Bradford. I'd little doubt of it. He sought to hold as much leverage over me as possible, to force me to move at his bidding like a puppet on a stage. "My sisters do enjoy the theater, and of course, my aunts will wish to accompany us as chaperones."

"I expected nothing less." The mocking smile I'd come to abhor played about his lips. "I expect the evening to be quite entertaining."

Our fountain murmured softly in the background, its calm only heightening my turmoil. "It was . . . considerate of you to make the arrangements." I straightened. If he forced his presence upon me, then I'd try to gain something from it. "Will you tell me of the business that calls you away?"

"It concerns you, as a matter of fact."

An icelike shard lodged in my chest. "Me? Or Kilmere?"

"Can't it be both?" The faintest of shadows pooled in his hands. "Kilmere weighs on your mind, does it not?"

"Of course. As I've said, I wish to honor Lady Dromley by tending it properly." I tilted my head. "And I find the deaths in the area quite the tragedy."

"They are a consequence of mortals meddling in what they don't understand."

I hesitated. Dared I inquire further? If I could obtain the truth, perhaps Mr. Burke need not explore the ruins after all. That decided it. "And have you enforced those consequences by killing citizens of Withern?"

"No."

I rocked back. I'd not expected a straightforward answer. Still, I must be sure. "Then have you bargained with or coerced another mortal or fae to do so on your behalf?"

"Indeed not, though I appreciate your attempts to give me credit." He laughed, a sound that held no mirth. "If you're quite done with your wild speculations, I'll give you a warning. Kilmere is dangerous, more than you can possibly fathom. By intruding upon its workings, your man Tibbons has done harm. Many will be forced to deal with the repercussions."

Tibbons? He was caught up in this somehow? Or was Lord West merely seeking to throw me off course? While fae couldn't outright lie, they were known to be masters of twisting the truth, of shading layers of meaning to manipulate belief and perception of what they spoke. But I could see no room for deception in his words, could find no double meaning. I brushed strands of Jade's fur from my skirts. "You expect me to believe he's responsible for these deaths?"

"Believe what you please." The shadows behind him darkened. "But consider how readily you leap to defend your fellow mortals. Is that wise? What gives you confidence he means well?"

No matter how much I wished to, I couldn't dismiss his questions. Mrs. Darrington had also noted that the deaths started after Mr. Tibbons went to Kilmere, though she'd attributed it to him reawakening the curse. "If you believe his motives false, why warn me?"

"So you might understand—no mortal can govern Kilmere. Any attempt will only lead to destruction."

"Then I suppose you suggest I simply surrender it to you now?"

"It would be in your best interests." He shrugged. "But watching you try to hold it will be a great deal more entertaining. Either way, in the end, the outcome will be the same."

Though he left it unspoken, his meaning was clear: Kilmere would be his.

I stood, hoping to end our conversation. "You've given me a great deal to consider."

"Then we shall revisit the matter upon my return," he said. "In the meantime, allow me to leave you this gift."

From his pocket, he withdrew a magnificent bracelet wrought of white gold. The delicate metalwork surrounded starbursts of diamond and pearl, which shimmered with a glow like moonlight. While breathtaking, the glittering confection pulsed with Other, as cold and hostile as its owner.

How much power had been woven into its swirled form?

Jade eyed it, her pupils narrowing to slits. And I shrank back. "You are very generous, but it's far too fine a gift. I'm afraid I can't accept."

"No? Need I remind you of the dangers of refusal?"

My pulse surged in my ears like the wind among rushes. "I—"

He advanced. "Allow me to put it on."

Jade yowled and sprang upon the mantel overhead. With deliberate precision, she wove between two tall candlesticks and then knocked off a large porcelain vase full of roses. The vase shattered on the floor, while the water spattered both Lord West and me. The ruckus should have brought servants rushing into the room to intervene; instead, a fog-like haze obscured the doorway—blocking sound perhaps? Or glamouring the room so it appeared all was well?

I glanced up at Lord West. "Perhaps you might return another time? I'd like to see to Jade. The glass may have injured her."

"Our business remains unfinished." His voice emerged as

smooth and cold as a mountain brook, and his gaze darkened as he regarded Jade. "I've no intention of departing until it's complete." He closed the distance between us, his towering form too close for comfort.

Jade must have agreed, for her hackles rose. With trembling hands, I snatched her up, willing her to remain still. I could not endure it if Lord West struck her as he had Asrina, and this time, if he did, we wouldn't have Wyncourt to shield us.

"I told you what your fate would be if you did not cooperate. For now, the choice remains with you. Accept this gift as a token of our courtship—or I will call on the Vigil before I leave town."

I didn't doubt he'd follow through with the threat. I raised my head to meet his gaze. "One could hardly call an unwanted object a gift. Nevertheless, I accept."

He lifted my arm, his fingers brushing the skin at my wrist. "Not a trace remains. It would seem you have remarkable fortitude."

Then I'd been right—his working was a test, and he'd sought to see if the injury he inflicted would linger.

"One with your resilience bears closer watching." He slipped the bracelet on. When he latched the clasp, biting cold numbed my skin. "I wouldn't want you leaving Avons while I'm away. Now I shall know just where to find you."

Then, like a winter tempest, he swept out the door, leaving me alone with the ache in my arm creeping toward my heart.

AFTER HIS DEPARTURE, I fumbled with the bracelet, seeking the clasp, but it had vanished. The band wove seamless around my skin, a jeweled shackle impossible to remove, one that burned as if my body fought against it.

Perhaps if I could work the salve beneath it, the discomfort would ease. I went to the compounding room and generously slathered some on, and the salve appeared to sink into the surface of the bracelet, its rich golden hue warming the cold light cast by the white gold. The burning sensation subsided to a dull ache confined at my wrist.

I sank into the chair. Though clearly whatever workings he'd placed on it remained active, I welcomed any relief. Still, what would come of it?

If Aunt Caris saw the bracelet, she'd be scandalized. It was far too fine a gift for a gentleman who'd only just expressed his interest—too fine even for a couple openly courting. It was better suited to a wedding present.

Perhaps Lord West had known it and appreciated the symbolism. Yet I refused to consider that he'd succeed in forcing me into marriage. I rubbed my temples.

Had Ibbie felt like this once? Not when she'd fallen headlong for her fae husband-to-be, but later, after they'd wed, when she recognized the trap that had closed about her?

The bracelet blurred beneath my gaze. Somehow I must hide it and all the questions it would bring—

"Miss Jessa?"

I jumped.

Holden hovered in the doorway. "Your chaperone has arrived."

I tucked my wrist into my skirts, attempting to conceal the jeweled band. Fortunately, he appeared unharmed by the glamour worked on him, though he'd not mentioned Lord West, so perhaps his recall had been affected. I shoved that unsettling notion away. "Has Aunt Caris returned?"

"Not yet. Do you want me to show Miss Twells to her room?"

"Thank you, but I'll see to her myself. I want her to feel at home." I stood.

"Yes, Miss Jessa. She's waiting in the drawing room."

With the bracelet still pressed into the folds of my gown, I made my way to greet her.

In the drawing room, Dreda perched on a winged chair, her nerves over the new situation evident in the tight way she clutched her small valise.

I pushed all thoughts of Lord West from my mind and hastened forward. "Miss Twells, I'm thankful you've come."

"It's I who owe you thanks." She tugged her bag to her chest, her expression earnest. "That you know the truth and still suggested your aunts offer me a position . . . I'm ever so grateful."

"I believe Sister Margery best expressed the truth when she commended your fortitude in the face of great trial." This time, I didn't have to force warmth into my smile. "Besides, you've spared me from a dour guardian by the name of Ermenhild, who I hear loves nothing more than issuing lectures."

An answering grin stretched across her face, revealing slightly crooked front teeth and tilting the smattering of freckles on her cheeks. "I won't give lectures, but I'm not one to cast aspersions on anyone's name, seeing as my full one is Aetheldreda."

"Truly?"

"I'm afraid my parents chose to hold with tradition. That name was my gran's before me, and hers before her." She relaxed her grip on the valise. "Please just call me Dreda, no need for Miss Twells."

"Then you must call me Jessa."

"I don't think your aunt would be best pleased with that."

"Aunt Caris won't mind," I said. "But perhaps you should refrain in hearing of Aunt Melisina."

"Of course." She caught her lower lip between her teeth. "There's one thing more. I don't want you to think I was ungrateful before. Sister Margery told me you'd left your address, and I wanted to call to thank you, only I was afraid you might regret involving yourself with someone who'd been fae-touched. I didn't want to cause trouble. But when she told me you recommended me to your aunts, I knew it must not be so—so I thank you for both the position and the . . . the other matter."

"I'm happy I was able to help." I shifted uncomfortably, the spindles of the chair digging into my back. I hoped she'd not taken the position solely because she believed she owed a debt. "I'm glad to have you, but I don't want you to feel bound in any way—"

"Indeed, I don't." Her hazel eyes widened. Though she had nearly two decades on me, she appeared younger, unsure. "Before—well, before, my brothers were most gracious to me, but I was the only one of my siblings to remain unwed. They offered me a place to stay in turns, as I could be of assistance, and they provided for me, for which I'm truly grateful. But I'd no place to call my own—no true home, not after Father died."

So she'd become a nonentity, a being that existed to serve whichever relations were charitable enough to take her in. As such, she'd be dependent on their goodwill and expected to do their bidding without complaint.

It wasn't an uncommon fate, and it was one Aunt Caris sought to spare us from by seeing us marry well. Of course, if I could steward the trust from Ibbie well enough, we might be spared whether we secured a favorable match or not—though it was the least of my concerns at present. "I hope you'll feel you have a home here, and you'll let us know if you need anything for your comfort."

My gaze fell upon her small valise. If that was truly all she possessed, then Aunt Caris would want to remedy it as swiftly as possible. "I'll show you to your room—"

But before I could complete the thought, Aunt Caris herself bustled in, offering her own warm welcome to Dreda.

I willed her to take no note of the bracelet, for it to remain unnoticed as we settled our new chaperone. After showing Dreda her room, Aunt Caris performed the introductions to Ada and Ainslie, as well as the household staff. Though Father was truly absent now, gone on a short trip, the rest of us then gathered for dinner. Only later, when I retired for the evening, did I realize.

At some point, I'd stopped tucking the bracelet within my skirts. And it had drawn no one's attention, garnered no remark. I pulled the bedquilts tight about myself.

Had Lord West glamoured it? Or . . . had I?

CHAPTER 12

As I'd expected, the next morning Aunt Caris insisted upon procuring a new wardrobe for Dreda and making it a family outing, so that Ada, Ainslie, and I could grow better acquainted with her.

I couldn't escape without drawing suspicion, so I donned my hat and gloves with the best grace I could muster. Asrina climbed upon my reticule, as though she desired the safety of its confines once more, and when I opened it, she curled up inside. With my shoulder free, Jade availed herself of her favorite position, and together, we joined the others in the carriage.

Through our stops at the dressmaker and the milliner, the situation with Lord West and Kilmere preyed upon my mind, the shackle upon my wrist an ever-present reminder.

If Lord West hadn't caused the recent deaths in Withern, then what had? A mortal poisoner, as Mr. Burke believed—or the curse of Kilmere? If the curse, then what was its origin? Did it spring from remnant fae-workings left from the Forgotten War or hidden objects of power from the same era? Or might some Otherkind lurk in its depths? Ibbie *had* spoken of delving deeper than was safe.

"What do you think of this hat, Jessa?" Ainslie lifted a

charming confection of pink and white lace and held it up to Dreda.

She flushed. "Miss Ainslie, that's best suited to a young lady coming out, not one such as myself."

"It is lovely, though," I said.

"But not proper."

While she and Ainslie debated the matter, my thoughts drifted back to Kilmere. Our lore told of venomous Otherkind. Could the solution be so simple?

If Lord West knew a powerful Otherkind lurked in the depths of Kilmere, perhaps that was why he'd said no mortal could govern it.

Countless Otherworldly entities were believed to possess the capacity to poison mortals, wyvern, basilisks, and other draconic beings among them. But such large entities surely would have drawn attention—and thereby received credit for the deaths, rather than legends of a nebulous curse.

No, it seemed if some Otherkind were responsible, it must be something subtle and skulking that could strike from the shadows. A bau, perhaps? Mother had told stories of these powerful creatures who pooled shadows to disguise their movements before pouncing upon their unsuspecting prey, their bite imparting poison.

Could such a creature hibernate? Could Mr. Tibbons have woken it? I'd have to ask him if he'd seen any traces of life within the ruin. I ached to investigate myself, to cast off the limitations binding me to Avons and speak to those who believed in the curse—to dig into their lore and examine Kilmere with my own eyes. But once again, Lord West had been one step ahead.

"This would suit you, my dear." Aunt Caris held up a leghorn-style hat trimmed with indigo silk flowers. "Would you like it?"

Her expression was hopeful so I murmured my thanks, then stepped back to watch my sisters and Aunt Caris. They clustered around Dreda, finalizing the choices for her attire. My chest burned. They belonged with each other in a way I did not. How could I bear it if they learned the truth?

Perhaps for now I could justify withholding it, when I did not fully understand what I was myself. But if fae blood *had* been passed down to me, could I continue to endanger them forever?

Somehow I offered my approval of the selections when asked and maintained my composure through luncheon, where I choked down a bit of food. Aunt Caris meant to take Dreda to the haberdashery afterward, but fortunately this time she accepted pleas of fatigue from Ada and me. She and Ainslie swept Dreda out the door, while Ada went to soothe her soul at the pianoforte and I fled to the gardens.

What now?

Speculating on the curse and how it might relate to Lord West's desire to control Kilmere could give insight on how to stop him, but I required a more immediate defense, and I'd come up short with every attempt.

The only thing that had appeared to give him pause was Wyncourt. He'd wanted to enter, but it seemed the demesne had kept him out—and possibly sheltered Asrina from the full impact of his working.

She perched where I'd set her on the edge of the fountain, soaking up the warmth of the sun, her wings motionless. I didn't want to consider what would have happened if we hadn't been at Wyncourt when he'd struck.

But was it Wyncourt itself or some working within? Could the two even be separated? I trailed my fingers through the cool water of the fountain.

If I explored Wyncourt further, perhaps I could learn how it dissuaded him—and if I might put it to any practical use. I could hardly keep myself and my entire family confined within its walls forever, however much we required protection from Lord West.

As soon as Aunt Caris relinquished her claims on Dreda, I'd return.

"I'm certain you'll find the gardens quite pleasant to explore." Aunt Melisina's voice, sweet and smooth as honeyed pears, drifted on the wind.

Company must be present.

On instinct, I shrank behind the fountain, but not before I caught a glimpse of Lord Bradford standing alongside Ada and Aunt Melisina. I lowered myself to hide beneath the stone rim.

"Won't you accompany us?" A note of pleading threaded Ada's words.

"I must consult with Caris on the menu for our upcoming dinner party first."

"Aunt, perhaps I should—"

"Don't discompose yourself, Ada," Aunt Melisina said. "I don't require your assistance. You need only enjoy your stroll."

By leaving them alone, Aunt Melisina must intend to give opportunity for Lord Bradford to come to the point—to ask for Ada's hand. Only a fool would imagine this suited Ada, and Aunt Melisina was no fool. That meant she didn't care how Ada felt, only about the accomplishment of her own desire: a match to make all Avons envy. The flamesward across from me murmured with an anger to match my own.

Body crouched low, Jade prowled around the edge of the fountain, and I stole another peek through the surrounding shrubbery. Lord Bradford had tucked Ada's hand in his arm, his gaze lingering rather lower than it should, while she appeared pale and strained.

"I've long hoped for a moment alone." His tone conveyed his satisfaction with the arrangement.

"Lord Bradford, you know I—"

"I know you care a great deal for your family and their views." His lips tilted upward into a satisfied smirk. "Therefore, I believe you will come to share their view of a marriage between us."

"I do care for them—"

"Then we are in accord."

They approached the fountain and stopped just short of it. Ada took the opportunity to free herself, but he stepped closer, trapping her against it.

"Come, you need not be shy, not with me."

"Lord Bradford, this isn't what I want."

"You don't know what you want. Women rarely do."

She inhaled sharply, looking for all the world like a bird caught in a snare—how I'd felt with Lord West. But Lord Bradford was not fae. I *could* stop him, and I refused to stand by and watch her suffer his unwelcome advances.

How might I best intervene? Aunt Melisina had an iron will. She doubtless kept watch over the situation from a window. If I showed myself, she'd do her best to fetch me in and allow him to carry on.

But if I could remove Lord Bradford from the situation altogether . . . Before I could think better of it, I bent to murmur in Jade's ear. "Can you make him go?"

Perhaps it was ridiculous to speak to her so, to give credence to the theory that something Other had given her greater intellect than any ordinary cat. Yet she'd shown evidence of it time and again, never mind her refusal to respond when asked.

A rumble sounded from deep in her chest, and her pupils dilated. Then she clambered up onto the lowest limb of the overhanging oak, from which she launched herself onto Lord Bradford.

He staggered forward under the unexpected weight, barked his shin on the edge of the fountain, and toppled in, while Jade gracefully sprang from his back and landed on the path beyond.

He rose sputtering and swearing.

Jade lounged at her ease.

"Oh dear!" Ada hurried forward, pressing her lips together, her eyes gleaming with suppressed laughter.

He stopped muttering oaths and drew himself up, as though

attempting to collect his tattered dignity. Then he glared at me. "What manner of foul beast do you permit to roam free? I've heard talk of your monstrous cat, but this—it's a menace!"

The distant snick of a door closing and the crunch of boots on crushed stone heralded Aunt Melisina's arrival. "Lord Bradford! I trust you're unharmed?"

"I'm fine." His jaw tightened. "But I cannot say the same of my attire." He crammed on his soaked hat and marched from the gardens with a muttered by-your-leave.

When he vanished into the depths of the house, Aunt Melisina whirled about.

"Do you know what you've done?" Her voice snapped like a whip. "He intended to make Ada an offer, despite the lack of encouragement she's given. If he never comes up to scratch after this, I shall hold you and that monstrous creature responsible, Jessa."

Jade stopped licking her paw and bared her teeth at Aunt Melisina. Before she could execute another attack, I scooped her up. "Better that she never receive an offer for the rest of her days than she entertain one from him. We'd intended to speak with Father upon his return, but you may as well know the truth now —Lord Bradford has at least three natural children and shows no sign of taking any scruple to care for them or his discarded mistresses."

"Mind your tongue, Jessa. It's not for young ladies to discuss such things." Not a flicker of surprise showed on her face.

"You knew?" Ada's voice emerged soft and shaky, and I clasped her cold hand.

"Why would you encourage him to further his connection with Ada?" I asked.

"What gentleman doesn't have his by-blows and dalliances?" For the briefest moment, she lowered her gaze. Then she pulled herself upright, bristling like a hedge of brambles. "What does it matter so long as the future is secure? If Ada marries him, she'll want for nothing. She'll be elevated far beyond her current position, as will her children to follow. However Lord Bradford chooses to occupy himself, she'll have the pleasure of their companionship and all of society open to her. What more could she want?"

I gripped Ada's hand tighter. Did that mean . . . Had Uncle Milton conducted dalliances of his own? If so, why would Aunt Melisina want Ada to endure the same pain? For I could not think her as untouched as she'd proclaimed. "She might want respect, friendship . . . even love."

"And will love keep you from poverty and affliction?" Aunt Melisina whitened to the lips. "I seek to spare you from that suffering—yet you throw all my efforts back in my face!"

"Father will never support it," I said quietly. "When he returns and Ada speaks with him, it will be the end of things."

She swept her gaze over me, assessing. "Your father *will* listen to me in this. I'll make sure of that."

Ada's mouth trembled, and she lowered her head, as if in so doing, she could conceal the hurt etched across her features.

I positioned myself before Ada, giving room for her to gather composure. Aunt Melisina's words had sounded like a promise—or a threat. What gave her such confidence? Even if Father were the sort of man to impose his will on his daughters, he abhorred men of Lord Bradford's ilk. I couldn't imagine any circumstance in which he'd agree.

Unless . . . would Aunt Melisina go so far as to threaten scandal to bend Father to her will? Did she suspect how deep my irregularities ran? She'd known why Father had sent me to her as a child. Would she threaten to reveal it now, if Father did not cooperate? No, surely that was too great a leap. I was allowing my own fears to inform my thinking, to center unrelated circumstances upon myself in an unwarranted manner. She'd not want to bring ruin upon our family, nor involve the Vigil, not when it could taint her reputation by association.

Aunt Melisina pushed past me and brushed a fallen wild-rose petal from Ada's gown. "I suggest you consider how you may show Lord Bradford your interest."

Eyes shadowed, Ada shook her head. "I cannot—"

"You can, and you will." She lifted her chin. "We're attending the theater with him tomorrow, and you'll give him every indication that you are pleased to receive his attentions."

Before Ada could object, Ainslie and Aunt Caris hurried down the path to join us.

"What in the Crossings has happened?" Aunt Caris looked from one of us to the other, while Ainslie hastened to Ada's side. "No sooner did we return than Holden told me Lord Bradford had been here and left soaked to the skin. And now you conduct an argument for all the world to hear?"

"Your neglect of proper instruction has produced the fruit that might be expected," Aunt Melisina snapped. "Talk some sense into these girls, while I see what can be done to mend what they have damaged."

With that, she glided down the path, her head held at an imperious angle.

Aunt Caris folded her hands. "Will one of you explain what happened?"

"It's all my fault, I'm afraid." Ada rubbed at her chest. "Lord Bradford came, and I didn't welcome him as Aunt Melisina wished."

"That can hardly be a fault. The trouble is that Aunt Melisina insists on subjecting Ada to his attentions when she doesn't desire them. And he's deplorable in every way." Ainslie spilled all we'd discovered, then looked to Aunt Caris. "You cannot support this, surely?"

"I did not know, nor can I condone such character." A sigh gusted from her.

Ada wrapped her arms about herself. "Aunt Melisina says all gentlemen conduct such affairs."

"Not all." The usual radiance of Aunt Caris's countenance dimmed. "But more than I like to consider."

"I cannot wed such a man." For once, Ada spoke firmly. "I can scarcely even tolerate his presence."

"I'll try to speak to Melisina, but she's been highly invested in this match—to the point of discouraging others who have taken interest in Ada."

"Why?" I asked.

"I cannot say why she favors Lord Bradford, unless it's merely that he offers the greatest fortune of the lot," Aunt Caris said. "But I will not have you thinking too badly of her. She only seeks to spare you pain by seeing you wed well. Melisina doesn't share her affections readily, but when we were growing up, she had a friend dearer to her perhaps than even us sisters. Her friend was swept off her feet by an impoverished artist of little standing and wed him against the wishes of her family. She was cut off, and just a few years later, she passed in childbirth for lack of care she could have received if only they were better situated. When she died, Melisina was crushed. It changed how she viewed things."

I didn't want to feel any glimmer of understanding for Aunt Melisina—but if she'd suffered such a loss, if she feared us enduring similar fates, then perhaps I could accept that she meant well, whatever hurt she caused. Only she'd not readily surrender her plans—and for whatever reason, she believed she could sway Father to her cause.

What leverage did she hold?

"In any case, I suppose I had best see if I can reason with her. If not, Alden will have to." Aunt Caris trudged back toward the house, her usual bustle absent.

Then Ada turned toward me. "Thank you, Jessa. If you hadn't come, I'm not certain what I would have done."

"Sent him on his way, as he deserved, I hope." Ainslie plopped onto the edge of the fountain, thankfully some distance from Asrina.

"I tried, but he refused to listen." Ada shuddered. "If Jessa hadn't intervened . . ."

"You would have done the same for me. Besides, it's Jade you need to thank."

"I suppose I should." She knelt in the grass next to Jade. "Your intervention was most welcome."

Though Jade still kept her distance, she condescended enough to offer a soft *mrow*.

Ada wrapped her arms about herself. "I wish Father were here."

"Aunt Melisina seemed very sure that she could sway him." I twined my fingers around a sprig of lavender, its soothing fragrance filling the air.

Ainslie frowned. "I wish we knew why."

As did I—on every front, I'd far more questions than answers. At least with Lord Bradford, Father could offer help. With Lord West, I was on my own, and if I didn't gain some answers soon, I feared he would have his way.

CHAPTER 13

Though I intended to depart as soon as was proper the following morning, Aunt Caris pulled Ada, Ainslie, and me aside shortly after breakfast to discuss the matter of Lord Bradford. As she'd made no headway with Aunt Melisina, she suggested Ada maintain a cordial demeanor until Father returned to settle matters—at least cordial enough to avoid a scene at the theater, since we were already committed to the outing.

In turn, Aunt Caris assured us she'd allow Lord Bradford no opportunity to approach Ada alone. After much debate, primarily from Ainslie, the matter was settled—though it did not appear we were in for a pleasant evening. Lord Bradford aside, I must still face Lord West, and I possessed no new means of resisting his plans.

I wrapped my hand around the pendant of my necklace, welcoming the pulse of warmth in response. If only it deterred high fae . . .

When at last Aunt Caris dismissed us, I sought Dreda. "Will you accompany me to Wyncourt this morning? I have some tasks to attend there, which will allow you time to do as you please."

"Then I shall bring some needlework. I told Miss Caldwell that I could rework several of her lace caps to best match the current mode, and it will give me time to finish them all." She collected the necessary items in a mending basket, and when we arrived at Wyncourt, Mrs. Peters saw Dreda swiftly settled in the drawing room with a lavish tea—despite her insistence that she required nothing.

"And what of you, Miss Jessa? Do you wish for refreshments also?" Mrs. Peters asked.

"No, thank you." I lowered my voice as we stepped from the drawing room into the corridor beyond. "Danvers said there have been continued reports of odd noises about Wyncourt, and I'd like to make sure all appears well."

That was true, as far as it went. While I sought anything that might aid in resisting Lord West, I also wanted to ensure Wyncourt was safe for its inhabitants.

Of the servants, Mrs. Peters and Danvers alone had known of Ibbie's habit of scripting runes on the walls of Wyncourt. While Danvers appeared to dismiss it as a mere oddity, evidently Mrs. Peters thought Ibbie'd had cause for caution, for she offered an appreciative nod. "I'd be most grateful if you checked about."

"You've no cause for concern, I trust?"

"Nothing I can put my finger on, only I have a peculiar feeling sometimes—I'm certain it's nothing."

"Still, if anything worries you, please tell me."

I took my leave of Mrs. Peters. Just down the corridor, the white-bonneted head of one of the serving girls winked out of sight. Had she overheard our discussion?

I shook off the notion as I ascended the stairs. I'd first encountered fae-workings in Edward's bedchamber, so it seemed the sensible place to start, yet I found myself reluctant to enter without Riven.

I straightened to my full, rather insubstantial height. I couldn't wait for help that would never come, not when Lord West intended to return tonight. A glamour-concealed door connected Ibbie's and Edward's chambers—the only access point I'd yet uncovered to his room—so I entered her bedchamber and marched over to where it remained hidden. This time, when I halted before it, the glamour melted away at once, leaving only a pattern of dark threads, fine as gossamer, woven above the latch.

I traced them with my finger. Despite my anticipation of the needle-like prick, I still flinched when it came. The drop of blood that welled in its wake unlocked the door, and I stepped inside, the musty, long-enclosed scent engulfing me.

Without Riven to cast a fae-light, I required some other source of illumination. I crossed to the heavily draped windows and drew back the curtains.

A swirl of shadow met my gaze.

Oh.

Was this room entirely disconnected from the outside world or simply shrouded by strong glamour? I fumbled with the gaslights on the wall, at last sparking one to flame. By its pallid glow, the chamber looked far gloomier than it had when illumined by fae-light.

Yet I'd no need to linger. If Edward had concealed anything of value, he'd most likely have hidden it in the chambers beyond the hidden staircase. So I crossed to the pair of bookcases in the corner and pulled the books in the same pattern Riven had.

The right bookcase swung back, and air tinged with a hint of decay wafted from the stairs beyond, though not nearly as strong as before. It mingled with the ancient, sharp scent of the stone from which the hidden stairs and walls were hewn, an unpleasant reminder of Lord West.

I steeled myself and stepped through the doorway, only to stumble to a halt. The stairs ascended as before, but another segment spiraled downward. How had I missed that last time?

Was it merely the openness of my Other senses, which I'd kept so tightly shuttered at the time? Or did Wyncourt itself extend further welcome? I hesitated.

Which way should I go?

If I retraced our former path, I'd have greater assurance of safety, since Riven had unraveled the workings that sought to claim our lives. But if I wanted to uncover further truth, I must descend.

I glanced down at Jade.

Though she prowled about, her movements wary, she didn't attempt to bar my way down, which offered reassurance.

Asrina, from her perch on my shoulder, brightened a bit, as if to light our way. Together we began a slow descent. With each step, I examined our surroundings for any hint of hidden danger, yet found none.

Did I have Wyncourt to thank for safe passage? I'd likely never know.

The stairs deposited us in a circular chamber lit not by gas lamps, but ever-burning fae orbs, which arced across the ceiling, casting a pale luster over the expanse below. The air warmed about me, as though in welcome. It seemed Wyncourt *had* wanted us to come.

A breathtaking mosaic of stone spread across the floor. Unlike mosaics of mortal make, where individual pieces composed a picture, the floor remained whole, not a single seam marring the magnificent starscape unfolding before me, the colors as vibrant as though the stone were a living thing.

In the center, a tremendous starburst held court, radiant and shimmering with silvery hues. I eased forward, and when I stepped over it, a sense of immense power rooted me in place.

Wyncourt itself burst into my awareness, bright and determined and yearning for . . . something? The multitude of workings woven through every stone, every arch and beam, tugged at my awareness, vast beyond measure.

I staggered away from the starburst, my senses spinning, and my gaze caught upon something concealed before. Across the chamber from where I'd entered stretched an arched doorway outlined with a spiraled star pattern. Silver-laced threads of black bound the door, dark and bold and beautiful.

Mesmerized, I crept closer. When I tried to study the strands of power, of what must be a fae-working of immense complexity, they blurred before my eyes, shimmering in and out until I could no longer trust my vision.

I stretched my hand toward the door, and a veritable gale of frigid air blasted my back.

Jade leapt forward, weaving between my ankles, driving me away from the door.

What in the Crossings?

Why draw me here, then bar me from entering? Unless Wyncourt wished me to connect to its heart, but not unleash whatever was hidden beyond.

Though I felt a bit foolish, I had to be sure, so I spoke. "Should I enter the chamber beyond that door?"

My words resonated in the vast space, one that should not be able to exist without displacing numerous chambers in the manor proper.

The starburst in the center of the chamber went black, an ominous signal. When I moved farther from the doorway, it radiated its silvery light once more.

I would trust its direction—I had little choice. The last hidden chamber I'd explored in Wyncourt had revealed ghouls. A far more complicated working concealed this space, so I did not want to contemplate what might be imprisoned beyond. Except I must know if the inhabitants of Wyncourt were at risk. "Are the servants safe?"

The light brightened further.

I'd take that as affirmation. If I could somehow communicate with Wyncourt here—and after all I'd experienced, speaking with a fae demesne didn't seem particularly odd—then I must ask about Lord West. This time, I remained on the farthest edge of the starburst design, rather than seeking the core.

Wyncourt once more surged into my awareness, this time more muted and manageable.

"Can you help me in the matter of Lord West?" I asked.

The starburst dimmed to the dullest of grays.

Was that a no? Certainly, all I'd beheld thus far suggested the power of Wyncourt rested in the workings woven into its very fabric, not something that could be used beyond its borders. It had been the slimmest of chances, but still I'd hoped. If it could not help with Lord West, perhaps it could offer other aid? "What of assisting me with contacting Lord Riven?"

It remained murky.

I sighed. Given I'd no true notion of how demesnes worked, I shouldn't be surprised that my guesses had missed the mark, yet—

"Miss Caldwell?"

I whirled around, my heart drumming against my chest. Had someone followed me?

I could find no trace of another living soul within the chamber, but an image took shape in my mind, that of the young, white-bonneted maid—and then the voice sounded again. "Miss Caldwell, are you here?"

While I stood within the star, I could gain some sense of her presence: she was traveling the corridor leading to the bedchambers. If she somehow managed to enter Edward's chamber . . .

With Jade at my side, I raced back up the stairs, securing the hidden entrance and flying into Ibbie's room just as the maid entered it.

"There you are, Miss Caldwell. Begging your pardon for the interruption, but I . . ." She subsided into uncomfortable silence, clutching at her apron.

"Is something troubling you?"

"Yes, miss." She took a deep breath, then plunged in. "It's like this. I'm the one that keeps the bedchambers, and I've told Danvers time and again about the sounds up here; they come from the walls, seems like. Danvers thinks I'm imagining it, that I've listened to too many tales of spectres and such, but it's not that, miss."

"I see." That sounded like Danvers; his no-nonsense personality made him well-suited to run a house the size of Wyncourt. "When did you start hearing these sounds?"

"After Lady Dromley died, miss." Her gaze lowered. "I feared 'twas the killer lurking, that we'd all be murdered in our beds and I must leave, but then Lord Riven came, and it all stopped."

"So you heard nothing when he was in residence?"

"No, miss, and I thought it was because no killer would want to confront a man like Lord Riven." She shifted her weight from one foot to the other. "But then Lord Riven went away and the sounds started again, but the killer was dead and gone, so it couldn't have been him at all, and I'm so afraid of what it *could* be. It's why I was wishful of speaking to you today, after I heard you talk to Mrs. Peters. I hope I've not done wrong."

"Indeed not. I'm glad you came to me. Do you have any idea what could make the sort of sounds you've heard?"

"I don't rightly know, but I . . . I'm feared someone is trapped somewhere inside."

"What makes you think that?" I asked softly.

She twisted her apron in a way sure to leave indelible wrinkles. "I've had such dreams, and I've tried to tell Danvers of them, but he says it's all stuff and nonsense and that I won't be excused from my tasks for making up tales."

I rubbed my temples. Her story appeared to confirm the theory that something was imprisoned behind the mysterious door below Wyncourt. I'd come seeking answers and instead found new problems.

Yet Wyncourt had offered assurance of their safety, which must mean whatever was inside remained bound. "Don't worry. I'll look into the matter, but if you feel you must leave, then I'll see to it that you're given a good character reference. I will say I agree with Danvers that you're safe here."

"Yes, miss." She bobbed her head and slipped from the room as the mantel clock chimed five times.

I'd lost hours in the depths of the manor, only catching glimpses of all it held within—and now I'd run out of time.

Dreda poked her head into the room. "Miss Caldwell gave me strict orders that we're to depart at five. I hope you don't mind."

I did, yet I could scarcely confess why. In just a few hours, Lord West would fetch me for the theater, doubtless with some new torment he'd devised—and I'd no hope of protection.

~

AFTER LIANNE FINISHED SWEEPING my hair into an elaborate affair of curls woven with starflowers, Aunt Caris bustled into my chamber. Her soft features warmed with pleasure as she regarded me, her gaze meeting mine in the mirror. "You look lovely. Lord West will be enchanted."

Despite my efforts, she must have perceived something of my fears in my expression. "Does something trouble you, my dear?"

So many things, but only one she might help with . . . that of my past. I turned to her. "I've been thinking about Mother more often of late."

"I understand, my dear." Sorrow laced her voice. "I'd wondered if you might feel her absence more when Lord West expressed his interest. It's natural you'd wish for her guidance as you contemplate your future."

I fiddled with an abandoned starflower. "Do you remember how she felt when she learned she was expecting me? She had two others so close in age, so perhaps—"

"She was delighted, my dear. She gloried in her daughters, to the point she was scarcely willing to let the nursemaids tend you." A soft smile crossed Aunt Caris's face. "I must confess, when Alden wed her, I thought she'd never take to motherhood. She was so lively, so very determined in all things. Yet nothing pleased her more."

"So she was never . . . low in spirits when she carried me?"

A faint shadow crossed her face. "There's no need for you to worry about such things."

"Aunt Caris, I'm no longer a child that I need my feelings spared. I'd like to understand, truly."

"Then I will tell you that her oppressive moods never worsened during confinement. If anything, she was her brightest with the three of you."

It fit with my recollections of how she'd called us her golden ones, how she'd always made herself available to us. Yet something had caused her melancholy—just as something had caused the abilities I displayed, which were unnatural to mortals. I could theorize all I wanted, but I needed more information. If Aunt Caris couldn't offer further insight, then perhaps Father would, though it pained him to speak of Mother, even now.

Aunt Caris stepped close and added a pin to secure a flyaway curl. "I know I'm a poor substitute for her, but—"

I clasped her hand before she could pull it away. "Don't say that. You've done nothing but love us well our entire lives, and I can't imagine where we'd be without you."

Her features softened further. "My dear girl. She would be so pleased with all of you—as I am."

Only because Aunt Caris did not know what I truly was. If I couldn't conceal it, if I had to see her affection turn to fear—a knife-blade of pain pierced my chest. I ducked my head, pretending to rummage for my gloves.

Then, blessedly, Gaile entered, providing a further distraction. "Lord Bradford has arrived."

"What of Lord West?" Aunt Caris asked.

"No sign of him yet, Miss Caldwell."

"He doesn't seem like the sort to arrive late." A slight frown crossed her face.

"Perhaps his business delayed him, and he'd no time to send word?" A little spark of hope flared within. Could I be so fortunate as to gain a stay?

Evidently so, for when we could delay no longer without

missing the performance, Aunt Caris consented to our departure. Along with many of society's finest, we entered the Crescent Theater. Gas chandeliers cast a brilliant glow over ornately gilded walls and white marble floors, a sparkling array of beauty to feast the senses.

Under other circumstances, it would have been a pleasant treat. But confined to a box with Lord Bradford, it proved a torment.

I sank back into the plush red velvet seat, watching the two of them. The music held Ada enraptured, but not so Lord Bradford—his attention rested on her.

Then he leaned over to whisper something to Ada, and his gaze dropped decidedly lower than her face.

I half-rose from my seat, and Aunt Melisina clutched my arm with a talon-like grip. "Sit. Now."

I'd promised Aunt Caris not to make a scene, so I subsided, chafing beneath the conventions that bound me. I forced myself to look beyond Lord Bradford—wait, was that Lord West? I leaned forward. In the shadows of a box across the theater lurked an indistinct figure, something in its bearing reminding me of him.

But if Lord West was here, why had he kept at a distance? Was this another test of sorts?

I sat very still as the music and dialogue swirled about me. At intermission, I hurried to get a better view of the spot where I thought I'd seen him, tucking myself behind a fluted pillar. If he was here, I wished to know it, yet avoid him taking note of me —were such a thing possible. Yet it seemed he was not. A party of strangers occupied the mysterious figure's box, and no pricking sense of Other hinted at Lord West's presence.

I whirled about to return to my family, and in so doing, caught sight of Mr. Ludne, the Vigilist who'd handled Ibbie's murder, greeting an unfamiliar gentleman.

Of all the people I did *not* wish to see. Only Lord West

would have been less pleasant. I shrank deeper into the shadows, willing him to take no notice of me.

The two men exchanged pleasantries, then the gentleman said, "With the Crimson Tattoo Killer apprehended, I thought you'd have welcomed the chance to return to your Vigil-house. I know you have no particular fondness for Avons."

"I find myself dissatisfied by several irregularities that came up during the case." Mr. Ludne's long fingers clutched his raven-head cane. "I don't intend to leave the city until I have the answers I require."

"You always were single-minded."

The two men fell into step alongside each other, their voices blending with the general hum of conversation. I hurried back to my seat, my mind whirling with speculation. If Mr. Ludne had suspicions about the affair of the killer, would he eventually trace them back to me?

Between such thoughts and those of Lord West and Kilmere and Lord Bradford, the play felt interminable, the applause it provoked overloud, the exchange of wit flat. At last, it reached its finale, and we could make our escape.

The cheery fragrance of sweet pinks, clustered in stone planters outside the doors, greeted me, and I breathed a bit easier as we trundled into Aunt Melisina's carriage.

When we emerged before our townhome, the gas lamps burned bright, casting great pools of light into the darkness. Yet a chill pricked down my spine. I hesitated on the stairs, surveying my surroundings. Then I saw it: a spiraled shadow resting in a pool of light.

Nothing nearby could have cast it; it was an impossibility. A sentinel left by Lord West, perhaps? As if in response, the bracelet burned bitter cold at my wrist.

Shoulders tight, I turned my back on the odd shadow and entered our row home.

If only it were Wyncourt.

CHAPTER 14

In the light of morning, I could almost dismiss the shadow as a phantasm birthed by night and my own fears. Unquestionably, the knowledge that as yet I possessed no means to escape Lord West had left me shaken. Perhaps it also made me see his influence where it did not exist.

Or perhaps he in fact watched and waited to spring some particularly unpleasant surprise. I couldn't simply wait for him to strike again. Whatever its cause, his absence offered me time, and I'd put it to good use.

What about the Cloister library? The old logbook I'd discovered there had contained hints of the Forgotten War. Why not also some reference to the defenses used then as well?

Unless Mr. Heard was right, and we'd never possessed any. Either way, the old tomes hoarded within might offer some direction.

Outside my window, a sudden gust of wind tossed the branches of the oak restlessly. Its song surged into my senses, its deep-rooted determination becoming my own. I turned from the window and left my bedchamber, descending the stairs to join my family. Jade kept close to my side, as she had all morning. She acted as though I'd abandoned her for days instead of mere hours to attend the theater last night. When we settled at the breakfast table, she perched vigilant on the chair next to mine, even going so far as to growl at Holden when he parceled out the early post.

We all had an assortment of letters and invitations, all except Dreda. She sat eating quietly, yet something in her downturned shoulders hinted at disappointment.

The sweet roll in my mouth turned dry. "Dreda, if you wish to write to your family, you're welcome to use the supplies in the secretary."

"Thank you, Miss Jessa." She sipped her tea, then returned the cup to its saucer with care. "But they're not much for letter-writing."

Because they did not enjoy correspondence or because they'd shunned Dreda after her affliction? Or had they simply forgotten her now that she was of no use to them? I could scarcely ask without causing greater pain, so I let the matter drop.

While Aunt Caris engaged Dreda in light conversation about the caps she'd remade, I slit open my first letter, skimming down to the signature.

It was from Mr. Burke, and it had arrived sooner than I'd expected.

Miss Caldwell,

> *You'll be pleased to hear the investigation of the local authorities continues to point to the suspect I mentioned when I called. The choice of victims—all old families in the region, whom he has reason to hold a grudge against—appears to confirm his involvement. Our suspect will shortly be taken into custody. I trust you'll keep this to yourself, but I wished to ease your mind.*
>
> *As of now, these deaths don't appear to relate to Kilmere. If you should have any further concern about the situation, only write. I intend to remain in Withern-at-Sea until our suspect*

appears before the local Magister and his guilt or innocence is conclusively determined.

With respect,
Mr. Burke

I folded the letter slowly. While he'd divulged more than I'd expected about the case, he'd said little about Kilmere. Surely if he'd discovered any sign of Other within, he'd have found a way to hint at it, whether or not it related to his case.

Unanswered questions churned in my gut. If only I could go to Kilmere—or at least ask him face-to-face. If I composed my reply with care, perhaps I could draw out a bit more.

I lifted the second letter, one written on the finest linen paper. It bore an inscription from Lady Hampton. My spirits lifted. When I'd written to some of Ibbie's oldest acquaintances, I'd only the smallest of hopes that I'd receive a response.

Miss Caldwell,

I have considered your request to discuss the matter of Kilmere. I must say I found a great deal that happened then peculiar. Some of it I'd prefer not to revisit, yet I feel it my duty to speak the truth.

If you call this afternoon at two, I would be delighted to receive you.

Best regards,
Lady Hampton

I rested the letter in my lap. Perhaps she might offer one of the missing pieces I required to understand the nature of the curse and in turn Lord West's interest in Kilmere. Ibbie couldn't have spoken openly of it, of course, but Lady Hampton's observations and memories could hold valuable clues.

If I called on her at two, I'd have time enough to visit the

Cloister library afterward, assuming they'd receive me after I'd led a Vigilist into their hallowed halls. Perhaps I still had a chance of constructing some defense—or finding information I might use to bargain further with Lord West.

I folded the letter. "Aunt Caris, what do you know of Lady Hampton?"

"She's become a bit reclusive in her old age, but she still comes to Avons every season—and her patronage is coveted." Aunt Caris inclined her head. "Why do you ask, my dear?"

"She was an old connection of Ibbie's, and she's sent an invitation to call this afternoon."

"How delightful." Aunt Caris stirred a half-spoon of sugar into her tea. "She rarely welcomes visitors, so that's quite an honor. I've already promised to call at Penwick Hall, but perhaps Dreda will accompany you?"

"I'd be pleased." She offered a shy smile.

Though I'd rather conduct the conversation without an audience, I could offer no reasonable protest. "I plan to visit the library afterward, so it may be a long afternoon."

"It's no trouble, truly. That's why I'm here."

I murmured my thanks and sat quiet as conversation swirled about me. A restless energy churned inside, a relentless desire to *do* something—though what, I did not know.

When we retired to the morning room after breakfast, Jade refused to calm. She prowled about the windowsills and sniffed at the doorways, as though seeking hidden prey.

At last, Aunt Caris set aside her embroidery. "Perhaps she needs to go out of doors?"

Jade glared at her.

"Perhaps we both do." I scooped her up and sought refuge in the garden.

Instead of the gentle cool of morning, early hints of summer heat laced the air, along with a stickiness that coated my skin. A distant, heavy, greenish scent signaled the approach of a possible storm, though only a faint smudge on the horizon hinted at gathering clouds.

I plucked at my bodice, wishing for a gust of wind like the one that had stirred the oak earlier, but no such good fortune came. So I fetched my collecting basket, then bent over the garden bed that skirted the glasshouse, one in which I grew medicinal herbs—rue, chamomile, lemon balm, and countless others.

Their multilayered fragrances laced the air, as rich as the songs that danced through my mind as I gently collected leaf and stem and blossom.

The repetitive motions brought some measure of calm, yet Jade remained restive. Did she know something I did not? With increasing frequency I glanced over my shoulder, seeking any misplaced shadows. When a sparrow chirred from the garden wall, I jumped.

The ivy climbing the trellis along the house rustled with an agitation to match my own, though no breeze stirred it. And the sense of pressure within mounted.

Within my skirts, Asrina shifted. Since she'd favored the security of my reticule, this morning I'd made her a nest of sorts in an inner pocket of my gown, where she might rest if she didn't feel inclined to cling to my shoulder. Now she nestled contentedly inside.

Yet before Lord West had assaulted her, she'd radiated strength and energy, never weary, never still. What had he done to her? If she didn't survive her injury . . .

I snatched up my collecting basket and pressed to my feet. I'd try the goldhearts. What had I to lose? Though I sensed their restorative properties did not extend to physical ailments, perhaps they'd lift her spirits.

I carried my selections into the compounding room and gently placed some goldheart blossoms in a jar with sweet oil. Then I placed the container on the windowsill, where the sun might draw out their healing properties—at least what little still shone in the rapidly clouding sky.

I eyed the gleaming bracelet and then slid a small tin of my amelior salve into my opposite pocket. Gowns with pockets were uncommon, but now I was glad I'd persuaded Aunt Caris to commission me a few.

When at last we reached the appointed time, Dreda and I rattled along in the carriage, Jade at my side, Asrina still concealed.

Dreda opened her mouth as if to speak, then subsided, studying her hands.

The heavy scent to the air strengthened, the heat thickening about us as I surveyed her. The role of chaperone or companion wasn't an easy one. She wasn't a proper servant, nor quite family either. Perhaps it left her uncertain how best to comport herself; perhaps she felt as awkward as I did at this moment. The carriage jostled over an uneven cobblestone. What might I do to set her more at ease?

"Dreda, I know you didn't want supplies for correspondence, but is there anything else that might make your stay more comfortable?" I didn't know much about her interests, but she'd likely received some instruction in the ladylike arts. "You're always welcome to make use of the pianoforte or other instruments as you desire. Or if you wish, I could procure some drawing books and supplies for you? If you've any particular interest, you've only to say the word, and—"

"You're very kind, but I'd not want to give your aunts the impression I mean to shirk my duties." Her lips firmed. "If I'm not needed as chaperone, then I'm sure I may be of aid to your aunt."

However much she demurred, she must desire something, even if her hopes were so deeply buried she refused to admit them. "Aunt Caris doesn't expect you to serve every waking moment. She'd not begrudge you having your own pursuits when you're not required to chaperone."

"It's best this way. My brother's wife always reminded me that no one wants a layabout or chatterer in their home, and I've seen its truth," she said softly. "Besides, I've no particular skill. Only that of being useful."

Her voice held a dull quality that spoke of hidden pain. If her sister-in-law had addressed her so, her place with them must have been quite uncomfortable.

"I'm certain that's not true."

"Your aunt has been very gracious, and I want to please her. Nothing else matters."

Which meant she feared losing her position, though I couldn't fathom Aunt Caris had given her reason to do so. Aunt Melisina, on the other hand . . . I gave her a reassuring smile. "She's delighted, I can tell."

Dreda bobbed her head and subsided back into silence. The sticky heat in the air settled unpleasantly over my skin, and I shifted against the hard leather seat. Perhaps I was simply unaccustomed to her companionship, but for all my efforts to set Dreda at ease, my own restiveness refused to subside; rather, it increased as we neared Hampton House.

Anticipation swirled in my stomach like river rushes caught in a crosscurrent as our carriage halted before an imposing edifice. It was crafted in the old style, all gentle curves and arched domes, the sovstone an even richer hue with the passage of years.

Together we descended from the carriage. A sudden burst of wind swirled the leaves of the white poplar trees that lined the street, revealing their silver undersides. Damp air, heavy with impending rain, pressed upon us, and my gown clung unpleasantly to my skin as we climbed the stone steps. I lifted the bronze griffin that served as a knocker and rapped firmly.

A moment later, the butler appeared, birch-bark pale hair crowning a narrow face. "May I help you?"

"I'm Miss Jessa Caldwell, and this is Miss Twells. We're here at the request of Lady Hampton."

"Ah, yes. I was told to expect you, Miss Caldwell. If you'll come this way . . ." He withdrew into the lavish entry.

Before I could follow, a sense of Other pricked up my spine. I couldn't resist one more glance over my shoulder.

There.

Upon the bottom step, a shadow rested, spiraled like a snake —only there was no form to cast it.

Jade growled, her hackles rising.

I *wasn't* imagining it.

I hurried into Hampton House and the safety of its walls— but aside from Wyncourt, no home in Avons offered protection. Was Lord West nearby? Did he intend to continue stalking me from the shadows, placing them in my path whenever he pleased in order to unnerve me?

Why not come out into the open, when he had the upper hand? Or was this simply another of his cat-and-mouse games, one meant to make me doubt my own perceptions—or to test the extent of them?

I crossed the polished white-and-black stone floor. Above our heads stretched a magnificent domed window, its patterned panes offering a glimpse of the glowering sky. On a sunny day, light must flood through it, kindling to flame the golden walls.

The butler led us down a passage wide enough to accommodate eight side by side, then he halted outside the double doors at the end. "I'm afraid Lady Hampton cannot abide the company of cats—they cause her great torment of body."

Though uncommon, in response to certain animals, some endured the most dreadful afflictions—rasping breaths, swelling of the eyes, and so forth. If Lady Hampton were one of their number, I could scarcely expect her to entertain Jade. And yet, I couldn't bear to part from her. "What do you suggest?"

He bowed slightly. "I could make her comfortable below-stairs until your visit is through."

Jade bristled, and the slightest of snarls escaped.

He edged away. "Perhaps she'd be more comfortable if Miss Twells attended her?"

"I'd be happy to help, Miss Jessa."

"Jade doesn't take kindly to anyone aside from me." Yet I needed to speak with Lady Hampton. I hesitated. "Might the two of them be situated somewhere closer?"

Perhaps that would console Jade.

"The parlor is just down to the left. Will that suit?"

"Very well, thank you."

The butler bent, as though he intended to scoop Jade up and carry her there. She glared at him, and her lips drew back, showing a hint of fang.

"There's no need to fetch her. She'll follow you."

Jade turned her glare upon me, then collapsed upon my feet.

"Please, Jade. Go with Dreda. I must speak with Lady Hampton, but I won't be long."

"Perhaps I might offer some . . . milk?" the butler stammered.

"No need for that. She'll go."

Please.

With a low growl, Jade rose and padded to stand alongside Dreda.

"If you'll come this way, Miss Twells and, uh, Jade." He escorted them to a room only one door down. "I'll have refreshments sent to you momentarily."

When he ushered me into the drawing room, an ache stirred within me. However much I needed to speak with Lady Hampton, it wrenched me to leave Jade. Perhaps her aversion to separation had influenced me more than I knew.

The butler stood in the doorway. "If you'll be seated, miss, Lady Hampton will be with you shortly."

He slipped from the room and closed the door, perhaps a precaution to keep Jade from joining us. Only where was Lady Hampton?

One of her advanced years might take time to descend the

stairs and greet a guest. Still, I'd have expected her to be waiting, given her summons.

Uneasy, I perched on the edge of a chair near the tea table, which was set for two. A bank of windows stretched just beyond, but the heavy velvet curtains were kept drawn. Some of the elderly favored the softer lighting of gas lamps above the bright rays of the sun—evidently Lady Hampton was among their number.

The lack of natural light muted the golden walls, giving the chamber a feeling of gloom, despite the lavish oil paintings and the intricate swirls and gilded carvings of the trim work.

Something was wrong.

The shadows in the corners were darker than they should be, given the gentle glow of the gaslight. And Lady Hampton *should* be here.

I scrambled from the chair, ready to flee Hampton House and face any scandal my departure might cause, should I be mistaken.

The far wall darkened till it resembled a midnight sky, and Lord West strode through. He made no attempt at glamour, and he was fierce as a winter wind—his dark hair longer, wilder, his eyes an impossibly brilliant black now tinged with blue, his features sharp-hewn and unnaturally perfect.

I'd not been mistaken—and it was too late. My blood surged into my temples, sharp and pounding.

Twin coils of shadow drove into my chest with the force of javelins, driving me back into the chair, binding me in place.

I was trapped.

Yet I could not reveal my fear. I lifted my chin. "What do you think you're doing?"

"Utilizing a bit of information I uncovered." The shadow-bindings tightened, bitter and biting. "I did warn you that you might not like the results of my investigation. That you'd regret not accepting my first offer."

He took the chair across from me. The tea things rested on

the table between us, little tendrils of steam fogging the air as we sat in some bizarre semblance of an ordinary call. It should have been Lady Hampton ready to pour out instead of a predatory fae—

Lady Hampton. I strained against the bindings at my wrists. "What have you done with Lady Hampton and her staff?"

"Only a mortal would be so foolish as to consider that at a time like this." The shadows behind him deepened. "You should be far more worried about your own fate, my sweet."

"She was innocent in this." I strained to sense some connection to the trees lining the streets outside, to anything beyond this room, anything that might allow me to resist. Yet his shadows formed an impenetrable shroud. He'd woven his trap well.

"You think that matters?" His sharp-edged laugh sliced the air. "Never fear, she's retired to her family seat for the summer, leaving her home empty."

"And the butler?"

"A man in my employ." His obsidian eyes narrowed. "Now I have a few questions for you, before our game reaches its conclusion."

Its conclusion . . . my death? What would that mean for Dreda and Jade? I was shaking now, beyond my ability to conceal. "If you had questions, there were easier ways of getting answers."

"None quite so entertaining." He leaned forward. "How long did you think you could keep the blood on your hands a secret? You killed in my world."

Uros. That was what he'd learned? Somehow that information changed things between us—now he was not obliged to restrain himself. Which meant Mr. Heard had spoken truth. Something governed the relations between our worlds—some rule I'd unknowingly violated. "I never sought to hide it from you."

"Of course. You weren't told what you surrendered in the

act." He leaned forward, gaze hungry. "Who bid you to strike the auvok? And what were you offered in exchange?"

"No one—" I stopped short. Might I bargain with the information he imagined I possessed?

"No one?" One of the shadows from my wrist crept up my arm, numbing as it traveled. His lips curved into a half-snarl, half-smile. "Don't think you can lie to me. If you didn't have fae protection, fae instruction, you could never have survived the Otherworld, let alone an encounter with an auvok."

"I've only spoken truth."

Yet he didn't believe me, which meant he couldn't compel or perceive truth, not like Riven.

Spikes of pain dug everywhere the shadow traveled, bruising deep as bone. "My patience has limits. Who did you serve?"

I struggled to draw breath. "What will you give me in exchange for that information?"

"A quicker, less painful death."

In my pocket, Asrina stirred. *Not now, please not now.*

Again, I stretched forth my senses as I'd practiced, but only encountered the cold, empty darkness. I made a bid for time. "Then you won't reconsider your earlier offer?"

"Why should I? Whoever reached you first has placed upon you sufficient workings to render you unmalleable." He arched a brow. "If you'd not forsaken all protection, your inheritance and the prospect of gaining another child would make you worth the trouble. And I've found you quite entertaining."

Another child? Then I wasn't his first victim. How his chosen companion must have suffered. The frigid cold snaked further up my arm; a lattice of shadows spread across my skin, resembling those on Asrina's wings.

"But now you're of no further use." His teeth flashed white in the gloom. "Your father will be far more biddable, particularly as he grieves the loss of his daughter. He'll be only too pleased to sell Kilmere to me in honor of your memory."

The pain sharpened; the room blurred.

Lord West leaned closer still, the cold, metallic scent of ancient stone filling the space between us. "And then, if I still desire a mortal bride, perhaps one of your grieving sisters might take comfort in my arms."

A wave of furious heat—like liquid sunlight—seared my body, burning so fierce and bright that not a trace of fear remained. And the room shimmered with all sorts of intricate lines, not the vague shadows I'd beheld before, but woven workings of power. I could see them all, though no means of their undoing. And something else.

At the doorway, another pulse of power lurked—this one also dark but laced with sparks like shimmering white stars. Friend or foe?

I sank deeper into the sensations, and I could feel Asrina. Her gentle pulses of light warmed my skin, thrummed deeper into my being—and gold-laced images flashed in my mind with each pulse of light: *Asrina moving, abandoning safety, needing concealment to act.*

Then she stirred within my pocket. If I did not distract him, Lord West would take note. What I attempted would be like poking a dragon in the eye with a stick and hoping not to be incinerated. Yet what choice did I have?

Asrina crept to the opening of the pocket; I couldn't wait any longer.

"You're a coward," I blurted.

"What did you say?" His eyes darkened till they became like shards of midnight.

"You. Are. A. Coward." I bit off every word. "You skulk among the shadows. You prey only on the weak, those with no means to resist. You can't even attempt to take my life without binding me to a chair so I can't fight back. Do you fear your power is insufficient?"

The ice-shards of pain tore at my arms, then the cords of power wrenched me to my feet before dissipating.

Quicker than I could blink, his hand closed about my throat. "Bound or unbound, I can kill you any way I please."

Slowly, his grip tightened. My ears popped as Other surged about me, strong as a winter tempest.

An image of the pendant flashed into my mind, tinged with golden light. Asrina sought the pendant, and she'd never reach it with his hand about my throat. She'd clambered up my back, waiting.

My vision dimmed at the edges. It was now—or never. I drew upon the heat surging through my veins, and it restored motion to my limbs.

I lashed out with one leg, kicking the tea table hard enough to upend it. The china fell, shattering against the marble floor. A shard flew up and sliced his cheek, drawing the thinnest line of blue-tinged blood.

He released me to skim his fingers across the cut. It closed. "Little *ashna*. You will pay."

The gathering storm of his power chilled the chamber. But Asrina had reached the pendant.

What now? My pulse drummed against my stays, beat a warning in my ears.

She clutched it—though it was half the size of her—and leapt across to Lord West, a blinding light flashing from her frame. The pendant shattered over the two of them, releasing a storm of blue-violet. The stench of burnt flesh filled the air, along with a lightning charge of power.

When it cleared, the pendant was gone.

So was Asrina.

Lord West stumbled back, cursing, ugly blue-violet marks seared into his skin. The working of shadows around the door wavered.

Then the door burst open, shattered into a thousand fragments beneath an immense beast of black, many times larger than any mortal tiger.

She stalked into the room, grace and power in every line of

her dark, lethal frame. The white starflower on her chest blazed with glorious splendor, and her roar shook the walls.

I could not move.

But Lord West did. Shadows spilled from him, toward Jade.

She ignored him, her glowing green gaze locked on mine. With unnatural speed, she bounded across the room. Her tremendous frame collided with mine, and the force of it drove me through the windows.

The glass shattered around us.

We crashed onto the footwalk in a jumble of broken glass and torn drapery. Stone bit into my shoulder and my hip, bruised my face.

And a silvery mist closed round us as Jade shrank back into the form of a cat. It cleared, but my ears still rang with the force of her roar.

Dimly, the shouts of passersby pierced the haze. The blazing song of the white poplars surged into my mind, their strength into my body, no boundary remaining between us. I staggered to my feet.

And more songs poured into me, a surge so strong it nearly swept me away.

Two gentlemen approached, peering at me with concern.

"What in the Crossings happened?" the taller said. "Are you well?"

"Of course not—she's clearly injured." His companion surveyed the house. "Were you staying with Lady Hampton? Let us fetch a servant."

"No . . . please."

"Had a shock, I'd say," the first muttered. "Can't imagine how anyone could tumble through those windows."

I had to escape before Lord West emerged, yet I could scarcely stand, let alone flee. And Dreda—

I scared her into the streets. She waits nearby.

No one else moved, no one else heard the rich voice. Nor

did Jade so much as twitch. She'd spoken into my mind. How? Never mind that now. She wasn't touched by Other.

She *was* Other.

And she concealed her nature no longer.

My vision blurred, and the voices around me came as from a distance. How long before Lord West visited his wrath on the crowd? Why hadn't he emerged?

He won't come. Not with the others here. You're the only unprotected mortal.

She didn't only speak into my mind; she read my thoughts. I clutched my arms about my middle.

What *was* she?

Several more stragglers stopped in the street.

No, no, no. I couldn't afford a crowd.

"Let us send for a doctor, miss," someone said.

With trembling fingers, I touched the mottled bruises on my arm. "I don't need a doctor. I just need to go home."

"Where's your carriage?" The nearest gentleman looked about.

The querulous voice of a lady came from behind. "What happened?"

"Someone attacked me." The metallic taste of blood coated my tongue. "I was knocked through a window."

"Shocking! Simply shocking." The lady rummaged in her reticule. "Watch her, she doesn't look steady."

My legs wobbled. She waved smelling salts beneath my nose. The sharp scent burned, clearing my senses.

And then Dreda broke through the gathering throng. "Miss Jessa! What in the Crossings has happened? I heard a commotion, and then your cat went wild. She chased me from the house."

"I'm sorry." My voice sounded peculiar, as though it came from down a long tunnel. Everything felt distant. "Perhaps . . . perhaps she sensed danger. There was an intruder. He came in while I was waiting for Lady Hampton."

"Someone check the house." A man spoke from the edge of the footwalk.

"No!" I stumbled back. A poplar beckoned, and I clutched its trunk, desperate for stability. "He will have fled."

"Let us be the judge of that."

An unfamiliar sensation of Other swept across my over-whelmed senses, cool and compelling at once.

Blight and rot.

Had Lord West's actions somehow drawn the attention of additional Otherkind?

We must remove ourselves.

I dug my fingers into the rough bark. Jade was right, yet if they went inside and found Lady Hampton absent and the drawing room in shambles, how could I ever explain? And if Lord West still lurked within—there was danger.

All my ragged emotions bled into my voice, weaving threads of Other I could not contain. "The intruder is gone, no one need enter."

All about me, the gazes of the bystanders fogged. What had I done? I'd sworn not to sway others, yet it spilled from me in my greatest vulnerability.

The gentleman nearest me nodded slowly. "No need. Of course."

My head spun. I'd bidden them against their will. It was unforgivable, and yet some part of me did not regret it—and that frightened me more than the rest.

The woman who had offered the smelling salts approached. "Allow my husband and me to escort you home. You shouldn't go on your own."

Jade stalked forward. *Decline them—it's safer to walk and remain in public view.*

The golden heat within was fading, my skin going cold, my pulse thrumming ragged and uneven.

You cannot delay.

This time, the words echoed with greater force within my

mind. I rubbed my temples. She'd always sought my protection. If she claimed it safer to walk, I'd do my utmost.

I hadn't the strength to traverse Avons, but we were only a few streets from Wyncourt. As though my thoughts summoned it to awareness, it burned in my mind like a beacon. "I can walk. I'm not far from home."

"But your injuries—"

Dreda stepped up, threading her arm through mine. "I'll see to her, don't worry."

Over the objections, I limped away, Dreda supporting me and Jade at my side. Every step sent pain jolting through my body. From the shadow-bruises left by Lord West's bindings to my scored side, everything throbbed. My breath came in unsteady gasps.

One of Jade's ears pricked toward me, a tentative motion. I stumbled. Everything had changed between us in an instant. I'd treated her as a pet when she was a fully sapient being, one who possessed strength enough to snap me between her jaws. She'd hurled me through the window with no apparent effort and—

I regret that I caused you pain. Her head lowered. *West is deemed powerful, even as high fae measure it. Our only recourse was flight.*

I was grateful for her protection, only I couldn't endure this sensation of being stripped bare, of every thought and emotion exposed. And even this, I could not hide from her.

She pulled ahead, increasing the distance between us slightly. A faint sheen of sweat glossed my skin, yet I felt frigid.

"Perhaps we should rest," Dreda said. "You look dreadfully pale."

I shook my head. "We have to make it to Wyncourt."

"As you wish." She tightened her grip about me, supporting more of my weight than was fair. She didn't cluck or fuss as Aunt Caris might have done, nor ask questions as my sisters certainly would have. She simply provided unwavering support.

"I'm sorry to have drawn you into danger. I never dreamt—"

"Save your strength, Miss Jessa." Her face was set, determined. "I took no harm, and you can hardly be held responsible for the actions of some footpad."

Yet I'd known Lord West lurked—I'd just never imagined what he'd planned. Distant thunder rumbled in an ominous sky, an echo of the turmoil within.

At last, we reached Wyncourt.

I limped up the steps, and Dreda lifted the knocker. We remained in plain view of the public, and yet I feared Lord West stalked in the shadows.

Jade leapt upon the stone planter. *He's not nearby. Not yet.*

On instinct, I reached for her, then hesitated. What if she'd resented being treated like a pet all this time, when her power and ability outstripped mine? How should I—

Danvers opened the door and inhaled sharply. "By the Crossings! What happened, Miss Caldwell?"

I opened my mouth, but no words escaped.

"Miss Caldwell was assaulted by an intruder at the home of Lady Hampton and thrown through a window onto the street. She's in need of care." Dreda spoke with an assurance I'd never heard from her. Evidently she was the sort to rise to a crisis.

"Come in, come in." Danvers called over his shoulder for Mrs. Peters, then turned to me. "Miss Caldwell, you must allow us to assist you."

Wyncourt rose up to surround me, warmth and Other alike swirling through the air. Everything faded to a peculiar washed-out gray as Danvers and Mrs. Peters fussed over me, installing me on a wide settee in the morning room, where they plied me with strong tea and insisted we needed to summon a doctor.

"Thank you all for your kindness." The room spun, and I struggled to steady my voice. "I don't need a doctor, just a moment to collect myself. I'll be fine."

"Your injuries . . ." Mrs. Peters wrung her hands. "Let us send for your aunt. She'll know what to do."

"No!" My voice rang out, far stronger than the situation

warranted. I couldn't hold together my fraying emotions much longer. As if it sensed my distress, Wyncourt seemed to shudder ever so slightly. "All I need is a moment to myself. Please."

Mrs. Peters and Dreda exchanged a glance above my head. "Of course, Miss Caldwell. I'll take Miss Twells belowstairs and make her comfortable. You send for us when you're ready."

When I was ready. I'd never be ready to face Lord West. Without Jade and Asrina, he would have killed me today.

Asrina.

Where was she? She'd shown tremendous courage, and I'd abandoned her, possibly to death.

My throat tightened, and my eyes stung. No, no tears—I couldn't afford to draw further attention from the servants, to give evidence that I was *not* fine, not in any way.

Still, one escaped to trickle down my cheek, hot and stinging. No more, not now. Perhaps I could afford emotion later, once hidden away. But where?

The bracelet Lord West had given me burned at my wrist. He could find me wherever I went.

The great mirror across the room reflected my own forlorn figure back to me, small and uncertain and battered. How had I thought I could resist him?

If—when—he returned . . .

Jade sprang onto the settee next to me, and I flinched.

She perched before me, statue stiff. *Do you want me to go?*

"No."

My Other nature troubles you.

I wanted to deny it, yet she would be able to perceive the uncertainty and confusion swirling within. I could hide nothing, couldn't avoid hurting her, however much I desired to. "It's only . . . What are you?"

I am kit-isne.

I sank back into the cushions of the settee. Clearly that had never meant cat. I shouldn't have leapt to that belief, nor allowed my own fear of Other to fuel it.

It wasn't your own desire only. I wanted you to believe me ordinary. Even suggested it.

"You've been putting thoughts in my mind?"

Ideas. Nudges.

I pressed my lips together tightly so they would not tremble. Even though I might possess fae blood, I was ignorant of so much, incredibly vulnerable to Other. "I see."

She remained unnaturally still, almost wary. *Will you send me away?*

"Of course not." If I lost her, it would be like plucking out some vital part of myself. "Only . . . please help me understand."

Understand what?

"Why you sought me. Why you've stayed. If—" My throat tightened further, and I could not bear to speak the words. What if some Otherkind had sent her to keep watch over me? What if our bond was not what I'd believed it? The shadow-marks on my arms throbbed. "If you want to stay."

Before she could answer, Other flooded the room. I braced for another attack. Yet instead of the shadows I feared, a glorious wash of light poured across the room, rich with the scents of sun and storm.

Riven?

CHAPTER 15

He surged into the chamber, a lightning charge of power swirling round him. It wasn't Riven as I'd last seen him, but a very fae Riven, with light coiling from his hands and only the slightest shimmer of glamour veiling the wild beauty of his features.

His gaze fell on me, and he became still. A sheen of gold displaced the dark green in his eyes, and the coils of light retracted.

Yet still the force of Other raked over my exposed senses, sharp as a blade, stealing thought and reason. Some wild thrum within my own veins rose to meet it, yet my body could support no more. I collapsed on the settee. "How did you know to come?"

Red-gold sparks kindled the air about him, and he folded his arms across his chest. "You mean since you *didn't* send for me when fae threatened your life?"

He was angry? Why? I might have expected this reaction if I'd sent for him idly, wasting his time on mortal affairs, but now? A sensation like knotweed snarled in my chest—Asrina. Had he sensed her death and come to demand an account?

He closed the distance between us, the light of a concealment glamour spilling across the room, protecting us from detection by the servants. "What happened?"

The knotweed tightened, the ache spreading up my chest. What debt would I owe now? Never mind that—nothing could repay a life lost. Rain lashed at the windows, a relentless torrent of deep grief. "I'm sorry about Asrina. I tried—I know you left her in my care, and I failed her."

"No. I entrusted you to hers." The sparks flared. "Why didn't you send her?"

I'd nothing left for another confrontation, not now, not when my pulse beat ragged and unsteady, and every part of my body throbbed from the power Lord West had forced upon it. Yet I must say something. The rain beat harder against the panes, washing the world beyond into a swirl of greens and whites and pinks.

"Help from fae comes with a cost—you told me that," I whispered.

"So I did. And what price did you imagine I'd require?" His eyes shadowed to the darkest of greens, yet his voice betrayed no emotion. "If you credit me with nothing else, I hope you believe I would have stopped short of your life."

"That's not what I—" How could I explain all I'd feared? Other poured from him, relentless as the summer storm beyond the glass, strong as that which Lord West had wielded. And it undid me. Any attempt at explanation withered and died like a blossom in early frost.

"I see." The sparks died; all trace of emotion vanished from his features. And mercifully, the onslaught of Other faded beneath whatever careful, meticulous control he exerted.

He hadn't yet exacted whatever he felt due over the matter of Asrina, and I couldn't begin to guess what he was thinking.

My arm throbbed, and when I touched it, my fingers came away tinted red. I'd sustained a gash on my right arm, yet its pain had gone unnoticed, paling next to the shadow-bruises.

He reached for my arm, and I flinched. I couldn't bear to be touched again, not by anyone. "Please . . . I'm fine."

"Very well." A muscle twitched in his jaw. "If you are—fine—then tell me what happened? What did your attacker want?"

"Kilmere, at first." Thunder cracked the sky, and I jumped, betraying weakness I hated. My thoughts scattered again.

Riven assessed me, then plucked a flask from a leather pouch at his side. "Take this."

I shrank from it. "I don't need it. Truly, I'm fine."

"You're one step away from collapse. This fae exercised little restraint." He set the flask on the table with a thud. "We've established that you'd rather suffer than accept assistance. But I require information, and I cannot wait for your recovery."

Jade leapt upon the table and sniffed at the flask. *I believe it safe.*

Safe for whom? It was fae-drink. If I had some fae blood, perhaps it wouldn't harm me, but if I was mistaken, if I took something that put me further under the sway of Other or released that which I concealed within . . . I scarcely maintained control as it was.

I shivered.

Jade hopped down and nudged my ankle. *You may pick me up, if you desire.*

It was hardly a warm invitation. The reminder of the distance between us, of all my uncertainties about her nature and her purpose, drew tears even closer to the surface. Yet I couldn't afford to crumble now.

Jade remained silent at my feet. Her fur bristled slightly. Was she offended?

As if from underwater, the distant rumble of Riven's voice reached me. I struggled to attend.

He vanished and came back a moment later with a decanter of whiskey I recognized as one Ibbie used when hosting. He splashed it liberally into the half-cup of tea sitting on the table. "Drink this, at least."

I lifted the cup, and when the light caught it, it glowed warm. The liquid inside burned all the way down, but somehow the sharpness cleared my senses, brought me back into my body.

We'd sheltered like this in Wyncourt once before, after the ghouls had attacked me. Only then I'd not had a high fae hunting my life. To escape the weight of Riven's gaze, I poured another cup of tea.

"Now tell me what happened." Riven drew a chair alongside me, his attention discomfiting. "Asrina told me a fae lord was about to kill you—"

"She's alive?" At once, the knotweed-like strictures unbound as though sliced with a scythe. I drew a full, heady breath. "The jewel shattered, and then she was gone—I thought she died."

"She's resilient." He spoke a few words in the fae tongue. With a radiant spark, a small passing opened, and Asrina emerged, her light undimmed, her wings unshadowed.

Dark clouds still clustered outside, but she brought the sun within, her lively warmth as welcome as the first day of spring. Though she was also Other, her diminutive form and less formidable abilities made her feel . . . safer. I held out my hand, and she fluttered gracefully onto my palm. "Well done, most lovely of sylphs."

She preened, her light shimmering with shades of rose and ivory, her glorious flame-like wings flaring out behind her. Despite the grave circumstances, I couldn't restrain a smile.

Then I turned to Riven. "I don't understand. Lord West cast some working upon her, and she couldn't fly. How did she reach you?"

"By taking a tremendous risk. In most cases, shattering the pendant would have killed her, yet the pyske who crafted it wove a protection-working for the bearer into the blood."

"The . . . blood?"

"Pyske blood holds great power, even more so when shaped by their affinities. They don't give such gifts lightly." His gaze rested on us, speculative. "Nor do sylphs often go beyond the requirements of their assignment. She chose to risk her life."

I gently curved my fingers around her. "I owe you a great debt."

Though it was a danger to say so, I didn't regret it. If she hadn't given Jade the opportunity to intervene, I would have never escaped Hampton House.

Her light pulsed a rhythmic pattern, casting a gold-tinged image in my mind of all my attempts to care for her, then her own attempt to . . . do the same for me? She launched off my hand, her light catching on the bracelet as she fluttered alongside my shoulder.

Riven tensed. "When did you get that?"

"Lord West forced it on me some days ago—"

"It needs to come off. Now." He reached toward me, then stopped. "May I?"

With that, something in me quieted. He might be fae, with all the attendant dangers of his nature, but he wasn't Lord West. He'd asked, rather than forcing his will upon me.

I nodded.

Shimmering threads of light wove over the surface of the bracelet, then the band shattered, falling to the floor in shards of metal and gleaming stone. The light blazed fierce across them, and they vanished altogether, along with some portion of my pain.

My mind cleared a bit more, and with it, I remembered: I'd brought the amelior salve. In silence, I worked it over the shadow-bruises.

Riven leaned forward. "Where did you find that?"

"I made it."

Again, I'd the disconcerting impression he assessed me with Other senses. I lowered my head and attended only to mending my injuries, my emotions tossed like willow branches in a tempest. What now? Asrina had fetched Riven, and he'd come, but he'd been angry—

If I must guess, he came prepared to deliver retribution. Jade's eyes kindled. *He expected to find your body.*

Did she read all my thoughts? If I were to simply think in response, would she attend?

I can perceive all your thoughts, but if you wish to hold a proper conversation, then form the words in your mind.

Very well. How long could I sit here communicating in the confines of my mind before Riven pressed me? I hurried on. *How do you know? Can you perceive his thoughts also?*

Like most high fae, he guards them with walls I cannot breach. But he is arbiter, and he has seen many bleak things. Your death would be the usual outcome of such an attack.

Even as the salve eased the pain of the shadow-marks, the reminder of my current plight stung. *If so, why would he bother to come?*

That is what I wish to know also. I have a possible explanation. As arbiter, he must watch for threats to his court. The unknown, the inexplicable, poses such a threat.

So he keeps watch over me to obtain the answers he seeks?

I do not know. Only I wonder.

It fit with what he'd said before he left last time: *I require answers about your abilities.* And when he uncovered them—if he could—what then? I tucked the tin of salve away.

"Perhaps we could start again from the beginning?" Riven said softly.

All I wanted was to hide somewhere dark and quiet, tucked beneath the firs of Thornhaven perhaps, somewhere safe where I didn't have to struggle to maintain control, to hide my weakness.

Yet Lord West waited, and whatever Riven's intent, he represented my best chance of safety. "I'd like that."

I did my best to offer a concise account of my dealings with Lord West, from his appearance before the Magister to our confrontation in Hampton House.

Riven remained still, only his eyes shadowed ever darker. When I finished, he said, "He gave the name Lord West?"

Jade's tail twitched. *Tell Riven he is known as Damir in our world.*

"Yes, but Jade says he's known as Damir?"

"Damir." A sudden gust hurled rain against the window. "How unfortunate."

"Why?"

"He's one of the more prominent and powerful fae in the Court of Silver, which most closely borders my own." His hands tightened slightly, and the gaslight gleamed on his green-and-gold ring. "Our courts have ever been rivals, and I cannot remove him without causing open war."

"I didn't expect that you would." I lowered my gaze to the scrolled ivory rug at my feet. "I know fae do not concern themselves with mortal problems."

"This isn't strictly a mortal problem; rather, it offers an opportunity to my court."

"I don't understand."

"Several decades ago, Damir acquired something of great value to my king. He was cunning enough to twist circumstances to his advantage and keep his involvement hidden. It is the way of our kind, and it violated no treaty between courts. Yet it caused a great deal of harm." Riven stood and began to pace the room. "If I were to uncover and thwart whatever he plans now in turn, my king would be greatly pleased—provided I avoid sparking war in the process."

A little spark of hope burned in my chest. If he was willing to help . . . "What do you propose?"

"An arrangement of mutual convenience. We each have use for the other." His features remained shuttered, giving no hint at his feelings. "You require protection, and I desire opportunity to move against Damir—which you provide. You hold what he wants. I provide the means by which you keep him from attaining it."

I sank back into the settee. My conflict with Lord West offered Riven an opening—a chance to use a mortal to snare a fae. Could I accept help on those terms? If he intended to make use of me to get at Lord West and to further the interests of his court, it would be an uncertain alliance. The moment our purposes failed to align, he'd abandon me to Lord West.

Yet what choice did I have? "I accept—but how can you be sure he won't attack again?"

"He is restrained in the same manner I am," Riven said. "That offers you a measure of protection as long as I'm present."

The fae machinations made my head spin, a world of politics and powers beyond what I'd dreamed.

Jade regarded me through slitted eyes. *To strike at the arbiter of the Court of Gold would be like striking its king. Riven is right. Damir will not act so. It would unleash the wrath of his own queen upon him, and his power is no match for hers. If either Riven or Damir attacked the other outright, it would lead to war—to many fae lives lost and fae-lands destroyed in ways that would take centuries to recover. While they ever play games of power, the monarchs of these courts have embraced uneasy peace. Neither wish to disturb the balance, not when—not now. If Riven is present, you will be safe.*

"But you cannot stay forever. You have duties in your court, which means any protection is temporary."

"Yes—unless we stop him altogether, a more difficult matter."

Which meant as yet even Riven didn't have a plan that would ensure safety for me and those around me. My thoughts drifted like dandelion down carried on the wind, unable to plot a certain course.

"I suggest we discuss it later, when you've made a full recovery."

"But there's nothing to stop him from coming when I retire tonight." He needed only wait until I slept, then steal into my bedchamber to finish me off.

Riven arched a brow. "As I said, he won't try to kill you in my company."

"But you . . . I . . ." Surely I misunderstood what he implied. "You plan to stay in my bedchamber?"

"Until we can devise a better plan." He appeared utterly unruffled. "A working would be an effective solution, but as your father owns the home, I require his permission. Unless you wish me to persuade him to give it."

"Of course not." I'd not subject Father to glamour again; it was far too risky. But to welcome a fae into my bedchamber, to become more vulnerable still—at the moment, it felt unbearable. There must be another way. "But you must see that you cannot stay."

The slightest charge pulsed the air between us. "Why not?"

Assumptions were made of a woman who rode in a closed carriage alone with a man or stood up with a gentleman one too many times at a ball. To share a bedchamber—whatever the reason—would create a scandal for the ages. And now those conventions provided a cover for fears that ran far deeper. I folded my hands, tucking them into my stained skirt. "It wouldn't be proper."

"You're suggesting you'd rather die than risk impropriety? Don't forget I witnessed your deeds in the Otherworld." He gave me a sharp look. "If you have something to say, just say it."

I went cold. Why did he have to be so perceptive? I ached to hold Jade, to seek solace in her warmth, but she remained as distant as I was unsure. So I sank down further into the silk-tufted cushions. Jade had indicated Lord West wouldn't act while I was in public, so perhaps . . . "If I shared a bedchamber with my sisters, would it provide sufficient protection?"

"All he must do is wait until they fall asleep, then draw them deeper in. They'd wake up to your body in bed." I flinched at the blunt words, but Riven offered no apology. "Whatever games he played before he has no use for now. He's taken the lives of many fae through the years—it will be a small matter for him to claim yours."

"Then why didn't he simply kill me and take Kilmere from

the beginning?" If protections existed, as his words had hinted, then I must understand.

"He was bound by certain . . . regulations. You own Kilmere. He couldn't simply take it without your consent. He could—and did—try to glamour you into agreeing, but you're unusually resistant to glamour." A hint of speculation crept into his tone.

I didn't want to think about the reasons for my resistance to glamour, never mind that Riven clearly was. With effort, I straightened. "He told me that he sought knowledge about what made me different, and when he found out I'd killed Uros, then he struck. He implied that in so doing, I'd forfeited some protection."

"I cannot speak of it further."

So whatever protections existed were to be kept hidden from mortals—yet I needed understanding of them if I was to keep my family safe. I hesitated, then asked, "Cannot or will not?"

"Cannot. Our sovereigns bind us—it's a geas as old and powerful as the courts themselves."

If so, was that why he'd left Asrina? He'd known I might be in danger after killing Uros, yet he couldn't speak of it? I shifted, and the muscles that had taken the brunt of my fall protested. "I believe Jade suggested the presence of others provides some protection?"

"I cannot speak to particulars. But you may find that if you're surrounded by other mortals, he takes care in how he acts."

It was as much a confirmation as I would receive, only new questions simmered to the surface. "How did he know about Uros? Only you and Nikol and Mr. Burke knew what happened."

"And Mocvar—and those beings aware within his realm, which are numerous." Riven gave a slight shrug, his shoulders straining against the silken jacket that presented the veneer of a gentleman. "Damir has a long reach. If he bent his mind to it, he could find a source."

"But—"

"You can't avoid the matter at hand forever, Jessa. Do I have your consent to stay?"

However uncertain I felt, the alternative was Lord West. I nodded. "Wait—you won't need to glamour my family?"

"Not in any meaningful way. The glamour of concealment poses no risk to mortal minds." He crossed to the door. "When night falls, Damir's power will be at its height. I suggest we depart."

Jade chuffed, and I could put forth no reasonable argument; indeed, if I didn't return home in time for dinner, I'd face more questions than I wished to answer, yet leaving Wyncourt felt wrenching.

I forced myself to stand.

Oh.

My reflection in the large mirrors across the room revealed alarming dishevelment, a state far beyond repair. Small wonder Riven hadn't believed my claims that I was fine. Lord West had been thorough.

My shoulders bowed. Even if I could conceal the remnants of my injuries, I couldn't hide the damage to my gown—the bloodstains and the rents left by the glass—and Dreda would certainly describe the assault to my family.

Even if Riven remained hidden, there would be a reckoning.

CHAPTER 16

When Holden opened the door to greet us, his usually unflappable demeanor deserted him. He rushed forward. "Miss Jessa!"

"Don't worry, it's not as bad as it looks."

"Not as bad as it . . ." He sputtered. "You look as though a carriage ran you down."

"It wasn't a carriage." Perhaps that would have been preferable.

"Never you mind, Miss Jessa. Just come in. Your aunt will wish to tend you at once."

My shoulders tightened. "There's no need."

But he herded us inexorably toward the morning room. Unlike Danvers, who had heeded my wishes as mistress of Wyncourt, to Holden I was still a child—perhaps I always would be, given how long he'd been with the family. The sense of Other emanating from Riven altered my familiar surroundings, overlaying them with fears that somehow my family would see through his glamour—and then all I'd worked so hard to conceal would come undone.

When we entered the morning room, Aunt Caris looked up

with a smile, which swiftly vanished. She went as white as a snow lily.

"Oh, my dear." She hastened to my side, clucking under her breath and dabbing at the dirt on my face. "How did this happen? What happened? You were meant only to see Lady Hampton."

As if by rote, I offered the tale of the assailant, and Dreda murmured her corroboration of my story, adding that we'd taken shelter in Wyncourt to allow me to regain my strength.

Not a single one of them glanced at Riven, who stood vigil along the door, light bending around him in a dizzying fashion.

Holden cleared his throat. "Shall I send for a physician?"

Very careful to keep all possible trace of glamour from my voice, I said, "There's no need. I'm only a bit bruised and shaken."

"I'll be the judge of that." Aunt Caris spoke with rare firmness. "Holden, send Gaile to my bedchamber with a basin of warm water. Dreda, thank you for seeing Jessa safely home. I'll take charge of her now."

Dreda and Holden withdrew, and she took hold of my arm. "Come, my dear. We will get you cleaned up and see if there's need for a physician."

Aunt Caris bustled me up the stairs and into her bedchamber. Jade padded alongside us, and Gaile followed a moment later with a steaming basin and linen towels. With care, Aunt Caris removed the pins from my hair, and glass fell to litter the floor about us.

Her lips firmed. "Gaile, sweep up this mess, if you please."

"Aunt Caris, I can manage on my own."

"No, my dear." Her eyes glistened. "You do far too much of that as it is. I begin to think the society Avons offers not worth the risks. First the killer, and now this? If a young lady cannot go calling in the full light of day without suffering assault—"

Her voice broke, and something inside me did as well. "Please don't worry. It won't happen again."

Not with Riven here. But if he must go . . .

Gaile swept up around us, and blessedly, Riven kept out of the room. Given the strong sensation of Other, he must be waiting just outside the door. Jade stationed herself before it, rather than draw close, as was her wont.

How could I mend matters between us?

Then Aunt Caris gently tugged away my ruined gown and gasped at the scoring on my side, where I'd not yet applied the amelior salve. I stood shivering in my shift, while she sponged at the dirt and abrasions. "When I think what you must have endured when that thief assaulted you—oh, my dear, are you certain you're all right?"

Her sympathy nearly undid me, but I clung to the thin veneer of calm. "Better now that I'm home."

When would it occur to her to ask after Lady Hampton? Once the first flush of concern faded, questions would be inevitable. What little strength I'd summoned after the administration of the whiskey-laced tea faded swiftly.

I withdrew the tin of salve and applied it liberally, then Aunt Caris wrapped me in one of her dressing gowns, her familiar, soft violet-and-lavender scent engulfing me along with it.

"Now, my dear, just sit and rest while I fetch you some clean things." She left the door ajar and bustled out into the corridor.

Jade crossed the floor, yet remained at a distance. When our gazes met, she looked away. I collapsed inward.

If she meant to go, what would I do?

She took a few steps closer. *It's not what I intend, but rather what you desire.*

Why didn't you tell me what you were before? Was she sent to cause harm? To keep watch? I tugged Aunt Caris's dressing gown closer.

I knew you would fear me, as you've feared the Other within yourself. Her unblinking gaze bored into mine. *When we met, you were afraid of everything about my world, of all my kind. Can you claim you would have accepted me?*

I don't know.

It was a risk I dared not take.

Yet she had revealed herself to protect me. Pain echoed through her words, and I knelt on the floor before her.

She remained still. *Our fates are tied together, at least as it concerns me.*

What does that mean?

Kit-isne *cannot long survive a severed bond.*

A severed bond? What did that mean? I rocked back onto my heels as Aunt Caris bustled back into the room.

"My dear, you should be resting."

"Yes, Aunt Caris, but Jade—"

"Your cat can take care of herself." She helped me into the clean gown. "Now, shall we send for a physician or do you feel up to joining us for dinner?"

"I'll join you."

Again Jade followed at a distance. The uncertainty between us plagued me, but I couldn't conduct one conversation with much clarity right now, let alone two, and Aunt Caris continued to ply me with questions.

In the doorway, I stopped short. "Father, you're back."

Lovell was here too, attending family dinner as he often did when Aunt Melisina occupied herself with society events. Only Ada and Ainslie were missing—they must be dining with friends. Riven took up a post across the room, where he could take full view of the proceedings.

"I returned only this afternoon, as your aunt sent word to me about Ada." Father frowned. "But what's happened to you?"

Aunt Caris poured out the story, and Father appeared decidedly shaken.

"You're certain you're unharmed, Jessa?" he asked.

"I've no injuries that won't mend."

"Still, we must send a report to the Magistry." The gaslight flickered on his spectacles. "Such a dangerous fellow can't be left to roam Avons unchecked."

"I'd like to deal with him myself, if he can be found." Grim lines tightened around Lovell's mouth. "Didn't you say that Lady Hampton sent for you? Was she harmed?"

He *would* consider the matter as though he drew up a report for the papers, attempting to fact-gather about all involved. "There was a . . . misunderstanding of sorts. She wasn't home."

Lovell sliced through a piece of fish. "So she sent for you when she meant to be out?"

"She . . ." For the dozenth time of the day, words deserted me. My fingers tightened around my fork.

And though she always kept silent in family settings unless directly addressed, Dreda broke in. "Sometimes ladies of a certain age are forgetful. Perhaps she didn't recall that she'd sent for Miss Jessa? Or she wrote the wrong time?"

I exhaled. Had Dreda witnessed more than I knew? Did she attempt to cover for me because she felt she owed me something? Whatever the case, I was thankful for her intervention. "It's possible."

Though far from what transpired. If only I could sort through in quiet what I ought to say, compose a story to allay concerns, and find a way to calm my disordered emotions. Instead the weight of their fears and questions pressed upon me until I could scarcely draw breath.

And through it all, Riven studied me as though he could see through to my soul and all the emotions churning within. Any hint of appetite vanished.

In ordinary circumstances, I'd escape to my bedchamber and the solace of silence, but now when I entered it, I'd still have to face Riven—and on terms of intimacy far beyond comfort. I dragged my fork through the savory cream sauce that topped the fish, scoring its surface with fine lines.

After Uros's death, when I'd thought fae-touch had claimed me, I'd trusted Riven with a truth I'd kept concealed from everyone else. Yet his thoughts and feelings remained more a mystery to me than ever, which gave him one more advantage in the situation.

I was so very weary of feeling vulnerable, but the situation presented no favorable options. Either I remained in the public spaces with my family, struggling to maintain my composure, pretending that every part of my body didn't ache, and possibly allowing them to perceive more than was safe, or I could retreat to the comparative privacy of my bedchamber, despite the fact it would no longer offer a true haven.

Lovell leaned forward. "Can you give a description of the fellow that attacked you?"

"I can't . . . not now. It's all . . ." I set down my fork. Riven or no, I couldn't remain any longer, couldn't allow Lovell to press and prod until I betrayed myself. "I'm sorry, but if you'll excuse me, I'm feeling fatigued. I think I might retire."

"That's wise, my dear. You must regain your strength." Aunt Caris patted my hand. "Shall I send up some tea?"

"No, thank you." I pushed back my chair and fled the room.

Jade and Asrina accompanied me; Riven followed in silence. Exhaustion weighted my limbs, and I stumbled over the final step. Did lack of grace indicate mortal blood ran stronger in me than fae? Never mind that now. On the threshold of my bedchamber, I hesitated.

Riven stood close behind, and the power inherent to his nature surged about me.

I froze.

How could I do this? He'd spoken of the arrangement in practical terms, a defense against Lord West, but I knew nothing of fae conventions. What if he expected something more in return for the protection he offered tonight? I spun around, the door at my back. "I can't—there's no room for you to sleep here."

It emerged as awkward and graceless and faltering as I felt.

"Tell me." He spoke low, but his words carried an edge.

"Should I be insulted that you'd rather face the fury of a thwarted fae lord than spend a single night in my company?"

The tone of his voice suggested he *was* insulted, and I struggled to even my own. "I meant no insult."

"Then you have no concern over the situation?"

He'd worded it so neatly that it was impossible to deny. But how could I explain the tangle of fear within—how overwhelming Other felt? How could a fae ever understand what it felt like to be mortal, if I even was mortal? How could I confess that when his power washed over me, for a moment it took me back to the grasp of Damir, to the shadow-cords he'd used to bind me in place? If I confessed, I'd appear as weak as fae believed all mortals. My breath caught.

He reached around me and opened the door. "Fae need little sleep. A chair will do. But the longer we linger here, the greater chance I will have to glamour someone."

He strode into the bedchamber, and I forced myself to follow, to attempt to reason. If he'd wished to take advantage of the imbalance in our circumstances, he could easily have done so before. Yet all the raw emotion of the day poured over me, driving out rational thought.

He crossed to the window and surveyed the drenched world of darkness beyond. "I'll wait here while you prepare for bed."

I stepped behind the dressing screen, and Asrina fluttered to perch atop it.

At least one thing on this dreadful day had gone right. She'd survived and regained her full health. Yet Lord West—Damir—still waited for his opportunity to strike. Instinctively, I reached for my pendant.

But it was gone.

Sharp and vivid, the acrid scent of burning flesh returned. The rage on Lord West's face. The force of his shadows, driving pain deep into my body.

I sank to the floor and buried my face in my hands. I shouldn't indulge in tears, not with Riven here, but I could not restrain them, not anymore. Though I did my best to keep quiet, my breath shuddered.

Perhaps Riven would take it as more evidence of mortal weakness. Perhaps it was. I must collect myself. I'd already taken far too long changing.

And I did *not* want him to check on me.

I struggled to my feet and pulled on my thickest dressing gown. Yet I remained as frigid as if the rain outside sluiced over my skin.

After I climbed into bed, Riven crossed to the chair before the hearth, the lines of his body tight in the flicker of the gas lamps.

I'd forgotten to lower them.

Jade padded over to them and gave a soft *mrow*, catching Riven's attention. With a quick motion, he drew their light to himself, and it vanished, shimmering into his skin.

I'd not needed another reminder of all I *didn't* understand about fae. Even in the dark, the tension in the air became a living thing, the weight of what remained unspoken pressing upon my chest. Had I caused offense? Broken some rule of fae etiquette in our interactions?

Exhaustion weighed upon me, slowing my thoughts as though they'd become mud-mired. I tugged the quilts up to my neck, breathing in the scent of sun and storm that Riven carried.

If he wasn't here, I'd be petrified in the dark, waiting for Lord West to come and finish what he started—to fight for my life and almost certainly lose it, as I'd not yet found an effective means of defense.

But I'd offered no thanks for his assistance. Perhaps if I did, it would mend whatever was strained between us.

"Riven?"

"What is it?"

"You should know—I did try to send Asrina to you when I couldn't find a way to stop Lord West, but he'd already injured her and she couldn't fly." It was easier to speak into the dark, since I couldn't see him. "I'm glad you came. And that you've stayed."

A long silence followed, so long that I wished to pull the bedcovers over my head—but could fae see in the dark?

When he spoke, his voice came as warm and gentle as a summer breeze. "You should sleep now, Jessa."

And even as he spoke, slumber claimed me.

I woke with a start in full night. I'd forgotten to draw the curtains, and moonlight poured through the windowpanes, creating squares of silver-white on the floor.

Riven sat near them, the light glinting across his features, and several sun sylphs fluttered about him, flickering in their distinctive communication pattern. I was safe.

But still, something felt wrong. What?

Jade. She didn't occupy her customary place in my bed. A soul-deep ache flooded my body. Where had she gone? If she'd vanished . . . I should have sought to make amends, only I'd been so weary.

She leapt upon the bedside table. *I'm here.*

Were you sleeping on the floor?

I didn't think you wanted my company.

An image of her formidable fae form flashed through my mind. I pressed it aside. *But I do. I don't want things to change.*

Nevertheless, they have. I did not wish to presume.

The vulnerability lacing the formal words pricked like the thorn of a thistle. What could I say? She perceived the turmoil within; there was no denying it. I shifted slightly, and the bedsheets rustled. *You know I have questions.*

It is your nature. A slight archness laced the words, a reminder that she knew me far better than I found comfortable.

How did you come to me?

She climbed onto the bed and curled her legs beneath her, regarding me steadily. *It is not a simple tale. Yet I owe it.*

You don't owe me—

I do. You will hear the truth and then decide. She hesitated, then continued. *Before I came to your world, my clan was attacked by a clutch of rock drakes. Aside from high fae, not many Otherfolk pose a threat to us, but the dragon-kind do. My bond-mate and I volunteered to lead them off. We killed several, but more came. More than we ever anticipated. The battle was long and bitter.*

I thought back to the wounds she'd borne when she took refuge in the glasshouse.

One of them sliced through Ti-dor's neck, a deep wound. He could no longer fight, so I dragged him through a Crossing. It offered a chance to throw them off, an opportunity to survive. In case of pursuit, we wandered as far from the Crossing as we could, but he'd lost so much blood. He died before morning, and I would have soon followed, but I found your glasshouse.

By chance?

Not chance. The essence of Other drew me. And then you chose to tend my wounds, but you did not know.

Know what?

That to survive, I had to bond with you. Otherwise, no matter how much care you took, I would have died before another full day passed.

She'd said *kit-isne* couldn't long survive a severed bond, but I'd not realized the extent. *So if you hadn't found me, if I hadn't had something Other about me—*

I would have been lost, like Ti-dor. I'd resigned myself to it, didn't want to survive losing him. A severed bond is . . . it does not bear speaking of.

A vast grief, like that which touched me after Ibbie's death, swirled across my senses. *And replacing a lost bond with another works?*

Not always. Nor was I certain I wanted it to, not at the very first, but then . . . Her eyes shimmered with their uncanny glow.

It doesn't matter. I chose, but you did not. So I will ask again. Do you want me to go? You need not fear that you will suffer from my parting—I alone am bound.

Was she volunteering to go to her death? How could she consider such a thing? I wanted to cradle her close, but I wasn't sure it would be welcome. *I have no intention of letting you go, so I hope you've resigned yourself to being stuck in the mortal world.*

Her body relaxed. *Then you should know that I've no objection to contact—*kit-isne *favor it for the nurturing of the bond, and we're rarely parted from our bond-mates. Of course, in the rare instances we bond with fae instead of other* kit-isne, *we do not force them into all our rituals. Fae do not take kindly to being groomed.*

So I imagine. I shifted to a more comfortable position. *I have one other question.*

Only one?

I smiled into the dark. *For now. Do you know of the protections in place for mortals? Those of which Riven could not speak?*

The same geas binds me. There are many things I wish . . . A low, pained rumble resounded in her chest. *I cannot.*

I understand. I wrapped my arms around her, her sweet-grass scent wafting around me, her warmth a comfort. And I lay in the silvery dark, considering it all—all that she'd suffered, all the dangers and hostilities of the Otherworld, all the threats Lord West posed.

And Kilmere.

Somehow it all came back to Kilmere.

Perhaps there is a curse, after all.

I flinched at the sudden intrusion into my thoughts. How would I ever grow accustomed to it?

Jade's ears twitched back.

I'm sorry, it's only . . . I faltered.

You hate that you cannot keep your thoughts and emotions hidden.

Yes.

Her muscles tensed. *Are you certain you do not wish to sever the bond? It is your right. You never agreed to it.*

No! Never think that. I couldn't endure losing you. I stroked her fur. The moonlight somehow deepened its darkness and set the white starflower patch on her chest to sparkling. *Only perhaps you needn't visit my thoughts all the time?*

Kit-isne *hold nothing back from their bond-mates.*

But I am not kit-isne. And I felt exposed beyond my ability to endure—ah, she would perceive that too. I sighed. *You said at times* kit-isne *bond with fae. Surely things are different in those cases. Might it apply to us also?*

That is not much discussed. Only the dangers of kit-isne *bonding outside their kind, for in such cases, the* kit-isne *bear all the risk.* For a moment I felt her uncertainty—or perhaps it was only my own—then she spoke again. *Since we are bonded, I cannot keep your thoughts from touching my own, not like I do with others. When* kit-isne *bond with fae, such boundaries flow from the fae, not the other way around. And you do not know what you are, let alone if you have the ability to put such boundaries in place. But I will create what distance I can. If you prefer, I will remain silent as before. You need not be reminded of what I am.*

Oh, Jade. That's not what I want. I can't deny that it will take me time to grow accustomed to this. But I will, if you'll only be patient.

Kit-isne *excel at patience.*

Somehow I had a feeling *kit-isne* believed they excelled in all things.

It is not belief, but fact. She arched her back, then stretched. *Do you want to discuss Damir?*

Perhaps. I fixed my gaze on the silver-tinged ceiling. *Even with Riven here, he'll not surrender his plans. And I can't expect him to stay at my side for days or weeks on end. Even if he does, if something goes wrong, if Lord West manages to kill me, then my family will be at risk. He'll force himself upon them, and there won't be anyone left to protect them.*

Then you must make sure pursuing them no longer offers him any gain.

But how? If I died unmarried and without a will, by default, my property would go to my father, but perhaps I might turn mortal law to my advantage? On some level, it appeared Lord West must abide by our conventions—purchasing land from its owner rather than seizing it by force.

Jade nestled close to my side. *You seek to use your legal system against him?*

If I can. A plan wove within my mind. If I could bring Father around—and Riven—then it might work to keep Lord West at a distance, at least long enough to allow us to explore Kilmere and find answers.

Because I couldn't stay away any longer, no matter what obstacles lay between me and the ruins. If I had any hope of ending this, I needed to visit Kilmere myself—whatever the risks —and unearth its secrets.

When I next woke, radiant sunlight streamed through the windows. Jade was curled up at my side, still drowsy. I eased away from her.

It was time to act upon the plans I'd concocted in the middle of the night, but I didn't want to have any sort of conversation while sleep disheveled—particularly not with a fae who appeared as elegant and polished as ever, despite having spent the night in a chair. At some point, he'd removed his jacket, and he now sat in his shirt sleeves, appearing unnaturally at ease, a stark contrast to the awkwardness I felt.

I'd rather bury myself deep within the bedquilts than come under his too-perceptive gaze at the moment—and perhaps he guessed at my sentiments. Though he must have heard me stir, he didn't turn toward me, but continued to converse with Asrina and another sun sylph, one with hair like blue flame. I took the offered escape and fled behind the dressing screen to make myself presentable.

What now?

I hesitated in the shadow of the screen. I couldn't begin to reason out Riven's actions, and my lack of understanding left me unsettled. He'd not taken advantage of the situation when he'd had ample opportunity to do so. He could have requested any bargain he desired in exchange for his help with Lord West, and I'd have had little choice but to accept it. I didn't know why he'd not required more, nor what his purpose was in offering assistance—not in full. Of course, fae couldn't lie, which meant at least part of it was the rivalry between courts and his desire to thwart Damir. Even so, it was a great deal of trouble to put himself to for what was otherwise a mortal affair, unless more remained concealed.

Yet I could not forever remain divided in mind. I must extend some measure of trust, must accept there were things he kept concealed, if we were to face Lord West together. If I constantly second-guessed his intentions, then I could not place my attentions on Lord West or Kilmere, where they belonged.

I finished weaving the braid around my hair and securing it with the pins I'd left on the stool the night before.

Jade padded over to me. *Are you certain you wish to take this course?*

I see no other. I adjusted my gown. *But when I speak to Riven . . . I'll not be able to converse with you both at once. I'm not yet practiced in this.*

And my head still felt slightly muzzy from the events of the day prior.

She stretched to her full length, arching her back. *Then I will keep silent. But have a care.*

I emerged from behind the screen and perched on the edge of the bed, as if it were ordinary to conduct a conversation with a gentleman within the confines of my bedchamber. "Do you need to sleep this morning?"

"Not now—we've more pressing matters to address." Fortunately, he matched my matter-of-fact tone. "Damir will not rest idle."

"I've had an idea about that." I plucked at a loose thread on the bedquilt. "He told me that after my death, he intended to glamour Father into selling Kilmere to him. As it stands now, if he kills me, he gains everything—which means my family will be at tremendous risk."

"Only if you die."

"Still, I'd prefer him to see as little purpose in pursuing them as possible—or in my death, for that matter."

"What do you propose?"

Understanding a bit more about the rules governing our worlds had opened a new possibility, yet I required Riven's confirmation. "If I made a will, must he abide by the terms?"

"He'd have to approach the new owner to acquire Kilmere upon your death, yes, but no other mortal would be able to resist his glamour." A little spark of light played between Riven's fingers. "The individual in question would be at risk."

"I know I can't leave it to another mortal. I'd hoped to will it to you."

Riven became entirely still, no flicker of emotion to betray his thoughts. The spark vanished.

I hurried on, my words tumbling over one another. "Not that I wish to place you at any risk, of course, but no one in my world can stand against Lord West. You can, and I'm certain he knows it, so I thought if I named you the beneficiary of Kilmere and the trust from Ibbie in the event of my marriage or death, it would dissuade him from trying to force either. He'd gain nothing from doing so."

Still, Riven kept silent.

Had I presumed too much? I forced myself to continue. "I know I'm asking a great deal, and perhaps this sort of involvement is what you must avoid. I admit there's much I don't understand, and if you don't want to be troubled—"

"Jessa." Glints of gold lightened the green of his eyes. "It's not that."

I pulled my knees to my chest. "Then what?"

"You should exercise more care in the bargains you offer." He fell silent, then at last continued, his voice low. "I owe fealty to a king who's not inclined favorably toward mortals."

"Then . . . would I be in danger if I left the estates to you?"

"Not at this time."

"Will you tell me if that changes?"

"Yes." He inclined his head. "But you've asked for nothing in return."

"Your assistance with the matter of Lord West is quite enough." The idea of pressing for more left me discomfited, as did the notion of bargaining in general, with all its hidden pitfalls. "Do you accept what I proposed?"

"On the condition that if we successfully deal with Damir, this new will is removed."

For all that he'd warned me against bargaining with him, he'd offered a concession decidedly in my favor, a very un-fae-like approach. "Then it's settled."

And somehow, with that declaration, my uncertainty eased, even though a gleaming binding mark appeared on my upper right arm. This time, the bargain had been of my choosing, and the mark represented safety, not a threat. I leaned back against the bedpost, and Jade rested her head on my lap, while Asrina came to rest on my shoulder, gold-tinged images of happiness pouring into my mind.

"Your notion of a will provides a start, but it won't prevent Damir from attempting to torture you into selling Kilmere outright, now that he knows he can." His eyes darkened. "Such things take time, however. It would be difficult for him to seize you and keep you from me long enough to execute such a strategy."

Torture me into submission? I'd not considered that possibility, yet Riven spoke of it as if it was something to be taken for granted. I skimmed my fingers along my arms, where the slightest trace of bruising remained. "I cannot sign Kilmere away without the permission of my father and trustees. He knows that. Does that mean they're at risk?"

"Not yet. Perhaps your conventions will serve to our advantage in this. You must have permission from all your trustees to transfer ownership?"

I nodded.

"Then make me a third, if you're willing," he said. "As with the will, it doesn't have to stand if we deal with Damir."

"I don't know if my current trustees will readily accept such a change—"

"If you tell them you're being threatened, will they act on your behalf?"

"If they were convinced it was necessary." Which would happen if Father insisted—they were far more likely to listen to his words than mine. Yet to persuade Father might well be as difficult as ridding a forest of a barberry invasion. Jade lifted her head to offer my chin a reassuring nudge, and I stroked her in return.

"Even if I secure the legal protections, what of my family? Will Lord West strike at them if thwarted in other ways?"

"He's cannier than that. Right now, it gains him nothing—and to target mortals involves risk. If he desires Kilmere as much as you say, he'll not chance spoiling his endgame for the pleasure of hurting them."

"But might he harm them to force me to submit to his wishes?"

"It's unlikely to occur to him that you might value them above Kilmere." His voice became flat. "Among fae, a family is more a unit of power than affection. Most refrain from the dangers of forming any true attachment—or revealing it, if they've done so."

"He's spent time in our world, though, so he must know matters are different for mortals."

"Time in the mortal world to wrest from it what one can and time engaging with mortals and learning their views are entirely different things. He's not the sort to do the latter." Riven folded his arms across his chest. "Based on his actions thus far, I'd say he believes they're expendable to you, otherwise he'd have threatened you into compliance by holding their welfare over your head long ago. He had no reason to believe you'd any knowledge of protections they might have. For now, that works to our advantage. Still, there are no guarantees in this affair, only calculated risks."

That wasn't what I'd wanted him to say. I wanted a promise that my family would be safe, that Lord West would be stopped before he harmed anyone else—but that was impossible to guarantee.

Riven was right, though—Lord West had not pursued my family. He'd not threatened them as leverage, only presented himself with the general charm of fae to win them over and gain access to me. Yes, he'd needled me about his plans for them at the very end, but otherwise he'd shown little interest.

And if I remained in Avons, seeking some means of defense rather than pursuing the answers that could free us, I'd lose my chance of securing their safety. Whatever protections we put in place, sooner or later Lord West would find a way around—and I must be ready when he did. "If I go to Kilmere, will they be at greater risk?"

"They should be safer. If Damir believes you threaten his plans for Kilmere, he'll focus on protecting his interests there—whatever they may be." He leaned forward slightly, and the scent of sun-warmed forest swirled round us. "Is that what you intend?"

"Yes—Kilmere brought Lord West into my life, and there must be a reason he wants it so badly. If we can uncover it, perhaps we can thwart his plans." I stroked the soft fur between Jade's ears, and she rumbled her approval. "There's also the curse. If the deaths that have taken place have something to do with Kilmere, I can't simply let the townsfolk suffer."

"There are rumors of a curse?" His attention sharpened. "Tell me what you know of it."

I recounted all the information I'd gathered—including the references in the faerie tale left by Ibbie and the dark hints given by Lord West. His gaze never wavered, nor did he appear shocked or troubled, as any mortal would before such revelations. The tangle of emotion inside unraveled as all I'd held in for so long poured out.

The smallest of golden sparks drifted about Riven as he considered. "You believe these deaths are Otherworldly in origin?"

"The peculiarities about Kilmere, along with the interest Lord West has in it, seem to support the theory. But I have constructed a number of possible explanations, all of which I possess insufficient evidence to confirm," I said. "I've even wondered if it were possible that some fae creature could have made its home in Kilmere and then struck out as people disturbed its rest."

"Possible, yes. But most low fae couldn't function centuries away from their world. They'd have no desire or ability to make a permanent home in yours." Riven plucked his jacket from the back of the chair, as if he intended to depart now. "However, if that's the case, it should be easy enough to determine."

"If I can convince Father to sanction the trip—and agree to the drawing up of the will and the alteration of trustees."

He lifted a brow. "Do you require such permission?"

"I'm not yet of age, so I must have his approval," I said softly. "And it's no small request, since I mean to disinherit my family in your favor."

Riven tugged on his jacket in a single graceful motion. "You have twenty years, do you not? I thought your world reckoned that full-grown."

"In the sense that I could wed and have a family, yes, but—"

"You still have no legal authority?" He stood. "Your world is a peculiar place."

"Peculiar it may be, but it's customary that women reach their majority at four and twenty—three years past the age required of men, because it's believed that our sensibilities are more tender, and we require more time for our reason to overtake our natural propensity toward emotion." I might not like it, but for now, I must work within it. I tilted my head. "Besides, you cannot say your world does not have its share of unusual conventions."

Of which I'd only caught the slightest glimpse.

His lips tilted upward. "I'll grant the point. But will your father consent?"

"I will do my best to persuade him."

Something shifted slightly in his features. If I failed, would he propose the use of glamour?

I hurried on. "Let's assume that he will."

Though it was a great leap.

"Then Kilmere is of next importance. If the protections are procured, I'll inform Damir, which will check him long enough for me to visit the ruin. Will you come with me, or do you intend to travel by mortal conveyance?"

After my excursion to the Otherworld, I'd learned that high fae could open passings between the worlds—despite the established belief that Otherkind could only travel through Crossings, which the Vigil kept well-guarded. I still had many questions about that, but this was scarcely the time. I brushed my hands together, clearing off the fur that had collected on them. "I cannot simply leave without warning. If I vanish for a day, or however long it will take to explore Kilmere, my family will worry—and that's if I can manage to slip out unnoticed. But if I wait long enough to persuade them that I must go, I'll have the time to investigate Kilmere as required and deal with whatever we find there."

"Very well," he said. "As soon as the matter of the will is settled, I'll see if there are traces of Otherkind, as you call them, about the region and within Kilmere proper while you make your arrangements. It might prove to be a simple matter."

Yet somehow I doubted it.

"Asrina will remain with you as a precaution," he said.

I glanced at her, all glorious with light. "And if Lord West seeks to incapacitate her again?"

"I don't think he'll strike again, not yet." His fingers tapped against his leg. "Once he knows I'm involved and you set protections in place, he'll have to reconsider his strategies. Still, I'll set a ward on her."

It all sounded well in theory, but if I failed to convince Father . . . what then? Riven might well suggest glamouring him —and even if he did not, I'd have to guard myself to avoid unintentionally glamouring another of my loved ones.

With Jade and Asrina as companions, I crept down the stairs and sought Father in his study, while Riven waited in the nearby drawing room.

As usual, he didn't stir at my entrance. I settled into the chair across from his desk. "Father, I need to talk to you about what happened yesterday."

That brought him up from his star charts with a jolt. He peered at me through his spectacles. "Ah, Jessa. You look much recovered. Are you well?"

"Still a bit sore, but I feel much better."

"Good, good." He set down the charts. "I thought I'd take the details from you and then go to the Magistry with a report this morning. If they've questions, they can come speak to you here."

"I'd rather you not, because—it was no accidental attack."

He half-rose from his chair. "What do you mean?"

"The invitation I received was a false one, meant to lure me into Lady Hampton's home, where an assailant waited. He made an attempt on my life, for the purpose of claiming Kilmere afterward." The words tasted bitter. "I have reason to believe Lord West is behind the attack."

Father collapsed back into his seat, his features suddenly haggard. "Jessa—I cannot—you are certain?"

I nodded.

His hands tightened slowly about a wood pen till it snapped, staining his fingers. "Lord West is behind it, you say? That any man would stoop so low—but it's all the more reason to involve the Magistry. He must pay in full for his deeds."

With nothing more than my word to go on, he believed me—and was prepared to go to war against forces he did not understand. My chest tightened. "You know how difficult it is for them to prosecute powerful men. And I do not have the sort of evidence they require. I did not speak of it last night, because I saw no way forward, but I've since thought of a way to thwart him, only I must have your consent."

He dabbed at the ink stains. "What do you plan?"

"It will sound peculiar, so I must ask you to trust that I've considered all the angles of the situation before coming to this conclusion."

Jade gave my ankle a reassuring nudge, and I drew a deep breath. This was the difficult part—how to say enough to sway him, but not enough to endanger him. I folded my hands in my lap. "Do you recall Lord Riven? He tenanted Wyncourt for a time, and he's acquainted with Lord West. He was the one who informed me of Lord West's true nature, and how he'll stop at nothing to accomplish his ends."

"I recall Lord Riven, but how will his information keep Lord West from making another attempt on your life?"

"Lord Riven has the power and position to discourage Lord West from pursuing the matter further—and there's enmity between them. I'd like to use that to my advantage by drawing up a will stating that Kilmere and the trust from Lady Dromley will go to Lord Riven upon my death or marriage. I'd also like to make him a third trustee, so that Lord West realizes he cannot force the trustees to consent to a sale of the property. I've spoken to him, and he's agreed, provided that you give your consent. Once Lord West gives up on the matter, the will can be revised."

Only he'd never give up, which meant we must find some way to force his hand. I refused to consider the difficulty of the task.

"That's rather extraordinary—irregular in the highest degree." He dropped the blotter he'd used to swipe at his fingers. The lines about his eyes drew deeper. "You trust him with this?"

"Yes."

Father fell silent.

Jade abandoned her post at my feet to prowl the room, as though she could not endure to remain motionless any longer.

Does something trouble you? I asked.

I share your father's concern. This plan requires a great deal of trust in Riven.

And you believe that a mistake?

I cannot say. Only that Riven is feared among his own people for the power he holds. He's not pressed his advantage, not yet, but I don't see him as a safe choice. Still, you require him to keep Damir away—thus the difficulty.

Jade was right. When in the Otherworld, I'd witnessed how Mocvar—powerful though he was—feared Riven. Was I mistaken to place so much trust in him? *You think he has another purpose in offering aid?*

I don't know. I wish I did.

So do I.

Father shifted, the chair creaking beneath him. "I don't like it, Jessa. To act so puts you at the mercy of a veritable stranger. The trust is a considerable sum, even apart from the value of the properties, and if this Lord Riven took it in mind to press his advantage, it might go poorly with you. Even the news spreading about could raise questions."

"Father, I don't believe—"

He held up a hand. "Let me manage the situation for you. Even if we don't have enough for legal action, I can make it clear to Lord West that under no terms will he ever receive Kilmere."

"Please don't—he's an exceedingly dangerous man." My arms stung, as though the shadow-bindings lashed them once more. "My assailant yesterday said that Lord West intended to wrest the properties from my grieving father. I cannot endure the notion that you'd be at risk, that he'd seek your life as well as my own, if you did not cooperate."

Father stood and rounded the desk to stand before me, an uncharacteristic display of emotion. He reached out to grasp my hands, and his own had gone cold.

"You don't have any reason to trust Lord Riven, and I have no better explanation to offer, only that I know this is the path that must be taken," I said. If only I could tell him the whole—but how could I choose to place him in such an impossible situation, caught between fae and Vigil and all the forces at work in this situation? I squeezed his hands tighter. "Do you trust me enough to believe I'd arrive at the best conclusion?"

He released my hands, a strange expression flickering in his eyes, something akin to pain. "You are very like your mother. It will be as you wish. We'll go this morning to the solicitor and to your trustees. One of the Magister's recorders shares membership in the Royal Society of Astronomers, and I believe he'd be willing to seal the documents today. Meantime, I shall inform Holden that Lord West is not to be admitted to our home under any circumstances. I cannot think he'd have the audacity to call, but we shall see you kept safe. If Lord West thinks he can inflict his will with impunity, he'll soon find he's mistaken."

I stood, and I laid my head on his shoulder, stealing a moment of solace. "Thank you."

Right or wrong, I was now committed.

CHAPTER 18

After securing Father's agreement, I'd told him I'd need a quarter of an hour to prepare to go out, and also that I'd already asked Lord Riven to join us this morning, in hopes that he'd agree. He'd grumbled slightly about presumption, but then admitted his presence would expedite matters.

I took my leave of Father, joining Riven in the drawing room long enough to inform him of how everything had unfolded.

"Good. I'll call at the front door in a quarter hour," he said.

I hurried up the stairs to fetch my hat and gloves, Asrina and Jade keeping pace. After collecting them, I slipped my reticule over my arm, thankful that Asrina no longer required it.

She fluttered at my shoulder, her light warming me.

And I hesitated. I'd endangered her once already. If she stayed as Riven bid, she might find herself at risk again. "Asrina, do you want to return to the Otherworld?"

An image flashed through my mind, of light forming a connection between us.

What was she trying to say? Riven had appeared able to communicate with her far more precisely than one would expect from vague images. Perhaps there was another way—after all, I'd not been able to perceive the images her light cast until recently. I regarded her blaze-bright form. "Is there a better way we might communicate?"

She nodded, then lifted her hands in a sort of beseeching motion.

I turned to Jade. *What must I do?*

Sun sylphs do not vocalize. They use the shifting of temperature caused by their light to create sound and form words. If you did not have something of Other about you, you would not be able to hear —but you do, so perhaps you may.

And the images she used before?

Are much like the language of hands your kind use for those who cannot hear, though even more limited in effectiveness.

I see. It was worth a try. I extended my hand toward Asrina, and she fluttered onto my palm. Then, in the same way I extended my senses to the plants around me, I opened them to Asrina.

"You listen, good, good, good." Her light pulsed rapidly, as words tumbled out. "I am bound to Riven; I will stay."

"Bound? What does that mean?"

"In the Court of Gold, sun sylphs must serve bond-terms to high fae. I did as a youngling, but no longer. With Riven, it is a bargain, a good bargain. He accepts those of my flight who have not yet served their terms, but does not send them idly into danger as some do. And he sets wards on the dwellings of our flight, so that *risnha* don't steal them. In exchange, some of us have bargained whole-life service."

My mind spun with the information, so rapidly imparted. "Still, if you don't want to remain, I could ask him to assign you some other task."

"I wish not to see the Court of Silver win. No, no, I'll stay."

"I—thank you, lovely one." Now that Riven was here, any risk to her lessened—and I could not deny I'd grown accustomed to her steady companionship, and the flicker of warmth and Other she brought.

She beamed and launched herself toward the doorway.

Jade followed more sedately. *That's not the only reason she stays.*

Did you read her thoughts?

Of course not. Without just cause, it's considered rude. And curiosity is not *just cause.*

Then why do you think that?

You've shown kindness to her, concern over her fate, even her injuries. To most high fae, sun sylphs—indeed, all you'd call low fae—are insignificant. Yet from the first, you've genuinely admired her beauty, and you've offered gratitude instead of demanding service. It must be a pleasing change.

I see. How very little I understood of the Otherworld. Certainly our lore reflected differing degrees of power between high fae and low, yet I'd never considered what sort of hierarchy might form—and what might be demanded of those less powerful.

I hastened to rejoin Father in the study, but he was not alone.

Aunt Caris stood before him, arms flung into the air. "You plan what?"

"I—"

He fell silent when I entered, Holden materializing on my heels.

I stepped aside so he could enter. "You first, Holden."

"As you wish, miss." He straightened. "There's a Lord Riven here to see you, Mr. Caldwell."

Father gave a nod. "Show him into the drawing room. I must finish speaking with Caris before we depart."

"I don't want to keep him waiting too long," I said.

Aunt Caris hesitated. Doubtless she'd not want to offend an eligible gentleman by not receiving him properly. "Jessa, Dreda's in the morning room. If you fetch her, the two of you may greet Lord Riven and offer apologies for the delay."

"Yes, Aunt Caris." Yet as I moved into the corridor, her voice drifted after me, rooting me in place.

"Alden, I cannot believe you've agreed to this. Only think if word gets out—"

"I've given Jessa my word."

"But *why*?"

"It's a chance to right a wrong, perhaps."

"What wrong has been done?"

Silence followed, at last broken by Father. "In the weeks before Kensa died, she worried about our safety. She had fears she could not explain—insisted we'd be better off at Thornhaven than Caldwell House, against all sense and reason. Who ever heard of Crossings offering a haven?"

"Oh, Alden."

"There had been a recent attack at the Fens Crossing, and I thought it too great a gamble to travel anywhere near one. I told her I'd not agree to the children going—it was too great a risk— but if she wanted to go herself, I'd not stop her. But in truth, I sought to take the decision from her hands. I knew she'd never leave them." His voice faltered. "She was so angry. So hurt. Yet she could give no reason for her insistence that we must go, so I stood firm. I've always wondered—if I'd just listened, would she have lived?"

If he'd driven a thorn through my heart, the pain would have been less. What had happened to Mother? Even the knowledge that Riven waited couldn't move me.

"You cannot blame yourself. Melancholy such as she experienced can lead to irrational fears, even the physician said so. And if she could not give an explanation for what concerned her, what were you to do?"

"So I justified it to myself. Yet she was so sure about what must be done. If she was right . . ."

Aunt Caris sighed softly. "I see why you feel you must give way to Jessa in this, but she's not Kensa."

"I know."

I strained to hear as his voice lowered, but a sudden surge of Other shattered my concentration—not Riven, but something else, something as cold as a winter night and terrifyingly familiar.

Lord West.

My pulse throbbed at my temples, and Jade bristled, glowering in the direction of the door as though she'd rip out his throat if he dared step through it. Whatever Father's instruction to Holden, it wouldn't hold up to Lord West's glamour. If he wanted admittance, he'd get it.

Forgetting Dreda, I fled to the drawing room where Riven waited. "He's here."

"I know." His eyes held the alertness of a hunting hawk. "A moment, and I'll ensure he's turned away."

"How?"

"By preventing him from glamouring your butler."

Shortly after Riven left the drawing room, the pressing sense of Other subsided, and I could breathe again. I'd not have to face Lord West today, not have to pretend I wasn't terrified by his presence. If Riven hadn't been here . . . It didn't bear considering.

Riven returned, and Father entered the room almost immediately thereafter, blessedly without Aunt Caris, who'd have been sure to ask why Dreda wasn't present. Before Father could consider the matter, I introduced Riven.

Father eyed him as though taking his measure—no surprise, given the circumstances. His right hand drifted to the wedding band he still wore. Did he recall Mother, even now? Did her memory fortify him to take this unusual step? Either way, he moved forward, giving a low bow to Riven. "We're grateful for your intervention in this matter." His lips tightened. "Holden just informed me that Lord West attempted to call. That he would attempt to gain entrance to our home, after what he did . . ."

Riven lifted a shoulder. "That is his way."

"Then all the more reason to put a swift end to his efforts." With that, Father urged us into the carriage before him. Once safely inside, I shrank back into the shadows.

When Riven and I had discussed our plans this morning, it had given me some sense of security, but all that had vanished when Lord West called. Whatever obstacles we placed in his way, he'd look to surmount. In my gaps of understanding, some loophole was sure to exist—and he'd not give up till he found it.

THE REST of the day passed in a blur. Between Father and Riven, the legal proceedings unfolded faster than I'd anticipated, with even my trustees giving their consent, despite the unusual proceedings.

I'd pressed so hard on my own that I was content to let them advance the arguments—and it suited my purpose better, for everyone paid them closer heed than they would have me.

When we returned to our carriage, Riven took his leave. And when he vanished from sight, I felt like a plant taken from the glasshouse and left exposed to the winter frosts.

But no, I couldn't afford to think so, nor to rely on him beyond the uncertain bounds of our bargain. He'd agreed to help for now, but I could not predict how long it would last.

We rattled along in the carriage, Jade perched on the seat beside me, surveying our surroundings as was her wont—yet something in the lines of her body suggested she took extra vigil with Riven absent.

When we returned to the residential section, the sweet-orange smell of the alchemical solution used to polish the door-stones drifted into the carriage, a familiar, homely scent that calmed my unsettled emotions.

We'd carried out the first part of our plan, and now I must persuade Father about Kilmere. "Father, I still have some concerns about Lord West."

He steepled his fingers. "I can see why. He's more brazen than I expected. That he would come into our home this morning defies reason."

"I don't feel he's given up, even with what Lord Riven told him." I stroked Jade. "I think I should go to Kilmere to figure out what he wants so badly. I suspect there's something of value he seeks to claim before another can discover it. But whatever the case, if I can find the truth, perhaps I can put an end to his interest."

It was the sort of thing of which Father approved—the examination of facts to draw conclusions, rather than reliance on others to interpret them. If he believed it would also keep me safer, then he'd not hesitate to agree. Or so I hoped.

"Your aunt may not favor such an excursion."

"If she does not wish to travel, perhaps Dreda might come as my companion? We could let a small cottage. Withern-at-Sea often has travelers come to enjoy the sea air and bathe in the waters, so it shouldn't be difficult to find lodging."

And I wanted my family as far from Kilmere and Lord West as possible. I'd rather not bring Dreda either, but at least she wouldn't look askance at any of my odd behaviors—and since the victims had only been among the old families of Withern, she shouldn't be at any risk.

Father rubbed his jaw, considering. "Very well—but you must make the arrangements with Caris. She's to have the final word on making sure they satisfy proprieties. I've no mind for another lecture such as the one I received after your botany expedition."

And she might not agree at all—it was likely that Father only had because of Mother. I couldn't let on that I'd overheard his wrenching confession, but I must try to learn what I could. "There's something else I'm wondering."

"Hmm." He was growing more abstracted, retreating from me even as we drew nearer to home.

"It's about Mother."

That brought him back, at least for a moment. He shoved his spectacles upward. "What about her?"

"Did she often travel?"

"More so before Ada and Ainslie were born. Afterward she preferred to stay close to home, unless visiting Thornhaven." His shoulders bowed inward. "She insisted we travel as a family or not at all."

Which was out of the common way. Did it mean she feared for us? Or that she genuinely didn't wish to be parted? Questions swirled within. If I was right, and I had been conceived as part of a bargain, then how would she have hidden such assaults at Caldwell House? Or had it happened at Thornhaven, with its proximity to a Crossing? If so, why would she have ever wanted to return?

It was too late to inquire further; we'd stopped in front of our row house. Together we descended from the carriage and made our way withindoors.

Once inside, Father handed his hat and walking stick to Holden and moved toward the study.

I followed, intending to secure the will—one of multiple copies—in his strongbox.

Already the liveliness brought on by knowing Lord West had threatened my life was fading from him; the prospect of his books and charts clearly beckoned, as did the escape from the heightened emotions he'd surrendered to. He sank into his armchair and lifted a sheaf of papers, soon becoming immersed.

I left him to his work and went to seek Aunt Caris. Unless I missed the mark, she would be the far more difficult of the two to convince, and I couldn't afford a delay.

I found her in the morning room, along with Lovell and my

sisters, who offered greetings when I entered. After an exchange of pleasantries, I settled onto a cushioned chair, and Jade hopped into my lap, the motion so familiar I could *almost* forget that she could turn into an enormous tiger-cat at will and wrench every thought from my mind whenever it pleased her.

She tensed beneath my touch.

I didn't mean offense—I'm sorry.

Some of the tightness in her body eased. *It is not your fault. You've had little time to adjust.*

But I will. I pulled her close, and she nudged my chin. Now, for Aunt Caris. I turned toward her. "Aunt Caris, I've been speaking to Father about visiting Kilmere. I'd like to check into some allegations made about it and consider reopening excavation. I know you have much to keep you in Avons, so I thought perhaps Dreda might accompany me?"

"Kilmere is near Withern-at-Sea, is it not?" she asked.

"Yes, which should make it easy to find suitable lodging."

"I suppose." Yet a small furrow puckered her brow. "But if this is about your concern for Kilmere—I thought a sum had been left in trust to see to matters like these. Surely your trustees would agree to send someone to look into whatever has gone amiss?"

"I believe they would, but it meant so much to Ibbie that I'd like to see to the matter myself."

Ada set aside the letter she'd been reading, and both she and Ainslie regarded me closely.

"You could be away for weeks." Aunt Caris stabbed her needle through the fine muslin. "What of Lord West? He might lose all interest."

Jade chuffed. *If only he were so weak-willed.*

I stifled a smile. "I'd not be disappointed if he did. We do not suit—and Father agrees."

"So he's said, though he's given me no clear reason why."

So he'd not told her the whole, only that he deemed Lord West unsuitable. How then had he justified the changing of the will to her? She'd clearly known of that plan, at least enough to object, and no wonder she had, if Father had kept back the full truth. Doubtless, he'd not wanted her to fear.

She drew the thread taut. "Whatever your father thinks, my dear, you should consider Lord West further. I've heard—"

Lovell lowered his gazette. "Haven't there been some unexplained deaths in Withern of late? Heard the authorities think there's a poisoner on the loose."

Aunt Caris paled.

Of all the distraction tactics, he would choose one that drew Aunt Caris away from Lord West but gave her reason to protest the entire trip. I frowned at Lovell, and he ducked behind his paper once more.

"Is this true?" she asked.

I shrugged slightly, as if it were of no consequence. "There have been some odd deaths, but as it happens, Mr. Burke has gone to Withern to investigate. He wrote that they've already taken a suspect into custody and that the entire matter appears to relate to long-held grudges between the old families in the region."

Aunt Caris tugged harder at her needle than strictly necessary. "He wrote to you?"

"It was a matter of business only. Since he was traveling to the region, I asked him for information on Kilmere."

A slight frown marred her amiable features. "I'm certain he's an upstanding soul, and he does come from a good family, but he's a stratesman, my dear—not at all a desirable acquaintance to cultivate."

I refrained from saying I'd found him more a gentleman than many who claimed that role and offered only a small nod.

Ada slid forward on the settee. "Regardless, that means Withern-at-Sea poses no danger. What if we were all to go?"

A smile lilted across Ainslie's face. "That's an excellent notion."

My breath hitched. Their attempts at support could

unravel all my plans. With only Dreda, I'd have considerable liberty to investigate—and I'd not have to worry about them attracting further notice from Lord West. Yet if they all came . . .

Ainslie continued, "You were saying just this morning that you thought after all we'd endured in Avons, it might be prudent to depart before the season ended. It's not as if it will last much longer anyway. In a few more weeks, nearly everyone will travel or return to their country estates."

Aunt Caris tied off a thread. "I *had* considered summering at the sea, and I do have an acquaintance near Withern. If I write ahead, I'm certain she could arrange lodgings."

I tried to halt the proceedings. "There's no need for the entire family to be discomposed on a matter of business—"

"I think a trip to the sea sounds delightful. We could enjoy new company." Ainslie nudged me, looking meaningfully at Ada.

Oh.

She meant to use this situation to remove Ada from Lord Bradford. How could I deny her the opportunity? Whatever my sentiments, it seemed I had no choice but to accept this new plan, as everyone discussed our travels with enthusiasm.

Ainslie reached for the writing supplies, her binding mark peeking out from the edge of her sleeve, a reminder she was as vulnerable here as anywhere. Perhaps it would be better that we were not separated, so I could keep watch over her.

But if Riven was right, and Lord West followed us to Withern . . .

I sighed.

"I think this will turn out to be fortuitous indeed. I'll confess I haven't been at peace about staying in Avons after what happened to Jessa, and it seems prudent to remove Ada from the path of Lord Bradford since she has no interest in him." Aunt Caris beamed upon us. "Yes, this will suit very well. It will take several days to put the household in order and make proper arrangements. I'll send word ahead to my friend to engage lodgings for us."

"Several days? I'd hoped to depart tomorrow."

"These things take time to arrange." Aunt Caris patted my hand. "But never worry, my dear, we'll depart before the week's end."

Which might as well be an eternity, for all the time it would give Lord West to marshal his forces.

CHAPTER 19

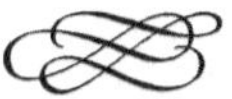

Where was Riven? The question plagued me the following afternoon, since he'd yet to return. Never mind that he'd made no promise as to when he'd come, my mind conjured a range of distressing possibilities, and as soon as I displaced one, another followed on its heels.

With difficulty, I turned my attention to the leather folio I'd fetched earlier that morning from Wyncourt, the one containing the documents on Kilmere that I judged most relevant of those Ibbie had collected. Nearby, Ainslie made her way through a stack of papers, and Lovell loafed on the armchair while Ada made notations on the latest musical score she'd obtained.

Across from them, Aunt Caris and Dreda rested on the settee. Dreda wound yarn, continuing to insist on taking additional duties rather than sitting at her leisure.

"Aha." Ainslie looked up from the paper. "This explains why the Dunmoors left Avons so abruptly. Miss Susan no longer wishes to wed Sir Rothmore, and he's filed a breach of promise suit."

"How dreadful. Her mother must be most distressed," Aunt Caris said.

"And she must have had a great deal of provocation to take such a step," Ada murmured.

What would it cost her family? If the Magistry settled in favor of Sir Rothmore, they could owe a considerable sum.

Ainslie turned the page. "If she'd been wise, she would have provoked *him* to end the engagement—then *she* could have filed suit, if she so desired."

"Either way, her reputation would be ruined," Ada said.

Ainslie peered over the edge of the paper. "Yet at least she'd have a sum to safeguard her future."

Dreda kept silent, steadily winding the yarn, her opinions concealed behind a serene exterior.

One of the pages in the pile I sorted was thicker than the rest. I ran my finger across it—it was in fact two stuck together. When I managed to ease the bottom one free, it depicted an intricate scrolled frieze—perhaps one copied from within Kilmere? It hadn't been done by an artist, for the details were rough and the rendering uneven. In the sketch, serpentine forms twined around elaborate blossoms. I held the paper closer.

Were those perhaps letters or sigils within the frieze? Perhaps I could borrow Father's hand glass to survey it more closely, but given the rough quality of the piece, even that might not produce any further evidence.

I stood to fetch it, only to be halted by the entrance of Holden, announcing Lord Blackburn had come to call. I'd not seen him since I'd talked with him in company of Riven. Had he come in response to my letter about the Dark Era?

Aunt Caris fluttered to her feet. "Does he wish to speak with Alden?"

"He says he's come to call upon the family."

"Then bring him in, but send for Alden as well," she said. "And tea."

I couldn't fault Aunt Caris for assuming Lord Blackburn had come to call on Father. After all, to her knowledge, none of the rest of us shared acquaintance with him. She could not know that he had *not* called on Father previously—rather Uros had, in guise of Lord Blackburn.

Would he recall my warning? What would he do if Father attempted to address matters they'd supposedly discussed? For that matter, what would I do if he openly addressed the Forgotten War, which I'd not so much as hinted about to my family?

Jade blinked up at me from where she sprawled across the end table. *You cannot control all things.*

I'm beginning to feel as though I can control nothing, and that the most trying of things are bound to happen at the most inconvenient of moments.

She let out a chuff. *That too.*

A moment later, Holden ushered in Lord Blackburn. Even at his age, his presence was imposing, once more putting me in mind of an age-weathered tree, one with its roots driven deep by adversity and therefore unmovable in the face of any storm.

He accepted the chair Aunt Caris offered him, and in the midst of introductions, Father joined us.

"Nice to see you again, Blackburn." Father situated himself across from our visitor.

"Caldwell. A pleasure." He offered the slightest tilt of his hoary head.

Father blinked, as though he came out of his usual state of abstraction with effort. "I've drafted those star charts you requested."

"Ah, yes." Lord Blackburn did an admirable job of disguising any bewilderment. "My thanks."

Still, perhaps I'd best try to smooth over the matter. "You and Lord Blackburn have spoken about your astronomy studies?"

"Yes. He's most interested in the anomalies in the heavens."

"I . . . As a matter of fact, I am," Lord Blackburn said.

Just how well had Uros imitated him? I shuddered at the recollection of his spider-form and his presence in our home.

Lord Blackburn warmed to his theme. "Anomalies of all sorts are occurring more than they should."

"Is that why you champion reform of fae policy?" Ainslie flashed her dimples, causing her question to appear more innocuous than it otherwise would. "To preserve the order of our world? Do you believe they're responsible for undoing it?"

A sigh gusted from Aunt Caris. "Will you take tea, Lord Blackburn?"

He accepted with a nod. "I make no secret of my views, Miss Ainslie. The longer we wait, the more risks we run."

"Yet the Vigil and Assemblage of Lords at large do not share your views." Lovell straightened from his lounged position, his gaze intent. "Do they lack important facts?"

"Perhaps. Or they suppress them."

A stillness fell over the room, his statement silencing us all. He held enough power that the Vigil couldn't come after him as easily—but no one was truly safe from their grasp.

Then he shrugged, as if to dismiss his own words. "In my position, one hears all sorts of rumors. Still, we all have a responsibility to seek the truth."

"Of course." Aunt Caris lifted a tray of pastries. "Can I interest you in a scone?"

He accepted both the scones and her determined change of conversation with grace, and as Aunt Caris was skilled in the art of proper conversation, it flowed pleasantly.

The longer he sat and listened, the more the craggy lines of his face softened. At last, he turned to Father. "You're a fortunate man, Caldwell. You've a delightful family."

Father lifted his cup. "The credit belongs to Caris. My wife was taken from us when my daughters were young, and she's had the rearing of them."

Lord Blackburn's mouth tightened. "It seems we share a loss."

"Caris and the girls are about to leave for Withern, but perhaps you'd join me to dine Tuesday next? We can discuss the star charts properly." Father ordinarily preferred the comfort of his books to the companionship of others, but perhaps their shared loss inspired him to seek connection.

"It would give me great pleasure." Lord Blackburn's eyes brightened.

Unease brushed along my neck, light as the touch of aster down. If Lord Blackburn pulled Father into his crusade for fae policy reform, would Father face danger from the Vigil . . . or the Otherworld? While a member of the gentry, Father couldn't come close to matching the wealth, status, or political clout Lord Blackburn wielded—and thus lacked protection.

Lord Blackburn continued, "Now, I must confess I've another motive in calling today. In life, Lady Dromley spoke highly of Miss Jessa—and of her interest in horticulture. I owe Miss Jessa a bit of a debt since she unearthed and returned something valuable to me, and I thought I might return the favor by taking her to tour the new display of exotic specimens in the Botanic Gardens before it opens to the public."

He regarded me. "Would you care to accompany me this afternoon?"

What was this? I pulled Jade a bit closer. Perhaps he had come in response to my letter after all, but did not intend to speak of the Forgotten War before my family. Or perhaps he merely intended a kindness?

"That sounds lovely." Pleasure radiated from every soft curve of Aunt Caris's face—evidently she deemed it a more than acceptable outing.

"Thank you, Lord Blackburn." I offered a smile. "It's very kind of you. I've followed the progress of the exhibition with great interest, and I'd be delighted to join you."

Though he was old enough to be my grandfather, a chaperone was still required. When Lord Blackburn stood, Aunt Caris gave Dreda a small nod, and she rose to accompany us.

We passed an easy ride in his spacious carriage, speaking of the new exhibition and other pleasantries. Though I was eager to see if Lord Blackburn would use the opportunity to address Otherworldly matters, a small part of me simply gloried in the display to come. For months, royal gardeners had worked to prepare the east wing of the great glasshouse in the Botanic Gardens for the new display. The gardens sprawled over several city blocks, and the glasshouse for exotic plants occupied its center, a building more immense than all but the dwelling of the king himself, one so large as to contain lawns and trees and a glorious array of living things.

Once we emerged from the carriage, I accepted his arm. The rich fragrances of all things green and growing filled the air, along with the scent of sunbaked stone. A surge of song came so strong that I had to draw the weave of the graceful trees within my mind tighter, an act I'd not required in some time.

Dreda remained several steps behind us, as was proper, while Asrina fluttered at my shoulder. Jade kept pace alongside, the fur on her ruff rising slightly. She sensed something.

What is it?

Something Other. Inside.

When I allowed the boughs of the trees to unfurl, the slightest hint of Other pressed against my senses. I almost faltered. I couldn't withdraw now, but what awaited within?

When we crossed the threshold of the great glasshouse, low, ominous notes thrummed into my awareness—not Otherkind then, but something botanical in nature, something that did not belong. It took all my effort to maintain a sedate pace, matching that of Lord Blackburn.

"What I said about owing you a debt was true, but it was your letter that inspired me to come." Though he'd kept quiet before my family, he evidently had no concern about speaking before Dreda. Perhaps to him, as with most of society, Dreda was all but invisible—a spinster companion who faded into the background.

"I'd wondered if that had moved you to visit." I attempted to press back the rich threads of song and attend to Lord Blackburn.

"Clearly you read the letters Lady Dromley procured for me," he said.

"I did—I hope that doesn't displease you." I kept my voice low, hoping he'd follow suit. If he did, perhaps the hum of activity from the gardeners would keep Dreda from overhearing too much.

"I'm not surprised. You don't seem like the sort to forsake an opportunity to gain knowledge. You're very like Lady Dromley in that. I expect she read them as well."

"I cannot imagine otherwise—she inspected every artifact that passed through her hands."

"And now it appears you've found something more. Your letter intrigued me. What did you uncover?"

To demur now, whatever the risk of Dreda listening in, would raise questions I did not wish to answer. So I inhaled the honey-spice fragrance of a sweet glory, its vine twining up an ivory trellis alongside us, and plunged in. "Before she died, Ib— Lady Dromley procured for me a history of the Vigil, which referred to a Dark Era in Byren during which the Otherworld invaded in force. The letters she'd set aside for you provided the first bit of corroborative evidence. Then I came across a logbook in the Cloister library with notes on a war between mortals and Otherkind. I thought you might find such records of interest."

The seams in Lord Blackburn's face drew into furrows of concern. "Indeed, I'm most intrigued, and I will seek access to the Cloister library. But I regret your involvement. May I suggest you leave the matter alone?"

"Do you believe such ancient history a danger in our time?" I kept my tone light, as if I were unconcerned.

"For such a thing to have been forgotten, those in power must have concealed it. And if so, they'll not welcome it reentering public knowledge."

Yet the authorities simply removing evidence wouldn't be

enough to drive all recall of a war from the populace. Altered memories suggested fae involvement, only why would fae want to conceal the war? I skimmed my fingers across a hanging broadleaf. "Then you believe the war happened?"

"I'm attempting to gather evidence, but it's proven exceedingly difficult." His eyes burned bright above the prominent crag of his nose. "You've had unusual success in that regard."

"So I have," I said. "May I inquire what you've found?"

He shook his head. "I'll not drag you further into this. I'd be doing you no kindness, much less honoring my friendship with Lady Dromley. Best you forget it altogether."

"Have you considered, my lord, that if you alone hold the evidence you collect, then anyone wishing to keep the matter concealed will have only to silence you?" It wasn't proper, wasn't at all what a lady would say, but I couldn't restrain myself.

Lord Blackburn halted before a magnificent fountain, his prominent brows bristling. "Miss Caldwell, you're a rather remarkable young lady."

"Not so very remarkable. Only concerned—as anyone would be—for the welfare of my family and my kingdom. It's a concern you clearly share."

"I do. But I've considered the risks, and I'm willing to take them. As I said, I've little enough to go on, certainly not enough to justify embroiling others in this affair. If I could prove things more conclusively, then perhaps . . ."

He did me the great favor of not treating me as a senseless young miss, and I'd press the advantage as far as I could. "Will you at least tell me why you believe the conflict was forgotten?"

"I have theories, but none that hold water. After the affair of the Crimson Tattoo Killer, the king approached me, more willing to listen, though he'd not explain why. Perhaps he thought if a mortal killer could wreak such havoc, what might a fae do? Yet without evidence, he won't act." His walking stick rapped against the polished stone pavers beneath us. "I'd hoped if I could find clear enough proof we'd once endured such a conflict, it might support my endeavor to reform our current policies. If we suffered the open wrath of the fae once, we could easily endure it again."

He was right. So why hadn't we? Some protections clearly remained in place, but the hostile incidents appeared to be increasing. What had changed? And why? Uros had spoken of destruction coming to our world . . . and it emboldened me to take a calculated risk in speaking more freely. "Do you believe it possible that we already endure some hostility from Otherworldly forces? I know you suffered the loss of your wife and son and that you believe Otherkind responsible for their deaths."

His fingers tightened on the head of his walking stick. "That time—it has become a haze in my mind. I believed so then, but the Vigil discounted it, said I was under the influence of grief and the laudanum administered for my shock. Now I scarcely know what is truth."

"So the Vigil denied your claim?"

"They investigated. Said it was an attack by highwaymen, nothing more." He resumed walking, his gaze fixed straight ahead. "Yet none were known to prey on that region, and their bodies had been . . . greatly disfigured. What motive would highwaymen have for such a deed? The farmer who found them said he'd seen strange prints on the scene, but when I went back to speak with him, he was gone. Everyone else refused to talk to me."

Had the farmer been taken by the Vigil? Or lured into the Otherworld? We rounded a corner, entering the east wing, and despite the serious nature of our conversation, Otherworldly melodies nearly unmoored me. The boughs within bent beneath the force of it.

I staggered to a halt.

"Are you well, Miss Caldwell? I forgot myself—I should never have spoken of such things to a lady. Please forgive me."

"It's not what you said. I just . . ." I straightened my shoulders. "I was accosted the other day, and I suppose I'm a bit on edge still. I thought I heard something . . . out of the ordinary, and it unnerved me."

"You should have told me. We could have taken this excursion another time, when you were not recovering."

"There was no need, truly." The low, threatening notes wove through my mind, yet I forced myself to summon a smile. "It's just what I needed."

We resumed our stroll toward the far corner of the east wing, and there I found the source, an oval niche in the wall containing a special display.

Above the rest of the plants therein towered a magnificent tree with many interwoven trunks, its silvery bark smooth, its glossy leaves threaded with pale veins.

It whispered menace, a quiet pulse of danger and displeasure. Clustered below the tree were thick waxy stems of unnaturally vibrant green that burned up to brilliant red tubular tops, in shape like the hood of a cobra, but speckled with white flecks. They swayed toward me, murmuring an offering to strike as I bid.

Jade rumbled low and wove around my ankles. Blessedly, she didn't speak into my mind, which could handle no other distraction.

Alongside these hooded-cobra blossoms bunched peculiar black flowers with long, whisker-like bracteoles that drooped far below the blossoms themselves and exuded the faint scent of rot, theirs a slow, creeping sort of song that threaded with the others in ominous harmony.

I clutched Lord Blackburn's arm. "Where did this display come from?"

"Oh, I believe it was a last-minute donation." He shrugged. "One they were exceedingly pleased to receive, since the botanicals are so rare as to be unclassified."

Unclassified indeed—this wasn't right. Would these Otherworldly plants cause harm? The donor must have some ulterior motive; I couldn't imagine any fae acting with generosity. I could see no reason for Lord West to present such a gift, but did that mean another high fae lurked within Avons? "It's remarkable."

"Quite. I expect it will increase demand for tours."

Only with effort could I keep the songs to a tolerable level, so I feigned interest in the rare orchid display on the far side of the wing, and he gladly squired me across the chamber.

As we left the Otherworldly display behind, the pressure within eased slightly. Yet snaking alongside the outer glass wall, a shadow followed our movements, a vine-like shape matching none of the botanical life within.

I edged closer to the center of the aisle.

I'd forgotten to ask Riven about the shadows—what their purpose might be and how Lord West wielded them. Did he still watch my movements? What if he decided to attack out of spite, even if it removed Kilmere from his grasp forever?

No, Riven believed otherwise, and indeed, I could not think Lord West so shortsighted. He'd said himself he must always triumph, which meant nothing less than claiming his objective would satisfy.

When we neared the end of the display, Lord Blackburn slowed. "Miss Caldwell, I must return to our earlier conversation. When it comes to Otherkind, there are endless dangers. I must reiterate my suggestion that you abandon any notions you might entertain of investigating further."

I murmured something noncommittal.

A frown creased his features. "I'm old, and I've nothing left to lose—everything that mattered to me has already been taken. But you have an entire life ahead of you. Don't throw it away in fear of the fae."

"I assure you, I'll do no more than is necessary."

"Very good." He gave a slight nod, then turned to lighter matters.

I stole a glance at Dreda. Her face was pinched. Clearly,

she'd heard his last remark about fae, perhaps even all that had passed before.

What would she do with her knowledge?

CHAPTER 20

In the stillness of evening, I sought Dreda. If she meant to speak of what she'd heard, it was better to know—and convince her to hold her silence, if she was willing.

I tiptoed down the quiet hall, the gaslights between my bedchamber and hers still kindled to light the way, the wool rug warm on my bare feet. And I knocked gently on her door.

She pulled it open. She'd already prepared to retire—her hair was down in long plaits and a white dressing gown wrapped about her slim frame. The smallest ink stain blotted one finger. Had she changed her mind about corresponding with her family? Or perhaps undertaken some sketching?

I ran my foot along the line of the rug. "I'm sorry to disturb you so late."

"It's no worry. I'm always available to you, Miss Jessa." Yet a slight pucker seamed her brow.

"I wanted to explain—about earlier, in the gardens . . . what Lord Blackburn said."

"You owe me no explanations."

"But I do. I haven't been fair to you, bringing you here without making you aware of the situation." The cool of night settled over the house, and the windows creaked softly as I braced myself for a partial confession.

"What situation?" The gas lamps flickered across her face, infusing gold across her pale features.

"That of Otherkind in our world. You know what it is to endure hardship at their hands, and . . . I believe many others suffer from affliction by fae. I want to understand why it's happening, and I work to that end." Just this small admission left me stripped bare. But even if she utterly rejected my cause, the risk of her making a report was negligible. If the Vigil ever found out she'd been numbered among the fae-touched, they'd claim her—study her, perhaps keep her confined, although she appeared cured. She'd want to stay as far from them as possible. Yet if she spoke with my family . . . My hands tightened, the nails digging into the skin of my palm. "As you may have heard today, Lord Blackburn shares this concern. His wife and son most likely perished due to an Otherworldly attack that authorities deny ever happened."

Her freckles stood out stark now against pale skin, and she clutched at the doorknob, as though she might shut out what I shared.

"If you stay, there's a chance of danger from these investigations, though I'll try to keep you out of it. If you wish to go, I'll understand, and I'll help you seek a new position." Jade settled on my feet, her quiet warmth bolstering me. "Whatever you decide, I trust you'll keep this in confidence—and forgive me for not being more forthright in the beginning."

"You've given me a great deal to consider, and no mistake." She fidgeted with the shuttle lace on her sleeve. "I won't deny it gave me a fright, hearing about the fae again. Remembering how it felt with that creature . . ."

"I'm sorry."

"I'm not. Pretending it didn't happen does no one any good. It still comes back to me, anyway, when I'm alone in the dead of night, how it felt . . ." Her delicate chin lifted, and the coils of her braids spilled back over her shoulders. "Unless I've missed the mark, it comes back to you too. Things that fae have done. Ways they've hurt our kind."

"I—yes."

"Do you plan to do something about it?"

I caught my lip between my teeth. What would she do if she knew I might carry fae blood? Would I figure in her mind—or worse still, the minds of my family—as a dangerous evil to be resisted? Never mind that. Whatever I was, I meant to keep mortals from falling victim to Other. I could offer that assurance at least. "I'll do all I can."

"That's good." Her eyes misted. "If there's a chance you can help others like you once did me, I'm for it. I've never had the opportunity to do anything that has . . . meaning. With you, perhaps I can."

"I'm grateful, but I don't want you blind to the risks."

"All of life has risks. But what you did with that creature—I know you'll keep me safe."

If she'd struck me, I'd have felt no worse. "Dreda, I'll do all I can, but I can make no promises of safety."

"That's quite all right, Miss Jessa. I've watched you, and I'd gamble on you any time."

"I . . . Thank you." We said our goodnights, and she left me standing alone in the corridor, the tall window at the end like a mirror of black.

Why did she extend such trust? What if I couldn't keep her from harm at the hands of the fae—what if I couldn't protect any of them?

I walked over to the window and pressed my face to the cold glass, beyond which the gardens rested. It could be worse. What if I turned out to be the very thing I feared, and I endangered them myself?

~

THE FOLLOWING MORNING, I bent over the paper with the image of the frieze, examining it through the hand glass. Perhaps the squiggles amid the serpentine forms were meant to be some sort of inscription, but they were so erratically copied it was difficult to tell. Of course, the source might have been damaged also.

I set aside the glass. If it had nothing more to offer, then what? Though Aunt Caris had only delayed me a few days, the wait to explore Kilmere felt beyond endurance—yet to leave now, heedless of her instruction, would jeopardize everything. I must be patient, but it would be a great deal easier if Riven would only return. At least today I expected Mr. Tibbons—a message had arrived ahead of him in the morning post, announcing his intended arrival and hopefully some answers.

I fetched my sketching materials and traced images across the page, which soon turned into figures at war as my mind wandered, dark forms fighting shadows.

If there had been open war, and the alchemists had sought an edge in the fight against fae, might they have found a way to imprison low fae within Kilmere? Riven had said none would stay willingly, but what if they'd been trapped and forgotten? A line jagged astray, and I took my rubber to it.

Or perhaps the alchemists had finally managed to conjure an artifact of great power, one which had unexpected effects . . .

Jade would know nothing about that, but she might have theories about low fae. *Jade?*

She stretched languidly in a sunbeam. *Yes?*

What did Riven mean when he said that low fae couldn't function centuries away from the Otherworld?

She began to lick her paw. *To survive, most of those whom you mortals call low fae require . . . ah, there's no true word for it in your tongue . . . let us call it the essence of the Otherworld. They can come to your world for a time, but unless it is close to a Crossing, they must return to their own—at least at intervals.*

That would explain why Otherworldly activity was concentrated around Crossings, through which this essence leached out into the mortal world. As I'd seen in Milburn, it appeared to even influence that which grew from the land. Small wonder the edgetowns offered riches to offset the risks.

I penciled a line darker. What other revolutionary revelations did Jade hold? And how many of them could she speak? A shadow-form took shape on the page before me, in shades of charcoal. *What would happen if a low fae was trapped here? Would it die?*

It depends on the circumstances, I suppose, but that's a likely outcome. You think that happened at Kilmere?

I don't know. Withern is far from a Crossing, so even if mortals once managed to seize low fae, Kilmere would be an odd choice of prison.

Her eyes tracked a swallow as it swooped overhead. *Such an act would be akin to playing with fire for your kind.*

Indeed, it would be far more likely to result in the deaths of the mortals in question than entrapment of the fae. But if the entire kingdom had been in danger, perhaps they thought nothing of the risk . . .

A charged sensation rent the air around us, a sure herald of Riven's arrival. With the gleaming remnants of passing about him, he strolled down the garden path. Though his stride remained unhurried, the slight charge to the air and the subtle tension in his jaw suggested all had not gone as planned.

I snapped my sketchbook shut. "Is something wrong?"

"It depends on how you look at it." He halted in front of me. "Come."

Without waiting to see if I'd follow, he moved into the glasshouse. Once I stepped inside, he wrapped a concealment glamour about us, a now-familiar shimmer tinting the air. In the safety of it, I spoke. "What did you find?"

"A number of powerful fae-workings around the borders of Kilmere."

I skimmed my fingers across the glossy leaves of a camellia, its touch soothing. "Left by Lord West?"

"No. They're crafted within the very rock upon which Kilmere was built—and they form a complete barrier." The sheen to the air intensified. "Lord West left faint traces of his passing nearby, but the workings themselves held no hint of his power. Rather, they were designed to keep denizens of my world out of Kilmere."

Jade's ears pricked forward, her interest clear.

Wait. Keep *his* world out? This knowledge upended my most recent theory—unless it was crafted to keep fae from passing in *or* out. But why would any fae willingly craft workings to keep away their own kind? "How very strange."

"Yes—and effective," he said dryly.

"You mean you couldn't enter Kilmere?"

"Correct."

"But you—" From all Jade had told me, Riven held tremendous power, even as fae judged matters. If the workings were strong enough to keep him from Kilmere, what did that mean? Mechanically, I tugged a withering leaf from the camellia. "Could you undo them?"

"Given time." The green of his eyes darkened to that of a fir forest. "And willingness to destabilize the entire region, not to mention destroy whatever remains housed within. If I shattered the workings, they'd pull down the entire cliff—and unleash destruction on Withern. It is in their make. Whoever crafted them did not intend the fortress to be breached, except at the cost of a great many lives."

The leaf fluttered from my cold fingers. "But . . . mortals have entered, both past and present, so the workings must not bar them."

"Exactly," he said. "Which makes them of even greater interest."

Of interest wasn't the term I'd choose—risk would be more

apt. What was hidden within? "You said you found traces of Lord West in the region. Was there any sign of additional Otherkind?"

"None strong enough to leave a trace. I spent some time examining a wide radius around the region and found nothing. But your world does not hold long to such signs—they grow cold and vanish quickly."

So Lord West had lurked about Kilmere. Presumably, like Riven, he'd been repelled. Which meant he must know about the workings. If he secured ownership, would that be sufficient to allow him entrance? If not, he must have some plan in mind.

"Miss Jessa?" Holden's voice drifted into the glasshouse. "Are you in the gardens?"

I moved beyond the glamour and into the doorway of the glasshouse. "I'm here."

He rounded the rose bushes. "A Mr. Myles Tibbons has arrived. He claims he's here on a matter of business."

Of course Mr. Tibbons *would* arrive now, when I most wanted an uninterrupted conversation with Riven. "It's about Ibbie's estate." I owed Holden no explanation, but reassuring him would make matters easier. "Will you show him into the gardens?"

"You wish to receive him out here, Miss Jessa?"

"Yes." If Mr. Tibbons was accustomed to working for Ibbie, then my occupation during our conversation would not appear odd to him—and it would keep us from listening ears. "You may send Dreda to join us."

He gave a nod. "I shall fetch her at once."

I snatched a collecting basket from within the glasshouse, along with a pair of garden shears.

Riven followed me out. "I'd like to question your Mr. Tibbons. If he entered Kilmere, his answers could be illuminating."

"As long as the questions don't involve glamour—or compulsion." Though I desired the truth, Mr. Tibbons didn't deserve to be forced against his will; he'd only been doing the job set out for him.

Riven lifted his shoulders, and the breadth of them tugged at his jacket. "You'll introduce me as before. Say I have a vested interest in Kilmere and its possible excavation."

We'd no time for further exchange, for Dreda strolled down the central path. She gave me as slight nod as she passed, perhaps in recognition of my desire to conduct this business with some privacy, then situated herself on the edge of the fountain, just beyond earshot.

And a moment later, Mr. Tibbons followed. He halted before me, in appearance as brown and sprightly as an upright hazel, his eyes bright and clear. "Miss Caldwell? I was told to seek you here."

"Yes, thank you. I trust you won't mind discussing Kilmere while I tend the beds?"

"Not at all."

Indeed, he appeared at ease out of doors in a way he might not in the drawing room. His calloused hands attested that he'd spent time working on excavations, not just overseeing them at his leisure—a stark contrast to the academic antiquarians of my acquaintance.

"Excellent." I snipped a sprig of lavender and placed it in the collecting basket, its soothing fragrance swirling around us. "Lord Riven, may I introduce Mr. Myles Tibbons, lately of Withern."

Riven gave a small nod.

And Jade sauntered forward to sniff at Mr. Tibbons's shoes, whereupon she promptly sneezed. *He smells of road dust and old stone.*

I stifled a smile. "Lord Riven has offered assistance in the matter of Kilmere, and we're both most interested in what you may have learned. Please start from the time you left Carlsdale."

"Of course. Lady Dromley requested that I locate as much

supporting documentation on the curse as I could, but she never spoke to me of her reasons. I'd wondered if she considered reopening the excavation but first sought reassurance that it would cause no further tragedy."

"Did she confide in you her theories regarding what happened there before?"

"She kept her thoughts close, only requesting that I find written accounts where possible." He nudged his hat back. "In Carlsdale, I'd no success obtaining the family documents that supposedly existed. I followed another lead to the Fens, but when I arrived, the gentleman in question returned to some family lands in Withern-at-Sea. I figured I might kill two birds with one stone, so to speak, and do a bit of exploration within Kilmere after I tracked him down."

An approach Ibbie never would have approved, though he'd have no way to know it. I breathed in deep, but this time, the lavender failed to bring calm.

Ever so slightly, Riven leaned forward. "Did you encounter anything or anyone unexpected there?"

"Can't say that I did." Yet even as he spoke, a slight haze appeared in his bright brown eyes, like frost over hazelnuts. "When I chased down the man in question, he'd no written documentation after all, only more of the same stories about a curse. He did say his granda always claimed the curse descended on oath breakers, yet he couldn't begin to explain what that meant."

Oath breakers . . . might there once have been a bargain involved?

"And you went into Kilmere itself?" Riven pressed.

"I did." He thrust his hands wide. "It's magnificent—I've never seen the like. If I could, I'd have spent decades there. It's expansive enough to support years of examining layer after layer. I was hard-pressed to tear myself away. I must confess I hoped I'd be able to disprove the curse, and that you'd grant permission to return and excavate further. Lady Dromley only spent a few months there before she lost her team. Who knows what remains to be discovered?"

Now I knew what had drawn Ibbie to him. He shared her passion for antiquities, but possessed the youth and physical strength she lacked, making them an excellent pairing.

"So Kilmere drew you to itself," Riven murmured, silky smooth. "What did you see there, precisely?"

"Ah, I . . ." He blinked, once, twice, then returned to his earlier statement. "It was magnificent."

Blight and rot.

Something influenced his recall. Could the fae-workings have tainted his memory? Could they be part of the so-called curse? I gripped my basket tight, the wicker digging into my hands.

Jade, would it be an easy matter for you to peek into his thoughts when he reflects on the exploration? If he's in danger, we must understand.

She padded to my side. *It should be. Yet there's some block within. When he considers Withern-at-Sea, there are large gaps.*

Abruptly, I turned away, ostensibly to collect more lavender, in truth, to conceal my fears. Clearly something Other had tampered with his mind . . . or had he been bound by a bargain? "Mr. Tibbons, I can offer no explanation, only a plea of forgiveness for my impertinence. Have you by chance recently acquired any scars?"

He shot me a questioning glance. "Carrying out excavations, one receives the occasional injury—but none recent."

The faintest trace of light rippled over Mr. Tibbons's skin— from Riven? Then it vanished, and Riven shook his head.

No bargain, which meant Kilmere was the most likely culprit. "I see." Mr. Tibbons didn't press me further, a remarkable fact. Perhaps he thought my question related to lore of the curse. I pressed upright. "I intend to go to Kilmere myself."

"So you are considering excavation?" The words leapt from his lips, quick and eager.

"I'm entertaining the notion, yes." I looped the lavender-filled basket over my arm. "In the meantime, I'd like you to carry out a charge for me in Avons. My trustees have assured me your salary may be drawn from Lady Dromley's estate, if you wish to continue working on her behalf."

A broad smile split his face. "Any chance of exploring the ruin, and I'm in."

"Very good. How are you when it comes to copy work?" I asked.

"I've done my share for Lady Dromley. If I was unable to obtain documents, she required exact replicas, down to the most obscure blots on the page."

"Then I shall request the same." Leaves rustled above our heads, a quiet murmur. "Upon the recovery of Mrs. Darrington, a friend of Lady Dromley's, I intend to ask if she will get you access to the Antiquary Society."

His eyes lit. "If you could do that, Miss Caldwell, I'd work without pay."

"I'll certainly do my best. If Mrs. Darrington secures you entrance, please copy whatever you can find within their archive pertaining to Kilmere or Withern-at-Sea." Doubtless Ibbie possessed the greatest portion of any information they held, but given her easy access to the archive, she might not have copied everything to her own records—and I'd not leave it to chance. "Once you've located what you can, bring the documents to Withern."

"With pleasure." After a polite farewell, he took his leave.

Dreda remained serenely perched on the fountain edge, knitting. Evidently, she did not intend to leave while Riven remained.

He turned to me. "Something clouds his memories of Kilmere. As I imagine you don't want me mucking about his mind, I cannot say the extent of it."

"Jade told me as much."

"Ah. You're getting on with your *kit-isne* better of late."

"You didn't tell me what she was." The words tumbled out before I could check them.

"She went to great lengths to conceal it from you. It wasn't my place to interfere with the bond nor the arrangements made between you."

For such a magnanimous statement, Jade offered the slightest incline of her head. *Perhaps he's more worthy of trust than his reputation suggests.*

A slight incongruity caught my attention. "Once before, you told me you didn't read minds."

"I don't." The pressure in the air around us shifted, taking on the charge of an oncoming storm.

He couldn't lie, but didn't want me to inquire further—nor would I dare, not when he wore such a forbidding expression. Yet I didn't understand.

The fur along Jade's neck lifted slightly. *Sometimes I forget how little you know.*

Will you enlighten me?

She wove between my ankles. *I can perceive what's within the mind of another, what they currently think and desire—what you might call mind reading. And I can speak mind-to-mind. What arbiters do is altogether different. They compel truth, and they may enter the mindscape itself, dredging past memories, forcing recall of what they will. Often they may force the truth from without the mind, but in cases where geas or glamour conceal reality, they force the truth to surface from within the mindscape—which usually shatters the mind in question. It's one of many reasons arbiters are feared.*

I bent to pick her up, hiding my face in her fur. *You are . . . certain of this?*

Jessa. I lived in the Court of Gold for several centuries before I came to your world. I am quite sure.

Does that mean he could enter the mindscape and command even another fae to do his bidding?

No. It's a unique blending of affinities that will only work to seek truth. One of several affinities that makes an arbiter. Affinities cannot be altered. You may strengthen them, allow them to atrophy, or forsake them altogether, but you cannot change their nature.

My stomach churned. Just how dangerous was Riven, truly? I'd so many more questions about affinities and how they worked and what fae did with them and . . .

Yet the air fairly crackled now, and the sculpted planes of his face drew tight. Did he guess what passed between Jade and me? He must know we talked, for I'd subsided into silence. Did he take offense?

"Do you wish to return to the matter at hand?" The words emerged cold.

Not trusting my voice, I nodded.

"Tibbons's condition suggests there's a reason the workings at Kilmere allow mortals to pass freely. It might try to influence them, perhaps coerce them to its will or make them more biddable to fae."

I pressed away the new, unsettling knowledge Jade had imparted. "If that were true, what would it mean?"

"That Kilmere is of fae origin."

Of fae origin? To my knowledge, fae had never lived openly among mortals, yet to construct a fortress the size of Kilmere would have taken years. What measures had they taken to conceal their nature—and how might it have impacted the people of Withern?

Small wonder Ibbie had believed Kilmere held keys to understanding the relationship between fae and mortals. If fae had established an outpost of this significance near Withern—and we'd forgotten it or been glamoured out of remembering—then it provided further evidence in support of a war between our worlds.

What would it mean if Riven was right, and something in Kilmere influenced the minds of mortals? If that were true, perhaps Mr. Burke was also correct. Perhaps a mortal had committed the murders, his mind clouded by the workings within.

I clutched Jade closer.

Which would be worse? The knowledge that a fae-working moved mortals to murder or that a malevolent force stretched out from the ruins to blight the town? A bird chirruped overhead, bright and clear, jarring me back to the present—and a new question. "If Kilmere might be of fae origin, then why would the workings keep Otherkind *out?*"

"Our courts don't exist in harmony—high fae are no more a monolithic entity than mortals. What one court possesses, they might wish to keep all others from obtaining." His expression remained distant, his fae nature closer to the surface. "We need to get inside. How quickly can you depart for Withern?"

"We leave in the morning, according to Aunt Caris."

"Good. I suggest you introduce me to the rest of your family now. Tell them I have interest in the ruins, and I intend to take lodgings in Withern that I might explore them with you. Otherwise, they may have inconvenient questions later."

He was right, and yet . . . I looped my fingers into Jade's thick fur. Of necessity, I'd trusted him with my own fate, but could I make that choice for my family—particularly after what Jade had said?

"Do you object?" His impassive demeanor gave no hint of his thoughts.

I looked away. "At Wyncourt, you glamoured my father, and—"

"It was for his protection, and it did him no harm."

"Yet you took the decision from him."

"And I'd do the same again, if the situation requires. I cannot promise otherwise." He spoke in the same emotionless tone one might use to discuss the weather, and it offered no hint of reassurance. "This is your family. It's your choice to further the acquaintance—or not."

Yet it was no choice, not when Lord West waited to claim

Kilmere and destroy us, not when fae-workings I could not hope to combat were woven into the boundaries of Kilmere, and who-knew-what-else awaited within. Riven knew it as well as I did. I required his help, and this was the most certain path forward, never mind my fears. "Give me ten minutes, then come to the front door."

CHAPTER 21

I should have asked Riven for more time, since ten minutes had proven far too short a measure in which to collect my scattered thoughts and emotions and gather some semblance of composure. With slow steps, I made my way back toward the house, where I went in search of Aunt Caris and my sisters. Even now, I did what I'd accused Riven of—I'd weighed the options and chosen the one I judged less dangerous for my family, without their consent. The knowledge brought a sour taste to the back of my mouth. Did I have the right to do so?

Jade nudged my chin. *What alternative do you propose?*

I can think of none—that's the trouble. Yet each time I took such a step, I became closer to what I feared being. Riven would appear on the doorstep soon, and then . . . there would be no going back.

Jade chuffed, her breath warm on my face, a small consolation. Then together we slipped into the drawing room, where Ainslie was offering a lively rendition of an encounter with a frail wisp of a woman struggling to contain a strong-minded pug within the millinery. She soon had Aunt Caris and Ada laughing with her account of the destruction said pug left in its wake. Despite the turmoil within, a smile sprang to my own lips.

Then Holden cleared his throat, and I jumped. "It's Lord Riven, Miss Caldwell."

I glanced up.

Just beyond Holden, Riven waited. Something had shifted in his expression. It was softer, more open, with perhaps a flicker of —longing? As abruptly as it had appeared, it vanished. When he strode into the room, only the elegant glamour of a gentleman remained.

"Lord Riven!" Aunt Caris's cheeks bore a residual flush from laughter, like the petals of a sunbloom. She beamed upon him, her displeasure over the matter of the will either forgotten or discarded before the pleasing prospect he offered. After all, she'd at one time announced her desire to form a match between Lord Riven and one of us. "How delightful that you've come to call."

"I would have taken the time to pay my respects the other day, had my errand not been urgent." He maintained the languid demeanor so many gentlemen favored, yet just below the surface, Other surged, pricking against my senses. "I thought it past time to call and receive a formal introduction to the rest of your family."

"Of course." Her hand fluttered to the lace at her throat, smoothed its folds. "You know Jessa from your dealings with Wyncourt and Kilmere, but these are my other nieces, Adamina and Ainslie."

He offered the proper greetings, and an undercurrent of fae charm lent a brightness to the conversation. Before it, Aunt Caris and my sisters were at their sparkling best—and yet, unlike Lord West, he did not press his advantage.

"Miss Jessa has informed me that you depart for Withern-at-Sea in the morning," Riven said at length.

"Indeed, we quite look forward to it," Aunt Caris replied.

I inclined my head. "Lord Riven has an interest in Kilmere, and as it happens, he also intends to spend some time in Withern-at-Sea. He's offered to aid in my exploration of the ruins, as he has expertise in this field."

"What a lovely idea." A speculative gleam entered her eyes as she surveyed him. "We shall be delighted to receive you at any time."

And with that, she put her seal on my choice. By allying with Other, I'd already embraced the forbidden, making a decision that would condemn me in the eyes of my world. But now, I'd joined the fate of my family with my own by willingly bringing another high fae into their midst.

Had I made the right decision?

BY THE TIME we departed the following morning, the sun burned hot. Even as she climbed into the carriage, Aunt Caris called out final instructions to the servants, at last subsiding onto the seat alongside Ada and Ainslie.

Dreda sat to my left, Jade to my right, and Asrina perched on my shoulder, casting her radiant glow over the deep blue of my traveling gown.

Our carriage clattered over cobblestones, the sound of its creaking wheels mingling with the lively noises of the city. I perched on the edge of my seat, as though I could urge it to greater speed.

Kilmere waited.

Even from afar, it drew me, and our days of travel chafed, though I kept myself occupied the best I could through the long hours in the carriage and nights we must stay at inns along the way.

At last, the salt tang of sea air wafted into the carriage, the first sign we neared Withern.

I looked up from my sketchbook, where I'd outlined the spiny form of the sea buckthorn that had sprawled outside our last inn. Perhaps I should add it to my herbalism guide, for the many benefits it offered to soothe everything from stomach to skin, despite its bristling spines.

When our carriage crested a hill, I peered down upon the town, a picturesque cluster of blue-roofed buildings, most of whitewashed stone, tucked into a tumbled stone landscape. It curved gently around the harbor, beckoning all comers.

Then I twisted back to glance to the north. On a distant clifftop at the edge of the sea, the ruins of Kilmere stretched dark and sprawling, overlooking Withern like a dragon prepared to spring on its prey. All I desired was to reach it as swiftly as I might—before it struck again.

Could I manage a trip today? Aunt Caris would surely insist we all get properly settled, but I'd try my best.

The others kept their gazes firmly fixed on the enchanting sea, its rich blues and greens kissing a pale sky.

"Oh, I'm glad we've come." A gentle smile crossed Ada's face, and she pressed her fingers to the warm glass. "A respite by the sea—it's perfect."

After perhaps another mile or so, our carriage halted in front of a charming country home that went by the name Willowere, built by one of the younger sons of Denby Hall several generations ago and now routinely let, since they did not require its use —though they did require the income it brought, most likely.

A message from Aunt Caris's friend had awaited us at an inn along the way, informing us with great pride that she'd let it on our behalf. She'd enumerated both its charms and its history and informed Aunt Caris she'd taken the liberty of arranging for the housekeeper, cook, and maid of all work that ordinarily served the tenants of Willowere to care for us during our stay.

Her high praise of Willowere fell short of the mark. If anything, she'd understated its charms. It sat on a gentle hill, which sloped down toward a lake surrounded by stately willows, whose soft melodies drifted toward me.

As for the cottage itself, abundant gardens surrounded it, and its stone remained a soft gray, rather than the whitewash favored within town. On either end, massive chimneys stretched toward the sky, and a generous bank of triple windows flanked the door on either side. Sprawling pearlflowers occupied the space beneath, their delicate boughs waving a welcome.

Our driver drew the carriage to a halt in front of the house, and the footman hastened to help us descend.

Aunt Caris led the way. She thrust open the door, then stopped short on the threshold. "What in the Crossings?"

When she stumbled back, I peered into the wide entry. In the hall and the chambers I could glimpse beyond, everything had been upended—furniture overturned, paintings knocked askew, glass shattered. I crossed the threshold, and my feet crunched on something—broken glass?

"My dear, come back." Aunt Caris beckoned to me from the doorway. "Some intruder may remain."

Jade, do you perceive anyone?

She picked her way among the debris on the wide plank floors, her ears flicking back and forth. *No, they've long since gone.*

"Please, come back." Aunt Caris gripped the door handle as though it offered a lifeline. "It may be unsafe."

I withdrew. There'd be time enough to survey the damage later. Yet what had we walked into? Willowere should have offered a haven, a safe place from which to investigate Kilmere, but this?

Ada pressed her hand to her mouth. "Who could possibly have done this?"

"And why?" Ainslie peered over my shoulder, her dark eyes absorbing every detail.

"It scarcely matters," Aunt Caris said. "Clearly, these lodgings are unsuitable, but I cannot think what we will do now."

With a flutter of its expansive wings, a raven landed on the hedge, surveying us with its beady eye. A harbinger, perhaps, but of what?

Before I could voice a response, a lean, long-limbed woman swept up the lane. A few strands of her hair escaped tight coils to sweep around her elongated face like tendrils of a horsetail fern. She halted abruptly before us. "Heard you were coming today, though I'd a mind to make it before you. I'm Mrs. Warren—I'm to keep house for you."

Aunt Caris murmured a feeble greeting.

Mrs. Warren glanced through the door and then back at us. "What's the meaning of this?"

Ainslie tilted her head. "I'd rather hoped you might tell us. We just arrived and opened the house to find someone has wreaked havoc within."

Her mouth pinched to a firm line. "Might have known."

"Known what?" I asked.

"It's what comes of meddling with the curse, miss. It meddles back."

"Meddling in the . . . curse?" Aunt Caris looked as though she wanted to sink into the ground. "What curse?"

I very much doubted a fae-working would enter a home and upend its contents. Regardless of the cause, might we be held responsible, since it had occurred upon our arrival? The sum for repair would be greater than I cared to consider. The raven on the hedge gave a loud *kraa*, and we all jumped.

"We've meddled in nothing," I said.

"Jessa." A warning note entered Aunt Caris's voice. I pressed the bounds of propriety by addressing the housekeeper in such a way.

The housekeeper ignored Aunt Caris, her lips tightening as she regarded me. "Aye, but you've come to survey Kilmere, have you not?"

"How did you know?"

"No secrets in a town like this." She shot a narrow glance at the five of us. "That Tibbons fellow said he worked on behalf of a Caldwell, and now here's a whole lot of you. Just look what happened after he arrived. What's to come next, I dread to think."

Ainslie had edged closer to the housekeeper as she spoke, absorbing every word as though she made mental notes which she'd use to compose a story—the very last thing I needed.

I shifted Jade in my arms. "If you refer to the deaths, the authorities claim to have apprehended the poisoner."

Aunt Caris blanched, yet before she could raise further objection to our exchange, the housekeeper spoke.

"They're fools if they believe such." Her fists went to her hips. "They'll soon see. The curse is naught to trifle with."

Jade pressed her legs into my stomach, launching herself toward the ground. She sauntered toward the raven.

"Yet you agreed to serve as housekeeper," I said.

She regarded me over her pointed nose. "I always keep house for those that stay at Willowere, no matter how misguided they be. But you've a mess to manage now, and Mina and I can't attend it, not in any timely way."

"That is quite enough discussion of rumor and accusation. We may not need you at all, if Lord Denby will release us from our contract." Aunt Caris folded her arms across her ample bosom. "I don't see how we can stay. Whether this curse is legend or fact, someone has gone out of their way to cause damage, which means Withern isn't safe—"

"Aunt Caris, you cannot leap to that conclusion. It seems most likely some thief broke in while the house was unoccupied and caused all this damage in search of his prize." Ada broke in, her voice surprisingly firm. She wanted to return to Avons no more than I did. "He can have no reason to revisit Willowere."

At Jade's approach, the raven hurled itself into the air.

Mrs. Warren frowned. "Never you—"

Whatever Mrs. Warren intended to say, the sound of hoof-beats cut it off, drawing our attention. Riven appeared on the path before the house. Though I'd sent Asrina last night to inform him of our imminent arrival, I'd not expected him to ride in on horseback, appearing for all the world like an ordinary gentleman out to explore the countryside. He halted alongside our carriage and swung down from his chestnut mount with his usual grace.

Aunt Caris hurried forward. "Oh, Lord Riven, thank heavens you're here. You shall advise us on what we must do."

The slightest flicker of surprise crossed his face. "May I first inquire why you're all clustered on the doorstep?"

She mutely gestured to the interior of the house, and he glanced inside. A faint swirl of gold wafted about him as he examined the destruction. What could he perceive that I could not?

A moment later, he rejoined us. "You found it this way?"

"Yes, and I'm of a mind to withdraw to an inn or perhaps leave Withern altogether. Mrs. Warren says it's a result of some sort of curse on the region, but whatever the cause, I cannot think it safe to stay."

Riven motioned to Mrs. Warren. "Go to Denby Hall at once and report this trouble to the lord. Ask for his immediate attention."

"He might not—"

"Now." Such was the command in his tone that she hastened to obey. Then he turned toward Aunt Caris. "I'm sure Lord Denby will see to the matter."

"But I'm responsible for the safety of my nieces. If some harm were to come to them . . ."

"Allow me to gather more information on your behalf." His calm voice appeared to soothe Aunt Caris. "If you'll withdraw to the inn for luncheon, the servants can tend to the cottage. I'll wait and speak to Lord Denby, see what he makes of it."

"But the curse . . ." She clutched at her reticule, as if she could use it to ward off any ill.

"May be only superstition."

As fae could not lie, he'd had to tuck the *may* into his words.

"Very well. You're most kind, Lord Riven."

Yet before we returned to our carriage, Lord Denby appeared alongside Mrs. Warren, puffing profusely. He was rather heavy-set, resembling a bottle tree, yet his demeanor was congenial. He'd seen our carriage ascending the hill upon our arrival, he told us, and had been on his way to give us welcome, only to be met by Mrs. Warren in the lane, and what was this tale she carried?

Aunt Caris shot a pleading glance at Riven, and he communicated the whole to Lord Denby. In short order, Riven had Lord Denby promising to send his staff to restore the cottage and replace any damaged items—no glamour required.

Lord Denby swiped surreptitiously at his brow. "I must express my regrets that you've received so inhospitable a welcome."

"You cannot be held responsible for the deeds of a local lawbreaker." Aunt Caris still clutched her reticule tightly, as though the thief might yet spring from the shrubbery.

"I told them it was due to the curse, my lord," Mrs. Warren said.

He drew himself up, his generous, affable mouth forming a stern line. "We cannot know that, Mrs. Warren."

Interesting—he didn't deny it outright. Did he also believe in the curse?

Oh.

Denby, of course . . . Mrs. Darrington had spoken of her friend, Lady Denby, perhaps his wife? She'd lost a relative in the recent deaths, which might be reason enough to make them fear the curse.

"Of course, if you wish to depart, I shall be happy to release you from our contract." His substantial jowls quivered. "Never let it be said that I'd put ladies to any inconvenience. Far better that I should be discommoded myself."

"There's no need for that, not yet," Riven interjected, in the smoothest of tones.

"He's right, Aunt Caris." Though I wanted nothing more than to send them away, in case some threat lurked, I couldn't do so without arousing suspicion. "We shouldn't be hasty—this may have only been a simple act of theft, or destruction by passing tramps."

"Regardless, perhaps we should send for the stratesmen." Aunt Caris eyed Willowere. "In case whoever broke in still lurks about and means some harm."

"No need for that, Miss Caldwell," Lord Denby said, a touch too heartily. "If you wish to stay, I'll see it put to rights and set my groundskeepers to looking about for any sign of an intruder. But whoever it was, I'm sure they've long since gone."

Riven's eyes narrowed, as though he mistrusted something Lord Denby said.

And I tilted my head to regard the lord myself. Did he truly believe the curse was behind this? If so, it would explain his reluctance to involve the stratesmen, who might then call on the Vigil—an outcome that could be disastrous.

I didn't want to expose my family or Dreda to possible dangers, nor could I afford to withdraw. I required more information. I surveyed the front door and windows—they bore no signs of damage. "Do you ordinarily keep the house unlocked?"

He harrumphed. "No, but one of our men opened it this morning in preparation for your arrival."

"And did you keep anything of particular value here?" This sort of damage appeared more like vindictiveness or a quest for some specific object than theft, but I couldn't ignore any possible angle.

"Willowere has the finest of furnishings," he said. "If someone was of a mind to steal some of the smaller items, I suppose they could fetch a goodly sum."

"Perhaps when your servants have restored the dwelling, you can inspect for any missing items." Riven surveyed him closely. "But perhaps it was not theft at all. Does anyone hold a grudge against your family?"

He stiffened. "None of our neighbors would stoop to something like this. And we should not stand here fatiguing the ladies further."

Indeed, Aunt Caris drooped in the sun.

Lord Denby spread his hands wide, his signet ring glinting. "You must all come partake of luncheon at Denby Hall."

"That would be a great imposition," Aunt Caris said.

"Not at all. We're already hosting several guests. A few more additions won't hurt, particularly when they're such charming ones." He smiled amiably upon her. "I hope this inauspicious beginning won't discourage you from enjoying all Withern has to offer."

"Well, I—"

"Of course, if you should change your mind about staying, you have only to say the word."

Aunt Caris faltered. "I'm not certain. I must consider what's best to be done."

"A woman of wisdom." Lord Denby nodded toward Mrs. Warren. "You'll oversee the maids and ensure everything is set to rights."

"Nothing will be right unless they leave Kilmere well alone." With that, Mrs. Warren stamped up the steps.

I eyed her retreating form. If others in Withern shared her views about my plan to "meddle" with Kilmere, it might explain the destruction within. Perhaps it was neither theft nor grudge against the Denbys, but rather an attempt to frighten us off, one that may have worked.

Though I wished I could send my family away, I couldn't let Aunt Caris force a retreat before I'd even reached Kilmere—or we'd never be free of the dangers stalking us.

CHAPTER 22

A quarter of an hour later, we reposed in an elegant bedchamber. Lord Denby had admitted us so that we might rid ourselves of travel stains and change before luncheon. To that end, we'd been provided with a steaming washbasin, fragrant lavender-and-lilac soap, and fine linen towels.

Lord Denby and Riven had departed, and a maid awaited to escort us to the drawing room once we completed our toilettes.

All the while, Aunt Caris wondered if she should remove us from Withern at once. In this my sisters lent me aid, saying we should leap to no conclusions, but rest here for the night and take fresh counsel in the morning.

Still, if Aunt Caris were to change her mind, what then? I couldn't leave, not without exploring Kilmere. Somehow I must find a way to persuade her to stay—or better yet, convince her and my sisters to go while I remained.

We emerged from the bedchamber into a corridor as cold and forbidding as the rest of the manor. Denby Hall possessed none of the winsome charm of Willowere; rather it adhered to a rigid formality of form, with deep colors and ancient tapestries and heavy furniture. It was old, perhaps even as old as Kilmere, and did not share the warmth of our affable host.

At the base of the stairs, a large oil painting depicted some Denby ancestor, a family crest with rampant serpents emblazoned on the shield he held.

Following in the footsteps of the maid, we swept into the drawing room, where the rest of the party had assembled. All turned toward us, and I shrank behind Ada and Ainslie, allowing them to absorb the brunt of the attention.

Jade kept close to my ankles, her presence steadying me as Lord Denby performed a swirl of introductions—his wife and his eldest son, Mr. Hale, and their guests, Lord and Lady Holloway and their daughter Lady Cadence, along with Miss and Mr. Redgrave, a brother and sister pair.

Lady Denby moved forward to greet us, as stiff and cool as a mum weathering the first frosts of autumn. Though she'd married into the family, she seemed to belong to Denby Hall, her black-brown eyes and ebony hair as dark as the furnishings within, and her manner as detached. "How fortunate it was that Lord Denby came to greet you and so discovered your misfortune."

"Indeed." Aunt Caris gave her a gracious nod. Next to Lady Denby, she appeared particularly warm and vital, her red-gold hair aflame and her gentle curves contrasting with the tall, stately form of our hostess. "Thank you for your hospitality, Lady Denby."

Her gaze fell upon Jade. "What an . . . unusual companion you have, Miss Jessa. Perhaps she'd like to wait belowstairs until we're through with our meal? Carrington can bring her down for you."

"As it pleases you, Lady Denby." Never mind how my stomach clenched at the thought of separation from Jade—in her home, she'd a right to choose which companions she'd accept.

It's not as before—and if you have need, you only have to think it, and I shall come.

"Nonsense." Lord Denby clapped his hands. "It will be a novelty, having such a great cat join the feast at our table."

"Very well, then." Lady Denby straightened. "We shall retire to the dining room for luncheon. Cook has kept it warm for us."

It was clear she didn't share Lord Denby's pleasure in unexpected guests, and I couldn't blame her. Our party of mostly ladies had thrown off her balanced numbers, and we'd delayed the meal. However, when she regarded Riven, she offered a warm smile.

And why not? From all appearances, he possessed everything society wished for in a man—wealth, title, and a striking appearance. Yet if she knew he was fae . . .

In the shuffle of preparation to remove to the dining room, Lady Cadence drew near to Riven. She gazed up at him through lowered lashes and murmured something soft.

As mortals went, she was lovely—her hair a rich auburn, her eyes a delicate green, and her features of porcelain. Yet for all the regard he gave her, she might as well have been an ancient dowager.

She looked at him with the air of one accustomed to gentlemen granting her every whim. He gave a small bow and then walked away.

A moment later, he offered me his arm. "Shall we?"

Lady Cadence watched us, her eyes taking on the hue of a winter sky. Then Mr. Hale approached her, and she turned a glittering smile upon him, sweeping off to the dining room on his arm.

Ordinarily, we'd have been seated with ladies and gentlemen alternate, but as our numbers were off, the arrangement became somewhat haphazard. I was placed at Riven's right, while Lady Cadence maneuvered herself at his left. Ada and Ainslie settled next to each other at the far side of the table, with Mr. Redgrave choosing a seat alongside Ainslie.

A large centerpiece sprawled across the table, obscuring my sisters from view, while multiple pyramids of fruit completed the blockade. I could catch only momentary glimpses between the foliage, sufficient to reveal Mr. Redgrave had already engaged Ainslie in animated discussion.

Servants placed a steaming white soup before us, and its rich creaminess warmed me. Having no desire to enter the various conversations about the table, I kept my gaze lowered.

But evidently, Lady Cadence meant to draw me in. She peered around Riven. "Miss Jessa Caldwell—where *have* I heard your name before? It seems familiar somehow."

"I cannot think how."

"Ah, I have it." She arched a delicate brow. "I believe you appeared in the Avons society column recently—there was some reference to your appearance before the Magister? But surely that cannot be true."

How had she recalled such obscure gossip? But then, gossip and scandal were the currencies that fueled society. I swirled my spoon in the soup. "I did appear before the Magister in regard to my inheritance from Lady Dromley."

"Shocking, that." From his position near Lady Denby, Lord Holloway took the offered bait. "No place for a lady, not with all those hardened criminals about."

"I wonder that you could endure the thought of your niece in such a harsh environment, Miss Caldwell," Lady Denby said.

"Perhaps Miss Jessa is accustomed to the less savory elements of society, Lady Denby. One mustn't assume." Lady Cadence delivered her insult in polished tones.

Jade tensed in my lap, as though poised to spring at Lady Cadence. I rested my hand on her back. This was one of the reasons I abhorred society. Its subtleties and veiled insults left me uncertain how to proceed—and all of it was a waste of time. I should be at Kilmere even now . . .

Aunt Caris dabbed her lips with a napkin. "It was all quite harmless, I assure you."

On the outside, she remained as unruffled as ever, but she must be distressed. After all, she'd warned me this might happen.

"I attended with her, of course." She set aside her linen. "Given the matter being contested, we were exposed to none of the unfortunates that often appear in court."

"Still, you must have been a great deal distressed to have one of your own entangled in a lawsuit," Lady Holloway said.

"It was indeed unfortunate that Lady Dromley's nephew did not share her character." Aunt Caris gripped her spoon as though it were a weapon, though she'd scarcely hope to wage war with Lady Holloway.

Before we'd arrived, she'd informed me she hoped to gain a welcome from her, as she led the society in Withern, but this was hardly an auspicious beginning. Would the prospect of rejection strengthen her resolve to quit the region altogether?

Regardless, I needed to change the subject, but I could scarcely bring up Kilmere or any of the theories of theft and sabotage that ran through my mind.

Miss Redgrave took a sip of her wine. "For my part, I cannot think of anything more tedious than to discuss such unpleasantries when we have a lovely repast before us."

"Hear, hear." Lord Denby raised his glass.

She offered him an engaging smile, which sparkled in her vibrant blue eyes. "How fortunate that you've retained such a skilled cook."

Lady Denby nodded. "She's been with the family since Lord Denby was a boy."

"And we dread the day she decides she's no longer up to the task," Lord Denby boomed. "Spoiled us all, she has."

Riven remained silent, his gaze taking the measure of each individual at the table. What did he seek? What did he make of our mortal conventions?

Lady Holloway inclined her head toward Aunt Caris. "What brings your family to Withern? Do you mean to enjoy sea bathing?"

"Indeed—we all wanted a holiday by the sea, and Jessa has a great interest in the area."

"Interest in Kilmere, you mean." Lady Denby summoned the next course with a flick of her fingers. "After Mrs. Warwick let the house on your behalf, she informed me you intended to explore the ruins—despite the dangers of the curse and the harm it might inflict on our town."

Riven gave her a sharp look.

I lifted my goblet, the glass cool against my skin. "I assure you I have no intention of causing trouble, but the ruins were left in trust to me, and I feel responsible—"

"No one can be responsible for Kilmere, let alone lay claim to it," Lady Denby said softly. "No more than one could harness the power of death itself."

Silence settled over the table. Perhaps Lady Denby did not hold us in distaste because we were unexpected guests, but because of my connection to Kilmere. If only Aunt Caris hadn't confided my intentions to Mrs. Warwick. But then, what reason would she have to keep them secret? She knew nothing of the dangers it held.

"Come now." Lord Denby motioned for another glass of wine. "No need to linger on such morbid things."

"Indeed not." Lady Holloway shuddered. "I don't know why so many persist in believing the superstitions of old."

"Not all old tales are superstitions, Lady Holloway." Mr. Redgrave leaned toward her side of the table. "Why do you believe the curse of Kilmere only legend?"

Lady Holloway faltered slightly, then rallied. "Because it's a ridiculous notion. Were there any shred of truth regarding the deaths and this so-called curse, the authorities would have uncovered it when they sought the poisoner."

"You give the authorities a great deal of credit, yet surely there are things they fail to understand at times, just like the rest of us," Mr. Redgrave said. "They seek the truth, but who is to say they've found it?"

Ainslie gave a nod of approval, but for my part, I'd rather Mr. Redgrave not press the point—however much I agreed with his remarks.

Lady Cadence lifted her fork, then arched one brow at me. "Whatever the case about Kilmere, I cannot imagine anything more deadly dull than exploring rocks and rubble for hours."

"Except perhaps tedious society." Riven inclined his head ever so slightly.

Across the table, Mr. Redgrave pressed his lips together as if to restrain a smile. Ainslie didn't bother with such a measure, but rather beamed at Riven.

And Lady Cadence flushed.

Blight and rot.

If she weren't of a mind to view me as an enemy before, she certainly would be now. If I could have reasonably fled the room, I would have—but I'd drawn enough attention to my supposed improprieties. Instead, I kept my attention fixed on the meal before me, grounding myself in the warm pulse of light from Asrina and the comforting bulk of Jade spilling across my lap.

When the interminable meal ended, the butler approached Lord Denby, murmuring something to him.

"Very good," Lord Denby said. "Miss Caldwell, Carrington tells me they've finished restoring order to Willowere. Shall I send you back in the carriage?"

Aunt Caris shook her head. "It can't be above a quarter mile, and we'd welcome the walk."

Though he pressed, Aunt Caris insisted there was no need. She must not wish to incur further debt to Lord Denby—or more properly, his wife, who appeared to wish us anywhere other than here. Did she desire our absence enough to sabotage our stay?

Certainly, her situation offered her the opportunity to employ someone to do so. The disquieting possibility followed me from Denby Hall.

When we rounded a bend, Aunt Caris let out a sigh. "Lord Riven, you must forgive us for involving you in our troubles."

"Think nothing of it." Riven fell in step alongside me. "I hope this hasn't discouraged you from remaining in Withern."

"I . . . I cannot say. I'm of two minds on the matter."

"Aunt Caris, however unfortunate, I cannot leave Withern with unfinished business at hand. We've come all this way." I navigated around a stone in the road. "Yet we don't all need to stay. If Dreda was willing to remain, the rest of you could return to Avons or visit another seaside town."

"Don't speak nonsense, my dear. As if I'd leave you with any hint of danger," Aunt Caris said.

"I vote we stay." Ainslie linked her arm through Ada's. "I like it here already."

"Or perhaps you're intrigued by Mr. Redgrave?" Ada suggested. "He seemed rather taken with you."

Instead of Ainslie's usual dismissal, a faint hint of color crept across her face. "He was merely kind."

Aunt Caris brightened. "Was he indeed? The Redgraves are an old family with strong standing before the king."

And if her tone meant anything, she considered Mr. Redgrave a promising marriage prospect, despite his lack of title —though she'd not speak so forthrightly with Riven in our company.

"I thought Miss Redgrave very pleasant also." I'd not forget her kindness in breaking into the conversation with Lady Cadence.

Aunt Caris became thoughtful, perhaps weighing the value of cultivating connection with the Redgrave family. "We could use the respite from Avons. We shall remain for now."

The prospect of a match had bought us time, and for once, I welcomed it—particularly as I was *not* the intended victim. Nor did Ainslie seem much troubled by the prospect.

"Then I trust you'll not object if I escort Miss Jessa to

Kilmere tomorrow?" Riven maintained an easy stride, as though he made a trivial request.

"You mean to explore the ruins?" Aunt Caris fidgeted with the ribbon of her bonnet. "Is it safe? Lady Denby seemed quite certain about this—curse."

"I believe we're equipped for whatever Kilmere holds," he said.

Aunt Caris slowed further. "Perhaps you might go first, just to make sure?"

"It wouldn't be the same without Miss Jessa." His rich voice filled the simple statement with shades of meaning.

"Oh." Aunt Caris brightened. "I see."

The faintest glimmer of gold appeared in his eyes. "I give my word I'll watch out for her."

Though Riven didn't use glamour, the natural charm of the fae—and that of an attractive gentleman—worked its own magic, softening Aunt Caris. "If you're quite certain."

"I am. I'll fetch Miss Jessa at nine tomorrow."

"Do you want me to accompany them, Miss Caldwell?" Dreda had remained almost entirely silent throughout our stint at Denby Hall—as expected of a spinster chaperone of no social standing—and her interjection caught me off guard.

"If you please, Miss Twells. I'd like to get us properly settled in, and then we must pay calls in the afternoon."

Ainslie released Ada's arm and snagged my own, while Ada, Aunt Caris, and Dreda continued ahead at a steady pace. "I shall join you also. I've been burning with curiosity about these mysterious ruins—and from what I hear, our friend P. Smith intends to write an article on it."

"No, you can't." I stumbled to a stop.

Ainslie halted also, frowning at me. "Whyever not? An ancient curse and a present-day mystery all wrapped into one? How could I miss such an opportunity?"

"Sharing about Kilmere will only bring down upon the ruins the worst of curiosity-seekers."

She waved a hand. "And why not? The greater the interest, the more likely you'll gain admittance to the society you were concerned about."

The slightest pressure gathered in the air about us. If I did not dissuade her, Riven would. I hurried on. "The ruins may not be all that interesting."

"Not interesting? I can't believe you'd make such a statement. Unless you're truly concerned about the dangers."

"I—"

Her eyes widened. "You are! You mean to go, but you think it's not safe. Lord Riven, surely you don't approve of this."

"I do. And Miss Jessa is right. There's no need for you to go to Kilmere." His voice softened, becoming warm and insistent as a summer breeze, glamour seeping into every word. "You'll put it from your mind and rejoin the others."

Ainslie's shoulders dropped, and her eyes clouded. "That's right . . . I . . . I have no need of Kilmere."

As though in a dream, she moved forward to join Ada. A trickling brook crossed the road ahead, leading into a charming copse, and they'd all stopped to examine it.

Riven and I continued past them, and my stomach churned. He'd warned me, but I'd hoped he'd never have cause to glamour my family again. And now that he had—I couldn't bear it. "Riven, I . . ."

"What? You wanted to take her into the heart of what may be an ancient fae stronghold, with all its attendant dangers?" He swept an arm toward my family, the motion sharp. "In such circumstance, I may not be able to conceal my nature. Then I'd have to strip the knowledge from her—a working with far greater risk."

"But I could have dissuaded her, if you'd just given me time."

"You truly believe that?"

No. If I were honest, at the best of times turning Ainslie from her course was as difficult as changing the path of a long-established river. She'd not have relented.

Yet every time he effortlessly glamoured someone, it reminded me that he—or any fae—could shatter their minds at will. It reminded me how defenseless mortals were against fae. And it reminded me of what I might become, if I did not take care. I fixed my attention on the long grasses alongside the road, their quiet whispers attempting to console.

Jade prowled alongside them, seeking some prey perhaps.

Riven slowed. "I'm not glamouring them for my own entertainment, Jessa."

"I know." The words emerged a ragged whisper.

"Then you're letting your emotions mislead you, keep you from what must be done." Faint and far off, the cry of a gull pierced the air. "If you give way to sentiment, you'll never survive."

"Yet if you allow no room for feeling, can you truly be said to live?"

The scent of sun-drenched forest deepened around us, traces of light swirling in the air. Yet whatever he intended to say was lost because Jade broke into my thoughts.

Jessa.

I hurried forward to join her. She stood where the lane split, the left branch leading to Willowere. And there a brace of hares had been laid across the road, their bodies contorted in an odd rictus, their eyes clouded whitish-gray, their teeth bared as though in agony.

Despite the sun beating down on my shoulders, my body went cold. They'd been left here, right in our path. Was it presumption to assume someone had killed them and left them as a warning, perhaps to frighten us from Withern? Lady Denby hadn't wanted us to use their carriage. Had she known we'd come across this? I swallowed hard, my mouth suddenly dry.

Riven sent a spark of light over their corpses, then shook his head. "They were poisoned, clearly left here on purpose."

"Someone wants us gone."

"Yes. The question is why? Do they seek to protect themselves or the secrets of Kilmere?"

Without a great deal more information, I couldn't begin to answer that question. Voices drifted toward us. My family and Dreda had abandoned their sightseeing and would rejoin us soon.

If Aunt Caris saw the corpses left before Willowere . . .

Without wasting a word, Riven surrounded the bodies with a brilliant flare of light. When it cleared, the road bore no sign they'd ever existed.

But I couldn't drive the images of their broken forms away so readily. Aunt Caris had agreed to stay, but at what cost?

CHAPTER 23

The next morning dawned with such a glorious rose-gold brilliance, I could almost forget that Kilmere awaited—and that some unknown individual sought to keep us from exploring there. Part of me wished to remain abed and hide from it all, but I couldn't afford to, not when the fate of my family—and the region—was at stake.

Only what would we find within? I removed my riding habit from the trunk. However dreadful it might be, surely not knowing was worse.

Jade sat on the windowsill, sedately washing her face. *I can think of a great many things worse than* not knowing.

Please, don't share them. I'm nervous enough as it is.

With a graceful leap, she descended from the window and wove between my legs. *Whatever we find, we face together.*

The knowledge heartened me as I donned my riding habit and leather walking boots. Soon I might have the answers I required, and perhaps in them, I'd gain protection from Lord West. If I could manage to thwart him without ever having to encounter him again, so much the better.

I gathered my hat, gloves, and collecting basket to place by the door. Inside the basket, I tucked Ibbie's hand glass, which I'd

271

fetched from Wyncourt before my departure. She'd made frequent use of it when studying her antiquities, and bringing it made me feel as though I carried some part of her with me. As she'd stood against fae malice with all the strength she possessed, so would I.

With Jade and Asrina at my side, I descended the stairs, the ache of loss throbbing in my chest. She should have been here. Of course, if she were, I would not be.

I stepped over a creaking floorboard and into the dining room, which was decorated in the same seaside colors as the rest of the cottage. The rich creamy sand tones on the wainscoting and the pale greens and blues of the ocean in the draperies and rugs combined to form a restful, charming palette, one which stood in stark contrast to the cold formality of Denby Hall. To my surprise, Aunt Caris awaited at the breakfast table, which already bore an abundant spread of meats, fruits, and pastries.

"Good morning, my dear." Aunt Caris offered a warm smile. "I suppose you're still determined to go to Kilmere?"

I slid into the chair next to her. "I am."

"At least the company will be pleasant." She regarded me over a porcelain teacup. "Lord Riven certainly appears interested in spending more time with you."

"He's eager to study Kilmere."

"Only with you." She returned her cup to its saucer. "He could have gone alone."

To explain that he couldn't enter Kilmere without me would raise questions impossible to answer, so I concentrated on filling my plate instead.

She offered me a sweet roll. "Are you more inclined to favor Lord Riven than you were Lord West?"

"In what way?" I asked cautiously.

"As a husband, of course."

I nearly dropped the roll. "I'd not considered either of them as matrimonial prospects."

"Yet it appears they've considered you. My dear, you're

twenty years of age. Perhaps I've done you a disservice in allowing you to keep so much out of society. It's hardly shocking that gentlemen would take note of you or express their interest." The fine lines at the corners of her eyes crinkled. "It's not for nothing that Lord Riven has followed you here, Kilmere notwithstanding. Only give him a little encouragement—or reconsider Lord West—and you might find yourself nicely situated."

Not for nothing, indeed. Lord West wished to murder me, and Riven to thwart his aims and solve the mysteries about my person. I shook my head. "I think you make too much of it. Lord Riven and I share common interests, that is all."

Her eyes lit as though I'd professed undying love. "That's more than enough to start."

Perhaps it was best if she believed I'd sparked some interest within Riven, for then she'd extend greater leniency toward any activities he proposed. So I simply smiled and said, "I suppose we shall see."

She let the matter drop, and I subsided into silence, consumed by thoughts of Kilmere. What awaited us there?

IN THE GOLDEN haze of the warming morning, Riven, Dreda, and I approached the ruins on horseback. Like a sentinel, the ancient stronghold stood atop a towering cliff that jutted over the cerulean sea. Although we'd only ascended halfway up the overgrown path that climbed the cliff, the weight of Kilmere settled upon me. In the early light, it cast a long shadow, and the pricking sense of Other strengthened as we climbed.

The mounts Riven had procured for us picked their way surefooted over the narrow, rocky trail. Jade perched before me in the saddle, while Asrina kept pace from the air.

An unkindness of ravens flew past us, their wings beating the air, their *kraas* harsh, and Asrina dropped close to me. Did they nest within Kilmere? What else might haunt its crumbling stones?

Whatever Kilmere held, I'd no intention of taking Dreda inside. And Riven concurred. I'd managed to secure a moment with him before his departure from Willowere yesterday, and we'd agreed to leave her in a safe place with some sort of protective working—and Asrina to signal if anything went amiss.

After we crossed a burbling brook, Riven drew his mount to a halt—the agreed-upon signal. Both Dreda and I pulled up as well.

"I have a suggestion." I turned toward her. "You know many believe a curse hangs about Kilmere. I intend to discover if that's true, but I'd rather not risk anyone else in the process. Lord Riven assures me he's found a place for you to rest in safety while we explore, as long as you don't object."

"I've no desire to venture into a blighted ruin." She rocked back in the saddle, and I caught a hint of the frightened woman the dread-aught had plagued. "Only your aunt wouldn't like it if you went alone, and I can't forsake my duty. With Lord Riven here, your reputation—"

"Will suffer no taint, as long as we keep this between us. Lord Riven has agreed to hold it in confidence."

"Still, I don't think your aunt would approve, and I've no wish to lose my position."

"I'll make sure you don't." I lowered my voice. "If you recall our conversation in Avons, about things that require investigation . . ."

She released the reins to rub at her arms, as though beset by a sudden chill. "This is . . . that?"

"I believe so, and I cannot drag anyone into danger unknown."

She swallowed hard. "If you are certain, then it shall be your way, Miss Jessa."

Riven led the way to a small clearing just off the path, bounded with alder. Stones scattered about the open space, a jagged outcropping alongside the brook offering a sort of seat. Were it not for the oppressive sense of Other emanating from Kilmere, I might have enjoyed lingering to sketch the clustered wood pinks dotted alongside the bank of the brook, which trickled through the clearing.

Once we rode deeper into the copse and the trees blotted Kilmere from view, some of the tension left Dreda's body. "Now I'm glad I asked your aunt for some mending. It will keep me occupied until you return."

"Or you could simply enjoy the lovely day?" I said.

She lifted her chin. "No reason I can't do both at once."

"We'll leave the horses with you and continue on foot." Riven swung down and secured the reins of his mount to a nearby tree, and I followed suit.

Dreda settled peacefully onto the rocks alongside the stream, Asrina perched just overhead.

Though Riven made no perceptible motion, light coiled out from him and wove between the trees, an intricate binding that fascinated me. Did the light itself carry his innate power, allowing his working to linger after he left?

I'd more questions than I'd ever receive answers for—and the contrast between the unfurling of his power and the glamour concealing it left me slightly queasy as my senses struggled to reconcile the two.

But when we left the copse, all considerations about fae power fled. The majesty of Kilmere seeped into my senses as we slowly drew near. In places, stone walls with magnificent arches that had once held windows and doors towered far above my head. In others, they tumbled across broken earth to mingle with moss-covered stones. Despite the less-hospitable air of the coast, glorious old-growth trees thrived alongside the deteriorating buildings, their power as ancient as that of Kilmere itself.

I breathed in the salt air, struggling to steady my pulse as we approached the boundary wall.

In some places, the broken stones still formed a chest-high

barrier; in others, they crumbled low, dragon-head ferns and scarlet tuft mushrooms springing up in their midst. Yet even in disarray, the wall formed a formidable barrier—for however aged the mortal materials, the fae-working had not faded. Etched into the very stone in shades of silver-white and old bone, it wove through the entire wall, bristling with hostility.

I strained to better perceive the jagged lines and discern their purpose. They slashed through the stone in sharp, intricate whorls that resembled daggers and shields, beautiful and fearsome all at once. I followed the lines as they sank into the earth.

How deep did the working extend—how far was its reach? What if it denied Riven entrance, even in my company, and I must explore alone?

A sharp *kraa* overhead mocked my fears. I'd already allowed myself to rely on Riven far more than I should, when his king could summon him back at any time. I had to prepare myself for the possibility—it wasn't safe to count on his presence.

I straightened and marched forward, stopping only a hand-breadth from the tumbled wall.

"Wait," Riven said. "Take my arm. It must be clear that I come as your guest."

I tucked my arm into his, then we strode over a low spot in the wall, Jade keeping pace. A concentrated current of Other rushed over me, strong as the waves crashing against the cliff below. It prickled down my spine, tingled across my skin—it permeated every bit of stone and soil within this place, a forcible drawing of Other power into my world.

I stood rooted in place, the waves crashing over me. Kilmere *was* a fae construct—and a hostile one.

Jade growled, deep and low, a rumble resembling that of her true form.

A cold force, older than the stone itself, prowled among the ruins, concentrated its bitter spite on me. The walls shook, ever so slightly, a low thrum arising from the ground, like the angry murmur of a disturbed hive.

The fur at the back of Jade's neck bristled.

Riven released my arm. "Cross to the lintel of the nearest tower. Touch it."

Without question, I hurried forward, Jade alongside me, and reached for the keystone of the nearest arch, though I had to scramble atop a stack of stone to reach it. A sharp gust of wind that stirred none of the trees beyond us swirled around me as I removed my gloves.

"Quickly."

I reached for the keystone and skimmed my fingers across it, as I'd once done with the walls of Wyncourt. Only here I received no welcome.

Cold bit my fingers, sharp as the fangs of a serpent, and pain pierced to my core. The barest image of broken bodies filled my mind, and I snatched my stinging hand away.

Another rumble sounded deep in the ground below, this time more pronounced, like the growl of some enormous buried beast.

Jade seemed to grow larger. Was she contemplating shifting?

Light flared from Riven, bathing my fingers and driving away the bitter sting. "It should have accepted you."

"What does it mean that it did not?"

"It wants to overthrow you." Gold flared along the workings in the lintel, and they sparked back, with ominous tones of black and ivory. "Yet you have rights of ownership. It must proceed accordingly."

Riven surveyed the ruin, with a distant expression that suggested he perceived far more than I could. Then he faced me, tension drawing taut the lines of his body. "You needed to touch one of the keystones to show that you're asserting your rights over Kilmere, but it appears it has liberty to choose, insofar as it follows its prime directive to gain power. From what I read in its workings, it may reject a master it demonstrates inferior. If it can prove you weak or unworthy—things will not go well."

Weak. Unworthy. What all fae deemed mortals. If fae had

crafted Kilmere, then what hope did I have? With a sinking feeling, I recalled what Lord West had said: *One of your kind can never hope to hold Kilmere. Not long, anyway.*

What of Ibbie? Had her fae husband given her some protections to allow the initial exploration? Or had it shown her first a friendly face, then turned against her? Perhaps it didn't matter, if she'd not sought to assert her ownership rights.

Jade perched at my feet, motionless, her green eyes aglow.

"What do you suggest?" I whispered.

He raked a hand through his hair. "You could return to Dreda for now while I gather more information."

"And allow it to rout me so readily?"

"It cannot reject you, not yet—"

Not until it proved me unworthy.

"And by bringing me as your guest, you've compelled it to allow me access." Ever watchful, his gaze swept the ruins even as he spoke.

What did he expect to find?

"You speak of Kilmere as if it's a living being." And indeed, I felt an awareness emanating from the stones around us.

Never mind curses, the sheer malevolence of this place could have done any amount of harm to the populace of Withern. I only wondered that any residents remained. I wrapped my arms about myself. "Is it a demesne like Wyncourt?"

He arched a brow. "You've been paying attention—but no. A demesne offers refuge and protection to its owner. It carries an echo of power from the one who created it. Shaped by the workings within, it takes on a life of its own. When the demesne is inherited, as with Wyncourt, it's a bit different—as is Wyncourt itself, being within your world. It does not follow the pattern, not precisely."

Then perhaps we suited.

"As for Kilmere, it's self-aware, like a demesne, but wasn't constructed by a single fae as a refuge and amplifier of power.

There are countless affinities woven into these workings. Many spent their strength here, from a variety of courts."

"Is that unusual?"

"Very." And it meant something to him, his expression suggested, but rather than share, he continued, "This was an outpost for conquest. What else it was remains to be seen."

I regarded the whole of it. Within its vastness, I was like a sylph before a wyvern—small and relatively defenseless. The ruined stronghold stretched across the surface of the tremendous cliff—which was unnaturally even, as if some great force had once leveled it—yet I sensed something *more*, something that burrowed deep, even into the roots of the earth.

And if I could not gain understanding, it would consume me. Spreading hawthorns bordered either side of the arch, and on instinct, I moved toward them. I had to try to understand.

Tucking my gloves into the collecting basket on my arm, I rested my palm against the fissured bark—and its awareness became my own, all its long years of digging deep into the rocky soil of the cliff, forging a path for its roots alongside fae-workings, even receiving nurture from them, encouragement to grow strong and sure, to join its strength to theirs.

The years stretched back, and images flashed into my mind.

Hundreds of mortals gathered before the fortress, every wall whole, every line and arch bristling with might. Fae lords and ladies of unrestrained power moved among them.

And—and Kilmere itself surged about me, severing my connection. My vision blacked at the edges, and I snatched my hand away.

Riven's brows drew together, dark slashes of concern. "Kilmere means to take your measure before it strikes. Have a care—and for now, don't touch anything."

What would it find? I did not even know my own measure, didn't understand what abilities I possessed, nor their source. I nodded, not trusting my voice.

I kept close to Riven, and Jade kept close to me as we picked our way through the rubble toward the central keep of the great fortress. Aside from a missing roof and windows, it remained mostly intact, its shadow a dark blot on the green sward before us.

The leaves of the trees rustled a warning as we passed, and the spiked seta of spindled moss on the tumbled stones bristled. On some level, I sensed the golden richness of Riven's power pressing back the cold malevolence of Kilmere.

If I'd been alone . . .

It did not bear considering. Even with Riven's power swirling about us, a bone-deep cold settled over me, driving spikes of pain into my temples. The spiraled sigils of the workings danced before my eyes, becoming deeper and darker, drawing me into their depths, seeking dominion.

Jade pressed against my ankle. *Be careful how long you look.*

Even as she spoke, a soft musical burble broke into my awareness, a sweet relief from the threats on all sides. I halted my progression toward the tower, turning my back on its dark menace, and made my way toward the familiar sound—one reminiscent of the fountains kept in every home to keep any nisi that might lurk about the household appeased.

Toward the seaward wall, a ring of smooth white rocks dappled with lichen surrounded a spring of clear water. It bubbled up in a way altogether unnatural for such a location. Doubtless it had suited the fae who constructed the place to have fresh water at their fingertips. Some way beyond, against the wall, a bounteous array of goldleaf basil—a rare cultivar— flourished, murmuring an invitation with its sprightly song.

Yet my attention caught on the spring. In the sunlight, it sparkled bright, untainted by the hostility of Kilmere. Suddenly thirsty, I knelt on the ring of stone and reached for the waters— but something caught my eye. Along the waterline, the pale green lichen had become dark and shriveled.

All that the water touched was dead. I sank back onto my heels. "Riven. Something's wrong here."

Jade sniffed at the edge of the water and recoiled. Riven approached, his eyes gleaming gold as he assessed it. "Basilisk venom."

I scrambled away from the spring and the danger it held. Our lore held that wherever a basilisk drank, the venom could linger for months or even years, claiming victims long after the serpent itself had passed. If I'd been in the Otherworld, I'd have been more wary. And I should have treated Kilmere with the same distrust. It operated by the laws of a realm not my own, and I'd best remember it if I wanted to survive.

I eyed the sparkling waters, deceptive in their beauty. "Does that mean a basilisk drank from this spring? Could it be hidden in Kilmere?"

"No trace of it remains. If it drank from the spring, it was some time ago—longer than your world retains signs of its passing."

"But it must have done so once, else how could the venom have come?"

A brisk wind churned in from the sea, stirring Riven's hair and tugging at his jacket. "Basilisk venom can be harvested, though at tremendous risk—which makes it rare and valuable."

"And you think some might be stored within Kilmere?"

"Given its nature, I find it likely."

I scrubbed my hands against my gown, as though the rock itself might have held some trace of the poison. "If so . . . could the workings in Kilmere have influenced mortals to use the venom against their own kind?"

"Yes, though we require far more evidence to say with any certainty that's what happened," Riven said. "If a mortal was coerced into acting so, it might prey upon his or her conscious mind with guilt."

"Thus the confession." My stomach plummeted as though I'd stepped off the cliff. I didn't want to consider that Kilmere could have corrupted one of the townsfolk, but it would be folly to ignore the possibility.

Still, there are others. Jade climbed atop a nearby boulder. *What of stasis, Lord Riven?*

"Jade said—"

"What of stasis? I know, she was quite loud in her request to be heard." Despite the circumstances, a faint hint of amusement flashed across his face.

Well, your walls are quite strong, and I wished to be heard directly.

"Just because I keep my thoughts my own doesn't mean I'll ignore you when you deliberately address me."

Good. What of it, then?

"No basilisk remains in Kilmere. Even in stasis, I'd be able to perceive its presence."

They'd lost me. "What is stasis, and why would the basilisk enter it?"

"It's a sort of deep hibernation—a self-protective mechanism used by basilisk in times of great duress," Riven said. "It's conceivable that it could have remained in stasis for centuries, and recently awoken. But to survive, it couldn't afford to linger here. It would seek a return to the Otherworld—to its bonded kin and its own territory. Unlike the Otherkind who venture into your world seeking easy prey, the basilisk has no such drive, only a near compulsion to protect its own territory and its knot."

"But could it have poisoned the townsfolk on its way back to the Otherworld, either by the venom left in this spring—or perhaps other places it drank from in the region?" I edged a bit farther from the spring. If the basilisk had left venom elsewhere, and Riven could track down the sources, the deaths would end and I'd be absolved of all responsibility. But how could we winnow truth from speculation?

My shoulders slumped as though the weight of Kilmere's stones heaped upon me, heavy as a burial mound. "Could you search the wells and springs in the area for trace venom?"

"It would take some time, but it's a simple enough task."

"If you're willing to attempt such a search, I could use the time to speak to Mr. Burke about the victims—and find out if any of them have been to Kilmere and perhaps partaken of the spring." Jade sauntered back over to me, and I lifted her, cradling her close. "Or, to the other possible theory, he may know if the confessed poisoner spent time here that would have allowed Kilmere to exert influence over his mind."

"It would be a start." Riven shook his head. "But be careful what you tell Burke. He already knows more than he should. And you might find the information you share has a longer reach than you desire."

Was this some fae disdain for mortals? Or something else? Mr. Burke had held in confidence all that took place in the Otherworld—I hardly believed he'd do otherwise now. I pressed a hand to my temples. "While we're here, we should search for the venom."

He shot me a piercing glance. "You wish to continue?"

"I didn't come this far to withdraw now." But again darkness encroached on the edges of my vision. Some trick of Kilmere?

Never mind that—if we found the venom, it would weigh the evidence more heavily toward a mortal coerced into preying on his fellows. To consider that a basilisk had somehow reawakened, perhaps one that had once preyed upon the region and created the original legend of the curse, would be bad enough. But if the workings in Kilmere had deliberately undermined the stability of an otherwise innocent man's mind, turning him into a killer . . . My shoulders knotted.

Though I wanted to flee back to the safety of the copse where Dreda sheltered, I forced myself to continue toward the nearest structure, a covered arch that still connected two outlying towers.

Then I stopped short.

Beneath the arch, a decorative frieze danced, some of the details obscured by the weathering of the stone. It matched the image I'd found in Ibbie's things, only now it became clear that the squiggles I'd struggled to decipher were in fact runes, skillfully woven between the serpent forms and blossoms.

Serpents . . . like the basilisk? I followed the frieze to a crumbling tower, which showed signs of mortal exploration—a few small chisel marks on stones near the base, where something had possibly been removed, and a section where someone, perhaps Ibbie's team, had excavated soil in an orderly grid, long enough ago that it was covered once more by plant life. I entered the tower proper, where a long rectangular stone stretched against the far wall, polished unnaturally smooth, in shape and size like a storage chest.

Riven surveyed the frieze. "This was an apothecary at one point."

What need did fae have of apothecaries? This was meant to appear as an ordinary stronghold to mortals, so perhaps it was simply part of the deception. "Ibbie studied this space before. I found a copy of the frieze in her things."

I moved toward the stone chest, running my hands over the surface. Again, biting cold met my touch, but my fingers passed over some sort of latch that I could feel but not see. I grasped it and tugged hard.

The song of the rowan alongside the arch surged into my senses, its rich strength pulsing through me. And the latch gave way, revealing a long line of vials. Two at the end were missing. "The venom?"

Riven pocketed one. "This section at the end appears to be. I'll examine it more closely once we've removed it from the ruins. This seems to be a well-stocked poisons chest."

The ground tremored, a low, angry sound. I'd forced into the open the smallest of its secrets, and Kilmere gathered its forces against me.

Another tremor followed the first, unsteadying me. I braced myself on the wall, and my hand came away damp.

Stained with deep red.

No, that wasn't right. It couldn't be. I blinked at it, my vision wavering. A glamour?

But no, all about me the stones oozed dark droplets like blood drip, drip, dripping . . .

A metallic, coppery scent assaulted me, and my vision narrowed till I could only see the stone and the drops of blood pat, pat, patting to the ground.

Hungry soil soaked them in, lusted for more. I sank to my knees, closed my eyes to blot out the rippling stones. "Riven, I can't see. Not properly."

Nor could I keep my voice steady, or my body from trembling. Jade curled her form around me, warm and vital and real.

"We need to go." Riven's voice came low, urgent. His hands gripped my elbows, and he tugged me to my feet. "Let's move."

A cry of anguish, shrill and piercing, sliced the air. Every bit of song from the trees and moss and lichen died, cut off by the sounds of agony. I shrank closer to Riven. "Do you hear that?"

"Not now, Jessa." A ripple like gold flame emerged from Riven, licked about my shoulders. "Later."

A haze gathered in the air about us, its gray tinged red, like smoke and flame. Through it, the form of the fortress appeared like a great draconic beast, rearing back for the strike.

Perhaps it was releasing the flame and smoke, the peculiar gathering warmth in the air—no, no, that didn't make sense. None of it did.

Don't dwell on it, Jessa.

Riven's grip tightened, and he half-lifted me over the boundary wall. Unfiltered sunlight poured down upon us, and my vision cleared.

Still Jade pressed at my ankles, urging me onward until we reached a bend in the road. Then my legs gave way, and I sank onto a fallen log. "What . . . what was that?"

"Kilmere sought to claim your senses—to test your strength." The muscles near his jaw tightened.

"Which it found lacking." I couldn't deny that in our first skirmish, Kilmere had routed me—with very little effort. Exhaustion weighed every limb, as though I'd run the entire way up the cliff.

"You weren't prepared. If it had drawn you too deeply into the glamour, it could have swayed you into hurling yourself off the cliff or disposing of your own life in another tidy way."

Which would mean the problem of an inferior mistress solved, at least from Kilmere's perspective.

"Next time, you'll know what to expect."

Next time? I shuddered. "Perhaps Lord West was right. I'm not equipped for such an adversary."

"I'll grant it's not . . . ideal."

I dug my fingers into the rough bark of the decaying tree underneath me. "But I have no choice."

Riven folded his arms across his chest. "You could abandon Kilmere now, but then you'll be in no position to thwart Damir. And he's not inclined to mercy."

My gaze drifted back to the ruin, which loomed above, dark and immovable. "But what defense can I possibly muster against —that?"

"You feel and hear the plants around you, so you've said. Next time, anchor yourself to them. They'll help tether you to what is real."

"And if Kilmere moves beyond illusion to outright attack?"

"We don't yet know its capabilities. I'll offer what help I can, but to Kilmere I represent a hostile force. It's extended only the most begrudging of admittances. If I try to undermine its workings, it will unleash its full defenses."

And he'd said before that would destroy not only Kilmere, but the surrounding region as well.

Jade perched on the log beside me. *I don't like it. And for all he says, I don't think Riven does either.*

Perhaps not. But either I return and seek the truth or I abandon the townsfolk to the mercies of Kilmere—and I surrender to Lord West. Not only that, but the fortress held secrets, knowledge I needed, knowledge Ibbie had wanted me to find. *I can't turn back.*

But nor could I face it again today, not with this bone-deep weariness oppressing me. I must collect myself to try again, consider all I'd learned so far, and find a new approach.

"There's something I don't understand." I brushed at some fragments of bark on my skirt. "Mr. Tibbons gave such a glowing account of Kilmere, the gaps in his memory notwithstanding."

"It would have had no reason to threaten him when it might beguile instead. You it wants to test—to either prove you worthy or destroy you. A mortal entering its borders need not face the same."

Perhaps then Kilmere had presented Ibbie with an enchanting aspect at first, inviting her deeper into its coils. How long before she'd beheld its true nature? Or had she ever seen it clearly?

Riven continued, "To maintain the guise of an ordinary ruin, Kilmere has decayed just like your mortal structures would have done, though it possessed power enough to remain intact. It funneled its energies belowground; its true self lies beneath the surface. To uncover what Damir seeks, to understand how it's preyed upon Withern, we'll have to delve deeper —and Kilmere will certainly resist any attempt to reach its heart."

Wonderful. The wind tugged at the ribbons of my hat, and the faint burble of the brook met my ears. I pressed to my feet. "For now, let's just fetch Dreda."

Even if I must return, I couldn't endure lingering in its shadow much longer.

Perhaps Riven perceived it, but he only said, "Very well."

As we distanced ourselves from Kilmere, my steps steadied and my thoughts arranged themselves in more proper order, though it seemed as though the ruin mocked my retreat.

The sound of the trickling brook strengthened, a reminder of the deadly spring. I looked down at Jade. *Do you think there ever was a basilisk within Kilmere? Or only the venom?*

Her ears twitched. *I think Riven is right. No basilisk would willingly stay here, in a world devoid of the essence it requires and lacking in bond-mates. The only way it could survive without its mate would be stasis, and once ended, it certainly would not stay. Unless there were more than one. Even so, they'd have to return to the Otherworld.*

They have bond-mates?

In this, basilisks and kit-isne *are alike.*

Forgive me, but I fail to see how you resemble a giant venomous serpent.

Jade sprang over an uneven root. *They're of our family of kinds, you might say. Like* kit-isne, *they have true-form and lesser-form. And they must bond.*

Do they also mindspeak?

They don't ordinarily deign to speak to the minds of any aside from their mates, and that they do mostly through the sharing of perceptions and feelings.

My foot caught on a rut in the path. *If they have a lesser-form, does that mean a basilisk could roam Byren with no one the wiser? Might it appear like some common garden snake?*

To a mortal, yes. But even in lesser-form, a high fae would detect its passing.

What else can you tell me of basilisks? Whether or not Kilmere had harbored one, it seemed prudent to be informed—and this at least was something I could control.

Among our kind, we tell a tale to our young: The Turn of the Serpent. Her green eyes glowed as she unfolded the tale of a basilisk bonded to one who turned *trasven,* a serpent who committed the gravest of misdeeds, treachery to the knot—the community of basilisks in which they made their home.

Once forged, the bond could not be unmade, not without death. The honest basilisk wrestled within herself, then she acted with honor. Knowing it would cost her own life, she slew her mate, whereafter she died in agony—the price she must pay for killing him. Her body was buried deep in the mountains, a memorial for all time, while the body of the *trasven* was destroyed. Each basilisk in the knot spat venom on it till its corpse dissolved and vanished into the soil below, ever to be trampled on by its kind.

That's . . . that's a horrible tale. You tell it to your kits?

So they might be wise in the choosing of their bonds. For once given, they can't be revoked without destruction.

Remind me never to ask you for a bedtime story.

She chuffed again, and a sense of her amusement traveled to me. Willowere beckoned, and I picked up my pace. We'd survived our first foray into Kilmere, and I'd time to find a way to deal with its workings in future. Now we just had to fetch Dreda—and hope she'd noted nothing untoward.

CHAPTER 24

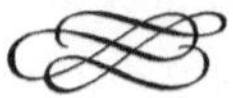

Alongside Riven, I entered the copse, then stumbled to a halt. Dreda sat rigid on the ground beside the brook, sheltered by a cropping of rock. Her eyes remained firmly shut; her basket was clasped before her like a shield. Had she come to harm?

Asrina flickered into sight, perching atop a nearby stone. "You're back, good, good, good. She's not well."

I hurried to Dreda and knelt before her. "Are you hurt?"

She blinked, as though rousing herself from some dread dream, then snared my arm in an iron grip. "No, not hurt, just . . . I'm sorry, Miss Jessa, I know I should rightly have kept watch, but I couldn't be in view of the ruins a moment longer. I thought I heard something strange, and then I looked up at Kilmere and what I saw—it was too much like—you know."

When the dread-aught tormented her. What else could have caused such distress? "You heard something . . . peculiar?"

"The most dreadful cries. I went to the edge of the clearing, because I feared you'd been hurt, and when I caught a glimpse of Kilmere in the distance, it looked as if something moved across its stones, all writhing and monstrous. Like the things that creature used to make me see. I want to help, don't want anyone else to suffer from the fae, but I suppose I've just no courage."

"The fae?" Riven crossed the clearing, his face grim.

"Oh, Miss Jessa." She gripped my arm harder, looking up wide-eyed at Riven. "Please, my lord, I don't know what I'm saying, I'm that upset."

"I think you know well enough. Miss Twells—"

"Wait, please." I recognized the undercurrent to his voice, the glamour about to settle over her.

"Emotions, Miss Caldwell. They don't lead to wise decisions."

"Allow me one moment." I staggered to my feet, helping Dreda regain her own. "You don't lack courage. Never think that. But I shouldn't have asked you to come."

"No, Miss Jessa, it's my job to accompany you. I'll do better next time, truly I will."

"Miss Caldwell, I require a word." Riven spoke in an imperious tone. "Now."

"Why don't you rest here a moment and collect yourself. It seems Lord Riven has forsaken his manners, but don't worry, I'll sort it. We'll be just beyond the clearing."

It was as unwise to provoke Riven as to rouse a clutch of slumbering rock drakes, yet I was exhausted and cross and of no mind to quibble.

He stalked onto the path, the familiar shimmer of the glamour that restrained sound forming about us. "Whatever your qualms about glamour, you need to forsake them. What she observed will prey upon her mind. Best to release her and have done with it."

At times he could be so frustratingly *fae*. I crossed my arms over my chest. "You cannot know that. And glamour over time *could* hurt her. Not to mention it strips her ability to choose from her—which she's had done enough already. How can I allow any further risk to her mind, however small?"

"You condemn my intent to glamour, yet in so doing, you

also wrest the decision from her, denying her the relief it may bring." Tiny sparks flared about Riven. "You cannot tell her the whole, so what else remains? Or have you confided more in her than is wise already? She spoke of fae. What does she know?"

I chose my words with care. "She knows that I'd like to protect mortals from any . . . trouble fae may seek to cause in our world."

"And she believes you can?"

No mortal could stand against fae, yet she *did* place an uncanny degree of confidence in me. "I suppose."

"Why?"

"If you recall, I found a dread-aught afflicting a woman and removed it."

"Miss Twells was its victim."

"Yes." My arms dropped to my sides. "But I don't think she fathoms that creature was only a mild nuisance in your world. It gave her far too great a confidence in me."

If she'd any notion of the true power of the fae, her faith would rightfully be shaken.

"And for that, you chose to reveal your knowledge about the Otherworld?"

I shook my head. "She knows little, truly, but a situation arose—I had to confide my purpose in her, at least in part. But I know she'll keep quiet. It matters a great deal to her."

"Perhaps, yet she might not retain control enough to do so," Riven said. "If she was afflicted by a dread-aught, the prolonged exposure to its saliva will have had lingering effects. The conflict between truth and glamour may well upset the balance of her mind. For that reason, I'll accede to your wishes. Even so, she'll remain more vulnerable to Other influences than most mortals, may even experience a relapse of hallucinations."

I pressed my hand to my stomach to still its churning. "Is there anything I can do to keep her well?"

"It matters so much to you?"

"Of course it does. She's done nothing to deserve her suffering."

"Then provide her protection." Riven spoke softly, but a hint of challenge laced his words. "A ward for her mind."

"A ward? I've no notion how to accomplish that." Along the path, a stand of blue buttons gently waved their blossoms. "I've done only the most minimal study of alchemy. They keep their secrets close."

"I don't speak of alchemy." He surveyed me, his gaze intent. "Use what botanicals speak to you on the matter. You have been practicing, have you not?"

"I—yes." I left out the disastrous encounter with Aunt Caris in the gardens, where I'd nearly lost myself, and my resolve to take more care since. "But what you're suggesting . . ."

It terrified me beyond reason.

"Some step must be taken to mitigate the risk—or you accept she may still succumb to what you mortals call fae-touch."

"Could you—"

"You'd have me form a bargain with her?"

"No, not in her condition." Only I'd presumed . . . hoped even, he might be willing to offer aid without one. A foolish notion. I shouldn't have let myself forget he was fae—and that bargains rested at the heart of their culture. But where did that leave Dreda? I rubbed my temples, weary.

"Then choose your plants. Craft them into something she can wear—and tell her to keep it with her at all times."

The dancing flowers blurred before my eyes. "Will you tell me why you believe I can do this?"

"No. Only that it's past time you tried, if you want the truth."

With that, he turned and walked back toward the clearing, leaving me to follow slowly. The truth? Did he mean . . .

You are greatly distressed. I wish to read your deeper thoughts.

However, I am not. Jade padded alongside me. *I let you know so you'll understand I exercise great self-control.*

A smile lifted the corners of my lips, pushing back my distress. *I appreciate your care. You've seen into my thoughts enough before to know what I fear.*

That you have fae blood.

Yes. Do you think it possible?

Possible. Her gaze tracked a red squirrel as it scurried into the underbrush. *Yet surprising, if so.*

Why?

As you've already considered, fae don't easily give up their claim on their children. Why were you allowed to remain in the mortal world, your nature hidden?

I have no answer, not unless my mortal parent found a way to conceal me. And if it were true—how could I bear it?

Clearly Riven considers the prospect, if he presses you to explore your abilities.

Oh.

Had his refusal to offer aid to Dreda, his insistence that I craft a ward, been a test? I'd long felt Riven did nothing without purpose, so it was a logical assumption . . . *Why not just say as much?*

Fae don't offer information freely—you know that, though Riven has shared with you far more than I ever would have expected. I believe he considers more than one possibility, and that there's a reason he takes care with what he says. But his mind is impenetrable, so I can offer no more.

As bone-weary as if I'd rooted out a field of tree stumps by hand, I stumbled back into the clearing to join Dreda and Riven. With Dreda present, I could speak no more of my fears or theories—about myself or Kilmere—but must keep them locked inside.

If Dreda took note of our silence, she did not comment on it. Perhaps her own weariness lingered. When we reached the cottage at last, I said, "I believe Lord Riven and I will stroll the gardens for a few moments."

Blessedly, she took the hint and excused herself to enter the cottage. As we'd stroll in full view of the inhabitants of the house, it could not be thought shocking. After securing the horses, we moved toward the side garden, only to be arrested by Aunt Caris's laughter, a lilting sound of pleasure.

A deeper voice addressed her, one smooth and laced with glamour strong enough to spark across my skin even from this distance.

Oh no.

I picked up my pace, rounding the corner of the house with Riven on my heels.

It was Lord West.

CHAPTER 25

My pulse surged at my temples. Even from this distance, the echo of his power washed over me, evoking pain. I had to get him away from Aunt Caris. What harm might he have already done?

Yet I couldn't move. Cold tendrils of fear, strong as cross vines, bound me in place. He shouldn't be here, I didn't want it, couldn't endure it. Yet I could give no sign he unsettled me; I must somehow appear still and composed. Reflexively, I reached for Riven, only just stopping myself from the impropriety of grasping his hand.

As though he knew, Riven placed his hand on the small of my back, and a shock of glorious golden strength surged through my body. Bolstered by his presence, I moved forward, rounding the corner. Jade stalked alongside me, her fur bristling. She seemed to grow slightly—and this time I knew it was no trick of perception, but her true-form about to break out.

But a peaceful scene met our eyes. Aunt Caris sat at a white wicker table spread beneath the trees, serving tea to Lord West, who appeared the perfect gentleman, his glamour disguising the monstrous power within.

When we drew near, Lord West stood, stalking toward me with predatory grace.

"West." Riven interposed himself neatly between us. "I can't say it's a pleasure to see you."

They stood face-to-face, two fae lords, Lord West as cold and dark and gleaming as the star of the north, Riven as vibrant and rich and warm as the summer sun—the splendor of night compared to the glory of day, both of them breathtaking, both forces with which I could not reckon. The air fairly crackled between them.

"Lord Riven." Lord West offered no nod of greeting. "I share your sentiments. When I learned you involved yourself in this affair, much became clear."

Aunt Caris passed a hand over her eyes, looking bewildered. Father had said he'd tell her that he no longer deemed Lord West a desirable suitor, yet she'd welcomed him with smiles to tea on the lawn beneath the gracious sweep of willow branches—he must have glamoured her thoroughly.

A flare of heat thrummed through me, burning away the tendrils of fear. How dare he drag her into this?

A mighty crosscurrent of power surged between them. I couldn't afford to have a fae conflict break out on the lawn of Willowere, with my family vulnerable. So I forced myself to speak, though my voice emerged softer than I wished. "What brings you here, Lord West?"

"If you recall, we once discussed that I always achieve my ends." Shadows angled across the planes of his face. "Nothing has changed. You still have a lesson to learn—and I have an acquisition to make. I wouldn't want you to forget."

A lesson. He'd meant to teach me the meaning of fear. My heart drummed fast and furious against my stays.

And Jade growled low, a flash of fang showing.

"I need no instruction." I couldn't let her reveal herself nor attempt to attack him—however much she desired it, however much he deserved it. With effort, I steadied my voice. "And you're not welcome here."

"Jessa!" Aunt Caris nearly dropped her cup. "You cannot intend to speak so."

"On the contrary, I've never meant anything more."

Her hand fluttered to the lace of her neckline. "Lord West, I . . . I apologize—"

"Have no fear." His lips curled. "I'm not easily deterred."

"Yet you'll go." Riven spoke with a quiet confidence that stilled any objection from Aunt Caris. Then he murmured something in the fae tongue, directed to Lord West.

"Is that so?" A cold smile lifted the edges of his mouth further. "Ladies, you'll excuse me. It seems I have business to attend." But as he passed me, he murmured low, "I shall see you again soon, my sweet."

When his breath whispered against my skin, I returned to that dreadful moment in Hampton Hall when his hands tightened about my neck, and I shivered.

Riven took a half step toward him, then halted, let him go in peace.

After he vanished from sight, a heavy sigh wafted from Aunt Caris. She looked far paler than was her wont, her features peaked.

"Are you well, Aunt Caris?"

"It's only the onset of a megrim—a bad one, I fear." She tottered to her feet, then braced herself upon the table.

"Why don't you lie down, and I shall bring you up some tea soon."

"That's very kind, my dear." Slowly, she made her way toward the cottage.

"A tea won't cure what ails her." Riven rubbed a hand across his jaw. "Damir pressed the boundaries harder than is wise."

"Did he hurt her in a lasting way?"

"He used a strong glamour. More than he should have—he must have needed it to override whatever your father told her.

Her pain comes from the struggle to reconcile the two." He angled his body toward me. "Do you have a handkerchief?"

"I . . . In my reticule." I withdrew the lacy square and offered it to him.

"It will do." Before I could even draw breath, lines of light, fine as spider silk, wove their way through the lace, then faded. "Place that over her head. It will ease her pain, clear her thoughts."

If I sprinkled some floral water on it, she'd accept it as a compress without question. But . . . Riven offered this to me without requiring a bargain. It was understood that all gifts from fae incurred debt, so I'd have preferred a bargain. At least then I'd have known what to expect. But since it was for Aunt Caris, I simply accepted. Whatever the cost, it would be worth it.

I tucked the handkerchief back into my reticule, struggling to weave together the fraying edges of my emotions. "Why would he have sought her, unless to try and sway me through my family?"

"As a show of dominance and an expression of his intention to vanquish you and your house."

"Is that all?" I sank onto the chair Aunt Caris had vacated. I wanted to tend her, but I needed answers first, as long as Riven was willing to offer them. "I know there's some protection over mortals—and that you cannot speak of it—but how can I leave them alone, even for a moment, if I know he might seek them, might toy with them for his own pleasure, even if he cannot strike them outright?"

"Because you seek their ultimate safety—and you have little choice."

That notion provided no comfort, not when I considered how pale Aunt Caris had looked. The willows murmured overhead, and I breathed in their vibrant strength. "When we were in Avons, you said that you could place some sort of working to keep Lord West out of our house, if only you had Father's permission. Can you do that here?"

"You've let this house with money from Lady Dromley's estate, correct?"

"Aunt Caris made the arrangements, but yes, the funds came from the estate."

"Then yours is the only permission I require, as long as the working ceases when your lease ends."

The woven spines of the chair dug uncomfortably into my back, and I shifted. "Will it require another bargain between us?"

His eyes darkened. "Consider it part of our agreement to thwart Lord West."

"Then please, will you?"

He nodded. "I'll complete it before I leave today."

I wanted to offer thanks, yet he'd warned me against it, so instead I traced the under-and-over pattern of the wicker and considered.

Lord West sought to unnerve me. Did he imagine, after everything, he could simply intimidate me into surrendering? Or perhaps it was just a reminder that he'd no intention of giving up, and time was on *his* side. The measures taken thus far were stopgap at best. And Riven couldn't remain indefinitely, even were he so inclined. Sooner or later, his king would summon him—and we'd be left vulnerable. Jade nudged at my ankles, and I lifted her onto my lap. "Do you think he knows the true nature of Kilmere?"

"Assuming he does, I very much wonder how he came by that knowledge." Riven reclined on the chair that had been abandoned by Lord West. "Apart from what objects of value might remain within, its nature makes it a prize worth winning. It would offer him a stronghold of sorts within your world, where he might operate with relative impunity. I'd say he knows."

My hand snagged on the wicker, a shard of wood jabbing through the skin. What destruction would Lord West bring in the region and beyond if not required to restrain his power within our world? Whatever the cost, he couldn't be permitted to seize it.

I wiped away the droplet of blood. "Then I think we must return to Kilmere sooner rather than later. But before we can think of returning, Dreda must have a ward—and I want to make sure Aunt Caris has recovered. Perhaps the morning after tomorrow?"

"Very well. That should also give you time to speak with Mr. Burke, while I examine the waterways of the region for trace venom."

After Riven placed his workings upon Willowere, I returned withindoors to prepare a tea for Aunt Caris, a blend of lemon balm and chamomile.

I hesitated over my satchel of simples for a moment, then added a pinch of dried goldheart to the infuser. A sense of rightness settled over me as its sweet-spice fragrance wafted up from the pot.

Jade sniffed at it, and her eyes brightened. *She will be well—she has you to look after her.*

I rubbed the soft fur between her ears. *Thank you.*

I placed the tea things on a tray and slipped into Aunt Caris's bedchamber. She reclined upon the bed, but she was not asleep, for a small shudder passed over her frame, and her breathing remained uneven.

Something twisted painfully inside my chest. "Will you take some tea, Aunt Caris?"

"Thank you, my dear." She struggled to press up from her pillows. "If you could help me—my head spins so."

I set the tray on the bedside table and gently propped her upright. Eyes closed, she sipped at the tea I lifted to her lips. When she'd finished the cup, I lowered her back down. "I'll stay with you until you're asleep."

"That's kind of you, my dear. But there's no need."

"I want to be here." I sprinkled some lavender water on the handkerchief and spread it across her forehead.

Aunt Caris relaxed at once, the tension leaving her form. "I'm sorry that you should all miss calling upon the Holloways this afternoon," she murmured. "Perhaps this will pass before it grows too late and—"

"You should just rest. There will be plenty of time to call upon them tomorrow, if you feel more yourself again."

As I waited for Aunt Caris to drift into slumber, my mind worked upon the problems before me. While the truth of my nature might be least among them, it plagued me as I watched her.

By virtue of whoever—whatever—I was, I'd exposed her to this danger. If I hadn't been able to resist Lord West's glamour, then he would have already claimed Kilmere and my family would be well out of it . . . but so many others would be suffering.

If only I could ask Mother what she had done, when faced with the impossible. How had she managed? Could she have kept any sort of record, as Ibbie had done?

To the best of my recollection, she'd not favored diary-keeping. But one night when I'd stumbled into her bedchamber after a bad dream, she'd been writing in a small leather book. Could she have chronicled her experiences, then hidden them?

If not, perhaps reviewing the letters she'd sent my aunts over the years could lend insight. When Aunt Caris recovered, I'd inquire.

Yet that would not help me against Lord West—nor give me insight on how to manage Kilmere. The game board had been set, the value of the prize determined—at least in part. Now we each gathered our pieces. How would it unfold? Would I find what I required before Lord West did? The beginnings of a headache clustered at my own temples.

At least we could further our investigation into the nature of the curse, which felt like a more manageable process. Riven would seek any trace of basilisk venom within the region, and I must send word to Mr. Burke this afternoon. If he reported the victims had been to Kilmere, then a new avenue of investigation opened. But if only the poisoner had, then what would Kilmere do now, with its chosen vessel in custody?

I didn't want to find out, but I'd a feeling it wouldn't remain a mystery for long.

CHAPTER 26

Although Aunt Caris slept through the afternoon and evening, by the time she arose the next morning she appeared herself once more, rosy-cheeked and placid, with only the smallest lingering headache. However, she didn't seem to remember much of what had transpired yesterday, other than that Lord West had come to call. Try as I might, I could not make her understand why I didn't favor him—she appeared to possess no recall of her conversation with Father on the matter. As I did not want to cause damage by ripping away whatever shreds of glamour entrenched the notion of Lord West as a favorable suitor in her mind, I let the matter rest.

Yet it preyed upon me.

As I attended her in the drawing room, I kept watch for any sign that the glamour influenced more than her memory on the one issue, yet so far encountered no trace. Perhaps we'd been fortunate.

She looked up from the morning post, her eyes sparkling a clear green. "Lady Holloway invites us to attend a tea at Holle Castle this afternoon. We must all go, of course. To do otherwise would be an insult to her hospitality."

It seemed our challenging beginning hadn't ruined our

prospects with her, as Aunt Caris had feared. Only I'd no desire to attend a formal tea nor to miss Mr. Burke's call—assuming he intended to respond to the message I'd sent yesterday.

The murmur of conversation between my sisters and Aunt Caris faded to the background. I couldn't escape this event, not without sufficient excuse, yet I must see Mr. Burke today. If he didn't come before luncheon, I'd find a way to seek him, however improper.

When Aunt Caris dispatched a servant with her acceptance, I excused myself to explore the gardens with Jade and Asrina. If I must wait for Mr. Burke, I'd use the time to seek plants for Dreda's safekeeping. I could think of no way to avoid her chaperoning my return to Kilmere, yet I could not let her do so at risk of her mind.

I wanted to preserve her against undue fae influence. Yet if I was right about my own nature, I couldn't make use of the plants intended to repel fae. I'd require a different approach—and I must utilize what grew in the cottage gardens, as I couldn't go farther afield just now.

Jade stretched out in the sun, regarding me steadily, but she remained silent as I sought to order my thoughts and sort through all the verdant threads of song. I moved toward the east bed, where gold runner vines released a determined thrum.

In combination with the protective zeal of the nearby snapdragons, might they offer her aid? A cooler melody twined between them, the star-of-night, which murmured of resilience and fortitude, steadiness and strength. Perhaps the three of them together would be strong enough.

Yet I hesitated.

It would be a tremendous risk to attempt to connect deeply once more—and it might accomplish nothing. But Dreda was vulnerable, and I'd dragged her into this situation.

I had to try.

Except aside from identifying my source plants, I'd no notion of what to do. I sank onto the grass—the deep blue of my gown should protect me from any revealing stains. The snap-dragons and star-of-night weren't far from one another. If I could perhaps coax one to grow alongside the other, much as I'd beckoned the ivy to curl up my arm . . .

In the canvas of my mind, I could see the three of them twining, the colorful, bristling stalks of the snapdragon bowing and bending, the bright star-of-night creeping among them, then the gold runner vines binding it all together, the chain linking the jewels of this necklace—one that would be gloriously fragrant but far too large and unwieldy to be worn. Not to mention the lack of longevity.

I released a quiet sigh.

What had Riven expected of me?

I stroked a snapdragon stem, the image of the necklace at the forefront of my mind, and it sparked with fierce strength under my fingertips. At its feet, from the root, the tiniest new stalks and blossoms budded forth in an instant—delicate and dainty, all gold-white and green. The song of these miniatures was far clearer and more vibrant than that of its parent plant, as if the power of the whole condensed itself into this tiny form.

I snatched back my fingers as though scalded. What had I done? How had I done it? I tucked my hands into the folds of my skirt.

Jade bounded to my side. *Have a care, Jessa. Someone approaches.*

I scrambled to my feet as footsteps crunched along the path of crushed shell that wove through the garden. A moment later, Mr. Burke appeared around the corner of the house.

He couldn't have seen my peculiar behavior. Nevertheless, I eased myself in front of the diminutive snapdragons. With his sharp eyes, he might take note of any irregularity.

He offered a slight bow. "Miss Jessa, I received your message. I hope you don't mind I've come so early."

"Not at all. I must confess I hoped you would." Though I'd

rather hold our conversation far from other listening ears. "Would you care to stroll about the lake?"

"It would be my pleasure."

We strolled down the path toward the lake, Jade padding alongside and Asrina bobbing at my shoulder.

When we'd distanced ourselves from the house, Mr. Burke said, "I take it you've had trouble of some sort?"

"I have some further concerns about Kilmere, and I'd hoped you could shed light on a few questions that have arisen."

"You explored the ruins, then?"

The muscles in my shoulders tightened in memory, and my fingers tingled as if the imagined blood still stained them. I nodded.

"When?"

"Yesterday. Riven noticed—"

"Riven?" His steps faltered. "He's here?"

I pressed my lips together, regretting the thoughtless remark. Yet his arrival to the neighborhood couldn't be hidden long, not since he'd already appeared in society. Mr. Burke would have found out in short order, and it was better not to act as if I'd something to hide. "He offered to help me investigate the ruins at Kilmere."

"And what does he want in exchange?"

"I . . . . It's complicated." The branch of a willow brushed against my neck, gentle and soothing.

"How can it be anything but complicated with fae?" His eyes darkened to a stormy gray. "May I speak freely?"

"If you wish."

"You cannot let yourself become further entangled with fae. If by some miracle you survive your dealings with Other, how long do you imagine you can keep it hidden? If the Vigil finds out, they'll strike." His words held an edge. "Fae only offer aid expecting a far greater return. If you allow Riven to draw you in you further, it won't end well."

"I understand your concerns." And I'd worried over each one myself. "But in this circumstance, I have little choice."

His hand flexed, brushing the blade at his side. "Is Riven coercing you?"

"No, it's not like that."

"What then?"

"It doesn't matter. I only—"

"What could matter more? If you saw fit to involve a fae, there must be a reason."

I swallowed hard against the desire to confess everything. Nothing about the Other nature of the problem troubled Riven, but a mortal would understand how overwhelming, how terrifying, all this felt. Yet how could I explain? It was ingrained in Mr. Burke to protect those in need. If he knew of the threat Lord West posed, he'd confront him, regardless of the danger. And that didn't even account for the risks of Kilmere itself.

His pace quickened, his steps becoming more clipped, a clear sign of frustration—he knew I was hiding something. He perceived far too much; he always had, which was what made him good at his job. And it meant I had to offer something. "Of course there's a reason. Many in Withern fear the deaths are a result of the curse, and I wanted to be sure that wasn't the case."

"That's why you've involved Riven?"

"Who better to seek an Otherworldly curse than high fae?"

"I can think of a good many choices less risky." He released a long breath. Perhaps he didn't believe me, not in full, but he didn't press further. "I'll share with you what I can, if you'll leave the matter alone—and tell Riven he's no longer required."

"I can't promise that, not until I'm certain Kilmere poses no threat." Which would be never, given the hostility within its borders. "But if you feel you cannot discuss the case further, I understand."

He blew out a breath. "You are extraordinarily stubborn."

"And you aren't?" Immediately I flinched—I shouldn't have let such an improper remark escape.

But instead of taking offense, he chuckled, breaking the tension. "I'll admit that accusation has been leveled at me before, most recently by my fellow stratesmen here in Withern."

"Why is that?"

"Because I'm not satisfied with the conclusions drawn in this case. Not in full."

The waters of the lake gently lapped the shore. "Then will you help me explore the possibilities?"

"Perhaps. What do you wish to know?"

"The victims—did they explore Kilmere recently?"

"I considered that angle. As best as I could piece together from the reports on their final weeks and my own conversations with their families, none of them had." He lifted a bough overhanging the path so I could pass underneath. "Many of the townsfolk fear Kilmere, believe it better left alone. Those that don't share their superstitions avoid it so as not to draw censure from their peers."

If all the believers in the curse were as outspoken as Mrs. Warren and Lady Denby, then it was no surprise most chose to stay away in the interests of preserving harmony—and perhaps their minds were not as free of fear as they claimed. But if the victims hadn't entered the ruins, then the most likely explanation became that Kilmere exerted influence over the poisoner—unless the basilisk itself had been roused by the incursion of Mr. Tibbons or some other unfortunate, and left traces of its venom as it passed to the Otherworld.

"And what of the man whom you took into custody?" I asked. "Did he share the views of his fellows?"

"Mr. Ellsworth. He claims he's not spent time there."

I tilted my head to regard Mr. Burke. He'd chosen his words with care. "But you don't believe him."

"Certain aspects of his accounts don't hold up—in my opinion, at least. Nor do I judge him of stable mind."

And I'd take his opinions above those of his fellow

stratesmen at any time. "Then you don't agree he's responsible for the poisonings?"

"It seems clear enough. He had means. Opportunity. And a reason to do so in the form of an old grudge, long nurtured." His jaw tightened. "More importantly, he confessed."

He'd confessed? I halted abruptly. "And you're satisfied with his statement?"

Something flickered deep in his eyes; clearly he wasn't convinced. "He was adamant about his guilt."

"If he's condemned, he'll pay with his life. So why confess to such a crime?" Unless he'd been compelled against his will and sought to rid himself of the burden. I could think of few things worse than being forced to commit murder. With difficulty, I managed an even tone. "Was he attempting to clear his conscience?"

"Such things happen on rare occasion." Mr. Burke folded his arms and looked out over the lake. "In this circumstance, it seems unlikely guilt motivated his statement."

"Why?"

"Because he claims that he's left poison elsewhere. That more in Withern will die, and his revenge will be complete." Mr. Burke's kestrel gaze swept over me. "I trust that none of this will go any further."

A small breeze rippled the surface of the lake, and I rubbed my hands along my arms to ward off a sudden chill. Why would Mr. Ellsworth say such a thing, unless he was compelled? Or—as Mr. Burke said—deeply bitter and slightly unhinged.

Jade perched on a rock, seemingly regarding the fish swimming in the waters below, but her ears flicked back to attend to our conversation.

"Did he give any indication of his intended victims?"

"No. And not for lack of effort to force the truth from him." Mr. Burke frowned. "The stratesmen here are not as—careful in their attempts to persuade him as I would prefer. But he refuses to speak another word."

"They used force against him?"

"When he wouldn't cooperate any further than confession. I understand the temptation with so many lives at stake—but if we become like those we protect society from, then who will protect them from us?" He rubbed at the back of his neck. "I threatened to report them to Avons, and they've left him alone for now, but it's not gained me any favor with the local force."

Small wonder he had faint lines of weariness drawn around his eyes. To have to watch over a self-confessed killer—it couldn't be comfortable. I forced myself back into motion. "You said he holds a grudge against some of the old families in Withern?"

"With good cause. When his wife was with child many years ago, she experienced a great deal of difficulty. They were land rich, with little ready money, and therefore lacked the necessary funds to obtain an expensive alchemical treatment they were told could help," Mr. Burke said. "Ellsworth went to several of the old families in the area to borrow on the land, but they hemmed and hawed until he was in a frantic condition, sure he'd lose both his wife and his child. When several of them finally agreed to help, he didn't take time to read the fine print, only took them at their word. Turned out the terms were such that it would be impossible for him to ever reclaim the properties. And due to the delays, even with treatment, his wife lost the babe. At great cost, the alchemists managed to preserve her life. When they returned, they learned they'd lost everything except a small farm passed down through his wife's family line. Needless to say, there's cause for a grudge."

"How dreadful," I murmured.

"Indeed. They did eventually have another child, a son, yet I imagine they've never forgotten their pain."

Could deep-seated bitterness have made him more vulnerable to the wiles of Kilmere? Or did I read too much into the situation? Perhaps it was only long-festering anger emerging—

but why now, if not due to Kilmere? "And you believe he could have readily obtained the poison?"

"I take it you haven't heard of their family garden? The locals call it Fellbane—it grows alongside their cottage and consists entirely of toxic plants. The botanicals there could provide poison enough to kill off the entire town."

"That's . . ." Words failed me. Who would fashion a garden of plants designed to bring pain and death? Had this been some long-standing plan after all? If so, did that mean the taint of Kilmere had long since seeped past its boundary walls? Perhaps more curious, how did the owners of Fellbane justify cultivation of said garden to their fellow townsfolk? I couldn't imagine a poison garden was a welcome addition to Withern. "I'd not heard, but then we've only been here two days, and our arrival was rather blighted."

"In what way?"

"A thief or some other trespasser ransacked Willowere before we arrived." I omitted the dead hares—no need to prompt him to look into the matter further.

"And no one reported it?"

"Lord Denby wished to avoid drawing the stratesmen into the affair, and as he attended the matter, we left it at that."

The furrow between his brows deepened. "Still, you could have told me."

"Perhaps, but the intruder was long since gone by the time we came—and I was much occupied by the exploration of Kilmere." I brushed a bit of residual dirt from my gown. "What did you make of the ruins?"

"I don't deny there's something menacing about the place. I can see why the rumors exist, but I found nothing to justify the theory of a curse."

Unlike Mr. Tibbons, he'd sensed some hostility. What did that mean? I surveyed him carefully. He showed no signs of glamour or enchantment, but what if it ran hidden beneath the surface?

"Did you find anything of interest?" I asked.

"Some signs of recent exploration, but I believe you said a Mr. Tibbons traversed the ruins of late?"

I nodded.

"Then likely he left the traces—or someone's not telling the truth about a recent excursion there." No trace of fog clouded his features as he spoke.

It seemed Kilmere hadn't attempted to snare him. Was it because of the wards he bore, wards that the Vigil had equipped the stratesmen of Avons with when the Crimson Tattoo Killer struck? Or because Kilmere had already chosen someone to enact its plan?

Mr. Burke's gaze sharpened as though he perceived the turmoil within. "You haven't rejected the possibility of a curse, which means you found something within to support the theory. What was it?"

I couldn't offer nothing and expect him to continue to speak freely about the case, but I must have care.

"Nothing conclusive." Jade nudged at my ankle, and I picked her up, glad to have her bulk as a shield. "Only I feel there's more to Kilmere than meets the eye. Our exploration was cut short, and we left a great deal unstudied. Perhaps I'll know more after we return."

His brows lowered. "What cut short your visit?"

I buried my face in Jade's fur. "I found it more taxing than expected. It seemed better to complete the exploration another day, when I was less wearied."

"You traipsed through the Otherworld for several days on end. What did you find so fatiguing within Kilmere?"

This was becoming uncomfortably like an interrogation, and soon he'd perceive far more than I wished. "I suppose all the events of the past few days simply added up."

"I'm beginning to wonder if you spied something I missed. Something that troubled you, perhaps?"

Warmth crept up my neck toward my face. I couldn't deny it, nor could I confess it.

"In any case, I'm coming with you when you return."

"I don't think—"

"Or I could go alone. Perhaps I should spend a few days there, see if it's really as empty as they claim."

"No!" A shock tremored my frame as sharp as if he'd shoved me into the cold waters of the lake. "That is . . . I don't think it wise."

"Then we shall go together. When do you depart?"

"Tomorrow morning. But Mr. Burke, there's no need—"

"It's not up for negotiation. If Kilmere poses some threat to Withern, I can't turn a blind eye."

And he had the authority to insist—or draw in those who could. But how could I tell Riven that we'd now have a stratesman accompanying us? We'd be able to accomplish little with an audience. Perhaps, if Kilmere appeared ordinary, Mr. Burke would be persuaded all was well. Only would the ruins cooperate? Riven had said they intended to test me, and if Mr. Burke were caught up in it . . .

I wanted to shout in vexation. Yet however frustrating it might be, Mr. Burke only sought to protect the people of Withern and to carry out his sworn duty—neither of which I could condemn, but both of which could endanger me. If he perceived the Other within Kilmere and involved the Vigil . . . I clutched Jade tighter.

I would like to be able to breathe, if that's not too much trouble.

Sorry. I loosened my grip. "We plan to set forth at nine, if that's agreeable?"

"I'll be here." He turned toward me, unusually hesitant. "I apologize for being so high-handed about the matter. The situation is . . . difficult."

"I understand that you do what you feel you must." I pursued my own convictions in the same way, so I could scarcely condemn him.

In silence, we turned back toward the cottage, and a new notion presented itself. If I could only speak with the so-called poisoner, perhaps I could detect any trace of glamour or fae influence that might hang over him. "Might I talk with Mr. Ellsworth?"

He shook his head. "I don't have the same authority here as I do in Avons, but even if I did, you know a lady would never be permitted to question a murder suspect—nor an uninvolved gentleman, for that matter."

Perhaps it was for the best. Even my visiting the Magistry had been seen as scandalous. If it became known that I'd entered the bowels of a prison and spoken with a confessed murderer, the shame might taint my family's prospects forever.

"What about Riven, then? You could introduce him as one with expertise in unusual deaths." Which was unfortunately true. "Surely in a case such as this, it wouldn't seem peculiar."

"And betray every oath I've taken?" His voice dropped low. "I'll not bring a high fae into a Magistry building nor into our proceedings of justice, not by choice. Not when I've vowed to look first to the safety of Byren."

"What if he could help ensure that safety?"

"Can you swear to me he has no other agenda?"

"No, but—"

"Then the best I can do is carry inquiries on your behalf. But as I said, Ellsworth isn't talking."

Even so, it was a more generous offer than any other stratesman would have made. I adjusted Jade. "I'd like to know what he believes about the curse and which poison he claims to have used."

"The second I can tell you, provided it goes no further. He says it was spire-bane."

That *would* fit the symptoms of the afflicted, yet it wasn't as if one could toss a leaf into someone's meal without it drawing attention, nor would the raw material be as effective as a distilled compound. "Did you ask how he formulated the poison?"

"Others have, but he's kept silent. I'll ask again. In the mean-time, have a care who you speak with about Kilmere. You don't want the wrong sort to take note."

Was he warning me against the Vigil taking an interest? Or someone in Withern itself?

From our vantage, I could just catch sight of the lane. A rider approached—Mr. Redgrave. Come to call on Ainslie perhaps? When the rider secured his mount and approached the front door, I turned my attention back to Mr. Burke and found he regarded me closely.

"Is there any chance you'll tell me what you truly fear?"

"I . . ." I hesitated.

Dreda emerged onto the lawn. "Miss Jessa, your aunt wishes to see you."

"Forgive me, I'm afraid I must go."

He looked as though he stifled an oath. "Don't forget you've given your word about Kilmere."

"I won't." Even if I wished to, I could feel it binding me like a shackle. Yet how could I bring him into danger? Heart aching, I followed Dreda into the cottage.

I trailed Dreda through the back door to where my sisters and aunt waited in the sitting room. With a deft touch, Aunt Caris smoothed an errant curl from my face. "What did Mr. Burke want, my dear? When I looked out the window and saw you strolling about the lake with him, it gave me quite a turn."

"It was just a matter of unfinished business."

"Well, never mind that now, Mr. Redgrave is here, and it will do us no good if he believes us in the habit of consorting with statesmen. I had Mrs. Warren stash him in the drawing room, for there's no clear view of the lake there, you know. Now that you've safely returned, we all may receive him properly."

She herded us down the hall, and together, we entered the drawing room where Mr. Redgrave waited. The sunlight streaming through the windows brought out the gold of his hair, a similar shade to that of his sister. Whatever Aunt Caris feared, even if he'd been in full view of the lake, I didn't believe he would have taken note of Mr. Burke. Although he stood and greeted us all with impeccable manners, his warm amber-brown gaze fixed at once on Ainslie. It was clear she'd captured his attention—and for once, she didn't appear to object.

Once we were seated, he lifted a large stack of papers from a leather folio and offered it to her. "You mentioned you'd missed the Avons gazettes since starting to travel. I have them delivered here so I can keep abreast of the news, however delayed, and I thought you might enjoy doing the same."

She smiled upon him as if he'd offered the moon. And why not? It was an act that showed consideration, and also revealed he was not overly concerned with proprieties, since he'd notably included not only the society gazettes, but the political papers as well. Just what *had* they discussed at Denby Hall, that he already perceived her desires so clearly?

Though Aunt Caris's brow furrowed slightly at the unconventional gift, she voiced no objection—she must be aware that Ainslie would appreciate this far more than the more conventional bouquet of flowers. After Ainslie offered her thanks, the conversation flowed readily, and his charming manners and ready smile won Aunt Caris over entirely.

At length, he asked Ainslie if she'd care to stroll about the lake, and her acceptance came as no surprise, nor did Aunt Caris's radiant expression when they left the room. Clearly, her sentiments about their stroll couldn't be further removed from her views on my own with Mr. Burke.

"Well, my dears, he seems quite taken with Ainslie. For that reason alone, our decision to stay was a wise one," Aunt Caris said.

"Indeed." Ada offered a small smile, then moved toward the pianoforte.

Although we'd no way to know if this interest on the part of Mr. Redgrave would last, the notion of Ainslie establishing herself away from the rest of us unsettled me—even though that had been the aim of our aunts for some time, and my own, as it hastened the day I could hide away in Thornhaven.

But unless I missed my guess, Ada felt as out of kilter over the matter as I did. Certainly the songs pouring from her fingers held a tempestuous edge.

I stood. "If you've no objection, Aunt Caris, I'd like to spend some more time in the gardens before luncheon."

"That's fine, my dear. Only don't linger too long—we must be ready to call upon Lady Holloway later."

With a nod, I slipped back out to the east garden where the tiny snapdragons had sprung from the soil. I'd almost believed them a figment of my imagination, but they still flourished at the base of their parent plant. I glanced over my shoulder.

Mr. Redgrave and Ainslie had reached the far side of the lake, and the willows provided a gentle screen between us. Though I'd rather have waited for more complete isolation, this might be my only chance to make another attempt at crafting a ward before my return to Kilmere.

Nevertheless, I hesitated.

Jade wove between my ankles with a soft *mrow*, pressing me to confess. I settled onto the lawn before the bed and beckoned her onto my lap. She acceded, and her sweet-grass scent wafted about me, comforting. *I'm afraid to explore this further.*

I know.

What if it consumes me? What if I lose myself? Or hurt someone? Or become . . . something I don't wish to be?

She nuzzled my chin. *I'll watch over you. If you start to delve too deep, I'll pull you back.*

How?

I have an assortment of methods from which to choose.

I recalled how she'd sunk her claws into me when I succumbed to the glamour of the water sprites in Milburn. *Perhaps we might select the least painful first?*

An impression of laughter wafted through my mind. *I've no need to resort to more barbaric tactics, not now that I can speak to you. I shall save tooth and claw for drawing the blood of our enemies.*

Let us hope that won't be needed. But please stand watch in case anyone approaches.

With Jade's steady presence to reassure, I turned my attention to the star-of-night and gold runners, my purpose held firmly in my mind. As I touched them, glorious green-gold threads wove about the flowers, drawing power from deep within roots and leaves, forming each plant into a miniature of itself.

And I lost myself in the sensations, the gentle movements of vine and blossom as they responded to my bidding. They surged forth in strength, exalting as they became more fully themselves . . . as *I* became more fully myself.

The thrum of warmth and light through my veins enlivened every part of my body as the soft brush of leaf and twig became something else, something Other, something that shimmered in the midday sun.

With a shock, I came back into my body. In my hands rested a delicate necklace that appeared for all the world woven of gold, yet it carried the intricate details of the living plants from whence it sprang. Fierce strength pulsed from it, all the individual melodies woven into one glorious song.

How?

My stomach churned, and I pressed a palm to my middle to still the storm within.

Stop. A hint of anger echoed in my mind. *Whatever you are, you must not despise it.*

I shouldn't be able to do this—I don't even understand what I did.

And if what I held signified fae blood, did I want any part of it? What would such an inheritance entail? Would I share in their immortality? Was that what made so many of them unfeeling, the centuries upon centuries they had to become cold to the world and all the suffering it held? I shivered. If so, what did that mean for me? If I gave room to these abilities, would their power or the accumulation of years change my nature, over time? Could I eventually become as distant and detached as the fae, my heart calloused enough to use mortals simply because I could?

Locking the fears deep inside, I struggled to my feet. Like one in a dream, I moved toward the cottage, ignoring the rumble of concern emanating from Jade, along with her gentle invitation to talk. Indeed, I did my best to seal my thoughts from her.

Jade *was* Other. If I rejected the notion that I might share in that nature, would it anger her? Would it strain the bond between us?

Somehow, I must find a way to manage my fears alone—and if the blood of the fae did run through my veins, I must not surrender to its dictates.

I ascended to Dreda's bedchamber and rapped on the door. When she invited me in, I spied a simple pen-and-ink sketch on the desk. While rough, it held a great deal of charm.

"That's lovely." I crossed the room to examine it more closely. "If you'd like, I have some additional supplies you could use."

"No indeed, it's nothing." She flushed and tucked it beneath a book. "I've no knack for it, and I shouldn't have spent my time so. You don't need to try and make me feel better, not after what I did."

"What you did?" I asked.

"With Lord Riven, speaking of the fae." Her shoulders slumped. "Did I cause trouble? I shouldn't have spoken so, I don't know what came over me, only I—"

"I've smoothed over matters with Lord Riven, so there's no need to worry. Only remember in future that to speak of the fae before the wrong person could endanger us both."

"I will—I swear it." She twisted the muslin of her skirts between her fingers. "Unless you mean to ask your aunt to send me away?"

"No, of course not. Nothing could be further from my mind." Had she tormented herself with the possibility? I lifted the necklace, willing it to appear inconspicuous—an innocent gift, no more. "But I would like to ensure you're better prepared for any oddities we may encounter."

"What's this, Miss Jessa?" Her eyes widened. "Surely it's far too fine for me."

"I believe it will protect you from undue fae influence." The chain pulsed warm against my skin. "But I must be forthright and say that I cannot be entirely certain. If it makes you uncomfortable, then you shouldn't take it."

"But you think I should?"

"I want to see you safe—that is all," I said. "The choice is yours."

"Very well, then. I accept." A small smile tilted the corners of her mouth. "I've never had anything half so lovely before."

She lowered her neck and allowed me to secure the green-and-gold chain about it. When she peered into the faintly foxed mirror, her countenance lifted. "It's magnificent. And I feel . . . lighter somehow. Since we traveled up to the ruins, I'd begun to feel as though they preyed on my mind. I even dreamt—well, it's of no importance now. But thank you."

On impulse, I wrapped an arm around her shoulder. "It's I who must thank you, for your courage and your help."

Unless I was much mistaken, we'd need all the courage we could summon and then some for our return to Kilmere. But first, I must strive to appear like a lady who held no secrets, who was ordinary in every way, at least long enough to pass muster at Lady Holloway's tea. Surely I could manage for a few hours.

OUR APPROACH to the imposing Holle Castle left me less certain. The towering walls of the sprawling manor, its vast turrets, and its tall, gleaming windows all conveyed the power and status of the family it housed. Small wonder Aunt Caris had said Lady Holloway led society in the region, when she could be parted from Avons.

If only I could make it through the afternoon without

committing some social blunder, then I'd count it a success. I trailed my family toward the grand arched double doors.

A dark-suited butler extended a cool welcome, then escorted us into an immense saloon in which a refined throng of ladies and gentlemen was gathered. This event appeared far grander than the simple tea I'd expected. I stopped short on the threshold, his drone as he announced us fading into the background before the sea of unfamiliar faces.

Across the room, Lady Cadence stood holding court, Mr. Hale and several unfamiliar gentlemen clustered about her. The chamber hummed with various conversations from other groups, all finely arrayed, and Asrina's glow brightened with interest as she regarded the sparkling scene.

Lady Holloway greeted us graciously, and as soon as she moved away, Mr. Redgrave approached. "Ladies, it's a delight to see you again."

After an exchange of pleasantries, he invited us to look at the sea view, but as I followed my sisters, Mr. Hale approached with a small bow, halting my progress.

Lady Cadence's glittering eyes followed him and hardened when they landed on me. Was she so displeased to lose a single one of her suitors? Or did she still bear resentment from our exchange at Denby Hall?

Mr. Hale drew uncomfortably close, blotting Lady Cadence from view. "Miss Jessa, I've regretted since making your acquaintance that we'd no opportunity for conversation. This seems an excellent time to remedy that."

Something in the way his pale eyes swept over me left me certain I did not wish to further any sort of relationship. Yet society allowed no room for cutting an acquaintance unless one wished to cause grave offense, and he'd done nothing to justify such a response. So I forced a smile. "You're very kind."

That was all the encouragement needed. He droned on about the enchantments of Withern-at-Sea, punctuating his remarks with increasingly uncomfortable comments about my person, comparing my so-called charms to those of Withern. Perhaps some would have been flattered by the profuse compliments—but no, I refused to think any of my fellow ladies could have so little sense as to believe the insincere remarks. Every time I shifted back slightly, seeking some means of departure, he closed the distance between us once more.

Jade gave a low growl, but he took no note. *I could* make *him give you space.*

Not now. We need this visit to pass without incident.

"As it happens, the Holloways have a remarkable conservatory," he said. "Have you seen it?"

I shook my head. The last thing I wished to do was follow him to some secluded location. I searched the room for Dreda, but she stood with Ainslie and Mr. Redgrave by the tea table, while Aunt Caris and Ada were on the far side of the immense chamber.

He offered his arm. "We must remedy that at once."

Before I could manage a response, Miss Redgrave swept over to us, her brilliant blue eyes inquisitive. "Miss Jessa, I hope you'll forgive the interruption, but I've been curious about your plan to explore the ruins since we met at Denby Hall. May I steal you away to hear the details?"

"Of course." I'd have agreed to anything to end the uncomfortable interlude with Mr. Hale, and he could do nothing but graciously step aside.

Miss Redgrave twined her arm in mine and steered me toward an out-of-the-way window seat. Rich golden draperies spilled down on either side, framing a striking view of the sea.

"There now." She settled herself on the brocaded cushions and looked at me expectantly. "An ideal place for a confidential chat."

Indeed it was, for we'd see any who approached, and the sheltered niche would muffle our conversation. I sank down beside her. Asrina settled upon my shoulder, her flame-like wings casting light upon the muslin of my gown, while Jade still eyed

Mr. Hale and muttered darkly in my mind. With effort, I wrenched my attention from her to Miss Redgrave.

She leaned closer. "I hope you don't mind the interruption, but you appeared less than pleased with Mr. Hale's attentions."

"Was it that evident?"

"Not so much that you need worry about gossip. But I feel we ladies must band together. No one should be forced to accept the attentions of a gentleman, and I've observed Mr. Hale can be quite persistent."

"Thank you. I'm afraid I'm not particularly skilled at extricating myself from such situations."

"You're quite welcome." She situated herself with the air of one settling in for a long talk. "As it happens, I truly am interested in your work at Kilmere. Is it as intriguing as it sounds?"

A tingle of unease swept over my skin. "I cannot say. I've seen very little of it as yet."

At least if Riven were correct, and it stretched far underground.

"But you do mean to explore further?" she asked.

Jade leapt onto my lap, and I stroked her head. "I feel I must. Lady Dromley, who left me the ruins, desired them properly stewarded."

"It's good of you to honor her." The sunlight spilling over Miss Redgrave enhanced her rather ethereal appearance, and several gentlemen stole glances our direction, as if considering an approach. She ignored them all, her attention locked on me. "I expect it will be very rewarding. There's something altogether fascinating about the ancient, don't you think? So many questions that might be answered, if only we better understood our past."

Her interest could only lead to danger, so despite the genuine warmth in her words, I kept my answer as impersonal as possible. "I'm afraid I'm no expert in antiquities, not like Lady Dromley was, but I'll concur the past is intriguing."

"Do say you'll let me accompany you when next you go? I've

been longing to ramble about Kilmere, only everyone here is too superstitious to give a proper escort." Her eyes sparkled. "Yet the stories intrigue me greatly, and I must see it for myself."

First Mr. Burke and now Miss Redgrave? A stab of alarm pierced my chest. "Forgive me, but I cannot agree, not when there's a chance of danger."

She gave the smallest of shrugs. "If you speak of the curse, I've no concern about such things. I'm not the superstitious sort, you see. Besides, to cower away from all possible danger means one might as well be dead, don't you think?"

"Well, I . . ." I faltered. "I'd feel dreadful if anything happened. I can't even answer for the stability of the ruins themselves. If you were to get hurt—"

She waved a hand. "I assure you I'm of sturdier constitution than I appear."

What now? How could I extricate myself without administering a direct cut? To offer even the smallest slight would cause a great deal of trouble, given she and her brother were house-guests of the Holloways—not to mention that Ainslie had caught her brother's eye, and I'd not willingly ruin her prospects. I turned my gaze toward the sea. "A stratesman has agreed to examine the ruins. If he deems it safe, perhaps we might consider an excursion there in the future?"

If I was fortunate, a few days would cause her to forget the matter entirely.

But her eyes brightened till they resembled the sun-kissed waves beyond the glass. "That is excellent news indeed. With a stratesman as one of the party, our safety *must* be assured. When do you go?"

"Tomorrow morning, but I—"

"Then it's fated to be! My brother Charles intends to go hunting in the morning, and my plans were all at ends, since Lady Cadence and I don't get on overly well. This will be the very thing. What time shall I join you?"

She'd boxed me in neatly. The pressure of all the people in

the room, the warmth in the air, the noise—it tightened my chest. "We'd intended to leave at nine."

"Excellent. I'm simply delighted."

And I was anything but. Somehow, I must contrive a way to derail the expedition, for how could I take her into Kilmere?

I was distantly aware of Miss Redgrave rambling about the time she'd examined the barrows in Hartford with her brother Charles and how the epigraphs there were most remarkable. I murmured something inconsequential in response.

Whatever would I tell Riven? We needed to explore the depths of Kilmere, not take a pleasure jaunt through the treacherous grounds. Perhaps I could keep them to the outskirts of the ruin or find some excuse not to cross the boundary stones? Mr. Burke might not be readily deterred, but perhaps I could at least hold back Miss Redgrave, never mind that it would prevent our original purpose.

If I canceled the plan or denied her outright, she appeared the sort to take it in mind to go herself or with her brother later—and that would be a far greater disaster. No, I must find a way to make Kilmere appear innocuous and uninteresting, a seemingly impossible task.

"Don't you agree, Miss Caldwell?"

I snapped back to attention. "Forgive me, I missed what you said."

"I quite understand. It's difficult to hear anything when so many occupy the saloon." She gave the slightest incline of her head toward Ainslie, who stood next to Mr. Redgrave, her animation and his interest evident even across the room. "I merely observed that they look well together, which brings me to a confession. I've another motive for wanting to accompany you to Kilmere."

I tensed. What now?

"Between the two of us, I'll admit Charles is quite taken with your sister. I've never known him to give a second look to *anyone* before, no matter how much Mother desires to see him wed, but he's not stopped talking of her since we met. So it would greatly please me to get to know your family and your interests better."

Her artless confession disarmed me. I surveyed her more closely. Was that intentional? Though she might appear as delicate as a porcelain doll, I knew what it was to be underestimated on appearance alone. "I would be honored to further your acquaintance also."

The stately approach of Lady Denby cut off any possible reply. "Miss Redgrave. Miss Caldwell."

"Lady Denby." I offered a nod. "Thank you again for your hospitality upon our arrival."

"I could do no less. Will you take a turn about the room with me?" Lady Denby held her head high, her expression forbidding despite her invitation. "Your aunt says you are fond of art, and Lady Holloway has an enchanting collection of oils along the west wall."

Would that Ada or Ainslie, with their easy charms, could navigate me out of this situation. But they were not here, and I could find no escape. "Of course."

As soon as we'd stepped away from Miss Redgrave, her voice dipped. "Miss Jessa, I must beseech you, if you've any scrap of feeling in your heart, forsake your exploration of Kilmere before you cost us more lives. Was it not enough that your Mr. Tibbons reawakened the curse?"

"My lady, I'm far from without feeling. I only wish to do what's best with Kilmere—and ultimately, what's best for Withern. I'm given to understand poison caused these recent deaths, and that they've taken the killer into custody. Surely you cannot—"

"The curse influences who it desires," she muttered. "We're not safe until Kilmere is appeased."

Appeased? What did she know? I followed her along the edges of the room. "And how might it be appeased?"

"Lives, always lives, so they say." She swept past a small throng of ladies, then whirled to face me.

Did she believe that claiming lives would sate the hunger of Kilmere for a time? What knowledge or rumor did the old families of Withern hide? I lowered my voice. "Lady Denby, I—"

"No excuses. You've been warned." She drew herself upright. "It's past time for you to leave Withern."

"Yet you have not evicted us."

"Lord Denby says your contract is binding."

Then might she have tried to frighten us away, given the depth of her fears? I eased closer to her. "Perhaps you might know who has tried to drive us off? With the disturbance of the house and the hares left dead—poisoned?"

Every line of her body tensed, her fine silk gown rustling as she stiffened. "Only heed my caution and leave Kilmere alone. Perhaps the curse will be satisfied with the lives already taken, if you do not rouse it further. If you will not leave the region, then simply enjoy your holiday by the sea and let it rest."

She knew who was behind the sabotage; I felt sure of it. If only I could convince her to speak of what frightened her so.

The butler stepped back into the room and intoned over the din, "Lady Stanford, Lord Stanford."

My head snapped up. Surely not. Why would Aunt Melisina and Uncle Milton come all the way to Withern, unless . . .

The butler continued, "Lord Bradford."

Aunt Melisina moved into the doorway, as elegant and graceful as always, with Uncle Milton at her side and Lord Bradford close behind. With evident pleasure, Lady Holloway swept forward to greet Aunt Melisina—of course, the two *would* be acquainted—while I remained frozen in place.

What more could go wrong?

CHAPTER 28

Across the saloon, I met Ainslie's gaze. As one, we moved toward Ada. If Lord Bradford let it be known he'd come to Withern-at-Sea from Avons due to his interest in Ada, it would be near impossible to prevent society from linking their names and making assumptions.

Which Aunt Melisina doubtless intended.

We must give Ada an opportunity to escape, before he could make his intentions clear. I snatched a glass of sherry from a nearby table, a plan taking shape in my mind as I joined her.

At my side, Asrina watched with interest. And Jade gave a soft *mrow. I like the way you think.*

Along with Uncle Milton and Aunt Melisina, Lord Bradford bore down upon us. He opened his mouth to speak.

And I pretended to trip, upending my glass of sherry all over Ada's lovely gown. "Oh, Ada. I'm so sorry."

She clasped my arm gently. "Think nothing of it. But I'm afraid I must excuse myself to tidy up."

The slightest huff escaped Aunt Melisina, and the lines around her mouth scored deep. As this was the second untimely accident resulting in the separation of Lord Bradford and Ada, she could have no doubt of the purpose behind it. Given the scowl Lord Bradford aimed at me, it appeared he shared Aunt Melisina's suspicions. Yet it didn't matter what they thought, only how it appeared to the rest of the room.

"No need to make a fuss over it, Ada," Aunt Melisina said briskly. "Not when we've come all this way—"

"The stain will set if she doesn't attend it." Ainslie shook her head. "It will never do."

"Besides, I've a bit of a headache." No one could deny Ada appeared wan. "Perhaps it's for the best that I return to Willowere."

Lord Bradford bowed. "I'm most disappointed to miss the pleasure your company. But have no fear, I shall call tomorrow."

I wrapped my arm around Ada. "I'll accompany you. I have a tincture that will ease the pain."

I gave Ainslie a speaking glance, beseeching her to detain Aunt Melisina—if such a thing were possible. Bright and determined, she threw herself into the gap with lively chatter about the tea and the views and the guests, drawing Aunt Melisina toward a bank of windows to admire the sea.

Meanwhile, Ada and I slipped out and ensconced ourselves in the carriage. We'd have to send it back to fetch the rest of the family afterward, but for now it offered a refuge.

Once the door shut behind us, Ada slumped against the leather seat. "I thought coming here would be enough to discourage him, particularly once Father addressed the matter with Aunt Melisina, but it appears she's ignored him. And as for Lord Bradford, I cannot fathom why he's followed me here."

"It seems to me he wants you because you do not favor him, because he's been told he cannot have you." Though Lord Bradford didn't possess the Otherworldly powers of Lord West, they shared a determination to obtain their desires, and a certainty that none could defy their will.

Ada's lips quivered. "Then how can I dissuade him? I'd thought Father would manage it, once he knew his nature."

"Perhaps we'd best write to Father and inquire. In any case, we've settled it for today, and we can speak with Aunt Caris upon her return."

But no sooner had I situated Ada in her room and administered the tincture—she truly did have a headache—than a clamor arose from downstairs.

The murmur of Mrs. Warren's voice drifted upward. I'd instructed her to inform any callers Ada was indisposed.

"That's of no consequence." Aunt Melisina's strident tones rang through the house. "Fetch them at once."

Ada pressed up from her chair.

"Wait—I'll go." I started for the door. "I'm the one who angered her.'"

"But it was on my behalf. She'll be in no pleasant state, and you should not have to face her alone."

"Nor should she be given the opportunity to force you into something you don't desire."

Besides, I needed to find out if Aunt Melisina had found a way to coerce Father into condoning Lord Bradford's suit—and if she had, I must plot a way to undo it.

Mrs. Warren stalked into the room. "Begging your pardon, but there's a Lady Stanford here to see you."

I straightened. "Thank you, Mrs. Warren. I'll see her in the drawing room."

When I approached, Aunt Melisina paced with an agitation she did not usually betray. This ruffling of her composure spoke volumes. Why was she so invested in this match?

Aunt Caris had told us why she desired us well married, and yet any number of gentlemen might provide an acceptable life. Why must it be Lord Bradford?

She whirled to face me. "Where is Ada? I've come to fetch her back to the tea. She can repair herself and return to greet Lord Bradford properly."

I stopped in the doorway, a knot of brambles forming in my stomach. "She feels unwell and won't be returning to Holle Castle."

"Pish." Aunt Melisina bore down on me. "I'll fetch her back at once."

"No."

She stiffened. "What did you say?"

"She won't be returning." The knot tightened within, the thorn-prick sensation of the brambles tearing at me. If I held fast against Aunt Melisina, she might never forgive me. But she'd left me no choice.

"Who are you to deny me, child?"

"Someone concerned for the well-being of my sister." I was trembling, yet managed to force out the words. "Someone who wonders why you are not."

"How dare you?" Her face whitened, her dark eyes glossing like black haws after a rain. "I've offered her nothing but the best, provided her and Ainslie alike with endless opportunity— all the right connections, every chance to secure their futures."

"But why must it be Lord Bradford?"

"Why not Lord Bradford?" She rapped the tip of her parasol against the floor. "Thanks to Alden's permissive ways, she's already discouraged several excellent candidates before him. If she continues in this vein, she may well miss her opportunity to wed altogether. She's not getting any younger."

"Yet his character is deplorable, and Ada doesn't wish to marry him. That should be reason enough to eliminate him as a prospect." As cutting as Aunt Melisina could be at times, I'd always believed she meant well. Why would she want to trap Ada into this? "Did you tell him she'd agree? Is he pressuring you in some way?"

Her breath caught, just the slightest hitch. There *was* something more. But rather than offer a confession, she gripped her parasol more tightly, jabbed it in my direction. "I'm shocked at you, throwing accusations in such an unbecoming manner. You've become unruly enough to ruin your sisters' prospects along with your own. I'd wanted to spare your father the heartache that must come from learning the truth—learning why he must rein in his daughters. But I shall hold my peace no longer, not when the ruin of our family might be at hand."

The brambles pierced all the way to my heart. Could she possibly know there was something Other about me? Would she truly shatter our family with the knowledge? Or did she refer to something else?

If I cowered beneath the threat, she'd only press her advantage. So I locked the pain deep within and held her gaze. "I would like to know what he's said about Lord Bradford. He doesn't approve of gentlemen sowing their wild oats."

"You shouldn't even know of such things, much less discuss them." Her hand twitched as though she might slap me, but when Jade leapt upon the table and glared at her, she stepped back. "Keep that creature away from me."

I ignored her. "Does Father know you've brought Lord Bradford here? That you continue to encourage a match between him and Ada?"

"Alden gave me permission to seek a suitable match for the three of you a long time ago. And I spoke to him before I left." She waved her gloved hand. "A bit of unfortunate gossip about Lord Bradford is easily explained away—and I have done so."

So she'd deceived Father? I lifted my chin. "Evidence of misdeeds is not so easily excused—and if needed, I'll search until I've found enough to make his character clear."

"If you insist on interfering, I will see you're sent back to Caldwell House and kept there," she snapped. "By the Crossings, your missteps since arriving in Avons have been egregious enough. And I shall make Alden see it."

"Do what you feel you must." Even the pulse of Asrina's light could not warm me. "I shall do the same."

"You're far too much like your mother," she hissed. "Have a care, or you'll share her fate."

I stumbled back, her words conjuring a vivid image of Mother's body sprawled lifeless on the dark stones near the fountain. My eyes stung. "What do you know of her death?"

"I know she was every bit as reckless and headstrong as you are—and such misconduct comes to no good end. It only brings heartache and suffering to all concerned."

In a flurry of rustling silk, Aunt Melisina swept past me and out the front door. I collapsed on the settee, shaking like a leaf in a summer storm. What did she know of Mother? Of me? Had she guessed that I might not be my father's child?

If she spoke of it . . . My throat closed around a sob. No, I couldn't consider it.

Jade nuzzled my arm. *I could bite out her tongue for you, however unsavory it might be.*

Oh, Jade. I let out a shaky breath. *What am I to do?*

Tackle one problem at a time. Unless you want me to go after her.

Indeed not. If she saw Jade's true-form, it would remove any doubt of my taint. But Jade's other suggestion held more merit. I needed to attend to what I could control, one problem at a time.

So I snatched up a pen and scribbled off a missive to Lovell. If Lord Bradford had some hold over Aunt Melisina, then he might put his investigative instincts to work and help us uncover it.

But would it matter, in the end? If Aunt Melisina followed through on her threat, she could shatter my world.

THAT NIGHT troubled dreams plagued my sleep, and I woke to a pillow damp with tears. Jade rested on my chest, her soft purr soothing, as I pressed back the dark remnants, jumbled memories of Mother, hateful slurs from Aunt Melisina, and bristling menace from Kilmere, always and ever Kilmere, lurking in the background.

I couldn't afford distraction, not when Riven, Mr. Burke, and Miss Redgrave would descend on Willowere in just a few hours, so I thrust aside the bedcovers and hurriedly dressed.

Rather than attempting to participate in light conversation over breakfast, I'd take refuge in the gardens and try to formulate a plan to protect Mr. Burke and Miss Redgrave.

Jade twisted onto her back, taking advantage of the spot of warmth I'd left. *Why do you rush so?*

I thought perhaps we could walk the gardens while we wait. I seized upon a new idea. *We've never properly examined them for traces of who might have committed the sabotage.*

She stretched and yawned. *Why not wait for Riven? He could conduct such a search far more effectively.*

Riven may not always be here to help. I must learn to manage on my own.

Jade chuffed, a sound of exasperation, if the sentiment tinging my mind was anything to go on. *I suppose you're not simply fleeing from your own emotions?*

Perhaps I am. Will you come anyway?

Where you go, I go. You know that. She trailed me down the stairs, and we tiptoed across the entry.

Through the windows, the rising sun cast a deep red flare over the bank of clouds to the west, toward the sea. Toward Kilmere.

I grasped the door latch.

Jade's nose twitched. *Wait.*

What?

I smell death. Her green eyes kindled with uncanny light, and she leapt upon the windowsill, tilting her head to examine the front steps through the glass.

Is there danger?

No longer, but what remains is not pleasant.

Steeling myself, I wrenched open the door. Across the steps splashed a scarlet spatter of blood and the twisted form of some smallish animal. Perhaps a fox?

Yes.

The word held an undercurrent of anger. Should the hapless individual responsible have lingered, I'd no doubt she'd find it difficult to maintain lesser-form. Clearly, this was another warning, meant to provoke our departure.

Jade prowled around the dead body, sniffing the trail of blood that led to our door, then she ranged farther afield.

Can you tell who left it, Jade?

She perched beneath a tall elm. *Many have passed here over the past weeks. I cannot trace with certainty the one who brought the fox.*

I crept past the gruesome form, considering what I knew of the matter. *At Holle Castle yesterday, Lady Denby attempted to warn me away from Kilmere. Perhaps my refusal prompted her to act? Though I can't imagine she'd do this herself.*

She has sons. And servants. Yet without evidence, we cannot stop whoever is responsible. She gave a pointed look toward the shrubs near the door. *Evidence you might obtain from the witnesses.*

I hesitated, then moved toward the pearlflowers. I trailed my fingers across those nearest the door, their willowy branches and white blossoms swaying gently toward me. Yet though they curved round my hands, eager and sprightly, they offered only snips and snatches, bits of indistinct conversation borne on the wind, swirls of fragrance, blurs of color.

I let my hand fall to my side. Perhaps the lack of a consuming vision should be welcome—only I needed to understand what had happened if I didn't want the sabotage to escalate.

Had I lost the ability to connect? Or was it merely that the flighty blossoms didn't attend closely enough to the world around them to convey their impressions? The tiniest of Otherworldly plants had spoken reams to me, but they'd carried the essence of Other within. In Milburn, to receive similar clarity, I'd needed to touch a linden—one old and well-established.

Perhaps the elm near Jade would do? I marched toward it, my purpose fixed firmly at the front of my mind, and skimmed my fingers across its craggy bark. A veritable flood of images ensued . . . there. I seized the one I sought.

A figure crept up the lane, dimly lit by moonlight and fully cloaked, a limp, bloody fox in hand. Certainly not Lady Denby, nor any other woman—it was far too tall and stocky.

Drops of blood spattered on the stones behind him; the hood of his cloak concealed his face. In the dim light, he tripped over a root and muttered an oath.

Then he approached the doorstep and deposited his gruesome bundle. When he turned to leave, the slanting beams of the moon fell across his face.

It was Lord Denby.

I snatched back my hand. Unlike his wife, Lord Denby had appeared so affable and welcoming. If he wished us gone, why hadn't he just refused us lodging? He must not have known our purpose until it was too late, and a gentleman never went back on his word. If he'd turned away a group of ladies at his doorstep, it would have blackened his name and his hospitality. But if we chose to leave, with none aware of his involvement, his reputation remained intact—it was a working of the curse, no more.

I turned to regard the bloodstained doorstep. If the smoke rising from the kitchen chimney was any indication, we'd lingered long enough that the servants stirred within the house. Which meant if I didn't act quickly, someone would discover the gruesome carcass and report it to Aunt Caris.

I walked back toward it, then hesitated. Somehow I couldn't bring myself to touch the broken form, a sacrifice made to force me to act.

Keep watch, and I'll remove it.

In a blink, Jade shifted to true-form, more magnificent even than memory suggested. The sun drew forth shimmering shades of indigo from the deep black of her coat, and her starflower gleamed. Before I could catch my breath, she snatched up the fox and vanished into the trees.

When she returned, a cat once more, I asked, *What did you do with it?*

Buried it beyond the wood line.

I thought perhaps you meant to eat it.

The fur at her ruff bristled. *I hunt for my food or receive that prepared and offered in my honor. I do not devour carrion nor the sacrifice of the dishonorable.*

I hastened to soothe her. *Of course not. I meant no slight.*

Her fur settled. I fetched a bucket of water from the well, then sloshed it over the steps to carry away the remaining blood. What now? At this early hour, I'd never gain admittance to Denby Hall, but I'd have to call on Lord Denby if I wanted this to stop—and stop it must, if we were to remain in Withern.

I returned the bucket to the hook on the side of the well, a charmingly rustic affair that one would never see in Avons. Yet for all the beauty of Withern, it hid a deep darkness. How much did the Denbys know? If I must confront Lord Denby about the sabotage, then I'd press him on his understanding of Kilmere as well. Only I must have a care in how I managed it.

The sharp cry of a gull resounded, and I jumped. I'd best move on before someone took note. I climbed the steps, the sun warming my neck. It would soon dry the stone, and no one would—

Mrs. Warren opened the door, with the air of one braced for unpleasantness. Had she known? Was she preparing to sound the alarm?

She startled, clutching her apron to her chest. "Miss Jessa! You gave me a tremendous fright. What's brought you out at this early hour?"

"I enjoy mornings outdoors—it's a quiet, peaceful time to explore."

"Aye, well it can also be unchancy." Her gaze lingered on the damp doorstep. "I trust there's naught amiss?"

"Nothing that can't be managed."

She shifted, straightening her apron. "Well, no sense dawdling out of doors, however fine the morning. Come along, and I'll see what Cook has prepared to break the fast."

At home, the servants placed a buffet in the dining room, where it remained between eight and ten in the morning. Since our arrival, the cook had done the same—but clearly, Mrs. Warren wished me out of the way. Perhaps she did know and thought Lord Denby hadn't had time yet to carry out his plan; perhaps she wanted to allow him an opportunity. Regardless, she appeared to have no intention of allowing me to explore the grounds.

I joined her in the entry, a sea breeze swirling through the open door to tug at our skirts. "Mrs. Warren, the curse concerns you a great deal. Will you tell me why?"

She took a half step back. "It's not my place to say, miss."

"Yet you took it upon yourself to caution us against it when we arrived. Won't you tell me why?"

She scowled. "Those of us who've been here since the beginning, we know to be wary."

"Do you mean your family has resided in this region since the founding of Withern?"

"Since its prospering, aye."

A sudden improvement of prospects suggested some sort of fae involvement. "Tell me about this prospering. When did it take place?"

"When they broke ground at Kilmere. When our fate became tied up with it." She shut the door with greater force than necessary, cutting off the pleasant breeze. "If you keep meddling with it, you'll destroy more than you know."

"How did Kilmere bring prosperity?"

"'Twasn't Kilmere, but the lady of the lord who built it. She brought in the sea-blossoms, which drew the bees. We couldn't keep hives enough to supply the demand for the honey, not even with the princely sums charged for it."

Sea-blossom honey—I'd heard of it, of course, but it was exceedingly pricey, treasured not only for its remarkable flavor but also its restorative properties. And Mrs. Warren claimed the lady who'd requested the construction of Kilmere had also brought in the sea-blossoms. Might she have been influenced by fae? Or had she been fae herself? If fae men could beguile mortal women into marriage, as Edward had done Ibbie, surely a fae lady could do the same to a mortal man, if it suited her purpose. Only . . . what had it been? According to lore, she'd died inexplicably at Kilmere. If she was fae, that made little sense.

Mrs. Warren cleared her throat, drawing me back to myself. "Forgive me. I was just wondering . . . Did your family live here when this prospering took place?"

"Not just then. We came soon after, brought in to help tend the hives. We've stayed ever since, serving in the grand houses long enough to see and know what happens to those who bring down the wrath of the curse." She folded her arms across her chest. "Mayhap you think there's no danger to yourself, since the curse only falls upon the old families—but I know what my great-granda told me, and his before him, and his before him, on back through the years. He always said Kilmere has fangs and strikes those it wishes."

"I see." My stomach dropped as though I trod the cliff's edge of Kilmere once more. Was the reference to its fangs a reference to the strike of the basilisk? Or use of its venom?

"Then you'll let Kilmere alone?"

"I can't do that." Because whatever evil existed within had already wakened.

"Then you will be responsible for every death to come." Her back stiff, she marched away.

CHAPTER 29

After breaking the fast, I sent Asrina to ask Riven if he'd come early to the gardens. I made sure to impress on her she must convey no imminent danger, only a matter in need of discussion. However much I dreaded the confession I must make, if he arrived at the same time as Miss Redgrave and Mr. Burke, the outcome might well be disastrous.

By the shore of the lake, I waited to unfold the plan I'd woven over the breakfast table, one I thought Riven unlikely to accept. I'd simply have to persuade him.

At half past eight, the scent of sun and storm heralded Riven's arrival. Without ceremony, he demanded, "What happened?"

After a deep breath, I plunged into a hurried account of Mr. Burke and Miss Redgrave and our altered plans, the storm-charged sensation building about me until I faltered to a stop.

"You mean to tell me you agreed to bring two mortals into a possible death trap simply to avoid hurting their feelings?" His voice emerged deceptively calm.

"There was more to it than that. I—"

"It doesn't matter." The glamour about us sparked a deeper hue of gold. "They cannot come."

"But they'll be arriving shortly."

"And I'll ensure they leave, since you failed to do so."

The remark stung. "You mean to glamour them."

"Little choice remains, since, as you said, you've already agreed they may come. They must be deterred another way," he said flatly.

"And you'd risk the soundness of their minds?" I turned away from him, pacing the shore within the confines of his glamour. "You were not present to witness their determination—they'll not be easily dissuaded. What if they shake off the effects of the glamour and choose to return on their own?"

"I will impress upon them otherwise." His words held the slightest growl.

As best as I could tell, the stronger the glamour imposed, the greater the risk of harming mortal minds. How much force would be required not only to deter them now, but to prevent any future interest in Kilmere? Yes, I desired their physical safety, but what good would that do if the glamour left them shattered or suffering the symptoms of fae-touch? Not to mention it would violate their wills, something Mr. Burke at least would not be swift to forgive.

I halted before Riven. "Mr. Burke already knows a great deal, and he wears wards provided by the Vigil. Unless I'm much mistaken, unlike ward-stones, those do provide some measure of protection against glamour, which means you'll have to use greater force."

"You're not mistaken."

"And you still believe this the best course, despite the risks?"

He closed the distance between us, his eyes darkening. "Have you already forgotten what Kilmere can do?"

In such proximity, his power swirled about me, muddling my thoughts. "I've forgotten nothing—and I know there's no good path forward. I merely seek the one least likely to cause harm."

"I'm listening."

So he said, as he stood with his arms crossed over his formidable chest, light coiling about him. A less approachable audience would be hard to find. I straightened. "As far as we know, Kilmere hasn't used force against other mortals, only beguiled them into doing its bidding. It wants to test me, but it has no need to strike at them. If I were to slip and twist my ankle at its walls and require a rest, perhaps you could escort Miss Redgrave and Mr. Burke on a swift tour to satisfy their curiosity. If they're convinced it holds nothing of particular interest, I hope they'll not seek to return. And since you'll be present, you can take note if Kilmere seeks to influence them."

And prevent it, I hoped.

"It could work—but the less time they spend in Kilmere, the better." His arms dropped to his sides. "All it would take is prodding at one of the workings to provoke a tremor, which would make the ruins appear unstable. Then I could encourage them to turn back. It's a risk, but I'll grant glamouring them holds one as well."

I released the breath I'd held. It wasn't a perfect solution—far from it—but at least it didn't involve tampering with their minds. Before I could check myself, I said, "Thank you."

His jaw tightened. "No thanks required."

Why were fae so prickly against the simplest of courtesies?

Because thanks admits a debt owed. Jade wove between my ankles. *For my part, I'd prefer you not offer them to Otherkind either.*

Even you?

Naturally, you may thank me—*I'll not try to come back later to collect any debts you incur.*

"Even if we manage to present them an ordinary ruin, we can ill afford this waste of time," Riven said. "There was no trace of venom in the springs or waterways of the region, which means someone brought it to the intended victims deliberately."

"I've drawn the same conclusion. Mr. Burke told me that

Mr. Ellsworth—the man they've taken into custody—confessed to the poisonings."

"Did he?" He inclined his head, a curt gesture. "Then that makes him of interest. It's past time I talked to him."

"They're allowing no visitors. I inquired of Mr. Burke."

"They'll allow me."

One look at his face assured me he'd not be dissuaded—and I must admit, we needed the information. But if Mr. Burke ever found out . . .

Riven glanced through the trees. "Your other guests approach. I suggest you fetch your chaperone so we can convene properly."

I nodded. "Aunt Caris has already given permission for us to take the carriage."

Less than a quarter hour—and several stilted introductions —later, we entered the carriage and took the road toward Kilmere. We'd leave our conveyance at the bottom of the cliff, from which we'd ascend to Kilmere on foot.

Dark clouds still clustered on the horizon, and the air alternately churned with gusts driven from the sea and fell into fretful stillness, as uneasy as my own soul. If I'd made a mistake in swaying Riven, if my plan failed to keep our companions safe, what then? Mrs. Warren's words of condemnation still played themselves in my mind, an echo that drew pain each time it returned.

Yet mortal will was stronger than fae imagined, and in the end, I believed Mr. Burke and Miss Redgrave would have sought their answers, unless Riven left them utterly broken. Better that their exploration of Kilmere happen when we could attempt to control it than when they were alone and vulnerable.

After Riven secured the carriage, we set off on foot along the rocky, ever-twisting path. A black feather drifted down from the treetops and settled on a bush before me, its form stark against the pale green leaves and pink blossoms of the creeping folia, a warning to turn back.

Yet we forged on, as we must.

Miss Redgrave fell in beside me and Dreda, leaving Riven and Mr. Burke to forge the path ahead in silence. Riven had reluctantly conceded to my plan, but both he and Mr. Burke had radiated disapproval upon the arrival of Miss Redgrave, though they could not voice their objections in front of her. Given the tense lines of their backs and the utter silence between them, they weren't best pleased by the company of each other, either.

In fact, the only one in good spirits was Miss Redgrave. "Isn't this simply delightful! A glorious morning, an enchanting seaside lane, and the prospect of an ancient ruin ahead. I can think of nothing more charming."

I eyed the winding path, the craggy rocks, and above it all, the stark outline of Kilmere, black against a darkening sky—it bespoke enchantment, but in all the wrong ways. A dead tree limb snagged my skirts, and I tugged it loose.

"Does something concern you, Miss Caldwell? You're very quiet this morning," she said.

"Forgive me. I passed an uneasy night, and I suppose I'm a bit weary."

She looped her arm through mine. "I'm sorry to hear it. My aunt swears by valerian for unsettled sleep, though the stench is rather unbearable."

Alongside us, Dreda remained grave, and her hand stole to her necklace, as if to assure herself it remained.

Miss Redgrave glanced at it. "Miss Twells, that's a lovely chain. The craftsmanship is quite remarkable."

"Thank you, miss." Her voice emerged low. "It was a gift."

"From an admirer?"

"Oh, no. Miss Jessa—" She cut off, then appeared to realize that would be more awkward and hurried on. "Miss Jessa gave it to me. She's been most kind."

"How very thoughtful of you, Miss Caldwell." Miss

Redgrave offered a bright smile. "I should like one myself. Where did you purchase it?"

Riven half-turned, and with the sun outlining his form, even his glamour only narrowly concealed his fae beauty. "What about the ruins appeals to you, Miss Redgrave?"

I breathed silent thanks for his intervention.

"I suppose it's the opportunity to uncover hidden secrets—such a thrilling thought."

"Not all secrets are of the pleasant variety."

"True, but that makes them all the more interesting, don't you think?"

He lifted a shoulder, then turned back toward Kilmere. And the wind picked up, raising the flesh on my arms.

"I must say, I don't find it fair for a man to be quite so attractive as Lord Riven." Miss Redgrave leaned in, her tone confidential. "Is there an attachment between you?"

"Not of that nature."

"What a shame. You look quite well together." She continued to make light conversation as we ascended, and true to her word, the climb did not leave her breathless, nor did she utter a complaint.

At last, we reached the top, and the shadow of Kilmere fell over us. Just before the boundary wall, an unsteady collection of rocks offered a promising spot for a fall. Above it, in the boughs of a tall fir, a raven sat upon her nest, her presence a plausible excuse for a detour in that direction.

I started off the path.

"Miss Caldwell, did you expect other visitors to the ruin?" Mr. Burke asked.

I turned to regard him. "No, it's my understanding the townsfolk stay clear of it. Why do you ask?"

"Because there's something—someone there." With sudden determination, he surged toward the wall. "They seem to be in distress."

"Wait." Riven moved toward Mr. Burke, but he'd already crossed beyond the boundary. Riven followed close on his heels —and they both vanished.

I froze.

Dreda gasped.

And Miss Redgrave's lips pressed into a tight line. "It would appear the rumors were not mere superstition."

No—it made no sense. Kilmere shouldn't have sought Mr. Burke. He'd already been and gone once in safety. Why snatch him now? My breath came quick, unsteady.

"I suppose we must . . . go after them?" For the first time since I'd met her, Miss Redgrave appeared unsure.

With Kilmere so roused, I could think of nothing more dangerous. I hastened toward her and Dreda. "Lord Riven and Mr. Burke are accustomed to navigating difficult situations—"

A keening howl pierced the air; another followed, equally chilling.

Dreda clutched at my arm, her fingers digging deep. "Miss Jessa? What's that?"

Jade's fur bristled. *Fang-wolves. Nothing else gives such a dire cry.*

Fang-wolves. It cannot be, not here.

Both Miss Redgrave and Dreda looked expectantly at me. "I believe . . . some sort of wolf."

"I'd not known wolves frequented these parts." Miss Redgrave gripped her parasol. "If you're right, then we should certainly move into the ruin. Better some rumored curse than death by mauling."

Yet I remained rooted in place. We might well stand a better chance against fang-wolves than Kilmere. Could we ascend the trees?

They're too canny for such tricks. They will come after you. And they've cut off our only line of descent. We cannot hope to make a stand here. We must enter Kilmere.

Even as Jade spoke, tremendous beasts poured over the crest

of the ridge, their shoulders nearly of a height with my own, keen intelligence sparking in the depths of their pale eyes. Thick silver-black fur bristled from their enormous heads, and their bared fangs gleamed stark against it as they snarled. Any one of them could fell the lot of us.

"Fang-wolves. This is indeed unfortunate." Miss Redgrave's voice wavered.

Dreda's fingers dug deeper into my arm. And Jade's shadow grew.

You cannot shift. I won't be able to explain—

Do you want to die?

Of course not, but I don't want you to risk your life either.

Let me draw some of them off. Enter Kilmere. Take to the high ground, the shelter of the central tower. Stone will hold better against their claws than wood.

No, Jade. If something happens—

Her green eyes kindled with inner fire. *Let me do this.*

Very well. But swear to me you'll return.

If it lies in my power.

My eyes burned, yet I attended to the others. "If we run, they will surely give chase. But if we back away slowly, perhaps we will attract less interest."

"I concur," Miss Redgrave said. "They've not moved to attack as yet. We may stand a chance, if we remove ourselves with care."

Indeed, the fang-wolves clustered in the clearing beyond us as if they awaited some signal. We edged over the wall.

The cold fury of Kilmere poured over me, mocking my weakness, my folly. Above the crash of the surf and the thrum of the pulse in my ears resounded the clamor of the wolves. I clutched at the wall, and the stone bit into my fingers. Around us, hostile air churned, before us, fury and hunger surged.

Miss Redgrave snapped a lever on the handle of her parasol, and it separated into two pieces, one of them a long dagger. Of all the unexpected turns. Well, at least one of us had a weapon.

"My brother is very keen on ladies protecting themselves," she said softly, as if to explain the peculiarity. "For all the good it's likely to do."

We continued our slow flight, and the strengthening wind ripped my hair from its confines, scudded darkening clouds across the sky.

They only await their alpha to strike. I scent his approach. It's time to run.

I snatched at Dreda and Miss Redgrave. "Make for the central tower, it's best protected. Go now!"

Even as we turned, the pack lunged forward. Jade snarled, then dashed toward them, holding lesser-form until she vanished in their midst, then springing into true-form like a creature materialized from mists. She met the fang-wolves in a clash of tooth and claw, their growls thundering through the air.

Though we ran, those who detached themselves from Jade came fast on our heels.

Miss Redgrave stumbled. "We won't make it to the keep, not before them."

She was right. The watchtower. I spun round, pulling Dreda up crumbled stairs onto a wide platform, presumably the floor of some long-vanished room. Miss Redgrave followed close behind, Asrina hovering at my shoulder.

Where was Riven?

The fang-wolves lunged up, snapping and scrabbling at the edges, their unnatural claws slicing through stone.

Dreda huddled against the back wall, but Miss Redgrave surged forward to stab one in the eye. It fell, crashing into several of its companions. She teetered perilously close to the edge, and I snatched her back.

The stairs. In only a moment, they'd find them, they'd claim us. Perspiration slicked my skin. Never mind the risks—I must act. As Miss Redgrave lashed out at the muzzle of another, I snatched at a young pine that swayed against the stone wall. Its vibrant strength coursed green and swift through my frame, burning as it went.

And a teeming mass of roots surged to the surface, snatching at the wolves, snaring them, binding them to the stone. Yet such was their strength that some tore through the bonds, heedless of the gashes rent into their flesh.

More fang-wolves surged from beyond the boundary wall. Jade tore through them, and all round her, their bodies crumpled, broken and unmoving.

Yet she could not defeat this many alone. Riven was gone, Mr. Burke also. And I must protect those in my charge. I sank deeper into the sensation of the pine, and a vast net of roots filled my vision, stretching far belowground, not only those of the pine, but all those twined with it.

As I urged them, they lashed their way to the surface, breaking stone, blocking the stairway with a tremendous coil of thick strands. I sank to my knees, my vision graying at the edges, the tangle of roots consuming me.

Their melodies came fierce and fast and furious, drumming of war in my ears, rending, tearing, seeking to break the bodies of the beasts . . .

My surroundings turned black, and tumult burned within, such a searing heat that every other sensation faded away before it.

Release the pine!

The song faltered before the strength of the command. No, I couldn't stop, if I did . . .

Jessa—you must.

Jade. She'd promised to warn me if I sank too deep, but . . .

KEL'S TEETH. DROP IT NOW!

Such was the force of her shout in my mind that my hands flew involuntarily to my head. I staggered back against the crumbling wall. The roots fell. The wolves surged forward.

I had to try again. Yet I couldn't move; my strength was spent. I vomited onto the stone.

And the entire cliff quaked and shuddered, rocks tumbling from the wall alongside us, the sharp scent of sun and storm flaring into the air. The wolves tumbled back.

Riven.

Whatever the danger of shattering the working that had snared him and Mr. Burke, he'd risked it. Or perhaps Kilmere wanted him here . . . wanted to force us all deeper into its snare.

If he used his affinities to drive away the fang-wolves, he'd reveal himself as fae. And stripping those memories from the others would be no mere trifle.

My head throbbed. But I . . . what had I done? Far worse— I'd exposed myself, revealed too much. Had they noticed?

It appeared not. Dreda's eyes were firmly clenched shut as she shrank against the rocks, and Miss Redgrave, positioned on the far side of the platform, attended only to the fang-wolves, lashing out at any who leapt toward the ledge. Yet it would not matter either way if we could not break free.

Sweat soaked my bodice, the harsh wind slicing through the damp, chilling me to the core. The last of the roots fell before the assault of the wolves, but Jade charged forward, holding the steps against their onslaught.

The stench of blood rose thick and choking, the musk from the fang-wolves' coats mingling with it till I could hardly breathe. Mr. Burke and Riven appeared, fighting their way through the clustered beasts.

Dreda buried her head in her hands; Miss Redgrave staggered back against the far wall, her dagger clutched tight. "Will they reach us in time?"

Could they, if Riven did not reveal himself as high fae? He was constraining himself to mortal abilities, holding himself to a pace that matched Mr. Burke's as they carved their way through the throng of wolves, opening a path toward us.

More wolves poured from the path into the ruins. How long could he reasonably restrain himself? Wolf howls swirled around us, and a fog settled over Kilmere, as though the dark clouds above descended into our midst.

Asrina burned like a beacon at my shoulder. "Bad, bad, bad, bad."

Her pulsing murmur pressed into my senses. Then, through the haze, Riven appeared at the base of the stairs. He wheeled round to slice through the neck of a wolf behind him, and the blood spattered his shirt. "To the tower."

"But that beast—" Miss Redgrave pointed to where Jade had stood in our defense, but she was gone, vanished into the mist.

At least she'd not recognized Jade in true-form. I tried to rise, but collapsed. Dreda snatched me up, her sturdy form supporting mine this time. We stumbled down the stairs, Riven and Mr. Burke plying their blades in defense.

And oh, Riven was using darting coils of light to bind and bewilder, so subtly coated in glamour that I'd almost missed them. The fang-wolves faltered, cowering before them.

In lesser-form, Jade materialized at my side as we fled into the central keep, where the walls still towered several stories high. Oh I hurt, every part of my being. I stumbled over a rock, collapsed to my knees.

A sudden, exultant shiver went through the stones, and then the earth gaped before us. With no purchase, we tumbled down into a deep chasm, hitting the bottom with painful force—and then the slab of stone that had drawn back closed over us once more. I struggled to regain the breath knocked from me by the fall, every muscle throbbing.

What now? I clutched at Jade, and Dreda buried her head in my shoulder. For a moment, we simply huddled together, shivering. We'd plunged into a frigid underground realm.

Then a faint crunching sounded at my left. A glow flared, and I flinched. Had Riven chosen to risk fae-light? Did he plan to strip them of their memories?

Jade nudged at my arm. *You should be more concerned with our survival.*

I couldn't argue, couldn't even properly order my own thoughts. Kilmere had laid a trap, and I'd tumbled right into it. It wouldn't let us go, not now, not ever, not unless I could force it, not unless I proved myself—how? I buried my face in the warmth of Jade's fur.

And Riven stepped back, revealing he'd only lit some sort of device on the wall. Its blue light played across the polished stone of an underground chamber. Kilmere had deposited us in a wide oval space that narrowed and stretched into full darkness on either end.

"Is everyone unharmed?" A dark bruise shadowed Mr. Burke's forehead, and his features were grim in the wavering light. "We must be sure no one was bitten."

Miss Redgrave limped to my side, her face very pale in the flickering light. "No bites here, Mr. Burke."

I considered asking if she still thought the curse a superstition, but that would hardly help our situation. Instead, I turned to Dreda.

She shook her head. "Nor here."

Still, she had a cut along her forehead from where she'd fallen against the stone. I offered her a handkerchief, and she pressed it against the gash.

All of this—their injuries, our danger—was my fault. If I'd kept to myself, as I'd known I should, if I hadn't asked Mr. Burke for help, if I'd endured the company of Mr. Hale rather than accepting the escape offered by Miss Redgrave, then neither one of them would have come—nor would Dreda. There would have been no need to choose between risking their minds by glamour or their lives at Kilmere. By virtue of the Other that snared me, I'd endangered them. I should have found a way to keep them from Kilmere, to come alone . . .

I couldn't stop shivering. Something warm and wet dripped on my hand. Jade. I examined her. A jagged tear in her side seeped blood.

I tensed. *Is it . . . a bite?*

Don't worry. Their bites don't infect Otherkind as they do mortals. I won't be long in healing. Still, an undercurrent of pain seeped from her mind into my own. *We were fortunate to come off so little scathed.*

Yet if we couldn't escape Kilmere, then our efforts with the fang-wolves mattered little. I clutched Jade close, careful not to tug at her wound. I'd allowed them to come, and now I must find a way out.

Riven strode back to the group. "This chamber offers no ready passage out. There's a long crevasse on the far end, but it's far too narrow to allow even the smallest of us to pass."

Dreda inhaled sharply, and even Miss Redgrave pressed her fingers to her lips.

Now wasn't the time to indulge in emotion—I must think. I looked toward the ceiling, which towered far above us in the darkness. "Could we climb back and somehow force our way through?"

"Kilmere wants us here. It has sealed us within," Riven said calmly. "It will offer no easy escape."

Indeed, the air had become close, almost stifling. The tang of something metallic, like fear and old blood, tainted my tongue.

And from the darkness to the right came a quiet trickle, the sound of . . . rushing water? The crevasse . . . surely it wasn't meant to usher in a flood? I stifled an absurd urge to laugh.

Of course it was. All of Kilmere was a death trap; why should this be an exception? An incoming tide swirled around my ankles, dark and cold.

Mr. Burke cursed softly. "We cannot simply remain, waiting for death."

Jade pawed at my hem, and I snatched her up. Death trap or not, I was of no mind to surrender. If Kilmere thought it could claim Jade and Asrina and all those I cared for . . . I would not tolerate it. Wearily, I staggered to my feet.

Riven gave a slight nod, and gold flared in his eyes. "I agree. There's still one possibility. This way."

He led us through the treacherous current of water to the far end of the chamber, then kindled another light mounted to the wall. What did he see?

Oh.

When I focused, it became clear. Etched into stone was the outline of an arched door—a rampant dragon across its surface. Yet no seam broke the rock. I bent to examine it more closely. Could it be an actual door, without joint or knob or hinge?

"I don't understand," Miss Redgrave said.

"This offers the only path out. Yet it's locked, and it cannot be forced by just anyone." Riven turned to me. "It puts me in mind of the door you opened in Wyncourt, Miss Caldwell. I suggest you do now as you did then."

I stripped off my stained gloves and traced the door with my fingers, but only cold, unyielding stone met my touch—no knob, no point of access whatsoever, no prick of blood to confirm ownership, only the same bone-chilling enmity with which Kilmere assaulted me at every turn, a hostility as marked as the favor Wyncourt offered.

And something else.

A sharp pain stabbed my temples, along with the faintest snatch of an anguished cry. I wrenched my hand away. "I fear it's not as simple."

Unruffled, Riven angled his body to block me from view of the others. How was he so calm? "No, it's not. Yet I have no doubt you're capable."

Miss Redgrave trudged toward me, eyeing the rising waters. "If you have some expertise in lock-picking, Miss Caldwell, do exercise it. I'm the last to cast stones—particularly in such a trying circumstance."

The echo of agony still resounded in my ears. What had I heard? What would Kilmere do to me if I persisted? Never mind that, I must find a way. Only with all of them looking on . . .

"Burke, will you take the ladies to seek any avenue of escape I may have missed?" Riven asked. Perhaps he sought to give me a moment to connect to whatever Other abilities I possessed, a notion which frightened me almost as much as the rising of the dark waters.

Despite his evident fatigue, Mr. Burke shot a sharp glance at Riven, doubtless aware that he'd not missed anything. Yet he did not object.

"Come, ladies." He offered them each an arm, as if they strolled a ballroom rather than a rapidly flooding cavern. "Let's see what we might uncover."

I bent my attention to the door once again. My vision swam—Kilmere meant to snatch it, leaving me vulnerable and bewildered. Already it blackened at the edges. My weary legs trembled against the assault of the cold waters, and I drew Jade closer. "Is this truly the only way? Can't you create a passing?"

"You forget this was designed against fae more than mortals—it's warded against such things, quite heavily." The light flickered across the chiseled planes of his face. "To create a passing, I must first undo all the workings woven into the fabric of Kilmere, and the use of such power would destroy Kilmere and Withern alike. I could bring us through—but those within Withern would die. Is that what you want?"

"No." If he were like other fae, he'd have already destroyed Kilmere to gain his own freedom. Yet he remained, accepted the risk of death. Why?

"Remember, Kilmere tests you. It took your measure before, and it believes you weak. Prove it wrong."

My gaze traveled to the huddled forms of the others, distant now, and I nodded. "I'll try again."

Ever so gently, his fingers brushed my arm, and the glorious warmth of a summer sun surged through my body. "Good."

If Kilmere meant to steal my vision and use it against me, I'd rob it of the opportunity. I closed my eyes, but I could not drown out my other senses. Every distant sound was amplified, the limp-step of Miss Redgrave and her quiet inhale of pain, Dreda's uneven breaths, ragged with fear, and the constant rush of water against stone, ever strengthening. It surged well over my knees now.

Riven was right. If I did not force Kilmere to cooperate, we would die—or we'd spend the lives of others to preserve our own. Neither was acceptable. I refused to have dragged Miss Redgrave and Dreda to their deaths in a recalcitrant ruin, to say nothing of Jade, Asrina, Riven, and Mr. Burke, despite the greater knowledge they'd had of the risks coming here.

Warmth built within, and I stopped shivering. Whatever I might be, whatever small abilities rested in my grasp, I'd spend to keep them safe—no matter the cost. Once more, I skimmed my fingers across the stone. Pain seared my chest, so sharp I thought it would rend me in two. With the shock, my eyes flew open—oh.

Sharp details came into view, workings concealed before now exposed. Strands the color of rust and old bone wrapped around the door, their patterns intricate and forbidding. They wove over two gilded handles, binding them shut, concealing their very existence.

When I'd failed to perceive them, I could do nothing, but now . . . I had a chance. And Kilmere *would* let us through. When I touched the coils of power, their drab browns and ivories sparked with green-gold, their forms altering, their patterns changing.

And this time, when I grasped the now-visible handles, the doors swung open. So simple, and yet my head throbbed as if I'd dashed it against the stone wall.

Riven caught my arm just in time to keep me upright. None of Kilmere's hostility had diminished; indeed, the temperature around us dropped further, and a sharp hiss emanated from the stone itself. I might have passed one small test, forced open one door in this vast ruin, but in so doing, I'd only provoked it further.

What horror would it show us next?

"Burke. Now," Riven called.

The others hurried over. When they came into view of the open door, Miss Redgrave clapped her hands. "Oh, well done, Miss Caldwell."

They surged through the waist-high water, clambering over the stones toward the doorway, from which a cold light spilled—not daylight, but something else.

Something Other.

CHAPTER 30

When we stepped through the door, it sealed behind us, locking away the flooding chamber. We'd entered a smooth, well-crafted tunnel with a floor of polished stone, set in geometric patterns. Unlike the cavern behind us, this was well lit by ever-burning fae-lights set into carved brackets on the walls. Only these orbs didn't share the glorious, rich hues that Riven crafted; rather, they were cold and remote and altogether hostile to mortal life. And in their depths, something silvery-white writhed.

I averted my gaze, looking down the relentless slope. We needed to return to the surface, yet this tunnel took us farther belowground, holding us to a course Kilmere had plotted.

Miss Redgrave pressed a strand of honey-colored hair from her face, appearing as bedraggled as the rest of us. "Well, it seems we've leapt straight from the kettle onto the coals."

"Miss Redgrave—"

"I think we've earned the right for first names, don't you? Please call me Elodie."

"Very well. Elodie." I adjusted Jade in my arms. "I'm so sorry to have brought you into this—"

"You didn't bring me, I forced my own way." She plucked

her damp skirts away from her legs. "It is a fault of mine, some would say."

"Fault or no, we need to move on," Riven said.

He was right—even as we stood, small filaments the color of sun-bleached bone stretched from the nearest orb toward Dreda. Her necklace sparked green-gold, and they recoiled.

"Yes, let's go at once." I twined my arm around her and pulled her onward, my cold, sodden skirts weighing me down. In their attire, the gentlemen had a decided advantage.

Beside me, Dreda shivered, and before us, the tunnel stretched down and out of sight, deeper into the unknown. I did not want to imagine the fate it had in store. If Mr. Ellsworth had indeed wandered the ruins, I'd no doubt it had bent him to its will. How would it seek to bend us?

No, us it would not wish to bend—but to break and destroy. I stumbled over a stone, scarcely maintaining my balance.

Jade chuffed. *You've spent too much strength—with the wolves, with the lock. In true-form, I could provide proper support.*

You're injured yourself. I'd never expect it, never allow it.

Nevertheless, I would.

My throat tightened, and I could find no further words. Asrina fluttered to rest on my shoulder, her wings trailing out behind, her presence a comfort.

We rounded a corner, and the tunnel halted abruptly before a solid wall. Did Kilmere arrange its parts as it pleased, rerouting chambers and tunnels in a never-ending maze? It began to appear so.

When Riven strode forward, the stones rent, opening a jagged crack just big enough for our passing.

"Well, that's not ominous at all," Mr. Burke muttered.

Yet it was either go on as Kilmere bid or return to the death-by-drowning chamber, assuming the previous door even remained. Still, I wavered.

"I'll see what's inside." Riven stalked forward.

Not to be outdone, Mr. Burke followed on his heels—and I

could not let them go alone. I pressed through the crevice and then stopped short.

Whatever I'd expected, it wasn't breathtaking beauty. Stonework that could grace a palace, carved in the wild sprawling patterns found in nature, star and sun, blossom and bough, covered the walls in glorious array. Every part of the oval chamber sparkled, a glow drawn forth by fae-lights in a variety of hues, each set in a sconce of silver that merged seamlessly with the stone. Sigils wove through and around the carvings, filling the walls with images so vivid that they appeared to live.

The air was thick, heavy with ancient workings and a rich copper-mineral scent that somehow sparked fear. Kilmere had brought me here for one reason—to impress upon me its might and force my surrender.

Yet I refused to be so easily routed.

I moved farther in to allow the others passage and tilted my head to better examine the space. A richly carved ceiling arched upward, and massive support beams of ivory curved across its surface, every line conveying grace and power as they bowed down to meet the polished floor, where—wait.

My stomach lurched.

I followed the arches back up to a central beam, far thicker than the others, that ran like a spine along the length of the chamber. And bile rose in my throat, churning and acrid.

Not *like* a spine.

The shape and structure were unmistakable now. The central beam *was* a spine, and the curved supports arcing down were the ribs of some creature immense beyond fathoming. I clenched my hands so tightly that my nails dug into my palm. What evil was this?

At my side, Riven had gone still, all trace of emotion vanished. He knew also.

Yet perhaps the others hadn't taken note. One look at Mr. Burke dashed that hope. His mouth tightened into a grim slash, but he said nothing. Perhaps we all knew and simply wanted to ignore that we stood within the corpse of some ancient Otherkind—and its tomb might well become our own.

A hiss echoed in my ears, almost mocking, and the crack behind us sealed shut. We'd no way out but through. Yet would Kilmere allow us some means of escape?

Wrenching my gaze from the bones, I forced myself to examine the rest of the chamber, which bore lavish furnishings to match the ornamented walls.

I moved deeper into the cavity. Surely the fae who'd crafted this place had some means of direct access and did not depend on random rifts forming in the stone. Unless their connection to Kilmere allowed them to form passings without danger.

Without a word between them, Riven and Mr. Burke began to examine the perimeter of the chamber, while I moved toward a large octagonal table resting in the center. The biting cold diminished, and an uncanny warmth seeped into the air as I approached.

The table was of a height to require standing, and it housed shelves on all sides, containing both books and scrolls. Across its smooth stone surface fae runes sprawled, bordered by rampant basilisk forms. *Jade, can you read this to me?*

With a tremendous leap, she landed on the tabletop and bent her head over the runes. *The most prominent line says "on this day, we are bound." Names follow, some of which I recognize— the Denbys and Ellsworths among them.*

In some way, the curse must relate to the record on this stone. *Does it give details?*

No, names only. And the seal of binding.

"Riven." My voice emerged slightly choked.

"I see." With a swift ripple of glamour, he concealed the runes on the surface. "Forget the stand for now. We have bigger problems."

Yet this was part of the reason we'd come, the answers we'd sought. My eye caught on a book below, its spine etched with matching basilisk forms. I seized it, then turned to ask Riven if he'd spied a way out.

Oh. I clutched the book to my chest. He hadn't just referred to our entrapment—something else had gone wrong.

Mr. Burke stood motionless and unblinking before a carving on the wall, strands of rust-iron weaving about him.

Elodie wandered about the chamber, her gaze unfocused, her voice dreamy. "It's so comfortable here, I should like to stay forever."

And Dreda had collapsed to the floor, vines of green and gold about her lashing against swirls of rust and bone.

Oh, please no. It shouldn't have bound them, not like this. Why did it claim them now? I swiped at perspiration gathering on my forehead. And why was it so hot in here? "What's happened to them?"

"They've succumbed to Kilmere, though Dreda not as fully as the others, thanks to your wards. They now perceive what it bids them."

My breath snared in my lungs. "Can you set them free?"

"We can't afford to try, not now."

"Why not?"

"Kilmere means to kill us—and soon. Do you feel how warm it's grown in here? It's toying with you. Warning you."

"Of what?"

"Dragon-fire."

My gaze returned to the bones binding the chamber. "But— it's dead."

"Not before some rather important things were wrested from it and given to Kilmere."

With difficulty, I dragged in a breath, my pulse thrumming unsteady in my ears. We'd escaped death by water, and now Kilmere offered immersion in dragon-fire. How very poetic. Perspiration soaked through the muslin of my gown. "Did you find a door?"

"Not yet—the workings in here are touchy, as ready to explode as one of the alchemical compounds of your kind."

Even so, Riven sent an exploratory tendril of light along the workings. The scent of old blood in the air intensified, and the walls brightened, the sigils on them shimmering in warning.

He shook his head, his shoulders tight. "Any further attempt to read the workings, much less breach them, and it will strike."

What then? It was on the tip of my tongue to ask Riven to get them out, no matter the cost, because I could not bear to watch them die. Yet in so doing I'd condemn those in Withern —including my family—to death. How could I weigh one against the other?

He stalked to the far wall. "These workings—they hide something beneath a number of concealments. Possibly a way out. Possibly something worse."

And he couldn't strip away the glamours without releasing dragon-fire upon us. Which meant I must try, even if I understood nothing of what I dealt with. In Wyncourt, touch had provided connection, offered understanding. Perhaps it would with Kilmere also—certainly it had provided it with means to strike at me before.

No matter that I feared it, I must try. What more did we have to lose?

I moved to the wall Riven had indicated, pressed my hand to the warm stones, and forced myself to open to Kilmere.

Images poured into my mind, as if all this time Kilmere had awaited an open channel of communication.

A tall fae lord with a shining star upon his brow bent over the central table, silvery strands of light weaving in the air around him, forming runes that spiraled onto the page of an open book.

In the corner, a small woman huddled, immobile, much like Mr. Burke. Snared by whatever visions she witnessed, perhaps.

At last, he straightened. He glided to the wall at which I now stood, then crooked an imperious finger toward the pitiable woman. "Come. It is time."

She struggled to her feet and stumbled toward him. "I'm ready, my lord."

He lifted a blade, then slashed her neck. Blood spurted across the wall, and her body fell to the floor, her life spilling out upon the polished stone. Beneath the splash of crimson, an outline of enormous double doors kindled bright.

As the blood seeped into the stone, sigils flared. The doors swung open. He stepped over her body, heedless of her pain, and vanished from sight.

My stomach churned as the images of the victim's blood pressed deeper into my mind, and bile burned my throat. Even as I pressed back the memories, the power of Kilmere surged into my senses. Taunting my weakness. Commanding me to claim this power of old, to open the blood lock—or else surrender and die.

And I knew. This was the choice it had brought me to make. It offered me a way to prove myself worthy—make a sacrifice of blood.

Now it was mine to choose. I blinked away the haze across my vision. Dreda stumbled toward me, the greens and golds now duller than the other threads weaving about her. "I'm ready, Miss Jessa."

No. No—it was unthinkable, this offer of one for many. I refused to become like the cruel lords of the fae, refused to bind myself to Kilmere in blood. My heart drummed against the walls of my chest, pounding like a bird might beat against its cage in a relentless struggle for freedom.

"Miss Jessa?" Dreda's voice wavered as she regarded me, a furrow of bewilderment creasing her features. Yet she did not flee, but stood waiting before the wall, just as the other woman had, so long ago.

Riven stalked over. "What is it? What does Kilmere demand?"

"I cannot—not this."

"Then we will die."

If I refused, would he allow himself to die here? Or would he rend the workings at the final moment, forging an escape at the cost of so many? No, I couldn't think that.

I must only consider my own course, and all those whose fate had become twined with my own. I closed my eyes, blocking out the arched bones, Dreda's pale face, Riven's imperious form.

There must be another way. Fae worked within the letter of the law all the time, altering its spirit to suit their purposes. Why couldn't I do the same?

To open the blood lock required sacrifice. Very well, I'd offer one.

Jessa. Jade growled low.

I need to try this. Don't interfere.

Such was the heat, the vivid stench of past death, that I could scarcely breathe. With trembling fingers, I skimmed the expanse of wall once more.

A flare of anticipation surged, a quickening of the stone beneath my touch, a hunger.

I looked to Riven. "May I have one of your daggers?"

His eyes darkened, but he withdrew a slender blade from a belt at his side and handed it over.

Then I lifted the dagger and slashed it across the full length of my left palm, the blade biting deep. Sharp, blinding pain burned in its wake, and blood rushed from the wound. Would it be enough?

I pressed my hand to the door, and rivulets of red rushed down the stone. In their wake, the slightest flares of scarlet and white scrolled over the surface of the stone, delicate tendrils that looked as though they attempted to form sigils, but they were banished in an instant by the blood workings flaring like stars in the night sky, shades of silver and old bone outlining the doors.

The exultation of Kilmere in quenching its long thirst surged over me, its pleasure in my pain so fierce that it almost didn't begrudge my failure to take a life.

Almost.

Even as it absorbed the blood, I sensed a current of anger, evident in the flare of its sigils—but they did not require life, only sacrifice. Kilmere had no choice but to comply, yet it had taken my measure . . . and found me wanting. I'd not gained any true mastery, only whetted its hunger.

The doors swung open, and cool, clean air surged into the chamber, carrying the scents of life from above. And still, blood poured from my hand.

Coils of light from Riven wound about my palm, stanching the flow. But he said nothing, only moved with ruthless precision to drive the others through the doors, his brows drawn into dark slashes.

In true-form, Jade assisted him, but even so, the others faltered, stumbled, struggled to return to the prison they'd only just escaped. I forced Elodie onto Jade's back and clutched Dreda close, while Riven dragged Mr. Burke into the open passage beyond, which was all dark beauty.

In exhaustion and pain and blood, we returned to the surface, to grassy expanses and sprawling stone walls and the resonant crash of the sea against the cliff. No fang-wolves remained, no fog lingered—nothing appeared out of the ordinary in this ancient fae stronghold. Yet I'd know no peace until we were beyond its bounds.

Exhaustion made each step a labor, but at last, we made it to the copse in which Dreda had sheltered before. Riven sequestered us within, then wove strands of power through the trees, crafting us protections.

Utterly spent, I collapsed onto a stone, cradling my throbbing hand to my chest. Whatever working Riven had placed upon it had stopped the flow of blood and eased the pain slightly, yet I'd cut deep—I'd had to be sure—and now I paid the price.

The quiet trickle of the brook offered a homely sort of

comfort, yet it couldn't drive back the horror of the chambers below the ground, not entirely.

Then Riven spun to face me, his eyes the dark green of an ancient fir.

Only the immense presence of Jade at my back kept me from shrinking away. "If you're thinking of saying I told you so, please don't—I know I placed them all at risk."

And it pained me beyond words.

His gaze lowered to my hand. "That's not what I was thinking."

Before he could say anything further, Mr. Burke muttered something incomprehensible.

"Will they be all right?" I asked.

"They're trying to come back, but they'll need help. What Kilmere planted in them will do far more damage than a mere glamour. I need to rework their memories. I won't press it if their minds don't take to my suggestion." He raked a hand through his hair. "But they're vulnerable and confused right now—I expect they will."

"Very well."

He raised a brow. "No argument?"

"I'm scarcely in any position to make one." The ache in my chest intensified as I surveyed the others. "Only I suggest that Jade return to lesser-form first."

She padded past me, all lithe grace and power, and dropped something at my feet. The basilisk book? *All the danger, and you fetched that?*

You wanted it. And it may be important. Swift as a bird on the wing, she shrank back into lesser-form. *Yet I have a quibble to raise.*

Now?

Since you insist on self-flagellation, yes, now. She ascended the stone, pressed her head to mine. *In Kilmere, you chastised yourself for accepting the help others offered. Do you think you're the only one willing to undertake dangers on behalf of those you care for?*

I fixed my gaze on my torn palm, and the gash wavered as my vision blurred. *I do not presume so, but—these dangers they did not expect. And whatever is . . . Other in me could destroy them.*

Perhaps. Or perhaps it will preserve them from what comes. It was your concern for all of us that strengthened you to fight free—and it was whatever about you that is not *mortal that gave you the ability to do so. You cannot attend to one side of the coin and ignore the other.*

What was I to say to that? A harsh *kraa* overhead broke my thoughts. A raven perched on a limb above us and eyed me with beady black orbs.

And Riven inclined his head toward it, then crossed to where the others huddled together. Light flared about him. "Wake up."

And they did.

Elodie roused first, blinking like one awoken from long slumber, her eyes haunted. "Where . . . where did they go?"

Mr. Burke gripped his sword, while Dreda clutched at her necklace, both unsteady on their feet.

"The curse . . ." Mr. Burke faltered to a stop, his ordinary assurance absent.

"No curse is required to attract fang-wolves." Glamour wove through Riven's voice, and it resonated with power. "It's unfortunate that we managed to tumble into the undercroft of Kilmere during the chase, but hardly unexpected given the instability of the ruins."

For a moment, my own head spun, and the memories of the darkness within Kilmere blurred and faded as the truth fell before a new narrative—a flight from the fang-wolves and a fall into an ordinary undercroft, such as any castle might have . . . I shook my head, casting off the strands of glamour.

A wrinkle furrowed Elodie's brow, as though she sought to recall but could not. "But there was . . ."

"A great deal of darkness. It was difficult to discern what lay within. Fortunately, we found our way out, and we can now warn others of the dangers, so they don't sustain similar injuries."

I wrapped my throbbing hand within the folds of my gown, dizziness assailing me as his voice washed over the clearing, warm and smooth as summer honey. "Nothing you thought you saw is worth recall, only you must never return."

Slow nods all around sealed his words upon their minds. And I drew a shuddering breath.

All this suffering because I'd not wanted them glamoured, and in the end, no other choice had remained. Yet this was to remedy an affliction forced upon them, while to glamour them sooner would have been to bind them to my will against their own.

There was a difference—one using power to control, the other wielding it to heal. Still, we'd had such a narrow escape.

Perhaps I'd been wrong.

In silence, we traveled down the cliff path. Even Elodie had little to say, and though she still limped slightly, she turned down all offers of assistance.

When we neared our carriage, Mr. Burke fell in alongside me, his eyes keen once more. "I trust you'll stay away from Kilmere in future? No matter how little credence should be given the rumors of the curse, fang-wolves tend to attach to a territory. It won't be safe."

"I have no desire to return." I cast a glance back over my shoulder. If I must go back—and oh, I hoped I could find another way—would I ever get free?

But I'd every need to do so. If I was ever to find a way to stop the curse, I'd have to venture within again—as soon as I could manage.

CHAPTER 31

Upon our return to Willowere, Mr. Burke and Elodie took their leave. Dreda drooped with exhaustion, and I felt as though I was a field that had been burnt to stubble, then harrowed and plowed till I was torn asunder.

A glance down at my garments suggested my appearance resembled said field—skirts all over damp, streaked with grime and blood, even rent in places. Somehow I must pretend all was well, smile to Aunt Caris and my sisters, act as though none of it mattered, as if the slightest of mishaps had taken place . . . except I'd no strength to feign normalcy, not now.

My entire body throbbed, and my hand pulsed in time with the irregular beat of my heart. One simple expression of concern from Aunt Caris, and I might shatter—then she'd surely demand the whole.

Halfway between the lane and the house, I hesitated. "Lord Riven, would you care to go out on the lake? Lord Denby has graciously left a small boat moored at the dock for our use."

Never mind the forwardness of my request, I couldn't face my family now. Nor would I be able to rest without some answers about what we'd faced today, despite my exhaustion.

Perhaps Riven perceived it, for he nodded. "As you wish, Miss Caldwell."

Some of the tension in my shoulders eased. "Dreda, will you ask Mrs. Warren to see to your injury? It should be examined. Or I could—"

"I've no need of assistance, Miss Jessa." Her fingers skimmed the cut on her forehead. "It's small enough. It only requires a simple poultice, and I can manage that. I'd not have you keep Lord Riven waiting."

I clasped the book tighter to my chest. "Still, I'll look in on you afterward."

When she vanished into the house, we strolled down to the shore, Riven slowing his pace to match mine. Despite all that had transpired, he showed no signs of weariness; indeed, he bore no residual sign of the battle at Kilmere, which put me at a decided disadvantage, given my own disarray.

At the lake's edge, Jade eyed the skiff. *I've had quite enough water for today.*

You don't have to come. Surely I'm safe with Riven.

With our fortune this day, some large Otherkind lurks below the surface of the lake, waiting to strike. I'll not let you go alone. Her tail twitched, and she gave a tremendous leap into the boat, which caused it to sway alarmingly. *Why do mortals enjoy these precarious crafts, anyway?*

I climbed in after her, and Riven shoved it into the water before striding in after it, the lake lapping at his high leather boots. Then he swung aboard. With effortless grace, he rowed the boat out onto the lake.

He'd no shortage of strength, but I possessed so little I could scarcely summon a clear thought. Even the book in my arms felt unbearably heavy, and I rested it on the bottom of the boat.

The ripples of the water left me dizzy and disoriented, the warm sun on my shoulders and face urging me to close my eyes.

The gentle murmurs of the willows along the shore washed

over me, soft and soothing. I leaned back in the boat, and the gentle lap of the waves blended with their song . . .

With a start, I returned to myself. Our craft sat motionless in the water. Riven had steered us toward the edge, where the willows skimmed its surface, and a blanket fashioned of their slender branches was draped over my body, their vitality pouring into me, becoming my own. The pain of my injury had greatly diminished, and most of my aches had vanished. In their shelter, I'd slept—for how long?

I sat abruptly, and they spilled away from me, caressing my arms and shoulders before returning to brush the surface of the lake once more.

Riven sat untroubled across from me, simply observing. How very awkward.

"How long did I sleep?"

"Three-quarters of an hour, perhaps?" He shrugged. "I've kept us hidden."

"I'm sorry, I should not have—"

"You did what was needed."

And he'd steered us to the edge—why? Because he'd known the willows would offer respite and strength? I couldn't bring myself to ask.

He picked up the oars once more, navigating us onto the lake proper as though nothing out of the ordinary had happened. "Tell me what Kilmere asked of you in the heart. My kind would never construct a lock that required their own pain as a key. So what was the binding?"

My mind clear once more, I described the scene it had shown me. "I theorized that it must accept the blood of sacrifice, no matter who offered it."

"That explains its displeasure. No fae—or fae construct— wishes its binding turned against it." His eyes lightened with a hint of amusement, despite the serious matter. "It wouldn't have expected you to circumvent its demand—that you did so means you still have a chance."

A chance for what? To survive, if we must return? I pressed the notion from my mind and trailed my uninjured hand over the edge, the cool shock of water welcome. "Does that mean every time the fae of Kilmere entered the . . . heart, they must have taken a life to leave it?"

Under the force of his downthrust, the oars shot us forward. "The act would have strengthened Kilmere each time—the greater the sacrifice, the greater the gain of power, which means they had every reason to do so, unless their supplies ran low."

To hear him speak of people as supplies . . . My stomach twisted. "You don't seem surprised by the nature of working upon the door. Are such locks common in your world?"

"No. We often use blood locks like the ones in Wyncourt, those that open for their owner alone. This is something altogether different." His grip on the oars tightened, and he fell silent.

Information was power. He'd said as much once. Would he surrender it without requiring an exchange? This *did* pertain to our dealings with Kilmere, so perhaps it could be considered part of our bargain. I drew my hand from the waters. "If I'm ever to deal properly with Kilmere, then I need to better understand its nature—how it was formed and why."

He secured the oars and braced his arms on his legs. "My people seek power, each vying for an edge against the other. At times, their methods leave a great deal to be desired."

At times? I'd not quibble, not when he might offer insight, yet everything I'd witnessed suggested they exercised no restraint in their quest for power.

"Our sovereigns have long since prohibited certain methods and workings for the well-being of all courts—if left unchecked, these forbidden arts destroy the fae-lands to which they connect, in the end. Which may be why the fae who constructed Kilmere chose your world." His brows drew down. "It's clear they availed themselves of numerous death workings, among other forbidden practices. The remains of the eld dragon confirm it."

"I don't understand."

But Jade clearly did. Green fire burned in her eyes, and her fur bristled.

And Asrina's light pulsed with tones of rose amid the gold, her displeasure evident.

"Kilmere brought us to its heart, which was formed from an eld dragon. Once taken captive, it would have been bound alive within the stone, impaled by their workings and subjected to tremendous agony while they stole the force of its life—its innate powers, the very vitality of its soul." His tone held no inflection; he might have recited from a dry textbook, rather than recounted horrors. "These they channeled into Kilmere while it suffered and died. The process would have taken weeks, perhaps months. Coupled with their own workings, it made Kilmere impregnable."

A pain pierced my middle, sharp as the dagger I'd wielded upon my hand. What I'd inherited *was* cursed, and in a darker way than I'd ever dreamt. How could the fae have conceived such a scheme, believed their power gave them the right to spend the lives of others as they willed?

With a slap, the oars hit water once more. "The dragon wouldn't have been the only source, though I assume it was the greatest. It's likely other such crypts exist within."

I lowered my gaze to the murky waters of the lake. "Then must it always be a place of death and suffering?"

"It would take tremendous power to alter its nature—even so, it might never change. It's rooted in death."

Yet something in me refused to accept it was beyond redemption. For if it was, what would that mean for all those caught in its snares? What would it mean for me? I must find some means of governing it before it spread its malice further . . . a task that felt impossible.

"Rather than dwell on what cannot be, you should consider what use you can make of it." His features sharpened, becoming more wholly fae, fierce and unfamiliar and altogether disconcerting. "To stop Damir, you'll need something as powerful and ruthless as he is. Kilmere offers that and more."

Despite the sun spilling over my shoulders, I went cold. "What are you saying?"

His eyes shaded darker; his face became devoid of emotion. "You must take control of Kilmere, force it to accept you. Then use it to end Damir."

"I cannot." The words emerged choked.

"It's the obvious choice. Before today, I wasn't certain you possessed the means to stand against Kilmere. Now you have a chance, and you must seize it." As if the sun on the waters was drawn to him, it rose in brilliant coils, its heat searing, its beauty ruthless. And still his expression did not change. "You will set a trap and draw him to his death."

I rocked back, and the boat quivered. How . . . how could he suggest murder? My hands clenched, sending a bolt of pain up my arm, and my eyes stung.

"You killed Uros." He spoke quieter now, yet his words pierced. "Would you do less this time to protect your world? If Damir becomes master of Kilmere, you know what he will do— what use he'll make of its nature."

"With Uros—it was different." And even so, the sensation of the cold heart pulsing within my hands still haunted me at times. "I didn't craft some stratagem by which I might deceive and ensnare him and then take his life."

"What then? You want to let Damir claim your family? Make them suffer? Use Kilmere to inflict his will on Withern and beyond?" The strands of light flared unbearably bright. "Do you want me to tell you what happens to mortals when they cross the will of fae? I've seen it time and again. Your lore falls short."

I flinched. "I cannot defeat him by becoming like him."

"Then you will not defeat him at all." His voice held an edge.

"Eventually, you'll find yourself at his mercy, and I assure you, he possesses none."

And if the alternative were to attempt to wield Kilmere as a weapon . . . I pulled my knees to my chest. If I did, the vastness of the power contained within would surely consume me, would seek to mold me in its image. It sought to gain power by taking from others. Would it drive me to do the same? Would it make me like those who'd created it, in the end? Would I become the danger I feared? No, I refused to accept it. "There must be another way."

"And what might that be?" Riven demanded. "My responsibilities are with my court. I cannot stay in your world forever."

"I know."

I'd known it all along. Riven provided only temporary protection. He bought me time to find a way to thwart Lord West, no more. I lowered my head to rest on my knees. If I failed, the cost would be tremendous—and if I succeeded, it could be even greater.

I traced the ragged edges of a scar in the wood seat. "Even if I managed to gain control of Kilmere—which I struggle to fathom—there's still the curse. Killing Lord West won't keep them from falling victim to it."

"But with full access, we'll find what we need more readily," he said. "The stand in the heart suggests the deaths in Withern are tied up in whatever bargain existed between the fae of Kilmere and the inhabitants of Withern."

"Yet it's not the only way to find the answers we require. To gain information from the townsfolk about the bargain, however difficult, would be far less risky than prizing it from Kilmere."

"If they've any recollection of it, perhaps." He leaned forward, power swirling about him. "How many lives do you wish to gamble with?"

He wielded truth like a sword, and it cut deep. "Please . . . don't press it further, not now. I'll think about what you've said. But I cannot—I need time."

Could I ever join to Kilmere without being consumed? Even Riven could offer no such promise.

The scent of sun and storm hung heavy in the air, pressing, relentless. Then ever so subtly, his features altered, losing some of their fae aspect. About us, light took on its ordinary form, the radiance of the sun resting gently on the waters. And he inclined his head. "Very well."

"I . . . I have other questions, if you're willing."

"Go on."

"The fang-wolves. How did so many come so quickly—and from where? Could Kilmere have drawn them?"

"Someone opened a passing and brought them through, drove them on at great speed."

"Then they are Other, as our lore suggests?"

"They have aspects of Other within them, but no, they're not of our world. Many centuries ago, your alchemists created them at the behest of your king—he wanted them to stand guard over Crossings, protect mortals from Otherkind. He was foolish enough to believe they could breed a lethal creature with elements of Other and keep it under control."

How had this been kept hidden? Did it correspond to the Forgotten War?

Riven continued, "Of course, they responded to the dictates of their nature alone and struck out at mortals as well as Otherkind, loyal only to their own packs. Your Vigil has worked to contain them ever since and has succeeded in keeping them mostly to uninhabited areas."

I rubbed my temples. "Those that weren't killed, will they prey on the town?"

"They've gone, along with the passing. Whoever brought them fetched them back."

"Might it have been Lord West?" If it was, it made no sense. If I'd died, then Riven would have inherited Kilmere, and Lord West would have known better than to think fang-wolves could fell his rival. Yet to think that *another* fae had taken interest in Kilmere . . . I shuddered.

"It wasn't Damir."

"Is there any room for doubt?"

"No. As mortals recognize the voice of a friend or foe, most fae will recognize the creator of a working, if they've encountered the individual before. This passing held no trace of Damir or any signature with which I'm familiar. If I were pressed, I'd say it most resembled those of my own court, but that should be impossible. I've familiarized myself with the signature of every fae of significance within it." He lifted a shoulder. "It's also possible there was a passing prism within Kilmere, and that's the trace I perceived—if so, it could be that of a fae long gone. If that were the case, it would have required a wielder."

So either way, someone else had been involved. If from without Kilmere, a fae. If from within, a mortal. Mr. Burke believed he'd seen someone, but that could have been mere illusion. Without returning, it was impossible to be certain. Still, we had one other bit of evidence.

"What of the book Jade fetched? Might it offer insight on the bargain?" I hauled it onto my lap, flipped it open to reveal fae runes. Jade could translate, or Asrina, but both would be slower than Riven. I extended the book toward him. "Will you see if it contains any references to a bargain with the mortals of Withern?"

He began to page through it, while Jade climbed into the spot on my lap that the book had occupied. *You've been very quiet.*

She curled up tight, and I stroked her fur. *I'm considering the strategy Riven presented.*

My hand froze mid-motion. *You cannot agree with it?*

West won't stop seeking his prize. When the time comes that Riven must go, West will make his move. I don't want you to suffer whatever he has in mind.

Nor do I, but—

Riven lowered the book. "This doesn't speak of a bargain. It addresses other aspects of the history of Kilmere—namely, its basilisk."

"Then one once dwelt in Kilmere?" Surely that must have significance.

"Yes, but not by choice." Sparks of light flared about Riven. "One of the lords who constructed Kilmere seized her from her knot, killed her mate, and forced a new bond upon her, one with a compulsion woven in it. It was a risky undertaking, for her and for him. He'd tried with other basilisks before and failed. Once, it almost cost his own life, because the venom was almost more than the antidote could counteract. But this time, he succeeded. She'd no choice but to do the bidding of her new mate, and she became a powerful weapon in his arsenal."

Jade sprang off my lap, her abrupt motion rocking the boat. *To violate the nature of bonds in such a way . . .*

Her speech became a wild flurry of fae oaths, and though I couldn't understand them, I agreed with the sentiment expressed.

Riven traced a finger over the runes. "This fae controlled her fully. He could bid her to assume stasis in lesser-form as he willed, and in such condition, he kept her bound around his neck until he required her—a reminder to any who might question his power of the death he controlled."

I drew a shuddering breath. "What do you think happened to her?"

"She was bound to this lord, so presumably she went with him in death. If he yet lived, Kilmere would seek no other master."

I reached for Jade, attempting to soothe her as she so often did me. "That explains the store of basilisk venom, yet others have entered Kilmere over the years. Why the recent outbreak of deaths?"

"Someone may have broken the terms of the bargain, whatever they were." His voice was grim. "It's possible death by poison was the consequence."

"If we discovered the details of the bargain, could we help them?"

"The terms would give insight, perhaps help—but the bargain cannot be undone without the consent of all parties involved. Mortal memories are frail, and centuries have passed." We came to rest along the shore, and Riven watched me closely. "Kilmere represents our best chance of answers."

"Perhaps, but in the meantime, if you speak to Mr. Ellsworth, it might shed light on how the curse is working." I sighed. "And I will confront Lord Denby."

"Denby?"

"I saw him leave another carcass on our doorstep. He's responsible for trying to frighten us away, and I believe it's because he knows more about the curse—and possibly the bargain—than he lets on." I rubbed the fur between Jade's ears, and she released a soft purr. "I'd also like to visit Fellbane and speak with Mrs. Ellsworth. Perhaps she'll confide in another woman, where she might not a stratesman."

Riven pulled the boat to shore. "We will see what account they give, then go from there. Persuade your aunt to come into Withern tomorrow afternoon. I'll make sure our paths cross and convince her to allow us a stroll."

In this case, it would require no glamour to sway her, since she desired a match between us. Yet for Riven to design a chance encounter, he'd have to know my location, and he'd said nothing about me sending Asrina to inform him. I'd long since known that Riven possessed uncanny methods of tracking individuals, though he'd said our world did not hold whatever traces he used as long as his own. Just how readily could he perceive my presence—where I was and where I'd been? Were there limits? "And how will you find us?"

He lifted a shoulder. "You're easy to locate."

It wasn't much of an answer, but it was all I was likely to get.

With Jade draped over my shoulders and Asrina fluttering alongside, I clambered ashore. I'd convinced Riven to wait while we investigated the mortal angle of the curse—but even if we obtained all the answers we desired, it would do nothing to stop Lord West. In the end, would Riven prove right?

As though Kilmere spread its shadow over me from this long distance, my skin chilled, and the ache from my palm spread up toward my heart.

CHAPTER 32

When I entered Willowere, Ainslie glided out from the drawing room. "Oh, there you are, Jessa! I thought you'd never return, and—" Her gaze dropped to my gown. "What happened to you? Did you take a tumble in the lake? Dreda said you went out with Lord Riven?"

I tucked my injured hand into my skirt. "I did end up drenched, but—"

Heedless of my reply, she hurried on. "Aunt Caris is quite distressed, and we've been at odds and ends all day. Her locket has vanished."

"How could it just disappear?" Aunt Caris wore her simple locket daily, and though she'd never shared her reasons, none of us doubted its sentimental value.

"She took it off and placed it on her dressing table before bed last night—you know she worries it will snag and break in her sleep—and when she went to put it on this morning, it was missing." Ainslie drew a quick breath. "She's interviewed all the household servants, and none of them know anything, or at least, so they claim. You saw nothing unusual when you rose this morning?"

How could I answer that? I followed Ainslie deeper into the

house. "Nothing that would suggest a thief had made his way inside." But could Lord Denby have instructed Mrs. Warren or one of the other servants to make things go missing? "What did the servants say?"

"Mrs. Warren claims it's further evidence of the curse, which appears to be her explanation for any calamitous circumstance." Ainslie lifted each cushion on the stuffed chairs in turn. "The others say very little, save to claim ignorance in the matter."

"Where have you searched?"

"Every conceivable place both withindoors and out. Now I'm examining them all again. Aunt Caris, Ada, and I have spent much of the day in the effort. Even Char—Mr. Redgrave came to help." She pressed a cushion back in place with more force than required. "Aunt Caris has no appetite for luncheon, and Ada persuaded her to rest this afternoon. I think the talk of the curse wears on her nearly as much as the loss."

I straightened the cushions Ainslie had left ruffled in her tempestuous search. This harassment wasn't the fault of a curse, but a mortal, which meant I could rectify it. But I didn't want to drag Dreda out again after her harrowing day, and I couldn't call at Denby Hall alone.

From her perch on my shoulders, Jade nudged my face. *You could take them into your confidence—ask for their help.*

Unlike the situation at Kilmere, I wouldn't be putting them in further danger by bringing them to Denby Hall—only what if Ainslie asked more questions than I could answer? She and Ada already suspected I hadn't been forthright about the events of the past few months. Yet given my only other choice was to wait for Dreda to recover, which meant a greater chance Aunt Caris would decide to abandon Withern . . . *Perhaps you're right.*

I'm always right. It just sometimes takes you awhile to see it.

I tweaked at her tail, and she twitched it against my ear. *Surely not* always?

I am kit-isne, *after all. My kind possess great wisdom.*

The arch reply brought a smile, despite my dread of the

confession to come. "There's something I need to tell you and Ada, but I don't want to chance Aunt Caris hearing—she doesn't need further worry. If you come to my bedchamber while I change, we can talk."

"How very intriguing." Ainslie's eyes sparkled. "I'll fetch Ada."

I hurried to reach the bedchamber before her so I might bind my hand. Already it was remarkably improved, as if the injury had taken place days ago rather than hours. Was this healing a result of the working Riven had placed on it? Or my own encounter with the willows? I slathered it with amelior salve and wound a clean bandage about it, tucking in the edges just as Ada and Ainslie burst through the door.

"Oh my, Jessa. Whatever happened to you?" Ada asked.

"I suffered a bit of a mishap. It's a long story, one that would take far too much time to recount now." I tugged off my soiled garments. "I'd hoped to speak to you both about what I witnessed this morning."

"Not a thief, you said?" Ainslie's brow furrowed.

"No—Lord Denby on our doorstep."

"Lord Denby?" Ada sank onto the edge of the bed. "What possible purpose could he have for lurking about?"

I pulled on a clean gown, summing up in short order the carcass left and my removal of it, leaving Jade out of the matter, of course. I finished with an account of the hares Riven and I had discovered on the road. "I believe Lord Denby genuinely fears the curse and therefore wishes us to remove from Willowere."

Ada smoothed the folds of her gown. "In that case, might it be better to go?"

"Even if we did, we'd not leave the trouble behind. Lord West is still bent on obtaining Kilmere, and I must understand why—and how to dissuade him." I attempted to restore order to my riotous hair. "Perhaps you could persuade Aunt Caris to return to Avons and allow Dreda and me to remain?"

"And leave you here to deal with an unwelcome suitor and an ancient curse?" Ada frowned. "I scarcely think so."

"If you did, you could avoid Lord Bradford." And that must be a point in favor of the scheme.

"I don't think avoidance will work, not any longer." She pressed up from the bed and crossed to the window, hiding her face. "Aunt Melisina has already been here today—but that's a tale for another time."

Ainslie wrapped an arm about Ada's shoulders. "Well, one thing is clear. We must see to Lord Denby. Such appalling behavior cannot go unchecked."

"Precisely my view." Securing the last of the pins in my hair, I unfolded my plan.

Ada shook her head. "What if he lashes out at you, Jessa? I cannot like it."

"Yet it offers our best chance, and I don't judge him the sort to strike at a lady. He values his reputation too much."

"I agree," Ainslie said. "And I'm certain if he tried anything underhanded, Jade would deal most severely with him."

She is correct.

"Yet there's one fault in your strategy," Ainslie continued. "I heard the servants talking—Lady Denby hosts a tea this afternoon, and she won't welcome additional guests."

"Then I suppose it must wait until tomorrow," I said slowly. I wished for few things less than a confrontation hanging over my head.

Ada clasped my hand. "Have no fear, we shall call tomorrow as soon as is seemly. In Withern, morning calls appear acceptable, so you'll not have as long to wait."

I thanked her, then excused myself to check on Dreda, who rested in her bedchamber, her fatigue evident but her speech clear. Perhaps she'd truly come through unscathed. Yet how could I possibly bring her back to Kilmere, knowing the ward I'd provided could not match its strength?

For that matter, how could I return myself, knowing all the horrors it held? If there was another way, I must seek it.

~

THE FOLLOWING MORNING, with Denby Hall looming above us, I questioned all my plans. If Lord Denby chose, he could make this exceedingly unpleasant—and much depended on him believing that I'd witnessed him.

He'd not hesitated to sabotage our stay. If he took things too far and someone was hurt—no, I must put a stop to it, and if I could, learn what he knew of the curse. For if none within Withern possessed the information I required, then Kilmere became my only option.

Ada gently lifted the knocker and rapped on the door. In short order, the butler ushered us into a well-appointed morning room, designed in a centuries-old style, with an immense, elegant fountain as the focal point of the room. Indeed, one must walk past it, admiring its beauty and significance, to find the settee and chairs, which were arranged in a half circle between the ornate fountain and a large bank of windows overlooking the garden.

Lady Denby occupied the settee, as poised as a queen holding court. At our approach, she offered a cool nod. "Miss Caldwell, Miss Ainslie, Miss Jessa, won't you be seated?"

Three gold cushioned chairs flanked the settee on either side, arching toward the fountain, and we settled into the trio at her left. I took care to place myself farthest from Lady Denby—no sense in provoking her unnecessarily.

"I trust you're finding your stay pleasant?" Her voice held no inflection.

Ada offered a serene smile. "We've found Withern even lovelier than expected."

Before I could broach the matter of her library, the excuse I intended to use to seek Lord Denby, the butler returned, ushering in Lady Holloway and Lady Cadence.

Jade's pupils narrowed as she regarded Lady Cadence. *How unfortunate.*

Lady Denby rose to greet them, clasping their hands warmly. Evidently, she reserved her hauteur for us. I couldn't entirely blame her, not when Kilmere represented a true threat.

After Lady Denby sent the butler for tea, she and Lady Holloway situated themselves on the settee. To my surprise, Lady Cadence took the chair directly across from mine. I'd expected her to seat herself near Lady Denby and ignore the lot of us, yet she fixed glittering eyes upon me.

Positioned as we were, closest to the fountain, the faintest mist settled over our gowns. The water burbled away, heedless of my discomfort, and I lowered my gaze, unwilling to be drawn into another confrontation.

"You've collected quite a pleasing house party this year, Lady Holloway," Lady Denby said. "We're obliged to you for adding so nicely to the society of Withern."

"Indeed, I find them all most congenial. We shall pass a pleasant summer here." Lady Holloway sipped from her cup of tea. "However, I must confess the society I find most pleasing came to Withern without my devising it."

"You speak of Lord Riven? Or perhaps Lord West? I've noticed he's been most attentive to your household."

Lord West? I straightened. Just how much had he integrated himself into Withern society?

"He certainly has—and I believe he has a very particular reason for his attentions." Lady Holloway nodded significantly at Lady Cadence.

Lady Denby returned the teapot to its tray. "Then you must be exceedingly pleased. He'd be an excellent match."

I clutched my cup, any desire to partake of it vanished. If Lord West chose to entertain himself with Lady Cadence while he waited to seize Kilmere and she accepted his advances, she'd be vulnerable to any of his schemes. I had to at least try to warn her. "Lord West isn't all he seems."

It was a graceless remark, and both older ladies frowned upon me. I pressed my lips together. Perhaps I should have kept silent.

"Any lady of good breeding would find him altogether charming." Lady Cadence spoke in honeyed tones. "I don't expect you'd understand."

Ainslie leaned forward, and I shook my head slightly. She subsided, and the other ladies continued to praise Lord West, while I wished myself in the garden beyond the windows.

As faint and soft as the mist of the fountain, the pricking sensation of Other swept over my skin, and the slightest spice scent wafted through the air, hints of cinnamon and ginger and something altogether unfamiliar. I returned my cup to its saucer, surveying the room in search of its source.

There.

Near Lady Cadence, strands of glamour rippled around the figure of a small fae, enabling her to blend in with the trickling water of the fountain. Only when I focused did she become distinct. A small form, no more than knee-high, perched on the broad stone rim of the fountain. A riot of bluish curls sprouted from her scalp, and her eyes were too enormous to be altogether canny.

Long, triangular ears stuck out from her head, pointing slightly downward at the tips, and bright metal bangles adorned every limb, enhancing the glamour by blending with the sun-sparkling water of the fountain.

She edged closer until she stood less than a handbreadth from Lady Cadence, who was describing in great detail a dress she'd made, oblivious to the nisi at her side.

I leaned forward slightly, the conversation fading into the background as the nisi caught her lower lip between sharply pointed teeth and extended a small hand toward the glittering gold-and-sapphire bracelet on Lady Cadence's wrist.

What an upset it would cause if she unclasped it, unless her glamour could keep Lady Cadence from taking note of its absence until later. Why would the nisi take such a risk? According to our lore, nisi adored bright objects, yet it would be far easier to snatch one from Lady Denby's vast stores than from the arm of a guest.

Never mind that. She was immortal—and if she'd occupied the Denby household for the span of her life, perhaps she recalled what they did not about the curse besetting Withern.

The small fae teetered on the ledge, stretching for the jeweled bracelet.

And I stood. Lady Cadence already thought me a hopeless academic—why not confirm her bias? "I'm much intrigued by the design of your fountain, Lady Denby. The scrollwork on it appears to date from the Ruskin era. May I study it?"

Both my sisters shot me questioning glances, but Lady Denby merely arched a sculpted brow. "If you wish."

"Thank you—you're most kind." With that, I slipped around to the back side of the enormous fountain, the rush of its waters dulling the conversation beyond.

Jade, can you get its attention?

She chirred, and a thrilling note of Other crept into her voice. The nisi rounded the fountain, darting over to Jade, her eyes wide.

I'd distracted her from her prize, so I must present something worthwhile in exchange, a token of friendship. What could I offer? Among the myriad of hairpins securing my curls, I'd several fashioned of gilt filagree, perhaps bright and beautiful enough to capture her attention.

I withdrew the one least likely to cause the whole to come tumbling down and held it out to her. Her lips parted in a fearsome sharp-toothed smile.

Then she winked from sight.

Well. That might have gone better.

Just wait.

A moment later, she returned with something brown and wrinkled—perhaps a nut of some sort?—cradled in the crook of her arm. She extended it toward me.

She proposes a trade.

Was this the nisi form of bargaining, perhaps? They did offer their services within a household in exchange for access to its fountains as well as its food, or so our tales told. I'd no notion of what she offered me, but it didn't matter, as long as it opened a path for conversation.

I held out my hand with the gilt pin, and she dropped the object into my palm before snatching up the pin and cradling it to her chest, her eyes bright.

Whatever nut or seed she'd given me sparked with Other, and I tucked it into my reticule.

She cast a longing look at the jeweled bag, but to part with that would attract notice from my sisters, where the absence of one pin would not. *Can she speak with me?*

Yes.

In that case, could you create a minor distraction? Though they might not make out the words, to stand behind the fountain seemingly talking to myself felt a bit *too* far to go with the eccentric academic persona.

With the greatest of pleasure. There are some mice in these walls, along with several rats. I believe procuring one will create a sufficient stir.

Jade prowled along the carved baseboard, then slipped out into the corridor. Less than a minute later, she returned, bearing an enormous dead rat.

Shrill shrieks followed, along with Lady Denby shouting for the footman.

Below the din, I murmured to the nisi. "What is your name?"

"Give no names to high ones, no indeed."

"Very well. Then may I inquire why you sought the bracelet?"

"Storm clouds gather. Must make strong the protections of my house. Need many shinies."

How very interesting. Did that mean that nisi used bright materials and jewels to create wards on the homes they inhabited? I shook off the thought; I must focus. "Then the Denby home is your own?"

"Yes. They know old ways. Fountain always prepared, food always left. Is quite satisfactory."

"And you seek to protect them against the curse?"

Beyond the shelter of the fountain, Jade led the footman in a merry chase, her satisfaction evident in every bound, every quivering lash of her tail. Lady Cadence huddled upon her chair, and my sisters looked on in bemusement.

"Protect what I can, but they remember not. Cannot make safe, not entirely."

"What is it they've forgotten?"

She brought her face close to mine, the spice scent strong. "Many debts owed, many years due. They forget, but not Kilmere. Never Kilmere."

"Miss Jessa, will you be so good as to fetch your cat?" Lady Denby's voice could have frosted over an entire garden.

The nisi winked from sight, vanished far too soon. I'd not be able to fetch her back.

"Forgive me, Lady Denby." I emerged from the shelter of the fountain. "Jade, surrender the rat, if you please."

She sauntered over to the footman and dropped the rat at his feet before returning to sit calmly at my own. Hurriedly, he snatched up the unfortunate creature and fled the room, while the other ladies resettled themselves.

Ainslie and Ada both offered sharp looks. Doubtless, they'd expect explanations for my behavior later. For now, I took the opportunity to present my request. "Lady Denby, do you have a library? Such spaces tend to calm Jade, and she's quite riled after the hunt. It seems best to remove her."

She sank back into the settee. "Excellent idea. You'll find it at the hall's end."

Clearly, she was ready to be rid of me. Jade ensconced in my arms, I slipped from the room. First I must stop in the library and select a book or two, so as not to raise suspicions. Then I'd beard the dragon in his den—if the outwardly affable Lord Denby could be called a dragon.

I made straight for the oldest-looking tomes and chose a slim volume entitled *The Keeping of Sea-Blossoms and Bees*. Asrina peered at its title with interest, her golden light shimmering upon it.

A bargain existed between Kilmere and some of the inhabitants of Withern, or it had at one time. Could the town's inexplicable prospering following the arrival of the sea-blossoms relate to this bargain? The lady of Withern who'd brought the sea-blossoms had also requested the construction of Kilmere, and I struggled to believe that a coincidence. Much did not add up. The nisi had spoken of many debts owed. What one bargain would result in many debts?

Never mind that for now. However much I might desire to shelter in the library, I couldn't afford to stand here pondering the conundrum, or we'd outstay our welcome and I'd lose my opportunity. I tucked the book under my arm.

Now for Lord Denby.

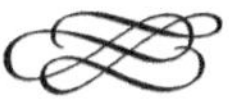

I might not know where to find Lord Denby on my own, but Jade had no difficulty leading me to him, her superior sense of smell allowing her to track him even in the large manor.

I halted in front of the door. While I intended to address him on a matter of business, it was still far from proper to seek him in the privacy of his study. I could only hope that given what I had to say, he'd have an equal desire to keep my visit concealed—and that Ada and Ainslie would distract Lady Denby long enough for me to accomplish my purpose undetected. I rapped at the door, and Lord Denby bid me enter.

When I appeared, he dropped his pen onto the desktop. "Miss Caldwell, what a pleasant surprise. Have you come about Willowere?"

"After a fashion." It was a reasonable assumption—what other reason might I possibly have to call? Mouth dry, I forced myself onward, leaving the door ajar behind me.

"Please sit." He gestured to the chairs before his desk, then looked over my shoulder as if to seek the servant who'd led me here. Finding no one, he returned his attention to me. "How may I help you?"

I set the book on my lap and rested my hands atop it. Where should I begin? Beneath his congenial, slightly patronizing gaze, I faltered.

With a single bound, Jade leapt atop the table, where she perched to glower at Lord Denby. He shifted, apparently ill at ease beneath her stare, which gave me the sense we were on more equal footing—and the courage to say what I must. "I have a rather difficult dilemma."

"If I may be of assistance, I'd be delighted to do so."

"I hope you can. You see, I watched you leave a carcass on the front steps of Willowere yesterday morning, meant as a warning, perhaps, like the others upon the road, or the destruction upon our arrival."

"What?" he sputtered. "That's . . . it's impossible. You must be mistaken."

"I know what I saw, Lord Denby."

"Now, Miss Caldwell, you're not to blame for any misperception. Such acts of sabotage are understandably upsetting to the delicate feminine mind."

"It was no misperception, my lord. I assure you my mind is as well-ordered as the rest of my senses." At my shoulder, Asrina flared bright, her warmth an encouragement.

He appeared taken aback. Perhaps he'd expected capitulation? Nevertheless, he drew himself up. "And you think anyone would believe such a wild tale from an unknown female?"

I lifted my chin. "I'm inclined to think Stratesman Burke would believe my testimony. We're well acquainted, and he respects my word, as I do his."

The faintest sheen of perspiration dampened his brow. "There's no need to bring a stratesman into this."

"I agree." I clasped my hands together tightly, and the wound on my left protested. "I understand that you'd rather us leave, that you fear the curse of Kilmere, but—"

His affable face hardened, the mask of amiability slipping. "You're selfish and senseless both. You understand nothing of the powers you'll wake if you excavate Kilmere. Years ago Lady Dromley thought as you did. She believed she could do as she pleased—and she paid a high price for her folly, as did many others. I'll not have your ignorance inflict suffering upon my family."

"I'm not willing that it should do so either." I lowered my voice. "So won't you tell me why you believe your family at particular risk of Kilmere's wrath? If you believe me ignorant, then enlighten me."

"I did not speak of my family specifically." Beneath his ruddy complexion, he blanched slightly. "All within Withern are vulnerable."

"All—or only those who have lived here since the founding of Withern?"

"What difference does it make?" he snapped. "If you keep meddling, death will follow."

"Yet they've taken Mr. Ellsworth into custody, so he can harm no others. Does that mean you believe him innocent?"

"I didn't say that." His eyes blazed. "Cannot Kilmere choose an instrument to do its work whenever it pleases? Whenever it's angered?"

His words echoed my own fears, and I rocked back. "Yet he claims he's spent no time in Kilmere."

Any remnant of his gentlemanly mask vanished, and he sneered. "But he did, all because he's softhearted for his wife. Were he not such a sentimental fool, he'd have left her sheep to appease Kilmere, rather than go in after them. Everyone knows it's wiser to allow it to take its tithe when it chooses. But my man saw him go up after them, then told me the tale in full."

If that were true, then what would happen if Mr. Ellsworth remained imprisoned? Would Kilmere seek another to do its bidding? The healing cut on my hand throbbed. "Help me understand. Your lore must suggest what wakens the curse— what angers Kilmere."

He stood abruptly. "Miss Caldwell, I don't know what you

think you're about, but I suggest you leave before I address your false charges as they deserve."

"You may do as you see fit." Somehow, I managed to keep my voice steady. "However, I did not think a gentleman of your standing would want his honor or good name tarnished by any suggestion of wrongdoing—which will certainly occur if this matter goes before the Magistry, whether you level a charge or I do. You know how relentless the gossips can be."

He leaned forward, bracing his hands on his desk.

"I see no reason we must be at odds." Aside from my intense dislike. I considered the best approach. He valued his reputation a great deal. He'd wanted to appear like a gracious and affable host, even as he worked to sabotage our stay. If I provided him a way out that allowed him to maintain his image, I'd little doubt he'd take it. "It's possible we've had a misunderstanding. Certainly there are aspects about the situation with Kilmere I don't comprehend."

"Not only about Kilmere." He collected his dignity, once more donning the air of a gracious host, albeit one grievously injured. "I assure you that you're altogether mistaken about the incidents at Willowere."

How could he lie so readily? It suggested that he knew more about Kilmere and the curse than he'd confess, yet he'd no intention of allowing me to pry it from him, so I must accept a partial victory, if I could manage it.

I conjured up a sweet smile. "Perhaps I am. If you give your word as a gentleman that you had nothing to do with the unfortunate incidents, then I must accept it for what it's worth."

Which, as of now, was absolutely nothing. Jade chuffed, her amusement flooding my mind.

"However, we intend to fulfill the term of our lease. May I trust you to ensure we have no more trouble? Surely one of your standing will know how to best address the matter."

"Can I not dissuade you from your course?" He settled back into his chair, his tone mild now, almost fatherly. "I'd want no daughter of mine to endanger herself or her family as you do. For your own well-being, won't you reconsider?"

"I appreciate your concern, but I'm quite resolved." I inclined my head. "I'd like to put all this unpleasantness behind us. I have no desire to involve the Magistry, but I must if another incident follows. May I have your word you'll see to the matter?"

He shifted uncomfortably. "As your landlord, I can do no less. I'll ensure you've no further trouble at Willowere."

Though I placed no value on his word, I trusted in his desire to protect his own reputation, and I sensed we'd have no more trouble from him. It would draw far more attention than he desired.

"I appreciate your assistance."

"Think nothing of it," he muttered.

I rose from the chair. "There's one thing more. A locket precious to my aunt has gone missing. The servants have no particular reason to confide in us, as we're little acquainted, but I feel certain they'll have more respect for you—and be more willing to listen to your instruction, if you bid them seek it. Provided it's found, I see no reason for word to spread of its disappearance or speculation on who might have taken it."

His well-padded jaw twitched. "I'll speak with them this afternoon."

"Thank you, Lord Denby. You've been most helpful."

As soon as we'd abandoned Denby Hall, Ainslie wound her arm through mine. "Well, what did he say?"

"Lord Denby strictly denied all involvement; however, he's agreed to put a stop to the matter."

"Of all the detestable—"

"Now, Ainslie." Ada glided along the path. "However

deplorable his actions, if this put a stop to his deeds, we shouldn't complain."

A smile flitted across Ainslie's face. "You would deprive me of the opportunity to relieve my emotions after such a tedious visit?"

"Was it truly that difficult?" I asked.

"Lady Holloway has a very high opinion of both herself and her daughter." The breeze ruffled Ada's dark curls. "Given she believes her word should be law, it was not particularly pleasant."

"And Lady Cadence bears you great malice for some reason," Ainslie said. "I was hard-pressed to hold my tongue."

"Well, I appreciate you both. If you'd not kept Lady Denby occupied, I'd never have managed to reach Lord Denby."

I glanced at Jade, who prowled about the tall stands of grass at the edge of the lane. *And I appreciate that you're the one who suggested it.*

Watching you force Lord Denby to agree to end his own activities offered ample compensation.

I pressed my lips together to avoid betraying our exchange with a smile.

Still, Ainslie looked between the two of us. "May I ask why you insisted on examining the fountain? And whatever possessed your cat to go hunting within Denby Hall? I've never known her to act so before."

"I cannot answer for her actions, but only feel thankful that they made Lady Denby more inclined to grant my request for the library."

"It did work out quite well." She adjusted the brim of her hat, watching Jade prowl about. "But—"

"I've been wondering about Mr. Redgrave." If I could distract her, then perhaps she'd forget the matter of my odd behavior—and Jade's. "You said he helped search for Aunt Caris's necklace? Might he have a particular reason to want to offer his assistance?"

The faintest rose hue tinged Ainslie's cheeks, and for once, she said nothing, leaving Ada to fill the gap.

"Oh, he most certainly does." Ada's lips curved upward. "Though he might have had an ulterior motive, he was very kind to Aunt Caris. He didn't grow weary of the search nor dismissive of her concerns, as many gentlemen might have done."

"You refine too much on it." Ainslie refused to look at either of us, keeping her gaze fixed on the horizon. "Certainly, it was a kindness, but from what he's said, he comes from a large extended family, much of whom lives in and around Redgrave Hall. Doubtless he's simply accustomed to attending to his own aunts and assorted relations."

"Doubtless." Ada somehow managed to conceal her smile, yet a little quiver in her voice betrayed her amusement.

If Mr. Redgrave truly meant to pay suit to Ainslie, as it appeared, then I must become better acquainted with him. Elodie had claimed he was keen to make sure ladies could protect themselves, which was unusual—as was she. I'd like to better understand them both, not to mention ensure Elodie suffered no ill effects from our excursion yesterday.

I skimmed my fingers along a stand of laceflower that bordered the road. "Perhaps we should call upon the Redgraves? Presumably Lady Holloway and Lady Cadence are still out paying calls, so we could visit undisturbed."

My sisters halted abruptly. Ainslie clutched my shoulders and peered deep into my eyes, her own sparkling merrily.

"What are you doing?" I asked.

"Checking to make sure you're indeed Jessa, not a changeling left in her place."

Her words twisted like a knife in my heart, yet I kept my smile firmly fixed. "Is it so shocking a suggestion?"

"Coming from you, yes." Ada shook her head. "Ordinarily you shun the very notion of paying calls."

"There's a first time for everything." I lifted my shoulders. "Our excursion to Kilmere yesterday didn't go as I'd hoped, and

I'd like to make sure Elodie does not regret her choice to join us."

"I think it's an excellent notion," Ada said. "As long as we make it a brief call. Aunt Caris wanted us back before two so we might attend our dressmaking appointment. Apparently, Aunt Melisina has arranged for new gowns for each of us. Lady Holloway intends to hold a ball, and she wants us at our best."

I'd no doubt she meant it as part of her schemes to match Ada—and I'd no desire to engage with Aunt Melisina again after our last skirmish. Though I wanted to plead weariness, our fitting would provide an ideal situation to accidentally encounter Riven in Withern. "If we fetch the carriage as we pass Willowere, we should have ample time."

We did accordingly, and when we arrived at Holle Castle, the solemn butler greeted us. "I'm afraid Lady Holloway is not at home."

Ainslie dimpled at him. "As it happens, we're here to call on Miss Redgrave."

"Allow me to see if she's in." In short order, he returned. "She would be delighted to receive you. This way, please."

When we entered a small drawing room, Elodie rushed over to greet us, her brother following at a more measured pace. The warmth in his smile when he greeted Ainslie tugged at my heart. How I wanted to believe him as kind and genuine as he appeared.

A low table held a polished silver tea tray from which hints of vanilla and sugar escaped, and the Redgraves urged us to join them for tea.

Ada accepted on our behalf, and while Ainslie, Ada, and Mr. Redgrave engaged in conversation, I sat next to Elodie.

As I did, a slight queasiness settled in my stomach. "I trust you're well?"

Jade's ears tilted sideways, as though whatever bothered me troubled her as well.

"I am now. I'm not one prone to megrims, but I felt as if my head would split in two by the time I returned to Holle Castle yesterday. However, I slept long into the morning, and I'm quite restored, as you see." When she leaned forward to pour the tea, a silvery-bright ward peeped from her bodice, one that did not resemble the useless ward-pendants peddled about Byren, but rather the one Mr. Burke had born, those he said alchemists provided to their Collectors—and like those given the stratesmen when the killer preyed upon Avons.

Was it possible they were Collectors? Surely not. The Redgraves were an old and venerated family, their head titled, their wealth long established. They'd have no need to risk their lives for the monetary gains offered by the Otherworld.

I swallowed against a swell of nausea, and Jade wandered to the far side of the room. "I'm relieved to hear it."

"Still, I must confess I've wondered about those fang-wolves. I never dreamt they ranged so far as Withern." Then she gave a light laugh. "But I'm scarcely an expert."

"You handled yourself well against them."

"Did I? I suppose the shock of it all impacted me more than I expected, for it's all a bit of a jumble in my mind." She stirred her tea. "How fortunate that Mr. Burke and Lord Riven were able to drive them off. I certainly shan't return."

I accepted the cup she offered. "If you don't mind, I wanted to inquire about your parasol blade. I found it rather remarkable."

"It *has* been of use on more than one occasion." A brilliant smile lit her face. "But don't tell Lady Holloway I said that. She'd be shocked that such a device entered her home, let alone that a lady wielded it."

"Are they easily procured?" Given the dangers gathering about me, I'd like a weapon at hand.

"If one knows whom to ask. I shall give you the name of its maker." She slid a honey cake onto her plate. "My family collects such peculiarities, so he's used to all sorts of unusual requests."

I sipped at my tea, the sea-blossom honey I'd stirred into it sparking with Other on my tongue. What did I know of the Redgrave family, aside from generalities? Some vague memory tugged at the edges of my mind, but I could not draw it forth.

"What do you think of the sea-blossom honey?"

"I find it delightful."

"Lady Denby informed me that in addition to its unique flavor, it has remarkable healing properties, and the locals of Withern use it in treating all sorts of ailments."

How very interesting. If true, that was another point in favor of the sea-blossoms having some root in the Otherworld.

With that, Elodie leaned forward to engage with Ada, drawing her into a discussion on her favorite composers. Unlike some, Elodie appeared to feel no need to prove her knowledge superior and listened with interest to Ada's account of the methodologies used by contemporary composers. Their conversation flowed about me, nearly as familiar and comfortable as that which we held within our own home.

Only I'd best remember that we knew very little of the Redgraves, and that I should not allow myself to become too much at ease. I swallowed against the lingering queasiness.

Ainslie set down her plate with a thunk, drawing attention to her conversation with Mr. Redgrave. "You cannot support the new mirror-crafting process, surely? Granted, it offers new positions to those who might require them, but it's the most dangerous sort, and they're not well compensated, particularly given the risks involved. I'll grant it produces a better glass—but at what cost?"

I blinked. I'd never seen her speak like this outside our family, and rarely within it. To Mr. Redgrave she revealed hints of her true self, her interest in the more serious matters of the world, which much of society would condemn.

"I have raised that exact question." He gestured with his free hand as though addressing an unseen audience. "Most say a better product—and better profits—are worth what they deem negligible risks."

"It's easy to call a risk negligible when you're not the one taking it," she said.

"As it happens, I share your perspective. My uncle has informed me of a forthcoming discussion in the Assemblage of Lords that will address the use of street children in the smelting process, at least."

"Truly?" Ainslie leaned forward, intent on his words—and clearly close to surrendering her heart. Perhaps it shouldn't be surprising, given that she rarely acted in half measures. "That's excellent news."

"It is a first step. Whether it will prompt action remains to be seen."

"You appear well-informed on political matters, Mr. Redgrave," Ada said.

"Not nearly as much as some. But my uncle serves in the assemblage, and he considers it vital that I understand the policies under discussion." He spread his hands. "I'm to take his place one day, so I hear more than I might sometimes wish—but he's right. If one has the position, one must take responsibility."

"You say you hear more than you wish. Do politics bore you?" Ainslie asked.

"Endless debates and powermongering trouble me." His eyes, a rich cinnamon-brown, darkened slightly. "Often the assemblage fails to do what it must. Words and promises mean nothing if action isn't taken."

Ainslie nodded. "Well said."

With a graceful motion, Elodie stood. "Miss Jessa, may I steal you away for a moment? I wanted to ask your opinion on a sketch I recently discovered. I hear you're a skilled artist, and I'd welcome your insight."

"I enjoy sketching and painting, but I can claim no expertise. Still, I'd be happy to take a look."

As I trailed Elodie from the room, Ada moved to the pianoforte and began perusing the music, allowing Mr. Redgrave and Ainslie to converse undisturbed. They didn't even appear to notice that the rest of us had moved away.

Elodie halted in the doorway, glancing back at them. "They suit well, don't you think?"

Jade bounded to my side, and I picked her up. "It appears they do, and I'm pleased they enjoy each other's company."

"Even so, it's a bit peculiar to think of losing one's sibling, isn't it?" She swept down the hall, the slightest hint of sorrow softening her features. "Charles has been the best of brothers. When our father died, he thought nothing of his own interests or grief, only threw himself into taking care of me and Mother."

"I didn't know you'd lost your father. I'm very sorry."

"It wasn't recent—I was quite young when he passed, just old enough to be devastated. Time eases the sting a bit, but still there are moments when I wish . . ." She looked away abruptly. "I shouldn't complain, when we've lacked nothing. Only, as I said, Charles has always felt he must look after us, even though Father left us well-situated, and our uncle was pleased to offer us a home in Redgrave Hall. I'm happy to see Charles think of his own interests for once."

"Your family seems close."

"Indeed, sometimes a bit too much so—there are so very many of us, after all, all involved in each other's affairs." Then, as though she regretted her frank speech, she fixed a smile on her face and began sharing a series of anecdotes about her nieces. "Ah, here we are."

She swung open a door, revealing a cozy chamber with floor-to-ceiling bookcases. "Before our visit to Kilmere, I wanted to see what I could find about its past. In the search, I came across a drawing within an old book. I thought perhaps it might interest you."

From the leaves of an ancient leather volume she withdrew a detailed sketch of a basilisk done in a walnut hull ink. Its enormous frame bristled with spines down the back, its ruff flared about its face, and its fangs were bared in hostility, as though it might leap from the page and strike.

Jade surveyed it, her green eyes glinting. *Someone knew of it.*

I kept my face as expressionless as I could manage. "How very remarkable. A skilled artist drew this. But was there no context as to its inclusion in the book? This appears like something one would find in a bestiary."

"The book details the history of Withern and makes no mention of basilisks, yet this was tucked between the pages, as if someone drew it and abandoned it there long ago." Elodie balanced the book in her arms. "It appears Kilmere was mired in tragedy from the beginning, which perhaps accounts for the legends of the curse."

Was some memory of what had truly transpired at Kilmere fighting to break free? Had she brought me here to gauge my reaction to a discussion of the ruins? Or did she know something more? I gripped the picture tighter, and the paper crinkled. "What tragedy occurred?"

"According to the book, Lady Firth—they called her the Lady of Ravens—requested the fortress built, but then died there even as the foundations were being laid."

"How dreadful." I eyed the book. How had Elodie so readily laid her hands upon it, when Ibbie had sought written accounts to little avail? Had she found it in the library, as she claimed, or had she brought it with her? "May I see?"

She offered me the book, and I skimmed the faded script within. It appeared to echo the notes Ibbie had collected long ago, but this account carried far greater detail. It described vividly the great beauty of Lady Firth and how she'd so captivated her husband that he counted the construction of the fortress but a small task, if it brought her pleasure.

As Elodie had reported, she'd become known as the Lady of Ravens, for after she wed Lord Firth, a large unkindness settled in the region—and they were known to come to her and feed from her hands.

She certainly sounded fae—beautiful and strange and bent on the construction of Kilmere.

Jade licked a paw and scrubbed it across her face. *Some fae have affinities turned toward animals. Perhaps she was one.*

I continued to turn pages, lost in the tale. According to the writer, one evening Lady Firth traveled alone to the site of Kilmere to survey its foundations, which were under construction—and she never returned.

Her frantic husband found her body broken upon the foundation of Kilmere, her blood spilled upon its stones—and he never recovered from his grief. In a poetic touch, the author suggested that ravens still nested about Kilmere because they mourned their lost lady.

I skimmed on, but the writer attended next to other members of the Firth family, who went into decline after the incident. I looked up to find Elodie surveying me intently.

I passed the book back to her. "How very tragic. No wonder the locals believe it cursed."

"For my part, after our ill-fated expedition, I'm prepared to believe it as well." She shuddered slightly. "In any case, I'd like to know what you make of the drawing. Do you believe it as old as the book?"

"Walnut hull ink fell out of favor centuries ago, so I imagine it is."

"How very interesting. I wonder why it was tucked away here." She tilted her head. "I suppose we shall never know."

"Oh, there you are, Jessa." Ada appeared in the doorway, with Ainslie alongside. "We must go, else we will miss our appointment at the dressmaker."

I could have embraced them for the escape they offered. I did not want to evade any more questions, but rather to consider the details revealed.

If Lady Firth had been fae, why had she died so? And what did it have to do with the curse?

CHAPTER 34

We returned to Willowere to find Aunt Caris and Dreda awaiting us in the morning room. Aunt Caris worked on her correspondence, while Dreda wound fine yarn.

"Ah, there you are, my dears." Aunt Caris sealed a letter and set it aside. "Just in time. I don't want to cause further trouble with Melisina by arriving late, not when she's offering such a generous gift."

"What would you like me to do in your absence, Miss Caldwell?" Dreda asked.

"You're to have a new gown too, so you'll come with us." Aunt Caris capped her bottle of ink. "You'll need something fine enough for a ball, and I didn't purchase anything of that nature before."

"Thank you, Miss Caldwell." Dreda bobbed her head. "I didn't think you'd want me to attend."

"With three unwed nieces to look after, I'll gladly take an extra chaperone." Aunt Caris patted her arm. "Besides, I believe you'll find it pleasant. Lady Holloway is known for her lavish parties, each outdoing the last."

She bustled us toward the door, and we opened it to find Mr. Tibbons approaching the cottage.

I halted in the doorway. "Mr. Tibbons, I didn't expect you so soon."

"Forgive the intrusion." He offered a bow. "It appears you're going out. Should I return later?"

"It's no trouble." I nodded at the others. "You go ahead, I'll only be a moment."

They moved toward the carriage, while I joined Mr. Tibbons in the front yard.

He lifted a leather portfolio. "I've brought all the records you requested, and something else too. When your father learned I intended to join you in Kilmere, he asked me to deliver this—he said he'd agreed to forward it from Lord Blackburn."

"Thank you for all your assistance." I accepted the letter and portfolio. What did Lord Blackburn want? Had he changed his mind about sharing evidence? "I would like to discuss what you've learned, but we're on our way to an appointment. Do you have a place to stay in Withern?"

"I intend to take a room at the *Sea Blossom*, if that suits you."

"I understand Withern is much occupied this time of year, so anywhere you can find a room is fine with me." I hesitated, mindful of the others awaiting me in the carriage. "Before you go, I have one question—how did Kilmere feel to you, when you explored it?"

"Feel?" His eyes clouded. "It's hard to describe. I suppose I was struck by its grandeur, intrigued by all it might hold. I could see why it had stuck with Lady Dromley all those years—why she wanted to return and fathom its secrets."

"And while you were there, did you notice anything out of the ordinary?"

"I can't say . . ." He trailed off, as though he struggled to remember, and then picked up on another vein entirely. "Should I continue making inquiries among the townsfolk or return to taking preliminary surveys of Kilmere?"

"Neither as yet. The townsfolk are uneasy, and I'd like to explore Kilmere a bit more myself before anyone else ventures inside. Why don't you enjoy a short holiday?"

"That's generous of you, Miss Caldwell, but I don't mind working, particularly not on a project as interesting as this."

"I assure you I'll put you to work as soon as I know what I need. I simply require some time to figure it out," I said.

Ainslie poked her head from the carriage and beckoned with a finger, restraining herself from calling out as she doubtless wished to do.

"Forgive me, I must go. Please take the next day or two to settle in and occupy yourself as you please. We'll speak more soon."

He took his leave, and I clambered into the carriage to join Aunt Caris on the back-facing bench. If Kilmere could no longer use Mr. Ellsworth, would it seek another who was already vulnerable—like Mr. Tibbons? Perhaps it would be best to send him away rather than put him to work, so he'd not be at risk? But what excuse could I give for dismissal? It was not as if he'd failed in his duties.

Jade settled onto the seat next to me, and our driver clucked to the horses, who swung into motion.

"What did Mr. Tibbons want, my dear?" Aunt Caris asked.

"Only to bring some records I'd requested from Avons." I longed to examine them right away, but it was impractical to sort through the contents of the folio while rattling along in the carriage—particularly since I did not want my family to glimpse the contents. However, I could more readily satisfy my curiosity about the letter from Lord Blackburn, so I slid my finger along the seam, opening it.

Miss Caldwell,

> *I have reflected upon our conversation at the Botanic*
> *Gardens many times since that day. When your father informed*

me you'd gone to investigate Kilmere, I felt I must write. Lady Dromley once suggested to me that Kilmere was built in the era of the now-forgotten war. If so, then perhaps it has light to shed on matters of interest to us both.

If you find records or artifacts within the ruins that might provide illumination on subjects of interest, would you consider selling them to me? I'd offer whatever you deem them worth, as I did with the antiquities Lady Dromley procured for me on occasion.

With regard,
Lord Blackburn

I folded the letter and tucked it into my reticule. Ibbie had helped him gather information in the past, and now I was positioned to do likewise—but knowing what I did of Kilmere, how could I agree? If I revealed to him any hint of the truth, I couldn't predict how he'd react. Yet he could prove an ally in my quest for understanding, so I didn't want to reject his offer outright.

What do you think, Jade?

She rested her head on my lap. *I think he means well, but he both fears and hates fae. If he has reason to suspect you're something Other—or something alchemically altered, as the case may be—he could prove a danger.*

I stroked the patch between her ears. Unfortunately, so could nearly everyone in my life. So what was I to do? I considered as we rolled along the road, the fragrance of the famous sea-blossoms filling our carriage—an almost intoxicating scent with an unsettling hint of Other.

Aunt Caris's voice broke into my thoughts. "I found it very promising that Mr. Redgrave called upon you yesterday, Ainslie. I only regret I was in too much distress over my locket to welcome him properly."

She colored slightly. "He understood, and I believe he truly didn't mind helping with the search."

"That bodes well indeed. Perhaps I'll have the pleasure of planning a wedding at last." Her hand drifted to the hollow of her neck, where her locket should have rested. A gift from a former love, perhaps?

Ainslie shook her head. "He's made no declarations as yet, nor would I accept one if he had. We've only known each other a short time, and it's far too soon to know if we'd suit."

"But you find him pleasing?" A hopeful note threaded Aunt Caris's words.

"I do." Ainslie's voice softened. "In every way."

"If only your mother were here. She would be as pleased as I am—more so, no doubt." Aunt Caris sighed softly. "I've kept her wedding gown and jewels tucked away, in case one of you wished to wear them when you wed."

Ainslie's gaze lowered, and her lips trembled slightly. "If that day comes, I'd be honored."

Ada gently clasped Ainslie's hand and then turned to Aunt Caris. "What was Mother and Father's wedding like?"

"It was lovely. Your mother had impeccable taste, and of course, it was a cause for celebration in all of Upper Northlea." A soft smile curved the lines of Aunt Caris's face. "Some—including my mother—had despaired of ever seeing Alden wed, so taken was he with his studies until he met Kensa. When he fell for her, our parents were delighted."

"What of Mother's connections?" I stroked Jade. "Did they support the match?"

"She had very few, so I cannot say. She didn't like to speak of her past, but it appears her parents kept her quite isolated. Then, when she lost them, she was alone in the world."

In that case, uncovering the truth would prove far more difficult. I brushed Jade's fur from my gloves. "Did she keep journals or anything from her past? Anything about her family?"

"She was a faithful correspondent, but if she maintained diaries I never knew of it. She tended to be a private person."

Ainslie shifted as though the bench had suddenly grown uncomfortable. "Why do you want to examine the past so closely, Jessa? As much as we miss her, it won't bring her back."

"I think I understand," Ada said softly. "It's natural to seek any connection that remains. To wonder what she would think and feel as we consider our futures."

As she spoke, I could feel again the sensations conjured by *ilusne*—Mother's gentle touch in my hair, her summer rose scent, her soft voice calling me *golden one*. Oh, how I ached for her.

If she were here, if I asked her outright, would she have told me the truth of my nature? Or would she still have kept her pain hidden? With difficulty, I returned my thoughts to Aunt Caris, attending mid-sentence to her commentary.

"—back in Avons. I believe Gillian kept all her letters too. Kensa and Melisina tolerated each other, but I don't think they corresponded much, if at all."

Jade nestled closer to me, her presence a comfort. "If you're willing, I'd like to see the letters when we return."

"Of course, my dear. I'll do my best to unearth them."

Though Dreda had kept quiet during our conversation, as was her wont when all of us gathered, a wistful expression had settled on her face. I knew she'd lost her father, and most likely her mother too. Did our conversation of loss spark her own pain?

The discussion moved to lighter matters as we entered Withern proper, and when we convened in front of the dressmaker, Aunt Melisina descended from her own carriage, sweeping toward us.

"I've ordered all of you new gowns, and though I gave her your measurements, Miss Penforth requires you present in person for the final fittings." Aunt Melisina unfurled her parasol to shade her face. "I only hope her work proves satisfactory compared to the skill we're accustomed to in Avons."

"That's very generous of you, Aunt Melisina." Ada straightened slightly. "But we might have made do with the gowns we brought."

"Not for a ball such as the one Lady Holloway plans." Aunt Melisina sniffed. "Despite the spectacle Jessa made at her last public appearance, Lady Holloway wishes all of you to attend. It will be three days hence, and you must look your best."

If she wanted Ada at her best, most likely she meant to orchestrate a proposal from Lord Bradford at the event—in such a public way that it would be difficult or impossible for her to decline. I couldn't imagine she'd given up, not with the calculated determination she'd exhibited in our last conversation.

As we strolled into the shop, Ada and Ainslie exchanged a glance. Perhaps they'd drawn the same conclusion. In any case, we'd best be prepared.

A woman as lean and upright as flowering bluestem greeted us, and she fetched out Ainslie's gown first.

As she donned the shimmering silver dress, Aunt Melisina clucked. "I declare, Ainslie, that scar hasn't faded at all. If anything, it looks as if it might have spread."

Had the binding mark truly altered? My breath hitched, as though the seamstress tightened my stays instead of Ainslie's. Did that mean the nature of her bargain had changed?

"You should consult with Dr. Fulton," Aunt Melisina said decidedly. "I once knew a woman who sustained a cut along her neck after a carriage accident, and instead of fading, it grew as the months passed, becoming most unsightly. You don't want to chance the same."

Were it a scar, perhaps her advice would be sound. But if she contacted Dr. Fulton, he'd be sure to note its peculiarities.

Ainslie offered a serene smile. "I'm sure you are wise, aunt. I will see what may be done."

I eased closer to her, examining the binding mark, which she ordinarily sought to keep hidden. It *had* altered from my recall. While its symmetry remained as striking as ever, its coils had spread further down her arm. I stumbled back and knocked a jar of buttons to the floor with a clatter. I leaned forward to pick them up, but the dressmaker checked me, motioning to her assistant.

"By the Crossings, Jessa." Aunt Melisina frowned. "What's come over you?"

"I'm sorry—I just need a breath of air." And even more so to breathe in the rich green life offered by the sea thrift and feather-lace ferns in the pots just out of doors. "If you don't mind, Dreda and I will take a turn about the block."

"Very well, but don't dally."

When we made our escape, I inhaled deeply of the sweet floral notes of the sea thrift, its melody bringing a measure of calm. "Thank you for accompanying me, Dreda."

"It's no trouble—Withern is lovely, and I'm glad for the chance to see more of it."

As was I, only I couldn't properly attend to the striking sea views given the tumult within. If Ainslie's binding mark had changed, that meant perhaps the fae who held it had sought her out since our arrival, and—

The sound of raised voices broke into my riotous thoughts, and a slim woman with flaxen hair came rushing out of the haberdashery.

She stumbled and nearly fell headlong before us. On instinct, I reached out to steady her.

Oh—she was weeping.

"Are you all right?"

"Do not pretend you care." The lacing of fine lines about her eyes suggested that she was of an age with my aunts, and the deep circles beneath her eyes bespoke ongoing distress.

What could I possibly say to bring comfort? Jade sniffed at the woman's skirts, and her ears twitched back. *She smells of rowlock and morsbane and other plants that share their nature.*

Poisons. Could this be . . .

Two ladies strolling down the footwalk toward us turned away abruptly, then made a show of crossing the street to walk on the other side, as if they could not bear to be in her presence. I heard one of them mutter *Ellsworth*. And the woman crumbled into silent sobs.

Clearly it was.

"Come." I gently steered her to an out-of-the-way nook between two buildings. Without my requesting it, Dreda positioned herself in front of us, sheltering Mrs. Ellsworth from view.

"You cannot get safely home in this state." I rested my hand on her trembling arm. "Is there someone I can send for you?"

"There's no one, not after—not anymore." She drew a shuddering breath.

"Are you Mrs. Ellsworth?"

She nodded, shrinking back as if I might offer a blow. How much had she suffered because of the confession her husband had made, because of what he might have done under compulsion? Her distress became my own, her tears a condemnation of my failure. And I couldn't keep silent. "I hope to find out the truth about your husband."

"The truth?" She shook her head, wisps of fine hair escaping from beneath her hat. "Don't mock me. Condemn me if you must, but don't hold out false hope."

"Do you believe him innocent?" I asked softly.

"What does my belief matter? He confessed, or so they say."

"Yet there are some elements missing from his story—like his trip to Kilmere."

She flinched as though I'd struck her.

"I heard you lost some sheep there."

"We've recovered them," she said. "It can have no bearing on the matter."

"Are you certain?" I blocked out the noise of the busy street beyond, attending only to Mrs. Ellsworth. "I don't want anyone to suffer for deeds not of their own choosing."

For the first time, she lifted her face and regarded me. "You don't want to see Elver hang?"

"Not if he hasn't acted of his own accord."

"Everyone else does—they can't wait for his death. The stratesmen told me it's as good as over, that as soon as he appears before the Magister, he'll be condemned."

"But perhaps you can change that. If you tell me what truly happened with Kilmere—"

She pressed her fingers to her lips. "I gave my word to Elver I'd not speak of it, not any of it."

"Won't you consider—"

"I promised!" The words burst from her with great force, then softer again: "I promised."

"If you cannot speak of it, will you tell me something else?"

Asrina's light flickered over Mrs. Ellsworth, soft and slow like a steady heartbeat, almost as if she intended to soothe, never mind that the woman couldn't perceive her.

She relaxed slightly. "What do you want to know?"

"I'm told you keep a garden the locals call Fellbane. Why?"

"You think like the others that Elver fetched poison from it." She pressed her hands to her head.

"No, I feel quite confident he did not. I only want to understand its purpose."

She sighed, a breathy gust of air. "That garden. So often I've taken refuge in it, felt safe in the reminder it offered: we're not defenseless. But now I wish I'd never vowed to my gran to keep it."

"Why did she ask for your word?"

"I cannot say, not for sure. But she'd maintained it, and her gran before her, and on back many generations. She used to say those who lived in the shadow of Kilmere needed to look to their own defense. But she was muddled then, not sure of herself. She made me swear never to root out the garden. And I keep my word." Her chin lifted, and the afternoon sun kindled the tearstains to lines of fire.

"So I see." I pressed her hand gently.

"There you are, Jessa." Ainslie hastened toward us, slightly breathless. "Ada's nearly done, and Aunt Melisina grows restive. She sent me in search of you."

Mrs. Ellsworth lowered her head, as if to hide. "I must go."

Then she scuttled into the shadows between buildings, taking the road away from Withern. In face of the pain Mrs. Ellsworth endured, I could hardly rejoice in the prospect of a ballgown—yet I didn't want to anger Aunt Melisina further, so I followed Ainslie back to the dressmaker.

Despite her feelings toward me, Aunt Melisina had spared no expense on my gown. Her unerring eye for fashion and color resulted in a stunning deep blue confection that suited me in every way.

Though she did not meet my eyes, she offered a small smile to the seamstress. "Very nice."

From her, it was extravagant praise. I slipped out of the gown and allowed Dreda her turn.

For Dreda, Aunt Melisina had chosen a simpler gown, yet it still had elegant lines and fine material, in a shade of rose that brightened her complexion and made her look more youthful. When Dreda beheld herself, a smile creased her face.

Aunt Melisina professed herself satisfied with them all, and she ushered us from the shop. As we exited, I turned toward the haberdashery from which Mrs. Ellsworth had fled. I did not know when Riven meant to happen upon us, yet I hoped it would be soon, for I longed to know what he'd learned from Mr. Ellsworth. All evidence suggested that he'd administered the poison, but could he be counted guilty if he'd acted against his will? I couldn't begin to answer that question.

Our aunts swept us along toward a local teashop, where we'd partake of refreshments. The quiet conversation of my aunts and sisters swirled about me as I nibbled at a fresh strawberry from the bowl before me.

Only a moment later, its sweetness turned bitter. An unmistakable sense of Other overshadowed me—not Riven, but Lord West. He strode through the door of the teashop and approached our table.

Jade bristled, and Asrina darted beneath the tablecloth. If only I could do the same.

"I'm pleased to find you all here—and looking so lovely." He tucked his walking stick beneath one arm, an ornate affair with the glaring head of a serpent forming the handle. "I trust you're finding your stay in Withern pleasant?"

One corner of his mouth lifted. Did he know how Kilmere had tested me? Almost certainly, for he'd warned me that a mortal could not hope to hold it.

Aunt Caris beamed at him. "Indeed, the sea air and the views are enchanting."

Aunt Melisina inclined her head. "They're pleasant enough, but I'm afraid my husband finds it rather dull. How do you feel?"

"Quite the opposite. I've found my time here invigorating. In fact, I've just made a valuable acquisition."

The soft chink of cup and saucer at once became overloud, yet not enough to block out his words.

"As you must know, good help is hard to find, but it seems there are those in Withern eager for new horizons." The corners of his mouth lifted further, baring his teeth. "One of the young men about town has just agreed to enter my service."

My hands tightened. The motion pulled at the gash in my palm, sending pain up my arm. "What sort of position have you filled?"

"One at my home estate." His dark eyes glittered. "He started yesterday, in fact."

I couldn't move, couldn't even swallow. If he'd lured someone into a bargain and dragged them into the Otherworld . . . what torments had the poor soul already endured?

"And only think—I have you to thank for it. If you'd granted me Kilmere at once, I should have never have engaged him."

Blight and rot. The vivid colors of the strawberries blurred before my gaze, turning into a pool of blood. How much more harm would I cause?

You've caused none, and you should not listen to him. Perhaps he'd not have claimed this particular individual, but if you'd given him Kilmere, he'd even now tyrannize the entire region, claiming anyone he willed.

Perhaps, but how long before he does worse?

Without thought, I sipped at my tea, its taste bitter on my tongue. Lord West meant to remind me that no matter what I did, he had every advantage. If I blocked him, he'd find other mortals to prey upon—and their fate would eventually become my own.

"I'll allow you to finish your repast. But I do hope to see you again, quite soon." He gave the slightest of bows, his gaze lingering a moment on me.

Even though he'd left, I couldn't stop shaking. How could I stop him—unless I gambled as Riven wished, risking a success equally devastating as the more likely failure?

CHAPTER 35

Where was Riven? It was all I could think of through the rest of our tea. Surely he'd come. Only what was taking him so long?

If he didn't arrive before we left the teashop, I'd send Asrina to him—no, he'd left her for urgent needs. My distress over Lord West hardly counted, not when he'd come and gone and done no harm.

Except to the captive he'd claimed.

I sat motionless, my hands clasped in my lap. How could I do nothing to stop him, when he continued to hurt mortals? Yet the only possible means of staying him was altogether untenable.

Dreda leaned over and spoke low. "Miss Jessa, are you well?"

"I'm afraid I feel a bit poorly."

"We could take another stroll, if you wish?"

"What are you murmuring about over there, Miss Twells?" Aunt Melisina arched a brow. "Do speak up."

She flushed, her freckles eclipsed in a tide of color. "Forgive me, Lady Stanford, I—"

"She only inquired about a personal matter." And I'd not let her receive criticism for her concern.

"This is neither the time nor place." Aunt Melisina swirled a spoon of honey into her tea.

"Aunt, you cannot—"

Oh, he was coming. The familiar charged-air sensation swirled about me, a change in the atmosphere heralding Riven's imminent arrival. As promised, he approached our table, charming my aunts with effortless grace.

Without hesitation, Aunt Caris released me to accompany him on a stroll through Withern with Dreda to serve as chaperone. As we approached the seawalk, she kept pace several steps behind us.

Riven wove the slightest shimmer of glamour about us to muffle our conversation, then he assessed me with a swift glance. "What's troubling you?"

"Lord West. He took one of the men of Withern, bargained with him, and forced him into the Otherworld." Doubtless he'd claimed many mortals before, but he'd chosen *this* man as a provocation. He'd taken him and then taunted me with it, a reminder that I was powerless to stop him. My eyes burned as though stung by the salt of the sea. "Shortly before you came, he stopped by our table to inform us."

A long silence followed. Riven continued at the same measured pace, only the slightest tightening of his shoulders hinting at any sort of response. Then he halted by the stone wall overlooking the water. "This surprises you?"

"Not truly, but I cannot endure the thought that someone else must suffer, caught in his snares." And that this one was my fault.

"If he must bide his time here, he'll entertain himself as he sees fit. You must accept it—or act." Though the words were blunt, his tone was gentle, a bewildering contradiction.

I braced myself against the cold stone, watching the endless ebb and flow of the sea. I could not ask his counsel, for I knew it: risk everything to claim Kilmere, and if I succeeded, use it as an instrument of death and destruction. An unbearable notion, if any other way remained. Yet this painstaking process of collecting information from mortals might take more time than we could afford—and might not provide what we needed in the end.

I traced a fault in the stone beneath me, the cracks darker than the rest of the surface. I wasn't ready, not yet, so I sought a safer subject. "Lord Denby informed me that Mr. Ellsworth spent time in Kilmere, and he appears to believe it coerced Mr. Ellsworth into poisoning the victims."

"Ellsworth may have entered Kilmere, but he wasn't the poisoner."

My finger snagged in a crevice. "If Kilmere didn't influence Mr. Ellsworth, then who . . ."

High above, a gull screeched, then plunged down into the depths, seeking its prey. Riven leaned against the wall, facing me. "We know Tibbons has been to Kilmere, and that the deaths started afterward. Further, no one else has fallen victim since he left Withern."

Even before he finished speaking, I shook my head. I couldn't bear to consider that he'd gone on my behalf and then succumbed to its compulsion. But something *did* cloud his mind.

Riven continued, "Still, we cannot discount the Ellsworth household. If Ellsworth went, there's a chance his family could have accompanied him. With Tibbons in Avons, we should start there."

"He's not in Avons, he arrived in Withern this morning."

"Did he? Then we must call on him."

"If he recalls nothing, how can we get the truth from him?"

"There are ways."

"That involve shattering his mind?" I dug my fingers into the stone.

"Not only that. If you wish, I can first make a search of his room and belongings. If he possesses basilisk venom, I'll be able to detect it."

I nodded slowly. "He's to report to me for further instruction on Kilmere. If I send for him tomorrow morning, you'll be able to examine his things without drawing notice. For now, will you tell me more of Mr. Ellsworth? He must be involved somehow, else why would he lie, when his confession means his death?"

"No glamour compelled him to make a false confession, nor did a bargain bind him. Beyond that, I cannot say, except that every word of his confession was a lie. When it came to Kilmere, he refused to say anything."

"Then you didn't . . . compel him to tell the truth?"

"He refused to consent. His mind is not stable—and he wants the truth hidden." Riven surveyed me, some indecipherable emotion flickering in his eyes. "Given his innocence, I did not think you'd have me drive him to the breaking point. Particularly when he may know nothing relevant to the case."

"Thank you."

He shook his head slightly, yet I could not bring myself to regret giving thanks where they were deserved. Perhaps it would be unwise with other fae, but Riven had yet to press his advantage. Still, best to hurry on and smooth things over. "What if he's protecting someone? That could give him reason to lie."

He's soft for his wife, Lord Denby had said. Could she have done it, rather than Mr. Tibbons? I flinched from the notion. Yet she'd been so distraught. Clearly she concealed something.

"You think he'd give his life to do so?"

"From what I've heard, he's deeply devoted to his wife and family. He was willing to give up all his lands to try to keep them safe."

"Possessions may be regained in time—one's life is another matter."

"Perhaps, but if he believed his wife or son had fallen prey to the curse and poisoned the townsfolk, he might have lied to protect them." We'd lingered overlong at the seawall, so I forced myself back into motion. "His peculiar story about leaving poison elsewhere would make sense if he knew that he *hadn't* done it, but someone else had, someone who would be compelled to kill again. Someone he wanted to keep safe from accusation."

"I'll concede it's the sort of illogical deed favored by your kind." Riven kept pace with me. "If we cannot locate venom with Tibbons, then we should call upon Mrs. Ellsworth and her son."

The recollection of her pain returned, vivid and condemning. Perhaps I couldn't do as Riven desired and seek to conquer Kilmere, but was there another way? In all likelihood it was the surest path to finding the truth of this bargain. If I delayed and others fell victim . . .

"I'd like to examine the one victim who still lives, Mr. Vershire, son of a local sea-blossom honey merchant," Riven said. "It seems he's hung on longer than the rest, but he's not expected to live more than another day or two. It's possible that some trace evidence remains that could direct our inquiries."

With difficulty, I wrenched my thoughts from Kilmere. "I cannot imagine anyone permitting us access."

"We don't need permission, only admittance. The man in question is in the care of Dr. Fulton, the town physician," Riven said. "If you distract him, I'll pay a visit to the patient and see if any evidence remains."

His plan didn't require that we glamour the doctor, and for that reason alone, I was inclined to agree. Even if the doctor was the surly sort, surely I could engage him in a few moments of conversation, long enough for Riven to examine the patient's chamber undisturbed. "We cannot be seen calling upon Dr. Fulton together, but perhaps if you accompanied me as you did when you first came to our townhome?"

"Very well. I'll take my leave." He offered a small bow before striding around the corner, a show to satisfy Dreda and any onlookers.

I waited for Dreda to close the gap between us, linking my arm through hers. "Do you mind if we call on Dr. Fulton?"

Her eyes widened slightly. "Are you feeling unwell?"

"No, I only wish to ask him a few questions about the curse and its victims."

She bobbed her head. "I see. I've no objection."

At that moment, Riven returned, shimmering threads of glamour drawn about him to conceal him from view. I obtained directions from a bystander and followed her away from the seawall and into the heart of Withern, where we halted before a charming two-story home crafted of white planks. The lady I'd spoken with had informed me the doctor resided here and when he didn't make house calls, he attended patients in the back. I hoped we'd find him at home.

Dreda and I strolled up to the door, and a servant appeared swiftly in response to my knock. I stepped forward. "We're here to see Dr. Fulton."

With the manner of one accustomed to all sorts of visitors at all hours, the servant moved aside. "This way, please."

From the brightly lit corridor adorned with nature lithographs, we passed to an antechamber with a number of chairs. The scents of dried yarrow, rue, and licorice teased at my senses, mingled with more pungent cleansers and—faint and far off, slightly acrid odors, those of sweat and vomit, suffering and death. Did my imagination conjure them, or had the agony of the victim pervaded the entire house? My stomach twisted.

"If you'll wait here, Dr. Fulton will see you shortly." The servant went into the room beyond, likely to notify the doctor.

Riven, who had accompanied us this far, now abandoned the antechamber in pursuit of whatever investigations he'd planned, and Dreda remained quiet, leaving me to my thoughts.

What did we know? Mr. Ellsworth had lied for some unknown reason. He hadn't administered the poison. And his wife and son may have gone to Kilmere. Mr. Tibbons certainly had. With Mr. Ellsworth innocent, Kilmere didn't need time to bend another mortal to its bidding. Whoever it used could strike again at any moment, unless I acted.

Jade climbed onto my lap, her warmth a comfort. *Do you consider a return?*

I fear I have no choice.

Yet perhaps there was some middle ground. If I must return to Kilmere, could I negotiate rather than attempt to conquer? *Could* one bargain with a malevolent, bloodthirsty fae stronghold? Or was such an attempt the greatest of follies?

A gentleman with long, graying side-whiskers and a solid frame strode into the room, glancing between me and Dreda. "Which one of you is the patient?"

"We're not here for treatment, but to discuss the victims of the recent poisonings."

His eyes, the shade of black currants, gleamed behind his spectacles, and the lines about them drew tight. "You'll forgive my bluntness, but I do not indulge in gossip about those in my care."

"Of course, I never dreamt you would." If only Riven had remained. Even without glamour, his natural charm would ease the situation. "It's just that I want to help, if I can. So many of the locals think it's a curse from Kilmere that has afflicted the dying, and with the ruin in my charge, I have concerns."

"Ah, you're the lass who intends to excavate the ruins." He stroked his side-whiskers. "I'm well aware of the rumors. I've treated several patients for nervous complaints brought on by fears of the curse alone. Why come to me? You wish your mind set at ease about their maladies and these recent deaths?"

"I suppose I do." I clutched my reticule tighter. "Do you attribute them to the curse, Dr. Fulton?"

"Before they found the poisoner, I'd have said there was a miasma about Kilmere, something in the air that doesn't agree with those who venture there." He adjusted his spectacles. "Now, we've no cause for such speculation. Ellsworth confessed to using spire-bane, a toxin for which there's no known remedy."

"Then you've given up hope for Mr. Vershire?"

"I'll do everything in my power to render him aid, but he

follows the same path his predecessors did, and I possess no antidote."

"Yet perhaps one could yet be found?" Perhaps Kilmere held information on that also, though I could not think why they'd want to spare mortals death. Still, if the venom was Other in nature, perhaps the cure was also—if one existed that could treat mortals. "Given the belief that these afflictions are connected to Kilmere, I feel in some way responsible, and I'd like to seek any cure that may exist in lore or herbalism—"

"You think I haven't sought the same, young lady?" The lines about his eyes deepened till they resembled the roots of a crows plant. "I've practiced medicine more years than you've walked this earth, only to see every effort come to naught for these unfortunates."

Jade tensed, as though poised to spring. I stroked her back, attempting to soothe her—and myself.

"Forgive me, I didn't mean to suggest otherwise. I can see how much you care." My voice dropped low. "And I can only imagine what you've suffered with each loss. Perhaps there's nothing I can do. As you've said, I'm young, and I lack your experience. But still, I mean to try. Isn't that a responsibility we all bear—to do what rests in our power to assist others?"

The rigid lines of his face softened, revealing a deep weariness beneath. "That's true enough, and I wish more felt the same. Forgive my hasty remarks. If you chance upon something you believe would help, bring it to me, and I'll investigate the matter."

Outside the antechamber, I sensed Riven once more, the pricking sense of Other strong. "Thank you, Dr. Fulton. You've been most helpful. We won't take more of your time."

Dreda and I, accompanied by Jade and Asrina, trooped from the room and out onto the footwalk once more. Riven waited there, and Dreda evinced no surprise at his presence, but simply fell in at a slight distance behind us. Bless her deliberate lack of curiosity.

When his glamour spread about us and I could be sure none would overhear, I turned to him. "Did you learn anything?"

"Very little life remains. No ability to respond, let alone recount anything that happened to him. It's clear basilisk venom is killing him, but the pall of death was so strong that it obscured any other trace."

The sea breeze sent salt air swirling around us, tingling across my face even at this distance. "When I spoke with Dr. Fulton, I wondered—from what you said before, it sounds as if fae can heal at times from basilisk venom. Does an antidote exist?"

"For fae, yes. Even so, too much venom, and they'll die before they can avail themselves of it. But it is Other in nature. For a mortal, the remedy itself would destroy them, hastening death."

I should not have considered otherwise; surely Riven would have suggested it before, if a known treatment existed. Still, I couldn't give up on Mr. Vershire, not yet. "Perhaps there's some record within Kilmere of a way to treat mortals who've succumbed?"

"It's conceivable, but the fae of Kilmere were far more concerned with taking lives than restoring them." His gaze raked over me. "And you've resolved against a return, have you not?"

"That was before Lord West claimed a mortal as his own." Before I'd scented death within the doctor's home, before I'd witnessed the suffering the Ellsworths endured—the weight of each crushing my soul.

The glamour about us deepened. "Then you're prepared to try to master it."

"I cannot, not yet." Even the mention plummeted me back into memories of the heart—the heat, the stench of blood, the images of lives stolen without sense or reason. My pulse throbbed at the base of my neck. "Not without understanding more."

Riven raised a brow. "You know its nature now. What more remains?"

I knew its nature, but I did not know my own. If I joined to Kilmere, whether I mastered it or it mastered me, I could become something bent on hurt, on destruction, endangering all those around me. I fixed my gaze forward. "I only mean to seek information on the bargain, something to help free those suffering. Perhaps greater understanding will reveal another path."

"Last time, you did something Kilmere did not expect. Caused it to reassess, allowed us time to withdraw." He navigated us around a shop display that spilled into the street. "When we return, that advantage will be gone. It won't sit idle while you seek out its secrets."

Unless I could upend its expectations again. My head throbbed in time with my pulse. Twisted bargains marked all the dealings of the Otherworld, and however much I disliked the notion, I might need to avail myself of one. "What if I led it to believe I intend to offer something it desires?"

His attention rested on me, sharp, focused. "What do you have in mind?"

We passed two boxwoods, standing on either side of a blue door in tall white planters. Their strong, purgative song swirled through my mind, and as their melodies flowed across my senses, a possibility took shape. *Jade, how directly can I speak with Kilmere?*

It has awareness enough to hear and understand your speech, though it cannot respond in kind. She trotted along the cobbled stones. *As best as I can understand, it communicates in impression and image, in sensation more than word. Yet it cannot read your mind, only judge your words and actions.*

Then it is worth a try. The song of the boxwood faded as we left them behind, yet something of their evergreen strength remained. "In Denby Hall I spoke with a nisi."

"A nisi engaged with you?" A flicker of interest crossed his features. "Did you command it?"

"No, only offered her a gift. She wouldn't accept without giving me one in return."

"And what did she offer?"

"It was a seed, I believe, but one I've never seen before." Even now, it seemed to call to me from my reticule, where I'd left it, as though it held the faintest of songs—one which waited to spring to full and vibrant life. It would bear closer examination later, but for now, I returned to the matter at hand. "After our exchange, she referred to many debts owed to Kilmere. Right now, it does not appear to be collecting them in an efficient manner. If I carefully suggest I might assist, provided I understand the terms of the bargain I'll be working to fulfill, would it take the bait?"

"There's a good chance. At its core, it's driven to see this bargain fulfilled. It stands to gain if you serve that purpose, particularly if you make no greater demand than understanding the bargain. After it uses you, it's still at liberty to discard you in favor of a stronger master." The lowering rays of the sun fell across his face, kindling green flame in his eyes. "Yet it's a stopgap measure at best. More information has value, but even if you pry the truth from Kilmere, you cannot stop it—or Lord West—without taking control."

"Perhaps . . . perhaps we could address one difficulty at a time?" Despite my best efforts, my voice wavered.

His gaze seem to burn to my very soul, exposing things I did not wish seen. At last, he gave a curt nod. "You understand we'll have to return to the heart. If any record of the bargain remains, it will be there."

And once in, I'd have to shed blood to leave. Pain ghosted up my arm. "I'll do what I must. But there's one other difficulty —I cannot take Dreda back, not now that I know the extent of the danger."

"Then we'll go alone."

And create the worst sort of scandal? I stumbled over an uneven stone. "Aunt Caris would never permit it."

"She doesn't need to know. We'll go late tonight, after the household retires."

If my absence was discovered, I'd be able to offer no explanation, but since it was our only option . . . "Very well."

"I'll come for you at midnight. Be ready."

Dread clutched at my heart, and I could only manage a nod. The ruins held the truth I required, or so I hoped. But they also possessed power I might be forced to accept—or die in the attempt to acquire.

No, I wouldn't consider it, not yet. Surely my offer would tempt Kilmere into revealing the truth of the bargain, perhaps even into offering some leverage I might use against Lord West.

I glanced over my shoulder, toward the cliff upon which the ruins lurked. Perhaps it would listen—or perhaps would merely mock me as it broke my body upon its stones.

Regardless, I must try.

CHAPTER 36

The hours flew by with discomfiting speed, until darkness settled over the gardens and quiet descended upon the house. Everyone had retired content, most particularly Aunt Caris, who'd discovered her locket wedged behind her dresser after I'd suggested we conduct another examination of her room.

Relief had suffused her features. "I cannot think how I missed it before. I'm certain I looked back there."

"Well, we've found it now—that's the most important thing." And the culprit had sworn to put an end to his harassment.

Could I find a means of forcing Kilmere to do the same? I sat alone in the stillness of my room, pondering that question, until the gleaming power of a passing rippled through the air, and Riven appeared.

If anyone discovered his presence, it would matter a great deal and very little all at once, compared to the threat of Kilmere. I lifted Jade from the chair and clutched her to my chest. Now that the time had arrived, I would have paid anything in my possession if I could only escape what must come.

Jade rumbled low in her chest. *You can still withdraw, if you choose.*

Do you truly believe that the best course?

She subsided into silence. Kilmere and I had become irrevocably connected, and she knew it as well as I did. Still, I stalled, standing in the center of the room, Jade held close to my heart. "I've been . . . wondering how much Ibbie knew of the nature of the ruins. Would Kilmere have ever permitted her to reach its heart?"

Riven leaned against the mantel, the picture of relaxed grace —as though our expedition concerned him not at all. "She might have found the door to the undercrofts, if Kilmere desired it, but on her own, she'd never have been able to undo the workings and gain entrance."

"But why did it permit her to explore at all?"

"It might have sought to exploit her, to extend its influence by working on her mind." His brows drew inward. "It's possible her fae husband offered some protections as well."

"Wouldn't he have explored Kilmere himself?"

"It's difficult to say. If the property passed to him upon their marriage, he'd have rights of ownership. If he mastered it, she'd have been kept safe as he dictated."

"And if she retained ownership?" I sank into the comfort of fact-gathering, of seeking information rather than considering the reality of what was to come: that I must again stand within the living-turned-dead—and that the ruins might not release us this time without greater sacrifice.

"He could have passed through the boundary with her, as I did you," he said. "I don't think he ever claimed it, not in full, else he'd have wielded his control over this region in unmistakable ways."

"What reason would he have had for restraint?"

"He might not have known what he held. The tale your Ibbie penned suggested he knew of the objects of power within, not that he understood its true nature. If he didn't trouble himself to examine it further, he'd never have perceived all it truly is."

"And you think it possible he'd have exerted himself so little?"

"Most fae think your world holds nothing of value aside from mortal thralls. Why would he bother to carry out the work on his own when he could command others, when he'd have no reason to conceive of an outpost of this nature?" Riven lifted his shoulders. "I've never heard even a whispered rumor of a fortress constructed by forbidden arts in the mortal world. Certainly, it's not common knowledge."

I tightened my grip on Jade. "Then how did Lord West discover its true nature?"

"I'd very much like the answer to that, among many other things." A slight frown crossed his face. "As for Ibbie's husband, it's possible he knew the nature of Kilmere, and merely bided his time. It's a forbidden power, and one that could have caused trouble for him in his court, if seized in the wrong moment. He might have intended to claim it at a strategic time."

"Might he have waited decades?"

"He might have waited a century or two and counted it as nothing. To amass power is as much about strategy as force, and fae do not suffer the same time constraints as mortals."

"Either way, he would have been required to rely on mortals to excavate for him and report their findings. What of the risk that they'd lie about what they found?"

"He'd not deem it a risk. Since your Ibbie was bound to him, he'd be able to force the truth from her. He'd have no reason to exercise restraint nor doubt she gave him a full account," Riven said. "Most of my kind would not believe mortals capable of resistance under those circumstances. But it appears your Ibbie had a great deal of fortitude."

Fortitude and stubbornness alike—she'd never have given him the satisfaction of breaking her, not while any spark of life remained. Only, what had it cost her? "If she—"

"Jessa." Riven pressed upright and crossed the room until he stood only an arm's length from me. "This won't grow any easier for the waiting. And postponing our departure increases the chance your absence will be exposed."

He was right, of course. I lowered my head. "Very well. I'm ready."

Yet nothing could be further from the truth. I'd never be ready to return to Kilmere, not if ten decades or more had passed. Despite the warmth Jade offered, despite the cloak I donned, I remained cold to the core.

Brilliant light flared about us, multihued strands weaving through the air, the pressure increasing, my stomach lurching as the power of the passing pulled us to the very border of Kilmere.

My head spun, and I clutched at the sturdy trunk of an oak, its strength steadying me. A sliver of moon sliced the sky above us. By its light, Kilmere appeared even more eerie, its tumbled stones jutting from the earth like jagged fangs.

In the distance, waves broke unending against the cliff, dashing themselves to pieces against the might of the forged stone. The salt tang of the air mingled with the bitter metallic taste of the workings, and I wanted nothing more than to flee, to run back to the confines of Willowere, to the warmth of Aunt Caris and the camaraderie of my sisters—but no. They were why I'd come.

I marched over to the boundary stones, positioning myself in the space between the fae domain and the mortal one. And I spoke into the stillness. "You want me gone, but you also have a bargain that requires fulfillment, many debts still owed. Your means of collecting them appears to be lacking—you need someone to represent your interests beyond your borders. Perhaps I can offer aid, if you grant us safe passage so that we might understand the nature of the bargain that must be fulfilled."

The hush deepened, as if Kilmere considered my words. Then the stones gently parted, a gap forming in the wall. Did that indicate consent? Or a new snare forming? Either way, I must go on.

In silence, Riven and I crossed the boundary, Jade draped over my shoulders and Asrina close between us. The immense darkness of Kilmere tried to snuff her light, but it flared all the brighter.

A disquieting moan rose from the stones about us, the echo of a mournful cry from some long-ago soul. And I shuddered. Kilmere might tolerate my presence for a moment, might seek to assess my intentions, but against the vast expanse of the ruin I was nothing—a tool to be used and discarded, a nuisance soon eliminated. I rubbed my temples.

It's planting ideas.

I know. Yet they felt so very real, so very persuasive. For all the hostility charging the air, it made no move against us— summoned no creatures bent on our destruction, formed no sudden rifts in the ground, conjured no dense fogs to bewilder us. Still, the moon and stars winked from sight, as though a wash of dark ink blurred the sky.

Riven took a risk, surrounding us with a ring of glowing fae-lights, their rich golden warmth bathing my skin and bringing a small measure of peace. Even that Kilmere allowed with only a low rumble as a warning: it watched and would act, if we violated its will.

Atop my shoulders, Jade tensed, as though she readied herself for defense. But what could she do—what could any of us do—if Kilmere chose to strike?

I followed Riven toward the central keep, stopping at the doorway. The walls towered far above my head, their sigils stark and ominous. It bristled with power, and I'd no desire to be thrust through the earth again, nor forced into another death trap.

"There's a passage down." Riven jabbed a finger toward the bleakness before us. "I suggest you seek it."

Why must he insist on pressing me to do things *he* could

do with the greatest of ease? Was it part of his attempt to solve my peculiarities? Or to prod me into taking control of Kilmere? Asrina flickered bright at my shoulder, her light a rapid pulse of encouragement, and I sought any sign of a way downward.

In the far corner of the vast open chamber, a staircase ascended to a now-missing floor. Where its landing met the ground, a dark shadow pooled, shifting in the gloom.

Oh.

The stairs continued below the stone, the shadows marking their descent. I moved forward, and this time, rather than tumbling through the earth, we descended into its depths on smooth, broad stairs.

Kilmere might have allowed its exterior to fall into ruin, but now that we made a proper descent, everything held the same dark beauty the fae had originally crafted into it, the stones meticulously polished, the fae-lights glowing upon the walls, the workings woven into vibrant paintings.

Our passage came with suspicious ease, as though Kilmere contented itself with drawing us deeper into its coils. What need had it to expend energy to force us to its heart, when we'd expressed our intent to return?

The staircase led to an octagonal chamber. Its floors were of pale polished stone, and its obsidian walls were shot through with gleaming strands of silver and gold. The roof formed an arched dome far above our heads, yet blessedly no bones provided support.

On each side, a passage led out of sight. *Can you scent which way to go?*

It shifts, but I believe we must descend using the right shaft.

Her guess would be far more accurate than mine, so we passed through that corridor, which moved ever downward. We soon found another door that matched the one we'd encountered in the death-by-drowning chamber. I could not discern if it was in fact the same door, only removed to this new location, or if the fortress possessed numerous doors with the form of the rampant dragon, all leading toward its heart.

In the end, it didn't matter—nor did I have to attempt to rework the lock, for the door swung open at our approach. Such was the nature of Kilmere that its welcome inspired only a desire to run as far and fast as possible.

I inhaled the sweet-grass scent of Jade's fur, her steady presence sparking my courage, and I forged on.

The air warmed slightly about us, and the walls began to pulse ominously, like the beat of an enormous, ancient heart, that of a patient predator waiting for some misstep on the part of its prey. My steps slowed, my feet dragging across the polished stone until we came to an intersection of ways.

I recognized the tunnel that we joined—it was the one we'd taken after our desperate flight from the heart, the one we must now descend. Straightening, I marched downward till I reached the double doors that led to the heart.

They stood open, as we'd left them, an invitation—or a command—to enter. My chest tightened, my breath shallowed. And I couldn't force my feet to move.

"Do you still mean to go on?" Riven spoke soft and low.

Mutely, I nodded. Without another word, he took my hand and placed it on his arm, as though we meant to enjoy a simple stroll. Then he strode forward, his strength bolstering my own.

The enormous rib cage arced overhead, and my own ached. How much had the eld dragon endured here? How long had it suffered before the mercy of its final breath? My vision blurred, and I forced my gaze away from the bones.

We were here for a purpose, so I moved away from Riven, never mind that I felt like a boat unmoored in treacherous waters. The thrumming power of the chamber beat against my senses, demanding obeisance. It waited, perhaps to see what I intended, but it would not delay much longer.

I moved toward the stand—it was a reasonable place to start. The runes were visible once more on its surface, and as I traced them with my finger, something shifted in the stone beneath.

"Continue," Riven said. "Follow the basilisk border."

So I did, the cold searing my flesh as I traced the writhing forms, completing the border. The stone sides slid back, revealing a shallow compartment in the middle containing a scroll bound with a band of silver.

When I unrolled it, a border of twined basilisks met my gaze, along with line after line of fae script, stark black against the pale parchment, unfaded despite the passing of centuries. The back of my neck tingled.

We'd found what we sought.

Asrina cast her light over it, the gentle glow transforming the words into ones I could understand, as it had once before in the Cloister library with the old logbook. Only now Riven and I read side by side, and the scent of sun-drenched forest washed over me, driving back the coppery stench of old blood.

Oh.

My breath caught. Here it was: in exchange for the prospering of Withern, for the wealth and resources transferred to the region by the introduction of the sea-blossoms and instruction on how to produce the honey, the inhabitants agreed to supply *people*. One from each family who'd dwelt there when then terms were struck, to be provided every twenty years, time without end. Old or young, hale or infirm, it did not matter according to the bargain, only that they would be presented to Kilmere—and thanks to the beneficence of the fae, there they'd receive immortality.

The light about Riven flared, casting deep shadows behind him. As his glamour faded, I shrank from glimmers of the wilder fae beauty and power that emerged. This bargain meant something to him; he understood perhaps far more than I. Yet he did not speak, and I dared not ask.

Whether through some trick of the light or the power woven into the bargain itself, the forms of the basilisks writhed across the page, their fangs flashing. I braced myself against the stand, and the hunger of Kilmere flooded my senses.

It craved the lives promised with a lust grown stronger through its centuries of waiting, the scraps of blood and life thrown its way only stoking its hunger, its desire for its power restored. Small wonder it granted me passage long enough to see if I would execute its desires in the broader world, enabling it to return to its former glory.

How soon would it perceive that I did not intend to claim the lives owed it? I rolled the scroll tight. This bargain meant more than I'd ever dreamt. It provided conclusive evidence that high fae had constructed a fortress and dwelt alongside mortals —a thing supposed to have never happened—and that they'd made binding bargains en masse.

Now that it was roused, Kilmere would see the bargain fulfilled one way or another. The walls of the chamber closed in about me.

And when Riven surveyed me, something in his eyes made me flinch.

"Are you satisfied?" he asked. "You now know what must be done."

"I understand." But even if I did as Riven desired and seized control of Kilmere, wielding it as a weapon against Lord West, this bargain would stand, would cause death and suffering unless I could find some loophole.

He paced the length of the chamber, surveying its workings closely and halting in places as though he perceived evidence I could not. Yet he made no comment on whatever he observed. How could he, with Kilmere listening?

I turned from him to look at the terms again, seeking some means of escape. I couldn't imagine the fae would have offered anything not to their own advantage. Why would they sweeten the bargain with the offer of immortality to those who presented themselves?

Oh.

Could they—surely not, but why else? I half-turned, seeking Riven. "This promise of immortality, the people surrendered to Kilmere, were they turned into . . ."

"Ghouls. Or wights."

Though his voice remained impassive, I rocked back, bumping into the stand. Men and women, determined to better their families and their communities, hopeful for new life, had come to Kilmere and been turned into monsters. It was unthinkable.

The basilisks blurred before my eyes, and when I wrenched my gaze away, the bleached bones of the dragon met them. More suffering. More death.

All for what?

To gain power?

My eyes slid shut, blotting the chamber of horrors from view. I wanted to flee this place, flee the reminders of the unspeakable cruelty of the fae. They'd found a way to damn the mortals snared in their bargain—either they kept their word and became mindless monsters or they suffered an agonizing death by basilisk venom. Either way, their lives were spent to strengthen Kilmere.

Riven crossed his arms. "Did you read to the end?"

I shook my head, unable to trust my voice. Surely it would be safer to have this conversation elsewhere, but if we left too soon, ignored something important, we might not be able to readily regain access. I needed to hear what Riven would say first.

"From these original thirty families have sprung hundreds of descendants." He might as well have been crafted from the same stone as Kilmere for all the feeling his words held. "According to the terms of this bargain, since they have not turned their family members over to Kilmere through the years, all of their lives are forfeit to the basilisk—or its venom."

Many debts, the nisi had said, but many lives would have been more correct. I could not let it stand; I could not change it.

Should I ever become proper mistress to Kilmere, I'd have no choice but to inflict these deaths, because I'd be caught in the binding as well.

I struggled to choose words that would not betray my sentiments to Kilmere and bring upon us death by dragon-fire. "When the fae left, there would have been no one in Kilmere to accept the tithe. What then? Can the bargain still endure?"

"Were it bound to a single fae, it would cease with his or her death, unless willed to another. This bargain joins with Kilmere. It still binds with all the force and power once woven into the ruin itself."

And the canny fae had crafted it so the destruction of Kilmere would also result in the total devastation of the region and its inhabitants, leaving them no escape. Given how they'd crafted the whole situation in their favor, why *had* they left? I didn't dare ask now, lest it upset Kilmere. Instead, I clasped my hands together so tightly that it sent pain shooting up my arms. "Reading this, I understand how the work has progressed so slowly. If the lives of all the original descendants must be claimed—but no others—that's not a task for one mortal, even with a supply of basilisk venom."

"Difficult indeed. Were Kilmere still under the keeping of a fae master, the work would be finished in days." He twisted the green-and-gold ring on his finger. "This will take far longer."

Which allowed me an opportunity to . . . what?

He continued smoothly, "But there's something more. Since the basilisk was integral to the bargain, there's a chance it remained here in stasis, even after the fae departed, particularly if they ever intended to return. It would have been a far more effective way to enforce the terms of the bargain, given the basilisk would be able to perceive the strands of the binding to target the proper individuals."

"But if the basilisk required the Otherworld and the fae it was bonded to for survival—"

"In stasis, it needs neither, but the moment it woke, it would have to find its bond-mate. If the fae in question were dead, it would need to bond with another within a few hours in order to survive."

A shudder passed through Jade's frame, and I stroked her soft fur. Such a fate had come close to being her own—the reminder couldn't be pleasant.

"Come." Riven returned to one of the places he'd examined closely. "I believe this sheltered the basilisk, but how long ago is difficult to say, given the number of workings in this space."

I examined the wall, which first appeared solid stone, graven with thick sigils. Yet as my fingers met the cold surface, a niche revealed itself, polished smooth and glittering on the inside. Certainly, no basilisk occupied it now, and I shuddered to think that one might have been imprisoned here in stasis for centuries. Yet if it had, it changed things.

It would mean that Kilmere had never required someone to carry the venom, but rather an individual to bond with the basilisk, that it might carry out the terms of its bargain. Either way, the mortal in question must have explored Kilmere. "If the basilisk did survive to be reawakened, wouldn't the bargain already have found swift fulfillment?"

"It would have been weakened by centuries of stasis. It would require not only a bond for its survival, but time traversing back and forth to the Otherworld to regain strength. If bonded to a fae, it would strengthen faster—conversely, a mortal would slow its recovery."

"Thus Kilmere grows impatient." How long would it believe I had something to offer to help it fulfill the bargain? How long did we have before the basilisk reached full strength and returned to destroy the townsfolk? And who had it bonded to?

Mr. Tibbons had come to Kilmere first, before any of the Ellsworths . . . and he'd not restrained himself to seeking lost animals on the surface. Had the basilisk itself clouded his mind, obscuring its presence to carry out its bound duty?

"It's also possible that the basilisk died long ago or passed into the Otherworld centuries back, and the bargain has sought another expression, coercing mortals to use the venom." Riven shrugged, as if it mattered little. "It would be within the original language."

"Which do you think more likely?"

"It's not a situation in which we should guess. We require certainty." His eyes lost their usual lively luster, becoming the cold green of sea glass. "It's time to press Tibbons, find the memories he lost. Then we can act."

I let the scroll fall to the table, and a cloud of dust puffed around us. "If you do that, it could hurt him beyond repair—leave his mind broken."

The air about us warmed, a reminder of the fury Kilmere might yet unleash. It did not want my concern, only my bondage to its will.

"I'm aware." His voice could have cut through stone. "That's where you come in. If Tibbons possesses the basilisk, you could claim it from him. You already have experience with your *kitsne*; you'll be a more effective bond-mate for the basilisk. Your abilities will bolster it to achieve its ends."

He carefully crafted words to support my original claim—at least, I hoped it was no more. I faltered. "Then I suppose we must find him."

"Yes, I believe we've uncovered all that's relevant here. It's time we go."

"Then I'll need your dagger again," I whispered. Kilmere might have allowed us access, but it wouldn't release us without some payment of the blood it craved.

My fingers curled inward, as if to protect my body from the pain that must come. Would Kilmere see it as a sufficient sacrifice, or would it now require more?

Riven slid the dagger from its sheath, but before I could move or even blink, he slashed his own hand, rivulets of crimson spilling over his fingers. He didn't flinch, nor give any sign of the pain he endured.

I checked the question that sprang to my lips as he pressed his hand to the wall. How could I begin to understand him? At times he appeared to embrace fae philosophies, to feel nothing for the suffering around him—and then this. Why would he injure himself to spare me? Nothing in our bargain required it.

As his blood ran down the stone, the palest lines of silver-white shimmered to the surface, shot through with scarlet, as I'd glimpsed once before. Not the outline of our exit, but threads of a working that yearned to rise to the surface, one banished by the sudden flare of the power controlling the door.

A tremor shook the chamber; the door swung wide. Riven turned to me. "Come. We shouldn't linger."

CHAPTER 37

When the light of the passing faded, I wasn't within my bedchamber, but the back garden of the *Sea Blossom*, with the waves crashing on the shore not far beyond. I stumbled, seizing the low stone wall for balance. Wait . . . did Riven truly mean to wrest the missing memories from Mr. Tibbons?

I couldn't allow his mind to be broken, if he'd acted with no intended malice. "Riven, why are we here? I thought what you said about me being a better bond-mate for the basilisk was a distraction for Kilmere?"

"It was distraction and truth alike. You'd be a more effective mistress and enforcer of the bargain, yet that's not why we've come."

"Then you seek Mr. Tibbons." The rasping cry of a nightjar sounded overhead.

"Yes. On some level, he's involved, and he must give account." Riven inclined his head. "Given your mortal conventions, I suggest you remain here while I seek him out."

How could he one minute shed his own blood to spare another pain, the next condemn a man? "You can't just decide to break him. I know that in your world—"

"If he's involved, hundreds will die. We require the truth. Do you deny it?"

"No, but—"

"It may not be necessary to force his memories, if a search of his belongings reveals the venom or the basilisk."

"And if not?"

"Then his memories of Kilmere must be drawn forth."

Jade had warned me of this ability of arbiters that even fae feared. The distant crash of the waves roared in my ears. "What if he's not involved at all?"

"His involvement is no longer in doubt, only the nature of it remains in question. If he's bonded with the basilisk to deal out death, then his fate has been sealed. Either we intervene now and spare others or it will break him once its task is done, forcing him to bear it to the Otherworld, where he'll become prey to the knot while it bonds with another of its own kind."

"I refuse to accept that." Nor had I thought Riven would, not when pressed. Tears sprang to my eyes.

"If you mortals had the privilege of more centuries, your perspective might change." His voice dropped low. "Do you prefer the deaths of many to the forced accounting of one?"

"There must be another way to get the information from him, if required."

"Not when he doesn't recall it. Something has a strong hold on him, that much was clear from the first." Riven raked a hand through his hair. "I'll do what I can to preserve his mind. I can promise no more."

"But you waited until now—"

"Because I required clearer evidence. While we were in the heart, I sought any traces he might have left—and found them," Riven said. "He descended, Jessa. Kilmere would have only one reason to lure him in and then release him."

"You didn't say anything then."

"It wasn't a wise discussion to have in the confines of

Kilmere. Yet it indicates he knows something. Witnessed something, at the least."

The damp night air settled over me with its attendant chill. I wrapped my cloak tighter, shivering. How could I reconcile the choice before me: the deaths of all the descendants of Withern's founding families or the forced shattering of a mind?

On the face of it, hundreds of lives held more value than one, but didn't each matter? And *I* was the individual responsible for bidding Mr. Tibbons to continue his quest. If he'd fallen victim to the basilisk . . . My stomach churned. "You won't interrogate him alone?"

"First I'll search his chambers." Riven stepped away from me, onto the path. "If it's necessary to address him, I'll bring him out."

When he left, I sank to the ground against the wall and buried my face in my hands. What if we'd gotten it all wrong? What if, despite exploring the depths of Kilmere, Mr. Tibbons wasn't the one? He'd still suffer the consequences.

Could I stop this? Should I? I couldn't draw a full breath, couldn't see a clear path forward. If Mr. Tibbons was guilty and the basilisk discovered, then what?

Jade perched at my side, peering alert into the darkness. *Then Riven will slay the basilisk, robbing Kilmere of its most effective weapon.*

I rested my hand on her head. *How do you know?*

I don't, not for certain, but it seems the best play. If Kilmere loses the basilisk—or the mortal through which it dispenses the venom, whichever the case may be—then it cannot claim its debts in Withern until it finds another to act on its behalf.

What she said should have brought relief. If we could bring about a temporary stay of execution for those bound to Kilmere, then it must be cause for rejoicing. Yet somehow the prospective death of the basilisk and the threat to Mr. Tibbons felt like a victory for Kilmere, not for us—because even if we spent their lives, the binding would remain.

There's something else. Removing the basilisk would weaken Kilmere's hold on the bargain, give you a stronger position for assuming control.

Was that Riven's aim? Above me, the branches of an alder rustled, its restiveness matching my own. *There's so much I still don't understand about Kilmere. What we learned today—why would the high fae ever have abandoned their stronghold, forfeiting the lives that belonged to them?*

I think . . . Jade gave a half-strangled chuff, a sound tinged with frustration. *There's much I am bound not to speak of to those outside my court. This is one such matter.*

She must refer to the geas that bound her and Riven—and all fae, if I understood aright—preventing them from talking of whatever protections mortals might possess against Otherkind, whatever rules kept our worlds in some sort of precarious balance. How did this relate? Or did it? Perhaps fae had many things which they were forbidden from sharing with mortals. If so, Riven might well have perceived and understood far more of Kilmere and its past than he was able to speak . . .

Her muscles coiled tight. *You should consider what else contains mysteries of the relations between worlds.*

Even those words entered my mind in a labored fashion, as though she must exert herself to speak them. Could she refer to the Forgotten War? It was what sprang first to mind. Had something happened during the war that had forced the high fae to abandon Kilmere? Without high fae in residence, Kilmere could not have turned the mortals into ghouls or wights—and without the basilisk active, it would have had no means of meting out the consequence for the broken bargain, at least not without a fae master. It seemed logical enough, but I had no proof.

If neither Riven nor Jade could speak of it, then I'd have to find another way to unearth the information in future. I rested my head on the wall, the coolness of the stone an unpleasant reminder of Kilmere.

A moment later, Riven appeared around the corner of the inn—and Mr. Tibbons wasn't with him.

"Did you discover venom in his chambers?" I pressed to my feet, hope blossoming as bright as forsythia in spring. If we'd no need to meddle with his mind . . .

Riven shook his head, the motion sharp. "No venom, no trace of the basilisk in the chamber. And Tibbons is gone."

"What?"

"He's left Withern."

I rocked back. Mr. Tibbons wasn't the sort to abandon his duties, unless some force of Other had swayed him. "Then . . . what do you intend to do?"

Riven said nothing. Only the quiet rustle of the alder broke the stillness. In truth, I did not know what I wanted him to say. Either way, Mr. Tibbons faced grave danger—with the basilisk on one side and Riven on the other. Yet if it were true that the basilisk had claimed him, then he could not go unchecked to continue dealing death. As if she sensed my distress, Asrina dropped to my shoulder, her warm glow bathing my face.

"Kilmere revealed the truth about the bargain, yet much remains hidden. I believe Tibbons's memories will provide the clarity we require. Certainly, if he's facilitating the execution of the curse, he must be stopped," Riven said. "Wherever he is, I intend to see him brought back—and the basilisk, if she hasn't hidden herself away."

"But doesn't she need to remain close? If she absented herself, couldn't he seek to break the connection?"

"She doesn't need proximity to ensure he stays bound. The serpent-folk of the Otherworld possess the ability to mesmerize. Their craft can't control high fae, but mortals have no means to resist—even apart from Kilmere, he'd be entirely hers to command. If she felt herself at risk, she could simply find a safe place and send for him when she willed. She remains hidden somewhere in stasis even now, perhaps using him as a decoy."

Thus the need to see his memories. I bent to pick up Jade, a convenient excuse to hide my face. "Then you mean to track him down?"

The sharp-edged slice of moon cast cold light upon his face. "No, I'm going to send Nikol after him."

"Nikol. But he—"

"He won't toy with Tibbons, if that's what concerns you. He owes me a debt, he'll bring him back unharmed."

Why would Riven so readily call in his debt for Mr. Tibbons?

Jade chuffed. *I don't believe he's acting on behalf of Tibbons.*

Then what? Never mind, it doesn't matter now. I pulled Jade closer. "But if you went—"

"Damir would press his advantage. You deem it worth that risk?"

"No . . . I suppose not."

"Then Nikol will fetch him."

I twisted my fingers into Jade's thick fur. "When he's found, will you send for me?"

"If you want—but I'll warn you, I mean to uncover the truth, whatever methods are required."

"Even so, I want to come."

"Very well then." With a swirl of light and a dizzying change of pressure, Riven drew us back to the haven of my bedchamber, moving away from me the moment the passing faded.

"There's one thing more. Though the evidence appears to condemn Tibbons, we can't afford to neglect the others who have entered Kilmere. It may well seek to use every means at its disposal to force the bargain fulfilled—there's no requirement that only one do its bidding." By the window, he halted. "I'll fetch you in the morning to speak with Ellsworth's wife and son."

Before I could object, he vanished.

~

I STOOD in the heart of Kilmere, holding a dagger crafted of a rose-hued metal, its jeweled hilt gleaming. In my hand, the dagger warmed until it cast a radiance that far outshone the fae-lights surrounding me.

From the shadows, Riven stalked to my side. "You found the dagger. I'd wondered if Kilmere would offer it to you, if you brought yourself to master it."

My pulse leapt. He'd expected this? No, he'd wanted me to take control of Kilmere as a defense against Lord West—as a protection. This wasn't right.

"I'll need you to give it to me." Coils of light flared about him.

"Why?"

"My king requires it. It's more important than you know."

"And what does he mean to do with it?" If the dagger somehow linked the power of Kilmere to the mortal world, then to hand it over could endanger countless lives.

"It's not your concern."

"Then I can't give it to you."

"Jessa." His eyes took on the dark hue of the forest by night. "That wasn't a request."

"Only assure me it will do no harm—"

"You'll surrender the dagger to me. Now."

The intensity of the glamour he turned on me made my head swim. Why wouldn't I just surrender it to him? I didn't have need of it. I should give it to—no, I couldn't. I clutched it tighter, backing away from him.

His face became emotionless, so very fae. And I trembled. If he meant to seize it, I had no hope of stopping him.

"I said I would tell you if things changed with regard to my king and Kilmere." The scent of storm eclipsed that of the sun. "Now they have. Surrender the dagger, surrender Kilmere, and you'll live. I'll make an excuse to the king for your survival, only you must stay far from here."

I froze. It wasn't only the dagger—now his king wanted Kilmere also? There could be no good purpose for fae to reclaim a fortress of ancient darkness, one which would give them a foothold in our world. The jewels on the hilt dug painfully into my skin. "Riven, I —can you give me your word he means only good by it?"

Silence stretched between us.

"The time grows short. But if you bargain, there's no need for your death."

My death.

"Please listen, Jessa." His voice dropped low, became slightly ragged.

Frigid air pebbled my skin. Would he truly kill me, if I resisted? Mocvar had feared him. Jade had told me she wasn't sure I could trust him—but I'd wanted to, I'd thought I'd seen something different in him than the cruelty that marked most fae. As I hesitated, power gathered about us, an unbearable tension. "I can't give you Kilmere, not if—"

He struck. Light coiled from his fingers and stabbed into my chest, burning agony in its wake.

And I . . . I reached for Kilmere, for the power it offered, its ancient workings sinking deep into my body, thirsting for his blood, for the power he could offer if consumed . . .

I collided with cold floorboards, the bedcovers tangled about my limbs. Sharp pain pierced my ribs, and the damp of tears stained my cheeks.

Jade burrowed against me, resting her head on my wildly pulsing heart. *Be still.*

Jade—she was here, in Willowere, and so was I. There was no Riven, no Kilmere, no dagger.

Only a dream.

Above my head, leaves whispered soothing songs and vines gently caressed my face. How? I blinked into the dim tangle woven about me, a barrier sufficient to ward off any intruder.

And a rap sounded at the door. "Jessa? Are you well?"

Ada, of all things. I swiped at the damp of my cheeks, then

pressed myself upright, only to collide with the cage of gold runners that had charged to my defense, their vines now as thick as sapling trunks, hedging me in so I couldn't break free. Could matters get any worse?

"We can't just stand here waiting." Ainslie addressed Ada. Of course she'd come too. "What if an intruder has broken in? That thud was loud enough to wake us both."

"I'm fine!" What could I do about the vines? I couldn't let them see, yet I couldn't think, could only see on the canvas of my mind Riven, wild and fae as he struck—no, it was only a dream. I pressed a hand to my aching ribs. "I just had a nightmare, and I tumbled out of bed. That's all."

I touched one of the vines, and it coiled around my finger, thrumming with a fierce promise to shield me from sight—to protect me, life for life. It was glorious, powerful, and . . . altogether unnatural.

Cold thorns of fear pricked my flesh. I couldn't let my sisters see; I must conceal it from them somehow.

The determination of the gold runners flared to match my own. They could conceal; they would protect. It was their purpose.

"Are you hurt?" Ada asked.

"No, I'm just . . . I'm fine."

A short pause. "You don't sound fine."

"She's not fine." That was Ainslie, swift and decisive. "Fetch the key, we need to get in."

Perspiration dampened my gown, every muscle tensed. I wasn't fine, not by any measure, but I must keep them out. If they entered, I could find no explanation to account for *this*.

Jade leapt upon my chest, and I snatched at her. She didn't protest the tightness of my grasp, only lowered her face to my own, so her scent drifted over me, all warm and sun-grassy.

The vines respond to your fear. You must quiet yourself.

I pulled in one shaking breath, then another, and another, pressing back thoughts of Riven and Kilmere and my family, until all I felt was the nearness and warmth of Jade and the steadiness of her breath. Then I reached for the gold runner once more.

An image of it surging from the garden bed below, climbing the wall and racing through my open window surged into my mind. So it had come. Would it depart the same way, if I asked?

There's no danger. You can go. I held in my mind a picture of it returning to the gardens and settling into its original placid existence. The leaves shivered, as though the gold runners contemplated.

Then slowly their vines unfurled.

"What's that sound?" Ainslie asked. "Oh, never mind, we're coming in."

Jade slipped through one of the widening gaps in the cage of vines and, with impossible speed, hurled herself against the door, slamming it shut before Ainslie could open it more than an inch.

"Jessa . . . what's happening?" Worry laced Ada's voice. "Let us in."

"Maybe we should fetch Aunt Caris?" Ainslie muttered.

"It was only Jade. She doesn't like it when I'm upset." That was true enough at least. "Give me a moment to settle her."

To Jade, I said, *Thank you for letting me use you as an excuse.*

Don't mention it. She lounged against the door, her bulky frame an effective stop.

The last of the cage shivered and broke apart, the vines sliding over the floor and retreating out the window into the gray predawn, where only a few remaining stars lingered in a faded black sky. Morning would come soon, and I'd scarcely slept.

I collected a few stray leaves left by the gold runners and sent them tumbling out the window. Then I wrenched open the door.

Ainslie's gaze immediately traveled to the tangle of blankets upon the floor. "It must have been quite the dream."

I wrapped my arms around myself, pain searing my chest

once more. Surely the nightmare had only been conjured by the oppressive nature of Kilmere and my own fears. Only Riven had warned me that he must heed the word of his king. What if he'd reported to him what Kilmere held after our discoveries last night? What if his king bid him to reclaim it?

Ada drew me into an embrace, her sweet orange-blossom scent wafting about me. "Jessa, what's wrong?"

"It was only a dream."

Oh, please, let it be only a dream.

"You're freezing." She pulled back. "And what's this in your hair?" She plucked from it a stray leaf, and a slight frown creased her face.

"No matter, it's far too early for man or beast to be awake. If it was no more than a nightmare, I propose we return to bed." Ainslie yawned. "And I propose we stay with you. The bed's big enough if we crush together."

I couldn't deny the comfort their familiar presence brought, the way their warmth and their voices chased away the worst of the images.

Yet even when we all trundled into the bed, I could not fully excise the pain of my dream. Its vividness, the peculiar clarity of every detail, the nuances of Riven's words haunted me. Could it be more than a dream? Perhaps a warning? My sisters' breathing became even, but I lay wakeful in the gloom. After a time, I cautiously shifted, clutching the blankets to my chest.

And Ainslie stirred. She murmured something, and I bent my head closer.

"It's hurting them. I can't . . ." The words trailed off into a soft moan.

On the other side of us, Ada remained still. I eased the sleeve of Ainslie's nightgown upward. The binding mark still appeared as it had in the dressmaker's shop, no further alteration. Might our proximity to Kilmere be troubling her also, since she bore a tie to the Otherworld?

We needed an escape, and I was no closer to finding one. Worse yet, my nightmare had introduced a new fear—that I might not only face the threat of Lord West, but also Riven.

What if Riven *was* here at the bidding of his king? What might he be forced to do?

The three of us emerged late to break the fast, just before the servants began to clear away the sideboard. Yet they made no comment; Mrs. Warren only offered to bring out fresh pots of tea.

Fatigue dragging at me, I settled into a chair, with Jade on the one next to me. In the full light of day, some reason restored itself. I'd no evidence to support the fears introduced by my dream or to suggest that its unusual vividness held any meaning, so I'd do my best to ignore them. Certainly, I'd enough to concern me already, troubles for which I possessed ample proof.

Even across the distance, Kilmere prickled at the edges of my awareness, as though invisible strands bound us.

Perhaps they did.

I poured fresh tea, the dark liquid pooling in my cup. Sooner or later, Kilmere would no longer accept my pretense at a bargain. And I must choose the course I'd take.

If Riven found the basilisk and ended her life, would it offer an opportunity to sever the bargain, if I risked the attempt to claim Kilmere? Right now, the bargain was bound to her as much as to the ruins, but if Riven removed her and I somehow managed to bring Kilmere under my control—could I break it?

When Riven held the bargain for Wyncourt, all he'd had to do was speak and release me, which implied that the holder of the bargain could choose to relinquish it. Yet this was altogether different. If Kilmere somehow accepted me as mistress—which I could not fathom—would it still hold its course?

I didn't want to ask Riven, didn't want to lend further fuel to his argument that I should attempt to take control, but I must consider it.

Jade sprawled out on the chair. *Will you accept my view?*

Of course.

It is opinion, not fact. But I'd say unless you remade the foundational workings of Kilmere, you could not change its nature nor break the bargain, even were it to accept your claim as mistress. As Riven said, it is rooted in a determination for death and conquest, and it would take tremendous power to change that. Jade's ears twitched. *If you determine you'll try to claim rights of ownership, you must accept that you could become bound in the bargain, rather than the reverse.*

I couldn't deny that even while arguing in favor of claiming Kilmere, Riven had suggested making use of its lethal nature, not changing it. That was the fae approach. Might there be another? If so, I could not perceive it, not yet. I stared unseeing at the pyramid of fruit on the table. Whatever the case, I needed to collect myself, and quickly, for I still must face Riven this morning. He was far too perceptive for my good, and I did not want him to ask questions.

I absently picked at a pastry, fruit swirling in variegated streaks through its folds. Ainslie, evidently also unsettled, abandoned her own plate and fetched the mail from the sideboard. After leafing through them, she disbursed the letters to each of us. In my stack was a message from Lovell.

I started to open it, but a familiar sense of Other prickled across my skin—Riven had arrived.

In the entry, Mrs. Warren greeted him. Forsaking the pretense of a meal, I hurried upstairs to snatch up my hat and gloves. I also collected my reticule and slipped the letter from Lovell inside for future perusal. Belongings in hand, I slipped out the door.

Mrs. Warren met me in the hall. "Lord Riven has come to see if you wish to take the seawalk in Withern this morning."

"I'd be delighted." I clutched my reticule tighter. "Tell him I'll only be a moment. I must fetch Miss Twells."

"Yes, miss."

In short order, I found Dreda, and we hastened down the stairs. At the last moment, I slowed, allowing her to descend first. I shouldn't give credence to a dream, even one that had felt so very real, yet when we joined Riven, I couldn't help but tense.

The weight of his gaze didn't help put me at ease; he watched me as though he could perceive every fear. And his eyes darkened. "Shall we?"

With a nod, I followed him outdoors. He'd brought an open carriage, a proper conveyance for him to escort ladies in. Despite our midnight wanderings, by day he maintained the required observance of proprieties.

Once Dreda and I had situated ourselves, Riven took the seat opposite us, and the driver urged the horses on. Dreda maintained her usual in-company silence, and I could find nothing to say.

Jade settled into my lap. *Well, this is uncomfortable—for the rest of you, at least.*

Thank you for that very helpful announcement.

Don't mention it.

We left the lane leading to Willowere and joined the broader road that led to the outskirts of Withern. Riven leaned back. "You're quiet this morning, Miss Caldwell."

"I'm feeling a bit fatigued." I offered a small smile, all I could muster.

It felt like a reasonable excuse, given our late-night excursion, but evidently he remained unconvinced, for he continued to study me. "Have you spoken to Lord West since our last meeting?"

Startled, I met his gaze for the first time since his arrival. "No, why do you ask?"

"I only wondered if he'd troubled you." He maintained a guarded tone; indeed, he could say little with Dreda alongside us.

Nor could I confess the truth, so I turned to regard the scenery, allowing the silence to stand. Before long, we halted in front of a charming cottage, iron muntins dividing its window-panes into a pleasing diamond array. The stone had a charming sea-weathered patina, and the newly painted white gate opened onto a crushed shell walk that appeared to invite visitors.

If not for the merciless battering of militant plants, I'd have thought we'd come to the wrong place. I coaxed the boughs within to form a tighter weave in an attempt to bring some relief from the angry songs lashing at my mind. Then I turned to Dreda. "If Mrs. Ellsworth admits us, you might want to stroll the sea-view portion of the property. She will be chaperone enough—and I'm afraid we must discuss Kilmere. She might speak more readily without an audience." Nor did I know precisely what Riven intended, and I'd not have Dreda exposed unnecessarily to something of which he'd want to remove memory.

"Ah." Dreda nodded. "In that case, I'd be delighted to explore. I'll be sure to keep clear of Fellbane."

Then she did know of the poison gardens, no warning needed. When we descended from the carriage and drew slightly ahead of Dreda, Riven spoke in a low voice. "Are you still concerned about Mr. Tibbons?"

"Of course." I pushed open the gate. "How could I not be?"

"But something else troubles you."

The shells crunched beneath our feet. Blessedly, there was no time for him to press me further, because we'd come to the door of the Ellsworth cottage. I maneuvered around the rambling roses spilling alongside it and rapped gently.

Mrs. Ellsworth opened the door. She held it as a shield between us, only just peering through the narrow slice of an opening. Her eyes widened slightly when she beheld Riven beside me.

"Mrs. Ellsworth, I'm sorry to trouble you, but I wondered if we might speak with you a moment?" I asked.

"I'm afraid it's not a good time for visitors."

Before Riven could press, I hurried on. "It's about your husband. I'm concerned for his fate, and we'd like to help."

She wavered, slow recognition crossing her features, then opened the door wide. "In that case, you may come in. I'll fetch some tea."

Riven strode into the entry. "There's no need. We won't be long."

After she ushered us into a small drawing room, I performed the introductions.

She gave a slight curtsy. "Lord Riven, I'm honored to have you call. What's this about Elver?"

Before I could answer, her son clattered into the room, a gangly youth, his thatch of burnished red hair blazing bright. "Why are they here? The stratesman told us to admit no one."

"Did he?" Riven raised a brow. "Which one?"

"Stratesman Burke." The boy thrust out his chin, challenging. "After two men came from the taverns in a rage, intending to force Da to talk by threatening us, he told us we'd best not accept any visitors."

"Raddie, he'd not mind this. I've spoken to Miss Caldwell once before." She turned to me, her expression beseeching. "Do you have a word of hope, Miss Jessa?"

"After a fashion. Lord Riven and I have some questions that might allow us to more effectively clear his name."

A quick inhale came from Raddie, and Mrs. Ellsworth sank into a chair. "Then I'll answer anything you want."

"You'll confess the truth in full?" The slightest current of power flowed in Riven's voice.

And I pressed a hand to my unsettled stomach. I'd thought he intended to ask questions, but he'd come here purposed to glamour them. Why bother asking before he forced the truth? He'd done something similar with Lord Blackburn, yet not Mocvar. Was it a concession to the rules between our worlds? Never mind that, she'd come under fae influence either way.

Mrs. Ellsworth hesitated, then gave a nod. "I give my word I will."

"And your son?"

"Aye." He drew up a chair close to his mother, his knobby limbs spilling over the edges. "But what's this all about?"

"Your visit to Kilmere." His words flowed smooth as silk, laced with glamour. "We know you spent time in the ruins recently. Give us the full account of what happened there."

I clenched my hands in my lap, forcing myself to wait and listen. If our conversation last night was any indication, he'd not relent, even if I protested, so I must trust he'd exercise care even when not required.

"It was a misty afternoon, with those fogs as sometimes come up from the sea—and favor Kilmere in particular." Though she'd told me she'd promised not to speak of it, the account now flowed easily from Mrs. Ellsworth. "We keep a small flock of sheep, for the wool, you know, and they'd gone astray in the mist. Elver was out, but Raddie had come back for luncheon, and I asked him to help me search for them. We spent a goodly time before we found their tracks leading up to Kilmere."

"Is that common? Animals going astray to Kilmere?" I asked.

"It happens from time to time. Those that wander there rarely return, which is why I wanted to fetch them back before any harm could come to them," Mrs. Ellsworth said.

Though he lounged on the chair with casual grace, Riven's gaze remained intent. "So you entered Kilmere?"

She looked away from him, as if shamed. "We did, the both of us."

"Da would have told us to wait for him," Raddie said.

Mrs. Ellsworth shook her head. "But if we had, my girls could have been lost."

Evidently, the force of her maternal nature, too abundant to be shared with only one son, overflowed onto her flock.

"Yet you said nothing of this."

She rubbed her hands together anxiously. "I wasn't supposed to tell. Say nothing, Elver told me, promise. Else they might think it was me. Some have never favored our marriage, much less the keeping of Fellbane. They'd welcome the chance to accuse me, he said."

How much had she endured, even apart from this recent trial? I turned to face her. "And what did you find there?"

"Little enough. I didn't think the mists would be so thick. I kept imagining that I'd heard them, but then we'd stumble along and find naught but more rocks and ruins. Kilmere's rambling enough, I suppose, but then—it seemed enormous. I suppose we must have traveled in circles. I . . . we lost track of time."

If Riven believed they'd forgotten something important, then he'd force the memories from them. I tensed, the spindles of the chair digging into my back.

His eyes gleamed. "How long were you there?"

"I don't rightly know. It was full dark when Elver fetched us out."

"And the entire time you sought your sheep?"

She nodded.

"Did you come across any other animals there?"

Raddie shifted, and the chair creaked beneath him. "Thought I heard a wolf once, thought it might have frightened the flock into scattering. Nothing else."

"What of you, Mrs. Ellsworth?" Riven was relentless.

"No, nothing living." She fidgeted with the folds of her skirt.

"Truly, we were all in a muddle—so much that I'm inclined to believe in the curse, though I'd not put much stock in it before."

"And did you poison anyone?"

The sharp accusation stole my breath, even more so the compulsion to speak truth—so strong none could elude it. They couldn't even voice the offense writ large on their features.

"Of course not. I'd never do such a thing."

Even without whatever capacity Riven held to discern truth from falsehood, I sensed her sincerity. I released a pent-up breath, as his intent became clear. He'd asked to eliminate the need to press her for further information. If her words rang false, then he'd require the memories—if not, they weren't needed, not for now.

"But you do have a grievance against the old families of Withern, you and your husband both," he said.

"They hated me from the beginning. I wasn't of their class, wasn't an old family like the Ellsworths. My family had only the cottage and gardens, and the small plot attached. Enough to make a simple living, no more." Her voice became choked. "When my babe gave troubles in the womb, they would have gladly seen me and her dead and then arranged a proper marriage for Elver."

Something inside my chest twisted. It was too easy to let myself forget: the lust for power wasn't limited to the fae. A very mortal desire for consequence had inflicted this pain on her. "And when at last they agreed to help, they deceived him, and you lost everything."

"Aye. Worst of all, the babe. If we'd consulted the alchemist sooner . . ." Her lips pinched tight. "But I've never poisoned anyone. I'd not wish my worst enemies to suffer as they are."

"And you?" The full weight of Riven's attention shifted to Raddie.

The boy blanched. "No, sir. I don't even like to go near to Fellbane, much less inside, and I've certainly never poisoned anyone."

"Very good." Riven stood abruptly. "You've no need to think further about this conversation."

They both blinked, and any trace of discomfort or offense vanished. Mrs. Ellsworth returned to our first topic, as though it was what we'd discussed all along. "You think you can clear my Elver, miss? They mean to take his life."

She'd lost so much, endured so much enmity. I could not bear she should lose her husband too. I clasped her hand. "I believe he's innocent, and I'll do everything in my power to make it known."

But what would that mean? We had evidence he wasn't the one responsible, but not evidence the Magister would accept. Mr. Burke might, if I took him fully into my confidence—yet that held its own dangers.

We took our leave, and once outside the cottage, I sought Dreda. There—she waited on a bench, a bit too close to the gated garden of Fellbane for my comfort. As we walked toward her, Riven said, "Shall we drive to Withern and take a stroll along the seawalk? I told your housekeeper of our intent."

As it would allow us to speak more freely about the case, I nodded. We fetched Dreda and returned to the carriage, but as we neared Withern, Riven tensed almost imperceptibly. Where the sunlight fell across him, it became richer and more golden, potent with power. What did he sense?

Dreda's presence did not permit inquiry, so I glanced down at Jade. *Do you feel anything out of the ordinary?*

She sat upright, pricking her ears. *No, not yet.*

Riven straightened. "Perhaps we could visit the town center first."

"I'd be happy to."

What had gone wrong?

When we left our carriage with the driver and descended to the footwalk, Riven set a pace brisk enough that I could scarcely keep up. Would that I had longer legs.

Jade trotted alongside. *I smell it now. Before, I thought it remnant scents drifting from Fellbane onto Dreda, but this is stronger, more distinct. Basilisk venom.*

I stumbled on an uneven stone. Did that mean another victim? In front of the milliner, a small throng had gathered, fear-laced murmurs spilling into the air. Riven pressed through the cluster, and the townsfolk parted before him, revealing a middle-aged woman sprawled upon the footwalk, her features tinted an alarming bluish-gray.

I felt as though a snarl of knotweed tangled in my chest, spreading roots until I could scarcely breathe. We hadn't acted in time, and now another would die. Did I have a right to continue avoiding Kilmere, when this was the result? Jade pressed against my legs with a soft *mrow.*

"It's the curse, I've said so all along," someone muttered. "It won't stop till it's claimed its due."

A tall gentleman wheeled to address the throng. "Has someone sent for the stratesmen? And the doctor?"

Another answered, "The Mulvurn lads went. Fast runners, they are."

For the briefest moment, a faint golden light limned the woman's frame. What did Riven seek?

He turned to me. "Stay with her as long as you can. I'll be back." Then he rounded the corner of the millinery and disappeared.

I edged to the side, where I could get a better view, and nearly bumped into someone who drew up alongside.

"Jessa." Elodie lightly grasped my arm, her features pinched. "Is it true that another has fallen victim to the curse?"

"It appears so."

She pressed her fingers to her lips. "How perfectly dreadful."

Even as she spoke, Mr. Burke and several unfamiliar figures appeared, along with Dr. Fulton. The doctor bent over the woman, while the stratesmen broke up the crowd with remarkable efficiency, herding them back, then drawing them aside one by one to ask questions. Though we moved along with the rest of the group, Elodie kept close to my side.

In short order, Mr. Burke approached the three of us. He offered a slight nod. "Ladies, I have a few questions for you."

"Oh, Mr. Burke, I'm very glad you've come." Miss Redgrave tilted her parasol to better shade her face. "What can you tell us about what's happened here? Do you believe the guests at Holle Castle are in danger? You know Lady Holloway isn't one to surrender her plans, even in the face of catastrophe, but it seems to me that those in her house party must consider if it's prudent to stay in Withern."

"It's for each individual to determine if they feel it wise to remain," he said.

She leaned forward slightly. "Yet it appears only natives of Withern have fallen prey? Does that mean we're in no danger?"

Though she'd couched it in socially acceptable terms, that statement revealed she'd put some thought into the victims. Was Elodie also interested in the case?

Perhaps Mr. Burke wondered also, for his eyes narrowed, became sharp and assessing. "I cannot speculate on the case, nor can I promise safety. Now, I'd like to hear what you witnessed."

"I'm afraid it's nothing worth reporting. I had planned to fetch some trimmings for a new hat, and then found myself in the midst of this crowd, and I saw the poor woman on the ground."

Mr. Burke's gaze fell upon me next, detached and businesslike. "And you, Miss Caldwell?"

"I also took note of the crowd." I'd best leave Riven out of the matter for now, though I hated to conceal so much from Mr. Burke. I glanced at the woman, who was still receiving attention from Dr. Fulton. "When I arrived, she'd already collapsed, which I assume is what drew everyone's attention in the first place."

"What of you, Miss Twells?"

Though she was pale enough that her freckles stood out

stark, she shook her head. "I know nothing more than the others."

Bless her, she'd also said nothing of Riven nor the change in plans he'd requested.

The woman began to convulse. Dr. Fulton barked orders to two men nearby, who lifted her and bore her in the direction of his house. An acrid stench wafted from her, and my stomach turned.

Somehow I must stop this.

Elodie looked past me to Dreda. "Miss Twells, are you well?"

Dreda remained silent and very pale, her attention locked on the suffering woman. Did she fear fae involvement? She was bright enough to have connected many pieces of what I investigated, even if she did not know the whole.

Elodie clasped her arm. "You should sit—come, there's a bench nearby. I'll lend you a hand."

Dreda allowed herself to be shepherded away, and I took a half step after them.

But Mr. Burke blocked my way. "Tell me about this stroll. I know you too well to think your presence here coincidence."

"In this case, it was truly by chance that I came to town. I'd intended to visit the seawalk." The weight of all I kept concealed from Mr. Burke bowed my shoulders. I didn't want to endanger him—but how long could I justify keeping him in the dark? About the curse he could do nothing, but the matter of Mr. Ellsworth was something else entirely.

A trace of Other raised the hairs on the back of my neck. I whirled around, seeking the source, and Lord West came into view, Lady Cadence on his arm. She beamed up at him, and something twisted inside me. She'd never listen to any warning I issued, but how could I stand by and do nothing as he preyed upon her? He'd already taken one from Withern, and if she surrendered herself readily, he'd have no reason to exercise restraint.

Across the distance, his gaze met mine. One corner of his

mouth lifted in a slow smile. Then Lady Cadence said something to him, and they strolled in the direction of the seawalk.

"Miss Caldwell, what's wrong?" Mr. Burke stepped closer.

I rubbed my hands along my arms. "It's nothing. I suppose with everything that's happened since our arrival, I'm a bit on edge."

His demeanor softened. "Forgive me, I should have called after the fang-wolves to ensure you were well."

"I'm fine, and I'm sure you've been much occupied with the business that brought you here."

"If there is something more—"

"Burke, over here." One of his fellow stratesmen beckoned him.

He glanced at the man, then back at me, jaw tightening. "We'll speak again later."

Which meant I'd have to decide how much I could safely tell him. Meantime, what was Elodie asking Dreda? Her pallor had been replaced by a flustered flush. I hurried over.

"Are you all through with Mr. Burke?" Elodie tilted her head, the ribbons on her hat fluttering in the breeze. "He's not a man I should like to cross; however, I believe an intimidating air is generally credited an asset to a stratesman."

I murmured assent.

Then Elodie stood. "I shall fall in with you and Miss Twells, if you've no objection. Given all that's transpired, I feel safer in company."

I couldn't protest without appearing rude, so I forced a smile. "We'd be delighted."

All of us fell into silence as we passed the millinery. With it behind us, Elodie took a shuddering breath, the calm facade she'd presented to this point wavering.

"That poor woman." Her lips trembled slightly. "It's unthinkable that someone would willingly inflict such suffering on another."

"Indeed, I'd hoped that it would come to an end." We halted

for a passing carriage at the street corner. What should I do next? Riven had wanted me to stay with the victim as long as I could, but Dr. Fulton would surely not allow any observers. Perhaps if I stopped by his house, I could at least gain knowledge of how she fared, but I must disentangle myself from Elodie first.

She'd sought information from Mr. Burke and quite possibly from Dreda, perhaps to soothe her own fears, perhaps for some purpose that remained hidden. I couldn't judge her for having an interest in the case, not when I did the same. Perhaps she also wished to keep her unladylike pursuits hidden. If I went on the offensive, would she retreat? "Elodie, I must ask—do you have a personal interest in seeking this killer?"

Her bright eyes widened, and the parasol dipped lower, concealing her features. "Whatever could I hope to do? I only hope that the stratesmen find whomever is responsible before he kills again. I thought they had, but this . . . Clearly, they were mistaken."

Then she did not know Mr. Ellsworth had claimed to have left deposits of poison elsewhere—or she sought to keep her knowledge concealed. "Clearly so. Yet you brought up an interesting point earlier about the victims all being descendants of the founders of Withern. What do you make of it?"

"I cannot say. I suppose it's for the stratesmen to make sense of, and one hopes they will sooner rather than later." She halted in the middle of the footwalk. "I've just recalled. I promised Lady Holloway I'd see if the haberdashery has her order of ribbon. You'll forgive my departure?"

"Certainly. Give our regards to Lady Holloway." Clearly my assumption was correct—she had something she wished to keep concealed. Yet for the moment, I must let it rest.

When she hurried away, I changed course, making for Dr. Fulton's offices. Could I gain admittance? The same servant we'd met last time opened the door, then shook his head. "I'm afraid the doctor cannot see anyone right now."

"I just . . . I need to speak with him about the victim. I can wait, if need be."

The servant pursed his lips, as though he restrained choice words, but he allowed us into the antechamber. "I'll consult Dr. Fulton. It's most likely he'll ask you to return later."

Yet after a few moments, the doctor himself emerged. "Miss Caldwell. Do you have any good tidings that may assist this poor woman?"

"Not those I'd hoped to have." I stood. "But I'd like a word in private, if I may."

"This way, please."

I turned to Dreda. "I'll only be a few minutes."

"Take your time, I'll be well enough here."

Clasping Jade, I moved through the open door, into a treatment room.

Dr. Fulton motioned me to a chair. "I assume you've come about the victim."

"Yes—seeing her collapsed and looking so poorly, it troubled me."

"You and many others. I expect my office to be flooded shortly. She's stable for the moment, but it won't last long." He scrubbed a hand over his face. "I suppose it's too much to hope you've uncovered any hint of a cure?"

"I'm afraid not." Sunlight caught on the bottled tinctures lining the shelves, giving them an amber glow. "How long does she have?"

"By my best guess, she was poisoned last night. Probably passed a miserable night, then sought to make her way here, only to collapse before she got that far." He pressed his spectacles further up his nose. "Which means another week of agony ahead, perhaps? Two, if she's exceptionally strong, like Mr. Vershire."

My shoulders drew inward. Whatever her forebears had done, she didn't deserve an agonizing death. "What of Mr. Vershire? Is he worse?"

"He's gone." His low tone betrayed his pain.

"I . . . I'm so very sorry to hear it." If the basilisk gained strength, his death would be the first of many to come in rapid succession, unless we could find her first. And even so, Kilmere maintained its claim. "If I learn anything that will help, I'll come at once."

His reply faded, for like a fog rolling in from the sea, a cold sensation of Other surged across my skin, one dreadfully familiar —Lord West. In my lap, Jade tensed. If I stayed with Dr. Fulton, his presence afforded me some protection, but Dreda was alone.

And I couldn't leave her to his mercies.

CHAPTER 39

I stood so rapidly that I nearly knocked over my chair. "Excuse me, Dr. Fulton. I've just recalled something—I must go."

"Are you certain?" He rose also, moving closer. "You don't look well—perhaps the shock of seeing the last victim. I could supply a tincture, if you'd like."

"No, truly, I must go."

I turned to leave and found the door, which had been left ajar, as was proper, was now shut, and I could not wrench it open. The slightest filaments of shadow wove about the lock.

Asrina burrowed against my neck, her tiny form shivering—and I could provide no comfort, not with Dr. Fulton nearby.

"I suppose a draft must have pulled the door shut." Dr. Fulton frowned. "Allow me."

When he turned, I snatched up Asrina and tucked her into my reticule atop the nisi seed, leaving the mouth open so she could come and go freely.

Dr. Fulton fumbled with the door, then threw his full weight into it, yet it refused to budge. "We do have occasional problems with the door sticking in summer—the heat and damp, you know."

The strands of shadow darkened to a forbidding black. In Kilmere, the lock mechanism had responded to me; these shadows answered only to Lord West. I must get to Dreda, and I did not care how ridiculous I appeared in doing so. "If we cannot force the door, then I shall depart through the window."

"The window?" He blinked rapidly. "Really, Miss Caldwell, there's no need for that. Just allow me a moment, and I'm sure I can manage it."

Once more he braced himself, and as he did, the strands of shadow abruptly withdrew. This time, when he slammed against the door, it flew open. "See now, all's well."

"Thank you, Dr. Fulton." Jade charged out before me, and I hurried after her into the antechamber, where Dreda stood conversing with Lord West.

Her features held a slight glow of pleasure, the influence of his glamour clear. Yet the pendant at her neck pulsed with a green-gold light—was it protecting her, or had it failed before a superior force?

Languidly, Lord West turned to regard me. "Miss Caldwell, what a pleasure to find you here. I've enjoyed becoming acquainted with your companion. You never told me how lovely she was."

Her flush deepened. Oh, please no—if I'd brought her to Withern to have her fall prey to Lord West . . . It was unthinkable.

"As it turns out, she's just agreed to accompany me on a stroll," he said.

Jade planted herself between me and Lord West, her fur bristling, and I drew myself upright. "I'm afraid she cannot join you. It would interfere with her duties as chaperone."

"You'd deny her this small pleasure?" His obsidian eyes gleamed, mocking me.

"It is not for you to interfere with the terms of her employment. She's obligated to fulfill her duties."

When I spoke, Dreda became still, her gaze lowered—had

my words wounded her? Never mind, I couldn't consider it now. I must separate her from Lord West.

"I'm afraid I have her agreement on this as well as other matters. You might even say it's binding."

My eyes drifted to her upper arm. A mark of gleaming silver wove about it. And the sound of his voice fell away before the rush of my pulse.

I'd failed her. Riven had warned me that the only way to stop Lord West was to remove him, and I'd been so afraid of the cost that I'd hesitated. Now he'd claimed Dreda—for what purpose? I stepped between them. "I don't suppose you'd consider other company instead?"

"Are you offering?"

"I am."

"What an unexpected pleasure." He held my gaze, his lips curving. "I've enjoyed far too little time in your company of late."

Jade growled low. *Don't go with him.*

I have to—I can't let him hurt Dreda. Just tell Asrina to find Riven. He'll come before Lord West can cause harm.

This time, perhaps—but there would come a day when Riven must go, and if I'd not dealt with Lord West before then, he'd certainly deal with me.

It is done.

Asrina darted away, and I smiled at Lord West. "I'd be pleased to take the seawalk with you."

It was open to the public, and at this time of day, it would be full of passersby. Of all my options, it was the safest. I clasped Dreda's hand and found it cold. Was she afraid? Could she sense something amiss? If I could just get her away from Lord West, perhaps I could help. "Do you mind?"

"No, Miss Jessa." Yet her voice was a whisper. "I know my duties."

Then she was hurt. I'd encouraged her to pursue other interests, and she'd no notion why I'd interfered between her and Lord West.

His lips curled upward in unpleasant amusement, and he extended his arm to me. "Come."

I'd no choice but to leave Dreda's side and take it, to endure the cold of his shadows snaking upward. My muscles tensed as they moved toward my shoulders. "Tell me what you know of this latest poisoning."

"That's a dark subject for a bright day."

"Nevertheless, what do you know of it?"

"I know that mortals who meddle with what they don't understand receive the due penalty for their misdeeds." He continued to walk, slow and unhurried. "You shall come to the same understanding soon enough."

It took all my effort to maintain a calm facade. Several paces behind us, Dreda followed, her feet dragging. She'd already suffered the afflictions of one Otherkind, and now something in their interactions had left her unlike herself. If only I could speak with her alone, offer reassurance and comfort. What had he forced her into? And *where* was Riven?

"Are you attending the ball at Holle Castle?" Lord West asked.

"My aunt has accepted the invitation."

"Excellent. You'll save me a dance." The corners of his mouth lifted, baring white teeth. "We've much to discuss, and unless I'm mistaken, we're soon to be interrupted."

"I have no interest in dancing with you."

"But you do have interest in the nature of my bargain with your chaperone." He drew closer, the scent of ancient stone assaulting me. "After all, many have suffered dreadful fates at the hands of servants with divided loyalties. How unfortunate if that became your end."

Had he coerced Dreda into acting against me? Or did he merely seek to inspire fear? If so, he succeeded. I sought a steady tone. "In the current circumstances, I don't believe my death works in your favor."

"Ah, my sweet." A smile spread slow across his face. "I've not forgotten the promises I made you. There are things far worse than death, things that would make you willing to release Kilmere to me—indeed, grant any of my requests, in order to gain relief." He bent lower still to whisper in my ear. "I've almost finished making my arrangements. Perhaps you think Riven will continue to protect you, but you'll soon find out the truth. You must know, once he's obtained what he wants, he'll abandon you and return to his own world."

Even as he spoke, Riven appeared from around a building, golden with light, Other surging about him like an oncoming storm. "West. You have something that belongs to me."

"Ah, Lord Riven. I thought I'd see you before long." Lord West released my arm. "I'll give her back into your keeping—for now."

When Lord West vanished, Riven wheeled to face me, his eyes kindling bright. "What possessed you to keep company with him? Even in public, it was a ridiculous risk."

The words came sharp as daggers, and I flinched. "The alternative was Dreda. He said they'd made a binding agreement."

Riven muttered an oath. "Miss Twells, come here."

Instead, she shrank into the shadows, and I couldn't blame her. Even with glamour veiling his power, he appeared ready to rend someone limb from limb.

"Riven," I said quietly. "Perhaps a request might better suit?"

The storm charge to the air lessened. "Miss Twells, will you join us?"

Reluctantly, she stepped forward. "As it pleases you, Lord Riven."

For the merest instant, his gaze flicked to the binding mark. "What did Lord West ask of you?"

"He . . . he wanted me to accompany him on a walk."

"And what else?"

She pressed a hand to her temples. "I . . . I can't recall . . . We didn't talk long."

"Don't worry." I gently touched her arm. "It's only that Lord West has a tendency to cause trouble, and I was concerned for your safety."

"Of course, Miss Jessa." She kept her eyes lowered. "I must ask your forgiveness. I should never have allowed him to distract from my duties."

I folded my hands in front of me, gripping them tight. She'd taken the wrong view of the matter, but without revealing the whole to her, I couldn't correct it. Far worse, Lord West had snared her in some unknown bargain. "On the contrary. Were it another man, someone honorable, nothing would have pleased me more than to see you enjoy a stroll."

At last she looked at me, some of the confusion leaving her eyes. "I understand."

Yet we were no closer to answers on how he'd bound her. I pressed my lips together to keep them from trembling.

Asrina flittered to my shoulder and patted it with tiny hands. "Why are you upset? Riven's here now."

In return, I stroked her wings, their delicate silk beneath my fingers a reminder of how fragile we were before Lord West, all except Riven. "You did well," I whispered.

But I, on the other hand . . . I'd told Dreda about the dangers posed by fae, and she'd trusted me to protect her. Instead, I'd exposed her to one far crueler than she could ever imagine—and I couldn't abandon her to his keeping.

In the distance, Kilmere loomed, its dark form resembling a dragon now more than ever. Blight and rot, what else could I do but face it? With his hold on her, with the threats he'd made, I'd run out of time to consider alternate paths. Only one remained.

Riven closed the distance between us. "Shall we still visit the seawalk before your return home?"

"I'd like that." Once we'd resumed our stroll and Riven had

secured a glamour about us, I gathered my courage. "Riven, I . . ."

The words died in my throat, as the bitter, metallic taste of Kilmere, that of forged stone and old blood, rose to choke me.

"What is it?"

I swallowed hard. "If I intended to try to claim Kilmere, how would I go about it?"

He became still, silent. When at last he spoke, his voice was low. "It will require evidence you'll be a worthy mistress, one that will enhance its power. If you showed it proof you'd fulfill the bargain on its behalf, it would concede more easily. Assuming that's not what you intend, then you must impress upon it your strength. It'll be your will against that of Kilmere. If you can overcome its tests, then you will have proved yourself."

How could I possibly demonstrate the sort of power Kilmere sought, short of offering what it craved? I skimmed my fingers across the lichens on the wall, their stalwart song filling my ears. Though tiny, they made their home upon the rock, drawing from its strength, and I in turn pulled from theirs. "Whatever abilities I possess, they don't come close to matching the fae lords and ladies of old. What possible impression could I make upon Kilmere?"

This time, Riven led us to the steps that descended from the seawalk onto the rocky shore, where the waves dashed ceaselessly against the stone. "When you see how it tests you, you'll know the response that must be given. As you did in the heart."

"And if I fail?"

He regarded me with darkening eyes. "Then I'll do what I can to bring you out alive."

Yet it wasn't likely that Kilmere would release me. If I could not impress upon it my worth—as it judged such things—then it would want nothing more than to be rid of me. I turned to look out over the sea, feeling as battered as if the waves tumbled me over and over in their depths.

It was madness to consider this. Yet Lord West would never relent, and I'd nothing else at hand with which I might stop him.

Riven had seen this end from much earlier. But perhaps it need not be as bleak as I imagined. Perhaps I'd succeed in asserting a claim, and perhaps my claim alone would convince Lord West his cause was futile. Perhaps I need not use it as a weapon against him. Yet the cold sensation from my dream returned, that of its power rising in me, its hunger becoming my own. And despite the brilliant sun above, I shivered.

With Jade at my side, I forced myself over the sea-worn stones of the shore, seeking sure footing. Dreda remained on the seawalk, content to look down on us from a distance.

And Riven strode alongside us, his grace unimpeded by the jagged terrain. "Do you mean to act?"

"I see no other way. Lord West has some claim on Dreda now, and he implied that he'd soon find a way to bend me to his will." At my side, Jade gave a low rumble. "I don't know what he has planned, but I can't let him take Dreda or anyone else. If he's gone after her, my family could be next."

"Then we should go tonight, after your family retires."

So soon—yet it wasn't wise to delay, however much I desired it. The scent of seagrass swirled amid the salt of the air. "I agree, but there's other business we need to attend beforehand."

"Yes. Not least of which is your chaperone. You'd be safest if you allowed me to compel her to speak of the bargain with Damir."

"It's clear she doesn't recall it, and I'll not see her hurt further."

"Then you're embracing unnecessary danger."

"I'm going to Kilmere." The words wrenched from me. "I'm doing as you wanted. Isn't that enough? At least allow me the comfort of knowing her mind remains intact. If I succeed, her bargain with him likely won't matter."

But if I failed . . .

"Very well." He rubbed a hand over his jaw. "There's something else—the reason I left you. I went to find and examine the place where the last victim was poisoned while the traces of what transpired were fresh."

I slipped on a slick stone, and Riven steadied me. "What did you find?"

"Signs of a basilisk."

"Then it survived."

He nodded. "But it left no trail coming or going. The only traces of its presence were at the scene, along with those of Tibbons. All evidence suggests he brought the basilisk there in stasis. Most likely, she compelled him to depart Withern afterward."

"I see." The jarring call of a sandpiper echoed across the rocks.

"I know you'd hoped otherwise," Riven said. "But it's better that we know the truth. Nikol is efficient. I expect he'll soon bring Tibbons back, and with his help, we should be able to locate the basilisk."

But what would remain of Mr. Tibbons after? The browns and grays of the stones beneath my feet blurred. On every side, Other hurt those I cared about—or those I was responsible for. I might not be able to spare Mr. Tibbons the reckoning to come, but there was someone I *could* preserve—Mr. Ellsworth. I turned toward Riven. "Before we go, we need to tell Mr. Burke that Mr. Ellsworth is innocent."

"And why is that?"

"If we don't, Mr. Ellsworth will die. His trial is set only a few days from now, and with his confession, they'll certainly hang him. If we can spare one innocent life, we should."

"Mr. Burke already knows too much about the Otherworld to be good for his health. You wish to draw him in deeper?"

"No, but I can think of no other way to spare Mr. Ellsworth from condemnation. And knowing what I do of Mr. Burke, this is the choice he'd make."

"And you trust him?" Riven asked, his voice silky smooth.

Did he know something I did not? "He's kept silent about my travels in the Otherworld, and he's shown me nothing but kindness. I'll grant it's a risk, but I think it's a necessary one."

"Fine, but we tell him as little as possible. Keep Damir out of it—focus on the basilisk angle only."

I couldn't argue, since to all appearances, Lord West wasn't involved in the poisoning—he only lurked nearby like a vulture, ready to prey on the advantage offered by the dead. "Very well."

"I suggest you send a servant and invite him to tea in the garden or whatever you mortals deem proper."

It wasn't proper for a lady to personally invite a gentleman for a tête-à-tête, but to request a stratesman call for information on a case? Certainly it was more reasonable than visiting the Magistry. So I nodded.

"Make it four this afternoon. I'll join you." With that, Riven turned, and we began to retrace our steps.

Each one came slower than the last, as weariness took hold. I didn't want to consider how Mr. Burke would react to the revelation of all I'd withheld. Could he be trusted to keep quiet the truth of the fae influence in Kilmere?

CHAPTER 40

"Astratesman here for you, Miss Jessa." Another rap followed, this one firm enough to suggest it was not the first. "Miss Caldwell, do you hear me?"

I pressed upright, the bedcovers tumbling about me. In face of Aunt Caris's concern after I'd come home and her insistence that I looked far too worn for her comfort, I'd agreed to rest, and when I'd lain down, I'd tumbled into deep, blessedly dreamless slumber. Could it be four already? A quick glance at the mantel clock confirmed it.

"Miss Jessa?"

I hastened to the door, where Mrs. Warren waited. "Please show Mr. Burke to the garden table and bring a tea tray. I'll be out momentarily."

When she left, I splashed cold water over my face to clear the residual muzziness. To bring true order to my disarrayed hair would take more time than I wished, since I didn't have any great confidence that Riven and Mr. Burke could hold a cordial conversation. Mr. Burke had objected to Riven's presence from the beginning, and Riven had only reluctantly agreed to confide any truth to him.

I wrapped a blue bandeau around the crown of my head to help restrain the effusive curls, brushed a few wrinkles from my muslin gown, and then hurried down the stairs.

I'd convinced Aunt Caris that I needed no caretaking, and she should follow through on her original plan to pay calls with Ada and Ainslie this afternoon. I'd further commissioned Ada and Ainslie to bring a note to Lady Cadence when they called on the Holloway family, warning her of Lord West's connection to the assault in Avons. I didn't imagine she'd believe me, but I had to try. Provided they took their time about it, I should be able to hold an uninterrupted conversation with Riven and Mr. Burke.

I slipped out the door. Within the gardens, a joyous rush of song greeted me: sprightly astilbe, vibrant wild rose, and decorous iris weaving together an enchanting melody. I glided toward the wicker table where Mr. Burke waited, and no sooner had I greeted him than Riven strolled around the corner of the house.

Mr. Burke's shoulders tightened. "You asked Riven to join us?"

"He's involved in what we must discuss."

"I see."

"Burke." Riven gave him a slight nod before settling with grace onto the nearest chair. "Sit."

Mr. Burke's lips pressed into a line, yet he complied. "What's this about, Miss Caldwell?"

"Will you take tea?" I hastily took my own seat and lifted the pot.

"No, thank you." He fixed me with an all-too-incisive gaze —no doubt he guessed I was stalling. "Just facts, please."

I poured a full cup for myself and swirled some of the seablossom honey into it, the faint sensation of Other tingling along my hand. "Then I'll come straight to the point: Mr. Ellsworth is innocent."

"You have proof?"

"Of a sort."

"The Magister will only accept proof of a very specific kind—they require concrete evidence, facts that are indisputable."

"I'm aware. It's one of the reasons I hesitated to speak of this." A sweet, slightly citrus scent drifted from my cup. Mr. Burke had kept hidden my involvement in the matter of the Crimson Tattoo Killer, but this was a great deal bigger, an ongoing threat to Withern. Would he feel obligated to speak of it?

"It's more than just Mr. Ellsworth, isn't it?" Mr. Burke's brows drew inward. "I can't help if you continue to keep me in the dark."

Riven toyed with a spark of light. "She doesn't need your help."

"I suggest you let her speak for herself," Mr. Burke shot back.

I stared at the lake, wishing I was floating on its placid surface, far from the growing tension between the two men. "I told you in the beginning that I feared some sort of Otherworldly involvement in these deaths."

"You did. You also refused to be forthcoming with your reasons." Faint lines tightened about his eyes.

"At the time, I had only suspicions. Now I have facts." I cradled the cup in my hands, its warmth seeping into my cold fingers. "Kilmere was constructed by fae and holds a bargain that allows a basilisk bound to the ruins to kill all the descendants of the original families of Withern, of which there are now hundreds. As soon as it regains full strength it will take them all, yet the bargain cannot be unmade without also destroying both Withern and its surroundings. It's not Mr. Ellsworth who poisoned the victims, but the basilisk at the bidding of Kilmere."

The words left in an alarming rush, and I felt no better for their passing. Above, the willows swayed, though no breeze stirred their branches.

And Mr. Burke tensed, his gray eyes darkening. "How long have you known the nature of Kilmere?"

"Since I first visited it. Knowledge of the bargain didn't come till later."

"And it did not occur to you that this was relevant information?" His voice snapped like the crack of a whip. "You allowed Miss Redgrave and Miss Twells to enter the ruins at risk of their lives? Not to mention the careless endangerment of your own."

Jade gave an ominous rumble, glaring at him, and I tugged her closer. "It wasn't like that, precisely—"

"Then what?" He scrubbed a hand across his jaw. "I take it Kilmere drew the fang-wolves? You're fortunate we encountered nothing worse."

I looked down into my cup. "Well . . ."

Mr. Burke muttered a quiet oath. "We did encounter worse, didn't we?"

"I'm sorry, I wanted to tell you from the beginning, but there were risks, and I did not know . . ."

"I risked speaking to you of official business when I should not have done so. I regret you did not find me worthy of the same trust." Then Mr. Burke turned to Riven. "I take it you glamoured away any recall of what truly happened."

I'd been so locked into my exchange with Mr. Burke that I hadn't so much as glanced at Riven. Now I did so and flinched. Though his glamour remained, concealing his power from the mortal eye, he'd drawn an array of sparks about him, gleaming like small blades of diamond—as though he prepared to go to war.

The sparks glinted in the sun. "I did."

"You had no right."

"It was for your protection."

"I don't need that sort of protection." The muscles in Mr. Burke's neck corded.

"In this instance, you did. Your mind was already taxed by what had transpired, by the attack Kilmere made against it." Riven leaned forward. "And it wasn't for your protection alone."

"Then whose?" Mr. Burke shifted, his gaze falling on me. "You thought I'd report what I saw?"

"You expect me to believe you'd have kept it to yourself?" Riven spoke in the silkiest of tones, which alone should have put me on guard. "Do you mean to claim that you're not giving information to the Vigil? Have a care how you answer."

My lips parted, but no protest emerged, for Mr. Burke didn't deny it. My body responded as if I'd been shoved from a cliff, a rush-roar of fear racing through my veins, and I leapt to my feet, my chair tumbling to the ground behind me. "You've been reporting about me to the Vigil?"

"It's not like that."

"Then what, pray tell, is it like?" Riven's voice was unyielding. "Who gives you orders?"

I braced myself on the willow, trembling. I'd trusted Mr. Burke—he'd extended friendship that went past the requirements of his job, or so I'd thought. The roar in my ears intensified. Had it all been a stratagem of the Vigil? Did they suspect what I was? I'd just given him all the information he needed to further their cause, and more than enough to lock me away, if he should speak it.

And Riven. He'd known that Mr. Burke engaged with the Vigil and said nothing? No wonder he'd asked if I trusted Mr. Burke. How much else did he keep hidden?

Mr. Burke stood also, closing the distance between us. "Jessa, please listen."

He'd dropped all formalities, yet I couldn't speak, couldn't even lift my gaze to meet his—because I didn't trust myself not to betray an unseemly amount of emotion. If he informed the Vigil of what I'd just said, all the lengths I'd gone to in order to keep the truth from my family meant nothing. I dug my fingers into the bark of the willow, and it crumbled at my touch.

"I have unanswered questions," Riven said. "And my patience wears thin."

"I owe you no answers, but I'll grant that Jessa deserves an explanation." Mr. Burke restored my chair to its spot. "Will you sit, Jessa? This may take awhile."

Reluctantly, I perched on the edge of the chair, and Mr. Burke returned to his spot across from me.

"I called on you in Avons because the Vigil asked me to investigate Kilmere and the curse—to determine if the responsible party was mortal or if their involvement was needed."

"And you said yes?"

"I agreed because if I did not, they would have sent someone else instead. Someone inclined to report any small oddities."

I lifted my eyes. "Then you thought there was something Otherworldly involved from the beginning, despite your claims otherwise?"

"Given all that transpired with the Crimson Tattoo Killer, I couldn't discount the possibility. Were it true, it would have boded poorly for you. I knew that Kilmere was important, and that it would take little for the Vigil to try to seize it. I thought to stay their hand."

Riven gave the slightest of nods, and the spark-shards vanished. He accepted what Mr. Burke said as truth, and given his arbiter nature, that meant I could rely on it also. I released the breath tangled in my chest. "You kept quiet about this, yet you condemn me for doing the same about Kilmere."

"I sought to keep you safe, as I'm sworn to do."

"Did it ever occur to you that I attempted the same? Are you the only one permitted secrets?"

He gave the slightest nod. "I'll concede the point. I should not have spoken as I did."

Yet I understood why he had—and I still withheld the full truth. Might he do the same?

"What have you told the Vigil about the situation here?" Riven asked.

"Very little. Jessa's admittance that you were involved put me in a difficult position. I've had to mislead my superiors in ways that would cause a great deal of trouble if they became known—and I do not favor such deceit."

"Yet you did not speak."

"I have a duty to protect the people of Withern, and I wasn't confident the Vigil would take the best course of action."

I tucked my hands into my lap, seeking calm. "So what now?"

He shot a glance at Riven. "If Riven will refrain from tampering with my mind—"

"That depends very much on what you say next."

"I intend to do what I believe right."

"And that is?" Riven inclined his head.

"Finish gathering facts, to start." Mr. Burke steepled his fingers. "Will you give me a full account?"

I reported as concisely as possible on the nature of Kilmere, the bargain with the townsfolk, and the trace evidence found of the basilisk, which confirmed that it remained an active threat. As Riven had requested, I left out the involvement of Lord West and his fae nature.

"I'll take that cup of tea now." Mr. Burke eyed the china cup. "Unless you have something stronger?"

"Not here, and I hardly wish to raise suspicion with Mrs. Warren by sending for port or brandy." I poured out a steaming cup, and he downed it in silence.

To my surprise, Riven didn't try to press him further, only waited, watching him closely. In the end, I spoke. "What do you intend to do?"

"My responsibility is foremost to the people of Byren. I don't think the Vigil is equipped to deal with this curse. If there's any hope of a favorable resolution, then it needs to come from the Otherworld, much as the problem did," Mr. Burke said. "I won't report what you've uncovered—but I think you're out of time. Despite my efforts to deter them, they're growing suspicious. Several citizens of Withern have contacted them, requesting aid."

"Then what?" I fidgeted with a loose piece of wicker.

"We can perhaps turn it to our advantage."

Riven lounged back in the chair. "Our?"

"Yes. Our." Mr. Burke met Riven's gaze squarely. "I have a condition for my silence—I won't be kept in the dark anymore. I'm certain Jessa means to act to protect the people of Withern, but it's not her responsibility to do so. It's mine."

"Then what do you propose?" I asked.

"I tell the Vigil that their presence is needed. That after this latest victim, I can only attribute it to the curse." Mr. Burke shrugged. "It's the only way I can imagine freeing Mr. Ellsworth. I'll tell them his confession was false, that he acted to protect his family—in fear of them having fallen prey to the curse. I'll need to get him to admit that, of course, by telling him what you've told me: that we have absolute proof of his wife and son's innocence. And I'll tell them that you came to me with fears the curse was real, so you'll receive no blame—no aspersions cast as to your involvement."

"But then the Vigil will come. They'll try to take Kilmere."

"That's the fault in the plan." His lips quirked. "I'll take suggestions."

I sipped at my tea, tasting none of its sweetness. Riven kept quiet, waiting, refraining from suggesting glamour—for which I was thankful. It was the obvious choice, but even if I accepted it, would it prove sufficient? Could he locate *every* person who'd had suspicions of Otherworldly activity in Kilmere and might petition the Vigil for aid? Even if he did, and even if he glamoured the Vigilists who were sent, how long before new fears would arise and new reports travel to the Vigil? Then they'd become suspicious once again—or aware of the incongruity between their reports and their memories, which would only raise more questions. And if they returned later, when Riven had gone back to the Otherworld, I'd have no means of protecting Kilmere. We needed someone with influence to intervene and check the Vigil, someone like . . . "Lord Blackburn."

Both men looked at me.

"With his name cleared, he has the ear of the king again, and he wants answers about the involvement of the Otherworld in our own, past and present. He asked me to consider helping him procure such information, as Ibbie once did. If I tell him Kilmere may hold answers and the Vigil seeks to seize it and keep the truth concealed, I believe he'd act on my behalf."

"It could work." Mr. Burke set down his cup with a thud. "If the king gives a dispensation, the Vigil won't be able to dispute it —though they might certainly try."

"You think Blackburn would follow through?" Riven asked.

"I think he hungers for answers as much as I do, and he's no friend of the Vigil, so yes, I believe so."

"The enemy of my enemy . . ." Mr. Burke muttered.

Did he see the Vigil as the enemy also? He'd come here at their bidding, and the Magistry and the Vigil often worked in tandem. At the orders of his superiors, he'd partnered with the unpleasant Mr. Ludne in Avons, when the killer stalked our city. Would he willingly do so again, if commanded? He was dedicated to his job. Or was he dedicated to justice, and his job simply gave him a means to express it?

"It's not a bad idea, but the time it takes for word to travel there and back may prove too great. I cannot stall long if you mean to preserve Mr. Ellsworth's life," Mr. Burke said.

Riven lifted a shoulder. "If Jessa writes a letter, I can see it reaches Avons swiftly."

I fetched my writing supplies and jotted a missive to Lord Blackburn. After I sealed it, I handed it to Riven.

He stood. "Unless Blackburn proves resistant, I can return within an hour. You'll stay with Jessa until then, I trust."

Something intangible passed between them, and Mr. Burke nodded. "I will."

It appeared Riven had decided Mr. Burke was to be trusted. Perhaps I'd not been wrong to insist we tell him the truth. I had every confidence he would fight to spare Mr. Ellsworth, now that he was convinced of his innocence.

But my ability to claim Kilmere, to keep it from Lord West and the Vigil? It felt as impossible an endeavor as roses blooming in the winter frosts. Unwillingly, I lifted my gaze to the distant horizon where Kilmere lurked.

And its cold hunger stirred in me once more. Ever eager, it waited.

In less time than I'd expected, Riven returned with a positive report from Lord Blackburn, who'd been intrigued enough to agree to my proposed plan. But would his help be enough?

I'd no time to ponder that, nor to discuss the matter any further with Riven or Mr. Burke, for Ainslie appeared in the distance, strolling up the lane toward Willowere alone. Her slow steps betrayed an unusual weariness.

I stood. "Forgive me, I must go greet Ainslie—and I don't want her to have questions about your presence here."

Both Mr. Burke and Riven took their leave, and I hurried down the path to meet her, Jade at my side. "Where are Aunt Caris and Ada?"

"They wished to stop at Denby Hall before returning home. Aunt Melisina accompanied them, but as I'm not particularly fond of Lady Denby, I thought I'd return to Willowere early."

She offered a reasonable explanation, yet her words faltered slightly, and a vague unease took hold of me. "Are you well?"

"Well enough, only a bit weary." Absently, she ran her fingers across her binding mark. "I suppose we've kept busier than I expected."

Busier than some might on a seaside excursion, but she maintained a far less hectic pace here than in Avons, where social events often kept her and Ada out late.

"Come rest in the garden." I looped my arm through hers. "I'll fetch my sketching supplies, and we can take tea together."

With a fresh pot of tea and my basket of sketching supplies, we retreated to the haven under the willows, one far more peaceful now that both Riven and Mr. Burke had departed.

Ainslie leaned back in her chair, her eyes drifting shut. What fatigued her so? Might it have anything to do with her bargain?

I withdrew a pencil, sketching first the binding mark Lord West had left on Dreda, then the more elaborate one Ainslie bore. Did the size and detail have significance? Or did these marks merely appear however the bargain-holder wished? A sense of Other swept warm across my hands, as if the mere recall of the marks held some of their power.

Whether Ainslie wanted me to or not, I needed to start collecting information, and the only place I knew to begin was with analysis of the marks. Next I sketched the bindings I'd received from Riven and Lord West, the rest of the world vanishing as I became immersed in the intricate details, the lines seeming to spark and shimmer on the page much as they had on my flesh, perhaps a flourish added by my own memories. These binding marks differed not only in style, but in color.

When I finished, I drew a deep breath, the gentle sounds of the lake and the birds overhead breaking back into my awareness. Might the color of the binding represent the court? If so, Ainslie's mark wasn't from the Court of Gold, where Riven made his home. It was closer in tone to the ones Lord West had inflicted. Did that mean a fae from the Court of Silver held her bargain? I'd no notion how many fae courts existed—but Jade likely did. Why had I never thought to inquire of her about the marks?

She scrubbed a paw over her face. *You've had several other things on your mind.*

True. I lowered my pencil. *What can you tell me of the courts?*

There are many, each desiring their own renown. Some are ever at each other's throats, like the Courts of Silver and Gold, while others hold very loose alliances. As for the binding marks, in appearance they're unique to the individual. The chosen colors connect to the affinities of the fae in question, which do often link to the courts.

How so?

She regarded me. *What do you know of fae affinities?*

Very little. What I do know comes from our lore, and much of that may be false.

Then I shall start with more basic information. Affinities may be elemental in nature—tied to aspects of the natural world. You've seen this when Riven wields light or Damir shadow. These particular affinities are common in their respective courts, though they may vary greatly in strength. Other affinities relate to the senses. As they join in an individual fae, affinities take on highly unique— and often unpredictable—expressions. She stretched out on the table. *In turn, fae binding marks often bear shades of their affinities, and—*

"Jessa?" Ainslie peered at my sketchbook. "Why are you drawing that . . . thing?"

"Because I don't think we can ignore it any longer." I snapped the book shut. "Ainslie, whoever you bargained with could come to collect at any time, and—"

"And all manner of ills could befall any of us at any moment, yet we do not live in fear." She brushed a fallen leaf from her skirts. "It's best forgotten, particularly now."

Despite her words, her tone was frayed at the edges, as though she'd spent much of her strength trying to persuade herself of that fact, as I had once done, when I tried to shove down and suppress my "fae-touch." Perhaps we were more alike than I'd once believed. "Why now in particular?"

"Because what I thought impossible appears to have happened. I never dreamt I'd find a gentleman who appreciated my mind as Mr. Redgrave does, one whom I could respect and whose company is pleasing in every regard." She gave a small shake of her head. "I cannot bear to think about fae and bargains and what might be—what I hope will never come to pass. I only want to enjoy what is."

"Do you imagine you can keep it concealed forever?"

Her eyes glossed over, brilliant with unshed tears. "I see no reason why the truth must be made known—and every reason why it should be concealed."

"Ainslie, I'm not suggesting we announce it to the world." Of all people, I understood the danger of that. "But I know someone who has familiarity with fae bindings. If we showed him the mark, perhaps—"

"If word gets out, it would doom me, and the rest of you alongside. Even if Mr. Redgrave chose to accept it—and so condemn his family and his own future—you know the Vigil would seek me. The rest of you would be guilty by association."

How could I argue, when her thoughts so closely echoed my own? I drew the sketchbook to my chest. "It would be a discreet inquiry, one that doesn't need connect to you—"

"I forbid it, Jessa." Ainslie stood abruptly, bracing her hands on the table. "Give me your word you'll speak of it to no one."

"Do you truly think you can make a future with Mr. Redgrave while holding this secret?" I asked softly. My connection to Other—whatever it might be—was the very reason I'd condemned myself to a solitary future. If she was bound to a fae . . .

She tugged her sleeve downward to better conceal the binding mark. "It may signify nothing but what's over and done."

"Ainslie, you know that's not the case. Why would a sign of the binding remain if your dealings were done?"

"I . . . I cannot say." She sank back into the chair, drawing her arms about herself. "I won't wed Mr. Redgrave under false pretenses, but everything is so new, so tentative, I scarcely dare hope . . . I just need time."

How could I force her to expose the truth when she wasn't ready, when I held my own secrets close in the same way, when the dangers were very real? I didn't think Riven would speak of my inquiry to anyone else, but I couldn't promise it. I reached over to clasp her hand. "I'll not take the choice from you, but I have concerns. Will you at least agree that if the binding mark alters again, I may seek help on your behalf?"

"Very well." Her chin lifted. "I daresay we're making much out of nothing." Yet her hand trembled as she stirred sea-blossom honey into her tea.

We sat in silence a few moments longer, until the carriage containing Ada and our aunts rattled up the lane.

"We should join them." Ainslie rose, then bent to press her hand to mine. "I know it doesn't seem like it, but I'm thankful for your concern, and even more that you've respected mine."

With that, we made our way into the drawing room. Ada joined us, collapsing on the settee.

Ainslie studied her. "What happened?"

"After we left Denby Hall, Aunt Melisina told us we must remain at home this evening. Lord Bradford intends to join us for dinner. Aunt Caris tried to protest it, but she completely overruled her." Ada broke off abruptly, abandoning the settee in favor of the pianoforte, a tempestuous song pouring forth, one that stirred all the tumult of emotions I'd wrestled so hard to restrain all day.

Jade's tail twitched, as though the melodies troubled her as well.

Ainslie leaned close to make herself heard above the music. "We must be rid of him once and for all. He cannot be allowed to continue tormenting Ada. Aunt Melisina said something to her the other day that she refuses to discuss even with me, something that's made her feel obligated, and I fear she's wavering in her resolve."

How could we—oh. "I wrote to Lovell about the matter, and I received a reply this morning. I'd entirely forgotten it in the events of the day, but perhaps it will provide what we need."

I hurried to fetch my reticule and withdrew the somewhat crumpled missive. "Let's see what he says."

Together we read the summation in Lovell's scrawled words, written with bold lines that indicated his anger. They contained all the indictment we needed to dissuade Lord Bradford—if only we used it properly. For once, the path forward appeared simple, a relief after the layers of intrigue and malice the fae wove about things.

Ainslie drew Ada back to the settee, and we shared the letter with her.

After she finished reading it, Ada collapsed inward, her hurt clear. "I did not think this of Aunt Melisina."

"I didn't either," Ainslie said. "But you'll agree to confront Lord Bradford?"

"Yes, although I cannot like what it requires," she said.

Nor did I—how could I relish the prospect of another confrontation in this interminable day, however straightforward? At least in this, Ada would take the lead.

A militant light entered Ainslie's eyes, as if she wished to have it out with Lord Bradford then and there. "You're far too softhearted. It's not as if we mean to expose him publicly, though you'd have grounds to do so, after how much he's troubled you."

"You'll both stay near while I speak with him?" Ada asked.

"Of course." Ainslie gave a decisive nod. "We shall be your witnesses and intervene if necessary—unless you want us to speak for you?"

"No, this should come from me. I've allowed Aunt Melisina to push me into this. It's time I took a stand."

Ainslie dimpled. "I couldn't agree more."

Over the next hour, we discussed how he might react and what she would do if he became too forceful and when we should intervene, until at last, Ada buried her face in her hands.

"Enough. I must think of something else, anything else, till he comes, or I shall lose my courage."

Of course, after her words none of us could conjure another conversational topic—or at least, I could summon none of which I could safely speak. So Ada resumed her tempestuous melodies on the piano, Ainslie scribbled down notes, perhaps for another P. Smith piece, and I worked on a reply to Lovell. His pain over the situation had bled into the letter, and I wished to offer what reassurance I could.

Finally, Mrs. Warren announced the arrival of Lord Bradford, his appearance far enough in advance of dinner that neither of our aunts were present. Ainslie and I withdrew to the back corridor, along with Jade and Asrina, leaving the door ajar to allow a limited view of the room. Then Ada gave Mrs. Warren permission to show him in.

Lord Bradford marched in, his boots echoing on the polished wood floor. "Miss Caldwell. I'm delighted to find you alone."

"My aunt told me you wished to speak with me." Ada kept her voice mostly steady, but a small quaver at the end betrayed her.

"Indeed." He strode forward, stopping far too close to her to be proper, the two of them framed side by side in the narrow gap between door and frame. "You can have no doubt of my desires, nor my intentions—much less the life I can offer you. I've waited long enough. I intend to send an announcement of our betrothal to the papers by the end of the week."

"But you've not yet asked for my hand nor given me opportunity to answer." Ada took a step back. "If you had, I would have informed you that I cannot marry you, now or ever."

His thin lips pulled back into a frown. "Then your father will answer for your actions before the Magister."

"You mean to sue for breach of promise?" Though pale, Ada stood firm. "That requires a promise made, and I have given you none."

He snatched up her hand and caressed it. "It's your word against mine. Who do you think is more likely to be believed?"

To provoke one as tenderhearted as Ada to anger was difficult, but he'd succeeded. I edged closer for a better view. Color suffused her features. "I suppose I shouldn't be surprised to find you a liar as well as a blackmailer."

"What did you say?" His voice altered, a strident note creeping in.

Jade's eyes glinted with evident satisfaction. *That needled him. I didn't think she had it in her.*

Nor did I think you took interest in mortal affairs. If I didn't know better, I'd think she wanted to champion Ada's cause, despite how prickly she'd been toward anyone besides me.

Her tail twitched. *They* can *be entertaining at times.*

"I'd hoped you'd hear reason." Ada raised her chin. "But since you won't, I must inform you that any accusation of breach of promise—or any continued pressing of your suit—will result in the truth of your activities coming forth."

He grabbed her shoulders with a grip that looked tight enough to bruise. "You dare to—"

As one, Ainslie and I swept into the room. If he thought he could assault her without repercussion . . .

Jade charged past us. She leapt onto the table alongside them, her claws digging into the finish, and snarled at Lord Bradford.

He stumbled back, releasing Ada and eyeing Jade with evident unease.

Ada rested a trembling hand on Jade's back, and for once, Jade did not spurn her.

Thank you.

Jade kept her gaze locked on him. *He should not have threatened those who dwell in my house.*

Ainslie interposed herself between him and Ada. "It's time you left."

"Time I . . ." Lord Bradford scowled at her. "I've condescended to offer for your sister, despite her small dowry and lack of title, and I'm repaid with insult?"

"You've received no more than you deserve, and she has far greater sense than to accept a gentleman who has taken bribes to change his votes in the Assemblage of Lords—or who has blackmailed numerous others to gain money to pay off gaming debts." Ainslie crossed her arms. "I understand the Magistry doesn't look favorably upon corrupted votes."

Mottled red spread up his neck. "How dare you—"

"You'll drop your suit, and you'll do it in such a way that her reputation remains untainted, or we will see that the truth of your deeds is known." I took my position at Ada's side. "Furthermore, you'll leave my aunt and uncle alone. I'd suggest a trip out of Byren, perhaps an extended one."

"You." His eyes narrowed at me. "You're behind this—you've sought to thwart me from the start."

"Do not think to cast aspersions on my sister." Ada drew herself up. "The only one you have to blame is yourself for refusing to heed my wishes. Please go at once."

"If you think you can order me about, you'll find you're much mistaken," he said.

With precision, Jade lifted her paw, her claws flashing, and sliced down his arm hard enough to rip through his sleeve and draw blood.

He recoiled, cursing and clutching at his arm. "Keep that beast away from me!"

I shook my head. "I'm afraid I cannot—at times she's quite outside my control."

Jade growled low in her chest and stalked toward him, the fur on her hackles rising. Combined with her bulk and generally menacing appearance, it was quite unnerving.

Still grasping his injured arm, he stumbled back farther.

You're enjoying this.

Quite.

"You'll come to regret this," he muttered, but it was half-hearted, as though he sought to save face. Then he marched from the room, slamming the door behind him.

"Well done, Ada." Ainslie pulled her into an embrace. "I don't think he'll trouble you any longer."

Nor did I. We'd one victory at least. Although we'd still have Aunt Melisina's displeasure to reckon with, Ada was free.

Aunt Caris bustled into the room. "What in the Crossings was that commotion?"

"Lord Bradford removing himself for good." Ada sank onto the settee, the tension washing from her features.

"There's a mercy. Melisina insisted she'd spoken to your father again, said he approved, though I could not think . . . It's no matter." She patted Ada's shoulder. "I meant to be back long before he came, but after I informed her we couldn't accommodate her and Milton to dinner as well as Lord Bradford on such short notice, Melisina devised a crisis, and I couldn't extricate myself. How did you finally persuade him of your disinterest?"

Ainslie dimpled. "With a skillful application of the truth. You should have seen Ada. She was magnificent."

Ada reached up and clasped both our hands. "I cannot take the credit—I had a great deal of help."

Ada and Ainslie and Aunt Caris settled into easy conversation, and a tangible peace settled over the room. With the three of them near and happy, I could almost press from my mind the knowledge that Nikol still sought Mr. Tibbons, that the basilisk still stalked the townsfolk, that Lord West had menaced Dreda and intended to force another encounter at the ball—and that my only chance of defending myself against him was to assume control of a blood-drenched, cursed ruin crafted by powerful fae. I clutched Jade to my chest and buried my face in her fur.

Almost I could forget, but not quite.

CHAPTER 42

In the confines of my bedchamber, I waited for Riven, the soft tick of the clock pronounced in the stillness. At midnight, he'd call, or more accurately, he'd summon me to fulfill my word, to bend Kilmere to my will—or be broken upon it. Remembered pain spiraled up my arm, and my resolve wavered.

Jade wove between my ankles. *It's not too late to change course.*

I think it's always been too late, from the moment I determined to protect what Ibbie left me—from the moment I set myself against Mr. Broward, and thereby against Lord West, unaware.

With her usual grace, Jade leapt upon the windowsill, balancing on the too-narrow-for-her ledge. *I'll keep watch over you.*

I know. It's my one comfort. I drew my chair up beside the window, and she climbed into my lap. I'd kept the gas lamps dim, and they mingled with the silvery glow of the waxing moon to cast deep shadows behind me.

If I allowed myself to consider further what must come, I'd certainly falter. Instead I reached for my sketchbook and slid my pen across the page, the ink a darker black than the moon-drenched night about me. I refused to allow myself to sketch Kilmere or any of the horrors it contained.

Instead, sea-blossoms took shape below my pen, followed by graceful willows. Outlining the sweep of their branches and listening to their song drift through the glass brought a measure of calm, but the moment Riven appeared in a fierce, forbidding flare of light, my heart leapt back into an uneven beat.

"Change of plans." With a single lithe motion, he crossed the room. "Nikol found Tibbons. He brought Tibbons the long way back to avoid exposing him to a passing in his vulnerable state. They're in a cave outside Kilmere—we'll go there first."

I'd allowed my pen to rest on the page far too long, and it left a dark blotch of ink behind. How could I endure witnessing his shattering? Given the only other choice was to abandon him altogether, to allow Riven and Nikol to interrogate him—well, it wasn't really a choice at all. I closed the book, blotting the ink stain from view. "Does he have the basilisk with him?"

"Unknown. But if he does, and we deal with her before Kilmere, it will give you an advantage."

And perhaps spare Mr. Tibbons the fate he'd otherwise suffer. "Then we should go at once."

With a swirl of power, Riven brought us through a passing into the entrance of a large cave, which was lit by silvery fae-lights. Their starlike glow bathed the ferns hanging over the opening and shaded the mosses below.

Only Nikol waited for us, lounging against a stone pillar, his silver eyes gleaming to match the fae-lights he'd kindled, his dark beauty ominous. There was no sign of Mr. Tibbons. Unease tingled down my spine. What had Nikol done with him?

"Any sign of the basilisk?" Riven strode forward.

And Nikol shook his head. "It's not on his person—and there's no trace of it nearby."

Of course there wasn't . . . it would have been far too simple that way. Every force of Other involved with Kilmere had shown itself canny from the very beginning. Why should the basilisk prove any exception? A tangle like that of thorns constricted my chest.

"I'll warn you, he's in no pleasant mood. You'll have to wrest whatever you need from him." Nikol tipped his head toward me. "And she won't be an asset. Mortals don't have the stomach for this sort of thing."

I ignored him, turning to Riven. "Before you . . . seek the truth, I'd like a word with Mr. Tibbons."

"What else remains to be said?" In the silvery fae-light, Riven's features appeared more forbidding than ever. "He cannot voluntarily give the information we require."

The thorn tangle tightened. "Perhaps, but if I can persuade him to cooperate, won't it go better for him?"

Riven gave a slight nod. "It's possible. If he can be swayed."

Nikol pressed away from the stone pillar, arching a brow at Riven. "I begin to think you've spent too much time in the mortal world."

"Just take us to Tibbons."

"As you wish." Nikol drew us deeper into the cavern. It opened into a broad chamber, lit with two silvery-bright fae-lights. They played over the stalactites, casting long shadows like daggers over the walls. In places, rope-like bundles of roots pierced the stone roof and stretched down toward the floor, gleaming where water dripped down their lengths.

At the far side of the cavern, Mr. Tibbons strained against the dark cords of shadow binding him to a thick pillar of stone. And my own arms ached in response—were these shadows tormenting him as West's had me?

A closer look revealed a bruise marring his jaw, blue-black and angry. A flash of heat quickened my veins. "Was it necessary to injure him?"

"I understood force was preferred above other means." Nikol shrugged. "Besides, he struck first."

"After you baited him, no doubt," Riven rumbled.

"As it happens, I did chance to insult a passing lady. Turns out Tibbons is quite the gentleman." One corner of his mouth lifted.

With so much at stake, I couldn't afford to allow him to bait me as he had the unfortunate Mr. Tibbons, so I picked my way across the uneven floor. "Please unbind him."

Nikol hesitated. When Riven gave a slight nod, he flicked his fingers, and the cords fell away. "If you want the trouble of catching him again, be my guest."

Mr. Tibbons surged forward. I stepped in front of him, and he stopped short.

"Miss Caldwell! How?" Forgetting propriety, he stepped within a handbreadth of me, his eyes sweeping down my frame. "Have you been harmed?"

"Not in the least. I'm here in hopes of freeing you."

"And since she's the only one here who cares about your fate, I suggest you listen to her—and cooperate." Nikol's distinctive silver eyes brightened. "Though it'll be vastly more entertaining if you do not."

Whatever Riven had said about Nikol not toying with Mr. Tibbons, he took far too much pleasure in his discomfort—and I was beyond weary of fae malice. The heat in my veins burned stronger. "You're not helping matters."

Even as I spoke, the roots in the cave writhed, pulling upright as though they sought a target to strike. Shaken, I stepped back, and they tumbled downward once more.

Shadows deepened around Nikol as he examined me. "I withdraw my earlier remark. Perhaps Miss Caldwell will prove useful after all."

"It's irrelevant to the matter at hand." Riven stalked forward. "Tibbons, we have some questions for you. I suggest you cooperate if you want to regain your freedom."

Mr. Tibbons thrust his chin forward. "I'll answer nothing, not when you've abducted me and quite possibly Miss Caldwell."

"Mr. Tibbons, it's not quite as it seems. I apologize for the handling of the matter, but the truth is that the situation here in Withern has grown dire." My fears surged forward, coloring my voice, and this time I could not check the rising glamour, no matter how I tried. "The authorities require information about what you've found in Kilmere, you understand. Of necessity, it must be done in secret."

"You mean they're Vigil?"

Shadowy figures abducting one in the night—I supposed it could fit. Certainly, his belief in it offered an advantage. Any odd abilities Riven or Nikol displayed he'd attribute to the alchemical devices the Vigil was rumored to possess in abundance. I lifted my shoulders. "I cannot confirm that. I trust you understand."

He slumped back with a groan. "Lady Dromley warned me they took interest in Kilmere—that I needed to take a care."

"I know it's unorthodox, but this is necessary, so please cooperate."

"I'll do what I can. But I've told you all I know, I swear it," he said.

The steady drip of water sounded in the distance, quiet and relentless. I drew a deep breath. "What of your departure from Withern? What prompted you to leave so suddenly?"

"I received word that someone had a document from old Withern that detailed the construction of Kilmere. They sent me a copy of a bit of it, and it appeared promising. The letter suggested the individual in question sought the highest bidder, and I thought if I reached them before any others, I could persuade them to sell."

I'd expected confusion at the question, some sign that the basilisk had swayed him into departing, but this . . . Who would want Mr. Tibbons out of the way? I studied him for signs of residual glamour. "I can see why that caught your interest, but why leave without a word?"

"I . . ." He scrubbed a hand over his face. "I sent a message to you."

"With whom?"

"There was someone . . . a servant at the *Sea Blossom*?" He drew a hand over his eyes, his words faltering.

There it was. The cold damp of the cavern seeped through my gown. Could the basilisk have muddled his senses on the matter? If so, who had sent the mysterious message?

"What did this servant look like?" Riven asked.

"He, ah . . . I believe . . ." He dragged his hand over his face once more. "I can't recall. And I still don't see the relevance of all this. What do you believe I know?"

"There's been another poisoning victim." Riven spoke without emotion. "Signs of your presence were found at the scene."

"That—it's impossible."

"Consider again." This time, an undercurrent of power laced Riven's words. "What were you doing last night, before you left Withern?"

"I returned to the *Sea Blossom* for dinner, then packed and departed. That's all."

"Miss Caldwell, a word." Riven strode back into the tunnel, leaving Nikol to stand watch. When we rounded the corner, he surrounded us with glamour. "He believes he's telling the truth."

"Is it possible?"

"No. The evidence was clear. Whatever has hold of him has claimed his true memories." Riven folded his arms across his chest. "It's time I forced the truth. We can make no further progress like this."

My eyes stung. At my side, Asrina pulsed with gentle warmth—after all she'd endured, she'd chosen to stay, and knowing she remained of her own accord brought me peace. How could we do less for Mr. Tibbons? "I'd like to tell him the truth first—the truth about what we suspect and what you must do."

"You imagine he'll accept having his mind broken to preserve the lives of others?" His voice held an edge.

"He might, if he understood the situation. Ibbie trusted him, and she didn't extend trust readily."

The glamour about us darkened. "He's in your employ. If you want to draw him deeper into the situation, it's your choice. But I will proceed whether he agrees or not."

Unable to trust my voice, I nodded, and we returned to the chamber. "Mr. Tibbons, I realize this will seem peculiar, but I believe you deserve to know what's at stake."

As succinctly as possible, I told him of the basilisk and the curse and his probable role in it all. Riven watched the two of us, his expression unreadable, while Nikol's skepticism remained clear.

When I finished, Mr. Tibbons went pale beneath his tan, his calloused hands tightening at his side. "You think it beyond doubt that some . . . Otherworldly creature has attached itself to me and forced me to poison innocents unaware?"

"That appears to be the case—at the least, it's clear you've come under Otherworldly influence." I ached to offer some consolation, but I possessed none—only painful facts. "Lord Riven has a way to obtain the truth, but it could hurt you."

His throat tightened as he swallowed. "What must he do?"

"He will exercise care, but he must bring back your true memories." My voice trembled. "And your mind may not . . . hold up to the strain."

He wheeled away, pacing the cavern, then at last he halted before Riven, his breathing ragged. "Do what you must. If somehow this curse has me a killer, if I murdered these people—I have to know. I can't ask others to continue to die on my account."

Even now, Riven betrayed no emotion. "It is a wise choice—your cooperation means better odds you'll survive unscathed. An anchor would give still greater opportunity."

"An anchor?" he asked.

"A connection point with someone you love and trust. The working that blocks your memories will urge you to resist, to fight me until your mind is shattered, and you can recall nothing."

Mr. Tibbons paled. Not for the first time, I wished Riven were not *quite* so ruthless in his honesty.

"An anchor will help you fight these fears. A family member would be best, but since we can't afford to bring anyone else into the situation, I suggest Miss Caldwell. She's the only one of us you share any acquaintance with, however limited."

A faint sheen of perspiration beaded on his forehead. "It's not something I should rightly ask—but will you offer your assistance, Miss Caldwell?"

"Of course." I doubted what help I could offer, since we scarcely knew one another, but it was better than nothing. I looked up at Riven. "What do you want me to do?"

"Take his hand. If he begins to grow agitated, try to soothe him. Convince him he's safe, that he must not fight the process."

Soothe him? While his mind was under assault? "I'll do my best."

However improper, I slipped my hand into his—it was cold, and it trembled, which drove all thoughts of proprieties from my mind. He was terrified, and rightly so. If I possessed any power to see him through safely, I'd lend it.

Coils of light wove between Riven, Mr. Tibbons, and me, and the cavern slipped away. An image formed before my eyes of Mr. Tibbons as a child. He played with his father in the shadow of an old oak, then his father rested a hand upon his head. Some exchange took place between them, soft murmurs that I could not hear. His father clasped his shoulder. "When the time comes, I know you'll do what's right."

What was I seeing? Was this what Mr. Tibbons had fixed upon, when he made his resolve? Did Riven's breach of his mind expose it to me also?

Strands of golden light shot through the image, and Mr. Tibbons's hand tightened painfully around my own. I clung to the picture of the child beneath the oak, willing Mr. Tibbons to remember the peace and comfort of that moment.

His grip relaxed slightly, then the light brightened. My awareness of my own body, my own mind, faded as the ruins of Kilmere appeared, vibrant and clear.

Riven was in—and he'd drawn me with him.

CHAPTER 43

I stood before the ruins, majestic even in decay, carrying echoes of splendor sufficient to haunt a man for a lifetime. If the lead I'd been given was right, I'd honor Lady Dromley's memory and the trust she'd placed in me by paving the way to explore them once more.

The lead.

A strand of light pulled a new image to the forefront, yet it appeared warped, shot through with shadow-like strands.

In the tavern, an aged man approached, his hat in hand. "Heard you seek information about Kilmere. That you've a reward to offer."

"Only if the information is sound." Lady Dromley had possessed resources in abundance, but I'd not squander that which she'd left in trust.

"It's sound, and I can prove it. I can tell you how to find the hidden heart within—it holds the answers you seek." Despite his wizened features, his eyes remained clear, as dark as the night beyond the windows. "I'll offer you a bargain, as a matter of fact. You investigate as I instruct, then pay me once you've found what you seek. It's an offer more generous than you'll find elsewhere."

Generous indeed. I'd be a fool not to accept, when this could *provide all the information Lady Dromley had once desired and more. If I could bring the evidence I uncovered to Miss Caldwell, perhaps she'd even let me begin excavation. "Very well. I agree to your terms. Let's have the information."*

A fog tinged the image, obscuring the man from view, then thick black strands webbed across it.

Riven sent a brilliant light skimming along the dark strands, and Mr. Tibbons thrashed in my grasp. Everywhere the light traveled, it burned, as the workings battled one another. The pain seared my own mind through whatever connection bound the three of us—yet it was only a shadow of what he endured. And he writhed against it.

The light subsided. Riven waited . . . for what?

Oh.

I spoke low and gentle. "It will be well. Only you must let him in. Your father believed you'd do what's right—so choose this course."

Mr. Tibbons stilled.

And Riven tried again, the smallest filaments of light working their way alongside the web of shadows, producing snatched fragments of word and image.

The aged man spoke. "Heart . . . blood . . . Seek the statue . . . Forget it all . . . . Meet at the milepost after, with payment in hand . . . You'll see only the ordinary."

Riven flared light across the interlaced strands that strangled the voice of the speaker, and fracture lines appeared.

Mr. Tibbons groaned.

And a bitter taste tinged my mouth. It would be so very easy for Riven to burn away the darkness, to expose the full truth and snatch it out before everything in the mindscape shattered into a million fragments. What would he do?

One moment, two, then the light ebbed once more. Thank the Infinite, he did not press. Half a heartbeat later, we'd skipped to a new image. Another figure appeared—a different guise, but the same tinge of compulsion in his voice.

This time, he gave Mr. Tibbons new information, offering to broker a deal for a document on the construction of Kilmere, each word dripping glamour.

Yesterday. We were witnessing what had transpired yesterday.

"What is your price for this?" I asked.

"A small task, no more. Just one thing you must do before you leave town."

A rending sound, new fracture lines, and we returned to the first image of Kilmere.

I stood before the ruins, majestic even in decay, carrying echoes of splendor sufficient to haunt a man for a lifetime. If the lead I'd been given was right, I'd honor Lady Dromley's memory and the trust she'd placed in me by paving the way to explore them once more.

I walked past the crumbled outer walls and toward the central keep. If there was any place secrets might be hidden, it was there. Besides, he'd told me I must go. Must fetch it, bring it out. How?

My—his—vision filled with fog, all interwoven with strands of the binding, glamour entangling the memories, weaving in confusion, deception.

Ordinary.

Ordinary.

So very ordinary.

Odd that it's so ordinary, after all the stories.

Ordinary continued to thrum through his mind, obscuring all else, until . . .

There—in the niche in the wall, just as the man had described it, a magnificent serpentine statue, crafted with meticulous detail, unmarred by the passage of time. Its eyes glimmered in the light, its stone scales were cold to the touch.

This would pay my debt . . .

With that, he spiraled away, back to the concealed-by-glamour fae who'd lured him.

I approached the borders of the ruin, the statue in hand, and he was there, waiting. How had he known to come?

Just outside the boundary stones, he stood watching, seeking his payment.

I crossed over to join him and passed the statue into his hands, though it gave me a wrench to part with it.

"Very good. Consider your debt paid." In his hands, the serpentine form shifted . . .

And a cracking sound, like that of a shattering mirror, echoed round me. The fine lines etched deeper, darkened.

Oh, please no.

My vision went black. Next I knew, Jade was pressing her nose to my cheek, her breath warm upon my face, and my eyes fluttered open, my senses reeling as I struggled to separate layers of reality. Somehow, I'd sunk to the floor of the cave along with Mr. Tibbons, who still held my hand in a deathlike grip. I leaned toward him. "Mr. Tibbons. Myles? Can you hear me?"

One moment, two, and still he did not move. The damp, musty scent of the cavern tightened my throat.

Then he exhaled, a long, ragged sound. "Miss Caldwell. What—what's happened?"

"You've come through a spot of danger." Gently, I extricated my hand. The dark forms of the stalactites blurred as I struggled to put the pieces together. Mr. Tibbons had surrendered the stasis-form basilisk to the fae who had instructed him to bring it from the ruin, the same one who'd lured him out of town, telling him there was one task he must do before he went. Given the evidence, that task was clear: he'd bidden Mr. Tibbons to carry the basilisk to its most recent victim.

He pressed his hands to his head, which likely throbbed even more than mine did. "I don't understand."

"You didn't bring the basilisk into Withern, only delivered it to someone outside Kilmere. Do you remember?"

"What are you talking about?" His voice emerged thready. "What's Kilmere? And how have we come here? Wait, I remember . . . the Vigil."

The scent of damp and stone strengthened, and I struggled to draw breath. After all this, had he broken?

"He's under a great deal of strain." Riven towered above him, and a note of glamour crept into his voice. "You should rest now. Sleep if you can."

"Sleep in the middle of a cavern while the Vigil stands watch?" He gave a tremendous yawn, and his eyes lowered. "Perhaps . . . perhaps I'll just rest a moment."

The instant he rested his head against the stone pillar, his eyes shut and his features slackened.

Unspeakably weary, I tangled my fingers in the hanging roots and pulled myself to my feet, their determined strength pressing back my exhaustion. Jade perched on my feet, her warmth anchoring me.

Even so, I found it difficult to meet Riven's gaze. He'd exercised far greater care with Mr. Tibbons than I'd expected, but now that I'd witnessed this power he possessed, his capacity to shatter minds . . . I couldn't afford to dwell on it, nor what it might mean for mortals, not now. "Will he ever regain his memories of Kilmere?"

"No. His mind seeks to protect itself. He may lose some adjacent memories also. I drew forth parts of what he actually saw, which wars against what the glamour compelled him to believe. With a bit of prompting, his mind has erased everything to do with Kilmere, eliminating the conflict that could rip away his sanity. He'll pull through."

Nikol sheathed the dagger he'd been sharpening. "Never thought he'd come out intact."

"He tried to cooperate with what will he could muster," Riven said. "And Jessa encouraged him not to fight. Both went a long way to preserve his mind."

But if Riven had forced a full account from him, he'd never have endured.

"You have enough?" Nikol asked.

"Enough to make it clear his every action in relation to

Kilmere, starting with his journey to Withern, sprang from compulsion and bargain."

"Who held the bargain?"

Riven shifted, and the shadow of the stone pillar fell across his face. "The fae in question was heavily glamoured. No amount of pressing would have revealed his identity, since Tibbons never possessed that knowledge."

Yet his grim tone suggested he shared my thought about the responsible party: Lord West. What other fae had interest in Kilmere? But when I'd questioned Lord West, he had said he'd not bargained or coerced another mortal or fae to kill citizens of Withern on his behalf—oh, of course, that was it. They weren't killed on his behalf. It was for Kilmere, part of a preexisting bargain—which provided the perfect cover. With the basilisk, he could have easily facilitated the murders with his denial remaining a technical truth. The roots around me shuddered.

"It seems clear that whoever has bonded with the basilisk forced Mr. Tibbons to bear it yesterday," I said. "Assuming it was Lord West, what was his purpose?"

"I'd imagine to distract us with Tibbons, which succeeded."

Nikol stood looking down on the slumbering man. "Lord West? Who's he?"

"Damir, of your court."

A fleeting expression of some emotion—perhaps shock?—crossed Nikol's features, quickly masked behind his usual nonchalance. "There's trouble. What's he after?"

"Kilmere. And Jessa, for standing in his way."

He gave a low whistle. "Good luck with that."

"We can't forget whoever opened the passing near Kilmere," Riven said.

"Do you think that a more likely candidate?"

Riven shook his head. "If anything, I consider it more likely that individual paid a debt to Damir and opened it at his bidding. He's the type to collect them."

The shadows about Nikol shifted. "As I've now fulfilled my own debt, I'll be going."

"It's not like you to avoid the prospect of conflict," Riven said.

"I'll admit, I'd like to witness the conclusion of this affair, but it's nearly time for the queen's high summer hunt. She's expecting me to return." He motioned to the passage out of the cavern. "Walk with me, Riven?"

Though Riven's eyes narrowed slightly, he followed Nikol toward the cave entrance. Unprompted, Jade crept after them, while Asrina and I kept watch over Mr. Tibbons.

A moment later, she returned, her tail twitching. *Your actions tonight drew attention from Nikol.*

What do you mean? I wrapped my arms about myself, attempting to stave off the chill of the cavern, more profound now that I'd grown weary.

When they left this chamber, Nikol commented that you'd made quite a display, asked what Riven's king made of you. Riven told him he should exercise more care with his words, then put up a glamour to conceal the remainder of their conversation—but I do not like his interest.

I sank onto a flat stone. Had Riven told his king about me? Beyond my tie to Kilmere, what interest could I hold for a king? Yet I'd not thought I'd draw attention from Nikol either. Perhaps fae disliked what they could not understand as much as mortals did. *Whatever the damage, it's done now, but I cannot think what he deemed worthy of notice.*

How the roots responded to you. What you perceived in Tibbons's mind. All things that should not be.

But that was due to Riven; he drew me in.

Jade curled up next to me. *Yes, but if you were an ordinary mortal, it would have broken you. To perceive the layers in the mindscape of another and retain your own sense of self—it's no easy matter.*

Another puzzle, one which I did not desire, which I could

not consider. I must summon what strength remained if I was still to confront Kilmere—and I needed to now, more than ever.

The cold of the stone sank through my skirts, numbing my legs. If it had been Lord West keeping the basilisk all along, then Riven was right. It wouldn't be enough to bring Kilmere under my control and hope that Lord West abandoned the notion of claiming it, not when he'd bonded to the basilisk who held part of the bargain.

I clasped my knees to my chest and rested my head on them. If I could, I must use Kilmere against him—it was his death or theirs, and the cost of failure had become unthinkable.

But how could I become like the fae before me?

CHAPTER 44

When we emerged from the cave, Kilmere overshadowed us, its stones black against the charcoal sky. The stars glinted hard and remote above it, and its hunger dug like thorns deep into my flesh.

Riven's presence offered little comfort, for he remained as remote and distant as the stars, given over to his fae nature, his power roiling just below the surface. Unbidden, an image of his light spearing my chest returned.

My chest ached as though the blow had landed true, and the ache turned to a throb as we approached the tumbled stones of the boundary wall, some jutting upward like fangs, others sprawling across the cliff like broken bodies.

Perhaps Riven perceived my fears, for he turned. "If Damir has the basilisk, she'll regain her strength far more rapidly than she would have with Tibbons. That makes tonight all the more important. We must act before he does."

"I understand." He was right, and yet I no longer had whatever advantage I might have gained with the elimination of the basilisk. I'd made the choice to attempt to claim Kilmere without expecting such leverage, and I'd not realized till this moment that I'd begun to pin my hopes upon it. Yet if Lord West did possess the basilisk, the cost of failure became even greater. I stumbled over a rock concealed in a shadowed depression. When I caught myself upon the wall, the slightest snatch of a memory of the basilisk in true-form impressed itself upon me.

Kilmere reminded me of its bargain, of my hints that I would help achieve it. Did it know a powerful fae lord had bonded with the basilisk already? It must not, else it would never have entertained my offer. For all it knew, the basilisk was gone, carried out by Mr. Tibbons, and I might help rouse her and bring her back. On the strength of that suggestion, I hoped to make it into the keep, but then I must reveal my true intent— and endure its wrath.

I held my station along the wall, every fiber of my being willing me to turn back.

Riven stopped alongside. "There's something you should know. Abilities of the sort you've displayed respond to intent. Understanding and experience help refine them and increase their power, but your purpose remains the driving force."

"What are you saying?"

He ignored my true question and continued, "Don't let Kilmere undermine your resolve, nor overtake your senses—or you'll not achieve your ends."

I pressed my lips together tightly, giving a small nod. Jade stretched herself upright, planting her front legs on my chest. In response, I lifted her, cradling her close, seeking what comfort I could claim. "Must we go as far as the heart?"

"I suggest the central keep and the keystone there. Until we know how Kilmere intends to respond, it would be prudent to avoid its depths."

A sort of pricking awareness emanated from Kilmere, as though it knew we'd come with a purpose, and it watched and waited for it to unfold, its predatory stones spread out like a snare, the wash of silvery moonlight insufficient to conceal their menace.

With Jade held close, I clambered over the wall. In silence, we proceeded toward the central keep, an unnatural stillness surrounding us. Not a single leaf stirred; even the crash of the waves in the distance faded away. What did Kilmere intend?

In the arched doorway, I removed my gloves, touching the wall alongside. It was how I'd made deeper contact before, how I must try again. Ivy coiled gently about my feet, its strength urging me onward.

Though the lichen warmed to my touch, the stone itself remained cold as frost. "I have come to make my claim."

An image flared about me of the basilisk and the scroll with the bargain. Then it deepened, and I saw myself as Kilmere did —standing before its vast expanse, small and weak. It offered me its own malicious strength in exchange for its bargain of old brought to fullness.

I stood in the ruins, the power of Kilmere flowing through me until I became an implacable force. No longer need I fear, not as long as I joined with its might. And as my will bonded to its desire, my face altered until it resembled those of the lords and ladies who'd once forged the stronghold, beautiful and cruel and unfeeling.

No.

I recoiled. I could not, would not become like them—not even to free myself of Lord West. "I claim you on my own terms."

The hasty words spilled from my lips, and the air about me plummeted in temperature. The stars were blotted out, the ruins vanished, and I sank into deep darkness.

Several tall, beautiful fae walked across the empty clifftop. "Is the eld near?"

"He comes."

A tremendous passing split the air, glittering silver-gold, and a band of fae appeared, along with the bound form of a dragon, immense beyond reckoning, snared not by natural cords, but by chains of raw power. The bonds seared his scales, and he gave no sign of life.

A fae lord strode forward, the trees swaying their limbs at his approach. "Let us begin."

Four fae took up their stations along the foundation stones of the keep. They knelt and touched the earth, and rents formed in solid rock as their power carved caverns below.

The dragon roused.

Thrashed.

Trumpeted his rage.

Yet he could not break free.

The fae lord stalked over to stand before its amber eye. "Be still —your time is at hand."

Then I plummeted down into darkness, my form melding with that of the dragon, its anguish becoming my own.

No, no, this wasn't right. I stood within the keep, I'd come to Kilmere of my own will . . .

The cords of power burned through scale into flesh. He strained against them, but all his might availed nothing. With their workings, the fae lashed him to the rock below, to the heart they forged in the depths of the earth.

A silver-haired fae stepped forward, flicking his fingers. And a jagged shard of stone shot through it—through me—piercing hide, muscle, sinew, leaving agony in its wake. Another followed, a third, a fourth. Time and again, the spears of stone bit and burned until they reached my core, the brilliant flame of power within.

And then, each spear-stone pulled.

I writhed, seeking escape. There must be a way out, must be. But I couldn't think, couldn't move, could only feel hot, cold, burning rending tearing . . .

No.

The distant murmur of the lichens brushed my senses. I must regain control. I was not this beast; I was not bound, not yet.

Yet the cold searing my bones promised I would be. Kilmere would break me, feast upon me. Then find a new mistress. It pulled me deeper.

I was bound, pierced, my life pulled spark by painful spark from my frame, roaring, fighting, broken, beaten . . .

Stop.

Cold crept up my fingers, into my hands, my arms. Before me, the dragon thrashed. Then its huge amber eyes opened, blood streaming from the corners.

Run!

I staggered away from the stone, returning to my body. My breath came in ragged gasps, my hands had gone numb, but my arms—how they throbbed. I sought to open my senses to the nearby rowans and heard nothing save the roar of my pulse in my ears.

Riven clasped my shoulders, his presence warm and living and vital in this place of coldness and death. "You can't let it pull you in. Look for the workings that bind Kilmere—you must seize control of them. As you did the lock."

About me, Kilmere gathered power, the scent of blood-stained earth choking. Why had I thought I could seize control, could change the nature of Kilmere, when I couldn't even begin to understand my own? Yet if I didn't try, I'd not survive—and so many others would die.

I turned, searching for threads of power like I'd seen in the lock—there. The faintest shimmer caught my eye, a swirled spiral arching from the keystone. Could I alter its color and form as before? I moved toward it, and my vision went black.

Three mortals descended to the heart, eager, afraid, curious. They huddled together, sheep to the slaughter. A fair, elegant fae lady beckoned them forward.

She motioned to them to lie upon tables of stone, and when they did, she rent their hearts from their bodies. Her workings consumed them as they screamed in agony . . .

This was Kilmere, built upon suffering and death, forged by mighty fae lords and ladies who'd bent their affinities to shape it, bound it to their wills, bound to it the will to dominate all others. Beside these mighty ones, I was insignificant as a gnat, an unworthy mortal, no fit master for this domain. It would soon rid itself of this fragile tie and find a partner to match its might.

No, those were not my thoughts, but those of Kilmere. What . . . what were my own? I clutched at my head, spiraled back into the mind of the dragon. Again spikes of stone pierced my flesh, each one wrenching power from the core of my being. I sank into the pain as it tore ever deeper.

And then I collided with the ground, breath driven from my lungs. In true-form, Jade towered over me, her sweet-grass scent driving back that of sweat and suffering. The stars spun above me, and the cold moon mocked my failure.

A bitter, metallic taste, like that of the old blood that had stained the stones, filled my mouth. Sweat slicked my hands, my neck, my back, yet I could not stop shivering. So many would die, all because I could not become what Kilmere wanted—and I did not possess power enough to make it something else. I couldn't muster the strength to rise from the earth, not even when a deep, rumbling growl issued from the stones beneath.

"Get up." Riven stood over me, implacable, relentless. "You must try again."

But I could not move. My arms throbbed. Deep blue-black bruises marred the length of them, each one a match for the spikes driven through the dragon's forearms. My pulse hammered at the base of my throat. The workings had power over my body as well as my emotions—and Kilmere reached for me, oh so hungry. It had tasted my essence, and it craved more.

Infinite have mercy.

I dug my fingers into the earth, struggling to press myself from the ground. I refused to believe that there was a place where death could reign unbroken, and yet . . .

Claws of stone broke from the ground. Jade charged forth to meet them, snarling, willing to give her own life before she let Kilmere take me.

I couldn't let her stand alone.

One of the immense dragon-like limbs caught her side, and

drops of blood spattered the ground. Where it fell upon the ivy below, a delicate working of ivory and scarlet wove through the vines.

As my fingers closed about the nearest shoot, it surged forward, vines sprawling in every direction, binding the claws of stone. Kilmere rumbled low and hostile, its force gathering.

And a vivid image flooded my mind.

A fae lady, dark and lovely, glided across the clifftop, ravens perched upon her shoulders. No stronghold yet existed, only the foundation stones for the great fortress. Around them, fae lords and ladies clustered, watching her approach.

A lord marched forth to meet her, a jeweled circlet shining on his brow. "Well? Where is your husband? We must have his blood to begin properly."

"As it happens, I'm no longer of a mind to surrender him." In the sunlight, the ravens' wings glinted blue-black, and she stroked the one on her right.

"Take another mortal later, if you find them so pleasing. This one's bound to the land, his must be the first sacrifice—it was the whole purpose of your marriage."

"Nevertheless, I prefer to keep him." Her chin lifted.

"Even at the expense of your own life?" About his feet, vines of ivy coiled, like serpents ready to strike. "By virtue of this marriage, you've also become bound to the land. Will you let yours be the first blood? You cannot resist so many."

Her golden eyes warmed with a glorious fire. "And if you claim my life for his, it will be your unmaking—"

Blinding strands of power closed about me, scarlet and old bone jumbling together, and then the irresistible force of a passing snatched me from the ground and thrust me, stumbling, into the brook clearing we'd sheltered in before.

Jade.

She was here, as well as Riven and Asrina, who lowered herself to perch on my shoulder, as if she wished to offer comfort.

"Worry not," she murmured.

Had Riven removed us? Ravens clustered in the branches above my head, wakeful and watchful when they should rightly slumber. And I collapsed onto the rocks. "How did you bring us through a passing? I thought you could not wield your power within the ruins?"

"It wasn't my passing, but one formed by Kilmere—or something therein." He jabbed his hand toward the ruins. "You did something at the end to divide Kilmere against itself. We should go back, press the advantage."

No! Jade shouted into my mind—and apparently Riven's as well.

He wheeled toward her, sparks flaring around him. "When it comes to Other, only the strong survive. Your mistress must be able to defend herself against Damir. Or she will fall."

And what does it matter to you if she dies, Lord Arbiter? Perhaps you press her because it suits you. You stand to gain. And I to lose everything.

"Have a care with your accusations, *kit-isne*. If I wanted her dead, I'd take her life here and now. Neither you nor anyone else could stop me."

The force of his words hit like a blow, and I shrank back.

Riven advanced toward Jade, the sharp scent of storm charging the air. "Do you have another plan for her protection?"

Jade lowered her gaze, and my breath caught. Always she defied the world, but now . . . she was afraid. *All I know is that she cannot go back now, not while she remains divided herself. She's spent her strength, but Kilmere retains its full might. If the counter-working opened a passing, it was to spare her life. We cannot count on such good fortune again.*

Jade perceived the whole of my weakness, and she exposed it to Riven. I pulled my knees to my chest, resting my head on them, even as he turned toward me, his eyes kindling gold.

"With all you've seen, you're still divided? You doubt the necessity of this?"

"Not the necessity—but Riven, I can't give Kilmere what it wants. Can't persuade it I'm the master it seeks." My voice broke. "I've seen those who crafted it, their power and their nature. I'm not like them, and I never will be."

"Not fae." His voice was flat. "Because that would be unthinkable."

"I did not mean . . ." I faltered to a stop. I couldn't deny it, because it *did* feel unthinkable, the notion of what I might do, what I might become, if fae blood ran through my veins.

He closed the distance between us. "Then what do you plan? Do you doubt Damir's resolve? The moment there's opportunity, he will break you himself and force you to surrender Kilmere."

I flinched, the words cutting deep. "I know."

Just as I knew he was right—I'd no choice but to try again. But Jade was right as well. I'd no hope of victory like this, and I could not see my way forward, not yet. I rubbed my hand over my eyes.

The fae-lights Riven had kindled about us revealed the bruises marring my arms. He shook his head. "I should never have let you waste strength on Tibbons."

"It was not your choice to make."

"But I knew what was at stake. You did not." The lights flared brighter. "If you don't intend to surrender to Damir, you must return and end this, but for tonight, take the reprieve given —the time to consider how you divided Kilmere and how you might exploit whatever weakness you uncovered."

A raven fluttered overhead once more. Weakness? I'd sensed no weakness in Kilmere, only implacable might. Yet it *had* sought to hide something. Why had I caught a glimpse of the Lady of Ravens? Why did Kilmere want to keep her actions concealed? Her past must hold something to put it at a disadvantage, but my exhausted mind could conjure no answers. So I simply nodded.

With the force of a summer tempest, Riven forged a passing about us. When he released the coils of power, we stood an arm's length apart in my bedchamber. His gaze returned to my bruises, and something flickered in his eyes. He raised his hand and rich light spiraled across my skin, sloughing away the pain. "Sleep and reclaim your strength. You'll need it."

With that, he vanished.

CHAPTER 45

I woke with a start, snared by stone—no, by Jade sprawled across my chest. Last night, I'd bound her wound with amelior salve and then stumbled to bed with her in my arms. Now the sun bathed us both, tugging me to wakefulness.

I pushed upright. Beyond the window, the trees swayed gently, inviting me to take refuge beneath their boughs, to rest where things were green and alive. I discarded my stained garment and donned a fresh gown, while Jade stretched on the bed.

How is your injury?

Improved—and it was the merest graze to begin with. The salve has gone a long way toward healing it. Another day or two, and it should be gone.

Thank you . . . for everything, always. I rested a hand on her head. *I'm sorry I could not stop Kilmere from hurting you.*

I'm not concerned about that, only what's to come. On what terms will you approach Kilmere? If you won't bend to its will, you must find some other means of swaying it. It cannot be left to chance.

I know. And I didn't have much time left to determine a

course. With Jade in my arms, I slipped out the back into the gardens.

In the branches of an elm, a raven stretched its wings, the glossy black gleam drawing me back to the revealed memory of the Lady of Ravens. How had I conjured the vision of her, when Kilmere did not desire it? And what did the ruin want to keep concealed?

If I could answer those questions, perhaps I could find my way forward. But beyond what I'd witnessed, the facts about her remained sparse, certainly not enough to shed light on her motivations. Why had she chosen to go against her companions—and her own initial resolve to snare a mortal in marriage and use him for her own ends?

Whatever the reason, she'd died upon the foundation of Kilmere. What I'd witnessed suggested she'd chosen it, that she'd acted to protect a mortal—a remarkable deed, if true.

I pressed my hand to the bark of the elm, its song of soft melancholy filtering into my senses. And I forced myself to *think* despite the lingering fog of exhaustion clouding my mind. In some way, could the Lady of Ravens be associated with the workings of scarlet and ivory that had appeared three times now? I'd witnessed them first when I'd given my own blood to unlock the heart, then again when Riven had done the same, and most recently, when Jade shed her blood for my protection. Each time, the appearance of the workings followed a sacrifice made willingly, not one claimed by force.

The mournful melody strengthened, driving pain deep into my chest. Was that the key to unlocking Kilmere? If so . . . it was unthinkable. I could not possibly take such a step, not if any other course remained. Yet perhaps there was another way to unlock those workings. If I could learn more of the Lady of Ravens and what Kilmere wished to keep hidden, then perhaps I could treat with it on different terms.

Last night, when we'd made our escape, I'd done nothing except take hold of a glimmer of hope extended. Could I find it again, such a fragile, determined spark amid the vast darkness? Not without some guidance, some confirmation that my theories were correct.

For the collection of such information, I could see two possible paths, both converging at the ball. Of all people, Lord West knew the most about Kilmere. Somehow he'd learned of its nature before his arrival in our world, which meant he might know those who'd crafted it, including the Lady of Ravens. His knowledge might prove the key, and I would see him there tonight—however little I desired it. As I would the Redgraves, and it was Elodie who'd first supplied information about Lady Firth, known as the Lady of Ravens. Might she know more?

Above, the leaves of the elm rustled and the raven gave a low *kraa*, one that heralded Riven's arrival. He strode about the house, offering no greeting. "Have you determined your course?"

"Perhaps." I rubbed my temples. "You suggested I consider how to exploit the weakness Kilmere revealed. I cannot do so without more information."

"Yet we cannot afford a delay."

His expression suggested he believed I stalled the inevitable, but I could not bring myself to speak of what I thought I'd witnessed, not without some certainty of its truth. If he were to dismiss it altogether—no, I must be more confident in myself first. "I agree. Lord West indicated he was almost through with his arrangements, and I don't think it was an idle threat, but the ball tonight will give me what I need."

It must, for no time remained. Regardless of his other plans, Lord West had already bound Dreda. If he approached Aunt Caris or my sisters, seeking to snare more whom I loved in his schemes . . . I wrapped my arms about my middle.

"Good. Find a reason to slip out early. We'll make our return to Kilmere then."

"I could plead a headache, perhaps." Like the one that encroached now, worsened by the notion of the upcoming ball and the confrontations to come. "Aunt Caris knows I don't favor such gatherings, and she'll likely excuse me without asking further questions."

"That will do." The distant voices of my sisters filtered through the trees, and Riven glanced toward them, the sun glinting in the green of his eyes. "I'll take my leave."

When he departed, I hurried toward the cottage. I didn't want company, not now, didn't want to don the pretense that all was well, so I ducked inside the back door and sank onto a trunk in the corridor with Jade at my side.

How could I ever be ready for what must come?

A soft sniff broke the silence, and my heart leapt. I'd thought everyone was out of doors. I crept toward the sound and found Aunt Melisina sitting in the drawing room, her shoulders slumped, her face buried in her hands.

She radiated pain. Despite all that had passed between us, I tiptoed forward. "Aunt Melisina? Are you well?"

"Go away, child." Her breath hitched, uneven. "You've won. Lord Bradford means to leave."

Though Jade bristled, I took another step toward her. "I know what he held over you."

"You cannot possibly know." She lifted her head, her eyes glittering with unshed tears.

"But I do." I stopped at a safe distance. "I know that he decided he must have Ada, no matter the cost. I know that when he discovered Uncle Milton had overextended himself in investments that hinged on the passage of an upcoming bill, he told him he'd ruin your family by voting against Uncle Milton's proposal in the assemblage and swaying others to do so as well."

"How?"

"It doesn't matter." I wouldn't add to her pain by telling her that Lovell had uncovered the truth—that was between them. "We've made sure he'll not carry through with his threats."

Her lips tightened. "Why would you care?"

"None of us want you or Lovell or Uncle Milton to suffer

from the acts of an unscrupulous man, whatever the reason." My hands tightened. "But your willingness to sacrifice Ada hurt her a great deal. She doesn't understand."

"I will . . . make amends, if I can." She pressed a lacy handkerchief to her mouth. "When Milton first suggested the match to me, I'd no notion what Lord Bradford held over him—you must believe me. I saw only the advantage for Ada, and I delighted at his interest. With Lord Bradford, she would have lacked nothing."

"And later—when you knew of his character and his dealings with women?" Jade stalked forward to sit at my feet, her presence bolstering me.

"At first, I reasoned that if he wished to wed her so badly, he'd treat her well. A man may deal with his mistresses or his opponents very differently than his wife, after all." She clenched the kerchief in her hands. "Later, I was . . . afraid. I've never seen Milton act so. He berated me for failing to secure the match, and I thought he'd . . . It doesn't matter. But he demanded I think of Lovell first, our son and his future, and I conceded."

Part of me wanted to shout that she should have protected Ada, no matter the cost. And yet in some way, I could relate to her struggle—her desire to protect Lovell, her vulnerability to Uncle Milton's demands. If he chose to mistreat her, the law offered little shelter. She'd seen no other way, therefore she'd become something she did not wish to be.

In light of the choice I faced with Kilmere, I couldn't condemn her. Only I did not want to repeat her mistakes. The golden gaze of the Lady of Ravens burned in my mind once more. What must I understand, before I returned?

Aunt Melisina lowered her head. "I regret what I said to you as well."

If she'd slapped me, I would have been less shocked.

"I stand by the fact you've a long way to go to become a proper lady—and that you influence your sisters in ways I cannot condone." She stared out the window, into the gardens where Ada, Ainslie, and Aunt Caris collected flowers. "But I know that you feared for Ada, and you wanted to protect her. I should never have faulted you for that."

An ache took up residence beneath my breastbone. "Even so, you wouldn't have said what you did about me—or about Mother—if you'd not already held those feelings long before Lord Bradford."

"It's true, your mother and I did not get on well." She straightened. "She made Alden incredibly happy, and I suppose part of me envied what they shared. It was never that way in my own marriage—nor indeed with most I've witnessed in society."

The faint sounds of laughter from Ada and Ainslie drifted through the open windows.

And Aunt Melisina continued, "Alden was so in love with her that he didn't mind her headstrong ways. She charmed even my father, who was notoriously hard to please. Certainly, he found fault with all his daughters. But not with Kensa, never with her."

How that must have stung. I ventured to sink onto a chair across from her. "You said she was headstrong. Why?"

Her fingers fretted with the edge of her crumpled handkerchief. "When she took to an idea, she'd not be dissuaded by anyone. You know she purchased Thornhaven and continued to make regular visits there, despite Alden's concerns about its proximity to Aelfgard Crossing. That was her way."

I sank deeper into the cushions behind me. Could Mother have been bound to Thornhaven? Had a bargain compelled her to return there until she produced a child? If so, how had she kept me from whatever fae might have sought to claim me? And why had she seemed to love Thornhaven? If it was the source of her pain, I couldn't imagine her doing so.

"I remember her visiting with us twice a year," I said slowly. "Did she go more often?"

"On occasion she'd go alone, but she preferred not to leave

you children." Aunt Melisina's lips parted, then she closed them firmly.

She was holding something back. If I wanted the truth of my past, I must press for answers. "There was something else that troubled you."

"It's of no credit to my account that I've spoken ill of the dead. I'll say no more."

"If you won't speak of what you know, then how am I ever to understand Mother? I cannot ask her all I desire—" My voice broke. Did she know something about my parentage, about the possibility of fae blood? "Please—can't you see the pain of not knowing is worse than whatever you could say?"

"At the end, she betrayed her vows to Alden." The words ripped from her, tinged with such pain I could not doubt them. "I might have forgiven her much, but never that."

My shoulders curled inward. "You witnessed this?"

"I don't know if you remember, but I was visiting when she died." All color left Aunt Melisina's face. "When Alden found her, he was shattered. Caris took him inside, and I said I'd wait with—the body—until the stratesmen came. But truthfully, I wanted to study the scene, because I feared some sign of her infidelity might remain."

"Why?"

"I hadn't been sleeping well, and I often remained up until all hours. Twice during my stay, I'd seen her venture out late at night. I'd watched as she met with a man in the gardens, then disappeared for hours each time. I could only assume that was why she'd gone out to the fountain that evening. All I could think was that if evidence of the affair remained, Alden would never have survived the double grief. And the scandal would have tainted all of you."

My throat tightened, and I could manage no response. Jade twined between my ankles, but even her closeness brought no easing of the pain. I'd wanted confirmation of my identity, but this . . .

"Crumpled alongside her was a letter, one that requested a meeting and addressed her with terms of endearment—no signature, only a mark at the end," Aunt Melisina said. "Perhaps I should have told Alden, but I didn't want to break his heart. And what good would it have done at that point?"

If whomever she had met with was fae—and was my father—then had he also killed her? Because she would not surrender me? The rich scents of green and growth from the gardens threaded about me, holding me upright. "Before she died, did you ask Mother about those meetings?"

"I did." Aunt Melisina lifted her chin slightly. "No surprise, she did not take it well. She told me I knew nothing and that if I breathed a word of the matter I'd come to regret it—that more would be lost than I could fathom."

More was already lost—the father and the family that I called my own. How could I endure it? Songs flooded in from beyond the windows, mourning and solace mingled. And I let my gaze drop to the scrolls on the rug below.

A long gust of air left Aunt Melisina. "You have no reason to believe me, given all that's passed between us, but it's the truth as far as I know it. I wanted to see your futures secured, to protect you all from the dangers of your mother's path—no more."

"I believe you've shared all the facts in your possession." But I'd never believe Mother had willingly abandoned her relationship with Father in favor of another . . . wait. "Was this what you meant to use against Father? Did you intend to tell him about the past?"

"I'd considered using it as leverage." Her eyes slid shut. "To show him he could not judge character and must allow me to guide this choice. I'd never have made it public."

Furious heat burned up my chest. "You would have hurt him so deeply just to get your way?"

Aunt Melisina shrank back. "I considered it—but I found I could not. He doesn't know, and he never will. Unless you choose to tell him."

The potted maidenhair fern on the mantel wafted its fronds restlessly, its leaves darkening. And I clenched my arms around my chest, wrestling to constrain my emotions. With all she already knew, I could not afford to betray myself further.

"You may choose not to forgive my deeds. If so, I understand." She straightened to her usual impeccable posture. "Either way, I give my word I won't speak of this again—to anyone. You need not fear it."

The fern shivered. I wanted to lash out at her, but what good would it do? I had the opportunity to forge a fragile truce and to keep what must remain secret hidden between us. I swallowed hard. "I'm thankful you told me, that I may better understand why you feel as you do."

"Then I suppose I'd best speak with Ada next." When she passed me, she hesitated a moment, then pressed her hand to my head with a gentler motion than I'd believed her capable of before she left the room.

Left my world in tatters. With what she'd witnessed, I'd little doubt I held fae blood, which meant . . .

I couldn't think of it, couldn't afford a distraction when I must engage Lord West tonight and then face Kilmere. My eyes burned, and I lifted Jade onto my lap, her low purr thrumming against my chest. If I must attend this blighted ball, must dance with him, then I'd draw forth whatever information I could—a test to confirm my theory.

Beyond the windows, ravens clustered on the lawn. Witnesses to my defeat? Or heralds of unfolding understanding? Right now, both felt the same.

In the heart, I'd subverted the working that required blood sacrifice. Yet surely to unmake all of Kilmere would require something more than a mere sprinkle of blood. Was there a way around this greater demand? Or must the price simply be paid?

CHAPTER 46

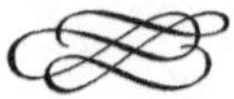

Through the carriage ride to Holle Castle, the conversations of my aunts and sisters, even Dreda, swirled around me, slightly stilted at times due to the lingering strain between Ada and Aunt Melisina. The spiced scent of sea-blossoms mingled with their perfumes, a reminder of how deeply Other had invaded my ordinary life and how impossible it had become to separate the two. If I understood rightly, I could never separate from Other, not fully, for its nature was my own.

How could I concede that I might be what I'd feared for so long?

My eyes pricked with unshed tears, and I pressed back the thought. I must uncover the truth about the Lady of Ravens and Kilmere, yet the notion of attending this gathering, of attempting to act at ease among the glittering members of society—and Lord West himself—sent a shiver through my body, despite the warmth of the evening. I was bound to my word to dance with him and bound to my purpose to gain the information I required, but otherwise, I'd keep to the sidelines as much as possible and avoid drawing notice until I could make my escape.

With that resolve to hearten me, we swept up the stairs into the glittering entry of Holle Castle, a chamber resplendent with gaslights that flickered off the gilded mirrors and polished floors. The butler conveyed us into the enormous ballroom, where the crush of people and cacophony of conversation plucked at my already strained senses.

Though I'd not yet set foot in the room, I wanted to withdraw. But as lively melodies unfurled about us, Aunt Caris looped her arm in mine and drew me into the bustle.

No sooner did Mr. Redgrave spy Ainslie than he approached, requesting a dance. A wild-rose flush crept up her cheeks as she accepted his arm. A moment later, an unfamiliar gentleman swept Ada onto the floor. When one began to approach me, Jade glowered at him until he turned away.

Thank you. I was in no mood to dance, beyond the one I'd promised Lord West.

Threading above all the other sounds and senses, Other swept across my skin. Riven entered the ballroom, his expression unreadable. It would be indiscreet to rush toward him, yet I required a word before we confronted Kilmere—perhaps even another bargain, although that remained unclear.

You keep your thoughts much to yourself today. Jade prowled alongside me. *And yet I uphold my word not to pry, despite our difficult situation.*

And I am grateful. I just . . . I have a great deal to sort through. And if she perceived the whole of my conjecture, she'd surely object to my course.

Her pupils narrowed. *As you say.*

With Jade on one side and Dreda on the other, I edged toward Riven, but to reach him, I had to stroll past where Lady Cadence held court, a small throng of admirers about her.

She did not allow me to pass her by, but instead fixed a bright smile upon me. "Miss Caldwell! I was just telling these gentlemen about your antiquarian studies that have drawn you to Kilmere. Do enlighten us on what you've learned."

An uncomfortable number of gazes turned upon me, and I fidgeted with my reticule. I couldn't speak of Kilmere's true nature, so I'd fall back on the more general precepts I'd picked up from Ibbie. While I couldn't match her passion, some of her knowledge had become my own, and I managed to rattle off a brief account of what antiquarians sought when they excavated.

"My. How very interesting." Her tone suggested that, in fact, she found it drier than dust. "I cannot keep up with the details you scholarly sorts do. I suppose you must spend all your time buried in books. However tedious, it must be preferred to gallivanting before the Magister."

Her barbs drew chuckles from the gentlemen surrounding her.

Jade growled softly, and I clenched my hands tighter about my reticule. Distracted by the pressing matter of Kilmere, I'd stumbled right into the social snare she laid. Better now, perhaps, to say nothing and let her lose interest.

Riven moved in our direction, drawing ladies' eyes as he traversed the room. In full formal wear, he appeared the sort of gentleman many swooned over—distant, aloof, and striking.

Lady Cadence fluttered her fan. "I understand that traipsing about ruins doesn't leave one much time to consider fashion. Come next ball, if you remain in Withern, you shall consult with my dressmaker, and we will find you evening wear that more closely resembles this year's styles."

Of all things, my aunts wished my sisters and me to appear to advantage—being branded a dowd, a bluestocking, and a wanton young lady all in the course of one short conversation would hardly further their cause. But neither would open conflict, so I managed a smile. "You are very kind."

The scent of sunbathed forest washed over me as Riven approached. "Will you dance?"

Though it was mid-set, I accepted his arm. At once, faint threads of glamour wove about us, muffling our conversation from listening ears.

We'd been this close before, in times of great danger, but something about this—was different. An uncertain warmth bloomed in my chest as the music swelled about us.

"Why did you allow her to insult you?" he asked. "At least, I judged she meant her words in such manner. You should not have let them stand."

I sighed. Did fae ever ignore plays for power, however small? Perhaps they could not afford to—there was much I didn't understand about their society. In any case, Riven wouldn't let me off without an answer. We blessedly broke apart, and when our hands met once more, I inclined my head. "What was there to say? She spoke no untruth."

"You might have countered with a number of others. You entered the Otherworld and faced an auvok; you strive against Kilmere despite the odds. You don't lack courage. So why let someone of so little sense or consequence steal your voice?"

"Because she was right—I've failed to conform to the expectations set for me. It's no surprise that people wonder and speculate." If I *was* Other, then perhaps they had just cause. I fixed my gaze on his shoulder, unwilling to reveal the turmoil within.

"What do their expectations matter?"

We took another separate turn. No surprise, he brought as much grace to the dance floor as to the battlefield. When the dance brought us back together, I said, "I must live in this world, therefore I must satisfy its conventions."

"Must you?" His voice came whisper-soft. "I'd suggest, rather, that you need to embrace what you are—cease hiding from it."

The final notes played, and I fumbled a step. About us, couples pulled apart, and he released his hold. "Riven, I—"

At my elbow, Lord West appeared. "I believe this dance is mine."

Riven stepped closer. "You're mistaken."

"He's not." The charge of power between the two snatched

the air from my lungs. "I agreed to one dance." And as much as I might dread it, I also required it.

All emotion vanished from Riven. He gave Lord West a slight nod, then withdrew, taking up a post by the windows. Though I did not imagine this dance would explode into open conflict, his watchful presence nevertheless brought comfort.

Lord West claimed my arm and led me onto the floor, sending a shadow spiraling along my arm as he did so. And something in me raged against it—the way he sought to inflict pain at every possible turn. A flare of green-gold sparked along my skin, driving back the shadow, and I missed a step. Yet Lord West missed nothing.

"How very interesting." His obsidian eyes gleamed. "It seems you've been holding out on me."

As he spun me around, his sleeve pulled back slightly, revealing the sleek brown-black form of a serpent coiled about his wrist—identical in detail to the statue Mr. Tibbons had fetched from Kilmere, though in this case, it did not stand rampant. The breath left my lungs. The basilisk was here, less than a handbreadth away from me. And if he woke her, she could leave untold suffering in her wake. I shuddered.

His grip tightened slightly. "You like it? It's a recent acquisition, one both lethal and beautiful."

"It's a fine piece of workmanship." Somehow I managed to keep my voice steady, despite the revelation. Since Riven had returned Mr. Tibbons to the *Sea Blossom*, Lord West must have concluded his plans for concealment had failed—or he believed himself so close to success that he didn't bother to hide the basilisk any longer. We parted for a moment, then rejoined as the dance demanded. "When did you learn there was a basilisk in Kilmere?"

"Before I ever arrived in your world."

"Who told you about it? And Kilmere?"

"Answers for answers, my sweet." Our hands met. "I'll

answer one question of your choosing, if you answer one of mine."

"Very well, but that's not my question." Above all else, I must understand what the Lady of Ravens had done—and if her path must become mine. This time, I didn't flinch when his binding mark wove across my arm.

"Ask your question."

I sought to form it as precisely as possible. "When the Lady of Ravens died, what was the impact on Kilmere?"

She'd said if they killed her, it would be their unmaking, yet Kilmere stood fast, all these centuries later. I must know what she'd believed, what seeds of power she might have sown.

"An interesting choice of question. I'm in a generous mood, so I'll give you more than strictly required. Perhaps you'll find her fate instructional. The so-called Lady of Ravens belonged to the Court of Ascent, those covenanted together for a single purpose. She was the one chosen to secure the site for Kilmere, through her marriage to a mortal." The shadows about him deepened. "For whatever reason, she became enamored with the mortal life, even more so by her mortal husband, and it led her into great folly."

"Must sentiment always be folly?"

"I think you know the answer to that—if not, her end certainly proves it," he said. "Why do you ask about the impact of her death on Kilmere?"

"Is that *your* question?"

He laughed, yet it held no mirth, only mockery. "Indeed not."

"Then you still owe me an answer."

When we met once more, he offered it. "Her death caused a great deal of trouble at the time, delaying the construction of Kilmere by several months and forcing the deaths of more than if she'd never taken her foolish stand. She fueled workings they could not eradicate, but it did not matter, because in the end, they were subsumed by the greater power forged in Kilmere.

And what is a few months to a strategy decades in the making? Whatever she intended, it failed. As did she."

Only I'd seen her workings reemerge in very specific circumstances. If I was right, that meant there was a way to remake Kilmere, but it required willing surrender of . . . how much? Never mind that or how it frightened me—for the first time, I had a tenuous plan that was my own.

"Now, my sweet, you shall answer me." His shadows obscured my view of the rest of the room. "I've come to believe that my earlier impressions of you were mistaken. What are you?"

Why were the fae so concerned with my nature? The bargain mark seared my arm, urging forth the knowledge I held, but I turned to a deeper truth, to the conflict running to my very soul. "I don't know."

My binding mark vanished, and Lord West's eyes narrowed slightly. "How unfortunate for you. Yet none of this is why I wished to speak to you. I've come to give you a warning."

I tilted my head. "Do you imagine I'd accept any warning you offered?"

"You're so very cautious about extending trust. Except when it comes to the arbiter."

"My dealings with him are no concern of yours."

"Is that a reasonable claim? After all, his involvement has protracted this affair a great deal," he said. "Yet he's not the one that will pay for it. Is it worth the price?"

"If you're so concerned, you could leave Withern and drop your pursuit of Kilmere."

"I'm sure that would please you, but I'm afraid I must decline—matters are just getting interesting." A smile lifted one corner of his mouth. "You appear to be quite the anomaly—and I begin to complete the picture as to Riven's interest."

He pressed for a reaction, and I sought to hide mine, taking refuge in another turn of the dance. All about us swirled brilliant gowns and floral fragrances, but his sharp, ancient scent overwhelmed them all.

"Do you know what an arbiter must do? Attend to matters of fae justice, yes, but also see to the stability of his court and the increase of its power, as it pleases his sovereign. Riven answers to his king, and his king has great interest in the current state of your world—and how to utilize the resources therein."

What resources could our world have to offer—oh. We had the only thing we'd ever offered the Otherworld . . . people to enthrall and torment. Did Riven's king seek a way to claim mortals for his own end, as the founders of Kilmere had when they'd formed ghouls and wights into an expendable army? Despite the warmth of the room, a chill stole down my spine.

"Even now, he speaks to another member of his court."

Surely not. I glanced over my shoulder at Riven, and Lord West had spoken true. He was addressing a woman unmistakably fae— her beauty and power glamoured, but unable to remain entirely hidden. As we spun among the dancers, their bodies obscured Riven and the lady from view. Why had she sought him? Or he, her?

"A mortal who displays Other abilities and a ruin of incalculable might—you must grant his king would take interests in such things. And Riven knows it." Lord West lifted a brow. "Why else would he adopt the pretense of offering aid?"

I couldn't let him see how his words roused all my doubts and fears. "Surely the enmity between your courts is reason enough?"

"I've no doubt he wants to spite me. But you, my sweet, are the true reward." Again a twist of his wrist revealed the stasis-bound basilisk, its eyes of stone staring. "He can afford to be patient and wait until he has what he seeks. Then your life will be worth nothing."

His statement pierced deep, echoing my own fears, pulling forth recall of my dream and betraying me into speech. "He's not like that."

"No?" He pulled me slightly closer and bent his head to whisper in my ear. "Why don't you ask him what happened to the last mortal family he drew into his sphere?"

His breath shivered across my skin, as cold as the stone of Kilmere. I wanted to wrench free, regardless of the scene it would cause, but it would give him far too much satisfaction. "I've no need to ask such questions."

But now—oh, I did. Because Lord West couldn't have spoken unless the words held some truth.

"Or perhaps you don't have the courage to face the facts?" The brush of his hands against mine left me cold.

"Don't pretend to be concerned with my well-being, not when you wish to take my inheritance and my life." I lifted my chin. "What was your warning? Speak it and be done."

"Keep an eye on your little maid."

Over his shoulder, I surveyed the room, looking for Dreda. There. My pulse slowed. She remained with Aunt Caris, the crowd of mortals a temporary protection for her. But for how long? When would he claim his bargain?

The dance ended, and he bowed, then stalked through the crowd and took the hand of Lady Cadence. Even she did not deserve him—but I was too late to issue further warning. She accepted his offer and flashed a triumphant smile toward me.

The moment her back was turned, I fled the crowd, seeking solace and safety.

CHAPTER 47

The soft song of sweet orange drifted toward me, arresting my flight, promising sanctuary. Other sprightly green melodies wove alongside, drowning out the conversations beyond. I changed course, following their living songs, and soon they drew me into a large orangery attached to the house.

Along the far edge a couple strolled, their presence a protection should Lord West decide to follow me. Jade and Asrina kept close as I ventured in deeper.

Everywhere, life thrived. Oranges and lemons and other fruiting trees clustered about fragrant blossoms and winding moonvines, all laid out in a pleasing array. But the beauty brought none of its customary calm, nor did the gentle songs wafting about me. On every side, large windows reflected back the dark of night, and the flickering lamps cast shadows into the arched roof overhead.

I collapsed onto a stone bench and wrapped my arms about my middle, a vain attempt to still the churning within.

What did West say? Jade demanded.

I didn't want to share it, yet the words sprang vivid into my mind. *Ask him what happened to the last mortal family he drew into his sphere.*

Jade hissed softly. *And will you?*

I don't know.

The truth would hurt me, else Lord West wouldn't have spoken. His pleasure made that all too clear. The branches of the orange overhead shuddered. I'd made an alliance with Riven because I'd had no choice. Yet I'd also wanted to believe his kindness and restraint genuine. Surely, they *must* be. But fae were masters of deception, concealing their every purpose and weaving layers of strategy to achieve their ends. How could I be sure?

He can afford to be patient, Lord West had said.

Perhaps that was true, but it must defy reason for him to go to such lengths to conceal his true aim. The cold of the bench seeped through my clothing. The fae in Kilmere had played such a game—feigning sympathy for the suffering and poverty in Withern, promising the inhabitants a better life, when all the while they intended to turn them into monsters.

Moonvines brushed my ankles, as though they meant to console, but their crisp, cold notes were like darts flung to my heart. I'd doubted Riven before—he'd tried to make me doubt him when we'd dealt with Uros, yet he hadn't abandoned the mortal world then. Never mind what Lord West said, why would he strike against us now? Except for a binding to his king, a danger of which Riven himself had warned me.

The blossoms overhead shivered, their edges darkening, and I drew a shuddering breath. I couldn't afford to speculate. I must be sure of his purpose. If I couldn't, my plans for dealing with Kilmere would wither before they bloomed.

Part of me welcomed the notion. I didn't want to return and endure what I feared I must, but—

He's coming, Jessa. One of Jade's ears twitched back.

My muscles tightened. *Lord West?*

No, Riven. She prowled down the length of the bench, her eyes narrowed at the door.

And Riven strode through it.

I shrank deeper into the curve of the bench, and the branches of the orange drooped low about me, as though they sought to conceal. I wasn't ready to speak with him yet, not with my thoughts and emotions tangled like brambles in a garden left long years untended.

Yet I could not hide from him. He approached, and the room brightened.

"What did Damir say to you?" His voice was low, almost a growl.

"You know what he is—he wishes to stir fear and confusion." And he'd done so. The only way I could see to break free of it was to bring his insinuations into the open. I inhaled deeply, but the spiced perfume of the blossoms failed to quiet my soul. I couldn't bring myself to ask about the mortal family, not yet, so I chose the other question that weighed upon me. "Who did you speak with in the ballroom?"

He stilled, the gaslights flickering across the planes of his face. "Why do you ask?"

"Because the more fae involved in this matter, the greater the risk."

"I still have duties to my court." He lifted a shoulder. "It's been dealt with."

Dealt with? By giving the information to a courier—all he'd observed of Kilmere, its nature and my failures to control its workings . . . I pressed my hands to my temples, attempting to drown out the vague speculations.

"That's not all that concerns you, I take it." His tone was flat.

"Lord West told me to ask you a question." And I must, or else forever remain plagued by doubt. I pressed to my feet. "What happened to the last mortal family you were close to?"

The gas lamps illumining the orangery flared a furious blue-white. But Riven himself showed no expression. Only his face altered, its glamour the merest mist, its cold beauty forbidding and inhuman. "My dealings with other mortals are no concern of yours. Nor are my duties to my king. None concern our arrangement."

I struggled to draw breath. The low-hanging orange boughs now curled about my shoulders, their leathery leaves brushing my skin. "I've brought you close to my family. It matters."

"To you, perhaps. But the past has no bearing on the business at hand. I'm here to keep Damir from achieving his ends." The faintest hints of gold sparked in his eyes, a gathering of power. "Unless that's no longer your desire."

"Of course that's what I want—"

"Then nothing else matters. It's as I said from the beginning. This arrangement is of mutual benefit."

If I was to succeed at Kilmere, if it required no small act, but the full price—then I had to be able to trust Riven to act in the interests of mortals. If I could not . . . I twisted my hands together. "Because you must use a mortal to interfere with him, since you cannot."

"Yes. I must *use* mortals, as you put it, just as you must *use* fae. For the time being, we each require the assistance of the other."

"And when you no longer require my assistance? What happens then?" My voice emerged just above a whisper, nearly drowned in the susurrus of rustling leaves.

"I owe you no information regarding my future plans."

"I'll concede you owe me nothing." The ache within spread like ivy tendrils, rooting deep into my chest. "But Lord West suggested—"

"I thought you wiser than to heed his words."

"Though what he said gave me concern, I don't trust him. If you tell me he merely sought to stir trouble—that there's no veracity to his insinuations—then I'll believe you." Yet his eyes darkened, and I knew. Whoever this family had been, whatever his dealings with them, their fate had been as bleak as those mortals who'd dealt with Kilmere. A bitter, resinous scent rose from the leaves. "It wasn't a tale, was it?"

"You want to know what happened to them? You think that will give you peace?" The gold in his eyes flashed as brilliant as lightning. "Very well. I killed them. All of them."

I stumbled back, bereft of words. All that remained in my awareness were luminous lights and white blossoms and dark truth. The orange leaves rustled in my ears.

And Jade rumbled low in her chest.

What now?

I didn't want to believe it, but his stark words left no room for doubt. I should say something, I must—only what? I felt as though he'd plunged the dream dagger into my chest, so sharp was the pain. It mattered because of Kilmere, and because of . . . so much more. Yet if I opened my mouth, I'd surely betray more than I desired.

When I remained silent, he turned and stalked from the room, leaving me to the quiet whispers of blossom and bough.

Heedless of possible witnesses, I sank to the stone floor of the orangery, and Jade nestled close. Numbly, I stroked her fur. I'd not be able to appear in company with anything like composure—and without Riven, what of Kilmere?

SOMEHOW I STUMBLED from the orangery back into the ballroom. At the edge of the chamber, near the windows, Aunt Caris and Dreda were speaking with a matronly woman. I made my way toward them, the lights and scents and sounds a nearly unbearable assault against my fragile emotions.

Only Jade's reassuring warmth within my arms checked a hasty flight. I must return to Willowere to rethink my plans—it offered the strongest haven, thanks to Riven's workings upon it —but I must do it with care. If something went wrong now, I didn't know if Riven would act on my behalf.

"My dear!" Aunt Caris studied me. "Are you well?"

"I'm afraid I have a dreadful headache." I offered my original plea, but it was no longer an excuse. Given an opening by my ragged emotions, all the rich plant life surrounding Holle Castle came surging into my senses. A tiny pinprick of Other even came from the reticule at my wrist, some spark from the nisi seed, perhaps. It all overwhelmed.

"Shall I fetch you home?"

"There's no need." Dreda bobbed her head. "I'm more than happy to accompany Miss Jessa."

My grip on Jade tightened. I wasn't at ease with Dreda's companionship any longer, but Aunt Caris beamed upon her and thanked her for her attentions. To insist upon Aunt Caris instead would only raise questions—and perhaps even put her in danger, if Dreda was forced by bargain to act against her will. We'd have our driver along, but even so . . .

Blight and rot. If Lord West meant to make me fear all those who surrounded me, he'd done his job well. I summoned a small smile and thanked Dreda. Once we returned to Willowere, I must find a way to elude her until I could get the truth of her bargain and free her from Lord West. If he caused her further suffering . . . My chest tightened.

Dreda offered the support of her arm, and somehow we made our way out of the crowded ballroom, with all its glittering splendor, and into the hush of night beyond the castle walls.

Our carriage awaited on the east side of the courtyard, only faintly lit by the gas lamps. In silence, we climbed in, but before we could secure the door, a voice rang out behind us.

"Miss Caldwell!"

Lady Cadence? What could she possibly want? My throat closed. If I fled without acknowledging her, administering a direct cut, my aunts and sisters alike would deal with the consequences. So I turned toward her.

A slight frown creased Dreda's face. "Miss Jessa, I don't think we should delay, not if you're feeling poorly."

Unease took root. Was there a reason Dreda wished us to depart at once, perhaps a compulsion from her binding? I hesitated. "We cannot simply ignore her."

Dreda clutched her necklace and shrank back into the shadows as Lady Cadence glided over to our carriage.

"Leaving so soon?" she asked.

"I've developed a headache."

"How unfortunate." She regarded me with clouded eyes. "I would have a word with you before you depart."

Jade glared at her. *I dislike this. Even if she means only to deliver further insult, it's the last thing you need right now.*

My temples throbbed. Should I demand the driver go on, never mind the aftermath? Or, given that Dreda had professed urgency, would that be playing into Lord West's hands? "What is it?"

"You think your beauty alone is enough to capture the attentions of Lord West, just as you believed me fool enough to fall for your ridiculous warning so you could keep him to yourself." She leaned in, her frame shadowing the doorway. "But he favors me, and I will show him it's right to do so. Then we will share a future."

All this over Lord West? "Lady Cadence, he's not who you think he is—"

"He's the match I've always sought, and he will give me the life I deserve." A small smile played about her lips. "Once I've shown him I'm worthy."

With a flick of her wrist, she dropped a small vial, which shattered on the carriage floor.

I reached for the stately boxwoods lining the courtyard, yet caught only the faintest snatch of their song before dark sigils danced before my eyes, stealing my awareness.

As from a great distance, I heard Lady Cadence say, "Driver, you may go."

Then all was lost.

CHAPTER 48

A drop of water splashed on my cheek, rousing me to a world of damp and cold, to the sharp scents of stone and malice. My eyes fluttered open to total blackness. Stone shackles bound my wrists and ankles to the rocky surface beneath.

Where was I? Near Kilmere. Its power gnawed at my awareness, prickled against my skin. We were near, but not within; otherwise it would have already consumed me. I tilted my head, and my face brushed something soft.

Jade.

She was bound beside me. Awake? Certainly none of her thoughts reached my mind. And I struggled to clear my own.

No sign of Asrina remained. Had she gone for Riven? Oh, please. Yet even if she had, he might not come. I strained against the cold bonds, but they only tightened further.

"By all means, continue to struggle." Lord West's voice cut through the stillness. "It will only cause you greater pain."

An uncontrolled shudder swept my frame. Of course Lord West was here. He'd sought me for so long, he'd savor this moment—and he'd make sure it hurt. Despite the futility, I struggled against my bonds.

A silvery fae-light sparked to life, revealing the truth of my situation. Lord West had deposited us into a tomb of stone set in the wall of the cave. Its jagged roof dipped only inches from my face, and its other sides boxed me in. Only one remained open so we could converse.

"Now isn't this cozy?" His teeth flashed white in the gloom. "I've grown tired of all the interruptions. I prefer to have you all to myself."

Though I strained, nowhere in the shadowed cave could I see Dreda. My pulse thundered in my ears. "What have you done with my chaperone?"

"Sent her back to Willowere, of course. When your aunts ask her what happened, she'll tell them that in your distress over Lord Riven jilting you, you fled back to Avons." He spread his hands, the serpent head flashing at his wrist. "She tried to dissuade you, but alas, you wouldn't listen to reason."

So that was the bargain he'd pressed upon her. Such a simple one, and not the dark deed I'd feared. For that, he'd used Lady Cadence, all the while directing my attentions—my fears—toward Dreda. My eyes slid shut.

"I'd thought to use her to bring you to me, but it was difficult enough to sway her even to this simple tale." The fae-light gleamed, casting dark shadows behind him. "No surprise that Riven provided her a ward. He would have known she was a liability. I only wonder that he did not eliminate her."

At least the necklace had provided some measure of protection, though not enough. Whatever my meager abilities, they in no way compared to those of Lord West. Yet he'd not guessed the necklace had come from me, which was one point in my favor.

He stepped closer. "Doubtless your family will be alarmed. Perhaps they'll even dispatch the stratesmen to go after you. How unfortunate that they'll seek you in all the wrong places."

He'd considered this well. Gathering information, biding his time, making arrangements. All part of his games—and despite my best efforts, I'd played right into his hand.

"I must thank you for making our interactions so entertaining. It's been too long since I've had the pleasure of working with mortals so closely, and I almost regret it will come to an end." His obsidian-shard eyes glinted. "Tell me, what did you think of your dream of Riven? Did you begin to realize then that you'd misplaced your trust?"

The shadows pressed closer about me, stealing breath. My dream, the one of Riven stabbing me, its unusual vividness . . . Lord West had sent that somehow, working to make me fear Riven, to plant a rift by any means he possessed. Our lore of high fae infiltrating dreams wasn't a mere tale, but another weapon Lord West wielded. Had he perceived and savored my fear even then? I dug my fingers into the rough stone. I'd not give him the satisfaction of asking.

"I want to be perfectly clear. No one is coming for you. Not your family, not the authorities, and certainly not Riven, not after what's taken place between you. Even should he eventually determine to seek you in his efforts to spite me, there's enough power laced in these workings to hide your presence even from him. Yet we have one other matter to attend." He lifted his hand, revealing Asrina shuddering in his palm. A lattice of dark cords spiraled over her skin, her wings, her entire body.

Oh, please no.

She'd feared him, and now . . . My vision grayed at the edges, and I sagged against the stone.

Don't react.

Jade. Despite the cold stone surrounding me, warmth bloomed in my chest. She was alive.

You can't let him know it matters, that you care about what's happened to her. If he knows he can move you by the death of others . . .

Then the lives of any I cared for would be forfeit. In the distance, the slow drip of water against stone echoed. And I choked back my fear. "Why imprison her, unless you're afraid of what Riven will do?"

"I fear nothing." Darkness spread over her form. "But she defied me before, and now she'll pay the price."

Asrina stretched a tiny hand toward me, then shuddered and fell still. Still, he pressed his power into her, until her limbs gnarled and her face distorted, leaving her frame unrecognizable.

Bile burned my throat, bitter and acrid. I could not move, could not breathe, could not wrench my gaze from her crumpled form. She'd not hurt him, not truly, could never have hurt him, yet it pleased him to crush her. A sob rose in my chest, and I wrestled it down with all the strength that remained. If I betrayed the truth, Jade might be next.

Yes. Doubtless he's left me alive because of what I can offer him, once you're removed. He's not one to cast aside a potential source of power. But if he knew your true sentiments—he'd not hesitate.

My lungs seized. I couldn't betray the truth.

Lord West discarded Asrina beneath a craggy overhang, throwing her aside like so much refuse. "Now, you answer to me alone."

Her crumpled body didn't move, not even the slightest gleam of light remained. He'd killed her. And if I spoke, my tears would spill. I remained motionless, bound in my tomb of stone, awaiting whatever horror he'd unfold next.

"You have two choices: hand Kilmere over to me now—or suffer and spend the force of your life increasing my power before your eventual surrender." The basilisk eyes on his arm gleamed. "I believe you're familiar with such workings from your exploration of the ruins. They're quite remarkable, really, and we're situated in such proximity that your pain is sure to please Kilmere."

The image of the dragon, of stone rending its flesh, of the burning torment in every line and limb of its body emblazoned itself on my vision.

"When you've lost control of your body and mind from the

agony you endure, you'll take any way out I offer." His voice dropped. "In the end, you'll give me Kilmere. The only question is—how much are you willing to suffer first?"

He left out what I knew to be true. If I signed Kilmere over to him this moment, he'd take my life—most likely as an offering to strengthen Kilmere and seal his mastery of it, which would make my death altogether meaningless. A bitter taste flooded my mouth. "I cannot give Kilmere to you."

"Yet you will." He stepped closer still. "Perhaps you doubt my sincerity? Let me give you a small taste of what's to come."

The slightest flick of his fingers and something pierced my shoulder, burning through muscle and sinew, then driving through the other side. He'd sent a spear of rock up from below, and the pain of the spike radiated down into my chest. Like licking flame, it reached for the core of my being, and blackness consumed my vision.

"If you'll excuse me, I have a proposal to make before the Holloway ball ends. Lady Cadence has proven quite useful, and once she's fully bound herself to me, she shall make an excellent offering to Kilmere. I'll be back in two hours. Perhaps you'll gain wisdom in the waiting."

With that, he sealed the stone about me.

I SANK into the sensations of deep darkness and cold stone and hot pain and salt tears and the creeping menace of Kilmere, the blackness never-ending.

Like the dragon before me, entombed in stone so long ago, I had no way out, only slow anguish until it pleased Lord West to bring about my end. He'd sent only one small power-drenched stone through my body, yet it had kindled a world of pain—and the worst was yet to come. Could I endure?

I gasped for air in great shuddering breaths that drew ripping pain from the wound in my shoulder.

Asrina was dead, her living flame quenched, her body discarded, all to satisfy Lord West's lust for power. I'd failed her. I bit my lip so hard the tang of blood, bitter and coppery, flooded my mouth.

Jessa. You must return to yourself.

Asrina might be gone, but Jade remained. The rise and fall of her chest formed a steady cadence, as familiar as the sweet-grass scent of her fur. With effort, I matched my breath to hers.

But nothing could ease the pain. And no one would come to set us free. I'd no leverage, no way out. Lord West had left no weakness in this trap. Should I be surprised? He was powerful even among his kind. What hope had I of resisting? If he was right, his tortures would induce me to surrender Kilmere to him . . .

No.

If nothing else, I *would* resist him until the end. I refused to allow him to claim Kilmere and inflict these terrors on others. Not even Lady Cadence deserved the fate he had in mind for her. And he'd claim so many others . . .

A flame of pain licked down my side, and I shuddered.

In the darkness, Jade stirred. *It isn't for you to face this alone. We'll find a way out, together.*

Together. My eyes burned. I'd tried so hard to find the ability in myself to resist Lord West, to master Kilmere, to protect the townsfolk from the curse. I'd spent my strength trying to avoid leaning on all others, even those who might have been willing to share the burden.

Because I'd feared.

Feared destroying their lives. Feared dragging them into unspeakable dangers. Feared the Other in me, a threat to them all.

Yet it wasn't only for the sake of those I loved that I hadn't taken them into my confidence—I could no longer pretend otherwise. I'd shrunk from the idea that their love would turn to fright, or even hatred, when they realized what I might be, realized I did not belong. It was easier to keep my true self concealed—to imagine a future in full isolation—than to take that risk.

I'd hidden from them, hidden also from myself. Now, I was trapped and truly alone . . . except for Jade. *I'm glad you're here.*

Even now, there's nowhere else I'd rather be.

Tears traced searing tracks down my face. *How can you say that?*

Because I am satisfied as to who you are. I know you better than anyone, and I trust you.

You should not have such confidence. I couldn't spare Asrina, and—

I share your grief at her loss. But she knew the dangers of warring against Lord West. Far stronger fae have faced him and lost everything. She knew, and she chose. Now let her death have meaning.

How? Lord West would never have abandoned me here if it were possible to escape. I struggled to press back the pain, to clear my thoughts. Like all fae, he underestimated those he believed mortal. He deemed me weak, believed I had no reason to resist, only to accept a quick death as a mercy. But I had every reason to fight back.

Was there a way out? The heat in my shoulder burned deeper. Even if I escaped, I still must face Kilmere, and I could not confront it alone, not with what it might require, unless I accepted the way of the fae and turned it into a weapon, becoming fierce and powerful in isolation. As Riven had suggested.

What of Riven? Even if I found freedom, I'd likely never see him again—and if I did, what was I to believe? What was the truth?

I swallowed against the metallic taste in my mouth. The facts could be construed to support either theory: that Riven helped because on some level he cared for the plight of mortals—which I wanted to believe—or that he engaged in some deeper game on behalf of his king and his court, as Lord West suggested, as Riven himself had not denied.

Yet why wait? If he'd wanted information from me or about me, he could have taken whatever he needed by force or compulsion, once I'd killed Uros. And if that proved I didn't know the truth of my own nature, he could have kept me in the Otherworld and made whatever tests and observations he desired there.

But perhaps his king had bidden him otherwise; perhaps there was more his court sought to gain. How could I know, when I understood so little of him, when he refused to open up?

To expose one's true self was a weakness—or so Riven had suggested, so the fae held.

So *I'd* held, on some level, for I'd hidden myself from those around me. A fresh wave of pain assailed me, and my breath caught. Would I ever have the chance to choose a different path?

I pressed away the thought, returning to the puzzle of Riven. His confession that he'd killed a mortal family still hollowed me. I could not fathom it, and yet there might be more to the story, more he'd withheld.

I'd witnessed his deeds, and I could not believe he'd murdered them. One could feign kindness perhaps, don it like a glamour, cloaking oneself in social niceties, discommoding oneself to make a positive impression. Yet when it was all stripped away, when the cost became blood and pain, life or death, then the truth emerged. One could adopt a pretense of kindness, but one couldn't feign mercy.

And I'd seen him act with mercy, more than once. The cold of the stone numbed my flesh, save for where the flames of the working licked across my shoulder and down my side, searing ever deeper.

Even if Riven could do nothing to free me, I'd give anything for him to walk into this tomb of stone. Perhaps that told me all I needed to know.

To trust would never be a safe choice—it always meant

opening oneself up to possible pain and betrayal. And perhaps it was more of a risk because Riven was fae, because of the power he held. Yet sooner or later, the risk must be taken or the relationship severed, not only from Riven, but from everyone else—even from my true self.

If I ever escaped from this prison, I'd take the risk. Perhaps Riven had already returned to the Otherworld, and I'd have no opportunity to try to mend things. But I could risk trusting the nature given me, even now.

Simply because I was something not altogether mortal—no, simply because I was *fae*—did not mean I must become like those who'd fashioned Kilmere. Protection from such a fate wasn't found in hiding from the truth of my nature, in doing my utmost to keep it from everyone around me, but in the hundreds of small choices I made each day—to exercise compassion, to trust, to hope, rather than grasp in fear.

These precepts of the Script formed a way forward, a surer safeguard than any I'd devised on my own. And perhaps they'd even strengthen me to forge a way out.

I have been doing my utmost to avoid intruding upon your deeper thoughts, but I must know. Are you at peace within yourself?

At peace might be a bit much, but I am resolved.

Good. Her eyes lit with green fire. *Then we can turn our attention toward gaining freedom.*

Is there any way I can undo his workings, as I did the lock within Kilmere?

That was meant to respond to its owner, which gave you an advantage. These workings are meant to bind captives, and they're crafted with great care against any outside force. You'd require strength far greater than his to break them.

Yet there must be a way out. I struggled to draw breath as the pain tore deeper. *I don't know how long we have before he returns. Will you be able to tell when he arrives?*

His scent is quite distinct, so yes.

It was a small boon, but I'd take it. What then? If I could

not sever the workings, then could I shatter the stone itself? Trees did, driving their roots deep over time. And when we'd faced the fang-wolves in Kilmere, they'd surged to the surface to defend us, rending through stone in an instant.

I'd no way to touch them, bound here—but perhaps I didn't need to. With all my remaining strength, I sought the songs of the trees. Faint and distant, they thrummed through stone, but even as I connected to their greening strength, something drove me back into myself, a sharp and painful severing of their songs. The workings about me flared to life, a barrier between me and the life beyond the stone.

If only I could touch them, if only they weren't so far distant, then perhaps . . .

Oh.

The tiniest of whispers touched my mind, a low murmur emanating from my side. How? I shifted slightly. Of course. The seed from the nisi. It was still lodged in my reticule, which the bindings of stone had pinned to my wrist.

To interact with living plants was one thing—to enliven a seed was another matter entirely. Yet it was here with me, no workings forming a barrier between us. And the very fae blood I'd feared gave me the power to wake it, or so I hoped.

What did this seed of Other contain? It was past time I found out.

CHAPTER 49

Within the seed swirled something Other, something that desired connection so it might thrive here as it would in its own world. Not yet a song, only the slightest whisper, waiting, hoping for life.

And with that tiny spark of Other, I forged a tenuous connection. Its desire and mine mingled, and the seed quavered within my reticule. Though I could not see it, I could feel the moment its thick shell split and its primary root shot downward. One heartbeat, two, and then a glorious golden light poured out between us, driving back the darkness.

My pain, its pain, our imprisonment—these were an affront. It existed for one purpose: to spread wide its branches under the heavens, to sink its roots deep in the earth, to flourish in freedom.

Roots surged about me, growing years' worth with every pulse of my heart, questing upward. A tumultuous melody surged about me, even as my blood spilled onto the stone beneath.

The song of the emerging tree drove back the pain. Stone crumbled at my right side. Wait, would we be crushed as it shattered?

The smallest breath of clean air invaded the damp must of the tomb, and I sought the vines growing without. Their sprightly songs thrilled at the request. They wove down alongside the roots, snatching at the crumbling rocks, pulling them to the side until Jade and I lay exposed to the night sky, with the white-gold boughs of an unfamiliar tree stretching over us, its trunk centuries wide.

What had I done? This would hardly escape notice, but with all that was at stake it mattered little. With the last remnant of strength I possessed, I coaxed the roots downward to twine around the shackles.

As they sank into the bindings, they shattered, and the roots delved further still, crumbling the base of the jagged shard of rock lodged in my shoulder. Though it still protruded like a spear, I could finally press upright. When I did, my wound throbbed with renewed rage, and blood oozed around the spike, staining my gown.

Jade leapt upon my lap. *Pluck it out. Even severed, the workings it contains will do you a great deal of damage.*

I forced my numbed fingers to close around the shard. Then I yanked.

The world blackened.

But the shard, its gray stone laced with dark workings and stained scarlet, fell into my lap. I seized it and cast it away, even as blood began to pour from the now-open wound. My vision blurred. Somehow, I needed to stanch the flow.

A handkerchief. In my reticule, I had one, but no—the growing tree had destroyed the bag, and I'd neither strength nor desire to search the wreckage of root and stone for the remnants. Instead, I ripped some fabric from the already rent hem of my gown, then wadded it and pressed it against the wound. With the motion, sharp talons of pain dug deeper.

Jade stared into the dark, her ears pricked. *We cannot linger. If West returns, you have no hope of eluding him in this condition.*

You could go for Riven. If he remained in Withern. If he would come, given how we'd parted.

I'm not leaving you to search for him. Particularly when we have no guarantee of his intervention. Beneath the spreading branches of white-gold, Jade shifted into true-form, the starflower patch on her muscled chest gleaming. *Lean on me.*

I wrapped my uninjured arm around her neck, hesitant to burden her too heavily.

You must allow me to bear you.

And I soon found I must, if we were to progress. Despite the pain it caused, I clambered upon her back, and she bore me onward, picking her way across the rocks and rubble, her steps as steady as if she carried no burden at all. Even so, the world swirled about me in an alarming fashion.

Then she halted. *People approach.*

Mortals?

She sniffed the air. *Your sisters. Burke. Others. A search party.*

Hope mingled with fear. How had they come to look here, when Lord West had bargained with Dreda to mislead them? It didn't matter now—if they sought me and blundered into Kilmere . . . *We need to catch their attention.*

We've almost reached the path. They'll find us. But I must diminish.

I slipped off Jade's back, then she shifted into lesser-form, and I staggered into the lane alongside her. When my legs refused to hold me any longer, I collapsed onto a broad rock. A moment later, lanterns appeared around the bend.

Mr. Burke's sharp eyes caught sight of me first. "She's here!"

Ainslie and Ada dashed forward, despite the hazards of the narrow, rutted lane, only to stop short in front of me.

"By the Crossings, Jessa!" Ainslie said. "How did you come to this?"

"You're all over blood." Ada raised her lantern, revealing shadowed eyes and strained features. "How badly are you hurt?"

"I'm not entirely sure." The lantern light revealed streaks of crimson traveling down the left side of my gown. My efforts had done little to stanch the flow of blood, and the pain worsened by the moment.

And there were so many . . . Why had they all come? In a half circle, they surrounded me: Ada and Ainslie, Mr. Redgrave and Elodie, and—Dreda.

She stepped closer, her freckles standing out stark on her pale face. "Oh, Miss Jessa. I should have stopped it somehow."

"You couldn't have known what was to come." But how was it that she hadn't told them the false account? My gaze drifted to her upper arm. The mark was gone; she was no longer captive. Somehow she'd managed to convey the truth, rather than the story Lord West had commanded. It defied comprehension.

Mr. Burke surveyed the scene, his eyes narrowing. "What happened?"

"A cave—there was a shard of rock . . ."

"A rock? And how did it find your shoulder?" His kestrel-sharp gaze swept over me, demanding answers.

"It was dark, I could see little—it's all a jumble." That much was true, for it already had become a blur of grief and fear and pain that choked me if I dared consider it.

Mr. Redgrave and Mr. Burke exchanged a glance. Clearly, my explanation satisfied neither of them, although it was *technically* true. Even I must admit the story wasn't overly plausible, but I'd no time to construct something better, and I didn't know Elodie or Mr. Redgrave enough to entrust them with the full tale.

Ainslie tilted her head. "But how—"

"Perhaps questions can come after we stop the bleeding?" Elodie stepped forward. "Your knife, Charles, if you please."

Mr. Redgrave handed her the blade, then peered down at my shoulder. "Looks more like a spear wound."

Why did he have to be the sort to take note? Wasn't Mr. Burke's keen eye enough? Most of the gentlemen in Byren would have been so shocked by an injured lady in indelicate circumstances that they'd not have given a second thought to the tale, much less considered the appearance of the wound and what might have caused it. Of course, Mr. Burke must attend to such things—by virtue of his nature and occupation both. But how would Mr. Redgrave know what a spear wound looked like? And why must Ainslie have chosen a shrewd man? I supposed if he wasn't, he'd never have captured her interest . . . Never mind that now, why was I even considering it? My thoughts drifted away from me like dandelion down on the wind.

"Whatever the cause, it must hurt a great deal." Elodie turned away and sliced a strip from her shift, which she handed to Mr. Burke. "Doubtless you've bound your share of wounds?"

He accepted with a nod, then bent close, and his very mortal scents of bergamot and clove comforted, despite what must come. "I'll take as much care as possible, but this will hurt."

Ada knelt before me, offering her hand, and I gripped it tight as he wove the cloth strip about my shoulder, then pulled it taut, the motion sending radiant bolts of pain outward.

"Can you walk?" he asked.

I gave a small nod. "I'll do what I must."

"Between the two of us, we can support her down the cliff." Mr. Redgrave's cinnamon-brown eyes warmed in the light of the lanterns. "If you'll permit it, Miss Jessa?"

Ainslie beamed her appreciation, and I'd no strength to argue about the indignity, so I simply nodded again. As it turned out, I couldn't endure contact on my left side at all, so I accepted Mr. Burke's arm alone, leaning on him far more heavily than was proper—and all the while wishing for Jade in true-form.

Every rustle in the dark beyond the edge of lantern light caused me to tense, my imagination conjuring visions of Lord West stalking us. But no, two hours surely hadn't passed, and I'd felt no encroaching sense of Other. At least that would offer a warning, if he came. In such proximity, I could not conceal my tension, however much I tried.

And the lines about Mr. Burke's eyes deepened. "I could carry you, you know."

"All the way back to Willowere?" I strove to maintain a light tone, and only half-succeeded. "Surely that would weary even the hardiest of souls."

"We've a carriage waiting at the base of the cliff." One corner of his mouth lifted. "But it wouldn't be the first time I've done such a task. Once I fetched a woman from the wreckage of a collapsed building. Her legs were crushed, and she needed to be taken to a physician for treatment. Given her isolated situation, there was nothing else for it but to tote her there, though she was easily twice your size."

He was rambling to distract me, I felt fuzzily aware, perhaps to assess if I could follow his words, a process that became more difficult with each passing moment. "Fortunately, I've only injured my shoulder."

"Yet you struggle to walk."

Talking hurt, breathing hurt even more, so I simply continued to place one foot in front of the other, the conversation about me drowned out by the whispers of the plants along the trail. When we traversed a particularly deep rut, I stumbled and nearly fell, despite the support Mr. Burke offered. Lord West had only injured my shoulder. Why had it left me so weak?

Jade pressed against my ankle, her bulk reassuring. *For fae-kind, being subjected to malevolent workings does damage far worse than any physical injury. And I fear some trace remains in you, despite the removal of the shard.*

Well, that was comforting—particularly since I'd no notion of how to rid myself of any residual workings. Quiet and low, the song of a fir threaded through my thoughts, drawing me back to the present. For now, I must simply make it to the bottom of the cliff.

Yet I soon stumbled again, and Mr. Burke lowered me onto a boulder alongside the path. "Either I carry you, or we wait here until Mr. Redgrave fetches a litter."

Mr. Redgrave examined me, a crease between his brows. "We don't know the extent of her injury, and a litter would get her to the carriage with the least amount of jostling. Yet I'm loath to separate our party."

A branch snapped in the woods beyond, and Mr. Burke's hand drifted to the blade at his side. "As am I."

"There's no need for anyone to take trouble." I breathed in the scents of fern and moss, their earthy fragrances pressing back the fog in my mind. "If I could just sit a moment, I'll be fine."

"Perhaps our definitions of fine differ." Mr. Burke shook his head slightly. "However, if you're determined, then I suggest once we reach the safety of the carriage, Mr. Redgrave should take his mount in search of Dr. Fulton. You'll need immediate care upon your return to Willowere."

"An excellent plan," Ada said.

Mr. Redgrave nodded. "I'd be happy to."

"Take a minute to rest, then we need to move on." Mr. Burke moved to the edge of the circle of light cast by the lantern, keeping watch.

An uncomfortable silence filled the clearing, the weight of unanswered questions oppressive. If I could not distract them, they'd press—and my resolve to begin trusting more did *not* extend to near strangers. I could only vaguely feel the fingers in my left arm, and my head swam, but I sought to form a question of my own. "How did you find me?"

"At the ball, I realized I hadn't seen you in some time." Ada gently rested her hand on my uninjured shoulder, as if to reassure herself of my safety. "Ainslie and I searched, and we came across Dreda. She said you'd disappeared, and she was worried."

Not at all what Lord West had bidden her to say. I glanced at Dreda. Her face was still drawn with concern. She'd found some loophole—but how?

"Aunt Caris said she thought you'd gone home with Dreda, but Dreda assured us that wasn't the case. She said you'd been separated, and she didn't know what had become of you." Ada's eyes glistened. "It was a dreadful moment."

"We knew you'd been worried about Kilmere, and we thought perhaps you'd found some pressing reason to return, never mind it was the middle of the night." Ainslie's voice faltered. "Since you'd gone without a word, we . . . we feared something dreadful had happened, so we enlisted Mr. Burke. Mr. Redgrave and his sister also volunteered to help us search. We thought we might need to split up when we came to Kilmere, if we couldn't find you quickly, so the numbers were an asset."

A chill pebbled my skin. By withholding the truth, I'd come so close to exposing them all to the dangers of Kilmere. If I'd not freed myself, they'd even now be wandering about the ruins while I was trapped belowground.

"Of course, we went to Willowere first, on the chance you'd returned, but when we didn't find you, we set out at once." Ada's lips trembled, and she pressed them together.

"Clearly, it's a good thing we did," Ainslie said.

I'd distressed them more than I'd ever desired, and their expressions promised I'd answer for a great deal later.

"It's past time we moved on." Mr. Burke moved back into the light. "Miss Jessa?"

It wasn't only my arm numbing, but my entire left side—and I could not force myself to stand.

Between West's workings and the strength you spent breaking free, you're not going to make it the rest of the way. You need to let Mr. Burke help you, since I cannot. Jade's eyes glowed. *I believe you* did *resolve to do so?*

However humiliating it was to be hauled about like a sack of dry goods, she was right. I sighed softly. "Mr. Burke, it appears I'll have to accept your offer, if it still stands."

"Good. That's the first bit of sense you've acted upon tonight." Though his words were light, his brows drew inward with concern. He lifted me, and the moon and stars above blurred with the black sky into an array of bleary gray.

A tide of dizziness swept over me, and I closed my eyes, yet I sensed each tree and blossom that we passed, their soft murmurs reassuring. When we reached the base of the cliff, Mr. Burke deposited me in the carriage.

He climbed into the driver's seat and flicked the reins, and the resulting jolt sent a fresh wave of pain down my side. This wasn't going to be a pleasant trip. The fog shrouding my vision darkened as the pain dug its talons deeper, and when we halted, I did not protest the assistance Mr. Burke offered.

Soon, the light and warmth of Willowere swirled about us. Mr. Burke carried me into the drawing room, where Aunt Caris and Aunt Melisina huddled together on the settee. As one they gave sharp exclamations of dismay.

"What in the Crossings happened?" Aunt Melisina surged forward. "Jessa, how came you to wander alone in the night?"

"Can't you see she's in no state for questions?" Aunt Caris reached toward me. "Oh, my dear . . ."

"You. Put her here." Aunt Melisina motioned Mr. Burke to the settee, and I soon found myself nestled into a mound of pillows. With a brisk snap, she unfurled her shawl and spread it over me.

Aunt Caris clasped her hands to her chest. "Someone must fetch the doctor. There's so much blood . . ."

Elodie stepped forward. "Charles went for him when we'd descended the cliff. If they've not come yet, the doctor must have been out."

"Oh, where can he be?" Aunt Caris added another shawl atop me. "If he does not come soon—"

"I'll be well, Aunt Caris. Don't fear."

Only the soft crackle of the fire broke the stillness that followed my pronouncement. Just how poorly did I look? I wanted nothing more than to sink beneath the shawls and escape all the questioning glances.

Ever my champion, Jade leapt upon the settee and curled up on my legs, glowering at all assembled.

Elodie broke the silence. "Jessa, I'm quite thankful you've been found, but you must surely wish to be with family and not entertaining outsiders at such a trying time. I shall keep watch in the entry for Charles and Dr. Fulton and give you your privacy."

I murmured my thanks as she glided from the room.

Mr. Burke made no similar offer, and I doubted he'd leave till he was fully satisfied with my account of the evening. He poured me a glass of brandy. "Drink this while you wait."

"Yes, my dear, it will do you good." After I complied, Aunt Caris tucked the shawls more closely around me.

Exhaustion threatened to tug me under, but I couldn't think of surrendering to it, not when Lord West might discover me absent at any time. If he came here, if he glamoured my aunts into admitting him, would their permission overrule Riven's workings and allow him entrance? My pulse hammered, and I struggled to sit upright.

"My dear, you must rest."

"Only if you promise."

"Promise what, my dear?"

"If Lord West comes, you're not to admit him, not even allow him to cross the threshold, no matter the reasons he claims." I glanced at those assembled in the room. "Please—you must swear it."

"Of course, my dear, if that's what you wish." Aunt Caris nudged Aunt Melisina.

A slight frown tugged at her lips. "Oh, very well. It would do no good for your cause if he saw you in such a state anyway."

Ada and Ainslie likewise murmured their assent, but Mr. Burke strode over to the settee, his eyes a stormy gray. Clearly I'd betrayed too much.

"While we await the doctor, I must ask Miss Jessa some questions," he said.

My aunts and sisters alike frowned at him, and Aunt

Melisina drew herself to her full, rather impressive height, her expression imperious. "You overstep yourself. She's in no condition to answer your questions. Perhaps we'll consider it on the morrow, if she's feeling sufficiently rested."

Unruffled, Mr. Burke held her gaze. "This can't wait—it is for her protection as well as your own. If some miscreant roams about—"

Aunt Caris gasped. "Do you mean to say someone inflicted this injury upon Jessa?"

"That's what I intend to determine." He moved forward, blocking them from my view. "I'll need you to clear the room."

"You cannot order us to leave. Do you know who you're speaking to?" Aunt Melisina snapped. "I am Lady Stanford—"

"And when it comes to criminal affairs, you have no authority." His tone remained even but unyielding. "This is a matter of Magistry business until I'm satisfied no crime has been committed."

Her lips firmed. "Then ask your questions with a proper chaperone."

"My only interest is to gain the truth, and you must leave me to do that as I see fit. Otherwise, I'll be obligated to take Miss Jessa down to the Magistry."

He wouldn't force me to leave, but Aunt Melisina had no way of knowing that. She sputtered her indignation.

I shifted, wincing at the motion. He'd guessed this had to do with Kilmere and that I couldn't speak of it before them. Despite my condition, he'd not let me off without an explanation.

"Please." The warmth of the brandy had already faded, and I drew the shawl closer. "Let's not argue any longer. I'm quite certain Mr. Burke intends no impropriety, and no one need know we spoke alone. Simply let him do his job, then we can put this behind us."

"She's right, sister." Aunt Caris gently clasped Aunt Melisina's arm.

And she gusted a sigh. "Very well—but see to it that you treat my niece with the *utmost* respect."

Mr. Burke gave a slight bow. "I assure you, I mean nothing less."

Then Aunt Melisina herded everyone from the room, casting one last frown at Mr. Burke over her shoulder as she departed. When she'd secured the door, he turned toward me.

"Did Lord West do this?" Mr. Burke maintained an even tone, yet his eyes darkened further.

If I confessed Lord West had assaulted me, then I must admit the truth of his nature, and there lay danger. Yet I'd vowed to take the risk of trust when appropriate, and certainly, Mr. Burke had shown himself worthy of it. Only I could not collect my thoughts; they felt like milkweed floss, all downy and drifting . . .

Mr. Burke thumped a chair alongside the settee with more force than necessary, drawing me back to myself.

"Jessa. I can't do my job if you keep withholding information."

"This—what happened—it's not your responsibility."

"I don't care if it's my responsibility or not, I don't want another death on my hands—nor would you, were the tables turned." His equanimity had vanished; heat laced his voice. "Was it Lord West?"

"Yes. He brought me to a cavern outside Kilmere and held me there against my will."

"To . . . force himself on you?"

I shook my head, and pain spiked down my side. "It wasn't like that. He was angry that I wouldn't sell Kilmere, and he intended to coerce me into signing it over, by whatever means necessary."

Mr. Burke stood so abruptly that the chair wobbled. "Then he has a great deal to answer for."

"Wait, you can't confront him. I—"

"I mean to do far more than that." His hands tightened at

his sides. "Even if you were a stranger to me, it would be my job to apprehend him and see that he faces charges for abduction and assault."

"Please, just wait." With my uninjured hand, I fidgeted with the fringed edge of the shawl. "There's more. I wanted to tell you before—but I was so afraid."

He sat once more, leaned forward with unnerving attention. "Speak then."

The fringes tangled with my fingers. Why was it so difficult to confess? "Lord West . . . he's fae. And if you try to stop him, he'll kill you."

"How long have you known?" he said quietly, and it pained me more than if he'd raised his voice.

"Since I first saw him in court."

He muttered an oath. "You should have told me."

"Perhaps so—but I'd already drawn you to the Otherworld once. To place you in this danger seemed beyond the pale. No matter what you say, it's not the duty of a stratesman to defend against Other." A flame of pain licked down my side, stealing my voice, and I drew a shuddering breath. "I feared what he'd do if you tried. Unlike Riven, he is everything our lore says of high fae. He lacks both mercy and scruple."

An image of Asrina's broken body filled my mind, bitterly vivid. If Mr. Burke—or anyone else—fell to him, how could I bear it?

"That's why you turned to Riven, despite the risks." His jaw tensed. "Where was he tonight? If you have some bargain with him, he's done a poor job of upholding his end."

"We had a . . . falling out of sorts."

"Then he's withdrawn his protection?"

"I . . . I don't know."

Mr. Burke's expression was grim. "If not Riven, what's to stop West from coming here tonight and finishing what he started?"

"He may not yet know that I escaped his snare. And Riven

placed wards on Willowere." My eyes slid shut. "While I'm here, I'm safe."

"And when you must leave?"

I'd yet to formulate a plan for how to get to Kilmere—somehow I must reach Riven and see if I could mend the breach, but with Asrina gone . . .

The door flung open, and Aunt Caris bustled into the room. "Dr. Fulton is here at last."

The doctor followed close on her heels, a leather satchel slung over one arm. The moment he entered the room, Aunt Caris whirled toward him. "Please tell me she'll be all right?"

"Allow me time to examine her, and I'll give you a full report." He hurried forward, his spectacles glinting in the gaslight. "Stratesman, I'll have to ask you to leave the room so I can conduct a proper examination."

"Very well. I'll return on the morrow to finish speaking with Miss Jessa." He glanced at me. "I trust you'll remain at Willowere until then?"

It seemed safe enough to agree, given I'd been rendered largely immobile, so I nodded, and with a small bow, he stepped from the room.

Dr. Fulton secured the door, then while Aunt Caris hovered over us, he took shears and sliced through the sleeve of my gown, revealing the gaping wound. From its center, small black filaments extended—the remnant workings?

I closed my eyes against the sight.

"Well, Miss Jessa, you've been fortunate. It's nasty enough, but a finger-width to either side, and it would have done far more lasting damage." He frowned. "But how did you come by such an injury?"

Trust did not mean confessing the truth to all and sundry, so I offered the same tale I'd given the others when they came across me. His lips pursed as he continued to examine the injury. Though he clucked over my condition, in his report to Aunt

Caris he remarked on my good fortune in the placement of the wound.

Yet good fortune had nothing to do with it. Lord West had been deliberate in his placement of the spike. If he'd struck something vital, it would have meant a quick death, and he'd only meant to inflict pain—to force my surrender.

I swallowed the bitter taste rising in my mouth. In my current condition, how could I reach Kilmere and evade him in the process? Never mind what I must face when I got there, that alone felt like an impossible task.

And one you cannot act on yet. Jade lifted her head and fixed me with an unblinking gaze. *Rest now, take fresh counsel in the morning.*

How could I, when Lord West might realize I'd gone any moment? I didn't want to consider his wrath.

But you know I'm right.

I sighed. *I do.*

"It'll take some time before you regain full use of this arm, but fortunately for you, our sea-blossom honey has remarkable healing properties." Dr. Fulton withdrew a jar of herb-infused honey from his bag, along with clean linen bandages. After slathering both sides of the wound with the concoction, he wove the bandages round it, securing them neatly.

Other sparked along the wound, seeking to soothe, and yet the flames of pain raged against it. If I'd had the strength, I would have fetched my amelior salve also . . .

Tomorrow.

When he tied off the last bandage, he stood. "I'll return in the morning to assess your condition."

"Thank you, Dr. Fulton," I murmured.

He turned to Aunt Caris. "She's had quite the shock. Best give her this sedative and see that she gets to bed. Her body requires rest to heal."

Yet when Dr. Fulton left, the rest of my family crowded into the room, the weight of unspoken questions heavy.

Perhaps they'd come to some sort of agreement not to pose any of them tonight, for when Ainslie spoke, she said only, "I thanked the Redgraves for their help, but told them perhaps they'd best take their leave so you can rest. They asked me to pass along their well wishes."

"It was kind of them to help search." I closed my eyes against the swirl of pain in my temples.

"Indeed." Aunt Caris pressed the glass containing the sedative powders to my lips. "Now you must get to bed."

I pulled away. "I don't need those." I couldn't afford to be so vulnerable, not now.

"Pish." Aunt Melisina shook her head. "They'll ease the pain and let you rest."

"She's right, dear, you need them," Aunt Caris said. "You heard Dr. Fulton. Take these, then we'll help you up to your bedchamber. As to what happened—we will speak of it in the morning."

I could argue no longer, so I swallowed the bitter powder.

"Ainslie and I intend to sleep with you tonight, so that if you want for anything, you'll have care," Ada said softly. "You shouldn't be alone."

"I—thank you."

With their support, I made it up the stairs and into my bedchamber. They cut my other sleeve, then slid down my soiled gown. To contemplate moving my shoulder enough to don proper nightwear felt unbearable, so I collapsed into bed wearing only my shift.

As we huddled together, Ainslie bent her head close to mine. "We know you didn't take a fall. And that something's wrong."

"You may not want us to pry, but you can't stop us from caring," Ada said. "Won't you let us help?"

The sedative powder muddled my thoughts, and shadows deepened around me. "Tomorrow."

And then the void claimed me.

CHAPTER 50

Blinding sunlight streamed through the windows and spilled over my face. I blinked against its brilliance, and Jade nuzzled my chin, her body stretched alongside mine. Ada and Ainslie no longer occupied the bed, but when I shifted, I found Aunt Caris seated in a rocking chair alongside it.

She stood and pressed her hand to my forehead as though she could measure my pain by doing so. "How do you feel, my dear?"

I murmured something noncommittal. If anything, the pain had grown worse, stabbing its way from my shoulder across my chest and down my side. Though I'd withdrawn the stone, the workings slowly wrought damage within. How could I rid myself of them? The only one who could answer that question was Riven, and to contact him by proper, non-Other means would require writing a note and entrusting it to a servant to deliver, a process that could take hours—if he even remained at the lodgings he'd taken in Withern. I could send Jade, but if Lord West came upon her—it was unthinkable.

"Dr. Fulton left a tincture for the pain, to be taken as need-ed." Aunt Caris stood. "Would you like some?"

"No, thank you." Bad enough that I'd been forced to take

the sedative last night and had slept past noon, I couldn't afford to lose any more time nor have my senses muddled further—no matter how great my discomfort. "When did he come?"

"Before we even broke the fast. He was a great deal concerned, but he didn't want us to wake you." She crossed to the beside. "Lord Riven called as well."

I shot upright, and the room spun about me as the pain clawed deeper. "When?"

"Last night, quite late—after you'd retired. I cannot think what possessed him to come at that hour. Perhaps the ball had just ended, and he meant to make sure you'd arrived safely home." The furrow between her brows deepened. "Naturally, I couldn't allow him entrance, given your condition, so I told him you were feeling poorly and could receive no visitors."

I sank back against the headboard. Despite all that had transpired between us, had he still intended to take me to Kilmere last night? If so, the presence of my sisters might have stopped him from entering my bedchamber and induced him to call more openly. I could only imagine that their company and the subsequent denial of admittance would be taken as a sign that I now spurned his help.

If so, he'd have no reason to return. Seeking calm, I stroked Jade's fur. "If he calls again, I must see him, no matter the hour."

Aunt Caris studied me. "I did not know your feelings were so engaged."

Warmth crept up my face. "It's not that—it's only that we had a falling out before I left Holle Castle, and I would mend it, if I can."

"I'm sorry that you've had trouble, my dear, but pleased that you mean to make amends." Aunt Caris adjusted my pillows and pulled the quilts higher about me. "Yet if you want a future with him—or any other gentleman—you cannot continue doing things like gallivanting about ruins in the middle of the night. You've surely received penalty enough for your misdeeds, but what *were* you thinking?"

"It was a situation that spiraled beyond my control, but don't worry, I have no intention of returning to Kilmere alone." Though I might have to, if Riven refused to offer aid. Because even if I confessed the truth about Kilmere to my sisters—a stomach-churning notion in the light of day—I couldn't drag them into a situation they were not equipped to face. Mr. Burke would be willing to go, but in this matter, he could provide no assistance, unless it was to perceive a solution I could not.

"Very well, only think on what I've said." Her hand stole to her locket. "Certain deeds cannot be undone—and a reputation, once lost, cannot be restored. But we will say no more of it. Allow me to fetch the medicine, in case you've need of it."

"No, I must get up."

"My dear, I cannot think it wise."

"And I cannot fathom lingering in bed all day because I've injured my shoulder." I forced a smile to my lips. "I don't want to become a layabout."

She chuckled. "I doubt we're in danger of that happening."

"Still, I mean to be about my day." If I was to try to rid myself of the remnant workings, it wouldn't be withindoors. "Will you help me dress?"

"Do I have a choice?"

"Of course, but if you refuse, I must try myself, the best that I am able."

She sighed. "I thought as much."

Between the two of us, we conducted a wrestling match with a fresh shift and stays and a clean gown. Perspiration broke out along my skin, and every movement sent shards of pain deeper into my chest, but finally, it was done. Aunt Caris had even sponged off the remnants of blood and grime from the night before, so I looked presentable.

Fresh crimson now stained the bandage where it was visible above the cap sleeve, and Aunt Caris eyed it with pressed lips. "I shall send for Dr. Fulton to examine you again this afternoon. Perhaps he can persuade you to take proper care of yourself."

My head spinning, I collapsed into the abandoned chair. "I think I'll just rest here a moment. The sun is very pleasant."

"As you should." She gave a satisfied nod. "Only ring for Mrs. Warren if you need anything, and she'll fetch me."

When she left, Jade curled up on my lap. As soon as I could summon the strength, I'd collect my writing supplies to craft a message to Riven. *I don't suppose you have any experience casting off fae-workings?*

I wish I did.

Before I could inquire further, a sudden pricking sensation of Other surged into the room. We both jolted upright. It could not be Lord West, not if Riven's wards held . . .

Rather, it was Riven himself, with the power of passing coiled tightly about him. A storm-crackle of power charged the air between us, and his expression betrayed nothing. No feeling. No concern. Nothing to offer a glimmer of hope that matters might be mended.

But he was here. Whatever his reasons, he'd returned, even without a request. Some of the tightness inside unwound. "I didn't think you'd come."

"So I understand, given I had to find out about Damir from Burke." His tone suggested he'd not welcomed the revelation.

"Lord West killed Asrina." My eyes burned, and I blinked back tears. Fae did not favor sentiment, and I needed to mend matters, not strain them further. "She tried, but he . . . snared her first. I was going to send a message to you—"

"Then I take it you wish to work together long enough to rid yourself of him? That you prefer the killer who shares a common cause to the one who does not?" He wielded his words like a blade, and I was too weary to deflect.

"Yes—no, that is, not like this."

"Like what?"

This wasn't how I'd envisioned the conversation. How could I open my soul when he was wholly Other in this moment, all brightness and power, with the merest hint of sharp-edged anger, buried deep? I pulled Jade closer. "I'd like to resolve our last conversation."

"We have business to finish conducting, no more." Whatever small hint of emotion I'd detected vanished. "Count our conversation a boon to us both. You received a reminder it's unwise to trust fae."

"And how is that of benefit to you?"

"Because I received one too—that mortals are prone to distraction and sentimentality. That they allow it to drive their decisions." He lounged against the mantel, his eyes glinting bright. "Nothing matters except the task at hand. You'd do well to remember that."

"I don't agree."

"No? We have one common goal. Stop Damir." His sharp gaze rested on my shoulder, lingering where the blood seeped through the linens. "And he's just made his move, so I suggest you stop wasting time."

I leaned forward, and my breath caught as talons sliced deep into my chest. Something flickered in his eyes, and that slight suggestion something more might stir beneath the surface gave me courage to speak. "I don't want to work together on these terms, using one another to our own ends—"

His lips firmed. "Then there's nothing more to say."

"Riven, please—will you just *listen*?"

"As you wish." His voice came lower now.

"Last night, Lord West meant to force my cooperation. He left me impaled and imprisoned in stone, and I had time to reflect on a great deal." It was more difficult than I'd imagined to speak to the fae Riven, the one determined to heed only the dictates of Other. Beyond the glass, gold runners encroached upon my awareness, their song militant, and I pressed them back. "After all I witnessed at Kilmere and in my dreams, after what Lord West said, what you said—it reminded me of the risks of trusting fae. And with so much at stake, I was afraid. I did not see my way clear."

He was perceptive enough that he likely knew most of this, but if I did not confess it, it would make all that followed ring hollow.

He folded his arms. "Then you were wise. I warned you from the beginning, if you recall."

"You did. Your words warned me, but your actions told me something else." However discomfiting I found the exchange, I'd come this far—I'd confess the rest. "Though I may not trust fae in a general sense, I do trust you. And I want you to understand that before we move on."

No longer did he lounge against the mantel; he pressed upright, a flare of gold about him. "You shouldn't."

"You can't stop me." I lifted my chin. "I can be quite stubborn, if the situation requires."

"Stubborn—and foolish to take such a risk, after what I told you."

"About that—I believe there's more to the story, and if you want to discuss it, I'll listen," I said quietly. "But one who sheds his own blood to spare another pain does not go about committing murder without cause. Of that much, I'm sure."

"Jessa . . ." He became very still, and I could read nothing in his face, but when he spoke again, his voice was slightly ragged. "You say you don't want the arrangement we had before. What then?"

"I know fae have no high opinion of mortals, but I'd prefer to think of this as a . . . friendship?"

Such a long silence followed that I feared I'd provided an insult. Finally, he crossed the room, stopping only a step from my chair. "If that is what you want, then perhaps you'll allow me to help with the residual workings in your wound? You cannot begin to heal until they're removed."

I nodded.

And he bent low, the scent of forest and sun swirling about us. With an impossibly gentle touch, he eased my sleeve down my arm and pulled back the bandage.

The wound looked worse this morning, thick spirals of black writhing away from the center and disappearing beneath my clothes. My stomach lurched, but I forced myself to watch as the tiniest threads of light traveled from Riven into the wound.

They drove out the dark filaments, which coiled in the air. Then Riven's workings forced them into his hand. Imprisoned there, the shadow-strands writhed.

The relentless, searing pain lifted at once, leaving only a dull ache in its stead. When I pulled in a breath, no flames of pain awaited to punish the motion.

Jade chuffed her satisfaction. *If you bear fae blood, you'll heal swiftly with the workings removed.*

Brilliant light pooled in Riven's palm, burning the dark filaments to ash. He studied me. "I know you were fond of Asrina. Her loss must pain you."

Blight and rot. Why did he choose now to express sympathy? This time, I couldn't check the tear that escaped, but I dashed it away before it fell. "She didn't deserve her fate."

"And Damir will give an account for it." Deftly, he rewrapped my wound. "There's something else that may yet be important. You spoke of a dream that made you afraid. Will you tell me of it?"

To expose my dream would be to reveal a bit of my soul, and I could think of nothing more uncomfortable. I'd already exhausted myself with the confessions made thus far.

He stepped back. "You're under no obligation to do so."

"I know, but I want to." Given that Lord West had sent the dream, it might hold more significance than I understood—I couldn't leave it out. Somehow, I fumbled through a recounting beneath a gaze that perceived more than the words I confessed.

"Had you heard of the dagger before you dreamed of it?"

"Never."

"Then your dream explains a great deal. Damir has liminal abilities. I imagine he was responsible for it."

"He said as much." I traced a finger down the carved arm of the chair. "But I did not know what he meant, not in full."

"Among other things, a liminal affinity gives the ability to influence dreams and other places where reality is in flux. He planted the constructs the dream would shape around, provided the power to bring it to life. When twined with your own thoughts and feelings, the dream took on a life of its own." A stray spark of light appeared between his fingers. "It was well-timed. Damir knew he'd see you at the Holloway ball, where he could work upon the seeds of fear he'd sown in your dreams. He knew how to make you vulnerable, and he seized his chance. Yet in so doing, he may have revealed one of the reasons for his interest in Kilmere—a gamble he'd be willing to take, for no mortal would know of the dawn-dagger."

"What is it?"

"An object of great power, long lost from our world. If he'd found evidence it was concealed within Kilmere, then it would explain his sudden interest. Perhaps the knowledge gives us an advantage, but I prefer to possess the facts in full before drawing conclusions," he said. "Tell me what passed between you when he took you captive. Burke said he'd abducted you but could offer little further."

"Is that why you came last night?"

"Yes. Burke called, and he had some choice words for me." Rather than offense, a small glimmer of amusement appeared. "He intended to provoke me to act, I believe."

"Then I owe him thanks for doing so." Particularly since I knew his sentiments about becoming involved with fae. "And you for returning this morning, despite Aunt Caris sending you away last night."

Since I could push it off no longer, I sketched out the tale of my abduction and what Lord West had sought. Riven remained motionless as I recounted the assault, but the scent of storm overtook that of sun.

When I'd finished, no trace of gentleness lingered in Riven.

"It is time to end him, you must know that now. You say he has the basilisk—perhaps that's our answer. You weren't prepared to wield Kilmere as a weapon before, and you're far weaker after your injury. The confirmation he keeps her on his person presents another opportunity."

I'd been so fixed on understanding Kilmere, on considering how to unmake its workings, that I'd not fully accounted for what must be done to deal with Lord West, so he did not seek revenge on my family afterward, if I was . . . out of reach. "What do you propose?"

"That we sway her to strike. He keeps her close, and she's fast. If she released the full measure of her venom, it would kill him before he had a chance to seek healing."

"And she would die also?"

"Yes, in a just and honorable death. By the laws of your land, her life is owed for those she's taken. By the laws of her own kind, her sacrifice would reclaim her lost honor."

A neat ending, but the notion of attempting to persuade even a basilisk to its own death left me unsettled. Was it justice to allow her to go free when she'd committed murder? She'd not acted of her own will, yet still, so many had suffered and died. I tucked my hands in the folds of my skirts. "She must know that, yet she's not chosen to act—not any time during the long years that she must have yearned for freedom."

"According to the account in Kilmere, her first master broke her and placed upon her additional bindings, using affinities Damir does not possess. He won't have the same hold, not yet." Riven paced the room. "We have a window of opportunity to reach her, to remind her of the ways of her knot, their value for honor. Her fierce nature must resent being used as a pawn. If any remnant of the basilisk spirit remains, she might be stirred to resist."

"It seems a very cruel redemption."

"Either way, the basilisk must die. Even if she's freed from a fae master, she's a key part of the bargain. As long as she lives, she's bound to it and has no choice but to execute its terms. Unless you want the original terms of the bargain to stand, she cannot live."

I pressed my lips together as an odd grief swept me. I didn't know her, yet if she had any likeness to Jade . . . "Of course I don't—the townsfolk are innocent in this. But so was the basilisk, when she was first forced into this."

"Not everyone can be spared."

Perhaps it was true, but I loathed it, loathed the bleak future before her. If she did not make this choice, Riven would end her life, so she did not end hundreds of others. Would she feel as I did, that if she must die, she desired it to have meaning? Perhaps, but I shied away from persuading her down that path.

Jade rumbled softly. *By the ways of her people, this choice offers her only chance at peace. Even if she freed herself and returned, once the truth became known, she might be cast from her knot.*

Even so, Jade's sorrow tinged my mind. Of all of us, she understood the pain of the basilisk the best—and all that it might mean to be coerced through a bond.

I closed my eyes for the briefest of moments. Even if the basilisk dealt with Lord West, Kilmere remained—but this path would give me time to attend fully to Kilmere itself, without fear of what Lord West would do before or after, time to talk through my plans with Riven and ensure that whatever price must be paid, it would not be in vain. I could not deny the removal of the basilisk would steal an advantage from Kilmere, perhaps allow the alternate workings to surface more readily . . . but I could not be sure.

Sunlight gathered about him, as if he drew in the beams in preparation for war. Could I persuade him? Before I could confess all I'd planned, I must gain some sense of his willingness to participate. In the distance, a raven *kraaed,* bolstering my resolve. "There's one thing more. I've been thinking about what will happen if I die and Kilmere passes to you."

The light around him fractured into shards. "That won't happen."

"Can you promise that?"

The muscles in his jaw tightened, but he did not attempt to argue further. Even were he willing to do so, he could not swear to my safety.

I drew a breath, venturing onward. "I have nothing to offer in exchange except Kilmere itself, but I'd like to make a bargain."

"A bargain?" Surprise shaded his voice, and no wonder, since I'd just rejected the concept of *making use* of one another.

"Were we the only ones concerned, a request would suffice, but as we are not . . . If we are bound by bargain, even your king cannot demand that you violate its terms—is that so?"

A spark of understanding lit his features. "It is."

"Would a bargain hold, even after death?"

"If the terms are defined as such. It's rare, but it can be agreed upon."

"Then if I grant you Kilmere, by my death or . . . for any reason, will you agree not to wield it to the detriment of mortals, whether or not I still live? And if it rests within your power, will you see that the ruins do no harm to Withern?"

"You make no small request." He toyed with the spark, light and shadow flickering in its wake. "Yet to prepare for all eventualities is wise. It shall be done."

A binding mark flared on my arm. Yet it had not come from Riven, nor did it appear the rich gold of the one he'd forged between us, but rather a softer shade, one tinged gently with the new green of spring. Had I crafted it, unknowing? As I'd done with the bracelet, I willed it to remain concealed.

"Such a binding won't be required, not if we focus our energies properly," Riven said. "Damir must be provoked to rouse the basilisk from stasis, then your *kit-isne* can help you reach her, bridging the gap between thoughts, while I distract him."

"But even if she's willing to remove Lord West, Kilmere still poses a threat."

He shook his head. "I know it's been difficult for you to consider what's required to master it. If she deals with Damir, you'll no longer have to govern Kilmere in order to protect yourself and your family from him—and with her death, Kilmere will be prevented from reaching outward to fulfill the terms of the bargain. With those provisions in place, it may be possible to craft a working outside the ruins to deter any from entering."

Even so, even if everything went according to plan—and when did plans ever unfold unhindered?—we'd still leave a weapon that the wrong fae could activate at any time, causing untold destruction. Perhaps Riven was correct, and we'd find another way to prevent it from doing harm. But perhaps he was not.

I drew a deep breath, preparing to confess my alternate plan, the one I feared most. "I've been thinking about the fae lady I witnessed—"

Riven drew a shimmering veil of glamour around himself just before Aunt Caris bustled through the doorway, her cheeks flushed like a wild rose. "My dear, a Vigilist has arrived—that dreadful Mr. Ludne, from Avons, you remember. He insists he must speak with you."

Of all times . . . My hands curled inward. "Can you delay him?"

"I tried, even told him you were injured and unfit for company, but he refuses to leave without speaking to you." She twisted her hands, which trembled slightly. "And he's . . . he's very angry."

Clearly, he'd frightened her. Heat surged through my limbs, as glorious as sun in the gardens. If he thought to threaten or intimidate her, he'd soon learn he was much mistaken.

I stood abruptly, and the room wavered at the edges as pain jagged down my side, sharp as the burr of a chestnut. I'd overestimated my strength. Never mind that, I'd not allow him to threaten Aunt Caris, not when my actions alone had drawn his attention. I gripped the chair to steady myself. "Allow me a moment to make myself more presentable. I'll follow you down shortly."

Aunt Caris hurried from the room.

And Riven drew back the glamour. "You should know—he has no authority to claim Kilmere. I called again on Lord Blackburn, and he's received the dispensation from the king."

"Then Mr. Ludne cannot claim it by force." I allowed the chair to accept more of my weight. "Why would he think to come here, breathing threats?"

"Because if he can intimidate you into agreeing, the dispensation means nothing." Riven raised a brow. "Perhaps he needs a reminder that he's to keep his distance."

The gleam in his eyes suggested he'd savor it. I shook my head. "If Aunt Caris sees you, she'll have questions. Let me try first."

"Very well. I won't reveal myself without cause, but I'm coming."

Jade bobbed her head, her approval clear. Then I slowly made my way down the stairs and into the drawing room, where Aunt Caris and Mr. Ludne waited. Riven settled into a chair at the far edge of the room, light refracting around him to conceal his presence from mortal eyes, while I approached Mr. Ludne.

"Miss Jessa." His iron cane bristled with cold to match his winterberry eyes. "I've come for Kilmere."

"It's unfortunate that you traveled all this way for nothing, but you cannot have it." I'd not surrendered it to a powerful fae lord, despite his threats, and I'd certainly not be intimidated into handing it over to this grasping man.

"And why is that? What do you seek to hide?"

"I seek to steward my inheritance, no more. And I do not think you have in mind any interests but your own." Though I'd rather not sit, I doubted my ability to stand for any length of time, so I took the chair next to Aunt Caris.

Mr. Ludne glowered at me. "You think you can stand in the way of the Vigil?"

"The king has already given his word on the matter, so my opinions scarcely matter."

"Oh, yes. The dispensation. Do you care to discuss how you obtained it? How you may have . . . influenced Blackburn to advocate for you?"

Aunt Caris inhaled sharply.

He couldn't know about my fae nature, could he? If he did, surely he'd have already seized me.

Jade bared her teeth. *I believe his mind is rather more . . . base, at the moment.*

What do you mean?

He suggests you've performed certain . . . favors for Blackburn.

What? Warmth surged up my cheeks. Yet as nettled as his insinuations made me, it was better than the alternative. I pasted on a smile. "I assure you I've exercised no undue influence over him. Lord Blackburn and Lady Dromley were friends, and he still seeks to honor her memory."

"If all you say is true, prove your good faith by allowing us to examine the property. If there's nothing you wish to conceal, what's the harm?"

"I shall be forthright." I straightened, meeting his gaze. "In Avons, I allowed you to bully me over Lady Dromley's estate—and as I recall, you found nothing. Now you've followed me here to harass me over Kilmere and make similar unfounded insinuations. I must conclude that you've some irrational prejudice against me, and this time, I'm not inclined to pander to it."

Though Aunt Caris's hand went to the lace at her throat, she gave no protest—a sign Mr. Ludne had so deeply offended her by his words and actions that she did not mind my unladylike bluntness.

"Pander to . . ." A flush swept across his pale cheeks. "You are very forward, indeed. And I wonder at you. If we began to examine your life, what might we find that doesn't add up?"

Jade's eyes were glinting green at the implied threat. *Allow me to draw some blood at least.*

Not now. I struggled to my feet. "I'm sure I don't know. But—"

A shadowed sense of Other closed my throat, stole my words, drummed my pulse against the base of my jaw. I could not mistake it. I turned away from Mr. Ludne, looked through the window.

There.

My sisters sat in the garden—with a newly arrived Lord West. They'd risen from their wicker chairs, standing close to each other, wariness in their eyes. How long before he tried to glamour them?

To make matters worse, Mr. Burke was walking up the lane. Evidently, he caught sight of Lord West, for he changed course from the house to the garden. If he attempted to apprehend him, after everything . . .

Lord West looked at me through the glass and smiled, the same cruel smile he'd worn while he crushed the life from Asrina. Then he turned toward Ada, a flash of black darting from beneath his sleeve.

My blood ran hot, then cold. I fled the room for the gardens, pain and weakness and weariness driven back by the furious tide of life in my veins, pulled green and gold from the plants outside the door.

Whatever the cost, it was time to stop Lord West.

CHAPTER 51

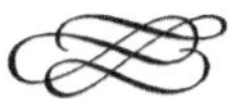

When I swept into the garden, all had fallen to disorder—Ada whimpered softly, and Ainslie wrapped a protective arm about her, while Mr. Burke jabbed a blade at something in the grass. In the center of it all stood Lord West, a mocking smile still playing about his lips.

I hurried toward them, willow branches lashing the air as I passed. Jade charged before me, while Mr. Ludne and Aunt Caris followed close on my heels. Why must a Vigilist have come today, when a high fae bent on vengeance attacked?

Riven stalked through the trees, maintaining the pretense that he'd just arrived at Willowere, and Lord West tipped his head. "You're still determined to spite me? I'm afraid you've chosen the losing side."

"Time will tell." Then Riven said something in the fae tongue, glamour swirling about him to obscure the words.

Mr. Ludne slammed his walking stick into the ground. "I demand to know what's going on here!"

Ada swayed, and Mr. Burke guided her toward the wicker bench. Then he spun toward Mr. Ludne. "Get a doctor and quick."

Perhaps he sought to rid us of the Vigil before fae power broke loose, but either way, I silently thanked him.

Mr. Ludne drew himself up. "If you think you can command me—"

Mr. Burke ignored him, bending over Ada to examine twin puncture marks on her arm. Even as he studied them, they vanished, and her skin became smooth and unmarked. The breath left my lungs.

Oh, please no.

No natural predator could erase signs of its bite—somehow, though not subject to the bargain, she'd been claimed by the basilisk. My heart thudded against my stays, and the branches overhead shuddered.

Even as my veins burned hot, the blazing songs of the gold runners and snapdragons flooded my mind. I'd hesitated to attempt using the basilisk against Lord West, and now it had poisoned Ada. But I'd hesitate no longer. Whatever it took, I'd remove him from my family before he could do more damage.

Mr. Burke's voice cut the air. "Ludne, if you fail to act and are so responsible for this woman's death, then I'll see you before your superiors, Vigil or no. Now *go*."

Mr. Ludne clenched his walking stick, then, his mouth tight, he marched away. One complication removed.

But where was the basilisk?

There. But I cannot yet connect to its mind.

A small serpentine form slithered back to Lord West, vanishing into the shadows pooled at his feet, while he and Riven continued to exchange words.

Lord West says the basilisk has the right to roam Withern, due to the original bargain, and as it does, it may strike who it pleases.

So that's how he'd circumvented whatever small protection sheltered our world from the wrath of the fae—by refraining from direct command to the basilisk and merely providing it an opportunity to attack. If Ada—no, I couldn't think it.

Has the basilisk returned to stasis?

Yes.

Which meant we'd no hope of reaching her, not unless we could provoke Lord West to rouse her again. I wanted him removed from my family first, but would Riven follow? Together we'd a far greater chance of inciting him to act.

Whatever you mean to do, keep me close.

I bent and lifted Jade, the motion reawakening embers of pain, kindling them to flame. Nevertheless, I drew in the rich strength from the willows and marched over to Lord West.

His scent engulfed me, and I choked down the acrid fear that rose. It took me back below the earth—but no, I'd broken free. And this time, I'd face him by my choice, not his.

To provoke him was far more dangerous than to rouse a dragon, yet it must be done—and I must show none of my fear. "Why have you come? What do you imagine this ridiculous scene will accomplish?"

One corner of his mouth lifted, a flash of teeth following. "It drew you out, did it not?"

"And to what end? You cannot touch me here." I inclined my head, drawing Jade closer to my chest. "Can it be that you've failed?"

"My schemes do not fail."

"And yet here we are."

"Not for much longer." His shadows closed about me. Then the world winked black, and I tumbled through a stomach-churning array of shadows that snatched me from one world into another, stealing my breath and the best of my hopes.

Unless Riven followed, I'd face Lord West alone.

WHEN THE FORCE of the passing faded, Other throbbed around me with such strength that no doubt remained—Lord West had brought me to his world. Why now?

Something else pricked against my mind, a hostile awareness, not as strong as Kilmere, but equally cold and ancient. I blinked to clear my vision from the passing, and an elegant chamber took shape before my eyes, crafted of intricately carved stone. Artifacts of silver and precious gems occupied shelves alongside an enormous hearth, before which stretched a claw-footed dining table.

Lord West had brought me to his demesne, the last place I'd ever wanted to find myself. The cold knowledge that he'd sealed me off from all aid seeped through me, shivering down my limbs. Could Riven enter the Court of Silver without provoking hostilities between the rival courts? I couldn't count on it. My shoulder spasmed, and I lost my grip on Jade.

She launched herself to the floor, growling low, but Lord West only chuckled.

"It's past time you enjoyed my hospitality." He gestured to the foot of the table. "Sit."

No sense arguing about something so trivial, not when I needed to put my energies toward reaching the basilisk. I forced my breath to steady. How could I provoke him to wake her without Riven present to offer a threat? I sank into the chair, its heavy carvings jabbing into my back, and surveyed the room for anything that might be of use. In the wide hearth, a kettle hung over an unnatural blue-silver flame, which required no logs to stay fueled, and before me sat a steaming cup of some foul brew. The stench that rose from it choked me.

Jade leapt upon my lap with her hackles raised. Every muscle quivering with the effort of restraint, she glowered at Lord West.

I clutched her close. *Don't try anything, not yet. Can you feel the mind of the basilisk?*

No, she remains in stasis.

I strained to catch any hint of life beyond these walls. If I could reach the plants that *must* grow beyond, could I draw them to act against a fae lord in his demesne? At least enough to provoke him into rousing the basilisk? No, his working muffled all sense of anything beyond cold stone.

Lord West pulled out the chair across from mine and settled into it. "Now, before we conduct our business, I would bid you drink."

The scent swelled about me, so caustic that the cup must contain some sort of poison. "If you kill me, then Riven takes Kilmere. And I cannot imagine he'd negotiate with you."

"Oh, this won't kill you, my sweet. It will only make you suffer such pain that you'll crave death. It comes on slowly, but it is strong."

My eyes burned. "I'm not bound to you. You cannot compel me to drink it."

"I think otherwise." He leaned forward, the lines about his eyes sharpening. "You see, I came to suspect something about you last night, something you confirmed when you rushed into the garden to see after your family. You could have remained safe behind the wards Riven provided in Willowere, but you chose otherwise, because you worry about the fate of those around you. Some might call that a fatal weakness. Certainly it's a peculiarity you can ill afford."

Jade had warned me against betraying my emotions, and I'd failed. I tucked my hands beneath the table to conceal their tremor.

"Drink it, or I shall take Solan to call on your family once more." He drew back his sleeve, exposing her. "As delightful as our games have been, matters within my own court require my attention. It's time to bring this to an end."

I couldn't allow him to bring the basilisk—Solan—back to my family. So I curved my fingers around the cup, its heat stinging. I wanted to fling it in his face, but I must stay the course, pay the price—and hope that I'd retain strength long enough to outmaneuver him.

I lifted the cup to my lips. The pungent liquid burned as it traveled down, and a foul taste lingered on my tongue.

"Very good. We begin to understand each other."

"Why bring me here?"

"I've wearied of Riven's interference. I intended before to present you to Kilmere, to seal my mastery with your blood at once, but this will do. He cannot enter here, and you cannot leave, so I shall have the pleasure of dealing with you at my leisure. I shall certainly not allow you away from my eye again."

My mind spun. He appeared to attribute my escape to Riven, and to avoid another such intervention, he'd chosen to bring me here, rather than risk a return to the borders of Kilmere. Perhaps that revelation offered an opening—I could needle him about his earlier failure to claim me for Kilmere, in an attempt to provoke him to rouse Solan. That plan felt like an unthinkable gamble, now that he'd snared me in his demesne, far from Riven. Still, what other hope did I have? I swallowed hard against the bitterness in my mouth. "I thought you did not fear Riven, yet here you are, running away. Perhaps it shouldn't be a surprise. I knew you for a coward from the first."

From the floor, shadow-bound stone formed shackles that snaked up my ankles, binding me in place, biting into my flesh. I choked back a cry—I couldn't betray my pain. He'd take too much pleasure in it.

Jade's hunger for his blood swelled within me.

And Lord West leaned forward. "You make free with your words. It shall be a pleasure to teach you restraint along with fear. And if you do not learn swiftly enough, then I shall remove your tongue."

I felt as though his stone embedded itself in my chest, every breath coming only with effort. I'd angered him, yes, but he still kept the basilisk bound. Dared I go further? "Even now, you prove the truth of my words. You keep me bound, you've made me prisoner to torture me where none can interfere, because you cannot consider ever facing anyone, even a mortal, on equal terms."

"There are no equal terms between us, mortal. You are nothing but a worm, unable to elevate yourself from scrabbling in the dirt for the entirety of your short, miserable life."

The bonds about my ankles tightened further, sending shards of pain up my legs. I clenched my shaking hands in my lap. I must focus, must bring him to the point of waking her. "Perhaps, yet I still have what you desire. And you still hide behind this basilisk, relying on her to do what you cannot. Solan, you call her—"

The entire demesne shook, and a shock of sun and storm burst over my senses, strong enough to infiltrate even the gloom of this place.

Riven.

Whatever the risks, whatever the implications, he had come —and I could breathe again, despite the dangers on every side. Together, we might succeed.

"Now that *is* a surprise." Lord West glided over to a midnight-black window, as though it did not matter that his plans had been upended. And why should he be troubled? Could a demesne even be breached? He'd said Riven could not enter. "It seems the arbiter values you more than I thought. Whatever his reasons for intervening before, he'd not venture into my court just to spite me. What does he know about you, I wonder?" A shadow coiled out from Lord West and caressed my face, chill and damp. "Perhaps you shall live after all—after I've broken you properly."

The demesne rocked once more, and the shadows about Lord West deepened. "First, I shall rid myself of this pestilence."

With the slightest flick of his fingers, the window became properly translucent, then stretched into a full door of glass, outside of which Riven stood, shards of light lingering from his passing.

"You've lost, arbiter." Lord West's sharp smile flashed in the gloom. "You may as well accept it. I did not disarrange my plans and bring the mortal here to permit your interference. Whatever value she holds, she belongs to me now, and Kilmere will follow."

I straightened, lifting my voice so it rang across the room.

"You're wrong. After what you did last night, I took precautions. I realized I couldn't protect Kilmere as I desired, so I documented transfer of ownership to Riven." In my mind alone —and just now—but he did not need to know it. If I crafted my story with enough care, I could lead him to the necessary conclusion—and my one chance at outwitting him. A knifelike sensation twisted in my stomach. A first sign of the poison? I hurried on. "Perhaps you have me, but I shall always have the comfort of knowing you lost in the end. As I recall, you said that never happens? I suppose there's a first time for everything."

It took everything in me to force out the defiant words, to provoke him to greater anger when he could cause me such pain. When he could hurt those I loved. But I held his gaze, even offered a small smile.

His lips drew back, baring his teeth, but before he could speak, Riven seamlessly continued my tale. "If I may suggest an alternative, I'm willing to bargain—if you allow me in so we may negotiate."

Whatever my relief that Riven played along, I must appear to feel the opposite. I strained against my bonds. "You were to keep it safe—you can't negotiate with him."

"I did warn you not to trust me, if you recall, but you were all too willing to give faith without cause." Riven wore the cold, forbidding expression of a fae lord now. "Quiet, mortal. This no longer concerns you."

I shrank back into the chair.

And Lord West drew a hand across his chin, thoughtful. "Nothing but enmity exists between our courts. Between us. You've been set against me every step of the way. Why should I believe that's changed?"

"Your court and mine will ever be at odds. But as it happens, you have something I need." Riven shrugged. "I knew you'd never deal with me, if given a choice. When this situation arose with the mortal, it offered an opportunity to get close to you—

and she gave herself right into my hands. Now there may be a way for us both to get what we want."

Something inside me sank. Riven couldn't lie, and I couldn't find the loophole in his words. I'd chosen to trust him, and if he acted against me—no, no, I'd rest in what I'd decided. If I divided my attentions now, if I doubted, we'd fail.

"How very interesting." Lord West chuckled. "You always were one to play the long game, but my question still stands. Why surrender what you fought to win?"

"Because it wasn't my ultimate aim. As I said, you have something I need. Now it appears I have something you need."

He'd said it *appeared* he had something Lord West needed, because Kilmere didn't belong to him. But he'd added no such qualifier to his statement that Lord West had something he needed. What did Riven want from him?

"Ah." He steepled his fingers, shadows coiling about them. "What is it?"

"I refuse to continue to bargain on the doorstep as if I were a peddling *erech*. Either admit me to negotiate properly or I leave."

"You think I'm fool enough to allow you into my demesne?"

Yet the lust in his eyes defied his words. He desired to possess Kilmere and claim victory, and he could never admit defeat by a mortal. No, he'd allow Riven entrance and then seek to grind my heart to dust in the face of Riven's so-called betrayal.

"I'm bound by my king not to touch you—as you are bound by your queen not to harm me," Riven said. "What do you have to lose?"

"One would have also surmised you were bound by your king not to enter this court so freely, much less assault my demesne."

"I merely sought to gain your attention, no more. If I meant assault, I would not engage in peaceful conversation."

"Very well." Lord West crossed the room to stand just before me. "You have proven unusually resourceful for a mortal. In case you have any ideas of using this negotiation to attempt escape, be assured any such effort will fail. In place of my eyes, you'll have those of Solan. If your *kit-isne* changes to true-form, if you try anything, Solan will claim you both."

The basilisk uncoiled from his arm and slithered down his wrist onto the floor, a small brown-black serpent. And then she shifted into a massive scaled creature with flashing fangs and a flared hood, one that bristled with menace.

I see her thoughts now. They are pain and chaos and torment. Images poured from Jade's mind to my own, snatches of death and destruction. *You must buy me time, if you can. It will be difficult to induce her to listen.*

With a flick of Lord West's fingers, the door swung open, and Riven strode into the dining hall.

I looked at him with all the pain I'd bottled up inside, the grief over those lost, the conflict I'd felt about the impossible choices made and yet to be made—all those feelings I channeled into my voice. "You . . . you made me trust you, and now—"

"On the contrary, I warned you never to trust fae. It was your choice to take that as a sign of my integrity."

"Mortal ladies. So very willing to have their heads turned." Lord West laughed, the sound jarring. "You're not so different from Ibbie, after all."

A peculiar chill spread over me. "Did you—know her?"

His lips twisted in a cruel smile. "Quite well."

Oh. *Oh.*

As when one discovered the final element of a cipher and the jumbled assortment of symbols formed words and phrases, so now all the little details formed one cohesive whole—and the meaning of everything that had come before became plain. I lifted my head. "You—you were Edward."

"That was the name I chose when I wooed her, yes. Ibbie thought herself strong, yet she was so easily deceived, like all mortals." He stroked his fingers across the wound on my shoulder, drawing pain. "I called her my dove, for she was like those from my world—not your pallid peaceful ones, but the moon doves of my court, fierce fighters that remain utterly unaware of their smallness and fragility. We cage them and use them for sport."

Far deeper than the pain in my shoulder was the spike driven toward my heart. All that Ibbie had suffered was the fault of Lord West—Edward. A furious warmth simmered inside, and even through the thick stone walls of the demesne, a thrumming of deep roots reached me.

Dimly I remained aware of Riven at the edge of the room, of his slight movement toward me, of Jade, striving to reach the basilisk, but Edward filled my vision, Edward, alive and well while Ibbie was dead. The thrumming of roots filled my ears— but no, to strike out now would undo everything. I couldn't overcome a fae lord in his demesne, not like this. I must prick at him another way. I raised my chin further, held his gaze. "She was far stronger than you ever understood."

"How little you know. I swiftly bent her to my will. She'd no capacity to resist, not when I was done with her." His fingers dug deeper into my wound, sending spikes down my side. "There are many ways a husband can make his wife suffer—perhaps I shall show you some of them, when I conclude my business with Riven."

Against the blinding tide of pain and fury, I strove to clear my thoughts. "And yet she deceived you about Kilmere, and you were taken in. You didn't know what you had access to then, or you never would have left it untouched. It took you decades to uncover the truth."

His obsidian eyes hardened. "She enacted no deceit—she was merely as ignorant as the rest of your kind. She uncovered several objects of power and was convinced it was all Kilmere had to offer."

"So she told you. But she left a written record of her deliberate deception, of the actions she took to keep you from its heart." I forced derision into my voice. "You were careless, trusting your own power enough not to bestir yourself to attend what you believed a menial affair. Your absence gave her liberty and allowed her to protect the truth. I suppose you might even say she won, in the end."

The temperature in the chamber dropped, and the stone walls darkened to an ominous shade. Oh, please, let this be worth it. If I could unbalance him, perhaps we'd succeed, but if I went too far . . .

He leaned over me, his breath whispering against my skin. "Ibbie may have escaped my wrath, but you have not. Perhaps I shall make you pay for her misdeeds as well as your own."

"Damir." Riven's words were clipped, his jaw tight. "If you're quite done playing, we have business to conduct."

"We shall resume this conversation later. I quite look forward to it," Lord West murmured. Then he straightened, striding across the room toward Riven.

I wrapped my arms about my chest. I'd done what I could, and now I must hope fae negotiations were as protracted as one might imagine. I could not allow myself to consider what would happen if we did not succeed. *Any progress?*

She will listen, perhaps. What do you want to say? I will relay her thoughts to you and yours to her.

Everything in me resisted the notion of persuading Solan to this course, but what choice remained? The circumstances had spiraled beyond our control. Riven was right about the justice in it, and yet . . .

The rise and fall of the fae tongue filled the room. What terms did they discuss?

Never mind that—I couldn't address the basilisk with my attentions divided. I needed to rely on Riven to distract Lord West, and I needed to rely on Jade to communicate with the basilisk. I wrenched my attention back to her. *I'm sorry. I'm ready.*

Within my mind, I rehearsed what I knew of Solan's history —the grim tale Jade had told of the basilisk and what I knew of their kind. And I chose my words with care. *Solan. I know you've suffered.*

You know nothing, mortal. You are weak, finite. When the time comes, I will break you as I have the others.

And please your master still more?

She surged upright, her form towering above my head, her eyes glittering, but offered no response.

No one should be forced to kill, much less abandon their family and all they love. I cannot undo the past. If I could, even now, I would give anything to break your bond to him, to undo his hold.

Words mean nothing. Only deeds matter.

What of your own deeds? Does it please you that you serve those who have caused you to suffer?

An angry hiss seared the air.

If it does not, why don't you sever the tie?

Do you know what the breaking of a bond is like? What price I would pay?

Raw anguish flooded from Solan to Jade to me, and the knives of pain stabbed deeper into my abdomen.

If I strike him, I will suffer the worst of deaths. The pain of a bond-mate tests endurance; to cause it is far worse. Fortunately, I have no need to act so, not any longer. We have bargained now. My freedom and return to my world, to my knot, once he has secured Kilmere.

I rocked back. He had checked our move. How could I expect her to strike at him when he represented all she most desired?

Her tongue flicked out. *You're not so unlike the fae; you seek to control me to gain your own ends.*

I want Lord West to stop threatening all those I hold dear, and I won't attempt to deny it. But I don't seek to control you. This is a choice I could never make for you and—

The basilisk hissed again.

Jade growled back.

What's going on?

She wants to look into your mind, but I won't allow it.

Why?

It's dangerous. She might mesmerize you.

Perhaps, but you shall be my safeguard. She needs to know if she can trust me—let her in.

Jade sat unmoving.

We can't drag this out any longer. Every moment that passes is a risk.

A heartbeat later, Jade conceded, and a cold fog invaded my thoughts. Jade had said basilisks preferred to communicate through images and emotions. Without her as an intermediary, what would—oh. I stifled a gasp, as every feeling and thought I'd had about the basilisk simmered to the surface. My fears, my pain over her plight, my torment over this request all became exposed. Then the cold subsided.

You mourn for me, Jade relayed. *You did not lie.*

Of course I do. What you've suffered is unthinkable.

In our world, those with the most power determine right from wrong. If you're strong enough, you set the terms. No one mourns the weak.

Tentatively, I reached out and stroked her scales. For the briefest moment, she sank into my touch.

Then her hood flared, its jagged spikes bristling. *I will not help you.*

I know. Perhaps I'd known from the moment she'd told us Lord West promised her deepest desire fulfilled. It meant Kilmere remained the only way.

The spikes lowered as she regarded me. *Your* kit-isne *tells me it was your sister I struck last.*

Yes. A tiny spark of hope kindled. If I could not sway Solan, perhaps I could still see Ada saved. Riven could carry back information about the cure, after I made my bid for Kilmere. *If you will not resist Lord West, will you at least tell me—is there any way to treat your mortal victims?*

That much I will offer, since you have seen me, truly. The remedy requires a fae to purify goldleaf basil, draw out its true essence. The plant is of your world, therefore mortals tolerate it, but the power to craft the cure comes from mine. Vivid images flooded my mind of a fae lord crafting such a potion—then forcing it down Solan's throat to torment her. As the antithesis of her power, the suffering it caused had been immense.

I'm sorry for all that's passed before. And I pray you find peace.

I choked down the bitter taste at the back of my throat. If I could remake Kilmere to protect instead of seize power, with Lord West inside, perhaps it would restrain him. If not, I must trust Riven to keep safe those I loved when I could no longer. For it was now clear—I must follow the path set by the Lady of Ravens.

The knives twisted deeper. *Tell Riven we must go to Kilmere. It's our only path forward.*

What do you intend?

I couldn't speak of it, not yet. *Just tell him, please.*

Evidently she did, for something shifted in the cadence of their exchange.

Then Lord West looked over at me, and his lips tilted into a predatory smile. "You'd make that a condition—that I sacrifice her within Kilmere?"

He wanted me to understand his words, wielded them to hurt me further.

Riven gave the slightest incline of his head. "It was within the bounds of our bargain that I not hand her over to you. This solution should satisfy both our interests."

"It will do quite well." Lord West drew shadows to himself. "We shall go and seal our bargain in blood."

Lord West's passing brought us to the boundary of Kilmere. The bone-cold sensation of his power chilled my skin, and his bindings coiled about me like chains. Since he could not deposit us within Kilmere proper, he wasn't taking any chance of my escape.

Yet even his power paled before the fierce hunger of Kilmere. Despite the full sun overhead, thick mists shrouded its walls, which jutted out cruel and dark amid the shroud of silver. The relentless thunder of the sea against the cliff sent a shudder through my body. It offered a reminder of Kilmere's terms—break others on its behalf or be broken by its might, just like the waves upon its stone.

Lord West prodded me onward, and I stumbled as the poison sank its claws deeper. Yet the pain represented a welcome tie to the land of the living, one I must almost certainly sever to remake Kilmere. To do so, I doubted a simple wound would suffice.

If I was willing to give what I believed was required—my life—would it be enough? Kilmere thirsted for it. If I touched the stones, if I offered myself, I'd no doubt it would accept, because it *must*. So its workings bound it.

Yet a deeper working lay buried within its foundations, and if I strengthened it, it must break free. The fae lords and ladies of old had feared such an alteration, had claimed additional lives to constrain its power, to bury it deep enough so it could not surface.

This was the key, if I had the courage to wield it. And I refused to shrink back.

Jessa, no. Green fire burned in Jade's eyes. *How did you conceal this from me?*

I'm getting better at hiding my thoughts, when I must. I did not want to pain you, when I didn't yet know what was needed. And if she'd sought to dissuade me, my resolve surely would have faltered. *Until we failed with Solan, I'd still hoped it would not come to this.*

Lord West nodded to Riven. "Lead on."

I made sure to keep step with Riven, forcing my leaden feet over the boundary stones at the same time as his, that it might appear he compelled Kilmere to accept Lord West. As we crossed over, Kilmere closed about us, fierce and exultant, the Other power within it slicing like hundreds of tiny blades across my flesh.

It sensed the presence of the basilisk, and its hunger swelled about me, as insatiable as the wyvern of old. One way or another, it meant to gain a new master this day. If I did not demonstrate my control of the situation, it would remove me as an obstacle—and choose one of these lords instead.

For now, it waited. Watched to see who would strike first, which power it should back, who offered the greatest gains. The stones about me thrummed with anticipation, dark voids against which the light of the sun vanished.

Riven glanced back. "We should complete this in the heart."

Satisfaction shadowed the air about Lord West as he strode forward. The exchange between the two of them faded into the background, drowned by the roar of my pulse, the strengthening murmurs of the trees, the mists closing about us—and the pain Jade exuded.

I won't allow this. When you said you had a way to control Kilmere, I thought you meant with your new understanding of your nature—not your life's blood. Does our bond matter not at all?

Oh, Jade, it matters more than I can say. You mean everything to me—and I cannot tell you how glad I am you're kit-isne, *and not the ordinary cat I once believed. But I must do this.* As we crossed to the keep, to the stairs that descended into the darkness, to the place where the eld dragon had suffered and died, her fear merged with my own. The bristling malice of Kilmere assaulted me, and I trembled. *Can you see another way?*

Her tail lashed angrily. *Claim Kilmere, as the fae of old did— and bid it kill West. Riven was right. You must.*

Within the octagonal chamber, Solan regarded us, her bead-black gaze unwavering, her eyes glistening. How did she feel about this return to her prison of so many centuries? Could she dread it as much as I did?

I forced myself onward. *He wasn't right, not about this. If I claimed Kilmere that way, then the cycle of death and destruction would continue unbroken—and even if I lived, I would no longer be myself.*

The cold of Kilmere snaked up my limbs, seeking to assert its hold. Already it encroached upon my senses as we traversed the underground corridors, distant screams of anguish ringing in my ears. Not long now, and it would seek to consume me, to subvert my senses and make its claim.

I must act before it did, take the path of my own choosing, the one the Lady of Ravens had walked before me. *Can you forgive me? I know this places you in an untenable position—*

She hissed. *You think I'm concerned with my future?*

Whether you are or no, I'm concerned with it. But Riven is here. He can forge a passing and take you to the Otherworld, so you can bond with another kit-isne *before it's too late. You'd be rejoined with your kind at last.* Our conversation was taking too long—even now we approached the heart.

I don't want my clan, nor another bond-mate. If you die here, I die also. I will not go.

Jade, please—

No. The word thrummed deep and sinuous through my mind. Not Jade's voice—had Solan spoken?

Yes.

Solan's reply resounded in my mind. Jade had reforged the connection between the three of us, and she now allowed the raw, ragged edges of her pain to seep into it, tearing at my heart.

Solan's hood flared. *No one—not fae, mortal, or* kit-isne—*shall show deeper devotion or more honor than a basilisk.*

What did she mean? The scents of ancient blood and stone surged about us, marking our entrance to the heart. A sacrifice would be made here, but not the one Lord West intended, nor Kilmere. I drew a shuddering breath and approached the stone wall, the arch of bones.

Then Solan surged past me, brushing her muzzle along my hand as she went. Like the flash of lightning in a summer sky, she struck Lord West from behind, her fangs sinking deep into his shoulder.

As she did, her voice echoed in my thoughts. *The only sacrifice given will be mine—as it should have been long ago. This I give willingly. It is my choice, mine alone.*

Darkness roiled and churned about them. Searing heat flooded the chamber, along with the choking stench of old death. The ground below us heaved, but Solan clung tight, pouring every drop of her venom into Lord West. The coppery scent of blood and sick-stench of poison filled the air, churning my stomach and coating my throat with bitterness. I struggled to peer through the dense shadows. Who prevailed?

A shudder passed through the floor, and I clutched at Jade. Then the cloud of shadow lifted, revealing their forms bound together. Solan remained coiled about Lord West, though he'd rent her body with his power.

Both were dead.

I could not wrench my gaze away from their broken bodies. The air about me swirled hot, then cold. Lord West would never hurt anyone again, but oh, the price that had been paid. Solan had sacrificed everything, and now her blood seeped across the stone and into the ground.

Kilmere quaked.

The door from the heart unlocked. Vibrant scarlet-and-white workings raced over dead stone, licking across it like living flame. The Lady of Ravens had awakened once more, all the power she'd poured into her workings flaring bright.

It was time.

Riven wheeled toward me. "What did you do to Kilmere?"

"Nothing." My breath caught, as the poison burrowed deeper. "It was Solan, and I promise I'll explain later, but now we must act."

Sigils of rust and old bone gleamed as the forces within Kilmere vied for control, and the stones about us trembled.

"You mean to take Kilmere while it's unmade from within." Gold flared in his eyes. "While it might be changed."

I could only manage a nod. We could afford no more delay —I'd not let Solan's sacrifice go to waste.

Well and good. Jade shifted into true-form. *But we will have words later about your actual plan.*

If we succeed in this madness, I will exchange as many words as you like.

About us, Kilmere shook, its very foundations in turmoil. If we attempted to remake it here, would it collapse around us and bury us in the depths? "We should surface."

With Jade as support and Riven as rearguard, I ran up the corridor toward the stairs leading to the keep. The walls shook on either side, a deep, wrenching rumble emanating from them —not a threat, not this time, but rather a war within. It could not seek to restrain us, even if it wished to do so, not with the workings of the Lady of Ravens dancing through its stones.

How long did we have?

We reached the central keep, and I turned toward Jade, perspiration slicking my skin. *Will you stand watch from the boundary? If I'm observed or interrupted, it could upend everything.*

And as much as I wanted her near, I could not leave the matter to chance.

Jade's tail lashed the air. *I'll keep watch and provide a distraction if needed, but don't take too long.* She marched down the path, then turned toward Riven, waiting—for him to listen? *I've almost lost my mistress once today, and last time, you nearly let Kilmere break her. If you allow any harm to come to her while I'm gone, I will spend my last breath seeking your life.*

"You need not worry, *kit-isne.*"

As she departed, the sharp scents of ancient decay and coppery blood surged into the air once more. No, that was past. And it would *not* be future.

My vision expanded, and the vast sea of workings came into view. How could I reweave all of this, strengthen that which the Lady of Ravens had left so it became an impregnable fortress— not of oppression, but of shelter for all who needed it?

I knew so very little. But I was not alone. Riven stood at my side, and this time, I wasn't afraid to rely on him. Instinctively, I reached for his hand, and his fingers closed around mine, warm and sure.

"You are certain you wish to do this together?" His voice came deep and low. "It will bind me in some measure to Kilmere."

"I'm sure."

The power of sun and storm surged through my body, driving back every remnant of pain. Glorious warmth and strength poured from Riven to me, and all at once, my vision deepened further. I perceived not only the workings stretched across its surface, but also those rooted deep below.

They stretched vast and darkly beautiful, through the tremendous cliff, on into the seabed and the lands beyond, consuming much of the stretch between the ruin and Withern proper.

The natural world faded, the fae-workings woven over it all that remained. A roselike bloom of scarlet and ivory flared across the keystone.

Together, we ascended the broken stairs toward it. And I pressed my hand, the one with the faintest white scar across the palm, to the stone of the wall. One part of me anchored itself in the ancient trees of Kilmere, in their thunderous songs of joy, another in the endless well of power within Riven, and the third —that reached for the other threads, the ones woven to protect, the ones sparking with love and devotion and sacrifice.

Oh, they were *beautiful*.

Slowly, I wound them about the rust-and-bone sigils, which vanished like smoke when enclosed with scarlet and white. Other threads too, new ones, became joined to the Lady of Raven's workings, these a vibrant green-gold, sigils that branched like deep-rooted trees and sprawling vines to stretch over the expanse of Kilmere.

Affinities responded to intention, Riven had said, yet I sensed his purpose alongside my own, his knowledge guiding mine, enabling the process to unfurl far more rapidly than I could have ever conceived.

Gleaming, living, vibrant color sprawled across Kilmere as all trace of the old workings vanished, until only the very first and very last remained, joined in an impossibly glorious whole.

Then I was sinking, pain rending my body as the power ebbed. It was done—and I'd nothing more to give.

With Riven's support, I made it back to level ground, my senses swirling. He lowered me down to the earth, into a bed of ferns, and I dug my fingers deep into the unfurling fronds, their determination becoming my own.

About us, shadows no longer clustered, and the air held the scents of greening life and fresh blossoms, the fragrances washing away the strain of the past weeks. I still could not fathom it had been accomplished, that after all the pain and suffering Kilmere had caused for generations untold, it no longer represented a threat.

It still held memories of pain—they ghosted the edges of my vision when I brushed against the stone—but they lacked their prior sting. Rather, the workings that reforged Kilmere remembered and mourned and then chose life anew.

The wind that teased the leaves held a jubilant tone, as though it celebrated with us. And then, like a cloud, ravens descended upon the ruin, their calls low and throaty. Could they remember their lady, all these generations later? Did they seek to honor her work?

They clustered about the central keep, fluttering among its

workings in swirls of blue-tinged black that gleamed in the sunlight. Then, their examination complete, they took flight, vanishing into the air.

The unkindness had departed.

Riven smiled, a slow and brilliant smile, one that warmed me more than the sun above us. "It was well done, Jessa."

I opened my mouth to speak, but the words died in my throat, cut off by a stabbing sensation in my abdomen. I stifled a gasp.

Riven leaned forward, intent. "The poison?"

"I think so." I yearned for Jade and her comforting presence. Would she be able to hear my thoughts over a distance? *Jade?*

The faintest whisper returned to me. *You succeeded.*

Yes. It's done. Will you come? Then a far more crippling wave of pain sliced through my middle, scattering my thoughts and stealing my breath. As if from a distance, I heard Riven speak.

"Damir gave you *fevren*. Its scent is distinctive." He withdrew a small vial from his pocket.

The wave ebbed slightly, leaving sweat dripping down my back. "What is that?"

"The antidote."

"You keep antidotes to poison in your pocket?" The *fevren* once more sliced through me, and I wrapped my arms about myself, struggling to maintain an even tone. "With so little space, how do you choose which ones to bring?"

"They're useful in my line of work, and I need not choose. This is a fae pocket—it holds realms of goods."

Oh. I could use one of those. Through the pain-muddled haze, I grasped at another thought. "You once said that fae remedies could harm mortals."

Jade padded through the doorway, and Riven stilled, the vial gleaming in his hands. "And what if you were not mortal? Would that be so dire a fate?"

Jade tilted her head to study me, her pupils slitting. They waited as I waded through waves of pain to form my response.

I might not fully understand how I'd come to bear fae blood, but I knew it to be true. My affinities had worked in harmony with Kilmere and with Riven, making it abundantly clear. Yet though I'd begun to come to terms with having a fae nature, I could not embrace the losses it would entail. "My family—I'll lose them all."

"Perhaps. Certainly you'll face difficult choices."

I swallowed against the bitter taste of the *fevren* rising in my throat. "How long have you believed I had fae blood?"

"For some time. I'd entertained various other possibilities. You might have been born in the Otherworld, in captivity—might have had residual fae-workings on you, if they'd experimented. But I've found no trace of that, nor of alchemical devices implanted within." In his grasp, the vial brightened. "As you exercised your affinities, it became clear, along with your resistance to the notion."

Another knife-blade of pain stabbed my stomach. Jade settled next to me, curling her tail about me for warmth and comfort.

Bending down, Riven extended the small bottle. "Do you wish to discuss the matter further or take the antidote?"

I accepted it from him and downed it in one gulp. The bittersweet liquid soothed as it worked its way down. If any doubt as to what I was remained, my body's willingness to embrace the fae antidote erased it. "Perhaps both?"

After all this time, Riven was finally willing to talk about my nature—perhaps because he'd determined I did have fae blood—and I'd not forgo my opportunity for answers, however great my pain. Besides, I could use a distraction from it. "Why didn't you say something sooner?"

"Given your fears, I thought you'd react in haste. If you rejected your affinities, it would place you in an even more vulnerable position." He situated himself on a stone across from me with the same easy grace one might a throne, placing us more on a level. "Then there's the fact that you've lived in the mortal world as long as you can remember, unaware of your true nature. Most likely that means someone deliberately concealed you here to keep you from harm."

"About that—I'd wondered . . ." Slowly, I spilled out my theory about my mother.

Riven nodded. "It's certainly possible she was forced to bear a child, though she would have been cunning indeed if she managed to evade a fae who sought to claim what he saw as his own. It's also conceivable that none of your family belong to you by blood, that an enemy of your fae family took you, stripped you of your memories, and hid you in the mortal world, though they would have had to place a powerful working on you to do so. There are other possible answers as well—it's too soon to narrow them down."

I burrowed my hands deeper into the ferns. I'd thought that speaking with Riven would bring comfort; instead, a world of discomfiting possibilities opened before me.

He continued, "I won't try to bind you to silence, but it would be unwise to speak of your nature until we find out how you came to be left in this world. The danger of mortal reactions will be the least of your causes for concern."

How could I begin to address all that troubled me in that statement? I decided not to try, but rather to attend to the more hopeful part—he'd said *we*. "You mean to help me find the truth?"

"If you'll allow it."

Why was he offering assistance? He'd said before that he required answers about my abilities. If I was part fae, then did that make me the concern of an arbiter, a matter he must report on to his king?

The bright song of the rowan trilled about me. Perhaps it didn't matter, because to uncover the truth required far greater understanding of the Otherworld and fae-kind than I possessed. Without his help, navigating the dangers would be difficult indeed. I braced against the wall, which now offered support, rather than threats. "I would appreciate it. But I must ask—why do you believe the threat of mortal reactions no cause for concern? Do you know what the Vigil would do, if they discovered—"

"Yes, and it pales to the dangers my world offers. How you came here with no knowledge of your heritage is matter for concern." His eyes shadowed. "Who hid you—and why? What lengths might they go to in order to ensure you don't return?"

I didn't want to consider the answers to his questions, nor all they entailed. If I somehow placed my family in more danger— *Ada.* Even now, she suffered. How could I have ignored her plight? She needed the cure the basilisk had revealed. I struggled to press myself from the ground, and the motion sent glass-shards of pain through every limb. I collapsed back onto the earth.

Riven frowned. "It's a swift-acting antidote, but not that swift. It will be several hours before you're back on your feet. You'd best resign yourself to a wait."

"But Ada—Solan told me of a cure for her, and I must try to prepare it."

"To do so, you must recover. It will have to wait."

I leaned back against the stones. It felt *wrong* in every way to sit here recovering while the venom worked its way deeper into Ada's body.

And yet, you saw from Solan the power that is required. If you have not healed, you will fail. And then her suffering will be all the greater. Jade lowered her head to mine. *May I remind you that I'm always right?*

I stroked her muzzle. *So you've said.* And since I could not move on my own strength, I must wait—just a little longer, willing Ada protection in her battle.

"Meantime, you owe me some answers." Riven leaned forward, his power charging the air. "Why did you return to Kilmere before suggesting Solan strike? Did you guess it would rouse these alternate workings?"

I pulled my knees to my chest. "I didn't come because of Solan—I'd tried to persuade her to act in the demesne, but she refused. She said Lord West had bargained with her, offered her freedom and a return to the Otherworld once he'd secured Kilmere."

"It was well played. The allure of freedom bought not only her forced obedience but a temporary alliance of purpose." His gaze sharpened. "If not to use Solan, what did you intend by coming here?"

"It's a long story."

"And one I'd like to hear."

So I confessed my vision of the Lady of Ravens, and all the information I'd pieced together of her workings and the power of the sacrifice she'd made, one that all the efforts of the fae lords and ladies after her could not fully eradicate. I ran my fingers across the ferns, and their green deepened, their soft fronds curling about my skin. "When our efforts with Solan failed, I'd thought . . ."

I couldn't say it, not with him looking at me like that. Yet I didn't need to.

"You meant to sacrifice your own life to trigger the workings and transform Kilmere." He stood abruptly, his eyes dark. "That's why you pressed for a bargain. Did you entertain the thought even then?"

"Yes. I feared the time would come when I'd have no choice."

"Even then, you could have sought to control it."

"If I had, it would have remained forever a threat. It needed to be given new purpose, for my . . . for the mortal world to remain secure." Soft sunbeams filtered over the age-darkened stones, and I lowered my gaze. "And for my own peace, I needed to know that even as I accepted my Other nature, I did not have to embrace all of its ways."

"And you what? Intended me to take note of the change and

rebuild Kilmere around your dead body?" The edge to his voice sliced against my raw emotions.

"It was hardly a plan I favored—but yes. I meant to explain it in full before Mr. Ludne ever came, not spring it on you unaware." Another shard of pain pierced my side. "I'm sorry I didn't tell you sooner."

"That's not what I—never mind, it doesn't matter." All traces of emotion vanished, and his voice became distant. "I need to tend the bodies, satisfy the Court of Silver with answers. You'll be safe enough with Jade for now, but don't leave this spot."

With that, he stalked from the keep.

For the record, I disapprove equally.

But . . . you'll forgive me?

Jade merely glared at me, her face only a handbreadth from my own.

You're right. Of everyone, I should have told you. Because my choice would have cost you the most. Earlier, I just—didn't want to think about it. Then, when it became apparent there was no other way forward, I needed a few moments to gather my resolve.

She chuffed. *What you said when we arrived at Kilmere, about being glad I was* kit-isne . . .

I meant it, despite my fears when I first learned the truth. Now I could not imagine you anything else.

Then you do not mind my true-form?

Not at all—in fact, I favor it. And right now, with exhaustion clinging to me like ivy on a brick wall, I wanted nothing more than to sink into her rich fur and let her warmth drive back my pain.

Then you shall. Her warm nose pressed against my cheek. *And I shall forgive you for leaving me from your counsel, as long as you don't make so free with your life again.*

I cannot promise what the future will hold, only that I will not conceal my purpose from you again. I curled up against her immense side, her steady purr filling my ears, the beat of her heart a soothing pulse.

About us, Kilmere had been unmade and reformed, and the full nature of its new making remained to be seen, yet its awareness filtered into my mind. It was still sharp-edged and fierce, as the Lady of Ravens had been, its immeasurable might undiminished, but it no longer sought to claim others, to soak the land in blood, but rather to strengthen and protect.

And in it, I was at peace—despite all my unanswered questions, despite all the threats that remained. I twined my hands in Jade's fur.

I might feel satisfied, but what of Riven? Clearly, he'd been displeased with my choice to act without sharing information with him—and I could not blame him, given I'd condemned him for doing the same when we'd dealt with Uros. In this case, however, I hadn't been unwilling to tell him, I'd merely lacked opportunity.

Perhaps it will do him good, not to always possess the answers. Her pleasure at the notion tinged my mind. *But what did you mean before, when you thought of your affinities working in harmony with Riven's?*

It's difficult to explain. I still don't quite understand it.

Then let me see what happened.

I allowed the memory to flow back through my mind, every detail vivid.

And Jade lifted her head from the ground, rumbling low in her chest. *I knew I shouldn't have left you alone with him.*

With difficulty, I pressed upright also. *Why? What's wrong?*

You once worried about the propriety of holding his hand . . .

Does hand-holding contravene fae standards as well as mortal?

She chuffed. *No, they are far more liberal when it comes to touch. Even if you'd flung yourself into his arms, they'd not deem it improper—only an act of great folly, for he could smite you for the offense.*

Fortunately, there was no smiting. I tilted my head. *What etiquette did I breach, if not that of touch?*

You asked to draw upon his power.

But—I said nothing.

You didn't need to. Your own affinities spoke for you.

I sank back against her side. *Do fae ordinarily share power?*

It's quite rare, because it's so dangerous.

Nearby, the rowan rustled restlessly, stirred by my unease. *How so?*

Because to ask another fae if you might share his or her power requires tremendous vulnerability. You cannot ask without first offering your own power. In such a position, the requestee has power to claim all. Riven could have taken everything from you, offering nothing in return. No fae wishes to initiate such an exchange and chance having their affinities ripped from them. Therefore, it's rare, even frowned upon—despite the great advantages it can offer.

Warmth flooded my face. I'd violated a fae standard I hadn't known existed, and somehow managed to contravene the conventions of both worlds in one act. Yet Riven had said nothing of it. *Since he clearly did not take advantage of the situation, what does that mean?*

That you owe him a debt.

And I already owed him more than I could ever repay. I sighed. "You cannot think he means me harm, not after everything that has happened."

I do not know what to make of his actions—they are not what one would expect. I would give much for a peek into his mind.

I buried my fingers in her thick, fragrant fur. *So would I. Yet I cannot take back what I did. Should I try to make amends in some way?*

Best not to bring it up. I'm sure he's aware you don't understand the ways of our world.

Yet I remained mortified . . . and so very weary. The soothing sensation of the antidote crept into my limbs, weighting me with drowsiness, and I drifted into a light sleep. Only the pricking sensations of a passing drew me to wakefulness. Riven strode back into the keep, and I had difficulty meeting his gaze. If he perceived my discomfort, he blessedly chose to ignore it—and it appeared he'd also abandoned his anger, for he settled easily alongside us.

I collected my courage and spoke. "Thank you for . . ." *Not stripping away whatever burgeoning affinities I possessed, for coming into the Court of Silver after me, for lending power to transform Kilmere . . .* ". . . for standing with me."

He didn't rebuke my offering as he'd done before, only nodded. "You're welcome."

"What did you do with Lord West and Solan?" I asked, stroking the starflower patch on Jade's chest.

"I brought their bodies to a place of convening, where I met with the arbiter from the Court of Silver," Riven said.

"He believed your report about Solan killing Lord West?"

"He would have preferred to do otherwise, but he could find no lie."

"Will your king be angry?"

"Far from it. He'll appreciate the subtlety of using a weapon against its wielder, as well as the result—Damir dead with no conflict between our courts. I could not withhold from the other arbiter that there were mortals present, not when truth was compelled, but I kept your identity out of it. Everyone knows Damir likes his playthings, but they don't think of mortals as individuals, particularly, and I doubt anyone will inquire further." He braced his hands against his legs. "There was posturing around my decision to enter the Court of Silver, but when I told the arbiter you were mine first, it settled matters."

"Yours?"

"We had a bargain long before Damir set his sights on you. As well as one when I entered the Court of Silver." Riven inclined his head. "It gave me grounds to act."

Jade's purr of approval resounded in my ears.

And now that Lord West was gone . . . "The young man from Withern that Lord West claimed. Did you perceive any hint of him in the demesne? Might we fetch him back?"

"We cannot venture into the Court of Silver again—we're

fortunate it caused no open hostilities between courts as it is. Even if we did, a mortal claimed by bargain would have been left with his estate, presumably to his son."

His son. He'd hinted once at having use for another child, and I shuddered to think what the boy—likely a man now—might have endured, what he might have become with Lord West as his father, and what might become of the mortal taken from Withern and held captive in the Otherworld, if he even still lived. Riven had once said not all could be spared, but knowing the truth and experiencing its reality were two entirely different things.

I leaned against Jade, her warmth bolstering me. "There's something else—about Lord West being Edward. I don't understand why he ever left Ibbie, and why he chose to come back when he did." Not to mention what it meant for Wyncourt, a demesne of his creation, and what might lie hidden in its depths.

"I imagine he tired of her—he'd taken what power and pleasure he could from the situation, and he'd no further need of her. Besides, it's never wise to be absent too long from court. You lose advantages, and he'd not tolerate that." The wind drove clouds overhead, shadowing Riven's face. "Moreover, he'd no reason to believe he could not return and take what he wished whenever he wished. If your Ibbie had left Kilmere to anyone but you, he could have reclaimed it with very little effort."

At least in protecting it, I'd honored Ibbie—and in some way, avenged all she'd suffered at his hands.

"Yet from some source unknown, he found information at an inconvenient time that revealed its true nature, as well as hints of the basilisk and dawn-dagger within. How that must have irked him, to know he'd once possessed it and let it escape his grasp." His hands tightened. "I'd like very much to know how he learned the truth."

As would I. The timing in which everything had unfolded, coming on the heels of so many Otherworldly incursions, appeared more than coincidental. "Uros said destruction was coming from the Otherworld to this one. I don't understand how that can be, if some protection remains."

"Certain elements are . . . quickly eroding." Riven spoke slowly, softly, as if he expected any moment the geas would steal his words. "The fault lies in your world, yet it may well have been sparked by my own."

In the distance, gulls released a piercing cry. Would open conflict between worlds arise again? I could not think mortals would come out ahead, yet somehow they'd not been destroyed before. I must understand what had happened, what might yet come. "It's not a plot of the rulers of your courts?"

"Not from my own. The king could not conceal such a thing from me." Bits of light wafted around Riven. "If I must make a guess, some individual or collective seeks to control worlds, to manipulate a conflict between them—to restore what once was. But I've no evidence to support this, not yet."

If that were true, then not only was my family in danger— my entire world was truly at risk. When Uros suggested as much, I'd thought it another of his lies, but if Riven believed it too . . . "I have to get home."

With Jade as a support, I struggled to my feet. I could move now without the blinding pain, and only a nagging ache remained at my middle. "But first, we need the antidote. Solan told me goldleaf basil could cure mortals of her venom, when properly crafted. When we first came to Kilmere, I saw it growing along the far wall, but it cannot be used as it is—she said it must be purified somehow. She showed me how one of the fae lords crafted it, but I didn't understand."

"Remember your affinities will respond to your intent," Riven said. "Collect what you need, then you may perceive the rest."

Since I'd nothing else to go on, I must try. We made for the seaward wall, where the goldleaf basil flourished. The plants spread broad and bountiful, the shimmering golden hues of their spreading leaves catching in the sunlight, their song ever sprightly.

If only I'd known then the remedy the goldleaf offered—yet there was still time, not only for Ada, but for the woman in Dr. Fulton's care. If I was right, we'd need a great deal of the herb to distill its strength into something potent enough to counteract the venom of the basilisk. The images from Solan had shown the herb collected into a large glass basin. Then the fae lord had done—something. Used some sort of working that teased a rich, golden liquid from the leaves.

Could I replicate it? I didn't have the least scrap of knowledge, but if I failed . . . all that I'd done would be for nothing.

I'd lose Ada.

I bound my fears deep in my chest, then stooped to collect the plants. They surged to greet me, their leaves brightening with an eager glow. Gently, I detached sprigs, and its sharp scent cut the air.

"Did you see where the fae worked to prepare the antidote?" Riven asked. "Was it within Kilmere?"

"Yes, Solan indicated as much."

"Can you find it again?"

"I can try." Somewhat reluctantly, I pressed my hand against the stone wall, and it sparked to life beneath my touch, Kilmere conceding my right to its knowledge. Its chambers unfurled in my mind's eye, a far greater expanse than we'd even begun to explore. "It was in a small chamber connected to the heart."

"You should fashion the tincture there. Use his tools. It might help, might hold some echo of his workings."

We'd have to pass through the undercroft again, traverse the remains of the dragon in the heart, and enter a smaller crypt alongside, but I refused to fear the depths any longer.

Life did not give way before death. Rather, death must surrender before life, always. The place that had imprisoned the suffering as they died would become a place that gave life to others—in some way redeemed.

With our bounty of rich leaves, we descended, and this time all the doors remained open to our passing, no locks, no tricks or deceits, no sacrifice in blood required. Threads of gold and white lined the walls, leading the way through passages of stone and into the heart.

Riven moved to explore one of the newly opened antechambers branching off the heart, perhaps previously concealed by other blood locks. Yet I hesitated.

The agony the dragon had endured still twisted my chest, but when I skimmed my hand across an ivory bone, I no longer sensed its struggle or its pain, only the quiet peace of one gone beyond. The new awareness within Kilmere, vibrant and living, beckoned to me.

As I leaned into the sensations, something warm and brilliant pressed itself into my awareness, as bright as a star buried within stone. Could it be that Kilmere held pleasant surprises that had awaited revelation until its malice was stripped away? I moved toward the gentle ripple of warmth, until I stood near where the heart of the dragon must have once rested.

There.

Scarlet sigils spiraled around a small door in the wall. Neither sigils nor door had revealed themselves in our previous examinations of the heart—instead, they'd chosen this time. A peace offering from Kilmere, perhaps?

As I eased the door open, some small part of me still feared a gruesome discovery. My breath caught. The niche contained not some gory relict, but a golden dagger.

Jade gave a low rumble, and I froze in place. Though the craftsmanship surpassed that in my dream, I couldn't mistake it. This was the coveted dawn-dagger that had presumably drawn Lord West back, that Riven would surely have to mention to his king, if he knew of its presence.

Had the fae who crafted Kilmere concealed it here for safekeeping?

No matter.

I slammed the door shut and braced my back against it, my heart thrumming. Better to leave it here for a time. I trusted Kilmere would keep it hidden and safe—and right now, I couldn't afford to remove anything that would draw more attention to me or my family. The ruins had attracted Lord West. What other foes might the dawn-dagger draw, if I dared take it into my possession?

Would it carry a trace of Other, a signature that would betray its presence? If so, I hadn't the knowledge or skill to conceal it, not yet. I needed time to navigate my bewildering new truths, not draw more Otherworldly attention by claiming a valuable artifact.

Riven emerged from the antechamber he'd entered, and I moved away from the niche, toward a second chamber, the one impressed upon me when I sought its location from Kilmere. Together, we entered the room.

Open stone shelving contained all sorts of implements— mortars and pestles of all sizes, large glass basins, small bottles, and the like. It reminded me of my compounding room, only on a far grander scale. I walked over to the collection of basins and selected a large one with a clear stoppered pipe leading from it. If I rested it on the stone shelf and placed a bottle beneath, I could collect the tincture as I'd seen the fae do in Solan's memories. I deposited the gold-tinged leaves within, and their pungent fragrance filled the air, driving back the scents of dust and minerals.

Then I looked at Riven. "Can you tell me what to do?"

"I've no affinity for plants. In this, you must find your own way. Seek the truest nature of what's before you."

Could it be so simple? Perhaps it was, for as I sought to connect with the leaves in the basin, a resonant hum filled my mind and threads of green wove about them, drawing forth a rich sap-like substance. It pooled in the bottom of the basin, then spilled out drop by drop into the bottle placed below.

The liquid looked a bit different from the image Solan had

placed in my mind, thicker, perhaps, and a bit more brilliant. Was that a virtue of her memory being hazy? Or a misstep on my part? Either way, I could do nothing but wait for the slow process to continue. "Riven, you said before that fae medicine could destroy a mortal body. If I've crafted this with Other power, won't it hurt Ada?"

"These plants aren't of my world—their essence should be compatible with your own, and you saw them used on mortals effectively. Further, you crafted them with the express purpose of mortal healing." He examined the row of bottles on the shelf. "There's a risk, yes, but certain death outweighs it."

With that, I must be content—but it was small comfort. When the bottle was full and the leaves spent, we made our way back to the surface. As we neared the boundary stones of Kilmere, Riven said, "There's another matter we must discuss, that of the authorities involved in this affair. The Vigil has been led astray, and if they seek to return, they'll see nothing out of the ordinary. But the Magistry's case remains unsolved."

With difficulty, I wrenched my thoughts from Ada and the victim kept by Dr. Fulton and the precious tincture I held. "Do you have a suggestion?"

"That Burke and I finish what's been started here by producing the snake that bit Ada and poisoned the other victims."

"How? You had to leave Solan with Lord West." I picked my way across a scattering of stones, Jade padding alongside, still in true-form.

"It will be an illusion. And it will vanish after examination, which will confirm to them that Burke was right about an Otherworldly culprit and ease any suspicions they may have that he conceals something." Riven halted just beyond the wall. "It will be suggested to them that the creature was responsible for the recent deaths and all those before, that it nested within Kilmere these many years, becoming disturbed by the recent incursions, and that it was the culprit behind the legends of the curse."

The tale held enough truth that Riven and Mr. Burke should be able to pass it off, enough perhaps to satisfy the Magistry and the Vigil alike, to protect the innocent and lay the blame in part where it was deserved. Even so, the enmity Mr. Ludne bore wasn't likely to be erased by it, not when I'd thwarted his will so directly. "Must I be involved?"

"I suggest you allow Burke and me to manage the authorities, while you see to the cure—and after, assuaging the concerns of your family."

A task I dreaded more than the prospect of facing the Magistry. They'd have questions impossible to answer. Riven had advised silence about my true nature, but how could I continue to keep the truth concealed? Yet if I told them, what then? If they didn't cast me out, they'd be embracing danger from both the Otherworld and our own. Remnants of the poison stirred within my stomach.

Never mind that now. Before I could consider unfolding the truth, I must see Ada cured. Within the bottle, the tincture glinted with a golden hue, rich and vivid and living.

Would it be sufficient?

When Riven brought us through the passing to the small copse of trees just outside of Willowere, I practically ran toward the cottage, my fist clenched around the antidote. Where had they taken Ada? Would she be at Dr. Fulton's or had they kept her at home? I could not imagine Aunt Caris surrendering her readily, even into the care of the doctor. I surged through the front door, and the sound of hushed voices drew me into the drawing room.

In the doorway, I stumbled to a halt. Far too many people clustered into the room for my safety—Mr. Redgrave and Elodie, Mr. Burke and Dreda, my aunts and Ainslie, all of them bent over some sort of map, discussing a search. For me?

At my back, Riven stood warm and steady, preventing me from fleeing the room, and Jade in lesser-form stalked in before me.

At the sound of her *mrow*, Ainslie glanced up. "Jessa!" She ran across the room and flung her arms around me. "We were so very afraid. Mr. Burke said if anyone could find you, it would be Lord Riven, but then the hours kept passing and . . . to have you gone, and Ada . . . It felt beyond bearing."

Aunt Caris bustled over and pulled both Ainslie and I close, her familiar warmth a comfort I might lose forever. My throat tightened.

In the background, Mr. Burke addressed Riven. "What of West?"

"He's been removed from the picture."

Only Mr. Redgrave appeared to attend their exchange. The ladies all clustered about me, and even Dreda offered an embrace after Aunt Caris released us. Though Elodie allowed Ainslie and my aunts space, she gave me a relieved smile. "I'm so glad to see you restored. When we heard what happened, Charles and I feared the worst. A man so unhinged as to abduct a woman in broad daylight . . ."

"It's unthinkable. Thank the Infinite you're safe." Aunt Caris brushed a curl from my face. "I should have listened when you spoke of your fears of Lord West, when Alden voiced his own objections, but I never dreamt he'd act so."

"You're not hurt, are you?" Ainslie pulled back to inspect me in all my disarray. "We could find no trace of Lord West or where he'd taken you, not even Mr. Burke, but he told us we shouldn't involve the rest of the stratesmen—"

"Quite right." Aunt Melisina sniffed. "Just think of the scandal."

Evidently Mr. Burke had won her approval with his discretion. Now he stepped toward us, his relief clear. "It was evident that Lord West had become unbalanced, if he would dare to conduct an abduction using alchemical devices to conceal his movements. Since Lord Riven has considerable experience with such cases, I felt involving others would only complicate the situation further."

Bless Mr. Burke for conjuring such a convincing tale, one that my aunts and sisters clearly accepted as fact. Yet Mr. Redgrave eyed me with a speculative gaze that left me unsettled. Which part of the tale did he doubt?

"Indeed, I owe a tremendous debt to Lord Riven." Whether he acknowledged it or not, it was the unsettling truth.

"We all do." Aunt Caris extended a hand toward him. "Thank you for finding Jessa, for freeing her. If you had not—" Her voice broke.

"I did only what needed to be done."

Before he could make a claim, if he was minded to, I hurried on. "There's more. It's no coincidence that the snake struck Ada in Lord West's presence. He kept it close and released it as it pleased him to poison the victims in Withern."

Aunt Caris paled. "To think, we allowed him into our home time and again, never knowing his true nature."

"Jessa did say she didn't trust him." Ainslie kept firm hold of my arm, as if she feared I'd disappear before her eyes once more.

"Not that he was a murderous abductor and attempted ruiner of women!" Aunt Caris pressed her handkerchief to her lips. "And now Ada—"

"How is she?" I asked.

"Gravely ill." Mr. Burke's brows drew together. "Dr. Fulton is with her now."

Ainslie blinked back tears. "We couldn't let him take her away. He sent us out so he could tend her, but we've kept watch, and to see her suffer so . . ."

Mr. Redgrave stepped so close to Ainslie that their shoulders almost touched. Her body curved ever so slightly toward his, as though she wished to take refuge in his presence, and her lips trembled. "He does not know what to do for her, no more than he did the others. And I do not know how we are to bear it."

Aunt Caris collapsed inward, as though her strength failed her, and even Aunt Melisina looked older in that moment, pale and worn.

"Perhaps we shall not have to," I murmured. "One good thing came of Lord West seizing me—he brought me to his dwelling, and there I saw a cure used for victims of the snakebite."

"You mean the man knew all along the remedy for the dying? And he watched them suffer for entertainment?" Mr.

Redgrave clutched his walking stick as if he'd like to beat Lord West with it.

"I believe ruling over their deaths satisfied him in some way." That much I could say in truth.

Elodie shuddered. "What a dreadful man. Did he come here to enact his perverse desires because he knew tales of the curse would confuse the authorities and conceal his deeds?"

"Who is to say what moves another?" I lifted the bottle. "Yet if this cure works, we can undo some of the harm he caused."

Ainslie's eyes widened. "If there's any chance, we must take it to Dr. Fulton at once."

Her arm locked in mine, she swept me from the room, and her hope buoyed my own. With our aunts close behind, we hastened into the bedchamber.

Ada lay on the bed, her breath ragged and a sheen of perspiration covering her gray-tinged skin. The sharp scent of sick pervaded the air, stronger than the aromas of the rosemary and rue compress Dr. Fulton had placed on her head. She moaned softly, then began to writhe beneath the bedcovers, clutching at her chest.

I stepped forward. Oh, please, let this work. "Dr. Fulton, I believe I've found what you sought—a remedy for the poison."

"How . . . how is this possible?" Behind his spectacles, the lines about his eyes smoothed. "You are sure?"

"As sure as I can be."

"If you as her family agree, then I will not stand in the way —but I cannot predict the results of some unknown remedy."

Aunt Melisina spoke. "It's this or we lose her. We'll take the chance."

I unstopped the bottle. The thick golden liquid held the sharp spice of basil, but something else too, a fresh, bright scent, like that of sunlight on an open meadow. It swept through the room, driving back the stale odors of sweat and vomit. I could not rouse Ada, so I allowed the smallest drop to fall into her mouth. After a moment, I repeated the procedure.

One.

Two.

Three.

She stopped writhing, became deadly still. Not a sound broke the silence. What did it mean? If I gave her more, would it choke her? Would it break the hold of the venom? Or what if I'd crafted something unsuitable for mortals after all, and only hastened her death? How was I to know?

Oh.

Beneath the pallor of her skin, a rich golden glow sparked. Could the others see it? Heartened, I ventured one more drop, then another. And her eyes blinked open.

"Jessa, you're here." A soft smile curved her lips. "You're safe."

Why had she worried about my well-being when death encroached upon her body, when venom burned through her veins? My voice emerged choked. "And now you will be also."

I wanted to linger, but instead I turned to Dr. Fulton, who appeared dumbfounded. "Have you another empty bottle?"

Wordless, he fetched one from inside his leather satchel.

I poured some of the tincture into it. "For the other who suffers."

With that, he accepted and flew out the door without so much as a by-your-leave, forgetting propriety in his haste to save his other suffering patient.

Then we clustered about the bed, Aunt Caris and I on one side, Ainslie and Aunt Melisina on the other, all craving the assurance that Ada was truly well.

When I glanced up, Mr. Redgrave waited in the doorway, Elodie alongside him. Unlike the others, he wasn't watching Ada. Rather, his gaze remained fixed on me. Did he have doubts about my story? About all that had happened? If he was as astute as he appeared, he must wonder about my abrupt disappearance and return with a remedy. It defied all natural expectations, and he did not have the emotions of my aunts and sisters to cloud his judgment, nor the knowledge of Other involvement that Mr. Burke possessed by way of explanation.

Ainslie looked up and caught sight of him in the doorway, and she broke into a radiant smile, which he returned. I wrapped my arms about myself. If he and Ainslie grew closer—if one day he offered for her and she accepted—what would that mean? If I confided my nature in her, would she be duty bound to confess it to him?

Before that time came, I must uncover the truth about the Redgraves. How else could I be sure Mr. Redgrave could be trusted with Ainslie? I did not believe the kindnesses they'd shown could be feigned, but a myriad of small details didn't quite add up—the unusual interest in Kilmere and determination to explore it, the parasol-sword and self-confessed family passion for collecting unusual weaponry, even the knowledge with which they approached the assessment and treating of wounds. When we returned to Avons, I'd seek more information about their family . . . and hope that whatever they concealed, it would do no great harm.

Yet what if Mr. Redgrave held the same resolve to uncover more about me? Jade wove about my ankles, and I lifted her, despite the protest of my injured shoulder. Each day it grew harder to conceal my Other nature, and I'd already roused the suspicions of the Vigil. If others began to perceive my peculiarities, it would only spell disaster. Yet I could do nothing about it now, only keep watch over Ada as she recovered—and rest in the knowledge the curse was broken at last.

THREE DAYS LATER, I sat on a wicker bench in the gardens absorbing the early morning sun and the quiet murmurs of the willows along the lake. Without the shadow of Kilmere tainting it, I could finally appreciate the charms of Withern, the slight tang of the nearby sea, the lush gardens of Willowere, and the sweet freshness to the air.

Jade curled up on my lap, and I stroked her head. Asrina should have been with us, her warm light bathing the scene.

To stand against the wielders of power has a great cost. And yet, I believe if she could have seen the outcome, she still would have chosen as she did.

I hope so. How long would it be before these losses ceased to draw such deep pain? Riven would say the answer was to hold all at a distance, to deny feelings their sway. Yet I increasingly had the sense he did not follow his own counsel.

Several hours after I'd healed Ada, I'd stolen away to the gardens to speak to him. He'd waited for me in this exact place so we might exchange words without an audience.

"You must go, I suppose."

"I've kept absent from my court long enough, and I need to give an account to the king of our dealings with Damir. I can keep him waiting no longer."

"And . . . do you mean to return?" He'd said he'd help investigate the truth of my nature, but I wasn't sure what that entailed.

"I'm given to understand there's a mortal custom of calling on one's friends."

"We do hold to such peculiar ways, yes."

"Besides, we have a great deal yet to solve." He hesitated, then said, "Before I go, there's someone who wants to meet you."

As he spoke, a tiny figure materialized next to him in a gleaming burst of light, in form so like Asrina that I could not draw breath. This sun sylph possessed hair of silvery blue, her wings a glorious iridescent hue to match.

She fluttered in front of my face, surveying me, then nodded. "Yes. I'll stay."

I pressed my fingers to my lips and shook my head. If I had to watch another sylph die . . .

Her wings flared brighter. Riven held up a hand as if to quiet her, then turned to me. "We need some means of communication. Other options may present themselves as your affinities grow. For now, this is simplest."

"I can't risk anyone else."

"Not even one who has volunteered as a companion in honor of her hatch-sister?"

A blade of grief pierced my chest. I'd resolved to accept help when offered, to allow others their choices. How then could I deny this sylph the opportunity to honor the memory of Asrina? "What's your name, lovely one?"

"Risha. In light messages, Asrina told me much of you." Her eyes burned with blue flame. "She told me that you are kind, that you change things. I want to see. To help. To remember her."

The blade twisted deeper. "And what if you share her fate?"

"Is always a risk, for sylph. This way, I choose the risk. I honor her, I make change come."

She was far bolder and more vocal than Asrina, but I should not compare the two, whatever their close connection. No one could ever replace Asrina, but if her hatch-sister intended to honor her, I must embrace that. "Then I accept, with deepest gratitude."

"Good, good." She fluttered to rest on the willow limb behind me.

Riven stood. "I must go, but Jessa . . ."

I looked up at him.

Light danced in his eyes, transforming them to the vibrant green of new spring leaves. "Next time don't wait till you've nearly been murdered by a fae lord before sending word. A maiming or minor assault would suffice."

The tension in my chest released, and I laughed. "Duly noted."

He looked as if he might say something more, but Aunt Melisina entered the gardens, calling for me. Since my so-called abduction, she and Aunt Caris had been determined not to allow me to slip long from sight, as though they feared some other miscreant lurked, waiting to snatch me away. As she drew near, Riven vanished into the trees, and soon after, the surge of power from a passing marked his departure from our world, an absence that left me oddly unmoored.

"There you are." Aunt Melisina surged through the boughs of a willow. Rather than chastise me for sitting hatless out of doors in the gathering evening, she settled onto the chair next to me and proceeded to share news of all the upheaval in Withern since the scandalous news about Lord West had broken.

"It seems Mr. Burke took it on himself to carry the news of Lord West's nefarious deeds to the Holloways, with Mr. Redgrave as support, since he's a good friend of the family," she said. "Lady Cadence has taken to her bed, by all accounts."

"I'm very sorry. She didn't deserve to be taken in by him." Yet she was fortunate his life had ended before he could claim hers. How narrow an escape she'd had.

"Indeed not. For all that she can be rather insufferable, she acted in good faith when she accepted his proposal." Aunt Melisina's lips tightened. "I called upon Lady Holloway this morning, and the events have near prostrated her also."

I didn't quite know how to respond. Aunt Melisina had never deigned to share gossip with me before, nor hold a conversation that didn't include some amount of criticism.

"At least the notion of the curse has been put to rest. Even the Denbys have let the matter go." She inclined her head toward me. "As a matter of fact, this afternoon Lady Denby asked me to tell you that she's glad you paid no heed to her advice."

That was more concession than I'd ever expected from any in Withern, but then, they'd no notion of the full tale, only the story we'd agreed to present of the snake held captive by Lord West. In truth, I still had more gaps in my own understanding than I desired, most particularly about my abilities and my future.

Even now, a day later, they plagued me, the number of questions about my affinities and nature growing by the hour. I leaned back in the wicker bench with Jade in my lap, listening to the soft melodies of the willows. So far, I'd excused myself from revealing the painful truth to my family because I did not want Ada to bear any shock that might hinder her recovery.

Yet now she was much herself again, and still I struggled. What would I say? How could I explain it? With my confession, I'd shatter their worlds as my own had been—shatter their view of Mother and our past. And of me. What would happen if they sent me away? Pain pricked my heart, as sharp as the thorns of the wild rose swaying across from me.

Do you think their love for you so small? Jade asked.

No, I think the test so great. All mortals fear fae. I have done so myself, thinking they could be nothing but the cruel figures from our lore. And many, perhaps even most, were. *How can I expect them to embrace this revelation?*

Whether they do or not, we will make a home together. She nuzzled my chin. *Though I know it's small comfort.*

It's more than a small comfort, but . . . I do not think I can endure a total severing of these ties. I sighed, and the branches of the willows swayed toward me.

Instead of my fears about what must come, for now I'd think of Kilmere, of what *its* future might hold, of what secrets might still rest hidden in its depths. Mr. Tibbons had called yesterday afternoon, and though he'd confessed to having spent several days laid low with an uncommon-to-him headache, I'd found him otherwise undaunted by his trials and determined as ever to explore Kilmere. Were his pains the price for extricating the truth of his encounters with Lord West? I hoped not. It was yet another question to add to my list for Riven.

As for Kilmere, Mr. Tibbons remembered only his interest in it and none of the exploration he'd done—to him, it was the same promising unknown it had been before he'd encountered Lord West and been driven to the depths. Perhaps he might be trusted to explore it in the future, but I must spend more time there myself first to determine the best path forward.

And it wasn't only Mr. Tibbons who was curious about Kilmere. I owed a great deal of information to Lord Blackburn as well, if only I could decide which pieces were safe to share. Though I'd no wish to provide an account to him, I'd become increasingly desirous of a return to Avons. So many unanswered questions remained—the mysteries of the Forgotten War, the Redgraves and the peculiarities surrounding them, Wyncourt and what lay concealed in its depths, even the odd display of Otherworldly plants supplied by the mystery donor to the Botanic Gardens. These and many others might more easily be investigated with the wealth of resources Avons offered. Yet Aunt Caris wished to wait a few days more to ensure Ada had truly regained her strength before undertaking the trip, and I couldn't deny the wisdom of such a plan.

Surveying the gardens, I toyed with a pencil from my sketching basket. Withern offered such rich botanical life, and I'd captured so little of it during our time here. Once I would have seized upon the opportunity offered by travel to expand my herbalism manuscript, but now . . . I'd hardly given the project a second thought since Ibbie died, since the knowledge of the Otherworld had upended my own.

An ache formed in my chest as I tucked the pencil back into the basket. However much there might be need for such a guide, I couldn't do the work justice, not right now. Perhaps a time would come when things felt simpler again, when my world would right itself and I could blend new knowledge with old to improve the whole . . . I must cling to that hope. Absently, I stroked the petals of a cheery primrose peeping over the edge of the bench and considered the choices before me until the crunch of boots on crushed shell broke into my thoughts.

Dreda appeared, walking sedately down the garden path. We'd yet to have an opportunity to speak in private, but perhaps now I'd get the answers I craved.

She sank down beside me on the bench, twining her fingers in her lap. "Jessa, might we speak a moment?"

I sat up straighter. "Of course."

"There's something I've been wondering. Something worrying me."

"Whatever it is, it's better to ask than live in fear." Only whatever would she say?

"Is Lord West . . . is he fae? I know the Vigil says high fae can't come to Byren, but he—I—please don't be upset that I've asked." The words came out in a tremendous rush, and she stared at her hands in her lap.

"Why do you ask?"

"When we spoke that time with Dr. Fulton, I felt so peculiar. That necklace, the one you gave me, got warm like a sunbeam, and then his words . . . They seemed so strange. Like they were full of shadows. And I remembered you said the necklace would protect me against fae influence." She clasped her hands tighter, the knuckles whitening. "Even so, it felt as if I could not fully clear my thoughts. And then Lady Cadence, her actions were so strange. I didn't want to speak of them to anyone, in case he'd snared her as I was once snared . . . I didn't know what to do."

"I see." The primrose shuddered beneath my fingers. "You're right—he was high fae."

"Was?"

"He's gone for good now. It's for the best that you kept Lady Cadence's deeds quiet, since she wasn't of sound mind when she acted."

She exhaled. "Then I'm very glad to hear he'll trouble us no more."

"As am I. While you're here, there's something I've been wondering myself. He said that he compelled you to give my family a false tale, yet you told them the truth when I disappeared after the ball. How?"

"When it came to it, I knew I must speak as he'd

commanded, because when I tried to think of holding back the words, the pain near split me in two—but I knew it wasn't truth, and I didn't want to betray you. Then a thought came to me. He'd said I must carry the tale, and somehow he'd muddled me enough that I'd agreed, but he'd not said how loud I must speak it." A small smile quirked her lips. "So I went to your sisters and whispered it real quiet. They couldn't hear it a bit in the crowded ballroom. And then I told them the truth."

Sudden laughter bubbled in my chest. "Dreda, you're a treasure."

She flushed and ducked her head. "I've been thinking something else, too. If high fae can enter Byren, then nothing in life is sure. I ought to have known it already, after my own fae-touch —but it seems matters are worse than I've feared."

"And I've dragged you deeper into them. I'm sorry."

"Please don't apologize." Her hazel eyes brightened. "You've given me purpose, and I don't regret it."

"Does that mean you wish to continue serving as my chaperone?"

She nodded. "Though what chaperoning I'm doing, I'm sure I don't know. It feels more like I'm conspiring instead."

"Perhaps you are. Either way, I'm thankful for it."

"Then it's settled. Only there's one thing more. If you're still willing, I'd like to have those drawing books you mentioned." Her smile widened. "I think it's time I started to learn something new."

I clasped her hand. "Nothing would please me more."

The sound of hooves on the lane drew both of our attentions. I peered through the trees and caught a glimpse of Mr. Burke riding toward Willowere.

Dreda pressed to her feet. "If I'm not mistaken, you'd like to speak with Mr. Burke alone?"

"If it's not too much trouble."

"No trouble at all. I was minded to walk about the lake

anyway." With a rustle of skirts, she departed, and a few moments later, Mr. Burke appeared.

He took the chair across from me. "Forgive the early call, but now that this case is considered closed, I must return to Avons. I didn't want to depart without a final word."

"Thank you. We're to follow in a few days, once Dr. Fulton deems Ada recovered enough to travel." I inhaled the scents of primrose and greenery. "May I ask what conclusions have been drawn by the authorities?"

"The Vigil immediately brought in king hawks to search the area for any other venomous snakes, though given the clear Otherworldly nature of the one discovered, it wasn't surprising that they found no others." His level voice gave no hint of the trouble he may have fielded. "They've concluded the presence of this creature concealed within Kilmere gave rise to stories of the curse, as it likely shared the long life of most Otherkind. Further, based on my report and his actions, they've judged Lord West the responsible party for reawakening and releasing the creature to prey upon the inhabitants of Withern. They say his unnatural interest in Kilmere—and possible fae-touch—drove him to a dark end. There's a young farmhand who disappeared during all this, and they're placing the blame for that on West's account as well."

"A very tidy resolution."

"Indeed." His features tightened. "But Mr. Ludne didn't seem as pleased as I would have expected. He hasn't made so bold as to enter Kilmere, since he has no just cause, but he seeks one. He and his men have spent an inordinate amount of time scrutinizing an ancient tree that sprang up seemingly overnight outside the ruins. It seems the town is abuzz about it as well. I've heard all sorts of speculation. Most say it's a good omen, one that signifies the breaking of the curse, but some believe it's a warning that Kilmere still holds dangers within. I assume Riven was responsible?"

"I . . . I cannot speak of it." Because if I did, I must confess the whole. My shoulders tightened. If Mr. Burke had any notion of my heritage, would he turn me in himself? He'd proven a true friend and one willing to work with fae, if the circumstances demanded, but if he believed me a threat to the people of Byren . . .

He did not press, only gave a slight nod. "I warned you against interacting with fae before, and I think it all the more vital now. You've made an enemy in Ludne. He'll be watching you closely."

"Thank you for the warning."

A sigh gusted from him. "But you have no intention of heeding it."

Warmth prickled up my chest. "It's not that I disagree, but —I fear it will be impossible. You must admit there's something happening now between the Otherworld and our own. We cannot hide from it or simply wish it away."

He regarded me with his kestrel gaze, as though he might prize out my secrets. "I'll grant that much. But it doesn't require your involvement. At least consider what I've said."

"I will." Indeed, I didn't think I could cast off the weight of his words readily—any more than I could shed whatever part of my nature was fae.

When he departed, a hush settled over the garden, but it was soon broken once more—if I'd wanted solitude, clearly I should have chosen a different location.

"Jessa?" Ada called. She hastened down the path, faster than was wise for her recovery, her features pale and pinched.

My pulse hitched. The primroses rustled, and in the distance the snapdragons pulsed. Something was wrong.

Jade's ears pricked, and the fur along her back bristled. *I sense no danger, but I concur.*

Ada stumbled to a stop before me, her breathing labored. "Have you seen Ainslie?"

"Not this morning."

"I woke in the night, and she wasn't there, but I thought

she'd simply needed to tend the necessary, and I went back to sleep. But now—she's still gone, and no one has seen her this morning."

After all that had happened, Ainslie wouldn't have left carelessly. However much I struggled to imagine it, I had to venture the question. "Do you think she and Mr. Redgrave might have—"

"Eloped? Certainly not. She may act on impulse at times, but as much as she cares for him, she's being cautious."

Nor did I judge Mr. Redgrave a likely man to conduct such a scheme. Yet any other possibility was far worse . . .

I tucked my trembling hands beneath the muslin of my skirt. I needed evidence, however I might betray myself by collecting it. "Have you spoken to the servants?"

"I don't want to stir gossip, so I made only the lightest of mentions that I sought her. It was difficult enough to keep knowledge of your abduction from spreading—another peculiar disappearance would sink us, even if the explanation proves ordinary."

"What of Aunt Caris?"

"She's still sleeping. All her worries have worn her out."

"If you can, quietly check the bedchamber for any signs of missing items that might show where Ainslie has gone—and examine the rest of the house as well. I'll search for any traces about the gardens."

Ada nodded and hurried back into the house, while I sought the best vantage point to gain a view of what might have happened, a veritable storm of worry clouding my thoughts. Where should I try first?

The elm.

It had offered the best perspective of the front door before. If Ainslie had left that way, I'd be able to witness it. With Jade at my side, I dashed across the garden. This time, when I touched the rough bark, I held the image of Ainslie in my mind. A veritable flurry of images poured into my own in response. I willed the most recent to surface, and one clear central picture unfolded.

In the full light of the moon, Ainslie crept from Willowere, moving as one in a dream. Her dark hair flowed unbound down her back, reminiscent of Mother. Her feet were bare, her white dressing gown billowed about her, and her exposed binding mark flared with a blinding silvery light.

She showed no awareness of her surroundings, only wandered down the lane, through the trees, and out of sight . . .

I wrenched away from the bole of the elm, a tremor racking my body. All the branches above shuddered as cold talons of fear raked down my spine.

The fae who held Ainslie's debt had come to collect.

ACKNOWLEDGMENTS

First of all, I want to take a moment to thank all the readers who have come along on Jessa's journey thus far—particularly those who have taken the time to share their love for these stories. I appreciate you all! And I'm delighted to have you accompany Jessa in her continuing adventures.

Every book I write comes from my heart, and *Ruins of Bone* is no exception. I penned this book during a time of major transition in our lives, when time was in short supply and stress levels high, but the story demanded to be told, despite the circumstances, and I couldn't be happier that it's finally ready to enter the world.

Through the whole process, my husband provided much support and encouragement. Thank you, CJ, for your love and for always wanting more of my stories!

It wasn't only my husband who provided encouragement along the way, but also the team involved in the production of the *Blood of the Fae* books. To Lauren, Kara, and Deborah—thank you for sharing your brilliance with me. Your love for story and language and attention to detail have made this a stronger book. None of you were daunted by the length of it, and all of you share my passion for this series. I couldn't be more thankful for each one of you.

Thanks also to Lena for the lovely cover!

To the fantastic family and friends have offered encouragement along this writing journey—I love and appreciate you all! Thank you.

To my beloved daughters—you're a gift to me, a joy and inspiration. I thank God for you every day.

And, of course, to the Author of my life . . . I'm always and forever grateful to you.

ABOUT THE AUTHOR

Sarah Chislon lives in Virginia with her husband and three daughters. When she's not writing, she's homeschooling her children and running a web development business with her husband. As an avid reader and a lifelong story-weaver, she delights in creating fantastic worlds and exploring them alongside her characters.

For more information on her books, visit her website sarahchislon.com—or sign up for her newsletter to receive updates and free bonus content.

facebook.com/sarahchislon

instagram.com/sarahchislon

bookbub.com/authors/sarah-chislon